TAIL of the DRAGON SERIES

SPECIAL EDITION #1, BOOKS 1-5

TAIL OF THE DRAGON

CLAWS OF THE DRAGON

BATTLE OF THE DRAGON

EYES OF THE DRAGON

FLIGHT OF THE DRAGON

CRAIG HALLORAN

Tail of the Dragon Series
Special Edition #1, Books 1 – 5
By Craig Halloran
Copyright © 2015 by Craig Halloran
Print Edition

TWO-TEN BOOK PRESS
P.O. Box 4215, Charleston, WV 25364

ISBN eBook: 978-1-941208-95-3
ISBN Paperback: 978-1-979168-21-2

www.craighalloran.com

Cover Illustration by Joe Shawcross
Map by Gillis Bjork

Publisher's Note
This book is a work of fiction. Names, characters, places, and incidents either are the product of
the author's imagination or are used fictitiously, and any resemblance to actual persons, living
or dead, events, or locales is entirely coincidental.

TABLE OF CONTENTS

TAIL

OF THE

DRAGON

-Book 1-

CRAIG HALLORAN

CHAPTER 1

"COME ON, BRENWAR. HURRY UP," Nath said, staring down over the rocky edge of a mountainside. Below, Brenwar's meaty mitts tugged hand over hand at the rocks. Sweat beaded his forehead. The brisk winds tore through his gray-streaked black beard. "I'm getting hungry."

Brenwar glared up at him. "I'll get there in my own good time. Why don't you go scarf down some cattle or something?"

Nath's golden dragon eyes widened. "Are you taking a poke at me?"

Brenwar didn't respond. The powerful frame of a dwarf continued his agonizing pace up the steep mountainside. Below him were endless miles of lush green countryside. It would be an hour before he caught up with Nath.

"Great," Nath said, turning his serpentine head away and facing the top rocks of the mountain. He took his anger out on Brenwar, but they both knew he was really mad at Selene. After all they'd been through to stop Gorn Grattack, a year ago she'd up and left. It still deeply hurt him she'd done that. No explanation. Not a word.

On all fours, Nath weaved his way through the trees like a great cat, his dragon paws leaving deep impressions in the ground. He sat back on his haunches and leaned his scaled dragon frame against the tall rocks, eyeing his prints. "I don't think I'll ever get used to that."

Nath was all dragon now, from his smoking nostrils to the tip of his lightning-quick tail. He was bigger than a team of horses, and though still graceful as a gazelle, he wasn't entirely accustomed to his huge body yet. He puffed out a fiery smoke ring. It floated high in the air before descending over a tree and turning it into ash. "I'm big. I'm astounding. I love it."

He clicked his claws together in admiration. Some were bigger than a man's arm. Sharper than elven steel. His scales were alabaster flecked with bronze now. A flame-red streak raced down from the middle of his horns to the middle of his back. His wings were red and folded tight over his back. He lifted his chin toward the sky, thinking it was true, what his father, Balzurth, had once said: "The land was made for men, the sky for dragons."

Nath's stomach rumbled. "Guzan, I can't believe I'm hungry already. I ate ten cows yesterday." He rubbed the scales on his belly. "I like food as much as anyone, but this is ridiculous." He snorted some air into his nostrils. His scaly brow started to crease. "Nothing worth eating up here unless I rustle up a thousand squirrels and chipmunks."

Nath pushed off the rocks and flattened himself so that his iron-hard belly hung inches over the ground. Head low and with his horns flared out over his back, he approached the rim of the mountain again. Brenwar had made little progress. "I'm going to eat," Nath called down to the dwarf. "Eh, so don't fall or anything."

"Like you care if I fall or not," Brenwar grunted.

"Oh, it's not you I'm worried about. It's the mountain." Nath's chuckles rumbled. "I'm off." He pushed off the edge and darted down the mountainside, zooming by Brenwar. Hearing his friend let out a startled curse, Nath spread his wings out and took flight, laughing.

The wind ripped through his earholes. A split second later he was soaring high in the sky. The mountaintops and farmlands, far below, looked like little more than a map on a table.

Nath let out an exhilarating roar. "Mah-hoooooooooooo!"

Cutting through the clouds, Nath spun, dove, climbed, and dove again. There was nothing like flying. Even the best days walking the land were not even close. Minutes into the flight, miles away from where he'd started, his keen dragon eyes spotted a herd of cattle roaming the land.

"Ah, dinner."

Circling lower toward the earth, he looked to see if any people were tending these cows. Nath took no pleasure in eating what people had rustled for themselves, unless it was absolutely necessary. So far, it had not been. Ranchers from all the races needed meat, but there were still plenty of wild herds for him to go around and feast on.

A flicker of movement caught his eye. There were men. Some on horseback and others walking.

"Blast my hide!" he said, hovering just below the clouds. "And I'm getting really hungry too. Wait a second." He sniffed the air. "Oh, I know that foul aroma. Those aren't men. Those are orcs." He clutched his claws and dove toward the ground with a broad grin full of teeth showing on his maw. "Perfect."

Nath's shadow fell upon the orcs.

Their necks snapped up. Their yellow eyes filled with surprise.

Nath buzzed over the tops of two orcs' heads, knocking them both from their saddles.

The horses galloped away. The orcs scrambled.

Nath let out a roar so terrifying the ground shook.

Orcs clasped their grubby hands over their ears and fell to their knees. One of them found the courage to rise to his feet and face Nath with his spear.

It's always the stupidest ones that are the bravest.

The orc, little more than a morsel in Nath's midst, marched forward. Its head hung low, and its spear was gripped with white knuckles. It was stout and sweaty, more so than the common orc. A brawler.

Really. Nath shook his head. *Being king, I really think I should be able to kill them. It would almost be worth doing if they had some flavor to them. Ew! I really hope I don't get so hungry that I eat foul beasts.*

The orc continued his march through the tall meadow.

If I were a man, I'd gladly pummel you with my fists, but I don't have time for that. He unleashed his tail. *Swat!*

The orc flipped head over heels and crashed into the ground.

Nath prowled over. Using his clawed hand, he plucked the orc up from the ground by the leg and dangled it in front of his face. Nath shook the orc a few times and flicked him like a toy far aside.

And to think I used to struggle with those smelly things. Oh well. Nath dusted off his paws. He turned and gazed over the rolling hills. The cattle were grazing again, not too far away. There were hundreds of them. Nath's eyes glazed over.

Thoom!

Nath stretched up his long neck. *What was that?*

Suddenly, mounds of dirt exploded near the cattle. Great men emerged from the ground, taller than trees and hewn from mighty frames as big as Nath himself.

Great Guzan! Giants!

CHAPTER 2

EARTH GIANTS. BIG AND NASTY was an understatement for their kind. The towering men stood more than twenty feet tall. They were built like mountains, and their faces were covered in dark, coarse beards. The ground shook as they closed in on the cattle and began snatching them up one by one. One of them, covered in furs for clothing, dropped a cow into his mouth and swallowed it whole.

"THAT'S MY DINNER!" Nath roared.

The giants froze and turned to face him, their eyes widening underneath their bushy brows and revealing an evil glimmer of yellow. The second giant stuffed a cow into his mouth, chewed it up, and swallowed. Then the pair of them rose to their full height and started to spread out, flanking Nath.

They're both as big as me. This should be interesting.

The cattle made their escape, pressing through the tall grasses and out of sight. The giants grumbled back and forth to each other, hands clutching in and out, eyes wary. It was only the dragons that ever rivaled them in size. The giants hated that. For the most part, they hated everything. They were the big bullies in Nalzambor.

Nath flashed his claws and let out another roar of warning. *I can at least give them a chance. They don't want to mess with this dragon.*

The giants pulled their shoulders back and closed in. Evil leers formed on their disturbing faces.

I expected as much.

Nath's golden eyes narrowed. He let out a small blast of fire.

Good.

The giants circled him. Their hands became monster-sized hammers. They started hooting at him. An odd sound. Weird, yet threatening. Brimming with confidence, their voices became louder. More disturbing.

Nath cocked his serpentine head. *Strange and ugly. I almost feel sorry for them. No wonder the dwarves hate them so. They remind me of oversized orcs.*

The ground rumbled beneath his feet. Hands and arms burst from underneath like massive tree roots. Powerful fingers locked onto his tail and jerked him backward.

Nath stumbled. *Blast!*

Another giant bearded head emerged from the ground and spat out a mouthful of dirt.

Nath tried to shake out of its grasp.

The other two giants leapt on top of him and began hammering away at his body.

Wham! Wham! Wham! Wham!

The first blow caught Nath square in the jaw. The next shots landed hard on his belly, knocking the wind out of him. Besieged by monsters just as big as him, he found himself in a fight for his very life.

The blows kept coming. Hard. Furious. All giants were brawlers. Fearless. Only the grave could take the fight out of them.

Great Guzan! I'm getting whipped!

Nath shook the stars from his vision. Out of the corner of his eye, he saw a giant fist coming down fast. Nath struck back like a snake, clamping his powerful jaws down on the giant's arm.

The giant let out a pain-filled yelp. Using its free arm, it started pounding on Nath's face.

That was a mistake.

Nath drew a deep snort of air in his nose and summoned his fire. The giant's arm that he clenched between his teeth erupted into flame and quickly turned to ash.

The giant staggered back, gaping at his missing arm.

That'll teach him.

The other giants were unrelenting. One still had Nath's tail locked up in its fists. The others continued to hammer away. Nath's scales shook under the force of the blows. A hundred mules didn't kick so hard. Every punch shook his dragon bones.

Enough of this!

Nath lashed out. His clawed forearms ripped through the skin and furs of one giant's chest.

It let out an angry grunt and locked onto Nath's neck. It put Nath in a headlock and started to squeeze.

The threesome thrashed on the ground, shaking the earth. The giants were great wrestlers. They had a natural knack for grappling. They tried to snap Nath in half like a twig.

Nath twisted and clawed. His muscles strained with effort.

Guzan! Nath's temper went red. *Blast it! I'm the King of the Dragons!*

With a tremendous heave, he ripped his neck free of the first giant's grasp. Rearing his head up eye to eye with the colossal man, he unleashed his inferno. A white-hot stream of yellow fire burst out of his mouth, covering the giant in flames.

In most circumstances, giants didn't burn. But in this case, Nath's fire, hotter than the hottest dwarven forge, could burn anything.

The giant's body turned into a pile of ash and bones.

Still seeing red with rage, Nath whirled on the giant that was still tugging on his tail.

Catching the fatal look in Nath's eyes, it dove for cover into the ground where it had come from.

Nath filled it with fire, and then eyeing the crater of flame, he let out a mighty roar.

"Mah-Rooooooooooo!"

A rustling caught his ear. His head whipped around.

The last surviving giant, the one missing its arm, was trying to dig its way back into the dirt. It caught Nath's eye, and its one good arm started digging faster.

Nath shot across the tall grass, spread his wings, and dug his back talons into the giant's shoulders. Wings beating, he ascended high into the air with the heavy earth giant in tow. He rose high above the clouds, ignoring the giant's angry cries.

Oh, be silent!

Nath was out of danger now, yet his temper had not cooled. He wanted to drop the giant. Let the evil creature plunge to its death. That would be a far more merciful fate than what he had bestowed on its comrades.

After all, the giants would have killed him. Skinned him. Eaten him if they could have. The great monsters were killers, said to be irredeemable.

Still, deep inside, Nath knew that would be wrong. He heard his father's words.

Take the high road.

He shook his head and glanced down at the giant. There was no pleading in its eyes, just anger. Hatred. It lashed out with its only hand again and again.

Sometimes I hate the high road.

Nath flew mile after mile until he came to a high and snowy peak and dropped the giant deep into the snow-covered banks. Without looking back, he returned to where the cattle grazed. Now even hungrier than before, he stuffed himself full.

Still, letting that lone one-armed giant live lingered. It was a knot nagging under his jaw.

CHAPTER 3

"YOU DID WHAT!" BRENWAR SAID, jumping to his feet. Nath didn't want to tell him about the giants, but the dwarf was always good at knowing when he was holding something back. "It was as if I'd gone looking for them. They just appeared. Erupted, rather, right in the middle of the field."

Brenwar gripped his war hammer in front of his chest and started to stomp around the woodland. "You can't fight giants without me. You just can't. It's wrong. Wrong." His hand tugged at his beard. "You should've come back and gotten me!"

"It was leagues away," Nath said, trying to sound reassuring. "Besides, they jumped me." He rubbed his jaw with his paws. "It wasn't an ordinary scrap, you know. They were tough. Caught me off guard, but I handled them." He puffed out a fire ring. "They're Nalzambor fertilizer now. Well, except one."

Brenwar turned and faced him. He lifted a brow. "One? What one?"

Nath inspected his dragon claws. *Is that a chip? Blast!*

Brenwar marched over and poked Nath in the leg with his hammer. "What! One!"

"Uh, the one I dropped off in the snowcaps. It won't be much of a bother now. And he's only got one arm left."

"You fool!" Brenwar blurted out.

Nath reared up. "What did you call me?"

Brenwar took a step back, glanced up at him, then glanced back down. "I apologize."

Nath sighed. Certainly Brenwar meant well, but things had changed. Nath was the ruler of the dragons now and had to be treated accordingly. An outburst like that would be costly in front of others. "You're fortunate no one else is around, aside from the trees."

"Punish me," Brenwar said. There was a sad tone in his voice. "It must be done. I never would have spoken to your father like that. And if I had, I'd have been ash."

"True. Either that, or he might have told you one of his hundred-year-long stories." Nath nudged Brenwar with his tail, knocking the stalwart dwarf over. "How's that for punishment?"

Lying flat on his belly, Brenwar said, "You're too merciful."

"Oh, am I? I guess I'll have to make the punishment more severe, then."

Brenwar took a knee and bowed his head. "As you wish, Sire."

Nath raised his tail to strike. Of course, he'd never harm a friend, even in the worst of cases. But still, he was the King Dragon now. Even on a rogue adventure, there had to be some form of order. Even for Brenwar, and the battle-hardened dwarven warrior knew that. Still, it made Nath uneasy. His stomach fluttered. He had subjects now, so things weren't the same as they had been. Brenwar and many others treated him differently now. It left him feeling isolated.

"First, Brenwar, tell me, why did you call me 'Fool'?"

"Er, the earth giants, well, they hold grudges. And they are tight knit. They'll summon all their clans to avenge their fallen. It would have been better if you'd killed them all."

"Has anyone ever made the right decision every time?"

"Your father did."

Nath huffed. It was hard to argue that his father Balzurth hadn't always made the right decision every time, seeing how Nath had never really seen his father do much of anything at all. However, of one thing he was certain: his father's word was without question. "Not that you have seen, anyway," Nath replied. "So, perhaps I'll revisit the snowcaps and finish what I started, then?"

"Don't bother, Sire," Brenwar said with an increasing frown. "He's long gone by now. I'm certain of it. Besides, we have things to do." His dwarven breastplate reflected the sun's light when he turned and faced what looked to be an abandoned temple of some kind. There, large piles of rubble and stone pylons had toppled over and become covered in overgrown brush. Brenwar started toward it, stopped, and said, "With your permission, of course, Sire?"

"Nath, Brenwar."

"Aye."

"And Brenwar, what about the earth giants. Is there truly a dire concern?"

"No doubt there will be," he said, pushing through the brush. "But it will take time. They aren't quick about such things. They'll plan, then strike. And all of Nalzambor will know."

"That sounds severe. I'd just as soon prevent it."

"Pah. If you wanted to prevent it ..." Brenwar's voice trailed off.

"Oh come now, Brenwar. Speak freely. Though I've often wished you had a bridled tongue, I value your wisdom."

Brenwar climbed up on a pile of busted stones and met Nath's dragon face eye to eye. "The giants couldn't have eaten all the cattle, could they?"

"Their bellies were quite formidable."

"You should have left well enough alone. Let them have their fill and moved on. But you couldn't, could you? Itching for a fight you were."

"And you wouldn't have been?"

"Of course. But I'd have planned it better. Let them eat, get fat, and be slow. They just bury themselves in the deep dirt again. They rest for years, even decades, you know. But now, they have a cause."

"Are you telling me my actions might have cataclysmic consequences?" Nath asked.

"Probably." Brenwar hopped to the ground and headed back into the ruins.

Nath lumbered in behind him. With ease he pushed the piles of rocks and fallen trees aside. "I think you're exaggerating, Brenwar. Just trying to teach me a lesson."

"We'll see," the dwarf said. "We'll see."

CHAPTER 4

BRENWAR TURNED HIS HEAD OVER his shoulder and gazed up at Nath Dragon. Over the decades, he'd gotten accustomed to Balzurth's mighty dragon frame. The king dragon's presence was warm and radiant, but one had to be mindful in his presence. Balzurth's very voice could shatter a man's bones.

Things were different now with Nath. His friend, covered in supine armored scales, had grown into nothing short of the magnificent presence that his father was. Nath was a beautiful work. A giant lizard that moved with cat-like grace. His voice was strong and reassuring. Nath was all the right things in one. Still, Brenwar's chest tightened. His heart ached. His best friend had grown up on him, and it wouldn't be long before he'd move on. Spend more time with his own kind. Brenwar was certain of it.

"Sire, er, I mean Nath, I'm going to venture into the bowels of the ruined mess, if that's all right by you?"

Nath's armored frame eased to the ground, becoming one with the mountainside. He eyed Brenwar and said with a yawn, "You do that, Brenwar. Just yell if you need me. Whew, those cattle sure were filling. I think I'll sit and listen to the birds for a bit."

"Well, don't fall asleep. The last time you went out, more than a month passed by." Brenwar hefted the war hammer over his shoulder. "And I'm not getting any younger. I've only a few hundred years still in me, if that."

"Oh, Brenwar, you'll never die. Your bones are too bitter for the grave."

"If you say so, Nath." Brenwar marched off. After he'd gone a few hundred yards, he began chucking away the stones that lay over some kind of buried entrance. With a grunt he pushed away a rock bigger than him and found himself gazing at a pewter portal wide enough for a large man to fit through.

It was round and marked in ancient script. He didn't know the writing. There were two handles on it. He clutched his beard. "I sense treachery."

"What was that, Brenwar?" Nath said from far away. "Treachery, you say?"

"Probably nothing, just a marker. I'm assuming there's another vault below. Probably filled with goblin bones or some other kind of stupid." He started to tug on the handles. "I got it." He strained and grunted. The pewter door groaned but didn't give. "Ugh!" Brenwar spat on his hand and renewed his grip on the handles. He put his back and short, powerful legs into it. "Hurk!"

The door didn't yield.

"Perhaps I can help," said Nath's voice.

Brenwar turned and jumped half out of his boots. Nath's nose was in his face. "Quit doing that!"

"Doing what?"

"You know, sneaking." Brenwar ran his eyes up and down Nath's huge body. "I don't know how you do that, but it's aggravating."

"Maybe you're losing your hearing, Brenwar." Nath tapped his dragon claw on his temple. "Too many blows to the head, perhaps."

I'd like to give you a blow to the head, Brenwar thought.

Nath's golden eyes narrowed on him.

Brenwar swallowed.

"Here, let me try," Nath said. He wedged one claw under one handle on the pewter portal and popped it off with a flick.

A rush of stale air burst out.

Nath dangled the portal door in front of Brenwar's eyes. "Here you go."

"I loosened it for you." Brenwar leaned over and peered down into the hole. He said to Nath, "Don't suppose you can squeeze down in there, too, can you?"

Nath took a snort of air into his nostrils. "Nothing but the malodorous dead down there. You might want to be careful." He flipped the pewter portal door like a coin and watched it land on the ground. He eyed the markings. "Huh, these runes have patterns similar to some we've seen before. How old is Nalzambor, anyway?"

Brenwar rubbed his forehead with his fingers. That same question had often been asked. No one knew the answer for sure, but the dwarven histories dated back a few thousand years—and no further than that. "So you're saying you can't read it?"

"No, I can't. But I can only assume that it's a warning. You'd better be careful."

Brenwar peered back into the hole again. The last time he'd crawled into one, he almost hadn't made it back out. "You could come too, you know."

"But it's so agonizing to change back into a human. You know that. Besides, we'd be able to cover more distance if you'd just ride on my back," Nath said.

"Dwarves don't fly."

"I could insist that you do it."

"Well, I'd prefer you didn't." Out of his rucksack, Brenwar produced a tiny lantern attached to a string. He tapped on its side three times, and its fire came to life. Hand over hand, he lowered it into the hole. "Besides, I like long walks. You used to, too."

With a matter-of-fact tone in his voice, Nath said, "Those days are gone, Brenwar. I'm a dragon now. And we have a lot of ground to cover in this search for my mother. At this rate, it'll be a hundred years before we even find a clue. Of which, well, we have very little already." Nath slumped down on his belly. "Oh, I don't even know why I'm bothering. If my mother really is out there, you'd think she'd try to find me."

"You can't think like that," Brenwar said, eyeing Nath. He noticed a deep crease forming between the eyes and horns of Nath's head. "I'm sure if she could, she would."

"It's futile. It's been a year, and we haven't found a thing."

"Nothing is futile, not for a dragon such as you, anyway. And we have found some things."

Nath rolled over on his back and gazed up at the sky. "Sure, a bunch of old pottery from civilizations long past. How exciting. Huff."

Brenwar's stomach started to knot. Sure, he didn't want to fly on Nath's huge dragon back, but he didn't want the quest to find Nath's mother to end too soon, either. He enjoyed his adventures with Nath, but now, he felt those grand times were fading. Times that would never come back again.

"If you like, you can scan for some other sights. I don't think we'll find much here."

Nath didn't reply.

So far, their journeys had been pretty exciting and eventful for Brenwar. He enjoyed traversing into places he'd never been before. And they had a great system going, too. Flying above, Nath would scour the mountain ranges and pick up anything interesting with his keen eyes. They'd already found dozens of ruins and temples that were long forgotten. Brenwar had even dug up some lost treasures, and he liked that. But their search for signs of Nath's mother was fruitless, and they only had one clue to go on. It was a message that Balzurth had left. It said, "What you seek is in the peaks." That was all.

"I'm going in," Brenwar said, glancing back at Nath. "Don't run off, now." He dangled his legs over and found footing on the iron rungs inside. He began his descent. Something shot out from below and snagged his leg. *Thwiip!* "What in the—*ulp!*"

CHAPTER 5

NATH SAT UP. "BRENWAR?" TILTING his head, he picked up the sounds of a violent rustling down inside the hole. "Brenwar!"

"Nath!" his friend bellowed out.

Nath leaned over the portal. Something big darted out and jumped on his nose. It was a tarantula-like creature, but it had scales and a dragon's tail. The fangs in its mouth dripped with venom that sizzled on Nath's scales. Its many eyes, deep red and beaded, glared at him. It struck, sinking its fangs into his nose.

The venom burned.

Nath's eyes watered.

He snatched the dragon spider by the tail and slammed it into the ground. "You little fiend!"

The monster, about the size of Brenwar, zinged spider silk into a nearby tree and started to scurry away.

"Oh no you don't," Nath said. Like a mighty whip, he unleashed his tail. He smote the dragon spider across its back and smashed it into the ground.

The spider spat a ball of venom on Nath, stinging his toes.

"Ow. Blast you, insect!" He snatched up the dragon spider in his claws and squeezed.

Its body squished and crunched.

Nath wiped the dragon spider off his paws and onto the grasses.

Its scaly skin was intact, but the goo was squished out of it.

"Yuck."

"For Morgdon!" Brenwar bellowed from inside the hole.

The ground shook.

Krang!

Wary-eyed, Nath looked back inside the hole. The lantern was out, but Nath could make out something still moving below.

Suddenly, the lantern was aglow again and Brenwar held it in his hand. His shoulders were sagging.

"Brenwar, are you all right?"

Brenwar started up out of the hole. He was moving slowly, even for him. He emerged. His armor was splashed with dragon spider guts. He staggered over and leaned against a rock. War Hammer hung loose in his hand, and his breathing was heavy.

"Brenwar, you don't look well." Nath took a closer look. Brenwar's skin was pale. Clammy. "By the Flames! Your hand!"

The skin on Brenwar's hand was purple and bloated.

"Just a little spider bite," Brenwar mumbled. I'll be fine."

But Nath could tell that the dwarf was not fine. His friend and oldest ally smelled of decay. Nath narrowed his eyes and focused. With his special dragon sight, he could see that the spider venom was eating Brenwar up from the inside. It was happening at a very alarming rate. Oh no! Brenwar's arm was beginning to disintegrate!

"Brenwar, the chest! Get the chest!"

The dwarf fumbled with his belt pouch. His eyes were glassy, his pupils wide and dark black. He collapsed face first on the ground.

"Brenwar!"

Nath's heart raced. He rolled Brenwar over and tried to open up his belt pouch. His claws were far too big. *I've got to change. I've got to change now! Guzan!*

Changing back into a man took time and a great deal of concentration. If he did it more often, it wouldn't be so bad, but it had been a long time since he'd been a man.

Think, Dragon. Think!

A thought struck him.

He let out a dragon squawk. A call for help. *"Ka-Kwak! Ka-Kwak! Ka-Kwak!"*

In times past, the cry for help wouldn't have done him much good. The dragons had ignored him for the first two hundred years of his life, but those fences had been mended. He was their king now. He nuzzled Brenwar's body close to his.

Brenwar's eyes blinked rapidly.

"Hold on, Brenwar. Hold on."

Brenwar's forehead burst out in beads of feverish sweat. He let out a painful groan. "Ooooh!"

I've got to change. I've got to change. Holding Brenwar tight, Nath closed his eyes and started to meditate. Despite all his power, Nath hadn't often taken the liberty of exercising his gifts. In truth, he had many that he still needed to discover for himself.

Right now, he could only hope some other dragons could come to his aid, because by the time he changed, it would probably be too late.

Brenwar's thunderous heartbeat had slowed.

Come on, Nath. Change. Change!

"Squawk-Chirble!"

Nath's eyes popped open at the unforeseen sound. A small dragon, little bigger than a dog, stood on its hind legs at his feet. It was a green lily dragon, rich forest green with a paler shade on her belly. Her eyes were lashed, a golden brown, and pretty.

Nath spoke to her in Dragonese. "I need you to open his pouches. Search for a small box in there."

"I'd be honored to assist the Son of Balzurth, my liege Nath Dragon," she replied in a very polished Dragonese voice. Her tiny paws rummaged through Brenwar's pouches and produced a wooden chest just big enough for a large ring. "Is this what you seek?"

"It is," Nath said, eyeing it. It was Bayzog who had shrunk it down to that size. There was a particular word that would make it grow back to normal size, and Nath hadn't been paying attention when it was said. "Ah, forgive me, Brenwar. I can't remember the word."

The green lily cocked her head and said in the direction of Brenwar. "Is this dwarf important to you?"

"Of course. He's my friend."

"Why?" she said.

"Oh, it's a long story and we're running out of time. He's been poisoned." Nath sighed. "I fear he doesn't have much time. Blast my scales. I can't remember the word."

The green lily turned and faced him with her little paws clasped together. She looked like a princess on her hind legs. "Is there anything else I can assist you with, Dragon Prince?"

"I need the chest open. I need a cure for that dragon spider poison."

"I'm sorry, I can't help you with that," she said. "It was a pleasure to meet you. May I be dismissed?"

"What? No! I need you to administer the potions once I get the chest open. Ugh!" He slammed his tail hard into the ground.

Boom!

Brenwar's heartbeat continued to slow and weaken.

If Nath could have perspired, he'd have been covered in sweat.

This is my fault. All my fault. Here I am the king of the dragons, and I'm not even paying attention.

He let out a roar. "Maaarrroooooooo!"

"Nath Dragon," he said to himself out loud, "what have you been doing?"

CHAPTER 6

THE CHEST POPPED OPEN.

It started to grow.

Nath gaped. What had he said that triggered it? "All I said was, 'What have you been doing?'" His thoughts were strained. A bright moment hit him. "Been! It was Ben! They sound the same. Ha! How simple! I'm such a fool." Relieved, he gave the green lily her next orders. "See those vials? I need the yellow one."

The green lily picked up one of the vials from the drawers that folded out like an old fisherman's chest. She held it up. It was yellow and milky in color.

Nath shook his head and said, "No, the golden one."

She picked up another and held it out for display.

"No, the more golden one."

She sighed and plucked out the last possible candidate.

"That's it, now carefully pour it over his lips. He has to drink it down, all of it. Plus, he needs another." His eyes scoured the chest that was still plenty tiny to him. "Oh, I need something to battle the poison. Which one is it? Which one is it?"

There were more than thirty vials, in a multitude of colors. Bright purples and lavenders. Velvety red. Orange that was swirled with black. Others cracked with tiny lightning in the bottle. In truth, Nath had little need for such things these days. There wasn't anything he knew of that he couldn't handle himself. "Ah, I think it's that one. At least I hope it is. Feed him that one."

The green lily slipped out a vial that was filled with a mix of pink and gray. "Are you certain?" she asked with a furrowed brow.

Brenwar's heart had almost stopped beating.

"I have to be," Nath said. "I have to be."

The green lily climbed up on Brenwar's chest, removed the cork, and pulled back Brenwar's lips with her free hand. Carefully, she poured the entire vial into his mouth. She replaced the cork and said to Nath, "May I go now, Sire?"

Most dragons had no attachment at all to the other races. Of course, much of that could probably be explained because of their persecution. Still, it rubbed Nath the wrong way. Fighting back the urge to rebuke her in some fashion, he said, "Yes, go. And thank you."

Her wings fanned out. Her lithe frame leapt from Brenwar's chest and into the air. A few graceful flaps of her wings followed, and she was gone.

Dragons. I hope I never feel as they do.

Brenwar coughed and sputtered.

Nath leaned down and propped him up against a fallen log.

His friend's heartbeat had steadied, but it was still weak.

Come on, Brenwar. Come on.

It was a long night. A long week. Brenwar hadn't awakened. He breathed, shuddered, and coughed occasionally. Nath stayed close the entire time. He pushed over some trees and started a fire. He did his best to keep Brenwar free of the chills. Still in the full body of a dragon, he wrestled in thought whether he should turn back to a man or not.

If I had been in the form of a man, as Brenwar requested, I might have saved him.

He lay near Brenwar, watching his every movement. Counting the heartbeats in his chest. They were slow and steady. A good sign. Good enough for Brenwar to awaken by now, but he hadn't. It was puzzling. Frustrating.

This is my fault.

Nath realized he'd taken for granted his own power and forgotten about the fragility of the other races. Perhaps that was why dragons were so distant from the men and women of the world. They just didn't last as long. They didn't have the same protection. Their thin skins were nothing compared to a dragon's steel-hard scales. Their lives could so easily be snuffed out in an instant.

He put his paw on Brenwar's chest and felt its rise and fall. There was a rasp in his breathing. Nath didn't doubt that the dragon spider's poison had gone straight to the heart. If anything, it was a miracle that Brenwar lived. He could thank his dwarven constitution for that.

Should I take him to Morgdon? To the elves, perhaps. They have the best healers, but Brenwar would want to kill me if I did that.

Nath batted the idea back and forth, a hundred times if not a thousand. Yet he remained where he was, certain that Brenwar would wake up. And he didn't want to fly with Brenwar, either. It might prove too much of a strain, and Brenwar would be furious if he did. "I'd rather die than fly," Brenwar had once said. Nath chose to honor that.

So Nath waited and waited. He pondered their mission. The search for his mother. His father Balzurth had told him that he'd have the power to find her, but he'd given only the one tiny hint beyond that. Traveling with Brenwar was slow, but for a dragon, a creature that seemed to have all the time in the world, it wasn't so bad. Nath wasn't even two hundred and fifty years old yet, and he had at least two thousand more years to go. But so far, this adventure hadn't been quite as exhilarating as the ones before. Of course, the battle with the earth giants had been nice. The battle with the dragon spiders not so much. He eyed the portal.

Dragon spiders. Of all the luck.

That was another mystery that Nath had to ponder. Dragon spiders were just as rare as dragons themselves. Even rarer. They weren't all good or all evil, either. In many cases, they were guardians of precious things and even used by the dragons themselves. Oft times they could be found guarding dragon eggs while dragons hunted. But it took a great deal of power to employ the service of dragon spiders. And Nath was certain that they weren't in the portal by accident. Something meaningful, perhaps more so for men than for dragons, was in that vault.

Not that it matters. I'm sure it won't have anything to do with my mother. Probably some withered lich's treasure hoard.

Nath studied the hard lines in Brenwar's face. He knew every weathered crease. He was certain he'd caused at least a dozen of them himself. He'd even seen three new ones form during one conversation. Nath chuckled. "Hah, Brenwar. You wouldn't have any gray at all if it weren't for me. It suits you well, though. Now, wake up. If you don't, I'm liable to do something stupid. And you wouldn't want that, now, would you?" He listened to Brenwar's heartbeat.

It was slow.

Thump-thump ... thump-thump ... thump-thump ...

"Boy, I think I can hear some giants nearby. Oh my, I can see them. Lords no! They are juggling dwarves!"

Thump-thump ... thump-thump ... thump-thump ...

"Oh my goodness," Nath continued, "I thought I'd never see the day. My, how the world has changed since you took your name. Your sister, Ellgall, is finally going to marry. But her groom isn't of the standard groomsman fare. No, she's different. Of course you always knew that. Aye, I can see him standing at the altar waiting for her now, except he's much taller than a typical dwarf. But I'm sure it will work out. I just never thought I'd see the day when a dwarven maiden, your sister Ellgall, married an *orc*."

Thump-thump ... thump-thump ... thump-thump ...

Nath's head hung low.

CHAPTER
7

NATH FLATTENED HIS BODY DOWN on the ground with Brenwar between him and the fire. He listened to his friend's heartbeat. He could feel it in his bones. Every beat seemed like the last, leaving him restless. And then—

Thump-thump-thump-Thump!

Brenwar's eyes popped open. His mouth parted. "Orc! Ellgall!" He sat upright. Bleary eyed, he looked around. "Where is the rotten beast?"

"Brenwar!" Nath said with elation. "You're back!"

The old dwarf scrambled to his feet, only to teeter over and bump his head on a log.

"You'd better take it easy," Nath said. With his tail he helped Brenwar to his feet. "Don't overdo it."

Brenwar blinked and slowly spun around. "Harrumph. I must have been dreaming. I don't see any orcs. Or Ellgall." He clawed at his beard, looked up at Nath, and said, "What happened?"

"The dragon spider's poison took you. About a week ago. I thought you were through."

The chestnut eyes under Brenwar's bushy brows popped wide. "A week!" His hands clutched at his beard. "Blast my beard! Why didn't you wake me up?"

"You know I certainly tried, Brenwar, but you were sleeping like a petrified log," Nath said, stretching his wings out a little and folding them back. "How do you feel?"

"Mmmmm, I'm so hungry I could eat an ogre."

"That can be arranged." Nath's serpentine head twisted around. His eyes scanned the surroundings. "I'd be happy to fetch some goats, or a stag."

"I can do it myself—Oof." Brenwar's face turned sour. He rubbed one hand through his beard, then rubbed his temples with his fingers. "Something feels funny." He held one hand in front of his face. It was the one the spider had bitten. There was no skin or muscle, only bone. "Gah!"

"Easy, Brenwar," Nath said. "I can explain."

"I'm dead, aren't I! You brought me back from the dead! Why did you do that? I deserve a proper burial. A grand tomb and plenty of rest!"

"You aren't dead, Brenwar. Again, let me explain."

Brenwar's eyes studied his one hand beside the other. His left hand was just fine, filled with strong, stubby fingers. The other, his right, was pure bone with big knuckles. He opened and closed it. His eyes filled with astonishment. He tipped his head up toward Nath. "What did you do?"

"Well," Nath said, coughing a little, "I may have gotten the potions mixed up a bit. Or perhaps the application was wrong." He made a remorseful face. "Seems I had you swallow what should have been applied, but it wasn't easy, and there wasn't much time. At least you live."

Brenwar's hard eyes filled with surprise. His brows clenched up and down. His eyes fastened on his skeleton hand. He mumbled something.

"What was that?" Nath asked.

In a low voice, Brenwar said something again. In Dwarven.

Nath's dragon lips turned up. "If I'm not mistaken, I think you said, 'like it.'"

Brenwar's eyes searched the area until they rested on War Hammer. He strolled over and picked it up with his skeleton hand. With a spark in his eye, he held it high in the air and said, "Wait until they see me in Morgdon! There's not a single dwarf in the great hall with a wound like this. Har!"

Taken aback a little, Nath said, "So you do like it?"

"Like it?" Brenwar growled. "I love it!" He brought the weapon's hammer-like head down, pulverizing some rocks. "Ah, the fear in the eyes that me and War Hammer will bring. Let's go find some giants!"

"Sure, but let's eat first." Nath eyed War Hammer. Handcrafted by Brenwar himself, it was a magnificent weapon. A hardened oak shaft hosting a burnished head of rune-marked steel. An axe head on one end and a mallet on the other. It was impressive, but something was missing. "You know, Brenwar, don't you think it's time that you gave War Hammer a real name?"

"It has a name: War Hammer. Mrrummaah in Dwarven. It's a fine name."

"I think that cleric of Barnabus was right. Something so exquisite needs a little more original name."

Brenwar scratched his head.

"For example," Nath continued. "It would be like me calling Fang Sword. Or you calling me Dragon. Er, well, bad example. Or me calling you Dwarf."

Brenwar's brow furrowed. Creativity wasn't part of his makeup. He found details such as the names of things mundane, not oft so important. Which was odd for a dwarf, because they had many sophisticated names. And some of them were almost as long as dragons' names for things. "What do you suggest?"

"Well, how about," Nath drummed his claws on his chin, "Crusher. It crushes a lot of things, does it not? Is there a word for that in Dwarven?"

"Hmmm, not really," Brenwar said, raking his beard. His rigid lips formed a smile. "But I can make it work. Mortuun..." The word went on for hours.

Finally, Nath said, "How about Mortuun for short?"

Brenwar grunted. "Aye. Now that you've made me go and think on it, Mortuun it is. Mortuun the Crusher."

CHAPTER

8

"**D**O YOU SEE ANYTHING INTERESTING down there?" Nath yelled down through the portal he had opened. Brenwar had climbed in an hour ago. Now that he'd eaten, he had a bounce in his step and had been eager to head back down. "Brenwar?"

Brenwar didn't reply, but Nath could still hear him shuffling through the tomb. There was a lot of scraping of stone over stone and the sounds of stone being bashed in with Mortuun, but apparently Brenwar hadn't found anything interesting.

"Watch out for dragon-spider nests!" Nath yelled back down. "You never know."

"And you'll never know," Brenwar fired back. His voice echoed up the tunnel, "unless you come down here yourself ... Sire."

"Humph." Keeping his ears tuned to the hole, Nath sat back down. He didn't sense any danger. Perhaps the dragon spiders had been the only "price to pay" for intruders trying to loot the ancient tomb. Quite adequate, for most intruders. And the dragon spiders could have been inside there for centuries. Maybe a millennium.

"I'm sure you can handle it, Brenwar Bone Hand."

Brenwar's rustlings came and went. There were tapping sounds on stones. Heavy grunts. Objects being shoved back and forth. It seemed Brenwar was deep in his search but not having much luck. It was possible that whatever needed to be found had been concealed by a spell. Nath could help with that, but the likes of Bayzog and Sasha would be better. *I wonder how they are doing. I bet Bayzog's had his nose stuck in a book ever since he returned to Quintuklen. What's left of it, anyway.*

Nath hollered down the hole, "Why don't you try a potion of finding or something?"

In a distant voice, Brenwar hollered back, "I don't need no potion."

The vault was deep. Nath figured it to be at least fifty feet straight down. And in some cases, the ancient vaults and tombs could go a hundred yards. They'd already come across a couple like that. And it was not that Nath was impatient. Pretty much all dragons were very patient, but Brenwar's searches could take months. Dwarves liked it down inside the earth.

Maybe I should change.

Nath grimaced.

But moving on two legs is so slow. And no wings? No way!

He scratched his dragon chin with his claw.

Hmmm, maybe I could turn into a man, and keep the wings?

He pondered the idea until the day turned into night and back into the day again.

Nah. Then I'd look like Sansla Libor. Or a draykis.

He sat upright. Cocked his head on his long serpentine neck.

Brenwar's booted feet were echoing off the portal's rungs and getting higher. His black-haired head popped up like a gopher out of the hole. Straining, he climbed out with a very heavy strongbox, half the size of him, in tow. Using two hands, he gave it a heave and dragged it out of the hole and onto the dewy grass. Breathing heavily, he said, "Found something."

"I can see that," Nath said, eyeing it.

It had handles on each side, like a chest, but there weren't any latches, key locks, or hinges. It was made of bright polished steel, which reflected the sunlight. To a mortal naked eye, it looked like nothing more than a block of solid metal.

Nath could make out a very narrow seam that looked like the lid. "That's one strange treasure chest."

"It was well concealed." Brenwar put his hands on his hips and stuck his chest out a little. "But I found it. No creature on Nalzambor can read the stones better than a dwarf. No sir." He held up his bony hand, marveling. "And none with a hand like this."

"Nothing compares to you, Brenwar. That's for certain. So the question is, how do we get this thing open?"

"Maybe we shouldn't open it at all," Brenwar suggested.

"Then why did you bring it up here?"

"Why? So you could look at it."

Nath rolled his eyes. "I am looking at it. I have to admit it's not like anything I've ever seen before. The craftsmanship is unique. Did anything down there give you any idea who created it?"

"I saw some markings. The tombs were all sealed, but I busted one open. There was nothing but powder and dust in there." He scratched his nose.

"Whatever fed on them, it fed on them long ago. There were worm holes, too, but most of them had refilled."

"How many tombs?"

"A few dozen. Judging by the size of them, I'd say they were men. Not for certain, but I'd say it's a tomb of the unknown." Brenwar started scratching his back with his bony fingers. "Mmm, that feels good."

Nath didn't really have his hopes up to find anything new. After all, there were plenty of strange things all over Nalzambor. They'd never find them all. And this location, well, it seemed much older than what he'd be looking for. As far as finding his mother was concerned, he should be able to find something, somewhere, that wasn't much older than him.

"Brenwar, are you certain that you've never seen my mother?"

"Of course not. I didn't come onto the scene until you were a mature young boy. Well, not exactly mature, but you know what I mean."

"Yes, I know," Nath said, drooping his huge dragon head down. "Surely my father knows where she is. Wouldn't he know?"

Brenwar shrugged his brows. "I think he likes to leave things a mystery until the time comes that you should know."

"You'd think I'd know enough already, but I don't know any more than I knew a hundred years ago." He balled up his paw and brought it down on the rectangular chunk of metal.

Whummmm!

"There must be a million peaks to search on Nalzambor." Nath hit the block again and again.

Whumm Whumm Whumm!

The odd strongbox hummed.

Mrrrruum mummm mummm!

Its cold steel finish swirled with life.

Eyes widening, Brenwar stepped back, readying his war hammer and setting his shoulders.

"What's this?" Nath said with wary eyes.

The steel box started to brighten, the sun's light feeding it with white-hot power. Its radiance became stronger and stronger.

Nath's neck coiled back. His scales tingled. There was power. Ancient. Ominous. Threatening. "You'd better get behind me, Brenwar."

"You'd better get behind me," the warrior said. He raised Mortuun over his head and rushed toward the strongbox.

"Brenwar, no!" Nath said.

CHAPTER 9

ATH'S TAIL LASHED OUT QUICKER than a snake just as Mortuun the Crusher came down. He was a split second too late. The war hammer smote the strongbox with all powerful authority.

Krang!

The burst of sound slammed into Nath and everything else in all directions around the strongbox.

Nath's claws dug into the dirt.

Brenwar was knocked off his feet and tumbled head over heels.

Trees buckled and branches snapped.

Nath's ears were ringing, but other than that, he was unaffected. "Brenwar, what did you do that for?" He surveyed the devastated landscape. "Brenwar?"

"Up here," said a gruff voice. Brenwar was hanging upside down from a tree with his feet caught in the branches. Angry and somehow with Mortuun still hanging in his grasp, he started chopping with fury. "Let go of me, leafmaker!"

Nath started to make his way over.

The branches gave way.

Crack!

Brenwar tumbled down through the air and hit the ground hard. "Oof!"

"Are you all right?" Nath said, brushing aside the bushes his friend had landed in.

"I'm fine," Brenwar said, rolling up to his feet.

"I wasn't talking to you," said Nath. "I was talking to the bushes."

"Hah."

Nath turned away and returned his focus to the chest. Someone or something sat on top of it.

Brenwar stopped in his tracks.

Nath froze.

It was a woman of sorts. Beautiful. Exquisite. No bigger than a child human's, her lithe body was adorned in pink, white, and black fabric in marvelous patterns that flowed with nature. There were wings on her back, transparent, that caught the light. Her eyes were black, her face expressionless. In a soft but strong voice, she spoke in a language that Nath did not understand.

"Pardon?" he said in Common, somewhat mesmerized.

"Who are you?" she asked in the same tongue.

"I'm Nath Dragon."

She rubbed her head with her dainty hands, tousling her long white locks. "And who is this one that smote me?"

"Brenwar," Nath said, edging closer. He eyed her up and down. He'd never seen anyone like her before. Her loveliness rivaled that of the most winsome dragon. "And may I ask who you are?"

She scoffed. "Hah." She fanned out her pretty pink nails and yawned. She hopped off the chest and started shoving it across the ground until it dropped back in the hole. A loud bang echoed up out of there.

Bang! ang ang ang ang!

Nath glanced at Brenwar and found the dwarf staring back at him. They both turned back to the winged woman, and Nath said, "Are you a fairy?"

"Hah!" she said. Her fingers began dancing in the air. Suddenly, the cover to the portal lifted up over the ground and dropped back over the hole, sealing the portal. She spoke indistinguishable words. The round cover glowed with hot light, and its edges sealed. She dusted off her hands and turned back and faced Nath and Brenwar with her hands on her hips.

"You're drinking in my beauty, aren't you."

"I'm just wondering who you are," Brenwar said.

"I am whoever I want to be."

"Why were you imprisoned in there?" Nath asked, narrowing his eyes on her. If she was a fairy, then she was a very powerful one. And fairies often tricked one into doing their bidding.

Approaching Nath, she rolled up on her toes and stood as tall as one of the claws on his dragon-clawed feet. It should have been funny, her being so small, but somehow it wasn't. "You should have gotten the answer to that before you freed me." She showed a smile full of bright white teeth. "But, still, I am grateful to be free from my bondage. So much so, I will share my name with you, and with it comes the answer to any one of your questions."

"You know the answer to everything? Hah!" Brenwar said.

"I do." Her eyes shifted up to the right. Her face creased in concentration. Her toes sank into the ground. "Ah, that's better." She faced Brenwar. "Yes,

I do, Brenwar Bolderguild. Five hundred and seventy-five years young, is it? Son of Ballor Bolderguild the Forgekeeper. Shall I go on?"

Brenwar looked like he had swallowed his beard.

"It's not often I've seen you stumped. Ha-ha!" Nath laughed. "And dare I ask what you know about me?" he said to her. "Oh, and what is your name, as you mentioned sharing it before."

"I am Lotuus, Nath Dragon. The Fairy Empress."

"Empress?" Nath lifted a brow. "That sounds important. I imagine there are many that have been missing you."

"In due time, I'll know." Her transparent wings fluttered and she rose up from the ground, coming to eye level with Nath. "Ah, you're the son of Balzurth. Seems I've been imprisoned longer than I imagined. It's so hard to tell the passing of time when I'm in a suspended state." Now her dark eyes gave him the once over. "You certainly are a magnificent dragon. It seems much has happened since I've been gone. So, please, ask me a question. I can sense something deep is on your heart."

"It was Brenwar who freed you, not me," Nath said, eyeing his friend. "Answer a question of him."

Lotuus chuckled. Her laugh was as light as feathers. "Oh, no, no, no. It was your touch, not his, that lifted the seal from me. You are magical, Nath Dragon. You are power without end. It was you who freed me. Not him."

"And you can tell me anything I want to know?" Nath withheld the suspicion from his tone.

She nodded.

He didn't want to insult her, but he doubted she could tell him the answer to any question. He didn't even think his father could do that. Hm. Come to think of it, his father had long ago told Nath there was a spirit world that couldn't be trusted.

Balzurth had said, "Be wary of their tricks. Seek wisdom, not shortcuts. The key to knowledge comes from the paths less taken."

Lotuus seemed harmless enough, though. What harm could come from playing her game? Nath thought he had nothing to lose and only something to gain. At least this was entertaining. She was so marvelous and pretty.

"Give me a moment," Nath said, putting his clawed paw to his huge dragon forehead to indicate he was thinking of a question.

CHAPTER
10

L OTUUS HUFFED.

Brenwar scowled. "Nath. Come."

Nath walked his monstrous frame over. "What is it?"

"I smell treachery." Noticing Lotuus spying on them, Brenwar turned his back to her. "Maybe she was imprisoned for the right reasons."

"Maybe she was imprisoned for the wrong reasons."

"I can sense your doubt," Lotuus said. "As the Fairy Empress, I find it a bit degrading. I tell you what. I'll let the dwarf have a question and you as well. After all, how hard can a dwarf's question be to answer?" She floated closer and stared down at Brenwar. "I bet I can guess your question myself. Let's see. Aha! You want to ask which ingredients make the best ale!"

Brenwar shuffled back. His expression was priceless. "No I don't. No I don't."

"Come on, dwarf, then ask me something," she said.

"All right, fine then. Where is Nath's mother?"

Nath's heart pounded in his horns.

"Oh, that's easy," Lotuus said, drifting back down to the ground. "She's in Nalzambor, of course."

Brenwar slapped his face with his bony hand. "Gah! Sorry, Nath!"

Nath's excitement deflated. His swaying tail came to a stop. "Way to go, Brenwar."

"She could've answered more than that," Brenwar whined. "She's a clever one, she is. They all are. I say don't waste your breath, Nath. She doesn't know where your mother is."

Feet barely touching the ground, Lotuus walked through the forest and sat down in a small bed of flowers. She plucked a purple flower and gave it a sniff. "Any second now."

Be smart, Nath. She might be the Fairy Empress, but you're the King Dragon.

He started to weigh the pros and cons of his question. Perhaps asking where his mother was would be a selfish question. Maybe there was something more important that he should ask, such as "What or who is the greatest threat to Nalzambor?"

That wouldn't be a bad one. I could just take them out now, before they expected it.

Nath reflected on what his father had told him about his mother again: "What you seek is in the peaks." He glanced over at Brenwar.

The grumpy fighter slowly shook his head.

Just because you blew it the first time, that doesn't mean I'll blow it the second time. Besides, we've been searching for a year. This is the best opportunity we've had. Just don't waste it, Dragon. Ask your question carefully.

He cleared his throat.

Lotuus looked up at him. "So, the King Dragon, ha-hah, is ready to ask the question." She rolled her eyes. "Oh, how I can't wait to hear it."

"I am ready," Nath said in a strong and confident voice. He lowered his massive horned head and came face to face with her. "Are you ready?"

Lotuus's black pupils enlarged. "Oh, certainly." She rose to her feet and shuffled back in the flower bed. "My ears are to hear. My lips to assist. It would be an honor, King Dragon. Please, go ahead."

Nath fanned out his huge claws and studied them with admiration. Each claw was about as big as Lotuus. He caught her eyes on his paw. He saw her swallow and drift back a little farther. "Come closer, Lotuus," he said.

"Uh, why?"

"I want to make sure you can hear me. I wouldn't want my question to be misinterpreted." He opened up his paw and lowered it to the ground. "Hop on."

"My hearing is excellent. I'm fine right here."

Nath took in a deep breath. The furnace inside his chest started to glow. He put a little thunder in his voice. "Hop on!"

Head down, Lotuus floated over, saying, "Yes, Majestic Majesty."

Nath raised her up to eye level and said, "I like the sound of that. Now, I think you were about to reanswer my companion's question. A lot more specifically."

"I was?" Lotuus said.

Nath's eyes narrowed. His claws started to close around her. "I'm certain of it."

She made a pleading look toward Brenwar.

His stern expression was the same as a petrified stump.

"Southern Nalzambor?"

"That's awfully vague," Nath said, closing his claws around her even more. "Perhaps a landmark to go with it."

Eyeing the claws that had closed around her like a cage, she said to Nath, "Am I being threatened?"

"No, you're being protected," Nath said with deadly reassurance. "Very dangerous creatures lurk about. And I'd hate to see anything happen to you, Fairy Empress."

"I see. And I thank you, but I am quite capable of taking care of myself." She placed her hands on his claws. "And I doubt any hostile forces would dare threaten me with you around."

Nath's dragon lip curled back. Not by his own will but rather as a reaction.

There was magic power in Lotuus's touch. Formidable. Mysterious. It was said the fairies and dragons were the earliest creatures in Nalzambor. Both came long before the other races. And Lotuus was much older than he was.

But he was a dragon and she was just a fairy. He turned up his inferno within.

Lotuus's hands jerked back, and she winced. "Borgash," she said.

"I beg your pardon," Nath said, "I didn't quite hear that."

"The lost city of Borgash. What you seek is in there." Shoulders slumped, she said, "May I go now? I long to see my kin."

"You've answered his question, but you have not answered mine," Nath said.

"But," Lotuus stammered.

"But," Nath said, raising a brow. "If you agree, then I'll hold my question for you to answer when I summon you later. Agreed?"

Her little body stiffened. Finally, with a scowl she said, "Agreed."

Nath opened up his claws. "Be well on your journey."

Lotuus spread out her transparent wings and said with a sneer, "Good luck staying well on yours." Her wings buzzed, and up into the air she went, disappearing into the sunlight.

"Clever," Brenwar said, toting Mortuun over his shoulder. "I hadn't seen that side of you before."

"You don't think I crossed the line, do you?"

"With a fairy? Har! There is no such line with them. I think you did well. And she still owes you one. I bet she hates that."

I bet she hates me, too.

CHAPTER 11

"**H**OW ABOUT WE GET YOU a horse, Brenwar?"

"No."

"Aw." Nath shook his head. He'd spent the last three days slugging through the lands with Brenwar in tow. He could have flown back and forth to Borgash ten times by now. Easy. "Well, you can't blame me for being eager. If you'd never met your mother, wouldn't you be anxious to get on with it, too?"

"Sire, er, I mean Nath…" Brenwar stopped along the edge of the stream and began refilling his canteen. "Don't put your faith in fairies. Trust in what you know and see."

"Are you saying since I haven't seen my mother, I shouldn't believe she's there?" He dipped his head in the cool waters and gulped in some water and a few small fish. "I've heard of many things that I've never seen, yet I still trust that they exist."

"That's not what I mean." Brenwar put the canteen to his lips, gulped down the water, and started refilling it again. "Just enjoy the journey. Like you used to. Sometimes there are clues along the way. You might have great eyes, but you still can't see everything from up there."

"I think it's best that I maintain a low profile. I can't exactly pass through forests like a cat anymore."

"You could if you'd change," Brenwar argued. "Pah! Forget it. Tell you what, if you want to go on forward as fast as you can, then go ahead. I'll catch up. Eventually."

"No," Nath said, wading into the stream. It was almost deep enough in the middle to cover his entire body. "Hmm, maybe this is a good way to travel."

"Humph."

Nath pushed up the stream. Brenwar followed along on the bank.

I do want to hurry on ahead, but I won't. I've learned my lesson.

Nath certainly had the authority to get Brenwar to do whatever he wanted, but he wouldn't use it. For one thing, Brenwar wasn't a dragon, so he didn't really have to listen to the Dragon King. But the dwarf had given an oath to serve Balzurth, and that oath had been passed on to Nath. And at the same time, Nath felt obligated to keep an eye on Brenwar. The dwarf had a noticeable hitch in his step that hadn't been there before Nath's last long sleep. Brenwar's pace was almost a half step slower than it used to be. The dwarf, though just as formidable as any that lived, was so much more fragile than Nath.

"What are you staring at?" Brenwar said, glaring at Nath.

"Oh, was I staring? Sorry, Brenwar. I was just admiring your hand. I think your kin will glorify it."

Brenwar's shoulders lifted. He held his hand high and gazed at it. "It is something. Ha! I can't wait to show them. I bet they start a statue of me right away."

"I agree." Nath had a thought. "You know Brenwar, Morgdon isn't so far away. Why not stop by for a visit? You haven't even been home since Gorn Grattack has fallen. For all you know, they have a statue of you already. It wouldn't surprise me a bit if Pilpin jumped right on it."

Brenwar came to a stop on the bank. His boots sank a little in the sands. Hard eyes fixed on Nath's, he said, "What are you getting at?"

"Nothing. I just thought maybe you, or we, should celebrate, before we dive too deep into other things."

A swarm of pink-feathered swans swam by and honked at Nath.

Haaaank! Hank hank hank!

"I'm certain what we're about to get into will be treacherous. You had one really close call already."

Brenwar's eyes narrowed into slits. His good hand became white knuckled on Mortuun's shaft. "You're coddling me."

"No, never."

"You are!" Brenwar set his shoulders and marched away from the stream and back into the woods.

Under his breath, Nath said, "Well, maybe I was." He eased his way out of the stream and spread his wings. He yelled after Brenwar, "Well, I could use some fresh air anyway." After gathering his legs underneath him, he launched himself into the air. In seconds he was hundreds of feet up and soaring like a big scaly bird. "That's better."

Below, he couldn't see Brenwar, but he knew the dwarf's scent all too well.

He was never hard to find, and Brenwar never tried to hide from anybody, either.

Nath spent hours up, traveling miles at a time, back and forth. He scanned the horizon and the landscape, too. He was very in tune with Nalzambor. More so than he used to be. His intuition was incredible. His senses were so acute he could tune into activity inside an ant hill.

Ah, it's great to be me.

He widened his circle, staying just within the belly of the clouds. He didn't want to terrify any townsfolk or farmers. They'd been through plenty, thanks to the likes of the armies of Barnabus. They were just getting their lives in order. Nath was privy to that. He could hear their hammers pounding. Saws cutting through the fallen timbers.

And stew was cooking somewhere always, not to mention the buttery biscuits. His mouth watered. Drool fell from his lips.

Now that, I do miss. I wish someone could make biscuits big enough for me. And it wouldn't be so bad gulping down a river full of stew sometime. I have to hand it to humans: they make the finest dishes.

A glimmer of movement caught his eye. A dark wink. A nasty twinkle. A small flock beat their wings nearby in a V formation. Thirteen of them.

Those aren't birds. Birds aren't that big, and they don't have tails like that!

Nath flapped his wings harder.

They have scales. Not the likes of which I've ever seen before, either. Great Guzan! What are they?

Closing in, Nath let out a squawk.

HrrAWk!

The dragon in the rear, the size of a long-tailed pony, turned its head. It was flat like a snake's, hornless, with slanted ruby eyes that glimmered with hate. It opened up its mouth and let out an angry hiss.

Hhussssssssss!

A pair of forked tongues snapped in and out of its mouth. It turned away and squawked up to the others.

Hrawk.

I don't understand what it's saying.

One by one, the other dragon heads turned and stared at Nath. Their pulsating red eyes bore into him.

Brash, whatever they are.

The dragon in the rear let out another frightening squawk.

Hrawwwwwwk!

In the blink of an eye, they stopped in midair in attack formation. Claws and teeth bared, they made straight for Nath Dragon.

Sultans of Sulfur!

CHAPTER
12

THE WICKED BROOD OF DRAGONS darted straight into Nath's path.

He spat out a ball of fire.

The lead dragon veered right.

Half of the ranks followed.

The other section of the formation went left.

The fireball sailed in between.

They're quick!

Screeching, the dragon brood flanked Nath and started to close in.

Let's see how fast they really are.

Nath pointed his head toward the earth, pumped his wings, and dove. He cut through the air, a scaly knife in the sky, reaching amazing speeds. Folding his wings behind his back, he dove faster. The wind whistled between his horns, making an eerie howl.

Eoo oo oo oo oo

I'm fast. I like it!

Daring not to glance behind him, Nath focused on the ground rushing up to greet him. He aimed his body like a giant missile toward the rocky hilltops, where the hill goats began to scatter.

Get it right, Nath, or you'll be dragon goo.

Chin out and horns back, he watched certain death coming to greet him. Jagged rocks waited like a mouthful of broken teeth, enlarging in an instant.

Now!

He spread his wings and pulled up, straining with all his might. Rocks scraped over his belly and tail.

Made it!

Soaring away, he glanced back over his wings. Three of the dragon brood had slammed into the hillside. Rock and debris exploded.

Boom! Boom! Boom!

Nath found the other dragons hovering nearby in the sky. Their eyes were full of malice. They let out angry shrieks, and their mouths glowed like red-hot flames.

Beating his wings, Nath hovered in the sky, looking down on all of them. "I don't know what you are or where you came from, but wherever that was, I'm going to make you wish you had never left." He unleashed a geyser of fire. It streamed out of his mouth and exploded, coating some of the smaller dragons in white-hot flames.

Their pain-filled screeches could have shattered glass as they writhed in the sky.

Eeeak! Eak Eaak Eeeeaaaaaak!

"That's only a sample of what I have in store for—Agh!"

From out of nowhere, razor-sharp talons dug into his back. A knot of four dragons latched onto him like leeches. Fangs bit into Nath's hard scales. Liquid fire dripped like venom from their mouths, causing him excruciating pain.

Nath let out a tremendous roar.

"RAWR!"

And then he turned loose his own assault. The end of his tail coiled around one dragon's neck and ripped it free of him. Using it like a club, he started swatting away at the others.

Whop! Whop! Whop!

He knocked one more off his legs, but two more latched on. Wings beating with fury, Nath fought to keep up in the air.

Rising higher, two more dragons darted in and attacked his wings.

Nath lost control and tumbled through the sky. Battling for his life, he hit the hillside hard.

Whoom!

"Enough of this!" Nath yelled in Dragonese. Eyes hot with fire, he unleashed his vision heat on the first dragon he saw. The beams of light turned the creature's dark armored scales to ash, leaving only a pile of bones. Ignoring the burning sensation of claws and teeth digging into him, he reared back his head and struck like a snake. His jaws clamped around another dragon's neck. With tremendous force, he bit down and broke its neck.

The dragon brood went into a frenzy. They struck and bit. Spat out small geysers of flame. They latched onto Nath's chest and coiled their tails around his great neck.

Unrelenting, Nath and the brood thrashed through the hill. Trees snapped under their weight. The branches caught fire.

Nath stomped one dragon's face in the dirt.

Another dragon spat hot flames in Nath's eye.

Nath snatched it by the neck and with his breath, he turned its head to ashes. He huffed for breath. The strain of battle was starting to take a toll on him. His inner flame was going dim.

Don't these things give up or tire? I've already killed six of them!

The evil throng battled on. Their teeth and claws were tiny razors digging deep in between his scales. They were merciless, and Nath was covered in them.

He bit one's tail and slung it off his back.

Another dragon whipped his eye with its tail.

"Argh!"

Nath made it pay. He slammed it into the ground and pulverized it under his paws.

Back and forth they battled, the dragon versus the drag-ons.

Nath matched their savagery with his own. They were strong and quick. He was stronger and quicker. But their numbers gave them the advantage. They stayed latched onto his arms. His legs. His wings. They started taking him apart a tiny piece at a time. Their fiery venom crept in between his scales and into his flesh.

Nath unloaded one more blast of fire, vaporizing two more of them.

Eight down! At least I think so.

His great strength had faded. He felt drained. His sight started to dim.

This can't be happening to me. I'm the King Dragon.

CHAPTER 13

FIGHTING TO STAY AWAKE, NATH's mind went through his known cache of abilities, but it was sluggish. Even the pain had begun to subside.

I have to get these things off of me before they drag me off somewhere. Or eat me!

He pushed up off the ground and belly-rolled over, crushing one of them underneath his girth. Still, his limbs became heavy. He flailed his tail but couldn't get a sense of where it was going. A dark shadow fell over them.

"Screeeeeech!" the dragon brood cried out in unison.

Guzan! What now?

Through blurry eyes, Nath saw a black-winged bulk drop out of the sky. It landed hard on the ground.

Oh no! They come in bigger sizes!

It closed in on Nath.

With tremendous strain and effort, he closed in on it.

One of the smaller dragons darted in between them and shot out some fiery breath.

The bigger dragon swatted it away with its tail and began pummeling it into the dirt.

Wap! Wap! Wap!

The bigger dragon finished it off with a blast of scorching fire.

"Huh?" Nath said, barely able to keep his eyes open.

The big black dragon's head whipped around just in time to confront another small attacking dragon. With its breath, it turned the little serpent into dust. Then the huge black dragon spoke to Nath in Dragonese. "Get up and fight, Lazy Bones!"

Nath's head perked up. His dragon heart began to race. "Selene?"

The big black dragon ripped a smaller one off his hide, smashed its bones into the ground, and said, "Do I really need to answer that?"

Charged up with renewed energy, Nath tore another small dragon away from his arm with his tail. He bashed it into the rocks until it moved no more.

Selene continued to rip them off of him and then crush them with her mighty paws or use her breath weapon and turn them into pixie dust.

In less than a minute, all the hostile dragons were dead.

"Gather them in a pile," she said.

"Why?" Nath said, shaking out the cobwebs inside his head.

Sarcastically she said, "Oh mighty King Dragon, will you please just do as I say." With her mouth she dragged one across the ground and into another, starting the pile. "And don't miss any."

Wary, Nath did as she asked. Strange dead dragons were piled up before them. "So, now what?"

Selene opened up her great mouth and covered them in flame.

The pile burned and popped. Nath fought the urge to cover his nose. The stench watered his eyes. The dragons burned—scales, horns, bones, and all—until there was nothing but ash left.

Finally, he said, "What did you do that for? Now I'll never know what they are."

"You almost weren't going to know anything else ever again, King Dragon."

Nath approached her with a smile.

Covered in black scales with a long, sensuous tail, Selene was the most beautiful dragon he'd ever seen. Her lashed violet eyes were radiant beneath her exquisite crown of horns, streaked with silver.

Heart pounding inside his chest, he said, "Thanks, Selene. It's good to see you. I didn't think you could stay away from me forever anyway."

"Hah!" she laughed. "Me, seeking you? Nothing could be further from my quest."

He frowned. "Quest? What do you mean, quest?"

Selene's violet eyes drifted onto the pile of ash. "Tracking down these vermin and killing them."

Irritated, Nath fixed his eyes on her. "So you know what they are, then?"

"Sadly," she said, neck drooping a little. "I do. They are called wurmers."

"Wurmers? What tongue is that?"

Without batting an eye, she said, "An ancient one. Long forgotten until … sometime around now."

Nath spread out his wings and winced. Turning his head around, he noticed one of his wings was dangling. "Blast!"

Selene's eyes widened. "That's a horrible wound. You should be more careful."

"Thanks, Selene. I'll remember that the next time I'm assaulted by a bunch of renegade dragons." He snorted. "Don't guess I'll be flying anywhere too soon. It should make Brenwar happy." He focused his attention on Selene. "You were saying these things had been long forgotten until sometime around now. So you knew of them?"

Sitting back on her haunches and clicking her clawed front paws together, she said, "Let's just say I've encountered them before."

Nath's eyes narrowed. "Is this something that Gorn Grattack had a hand in? That you had a hand in?"

"Yes and no."

"That's not an answer, Selene. And I don't like it. What do you know about these creatures? And how in Nalzambor did they get here?" He brushed his tail through their remains. "And is it bad that I killed them?"

"Don't fret, Nath," she said. "The wurmers are more dragon-like than dragon. They aren't flesh and blood like other life on Nalzambor. That I'm certain of."

Nath eased his tone. "Well, that helps a little. Keep talking." He half flapped his broken wing. "I'm not going anywhere soon."

"The wurmers are a creation of other evil mages and clerics who preceded Barnabus. They hated dragons, and through their collective efforts they created a creature to slay dragons. They used dragon parts and magic and turned them into bloodless, living things, like insects."

"Oh, I see," Nath said. "Isn't that pretty much what you did with the draykis? How many of them are still running around?"

"I'm pretty sure there aren't any."

"Pretty sure, well," Nath said, rolling his eyes, "that's reassuring."

"Don't be smug."

"I'm sorry, Selene, but this stinks of your old dealings, and let's face it. You haven't been around. There's no telling what you've been doing or who you've been doing it with."

Selene's eyes became bright as fire. "Nath! How dare you suggest?"

"I'm the Dragon King, and I'll suggest what I will. I have an entire world to protect."

"Well, you weren't doing a very good job of it a few moments ago—unless you were going to protect it as new fertilizer!" She spread her wings. "Good luck to you. I'll resume this quest on my own." Her feet started to lift from the ground.

CHAPTER 14

N ATH SNATCHED HER TAIL AND pulled her back down. Calmly. "You aren't going anywhere, Selene. Sorry. Just tell me more."

The flames behind her eyes subsided, and she continued her story.

"Yes, the Clerics of Barnabus sought to employ the wurmers in our cause, but dealing with them proved difficult." She sighed. "Very difficult."

"How so?" Nath said, brushing his tail against hers.

"They're mindless things that don't discriminate. They'd attack any dragon, good or bad. Both Kryzak and I tried to find ways to control them, but everything failed. I even have some scars to show for it." She ran her claws over her side. There were some gashes in her scales that had never fully healed. "Kryzak actually saved me. After that, I came up with the draykis. They were my creation. I could control them. But the wurmers, they come from another time. A different magic. I told Kryzak to destroy them. Their larva. Their nests. I was very disappointed when I found out that he didn't."

Nath reached over his shoulder and plucked a torn wurmer claw out from between his scales. Eyeing it, he said, "They are nasty things. How many have you hunted down?"

"Thousands."

Unable to contain his surprise, Nath said, "Thousands!"

"Give or take a few hundred," she added.

"You should have sought me out, Selene. How many of these things do you think are out there?" He stomped his paw into the ground. "And being the King Dragon, I need to be informed of any dire threats to this world."

"Don't stiffen on me, Nath. If you were so worried about any threats, you'd be back at Dragon Home. Instead, you are on a personal quest—which," she said, eyes saddening a little, "I don't blame you for."

"Regardless, Selene, you should tell me, especially when you are putting yourself in danger." His tail glided up around her shoulders. "I wouldn't want anything bad to happen to you."

Her eyes drifted down over his tail and then found his. "Really? And why is that?"

Nath swallowed. Nothing in Nalzambor intimidated Nath, but Selene did. Not as a threat but as a woman. A grand one. And his attraction to her was powerful. But he didn't know how to tell her that. "Because ... you're my friend."

Selene's eyes drifted away, and she let out a huff of smoke. She walked out from underneath his tail. "Oh, I'm elated to know that. And as for the wurmers, the amount I've destroyed isn't so big. As a matter of fact, these are the biggest I've seen." Her brow creased. "I've mostly found unhatched nests. You see, the wurmers start out in a larva stage. Much like insects. I find them and destroy them."

"How many more do you think are left?"

"Hard to tell. I found one of the original lairs, but I think there are many more. Especially after seeing a group as big as this flying around." She swatted her tail through the charred remains. "But these are drones. Which is good. The females lay the eggs. One female, rather. Perhaps a queen for every nest."

"So they are like the bees?"

"No. Bees produce honey; wurmers produce death." She continued, "Nath, now that the Clerics of Barnabus no longer hunt them, the wurmers will multiply fast. If they get out of control, they'll swarm all of Nalzambor like locusts. Nothing will remain."

Nath tried to get close again, but Selene shifted away. Aggravated, he said, "If it's so serious, you should take some other dragons with you, then."

"It's my responsibility. I'll handle it on my own."

"I insist," Nath said.

"I still have allies aside from yourself," she said.

"Really, who?"

"You focus on your mission, and I'll focus on mine," she said. "And I wish you well on your quest to find your mother."

"Selene, don't rush off. Please. You just got here."

"The wurmers are serious business, Nath."

"Just for a little while. Please?" he said, forming a long face. "All I've been doing is traveling with Brenwar, and it's not the same ... as it used to be. It's hard being a dragon when all your friends are mortal."

"That's why dragons don't get so close to the mortals. But you'll get used to it."

"I'm not sure that I want to get used to it."

"You can't have the best of both worlds. You are meant to rule the dragons, not the other races as well. They'll be just fine without you, Nath."

"I suppose."

"And if you spent more time among your kind, I'm certain you'd be enlightened." She ran her tail under his chin. Her eyes smiled into his. "But I envy you, Nath. You understand what it's like to be both man and dragon. And you have true friends among all the races. Consider it a precious gift. It will give you wisdom that others have never had."

"If you say so." He flexed his bad wing again. "Honestly, please stick around. Not being able to fly is going to be hard enough. And I'm never going to hear the end of this from Brenwar."

"You're such a child sometimes," Selene said, "but lucky for you I like it. So I'll come along, but only for a bit."

Yes! Pulling his shoulders back and heading back down over the hillside with a bounce in his step, Nath said, "Well, come on, then."

On foot it took a few hours to get back to the general area where he'd last seen Brenwar. Putting his nose to the dirt, it wasn't long before Nath found his oldest friend's scent. "It won't be long now." But an hour later, Nath lost the scent. A sinking feeling crept into him. "Selene, do you smell anything?"

She shook her head. "I sense nothing."

CHAPTER
15

THE VANISHING OF BRENWAR MADE for a long day—and days were usually nothing to a dragon. Nath ripped another tree out of the ground and flung it away.

"Nath," Selene said, "You can't check underneath everything. Least of all the roots beneath the trees. I'm certain there's a reasonable explanation for it." She stroked his back with her tail. "Take a breath and let things come to you."

Nath pushed some moss-covered boulders aside. Worms and insects scurried deep into the dirt. "Ah!" He rolled the rocks back into place. "Blast!"

"Nath, we will find him," Selene said, being reassuring. "I'm certain of it."

He wanted to agree with her, he really did, but Brenwar's disappearance left him feeling empty inside. Guilt swelled inside him. He couldn't bear the thought of losing his friend again. After all, Brenwar had almost died once already. Looking at Selene, a thought occurred to him. He couldn't help but let it out. With wary eyes he said, "It's been a strange series of circumstances."

Selene sat back on her haunches, crushing the brush underneath her tail. "What do you mean?"

"Well, let me put it together for you. I get a clue about where to find my mother. Not long after that, the wurmers show up, followed by the sudden appearance of you, and now Brenwar disappears."

Selene's dragon face darkened. "Are you suggesting I had something to do with this?"

"A wise king wouldn't rule out the possibility."

"A wise king wouldn't insult his friends!" she fired back.

"Oh yes, a friend who created the draykis, who was willing to let loose the wurmers on dragonkind." He shook his head. "Huh. Not to mention that you don't want any help. Look, Selene, you have to admit, is that not the least bit suspicious?"

She leaned toward him and said with her razor-sharp claws extended, "I ought to rip your tongue out. I just saved your life, you fool."

"Fool!"

Nose to nose, she added, "Do I need to say it in the seven languages to you?"

He bared his teeth. "You do not speak to me that way!"

"And you shouldn't speak to anyone that way."

"Hah! Like you care! This, coming from someone who killed if someone batted an eyelash at you. And you dare to judge me?"

Air rife with tension, Selene cut loose. Her tail lashed out, smiting Nath across his cheek.

Whap!

Nath shook it off. His eyes blazed with fury. He rose up to his full height, towering over her. "Why did you do that?"

"Because if you unleashed one more insult like that, I was going to try and kill you."

"Really?" Nath growled.

"Really!" Selene said, bumping her horns against his.

Clack!

Nath's temper boiled over.

Somewhere deep inside him, his conscience said, *Nath, what are you getting so mad for?*

He couldn't control it, though. His inner volcano was erupting. The fires in his chest wanted to explode. "You better get out of here, Selene. I think I've had enough of you."

Taken aback, she scooted away. There was hurt in her eyes. She spread her wings. "Fine. Fine, then, Nath. Good-bye." In one powerful flap, she took to the sky.

Nath clutched the horns on his head. *What am I doing?* "No, wait! Selene, come back!"

She was little more than a speck in the sky now. An ash drifting away.

He spread his own wings and cried out in pain. "Ow! Blast my busted wing!"

Hours later, Nath had made his way deep down inside a ravine. He'd pushed himself far into the brush overhanging the creek. His temper had long cooled, and now he hid from the world with a belly full of regret.

What in the world got into me? That was no way for a king to behave. Selene was right about that.

Sulking, he raced through the scenarios on how to make things right.

How am I supposed to apologize to someone who will probably never want to see me again? I can't fly. I've lost Brenwar. Now that's two people I have to find. Him and my mother. Not to mention there is another threat to Nalzambor. What do I do?

He closed his eyes and let it all soak in. Everything had happened at once. A sudden storm. A turn of the tide. At the moment, missing Brenwar hurt even more than losing Selene. Brenwar was his rock. The dwarf would have something to say that Nath needed to hear. But hadn't Selene?

Aw, I mess everything up.

Things were different than before now that he was a dragon. He was still getting used to it. He needed to focus on the best way to find Brenwar first. Another part of him wanted to be with Selene.

Think, Dragon, think!

He recalled a conversation that he'd had a long time ago, before he and Bayzog had parted. The part-elven wizard had given him some advice. "When in doubt, ask yourself what your father would do."

Yes, what would my father do?

He envisioned Balzurth's mightier red dragon frame sitting on the throne within the great treasure chamber. His father's eyes were often closed, but he was always aware of everything around him. Not even a mouse escaped his attention.

Come on, Nath, you're the greatest tracker in all the lands. At least you used to be. Think of your father. Think of something. How hard can it be to find Brenwar?

He thought back to when he was much younger. Back when he spent more time with his father. It was just the two of them most of the time: hunting, fishing, and feasting together. Both of them would lie down with a bellyful and count the stars in the sky.

But every once in a while, another dragon would come by and share news with Balzurth, speaking into his father's ear. Balzurth would nod, grunt a little, and send the dragon messenger on its way. Those were good, good times.

Nath's eyes snapped open.

I've got it!

CHAPTER 16

NATH RETURNED TO THE SPOT where he'd lost the scent of Brenwar. There was nothing extraordinary about it. It was just another stretch of woodland and heavy brush.

All right, someone around here must have seen something.

He stretched out his senses. The pulse of life was all around. The birds perched high up in the trees. The vermin that scurried over the ground. The insects that crawled underneath the moss and through the branches within. All Nath had to do was ask them.

Nath opened up his paw and sat it down on the ground. Creating a gentle hum in his voice, he beckoned to all the life that was around. His melody gently massaged the leaves in the trees. Everything that crept or crawled stopped in its path.

Come now, come. Come and help me out. I seek. Help me find.

He kept at it for minutes. There was hesitation. Fear. Curiosity. Not one creature came forward. Nath continued, however. Even though he was a friendly force, he still looked like a giant predator—for dragons fed on all kinds of things. The world was their buffet. Some ate bugs, others fish of the waters and the fowl of the air. Some dragons only ate the flowers and leaves.

Come, Nath beckoned. *Come.*

Nothing came.

Blast!

Nath sat down, shaking his head. He didn't have anyone left to help him. No friends in sight, and he couldn't blame them. He'd run Selene off. He'd acted like a lousy king, and even the creatures of the forest knew that. He'd lost all credibility.

I'm a sad excuse for a Dragon King. And I thought things would be easy once I was a dragon. Out of the corner of his eye he caught some movement. *What's this?*

A raccoon approached, head low. It was a big one, bushy, with chestnut brown spots and rings instead of black. It stopped short of Nath's paw.

Nath hummed out a welcoming sound.

The raccoon lifted its head.

Now came the tricky part. Animals and insects couldn't speak, but they had their ways of communicating. Nath summoned his magic and released a spell. He had several he could recall that he'd learned when he was younger and walked the lands more. Speaking with animals was one of them, and it had helped him rescue many dragons.

"How are you?" he said in words the raccoon could understand.

It spoke back. "I am well, Mighty Dragon. How may I assist?"

"What is your name, little friend?"

"I'm called the Ringed Goose by my family," it said.

"I lost a friend, a dwarf. Bones for a hand and black bearded. Have you seen him?"

"Yes," the raccoon said. "He was here yesterday. He marched through and then was taken."

"Taken by what or who?"

Tiny clawed hands together, the raccoon looked back over his shoulders. "I'm scared to say for fear that me and my family might be eaten."

"I won't let that happen," Nath said. "Please, help me. He's my dear friend, and he means as much to me as your family to you."

The raccoon nodded. "A black, black dragon dropped from the sky and took him."

No! Not Selene!

"Can you describe this dragon in better detail? Did it have blood-red eyes and rough, dark scales, perhaps?"

"The scales were such as yours," the raccoon said.

"Did it have horns on its head?"

"The raccoon rubbed its chin. "Yes, I think so."

Nath's heart dipped. "Now think hard on this. Did you see the dragon's eyes?"

"Oh, most definitely, they were the prettiest and deadliest violet I ever saw."

Head filled with troubles, Nath burrowed his way into a nearby mountainside and blended in with his surroundings. The raccoon's news was deeply disturbing. Selene had betrayed him once again, it seemed.

After all we have been through, she's turned on me? Why?

His heart ached.

And why take Brenwar? She wouldn't kill him, would she?

Of course, if anyone wasn't as blind as Nath, it was Brenwar. Nath cared deeply for Selene, Brenwar not so much. He wasn't a very forgiving sort. And if the seasoned soldier suspected something, he wouldn't hesitate to let Nath know about it.

I can't believe this is happening. And it couldn't be more perfect. Here I am grounded with a busted wing.

He curled deeper into his spot. Mind filled with doubt, he ran over countless scenarios. Did Selene want his throne? Did Gorn Grattack still live? Was she trying to prevent him from finding his mother?

It seems my suspicions were right all along. That Selene. She's such an actress. I should have known better. Fine, I'll wait it out, Selene. My wing will heal soon enough, and then I'm going to hunt you down like a draykis.

Burrowed deep in the earth, he settled in and used his energy to heal up. All around him the plant life perked up, starting with new growth. Hours went by that turned into days. Before long he was covered in the brush and flowers. The varmints of the forest didn't notice him. The birds started to nest. The smaller creatures burrowed. Life traveled all around him and over the top of him. He was part of the mountain now. Many dragons did that.

He opened his eye.

His wing no longer hurt.

That ought to do it.

Red birds with long white tails were chirping in the thicket that covered his eyes. The sweet music turned to a squawk as Nath shifted his bulk, loosening the dirt. The wildlife that covered him scattered.

Sorry.

With a heave, he pushed his way out of his burrow and shook off the leaves and foliage. He pressed his way through the forest until he found a clearing. He stretched out his wings.

Ah! That's much better! Here I come, Selene.

CHAPTER 17

LYING HIGH, NATH SET OFF in the direction Selene had been flying. She'd be hard to find if she wanted to be. She could transform, become big or small like he could. But her scent would linger. He had that to go on.

You won't escape me, Selene. I won't let you get away with this.

Of course, for all he knew, he might be playing right into her hands. A trap might spring. After all, she'd had plenty of time to set it. He wouldn't be one bit surprised if she'd left him a clue of some sort.

He dashed in and out of clouds filled with lightning and rain. He swooped over the land and his belly grazed the ground. There was plenty of ground to cover, but he sensed she was near. And he figured chances were that if he could find some of those wurmers, then he'd be about to find her as well.

Rising back into the air, he noticed a broken form unmoving down in the valley. There, a dragon lay still. He was citrine yellow with a red stripe across his back. Little bigger than a pony, the yellow streak dragon was dragging his belly through the sloppy rain with his head hung low.

Nath dropped out of the sky and down in front of him. "What happened, brother?"

"They're dead," the yellow streak said in a ragged form of Dragonese. His body had deep cuts in it, and some of his scales were missing. "All dead. I couldn't save them. I'm sorry, Nathlalonggram …agh." He collapsed on the ground.

"No!" Nath cried out in alarm. The dragon's heartbeat was quickly fading. Nath scooped him up in his arms. The yellow streak's life was gone.

Chest puffed out, Nath picked up the dragon's trail. The rains were washing it away in the mud, but Nath's keen eyes still picked it up. He followed the tall grasses that were matted down. The dragon's path wound through a valley, and Nath found bits of blood along the way. His nostrils flared.

That doesn't smell good.

He pressed on. Up ahead, a small plume of smoke twirled in the rain. Patches of fire were burning the trees.

Oh no!

Dragons were scattered all over the ground, yellow streaks, a large family. Their bodies lay still, their scale hides ripped and torn. Wings broken. Teeth and horns busted. The battle must have been fierce.

Nath stopped short of the battleground and scooped up a small dragon that didn't even fill his hand. She was so young and beautiful. Her neck was broken. Nath's eyes watered.

Lightning streaked across the sky and thunder cracked.

He let out a roar.

"Maaaaaarrrooooooooo!"

Someone is going to pay for this!

He stepped in a pile of ashes that had begun mixing in with the mud. It was familiar. Scraping some of the goo up onto his finger, he eyed it closely and gave it a sniff.

It's from a wurmer. Hah, seems the yellow streaks put up a fine fight and took some of these dark fiends with them.

He picked his way through the carnage. There were scales and teeth he hadn't noticed before. He sifted through them with his hand, feeling the texture and absorbing the scent into his scales. The wurmers couldn't be far away. It wouldn't be hard to find them now.

And once he found them, he'd find Selene.

Selene has a lot of explaining to do.

One by one, he picked up the fallen dragons and laid them down side by side. He even returned and brought back the first one he'd encountered. There were seven in all. The father went first, being the biggest, and the mother, going down to the sons and daughters being the smallest. With a heart full of sadness, Nath dug into the soft dirt. His powerful hands scooped out the dirt and rock and pushed it aside, and the first grave was made.

This hurts.

He had thought these days were done. That there would be peace on Nalzambor for a long time. He slung a pile of mud aside.

This shouldn't be happening! Why can't everyone and everything behave themselves?

He kept digging, taking his time about it. And he started singing, a sad and ancient tune. It was one he had learned from his father when he was a boy. The other dragons used to sing it as well. It was about the first dragons who had fallen during the first dragon war.

Their scales were cherry, the fairest of their kind.

They drank deep of the waters and flew high in the air.

Fire came. Lightning struck. They tumbled through the sky.

It was the end of the crimson dynamos and the beginning of Nalzambor's despair.

There were hundreds of segments to the song, but Nath only made it as far as fifty. He'd finished his work, laid his kin in the graves one by one, and started covering them in dirt.

When he lifted his sagging head, a change in his surroundings caught his eye. He was encircled by the creatures of the wild. Mighty elks with curled horns. Chipmunks and rabbits with tiny bright fairies riding on their backs. There were owls in the branches. An old and aging centaur woman too. The woodland creatures closed in and began pushing the dirt into the graves as well. Beavers and pixies. A pair of bears bigger than Brenwar. In moments, the dragon graves were covered and new grasses and flowers were planted.

"Thank you," Nath said to them all.

Quickly they were all gone, leaving Nath alone in the rain.

CHAPTER 18

NATH SCOURED THE AREA FOR leagues. He did it in the air and on the ground. The scent of the wurmers was strong. Flying through the sky, he caught a distant flicker of movement down below. There was a clearing on a hillside. Its peak was covered in rough stone and loose shale. A plume of smoke rose into the air and dissipated.

I'd better check that out.

Wary eyed, he glided down and landed soft as a dove on the ground. The shale squeezed up between his clawed toes. He spied a faint series of caves in the light of the dusk. They seemed to breathe with life of their own. Warm yellow smoke oozed out of them. There were no other signs of life nearby.

Could be a lair.

Head low, Nath crept in for a closer look. His nostrils widened as he took in a deep draw of air. The yellow smoke smelled like acid. It was like the Lakes of Sulfur farther south, which had been formed by the lava rivers. They made great places to hide for dragons, who could handle the heat, much more so than men.

But this was different. This was in the forest.

Strange.

He inhaled again. There was more than sulfur or acid. The wurmers' scent was there, mixed in with the pungent cover.

Hah! I have them now!

The tufts behind Nath's earholes fluttered. He could smell them but not see them. The mouths of the caves were too small for his great girth. He climbed behind them, hung his head over the lip, and listened for any sound. There was a roar of wind that whistled through the jagged rocks. Deeper, he could hear something else. In a part of the world deep in its bowels, there was a groaning. Something flowed. Beat. Pulsed.

Nath rubbed his razor-sharp claws under his lip.

Hmmm … can't help but be really curious. Perhaps I should change so I can go down there and check it out. No. Now is the time for patience. He envisioned the broken bodies of the yellow streak dragons. *Soon I'll have vengeance.*

Nath focused on blending in with his environment. His body became one with the natural surroundings. Part of the rock and soil. His thoughts wandered. What if Selene was down there? And Brenwar?

What if it's a trap? Another one of Selene's clever setups?

The hours went by, and darkness fell over the hill. Above, the moon's light was dim in the drifting and dreary clouds.

The caves gave off the faintest illumination. The smell of sulfur remained strong. Nath let his eyes close. He sank his talons deeper into the hard earth. He could feel all of the life of Nalzambor. The heartbeats of the sleeping creatures nearby. The feet of ants marching over the dirt. There was something else too that he felt. Distress. Nalzambor seemed worried.

The hillside suddenly quavered.

Thoom.

It was faint. Undetectable by many creatures of nature. The shale shifted the slightest bit.

Thoom.

Nath's eyelid slid back.

Thoom. Thoom. Thoom.

The bellies of the caves were coming to life. Angry sounds and shrieks erupted from within. Something was coming out.

Thoom! Thoom!

Shale and dirt poured out over the rims of the caves. Creatures who had been lying peacefully in the forest scattered. One of the caves glowed with bright orange light, and the roar of a dragon echoed.

Something fights within!

A slender black dragon snaked out of the hole.

Selene!

She was smaller. More svelte. The scales on her dragon chest were heaving as she backed away from the mouths of the caves.

Nath's claws pulled up out of the dirt.

I've got her now!

Selene snorted fire and smoke. Her long neck swayed from side to side. Her violet eyes were intent on the caves. She continued her retreat.

What's going on here?

One by one, wurmers emerged from the shadows of the caves. Ten of them, claws sharper than swords that twinkled in the night, flanked Selene.

This should be interesting. I'm no fool. I'll just wait and see what she says to them. She probably has them wrapped around her finger like she once had me.

Striking with uncanny speed, the wurmers plowed into Selene. Her body was covered in the scaly fiends. Only her whipping tail could be seen.

Selene!

"Maaaaaaarrrroooooo!"

With a fearsome roar, Nath tore his body out of the rocks and pounced into the fray.

The wurmers let out shrill cries.

With a bone-crushing stomp, Nath silenced several cries. Fully healed now, Nath tore into the wurmers. Fueled by his vengeance for the yellow streaks, he cut loose. Plucking wurmers from Selene like ticks, he pinned them to the ground.

They nipped and clawed at him.

Nath responded in fiercer kind. He took in a lungful of air and blasted them with flames that ended their existence.

"Save your breath!" Selene cried out. There was desperation in her voice. "Save it, Nath!"

"Hah," he said. "Like I should trust you." His tail coiled around a wurmer's neck. He lifted it up and slammed it repeatedly into the ground.

Wham! Wham! Wham!

"Nath!" Selene cried out. "Help me!"

His head reared up.

Four wurmers had latched onto her. Two of them sank their teeth and claws into her neck.

Her violet eyes popped open, filled with pain.

The hot glow of the wurmers' powerful maws ignited with fire. Lava oozed out, down Selene's neck.

She let out a horrifying howl that split the air in the sky.

"Haaaaaaarrrrrrrrllllllllll!"

Nath's scales stood on end.

Selene's supine body went limp, and the light in her eyes faded.

"Noooooooooo!"

CHAPTER 19

NATH'S GOLDEN EYES BURNED LIKE fire. Staring down the wurmers, he unleashed a blast of power from his eye sockets. The rays of light cut through one of the wurmers on Selene's neck, killing it. He let loose on another. Eye beams blasted into it and turned it to ash and powder.

The remaining wurmers detached themselves from Selene and launched into Nath.

Fueled by a desperate sense of urgency, Nath's massive body became a juggernaut of battle. He bit down on one wurmer and crushed it in his jaws. His claws smashed a second one into the ground until its bones became dust.

Die, you scaly vermin! Die!

The third wurmer pounced on Nath's head. Its razor-sharp talons tore at his eyes.

He reached up and grabbed the wurmer and squeezed it between his dragon paws.

A hot stream of fire shot from the wurmer's mouth, covering Nath's face.

"Argh!" Nath roared. "Enough of this!" He crushed it like a beetle in his hands and slung its corpse into the woods. Still tormented by the burning oil, Nath buried his face in the ground. The flames extinguished.

Need to be smarter than that, Dragon.

Shaking his head and slinging off the dirt, he quickly scanned the area. All the wurmers were dead.

A soft, weak, and desperate voice caught his ear.

"Nath." It was Selene. She lay flat on the ground, trying to push herself up. Her neck was sagging. Her chin rested on the ground. "Use your fire."

"On what?" he asked. His eyes narrowed on her. "You?"

"What do you mean?"

"I'm no fool, Selene. I'm certain this is some clever ploy to trap me. Where's Brenwar?"

Irritated, she pushed herself up off the ground. Her neck still drooped, and it had horrible gashes in it. Strength returned to her voice. "You are mad!"

Glancing at her wounds, he replied, "I see you are feeling better."

Selene, smaller and standing beneath him, looked up at him and said, "I can't believe you."

"Don't play games, Selene. Where is Brenwar?"

"I don't know where that bearded man-goat is! If he's lost, then it's your fault, not mine!" She craned her neck and winced. "Now, will you listen to me? We don't have much time!"

There was truth in her voice. Nath felt it. He'd always been able to discern the truth from a lie. But Selene had fooled him before. Still, her neck was in bad shape. Blood seeped between her claws that held it. Finally, he said, "What do you want me to do?"

"That's a wurmer lair," she said, pointing at the caves. "I went in and found the larvae, but the wurmer guardians found me before I could act. The wurmer eggs aren't too deep, but there are hundreds of them. You need to stick your head in there and turn loose the heat. Do you understand me?"

"And turn my back to you?" Nath objected. "I don't think so."

"Dragon King," she said, softening her tone, "you must listen. I'd do it myself, but I've nothing left. I can barely stand."

"Tell me where Brenwar is first."

"What in all of Nalzambor makes you think I have that dwarf?"

"Someone saw you fly away with him," Nath said.

"Someone who?"

"A raccoon."

Selene's jaw dropped. Then, with incredulity, she said, "A raccoon? Are you being serious?"

Taken aback, Nath said, "Yes."

Selene started to laugh. "Ha ha! Please, you are making me laugh! And it hurts. Heh heh! The Dragon King and his raccoon advisor. Haw!" She sucked her teeth. "Oh, it hurts."

"Stop it," Nath said.

"Ha ha! I wish I could," she said, slapping her tail on the ground. "Heh heh heh! But I can't. So, where is this advisor?"

Feeling like a fool, Nath filled his chest up with fire. He glared at her, turned, stuffed his head inside one of the caves, and unleashed his flames. The white-hot blast vaporized everything in its path. Nath let it all out. His anger. Humiliation. Frustration. His fire stopped. He pulled his head out of the hole and found Selene.

She had a wry smile on her face. "Well done, Dragon King. I'll be right back." With a hitch in her gait, she slipped back into one of the caves.

Nath sat down on his haunches. His head was light, and he saw spots in his eyes. He'd never let out so much fire before. All the cave openings were smoking brown now instead of yellow.

Huh, didn't know I had that in me.

A few minutes later Selene emerged. "That took care of it," she said. She held out her dragon palms, revealing an amber stone a little bigger than an egg. Something dark green wiggled inside. "Wurmer egg," she said. "It survived, but I dug it out. There's always a remnant that will survive if you are not careful."

The larva inside spun and rolled. It radiated evil. Its thrashings were revolting and vile.

"What are you going to do with it?" Nath said.

Selene squeezed it into goo in her claws. She rubbed the muck into the dirt. "I just wanted you to see it, so that you would know."

"Thanks. I still need to find Brenwar, though." He averted his eyes. "And I ..."

"Nath, I understand why you might not fully trust me. After all, I did try to destroy you once. But I won't again. I promise." She sighed. "You gave my life meaning. Once I accepted it, I knew I couldn't go back. I'll die first. Trust me or not, you won't get any trouble from me." She sagged and swayed. "Ugh."

"Selene!" Nath said. "You are not well."

"It's the wurmers' poisoned flames. It will fade away. I just need to rest."

"You rest, then. I'll watch out."

"I'll be fine. The threat has passed." She lay down in the grasses by his feet and closed her eyes. "Besides, you need to go and find Brenwar."

Nath's eyes grazed over her form. She was so beautiful adorned in her sparkling black scales. Supine. Graceful. Mesmerizing. *She's amazing.*

"I can feel your eyes on me," she said with her eyes still closed. "Do you like what you see?"

"Huh?" Nath stammered out. "The truth is, you aren't half bad for a dragon."

"You're supposed to increase in charm as you get older, not lose it."

"Well, unlike you, I won't be older for a much longer time."

"Whatever you say, Dragon Boy."

"Boy?"

CHAPTER

20

S ELENE SLEPT A WEEK, JUST as he had when he'd been poisoned by
the wurmers. During that week, Nath found that his patience was not
tried at all.

Too soon, she was up again. "I'll help out with Brenwar," she said.
"Besides, I'm curious about this raccoon you met."

"Curious why?" Nath asked.

"Because I don't recall any raccoons being in that area of woodland. It's
possible but atypical."

"The woodlands are full of varmints. Especially the raccoons."

"Did you see any others?"

"No," he said.

"But you do know that raccoons travel in families typically, don't you
think?" She stretched out her wings and yawned. "Tell me more about this
raccoon."

"He was big for a raccoon. White with brown eyes and brown rings."

She rolled her eyes. "A brown raccoon? You're certain?"

"Sure."

"Have you ever seen a brown raccoon before?"

"No, but there are plenty of things I've never seen. And what makes you
such an expert on critters anyway?" Nath expanded his wings and took flight,
and then he yelled back down, "Oh, come on. I'll show you."

Selene jumped into the air and flew after him. "Oh, I can't wait."

Nath and Selene were back in the woodland where he'd lost the scent of
Brenwar. Pushing between the trees and bending them aside, he sniffed the air.

"Let me guess, you lost the raccoon's scent too."

"Just give me a moment."

"Sure, take all the time that you want." She shrugged her eyes. "But I smell many things, and a raccoon isn't among them."

Selene was right. Nath didn't smell a single raccoon, but there were plenty of squirrels, chipmunks, and other such things. If dragons could blush, his cheeks would be red. It was embarrassing. He'd missed something again.

"Just keep looking," he moaned.

The search continued, but it was futile. Though the woods were big, Nath was still too big for them. His presence unsettled everything. Finally, he eased back into a clearing and waited for Selene to return.

I hate being wrong, and I don't much like her being right, either.

Selene emerged into the clearing. "Giving up so soon, are we?"

"There has to be an explanation for this." He dropped his horned head into his hands. "Selene, have you ever encountered a fairy empress?"

"No, I can't say that I have. Why, have you?"

"Brenwar and I found one in a tomb. Her name is Lotuus."

"Tell me more, Nath. Don't leave out a detail."

Nath filled her in from start to finish, leaving them both in silence.

"I'd say there is a very good chance that *Lotuus* is behind this." She smacked Nath's leg with her tail. "And you didn't even consider this before? Instead you blamed me."

"But the raccoon said—"

"Oh hush it, Nath. Besides, I've forgiven you already."

"You have? Why?"

"Why? Because you saved my scaled back at those caves, that's why. If you hadn't shown up, I might very well have died."

"Well, I'd hate for that to happen, even though you are difficult ..."

"What!"

"And irritating."

"You think I'm irritating," she said, rising up to full height.

"Not to mention beautiful."

"Oh." Selene's composure softened. "Now that's more like it." Slowly, she approached and nuzzled into his chest.

Nath's heart pounded harder and faster. Swallowing, he eased his tail around her waist and pulled her closer.

She kissed him on the cheek and said with a soft look in her violet eyes, "You're learning, Nath."

"Oh please," said an unfamiliar voice. "I don't think the two of you are married."

Nath and Selene stiffened into upright positions and eyed the owner of the voice.

A big raccoon, chestnut ringed, stood atop a small boulder, checking his claws.

"You!" Nath said.

"Me," the raccoon said, touching his chest. "Yes, I suppose it is me. What about it?"

"Where is Brenwar?" Nath demanded. Silently he snorted the air. The raccoon still didn't have a familiar scent. "Out with it now."

"I told you," the raccoon said, pointing at Selene. "She has him."

"I certainly do not!" Selene said.

The raccoon giggled. "Well, I might have been mistaken. These eyes aren't quite what they used to be. You'll understand when you get to be as old as me."

"Enough games, raccoon." Nath stomped his paw. "Tell me where Brenwar is!"

"Who?"

"You know very well who, you trickster." Nath crept closer. "The dwarf. Black bearded with a skeleton hand."

"What's he doing with a skeleton hand?" the raccoon said.

Nath slammed his paw down, shaking the ground. *Boom!* "Tell me where he is!"

"Eh, easy, big dragon. You might hurt something." The raccoon scratched his head. "Boy, you really aren't getting this, are you?"

"What do you mean?" Nath said.

"Come on, you know better than that."

"You are that trickster, Lotuus."

"No," the raccoon said, shaking his head. "I don't know who you are talking about."

Nath lowered his snout over the raccoon's face and sniffed him again. *Hmmm, he has no scent at all. He has to be made of magic, but who and what is he?* He snorted again.

"Hey, easy," the raccoon said, hugging the boulder. "I don't want to venture into your nose."

"Humph!" Nath said, eyeing the raccoon with continued suspicion. He stared deep into its eyes.

There was something there.

Something familiar.

"Gorlee!"

"Hah!" the raccoon slapped his knee. "It's about time. *Ulp!*"

Nath snatched the changeling up in his claws and squeezed. "Why the games?"

Eyes bugging out of his head, Gorlee shifted his shape into the human form of Nath Dragon. "I'm a changeling, remember. We don't do things the easy way. Besides, I needed you to track down Selene and bring her back." Struggling in Nath's clutches, he said, "Do you mind?"

Nath set him down and said to a human-looking version of himself, "So Brenwar is safe, then?"

"Yes, he is. He's back in Dragon Home. He's pretty slow, so I sent him back with a teleportation stone, but the two of you can fly there."

"Why would we do that?" Nath said

"Because Balzurth sent me to get you."

Nath's blood thinned under his scales. "My father is back from beyond the Great Mural?" He looked at Selene. Her eyes were as wide as moons. He turned back to Gorlee. "Why?"

"He didn't say," Gorlee said. He walked over to Selene and patted her on the back. "How have you been doing, Selene?"

"Fine," she said, glowering at him.

Gorlee backed away and slapped his hands together. "Glad to hear it. Now, which one of you grand beasts is flying me back to Dragon Home?"

For the moment, Nath's tongue was tied. Going home was one thing. Being summoned was another. He felt like a child again. *What is this all about? I can't stand it.* He lowered his head. "Get on, then."

CHAPTER 21

DRAGON HOME. ON THE OUTSIDE, things had changed. Dragons soared the nearby skies now. Colorful families of the scaly beasts huddled in the peaks. The deep valleys at the bottom of the mountain showed glimmers of the families hunting and frolicking with one another.

Lava flowed in small streams down the mountainside. The caves smoldered and sputtered out smoke.

A pair of blue razor dragons darted by, making friendly squawks. Several heads popped up at Nath's flying approach. They squawked hellos and welcomes. Fire Bite dragons the size of piglets swarmed the air and blew hot puffs of fire at him.

Nath was elated. In all his days before, he'd never received so much as a welcome, but he was accepted now. He was a friend. A fighter. A champion. He was their king to command them.

"They sure are making a fuss about you," Selene said as they flew, eyeing two columns of silver dragons that were guiding them toward the great mountain. "I guess they don't know any better."

"Funny, Selene. Hah-hah."

They dropped into the largest mouth of the cave and landed. The massive cave led to a very tall and wide passageway. Gorlee hopped down onto the carved stone path. "It's an awfully big place, isn't it?"

"You might want to shift shapes, Gorlee." Nath's heart was pounding as he eyed the passages that led to the throne room. "We wouldn't want to confuse anybody."

"Good idea," Gorlee said, "But who should I be?"

"Why don't you try being yourself for a change?" Nath suggested.

"Seems boring, but why not?" Gorlee made a face. "Uh, Nath, what do I look like?"

Nath gazed at the huge chamber doors towering over his frame. He studied the dragon images inlaid in the brass. Selene stood at his side, and Gorlee stood down between his feet. The changeling's skin was hairless and pinkish, his head bald, and his eyes big green baubles in the sockets. He was odd looking and lanky and wearing a set of loose cotton robes.

Nath raised his paw up and started to knock. "Wait a minute, this is my throne room." He shoved the door open and gazed upon the heaping piles of gleaming treasure. "After you," he said to Selene.

Inside, coins jangled and shifted under his feet. The throne room with its high columns didn't seem as big as it used to. Of course, he'd spent most of his time the size of a man before. At least that was how he had departed it last. He eyed the great throne, a backless chair plenty big enough for him and crafted from the finest metals. He made his approach, head moving side to side. "I guess I'll have a seat and wait then."

"Hold it right there," said a gruff voice. From behind one of the throne's legs, a stout black-bearded figure stepped out.

"Brenwar!"

"Aye," said the dwarf. "No need to get all emotional."

"I'm just glad you're well," Nath said, leaning down. "I was worried."

"Humph." Brenwar lowered Mortuun to the treasure floor and rested his hands on the butt of the shaft. He stood at attention, eyes forward. He didn't blink.

Nath looked at Selene and gave a shrug.

Her eyes were fixed on the gigantic mural behind the throne.

The painting always changed. The dragons and clouds in the sky moved in an endless and timeless scene. The changes were slow and subtle. It was like watching a very slow and massive hourglass with the sand draining. It took its time, but eventually it changed.

"So, I guess the waiting part begins. Say, Gorlee. Gorlee?"

The changeling was nowhere to be found.

"Well that's just great," Nath said. "He probably has the right idea, though. Wouldn't surprise me if we stood here for days." He tapped his claw on the treasure-coated floor. "Or weeks. And just when I was about to close in on my mother."

"Always be wary. Plans change. Be prepared for the unexpected," Selene said.

"I suppose."

I wonder what Father has in store for me now. He told me it would be fine to chase after Mother. Perhaps I should have completed the mission by now. Of course, I would have if Brenwar didn't slow me down.

"So, Brenwar, as I understand it, you teleported, but you won't fly? Didn't you use the old 'Dwarves don't teleport' line on Gorlee?"

Brenwar didn't move.

Oh great. He's assumed the position. Guzan, I'm liable to be standing here for weeks.

Nath gazed around the treasure room. There was nothing worse than waiting, even though he was a dragon and extremely patient. But this was different. He was waiting on his father—again—and he couldn't help but feel like he was in trouble. Still, he was looking forward to seeing his father again. He realized he might not see him again for a long time. It did his heart well.

But for Balzurth to come back, there had to be trouble.

Oh, I'll just give him a hug. Certainly he'll be as happy to see me as I am to see him.

Selene's tail swished into his. "I'm not sure I like this. Her eye grazed the vaulted ceiling tops. "Reminds me of my days with Gorn—"

"Let's not utter his name here," Nath interjected. "He shouldn't ever be mentioned in these hallowed halls."

"Noted," she said. "Let's just pray this has nothing to do with him or his ilk."

"I'm certain his existence is entirely wiped out," Nath said, with a sneer. "I felt it myself." He locked his eyes on Selene's. "You haven't sensed him again, have you?"

Flatly, she said, "No. But evil is so hard to destroy."

"As if we didn't already have enough of a problem with the wurmers."

The mural warbled, and a massive dragon stepped through. Balzurth came. The great horns on his head seemed to stretch to the top of the ceiling. The great muscles underneath his deep-red scales, flecked with gold, appeared more powerful than ever. His voice had as much thunder as it ever had. The room quavered, and the piles of coins shifted when he spoke.

"Welcome home, Son."

Nath pulled his wings back. "It's good to be home, Father." He stood eye to eye with Balzurth and butted horns with him. "You look as grand as ever."

"And you are quite the specimen of a great dragon yourself." Balzurth turned away and faced the other dragon in the room. "Hello, Selene. How are you?"

"Quite well, King Balzurth."

Balzurth's golden eyes examined her black-scaled body. "I sense that is not entirely true."

"What do you mean, Father?" Nath asked with surprise. "Selene is just as spirited as ever."

"No, no she isn't, Son. That's one of the reasons I brought you here."

"It is? Why, what is wrong?"

With a sad look in his eyes, Balzurth said to Nath, "Your friend Selene is dying."

CHAPTER 22

"DYING?" NATH SAID. HE SWATTED her gently with his tail. "I've never seen her better. You're fine, Selene. Tell him."

She looked up at Nath with weak eyes and shook her head. "No, I'm not. My time in this world has run its course." She turned and faced Balzurth. "How did you know?"

"I've always known. It's what Gorn does. If he goes, all of his closest acolytes go with him. It's in their bloodstream." Balzurth stretched his tail out and brushed it over her cheek. "You've been living on borrowed time, and now your time has come."

Nath's heart sank in his chest. "What? No. This cannot be. What are you talking about, Father?"

"Selene is a dragon the same as most, but more gifted, born black. Gorn found her at birth and took her under his wing." Balzurth cleared his throat. "He cursed her blood and blended it with his. She can't live in this world without him."

"I thought Gorn was a spirit."

"He was, but all evil spirits can taint things." Balzurth stepped around the throne and put his wing over Selene.

Tears dripped from her eyes.

Nath's eyes started to water. "What are you going to do?"

Balzurth then said to his son, "She's made the right choice: good over evil. She's one of us, and I'm taking her with me where she can live well—beyond the mural."

Nath was numb. Despite their battles, he'd become as close with Selene as anyone. Now she was going to be gone! He probably wouldn't be able to see her again for at least a thousand years. He turned and faced her. "Is this what you want?"

"This is the only choice I have." She shrugged. "But it's hardly a bad thing. It's just happening so suddenly. Quite frankly, I'm not ready. I feel my work here on Nalzambor isn't finished. That's why I've been working so hard to eradicate those wurmers. I'm partially responsible for that mess, and I knew I needed to clean it up. Now, it's going to be a burden for you and the rest of the world to deal with."

"Does she have to go right now, Father?"

"We need to be prudent about it, Son. I sense the poison could strike her heart at any moment. Can't you sense it as well?"

Nath shut his eyes. His heightened senses reached out. Selene's heart fought for every beat. She was strong, but the fight in her was weakening. There was a deep sadness in her, too. "Can we not heal her?" Nath suggested. "Perhaps the Ocular of Orray can help? It removes curses."

Selene brushed his cheek with her tail. "It's been tried. It worked for a time, but that time is up. Nath, don't be so sad. Without you, I never would have made it this far. I'd have been dead with no hope of life beyond the mural."

Nath stomped his paw. "Why didn't anyone tell me this until now? We could have been searching for a solution."

"Nath, you have to live your life and I have to live mine," Selene said. "Just let it be."

"Come now, Selene," Balzurth said. "We must go now. A new life will begin beyond the mural."

"Can't she leave, be cured, and come back?" Nath said to Balzurth.

"Only I can leave and come back, Son. And it's quite taxing to do so. Now, say your goodbyes so you can resume your quest."

Nath clasped Selene's claws in his. "We can beat this, Selene. There must be a way."

"This is my choice, not yours," she said. "And I fear I've done much more harm than good in this world." A giant teardrop dripped from her eye and splashed on the treasure. "Will you rid Nalzambor of the wurmers for me?"

"No!" Nath retorted. "You need to do that yourself. But I will help you." He turned on Balzurth. "Father, you've told me countless times that there is always a way to solve anything in this world. So tell me how to solve this. Please. What can I do to help my friend?"

Balzurth's voice darkened. "Don't ask questions you don't want the answers to."

"So there is a way?"

"One that comes at too great a price," Balzurth said.

"No price is too great, Father. I'd give my life for hers."

"Nath!" Selene said, gasping.

"Oh, don't be so dramatic, Son." Balzurth rolled his eyes. He leaned over and poked Nath in the chest. He ran his paws over Nath's horns. "You are as fine a dragon as there ever was, Son. Are you willing to give that up?"

"What do you mean?" Nath asked.

"Oh, you say you'll give up your life, but let's qualify that. Will you give up your life as a dragon?"

Nath swallowed. "I can't stop being a dragon, can I?"

"You'll always have a dragon's blood, as you did before you changed. But what if you gave up all of your other powers? The gift of flight. Your iron hide. Your humongous girth and awesome power. Hmmm?" Balzurth poked him again. "Can you give all of that up? Not to mention the crown of the dragon kingdom?"

Nath shrank inside his scales. "I can't give that up. I'm the Dragon King now."

"A Dragon King that has only spent minutes on the throne," Balzurth said. "You know, I was seven hundred and fifty-some years old before I assumed the throne from your grandfather, and it took another five hundred years to get used to it."

"But, it's my destiny to be king, is it not?" Nath said.

"Oh, destiny can wait. In the meantime," Balzurth said, taking a seat on the throne. "I can keep an eye on things."

"Nath, you can't do this. Not for me. I'm not worth it," Selene said, stroking his cheek with the back of her paw. "You love all of your dragon powers. It wouldn't be right for me to be restored and you to be the lesser of what you were before."

"You don't want to leave, Selene. I can feel it. And I don't want you to leave, either. Deep down inside, we both know we aren't to be separated."

"But it wouldn't be fair for me to have my powers and you to not have yours."

"Ahem," Balzurth interrupted. "Oh, but you would pay just as big a price as he, Selene. You both would be affected. You both have to want this. There is no other way."

"So, we'll be made human again?" Nath said to his father.

"I can't say exactly how it will work out. All I can say is that your powers will be severely limited. Notably so."

"Does this mean I can never be king?"

"You're a king already, Son. Always have been. Always will be. But, if you do this, you'll have to assume the title of Dragon Prince again. At least for now. And that won't be easy."

Nath looked down at Brenwar. The dwarf's eyes glanced up at him and quickly looked away. His friend seemed so tiny. Vulnerable. Nath didn't want to feel that way again: mortal.

"Now's not my time, is it, Father."

Balzurth sat there, deep in thought. His thinking lasted for days.

Nath and Selene stayed right there with him, figuring it was a good thing Brenwar had frozen, or the dwarf might have become bored.

At long last, the old Dragon King made his pronouncement.

"As a man, Nath, you defeated Gorn Grattack and ended the Great Dragon War, but I think Nalzambor still needs you, as a man. And the world needs Selene, too. And … you two need each other, I believe."

Nath's eyes found Selene's. "As I understand it, life is awfully nice beyond the mural."

"And life as a king can be just as delightful," she replied. "I wouldn't give it up for the likes of me."

"Well," Nath smiled and stared deep into her eyes, "then it's a good thing that you aren't king. Father, I'm ready."

Balzurth nodded. "What about you, Selene?"

"Can two bad decisions produce something good? I guess there's only one way to find out. I'm ready."

Balzurth leaned forward. "So be it. Now, clasp hands, close your eyes, and repeat after me."

CHAPTER 24

N ATH'S HEART POUNDED IN HIS skull. Darkness surrounded him.
Guzan! What's happened to me?

The last thing he remembered was his father saying some words. Ancient and mystical. Powerful and transforming. The words had felt like they were separating his bones from the marrow. They penetrated his very core. The essence of his being. He struggled. His eyes wouldn't open. His limbs wouldn't move. His entire body was hemmed in by warm goo.

How am I even breathing?

His heart beat faster and faster. It thundered in his ears.

Settle down, Nath. Certainly your own father wouldn't do you in. Would he?

Blood racing through his numb limbs, his body started to tingle. His strength grew. He pushed with whatever part he could feel. He hit something stiff. It was smooth to the touch.

What sort of prison is this? What has become of me?

Feet gathered into his chest, he stretched out. He kicked at the wall that held him fast.

Something cracked.

He kicked again and again.

The ooze around him began to spill out from the hole, and light crept over his eyelids.

Excited, Nath unleashed all of his limbs at once. Busting out of the strange shell, he started into a fit of coughing.

Yuck! What is this?!

Gagging, he spat up fluids until he could spit no more. Using his hand, he wiped the goo from his eyes and squinted them open. The light was painfully bright, and the surrounding sounds were muffled. A stiff breeze chilled his warm bones. Using his fingers, he cleaned out his nose and earholes. He rubbed his lobes.

"I have ears!"

"Yes you do, sleepy head," said a muffled voice. "And a tongue, too!"

Nath shook his head like a dog and wiped all he could from his eyes. On opening them up, he found Brenwar. "You're much bigger than before," he said, spitting ooze from his mouth. "So I guess that means I'm much smaller?"

"Well, you certainly aren't any smarter," Brenwar added, "but if I were ever happy, I'd be happy to see you."

Nath took in a deep gust of air. He was in the woodland, and a stream trickled nearby. His feet stood on large chunks of reddish-green shell and goo that reminded him of an ... "Was I in an egg?"

"It looked like an egg to me, hatchling," Brenwar said with the grimmest of smiles.

Nath stretched out his arms and hands. They were that of a man, but they still had scales. Black scales and golden-yellow claws. Eyes wide, he twisted his head over his shoulder and spun around. "No tail. No wings." He thumped his chest with his fist and forced out more coughing. "I feel so weak. Vulnerable."

"If you were smart, you would've asked to come back as a dwarf. We never feel that way."

Nath stared at his hands. His body. His chest was skin with a slight mix of scales. The same went for his legs. He felt his face. His sensitive touch revealed nothing but smooth skin on his face. He smiled when he felt his long hair.

He let out a breath and gazed up at the birds chirping in the trees. One darted into flight, and others followed. He became aware of a hole inside of him. He used to tower over the trees. Over everything. Now he looked up to it all again. He held his head and sat down.

"What's wrong?" Brenwar asked.

"This will take some getting used to, that's all. Where are we, anyway?"

"South of Dragon Home."

"Say, where's Selene?"

"Getting something to eat," Brenwar said, eyeing the streams. "Been gone since dawn."

Nath jumped up. His head spun and his legs turned to jelly. He crumpled down on the ground. "Oof. I am weak."

"And whining. Now get up." Brenwar offered his arm. "Get up now."

Nath took Brenwar's arm. It was like grabbing an iron rung that pulled him up. "Hah. I guess my strength will come back soon enough." He surveyed his colorful surroundings. "So Selene is well, then? How long has she been up?"

"Two days."

"She got out two days before me? Really?"

"It hardly matters. You always slept too much."

Combing his fingers through his hair, Nath then asked, "So how long since we left Dragon Home?"

"A few weeks?"

"Brenwar ..."

"Give or take a few months."

"Are you jesting?" Nath said in shock to Brenwar.

Brenwar eyed him.

"Guzan! A lot can happen in a few months." Strolling over the grasses, he noticed he had toes and not clawed feet. He waded into the waters and rinsed off. The goo was quickly shed from his muscular frame and washed away with the waters.

Brenwar handed Nath an off-white suit of commoner's robes and some boots.

Once he was dressed, Nath scooped up a handful of water and drank. "I guess I'll have to get used to drinking from cups and goblets again."

"And routine bathing will probably be in order," replied a voice much softer than Brenwar's.

Nath whipped around and found himself staring at Selene. She stood on the bank wearing commoner's robes like his. Her hair was long and jet black, her eyes violet fire. Behind her back, a long black tail swished over the grasses.

"How do you feel?"

Shrugging her eyes, she said, "As mortal as I ever felt."

"Yes," Nath agreed, "me too. Exciting, isn't it?"

CHAPTER
25

TRAVELING ON FOOT, NATH, SELENE, and Brenwar made it within a league of the Lost City of Borgash. Standing atop an overlook, Nath squinted his eyes toward the distant city. Its once-tall spires, now rubble, lay all over the barren and broken land.

"I don't see a sliver of life in there," he said, fading away from the edge of the overlook and standing alongside Selene. "What about you?"

"Though my vision is not what it was, I still see a few things that scurry."

"You do?" Holding his hand over his eyes to shade them from the bright sun, Brenwar leaned forward on the overlook. "My eyes are as good as any. I see nothing."

"Look closer. Scorpions crawl along the sand underneath that archway."

Brenwar scowled. "Poor eyesight, my hide. Pah!" He marched back and grabbed his gear. "You still see better than the eagles."

"I would hope so," Nath said. He had the urge to pick up a weapon, but there was nothing to grab. He and Selene had nothing on aside from their commoner garb. It was odd. The clothing itched a little. It was nothing like being covered in dragon scales. He sat down, took off his boots, and dumped debris out. His feet were swollen, pink and tender. He started to rub them. "Sultans of Sulfur! Is that a blister?"

Selene giggled. "Exciting, isn't it?"

"No, it's horrible. My feet hurt, and I swear there's a kink in my neck. And I can only imagine that my hair is a mess." With a sour face, he eyed the blister and extended his index finger's claw. Wincing, he sliced the blister open. "Ow!"

"Oh my, that's embarrassing, you scaly child," Brenwar huffed. "Perhaps I should get out a healing potion for you."

"Would you please?" Nath said, more ordering than asking.

"Absolutely not! That's not a wound."

"But it could get infected," Nath whined. "Great Guzan, what am I saying? I'm worried about a bloody blister. Shame on me." He punched the ground he sat on. "Shame on Nath Dragon!"

Playfully, Selene said, "I could carry you."

"No, we'd better make a stretcher and drag him," Brenwar offered.

"Be silent, both of you. Blast!" Nath got up and hopped away from the pair of them until they were out of sight. Being smaller and weaker was a horrible thing. He missed the grand power he'd had. The ability to fly. The power to take on anything. He'd been the most powerful creature in all of Nalzambor, and now he felt like nothing. "I can't believe I did this to myself."

Selene appeared from underneath the low-hanging branches and said with a guilty look on her face, "Having regrets?"

"Yes," he said.

Selene frowned. "I see." She turned away.

"No, wait, Selene," Nath said, hustling over and grabbing her arm. "Not about you. Certainly not about that. But losing all of that power. It's going to take some getting used to."

"You know, Nath, the first time I met you, there wasn't an ounce of doubt in you. You weren't scared of anything. And you were less powerful than you are now. Ask yourself, what is different?"

"About five tons of brawn and scales."

"Seriously?"

"Come on, Selene. Certainly you should understand. Don't you feel weaker?"

"Physically, yes. Mentally, no. I still have my wits. Have you lost yours?"

He kicked a fallen branch. "No. But I liked being a dragon. Now I might not ever be one again."

"You're still a dragon, Nath Dragon." She brushed her long locks behind her back. "Just a little smaller. You'll get used to it." She extended her hand. "Now let's go find your mother."

He took her hand in his. It was warm to the touch. Invigorating. The bounce returned to his step. After thinking things through, he came to a simple conclusion.

I'm a man once again. I have to live with the decisions I make.

Brenwar had already begun to forge ahead. He'd slid halfway down the steep hillside and had begun a determined trek into the valley.

The Lost City of Borgash was lost from sight and the wind picked up, howling through the half-dead trees. The area surrounding Borgash was eerie. It was heavy in overgrowth. Vines and roots jutted up like massive snakes, shooting from the ground and twisting around the trees. The berry bushes were barren. The leaves brown. The mosses weren't green but rather a sickly yellow. Soft and spongy on the ground.

Nostrils flaring, Nath broke the silence, "I'm not so sure about that smell. Not to be crude, but it smells like a giant defecated." He covered his nose. "It's foul."

"It's no more offensive than your words to my ears," Brenwar said, climbing into a corridor of fallen boulders. "Yer giving me a headache."

"Mind your tongue. I'm still—"

Selene tugged on his arm.

"What?" Nath stopped and looked at her.

"You might want to let that argument go," she said. "Things have changed, remember?"

"But I'm still the—"

"King? Prince? Does that really matter now?"

"I suppose not. It's just that—"

Selene pressed her finger on his lips and gently shushed him. Her nose twitched. Her eyes darted from side to side. "Let it go. We have more important things to worry about."

"Like what?" Nath asked.

Brenwar let out a yell. "Goblins!"

CHAPTER
26

HAVING SNAKED THEIR WAY INTO the path between the rocks, Nath and company found themselves pinned in now. Brenwar stood face to face with a knot of goblins pressed into the path.

Little taller than the dwarf, they stood brandishing crude swords, spears, hatchets, and knives. Their dark hair was matted and greasy. Carved bone jewelry rattled on their chests and necks. Their yellow eyes were wide with evil.

"Perhaps that's what I smelled," Nath said, lifting up his foot and standing on one leg.

"Uh, are you going to stomp them?" Selene said.

Nath put his leg down and gave a shrug. It was instinct. He'd gotten used to crushing many things under his powerful legs. Now all he had was muscle and claws. "Brenwar, let's see if we can come out of this encounter peacefully."

"Never," Brenwar said back over his shoulder. He held Mortuun out in front of the goblins' eyes. "If you value your lives, you dirty things, you'll be stepping aside."

The goblin in front, a small, hunchbacked knot of muscle, licked his lips and showed a mouthful of jagged teeth. "Dwarf. Mmmm. Lots of meat under that beard. Should be fun to kill. Delicious to eat."

"We'll see about that," Brenwar said, raising his war hammer high over his head.

Nath turned his ear upward. Scuffling clamored off the rocks that hemmed them inside the path.

Several more goblins appeared. Spears were poised in their sinewy arms. Their beady eyes hungered to attack. "I don't suppose you are open to negotiation?" Nath said in Goblin.

The lead goblin spat a wad of dark juice, wiped his mouth, and said, "We've not eaten in days." It set its eyes on Nath, then they shifted to Brenwar. "This dwarf should suffice. Leave him and you may pass."

"Let me think about that."

"What?" Brenwar said.

Nath made a quick count. There were ten goblins that he could hear and see. Their eyes were feverish with hunger. Desperation was in the leader's voice. Hearts pounded behind their bone breast-plated chests. *I can't believe I'm wasting my time with this. If I was still a dragon, they'd be fleeing into the hills. This is beneath me.* Summoning the authority in his voice, he said, "Tell you what, goblins, let us pass and I'll let you live."

The lead goblin made a face like he'd swallowed a large bug. In the next instant, his expression darkened and a rage-filled order burst forth from his sweaty lips. "Attack!"

Brenwar ducked underneath a slicing sword and charged straight into the leader.

Behind Nath, Selene's tail licked out and swatted two goblins across the face at once. Both tumbled headlong into the path.

"Nice move," Nath said, spinning around and snatching a spear that was flying toward his neck.

The goblin that threw it gaped, wide eyed. It went for the knife tucked into its belt.

Nath spun the spear around and busted the goblin's hand. "None of that, now!"

Clutching its hand, the goblin cried out in pain.

Nath slugged it across the jaw with the butt of the spear.

It stumbled into one of the boulders, knocking its metal helmet off. "That will ... *oof!*"

A pair of goblins flung themselves into Nath and drove him headfirst into the ground. One wrapped around his legs and started biting. The other goblin locked one arm around his neck, squeezed, and started stabbing at Nath's chest with his free arm. The blade bit deep.

"Argh!" Nath twisted the knife free from the goblin, dipped his shoulder, and, with a heave, slung it off his neck. He turned his attention to the one latched onto his leg and biting it.

Its teeth sank deep into his calf.

Now realizing he still had his boot in his hand, Nath started beating the goblin with it. "Get off of me, you dirty tick!"

Selene's tail coiled around its neck and jerked it free. She hoisted it high in the air and slammed it into one of the nearby rocks. *Thud!*

Ahead, Brenwar had a goblin pinned down by the neck. He hammered it in the face with his fist. "Eat me, will you? Eat this!" *Wham! Wham! Wham!*

Chest heaving, Nath caught a flicker of movement out of the corner of his eye.

Above, on the rocks, a goblin and its spear were poised to attack.

Nath sprang high in the air, landing right beside the slack-jawed goblin. It made a desperate lunge.

Nath caught the spear and ripped it away. He cracked the goblin upside the head with the shaft, breaking the spear. *Whap! Whap! Whap!*

The goblin fell to its knees and begged for mercy. "Please, stop! Please stop! No more hungry. Please!"

Nath picked it up by its ragged armor and trousers, and with a heave, he tossed the goblin far into the woods.

The party of goblins that survived quickly grabbed all the fallen weapons and fled in all directions, leaving Nath, Selene, and Brenwar alone once again in the crevice.

Looking up from the path at Nath, Selene said, "You're bleeding. Are you going to cry about it?"

Blood pumping through his battle-charged veins, Nath smacked his fist into his palm and replied, "Let's go find some orcs."

The Lost City of Borgash was anything but lost. However, it was a wasteland. Nath and company entered from what was left of the main gate that led into the city. A rusting portcullis—big enough for giants to enter—was torn asunder. The rocks that held it were half rubble, but many still stood firm. There were markings. Carvings in the stone.

Nath ran his fingers over the edges. "What do you think, Brenwar?"

"Well before my time. Not much in the dwarven archives, either." He ran his hands over a fallen stone column. "Clearly not made by dwarves, or it never would have fallen. Har. Probably elven or orcen."

"What about you, Selene?" Nath asked. "Any ideas?"

She ran her hands up and down her arms and shivered a little. "It's eerie. It's always been my understanding that there was an invasion and the people just disappeared. But that was hundreds, maybe thousands of years ago for all I know. I don't think anyone really remembers. Besides, there are several cities that have come and gone just like this."

"This was no small city," Brenwar said. He climbed up a pile of vine-covered rubble. "It rivals the likes of Quintuklen. If there is a clue about your mother here, it will take days, maybe weeks to search it out. And with the air so foul, it will take some getting used to."

"At least we're here, so let's get started. Perhaps we should split up," Nath suggested.

"There's danger here, Nath," Selene said, covering her shoulders with her hands. "I've no doubt we aren't alone. And there's a reason not many venture too deep into Borgash."

"Really, why is that?"

"Because most that go in don't come back out."

CHAPTER 27

B ORGASH WAS BIG INDEED. THE abandoned city stretched for miles
in all directions. Most of the city was nothing more than part of
the landscape, but in places there were remnants of once-thriving
stone buildings.

Nath climbed up a series of vines where dead-looking trees sprouted
up like massive pylons. The bark was petrified and swallowed up by the
prickling vines. He sauntered out on one of the branches and spied on his
surroundings.

Not too far off in the distance, Brenwar stood on the ground, moving
large rocks and boulders back and forth.

That should keep him happy. Well, "content" might be a better word.

Selene was nowhere in sight. Nath felt a little guilty about that. He'd
insisted they split up. They didn't need to watch over him anymore,
dragonman or not. If anything, Selene needed an eye kept on her. After all,
her roots had once been steeped in evil.

They'll be fine. This place seems harmless enough. He reached up, dug his
claws into a branch, and pulled himself up to greater heights. From his perch
up in the dead and leafless tree, he could see all around, and so far as he was
concerned, there wasn't much to look at.

I can see why no one leaves. They die of boredom.

He stretched his arms out and spread them wide. *Oh, if I could only fly!*

You can.

Nath froze with chills going up his spine. Finally, his lips moved. "Eh, is
someone there?"

There was no reply. Just the soft howl of the wind. Nath spun around on
the branch and looked everything up and down. There was nothing in the

tree. No birds. No nests. But there were some holes bored into the wood. He shook his head. "I must be hearing things. My own imagination, perhaps."

Glancing back down at the ground, he noticed Brenwar was gone.

A chill wind slid over Nath's neck, standing his nape hairs on end. His body tingled, but not in a good way. He felt unseen eyes all over him. The warmth of the setting sun on his face began to fade. Shadows from distant mountains changed the look of Borgash's landscape. Nath rubbed his neck. *Perhaps splitting up wasn't such a good idea.*

Too impatient to scramble all the way down the tree, he hopped down the last twenty feet and landed soundlessly on the soft ground.

Not bad. Couldn't have made such a subtle landing before, I'll admit that.

He was headed in the direction he'd last seen Brenwar when Nath tripped and fell. "What in the world?" Glancing down, he noticed his feet were tangled in some vines. He started ripping the vines from his boots. "Stubborn things."

Finally, his feet were free, and he carefully backed away. Glancing up, he noticed the tree he'd just climbed from was different. The branches were bent downward, seeming to come right at him, but still stiff and frozen.

"Odd. Very odd." He took off at a trot, traversing the jagged landscape of the fallen city, and found himself standing where he'd last seen Brenwar. There was no sign of the dwarf. No tracks, either. "Oh, I'm not losing you again."

By taking in a whiff of air, Nath found that Brenwar's dwarven musk lingered. On cat's feet, Nath picked his way through the foliage and growing shadows. If Brenwar had passed through the direction Nath was headed, there wasn't any sign of him.

I don't like this. I don't like it at all.

Nath stopped and turned. Behind him, the grasses he had trodden on didn't show the slightest sign that he'd passed through there at all. He squatted down and pressed his palm into the moss- and grass-covered ground. After he lifted his hand there was an impression. It lasted only a moment, and then the grass and moss had returned to their prior places. "That's new."

Glancing up at the setting sun, he noted there was little light left in the day. With a twitch in his nose, he hustled after Brenwar.

Great Guzan. What if this place has eaten him?

Pushing through the overgrowth, Nath noticed that every fiber of life he touched seemed to scrape and pull at him. His boots got stuck in between some more vines, and he ripped his foot clean out of the leather. He reached down only to find the ground and foliage swallowing his boots up. "Sultans of Sulfur!" He grabbed them just in time and hopped over more vines while he put them back on.

Keeping to the trail of Brenwar's scent, Nath sprinted away.

I've got to warn Brenwar! Find Selene!

Jumping over fallen stone after fallen stone, he emerged in a barren spot of land and came to a sudden halt in front of a living and gaping hole.

His eyes were locked on Brenwar's.

The dwarf was bound up in the new tendrils of a vine just outside a monstrous maw in the hole, encircled with teeth. On the other side of the expansive monster, Selene was corded up and being dragged into the gurgling hole.

"Selene!"

CHAPTER
28

THE GAPING HOLE OF VEGETATION groaned. Deep in its middle, a ring of teeth chomped up and down. The vines gripping Brenwar and Selene dragged them downward toward the bone-crunching hole.

"Hold on!" Nath yelled.

There were no replies. Selene and Brenwar's mouths were encircled by vines. Their eyes were pleading and filled with desperation.

"Blast! If I was bigger, I'd rip this thing out of the ground!" Nath's eyes searched for something, anything that might aid his friends. He dashed around the rim of the monster. "Selene! Give me your tail!"

Her tail whipped out. Nath stretched his fingers as far as he could, but there was still a considerable gap around him.

Suddenly, more vines burst forth from the monster's mouth. Like venomous snakes, they came right for him. He backpedaled. His feet were snagged by a tangle of vines and grasses. "Blast!"

Selene and Brenwar continued to descend deeper into the hole. All of their struggles were in vain.

"No!" Nath ripped free of the foliage.

The tendrils from the mouth reared up and encircled his arms. The vines tugged at him with tremendous force.

Nath tugged back with all his might. He ripped a tendril clear of the monster's mouth. *Snap!*

The ground shook.

The monster let out a shrill cry. *Eaaerrrrrrrr!*

Nath ripped out another vine. *Snap!*

The earth buckled beneath him.

"Hah! You don't like that, do you."

More tendrils burst forth from the monster's mouth. Dozens of them surged for Nath all at once.

"Not good!"

Striking fast, the tendrils ripped at Nath's legs.

He leapt backward and bounced off a boulder.

The tendrils snaked over the rim and pressed after him. The other grasses and vines came to life, holding him fast.

"This entire place is alive!"

While he was pushing himself out of the tangles, the boulder in front of him inspired an idea. He darted to the other side, wrapped his arms around it as best he could, and hoisted it up onto his shoulder. "Argh!"

The tendrils coiled up his legs and squeezed.

Sweat beading on his brow, Nath fought for balance and shuffled forward. The skin on his legs started to burn. The tremendous weight of the stone strained every muscle in his shoulders and back. Using the tugging of the evil vines, he continued the slow march forward.

"This is it, monster," Nath said through gritted teeth. "I've got a bellyful for you." Standing on the rim of the sunken maw, he hunkered down. With a heave, he launched the huge rock off of his shoulders and down into the mouth.

The boulder smashed right into the snapping mouth.

The ground rocked and reeled.

The earth let out an uncanny shriek. *Rreeeeeeeeeee!*

The tendrils uncoiled from around Nath's legs and darted back down into the hole.

The rock covered the mouth entirely.

The tendrils attacked it. They bounced off the gritty surface over and over like snakes gone mad.

Without hesitation, Nath slid down the side of the hole and yanked Selene free of the tendrils. She was gasping for breath. Nath carried her in his arms and set her down on the rim.

Below and butted up against the rock covering the mouth was Brenwar. There was a disgruntled look on his face. Nath scurried back into the hole, broke away the clinging tendrils, and fetched him up and out of the hole.

"Is everyone all right?" Nath asked.

The ground tremored beneath them.

"By Mortuun! The cursed ground here is living!" Brenwar said. He raised the war hammer high.

"Stop, dwarf!" Selene said, staying his hand with hers. "This isn't some mountainside you can cave in. This evil breathes." She shoved into him. "Let me handle this."

"How dare you!" Brenwar growled, pushing back.

Selene's hands flared up with fire.

Brenwar's eyes became moons.

"Selene! How can you do that?" Nath said, gaping.

"I've been a priestess, have I not? My ability to craft magic is not gone. Does it make you uncomfortable?"

"Just a little surprised is all."

She shook her head and turned away. Mystic tones and arcane words spun from her lips. Fire rushed from her fingertips, driving hard into the monster.

The ground screeched.

The gaping hole spread with flame. The tendrils writhed, popped, and crackled. The expanse became a burning pyre where vegetable turned to ash. The rock inside its mouth collapsed out of sight. Gray ash drifted in the wind.

Leaning over the edge, Brenwar said, "All we had to do was set it on fire?"

Selene dusted her hands off. "Mystic fire. But I took a chance."

Nath eyed her.

"What?" she said, eyeing him back. "I'm a lifelong spell crafter."

"Then why didn't you use your craft before?" Nath asked.

"The same reason the dwarf didn't get in a swing of his hammer. I was surprised."

Nath nodded. "If you say so."

"Nath, now is not the time to doubt me again."

"Well, maybe if you didn't have those black scales, we wouldn't doubt you," Brenwar interjected.

"Black scales. Are you jesting, dwarf?" She pointed at Nath. "Have you not noticed his too?"

"Aye, I have, and I don't like them. Black is a sign of evil."

Nath put his fists on his hips. "Well, your beard's black. Does that make you evil?"

"What?" Brenwar clutched at his beard with his skeleton hand. "Why no." He rapped Mortuun's shaft down on the ground. "Like I said, 'Black, isn't it glorious!'"

The three of them had a little laugh.

Nath then turned to Selene. "I have to admit, I'm envious. It seems you have much of the power you once had. I don't appear to have anything."

Selene cupped his face with her hand. "Nath, be patient. I couldn't have lifted that boulder."

His eyes brightened like gold stars. He flexed his black-scaled arms. "No, I guess you couldn't."

"I could've," Brenwar said, staring down at the hole.

"With the gauntlets, sure, but look at that thing. It must have been a ton if not more."

"It wasn't that big," Brenwar said, still staring into the black hole. He reached down and found a piece of broken vine. He waggled it in front of Selene. "Do you mind, snake tail?"

"Oh," she said with smoldering eyes, "you are a bold one, Bolderguild." With a snap of her fingers, the tip of the vine was encircled in flame.

Brenwar tossed the makeshift torch into the hole. It landed with a crunchy sound that echoed upward. "By Morgdon, that hole is full of bones!"

CHAPTER
29

NATH STOOD INSIDE THE HOLE, surrounded by bones piled as high as his chin. Beside him, Brenwar pushed through the skeletons, making a path.

"Guzan, there must be hundreds of them," Nath said. He picked up a skull and held it before his eyes. "Look at these high cheekbones. This one is elven."

"It seems the creature took all kinds," Selene said, holding up a round skull with heavy bone. "I'd say this one is dwarven or orcen."

Brenwar snatched it away. "Orcen? Pah! It's dwarven. And it needs a proper burial."

"Don't be silly, Brenwar. We can't pick through all of these bones to bury your dead. They've probably been at rest for hundreds of years." Nath plucked up a sword out of the pile then dropped it again when he saw that its metal was long rusted through. There were hundreds of decaying things scattered all over. "The dead are at rest. Let them rest."

Brenwar tucked the dwarven skull under his arm. "I'll bury him if I want."

"Fine, Brenwar. Fine." Wading through the bones, Nath sauntered up to Selene. Her tail was brushing the piles aside. "So, what do you make of this? Do you think this monster is what made Borgash extinct?"

She held a head in front of her that still had some hair on it. It was long and showed canine teeth. "A gnoll. A shame they aren't all gnolls, but no, I don't think this monster was the demise of the city. All of the races seem to be represented here. This is just hundreds of years of victims. Treasure hunters, perhaps? Travelers. All victims of the guardian."

Nath cocked a brow. "Guardian?"

"One of many in this valley, I'd say. And if I'm correct, this plant monster is called a devourer, though this is the biggest one I've ever seen."

"Where did you see them before?" Nath asked.

She dusted off her hands and faced him. "I don't think that really matters now. Excuse me." She brushed by him and began shifting through the char that used to be the dangerous plant. "Ah, see this?"

"Guzan!" Nath said, jumping back. "Kill it!"

Out of the ground, a tendril with a white bud on the end was writhing about. Selene seized it with her hand. "These devourers have strong roots and grow back quickly. You have to destroy the root." She started to tug on it. "A little help, please?"

Nath wrapped his arms around her waist, dug his feet in, and started to pull her back.

"This isn't exactly what I had in mind," she said.

"Oh, hush and hang on." Feet digging in, he started to pull her back harder. "Guzan! How deep is this thing?"

Puffing for breath, Selene said, "I thought you were strong!"

Nath set his jaw, leaned back, put all of his muscles and weight into it, and said, "I sure hope you don't break."

"I won't!"

"Grrrrrr!"

Rip! The plant gave.

Nath stumbled backward and crashed into the bones. Selene was on his lap, holding the squirming tendril. At its end, a huge red tuber, bigger than an ogre's head, pulsated like a heart.

"That's creepy!"

Brenwar charged up with Mortuun.

"No, dwarf!" Selene said, stretching out her arms.

Mortuun the Crusher came down with ram-like force.

Splat!

Slime and goo covered Selene and Brenwar.

Jumping to her feet with fists balled up at her sides, she screamed at Brenwar, "Fool of a dwarf!" Her tail rose up behind her. "I'm going to kill you!"

Brandishing his war hammer, Brenwar fired back a warning. "Watch yerself, dragon lady."

Nath, shielded behind Selene, chuckled. "You two just aren't ever going to get along, are you."

Combing the gunk out of her long black hair, Selene walked away. "Probably not."

"You really should try being a little nicer to her, Brenwar."

Brenwar's eyes widened. "Me? Why?"

"She's a woman."

"With a tail, and not so long ago, she tried to destroy me, you, and the rest of the world."

"We're past that now, so try to put forth a better effort." Ignoring Brenwar's frown, Nath glanced up out of the hole at the darkening, star-filled sky. "It's going to be blacker than my scales before long. Hmmm." He picked up a skull and chucked it into the black expanse that surrounded the hole. The sound of it skipping off stone echoed back. "That's interesting. Uh, Brenwar, we could use a torch or something. Do you have your tinderbox handy?"

Selene slipped in between Brenwar and Nath. "So primitive." With a snap of her fingers, her hand glowed with a warm green light. Its wavering glow illuminated the entire hole and beyond.

Gaping, Nath said, "Looks like the Lost City isn't so lost after all."

CHAPTER
30

DEEPER INTO THE BOWELS OF Borgash they walked. It was an underground city with a sky made of dirt. Selene's light cut through the dimness, revealing remnants of paved streets and buildings. Dirt and a slick coat of grime covered most of the area. The sky of dirt and roots was suspended above them, looking to collapse at any time. Somewhere, water trickled inside the eerie expanse.

"What do you think, Brenwar?"

The warrior held a small torch now that gave off a warm, glowing yellow light. He climbed up on a half-covered statue of a centaur and poked at the dirt ceiling with his hammer. "Hmmm, seems to have held hundreds of years; no reason to believe it won't hold a few hundred more." He hit it harder with his war hammer.

"Is that really necessary, dwarf?" Selene said, backing up into Nath.

"If it falls, I'll dig us out. It just might take a few years."

"Come on," Nath said. "If there is anything to be found, I can only assume it's below ground and not above."

Venturing deeper into the buried realm, Nath rolled his shoulders. The tightness in his back remained. Something lived here. Something dark. He dusted off his nose with his thumb. There was a stench, too. Not dirt or mud. Not bones or rotting flesh. Something unnatural. A lurking of Evil.

There were plenty of normal creatures that lived beneath the ground. Dragons were one of them. Gnomes and dwarves were well known for making league-long holes. But not too many creatures lived without daylight for very long. Hibernated, yes. Lived, no.

"What's on your mind?" Selene asked.

"Everything feels wrong." He kneeled down and began brushing off some caked dirt that covered a fallen statue. On uncovering its oversized visage, he discovered a monstrous face with multiple eyes and a mouthful of fangs. "Seem familiar?"

"I've never seen a carven image the likes of that before," she said, but..." She backed away and began clawing away hunks of dirt that covered the stony walls. Her efforts revealed painted images. Runes. People. Monsters. Violence. "I'm starting to think the devourer is here for a great reason."

The way she spoke made Nath's skin prickle. "You said it might be a guardian. A guardian of what?"

"A guardian that not only keeps things from getting in," she said, moving away from Nath. She kept the light of her hand pointed at the dirt ceiling. There was a higher spot above. The roots moved away from her light. "Nath, you know how you said this place was evil?"

"Yes."

Selene started back toward him. Standing by his side, she said, "I'm pretty sure you're right."

"Brenwar, did you hear that? She said I was right. See, Selene can be sensible."

Selene jabbed an elbow into his ribs. "Don't be foolish. We need to go."

"Really, why the rush all of a sudden?"

Selene knelt down beside the cruel and unusual face that Nath had revealed. She pointed at it and said, "Because I think I know what this is. It's an image of an old titan."

"Titan?" Nath said, making a quick shrug. "What's a titan?"

"The race that enslaved man. That tried to enslave the dragons as well." She started packing mud back over its face. "The race that would stop at nothing to enslave Nalzambor."

"Step aside," Brenwar said. With a quick swing of his hammer, he busted the image of the old titan face. *Bang!* "Humph. That's better."

"Will you quit hitting everything with your little hammer?" Selene said.

"We don't hesitate to deface the titans where I come from," Brenwar said, resting Mortuun back over his shoulder. "Ever."

Brenwar's tone was serious.

The truth was, Nath had never heard of the titans before today. He'd gathered from Selene that they were legend more than anything. Men and women of great renown, worshipped like deities, who had deceived the races in times past. Judging by the age of that statue, it had happened long before his time, just the same as Borgash. "So, are we staying in or going out? I'm opting for in. I'm not going to find my mother by being cautious. But if you don't want to venture any farther, I understand."

"Oh, please," Selene said, rolling her eyes.

"Shaddap," Brenwar added, holding his torch out and venturing deeper into the passage.

"It seems we're all in again. Great." Nath glided to the front. He could feel the heat from Brenwar's torch on his back. Using his keen eyes, he had little problem making out the deeper outlines of the cavernous passage. Here and there the old roads were revealed. There were still standing walls and columns with markings on them. Old wooden stables were petrified. The air was dank and musty. It would take days to search all of the cave city. Maybe weeks. They might have to dig, and digging wasn't very much fun.

"Seems like a strange place for your mother to be," Selene said. She stood by some stalactites and stalagmites that had formed around a small pond near her feet. "I'm not so sure that I'd trust a fairy. Certainly not a fairy empress."

"You didn't have to come—not that I'm unhappy that you did come—but this is all we have to go on for now." Nath came across a wide staircase of stone that wound deeper into the ground. Squinting, he swore he saw a wink of light down there. "Say, Brenwar, what do you make of this?"

Brenwar sauntered over and peered down the steps. "Looks deep," he said, bobbing his head. "I like deep."

A wink of light flashed.

"Did you see that?" Nath said in a whisper.

Brenwar replied in kind, "Aye, I did." He started down. "And I hear water, too."

"Coming, Selene?" Nath said.

Holding her glowing hand out, she stood behind Nath and said, "You first."

Nath took a breath and headed down after Brenwar.

One thing is for certain. Being small leads to many more interesting places.

The stairway was well over a hundred steps down, its hard surface slick with damp mud. Nath had been in caves all of his life. Even Dragon Home had been bored out of a mountain, and there were prisons more than a hundred feet deep. But this was different. It gave him a mysterious feeling that he couldn't shake. It clung to his scales. Rushed his breath.

"Bottom," Brenwar said. He stood inside a chamber the size of a small cathedral. The light did little to capture the full grandeur. Square columns and great arches held up the expansive ceiling. Colorful murals above glinted in the faint light cast from below. "Sound craftsmanship."

"Dwarven?" Nath asked.

"Not that sound."

A bright light, distant and wavering, appeared far away from them. Humanoid in shape, it glided forward. Nath's breath became icy. The shade closed in, getting bigger. Towering over them all, it came to a stop. Faceless, robed, and ethereal, its haunting voice froze Nath's bones.

CHAPTER

31

THE APPARITION SPOKE, TURNING BLOOD to ice water.

Nath felt Selene's arm entangle with his. Heart pounding in his chest, head gazing upward, he found it hard to keep his eyes fixed on the monster.

Haunting sounds came from its ghostly lips. Its language was unnatural and changing. A howling shriek burst from the veiled face of the apparition.

"Hoooowwww-eeeeee-hooooooowwwwww!"

Nath's knees buckled. His legs turned to jelly. Hair billowing, he covered his ears. Beside him, Brenwar dropped to a knee. Selene's sharp fingernails dug into his arms. "Selene, what do we do?" he asked, trying to shout over the howling shriek.

Shouting in his ear, she replied, "I don't know!"

The apparition's wispy veil lifted. Its face contorted and twisted, showing brief glimpses of all the races. Its shrill voice changed. The tones lifted high and fell back low. Its long-ranging arms stretched toward Brenwar.

The battle-hardened dwarf recoiled. His thick limbs remained rigid.

"Move, Brenwar! Move!" Nath yelled. At least he thought he did. He couldn't tell now. His own limbs were stiff and frozen. His tongue seemed to cleave to the roof of his mouth. Fighting against his frozen bonds, he reached down, grabbed the dwarf by the collar, and jerked him back.

The apparition's hands wavered to a stop. Its face settled into an image more readily seen. Its features sharpened. High cheekbones. Pointed ears. It opened its thin lips and spoke its first intelligible words in a deep and hollow tone. "Who are you?"

That's Elven! Nath's unseen shackles melted away. *An old dialect, but it's Elven.* He spoke back in the best Elven he could. "Nath. Nath Dragon."

The apparition's face shifted from elven to the face of a dragon. It spoke again, this time in Dragonese. "You are odd for a dragon."

Nath looked at Selene, only to find her eyes as wide as his. He turned back to the apparition and replied in Dragonese, "It's a long story. And who might you be?"

The haunting figure diminished somewhat in stature. Its foreboding presence eased. Its long hands stretched out again, cupping around them all but without touching. "Blood runs through your veins. Life-giving blood. Ah, so desirable. So delicious. How fortunate you are to live."

"Who are you?" Nath said. "What is your purpose?"

"Ah, to live again. To breathe. To taste." The ghost's hands lashed out and enveloped Nath. "So wonderful!"

Nath's head jerked back. His blood turned to ice and fire. A flood of memories washed through his mind, not his but someone else's. The apparition's. There were battles. Great titans ruling man and fighting dragons. Death. Life. Loss. Destruction. "Stop it! Stop it!" Nath screamed.

A blinding light flashed. Pain split through his skull. In slow motion he saw himself fall and crash into the cathedral floor, unmoving. Someone rolled him onto his back. Selene stared down at him. Her lips were moving, but no sound came out. Brenwar appeared. Gruff. Angry. Confused. He reached down and started smacking Nath's face.

Will you quit that?

Nath coughed. Finding a small reservoir of strength in his weakened limbs, he tried to sit up. Brenwar and Selene propped him up.

"Nath," Selene said, cupping his face in her hands. "Nath, can you hear me?"

Blinking away the pain behind his eyes, he said, "Yes, stop yelling. What happened?"

Brenwar pointed down at the cathedral floor and said, "That happened."

A man in white robes danced on the cathedral's floor, his bare feet slapping it. Hands on his towheaded hair, he side-stepped back and forth and was singing in a complicated common tongue that the old-timers used in more remote farms and villages deep in the valleys.

"Who is that?" Nath asked. He took Brenwar's arm and allowed the dwarf to help him to his feet. He stretched his aching back. "Gads! I feel like I've aged a hundred years." He caught Brenwar and Selene glancing at each other. "What?"

"Nothing," Selene said, showing an uncertain smile. "How are you feeling?"

Rubbing his head, Nath said, "I haven't been sleeping a hundred years, have I?"

"Why, do I look a hundred years older?" Selene said.

"No, it's just the pair of you have some very peculiar looks on your faces." He rubbed his beard and said, "Gads! What happened?" Nath clutched handfuls of red beard in both of his clawed hands. "I'm not a dwarf, am I?"

"What?" Brenwar growled. "Now you're dreaming. But the beard is a good look for you. Other than that, you look normal, aside from a few new wrinkles."

"Be silent, dwarf!" Selene said.

"Wrinkles!" Nath cried. He felt his face. His skin was tighter, and there were creases in his forehead that had never been there before. "What did that thing do to me?"

The dancing man in the robes came running up the stairs, leapt up the last few, and said, "Apologies and thanks!" He grabbed Nath's hand and shook it vigorously. "I could not help myself! Tee-hee! I breathe again!"

Nath's nostrils flared. The man was taller than Nath and big boned, but there was nothing powerful about his build. A strange, big man, a hair over seven feet tall. Human, but odd for that kind. He seized the man's wrists. "I'm only going to ask you this once. Who are you and what did you do to me?"

"Azorath is my name, I think. Azorath, the gatekeeper of Borgash." He grimaced. "Your grip is iron, liberator. You need not fear anything else from me."

"What did you do to me?"

"I merely stole some years from your life force." Azorath blinked at him. His eyes were black glass and spacey "Please, do not fret, you have plenty. A hundred years or so won't hurt you."

"A hundred years!" Nath started pushing Azorath back down the steps. "Give it back!"

"I fear I cannot! I admit, I would not. The flesh of life is in me again!"

"The flesh of life will be gone from you if you don't undo this."

"You would not kill me, Nath Dragon," Azorath said with a feeble smile. "It's not in your nature."

"It's in mine," Brenwar said.

Selene confronted the man. "It's in mine as well."

"Er ..." Azorath's eyes danced back and forth among the three of them. "Slaying me won't change a thing. It was worth it. And so will your sacrifice be as well, Nath Dragon."

"I didn't sacrifice anything," Nath said. "You stole it."

"The moment you ventured into the bowels of Borgash, you sacrificed everything to find your mother." Azorath tapped his finger to his head. "And I know where she is."

CHAPTER 32

Azorath led now. Nath, Brenwar, and Selene followed. The former shade, now a man, picked his way through the subterranean levels of the fallen city. They climbed over huge chunks of road that had been heaved up. Passageways that weren't made by men. Their eerie guide talked the entire time.

"This was the square here," Azorath said, running his hands over a piece of twisted metal. "Many celebrations and ceremonies. Weddings. Feasts. Grand times, at least until the titans came. They had a different way of celebrating. They killed and ate people. Pitted one against the other. Horrible times, but the dragons liberated the races." He pointed at Nath. "You understand that. A brave and noble thing, fighting for the weak and saving them from the strong."

"Yes, you've said that before, shade," Brenwar said. "How much more walking and talking? You say you know where Nath's mother is. How much farther is she?"

"Almost there," Azorath said, climbing down over a ledge and stopping before a stream of water that trickled. He pushed his hands down in the water and giggled. "I have not drunk nor eaten. I thirst!" He stuck his face in the water and drank. "Ah!"

Brenwar stepped into Nath and Selene's path. "That thing is not right. Don't trust it."

"I know, Brenwar," Nath said, watching Azorath continue to drink and giggle. "But if he knows anything, we have to take that chance."

Brenwar shook his head and followed after Azorath.

"You've been awfully quiet, Selene. What do you make of this?" asked Nath.

She rubbed his shoulder. "It's not for me to decide. It's your quest. You lead, I'll follow."

Nath nodded. Despite the creepy feeling he couldn't shake out from under his scales, he found a ring of truth in Azorath's words. He wanted to believe the strange man knew where his mother was. *Why am I trusting someone who just sucked a huge part of my life from me? How did he know I was searching for my mother? Did he steal my memories as well?"*

After finishing off another handful of water, Azorath continued. "You're probably wondering if I'm the only survivor left of this once-great city."

"No," Brenwar said.

"Sure you are, so I will tell you. Yes, I am." Azorath ducked between two buildings that had collided and formed an unnatural archway. "I was chosen to be the gatekeeper. To be the last. You see, the titans were defeated, but their dark ways were not. Borgash broke out in civil war once the deity-like beings were out of the picture. This faction fought with that one. Everything began to come apart at the seams. The wizards and priests battled for rule and order. Earthquakes broke out. Tornadoes screamed. It went on and on until everyone fought and no one survived. It was madness."

"Still don't care," Brenwar said. He shoved Azorath forward. "Now get us to where we need to be getting."

"I can't help but share my speech. It's been so long since I spoke to anyone. Forgive me for enjoying your miserable company." He ducked his head underneath a low archway that led into a tunnel. "I find it delightful."

Nath rubbed his temples.

I feel like a fool. Just don't look like one, Nath. Be wary of a trap.

He trod over the grime-slickened stones, keeping Azorath in sight. The lanky man had a spring in his step. His whistles echoed, too.

That doesn't make my head much better.

Finally, the gatekeeper came to a stop in front of an archway that was broken in half. Above it, two massive rocks had collided. Pitch blackness was on the other side of the archway. "Through here," he pointed. "Answers to the questions you seek." He reached for Brenwar's torch. "May I?"

"Get yer own."

"Brenwar," Nath said, "please, oblige him."

With a grunt, Brenwar handed the torch over.

Azorath waved it back and forth and erupted in a short series of giggles then said, "I can't help it. I feel the warmth from it. It's delightful." He stuck it through the archway. The flames vanished in the blackness. He pulled it back out, and the flames were still alive. "I warn you. It's very dark in there, but not far." Showing a row of big, smiling teeth, he said, "Who goes in first?"

Nath didn't move, and neither did Selene or Brenwar.

"I see," Azorath said, "then I guess it will be me." He hopped into the blackness and vanished.

Selene let out a sigh.

"What was that for?" Nath said to her.

"He bothers me," she said.

"Me too," Brenwar agreed.

"Nath, now that he—or it—is gone, I'm more prone to speak freely. I'm not so sure there is anything to be gained from this venture. You don't have any evidence to go on about your mother, just the word of a fairy, and now this creature. They are both far from trustworthy."

"Aye," Brenwar said.

"I've considered that," Nath said, "But what if my mother is down inside this horrible place? I can't bear the thought of that. Not to mention I want my years of life back."

"But why would she be?" Selene said. "This place fell more than a thousand years ago. Your mother gave birth to you maybe two hundred and fifty years ago. Why would she come here?"

"Those are good arguments," he said, "but my gut tells me that I need to at least eliminate the possibility." He stepped up to the arch and stuck his hand in it. It felt like he had stuck his fingers in ice. "I'm going in." He extended his free hand. "Anyone else?"

Brenwar came forward. "I'm going, but I'm not holding your hand."

"I will take it," Selene said, taking his hand in hers. "But don't get used to it."

Head ducking down, Nath led them into the archway.

CHAPTER

33

EMPTINESS. THERE WAS NO WORSE feeling than nothing at all.
Guzan, what madness is this?
He tumbled through the blackness, yet there was no wind in his hair. Selene's touch was gone. His heartbeat was missing. Only his thoughts remained. A mind without a body. Soundless, he drifted in nowhere.
I've been deceived!
Struggling to find his own self, he noted a small window of light. He swam toward it. It became bigger, brighter, and it swallowed him whole. Wind rushed by his ears. His arms and legs flailed. "Gah!"
He crashed into a soft bed of sand. He spat the sand from his mouth and shook it from his hair. A shadow fell over him. He glanced up.
"Incoming!" Brenwar yelled. The dwarf landed on Nath's chest.
"Ooof!" He pushed Brenwar off and helped him to his feet.
Brenwar shook the sand from his beard. "This is a fine place."
They stood on a huge bed of cool, wet sand. Water trickled from all around, running down slick, polished cave walls. A soft green light illuminated the cavern like a spectral sky. It was humid and sweaty.
"This will probably be a regrettable decision," Selene said. She was standing behind Brenwar and Nath, dusting the grimy sand from her clothes. Her black hair was matted to her face. She parted it and brushed it back behind her shoulders. Hands on hips, she said, "So, where is your friend?"
Nath shrugged. There was nothing in the cavern but them, and the archway they had entered from was gone. "Any idea how deep we are, Brenwar?"
Brenwar rumbled a reply. "I can't say."
Nath kicked the sand. "Just great."
"Oh, stop being so grim. I was only scouting ahead. Frankly, I didn't

think you would come." It was Azorath. He lumbered up a sandy hill where water ran like a stream below. "Time has a funny way of working down here, and it's been quite some time since I've been in this area. And with a body?" He felt himself. "Tee hee!"

"Listen, Azorath, enough of the games. Take me to see my mother like you promised," Nath said.

"I don't recall promising anything. But if it makes you feel any better, I promise to show you your mother."

Nath didn't reply. He'd spent almost all of his natural life wondering who and where his mother was. Other dragons knew, but he never did, and his father had never told him. Deep down it bothered him, severely, but he never dwelled on it for long. Now, to think he might find the answer to his question? He wasn't sure he was ready. He pulled his shoulders back, marched forward, and said, "Lead the way, then."

Shuffling over the strange landscape, they moved forward at a depressive gait. Never in his life had Nath felt so displaced. His surroundings were so unnatural and odd. Light without a source from above. An eerie tingle in the air. His heightened instincts choked back and waited to cry for danger. He had to see it through, though. Have faith that his heart would lead him to his mother.

I hope I am not deceived.

He recalled his father, Balzurth, often saying, "Be careful of your heart's desires. Sometimes it can deceive you. Seek wisdom first. It will always prevail."

Azorath slogged into the ankle-deep waters and forged away. The strange man's shoulders swung left to right as he moved. The oddness about him made Nath wonder about the people that had lived in Borgash and the culture they'd shared. He felt Selene take his hand in hers. Softly he said back to her, "You must feel as out of place as I do."

"I'd be lying if I said I didn't want to see Nalzambor's sun again. It seems we've been in here for weeks already."

"Almost there," Azorath said, picking up the pace. "Oh, that was quick. It seems we are already there. Now gaze, my liberators. Gaze at the Great Wall of Dragons!"

Selene squeezed Nath's hand and gasped.

Ahead was a great wall indeed. The most magnificent wall that Nath had ever seen. A wall made of dragons. It was expansive, too. It stretched up several stories high and was just as wide. The dragons were a tight cluster of scales, claws, tails, horns, and teeth. They were a colorful mix of stone and marble. Every detail was just as realistic as the next. Dragons, great and small. Nath could tell what they were by the shapes of their heads. There were dragon breeds from the large bull dragons to the smaller fire bites. Finding his breath, Nath said, "Who created this wonder?"

"Why, the dragons did," Azorath replied. He had his hands clasped behind his back and was studying the wall with adoration. "Quite the sacrifice, isn't it?"

"I don't take your meaning," Nath said. "Are you saying that dragons carved this?"

"No, no, you don't understand. Come, come," Azorath said, beckoning with his hand. "Touch it. Feel it. That is the best way to answer your question."

"I don't like this," Selene said, not hiding the concern in her voice.

"I've never seen stonework so grand as this," Brenwar added. "Not outside of Morgdon for certain."

Nath's heart beat faster. Drawn to the great wall, he ventured forward and stretched out his hand. With the slightest tremble in his claw-tipped fingers, he laid his scaled palm on the wall. It was warm to the touch. His jaw dropped, and then with amazement he said, "Sultans of Sulfur! It's beating!"

CHAPTER 34

"**I** CAN'T BELIEVE THIS," NATH SAID with incredulity. "Selene, you must feel it."

The raven-headed woman hesitated. "I don't know about this, Nath. How can they live such a fate? I don't understand."

Nath swallowed. Sweat dripped into his eyes, and his heart continued to race. Hundreds of heartbeats, slow and steady, thumped through his palm, igniting his entire body. So many dragons clustered together as one. *Why?*

Finally, Selene stretched out her hand and touched the wall of dragons. She took in a sharp breath. Tears swelled in her eyes. Her normal calm and cool expression switched back and forth between sorrow and joy. "This is madness. But I don't sense any torment. Do you?"

Nath searched his feelings. He searched the feelings in the life within the dragon wall. There was no sadness. Just duty. Honor. Comfort for one another. "They aren't alone in this. They have united together. But why, Azorath?" He tore his hand away. "Why?"

Rubbing his chin, Azorath said with sad dark eyes, "They formed a barrier to keep the titans within. Never to escape again."

"Didn't they kill them all?" Nath said.

"The dragons showed mercy in hopes that one day the titans might redeem themselves." He sighed. "There was a time when they served the world for good, not evil. At least some of them. That is how I remember it, anyway."

Eyes fixed on the dragon wall, Nath said, "The price is too high. These dragons have lives to live. Certainly there must be a better way to seal those foul monsters within."

"I don't know the answer to that," Azorath said, "but dragons live a long time. And I've seen dragons take other dragons' places." He walked up to the wall and touched the face of a red rock dragon. Running his hands over its curled tail, he said, "See, this one is new. I'd guess he came here not fifty years ago, when another one left."

"You're telling me the dragons know about this, but I don't? How can that be? Selene?"

"I don't know either, Nath. It's a mystery to me," she said.

"It's a big world, and it's full of surprises." Azorath placed his hand on the wall. "How sad, I don't feel what you feel. It just feels like a wall to me. Interesting."

"You were a shade before. Have you ever been on the other side?" Nath asked.

"No, not possible. Nothing can pass through it. No shade, spirit, titan, nor dragon."

It made sense enough to Nath. Staring at the dragons, he began picking out the details of their faces. He knew every breed. Beyond the color of their scales, each dragon breed had a unique design to its claws, horns, and even the flecks of their iron-hard scales. There wasn't any type that he didn't recognize. "I have no idea what my mother looks like or what type of dragon she is. Have you seen her, Azorath?"

"I've seen many dragons come and go."

"You said my mother was here. How would you know that if you hadn't seen her?" Nath's brow furrowed. "Show me which one she is."

"Ask them yourself. It might take me years to sort through all of them. I'm not so bored that I note every detail."

"This smells, Nath," Brenwar said. "Smells really bad. This Azorath is a liar. A stealer. I wouldn't trust another word he said."

"Don't be such a dwarf," Azorath said. "I haven't done anything you wouldn't have done given my situation. Again, I'm grateful. I have flesh again, but I do miss my people."

Nath spread his arms out, held them in front of the wall, and said, "I'm going to ask them."

"Be patient, Nath," Selene said, walking in front of him and staying his arms. "We need to learn more about what we're dealing with. Let's study the histories and research it."

"You felt it, too, Selene. We can't just let them live like this. We must see what they need. Maybe we can help them."

"They might not want help," Selene said. "It seems they made their own decision."

"That's only a guess."

"It makes no difference to me. You wanted to find your mother. I care not if you find her or not. But if I could find my mother, I'd probably venture the extra step," Azorath said, stretching his arms and yawning. "Oh my, did you see that? My limbs tire. What a feeling!"

Nath glanced at Brenwar. The dwarf's stern expression didn't offer any advice. He found Selene's eyes. Beautiful and mysterious, there was doubt lurking deep within. It wasn't like her at all. Perhaps it was guilt. She'd unleashed something terrible with the wurmers. Sounding as reassuring as he could, he said, "It's only a question."

"Then I hope you are prepared for the answer." Selene stepped away and found a place behind him. "You might not like it."

Nath placed both hands on the wall. Life flowed through the structure like a living stream. A powerful network of dragons forming a cohesive unit. It was a marvel the likes of which he'd never seen. Without hesitation, he spoke to it with thoughts instead of words.

"Brothers and sisters, I am Nath Dragon, and I am searching for my mother. Is she here?"

The wall trembled. Dragon thoughts assaulted his mind. They probed. They questioned. Nath felt every bit of them. Patient and strong they were. Formidable. Dedicated. His body shook.

"Go away, Son of Balzurth," they said. "Go away!"

Nath felt them holding back. They protected something. Something that wasn't beyond the wall. He didn't back off. "I want to know where my mother is," Nath fired back. "I am the Dragon Prince. I demand it. Is she here or not?"

Boom!

The dragon wall shook, juttering Nath's arms. Something had slammed into it from the other side. Nath grimaced. He could feel the dragons' pain.

Boom!

The wall shook again.

"Go, Nath Dragon, go. We cannot afford this distraction," they said with fierce desperation. "We must stay focused."

Nath held on and said again, "Is my mother here or not?"

"I am, Son," said a female voice.

Every fiber of Nath's being came to new life. The warmth of her voice enveloped him.

"Mother?" he said, tears streaming down his cheeks.

"Son, you must go. You endanger all of us. You'll see me when the time is right."

Boom! Boom! Boom!

Something raged on the other side of the wall. It was fierce. Unrelenting.

Nath sensed confusion among the dragons. There was pain and worry. How often did the dragons have to endure this?

"Mother! Let me help you! Let me see your face!"

"Nath, you must go before it's too late. Trust me!" Her words were no longer soothing but worried. "Flee this place with urgency!"

"I cannot let you suffer!"

Boom! Boom! Boom!

Brenwar rammed into him, knocking him away from the wall. "We have to go! This entire place is coming down!"

"Noooooooooooooooooooo!" Nath screamed, clutching at the wall. Selene and Brenwar hooked his arms and dragged him backward. Gaping, Nath watched the entire wall of dragons come to life. Their colors returned. They moved and shifted. Eyes snapped open. Dragon jaws grimaced. They squeezed into as tight a knot as they could.

Boom!

The entire wall buckled.

"Perfect," Azorath said. He found Nath's eyes. "We thank you for the long-overdue distraction."

Boom!

The center of the wall of dragons burst open. Dragons were flung from the air. Something evil and colossal emerged.

CHAPTER
35

THE TITAN WAS THE BIGGEST man Nath had ever seen. His head had two faces: one in front and one in back. The massive man was chest and shoulders on both sides, his body bronze and brawny. One face sneered. The other was shouting, "I am free!"

Nath's mother shouted an order. "Dragons, attack! Force Isobahn back behind the wall!"

Hundreds of dragons converged, coating the titan.

The huge man—so big he held a bull dragon in the crook of his arm like a pup—slung them off one by one.

The dragons released fire. Lightning. Everything shook. They flung themselves into the titan, driving him back inside the wall.

Nath watched the battle in awe. The dragons, with all their skill and grandeur, were no match for the titan's relentless power. His massive fist swatted the dragons down like flies. His feet stomped them between his toes. Isobahn was no man. He was pure monster.

"We have to help!" Nath said.

"Aye!" Brenwar said, spitting in his hands and rubbing them together. "Step aside. That giant is mine!" After a few seconds of winding Mortuun in a huge windmill circle, he released the hammer with all his might. The hammer flew and struck the titan between the eyes. A clap of thunder rang out.

Kapow!

Isobahn the titan teetered backward.

The dragons rallied with triumphant roars.

"Push him through, brothers and sisters. Push him through!" Nath's mother said.

Moved by his mother's words, Nath, little bigger than the titan's finger, charged. He hurled himself along with the throng of dragons and scaled up the titan. Clawed hands digging into its coarse flesh, he raced up its belly, up the shoulder, and launched both fists into one of its eyes.

The titan groaned and fell like a collapsed tower.

"Get out of there, Nath!" he heard his mother scream.

Fire and lightning blasted into Isobahn. The titan rocked and reeled. Dragons by the hundreds, all shapes and sizes, piled onto him.

Catching friendly fire, Nath dove away.

Guzan! Where am I?

The other side of the cavern glowed with a burning red light. Streams of lava flowed from the deep. Steam and sulfur tainted the air.

Nath's eyes watered and burned. Blinking, he watched the dragons reforming the wall.

"Run, Nath! Quickly!"

Nath sprinted for the wall. The dragons were reforming it with incredible speed. He took a quick glance over his shoulder. The titan was back on its feet. Its massive hand reached down and scooped Nath up from the ground.

Nath cried out. "Ahhh!" Pain exploded through his body. His breath fled. His face purpled.

The titan opened up its mouth and started to shove him in.

Sultans of Sulfur! I'm being crushed and consumed. Nooooo!

A gold dragon appeared. It slipped into the jaws of the titan's mouth and unleashed a firestorm down the titan's throat.

Nath slipped free of the titan's loosened grasp. He hit the ground with a thud. Reeling, he forced himself up to his feet, cried out, and fell. His leg was broken. He spat blood and clutched his sides. His ribs were busted.

How many bones did that monster break?!

Setting his jaw and ignoring the pain, Nath hopped on one foot toward the wall.

Behind him, the gold dragon, the most magnificent winged serpentine he'd ever seen, continued to let the titan have it. The monster's head was nothing but flames.

Still, it fought on, swatting oversized fists at the dragon. None of the heavy blows hit the mark. Roaring, it lowered its shoulder and charged for the wall.

Hobbled, Nath hopped as fast as he could.

The titan's foot overshadowed him and came down.

I'm going to be goo!

A golden streak whizzed in and scooped him up just as the giant foot came down.

Whoom!

Nath found himself being sped toward the small hole that was left in the wall and whisked through. The golden dragon gently set him on the ground and turned to face the wall. The dragons filled it in with their armored bodies. The final link was set. Their colorful skins and hides began to harden just as the titan on the other side rocked against it.

Boom! Boom! Boom!

"We are safe now," the golden dragon said. "The wall is secure."

Finding Selene and Brenwar back by his side, Nath used them to get back on his feet. Then, gazing up at the dragon, he said, "Who are you?"

"I am Grahleyna, Nath. Your mother."

Three horses tall, she towered over him. She was wondrous. Her pearl-white horns curled over her head, and long black lashes flicked over her golden eyes. Scales twinkled at the subtle movements of her muscles underneath. Nath reached over to touch her. Limping over, he wrapped his arms around her massive leg.

Grahleyna chuckled. "Oh, Nath, let me make this easier for us." With an utterance of mystic words, she began to diminish in size. Standing gold eye to gold eye with him, she said, "This is better. Is it not?"

She was a fair-skinned, golden-haired woman with a pearl crown on her head. Trembling, Nath reached over and hugged her with tears swelling in his eyes. Her embrace was warm as a campfire. "I was never sure if you were real until just now."

She stroked his hair. Tears ran down her soft cheeks. She sniffed. "I'm sorry, Nath. I never meant to leave. And I never intended to be gone so long, but I had to do what needed to be done. It was my turn, and the timing was bad. Besides, I didn't have any way of knowing that you were the one."

He eased back. "What do you mean?"

"There were many eggs. Some hatch in days, others decades. You certainly know that you have brothers and sisters." She squatted down and put her hands on his broken leg. "They just hatched dragons, and you a man."

Nath's leg tingled with tiny charges of fire. The pain eased. He shifted his weight on it and said, "It's better, but wait a moment. You said hatched."

"Yes, why?"

"So, I was born in an egg?"

She combed her fingers through his hair and said, "Certainly. How else would you be?"

"Hah! I knew you were hatched!" Brenwar said. "I knew it!"

Nath didn't want to think about it. Even though he was a dragon, he didn't care for the idea of being hatched. He never had, for some reason. Moving on, he asked his mother, "So, can you come with us? Or do you have to stay and help form the wall?"

Boom!

"Oh," she said, glancing over her shoulder, "Isobahn is secure. He's not the one we need to worry about. It's the others."

CHAPTER

36

"I DIDN'T SEE ANYTHING ELSE," NATH said to his mother. Brenwar and Selene looked around with wide eyes, too. "Azorath? What has become of him?"

There was a shuffle of movement underneath one of the dragons who had fallen to the wrath of the titan. It was a gray scaler, little bigger than Nath. A hand stretched up and around its belly. Brenwar jogged over and rolled the dragon over. He jerked Azorath's haggard form up to his feet. "Here is the wretched deceiver."

Clutching his chest, Azorath said, "I need to get used to this mortality. I think parts of me are broken. Weee! Ow! I hurt." His spacey black eyes drifted over to Grahleyna. "I see you found your mother. I told you so, Nath. Giving me life was worth it, now. Wasn't it."

"You took what wasn't yours, Azorath."

"Oh, you'll be fine," he said in his mysterious way. "Besides, with the titans free, you probably shouldn't plan a life of longevity. But I'm certain yours will be fuller than a hundred lives, for a spell."

Nath stepped toward Azorath and took ahold of his neck. "What do you mean?"

Grahleyna took his arm and pulled him back. Resting her hands gently on his shoulders, she said, "Finding me came at a price, Nath. You see, Isobahn was a bodyguard of the true threat. Now, the others escape. Crafty spirits they are. They couldn't penetrate the dragon wall, but little more than ethereal in form, they easily escaped when the wall was breached."

"So we can't see them?"

"They are harmless until they take host in other bodies, and that could be anybody," his mother said. "They prey on the weak. Divide and conquer. The threat they pose is not easily seen. That's why Borgash fell. The men and women were so divided that even after we vanquished the titans, they still fought among themselves. Once you plant the bad seed in men, it doesn't take long for their lives to unravel."

"How did you trap them before?" Nath said.

"In this last case, we trapped them, body and spirit, behind this barrier. Several brave dragons fought them on the other side, hoping to wipe them out of existence, but their valiant efforts failed." She rubbed his shoulder. "It's difficult to destroy evil. A remnant always remains."

Nath's throat tightened. Did Gorn Grattack still exist? Had Nath not wiped that monster out entirely? "Mother, there has to be a better way than this." He stretched out his hands toward the wall.

"Don't," she said, "else you'll have Isobahn trying to bite off our heads again. It's best such darkness lies in the deepness from where it came. Nalzambor's bowels can hold them without help. And the dragons understand their sacrifice, but a time may come when it has to be made permanent. That is a fate they must choose on their own." Grahleyna put her arm around Nath's waist and led him away. "It was destined that they should be let loose for a season anyway."

"Let loose? Why?" he said, incredulous.

"It's just the times we live in."

Long faced, Nath felt his blood seep into his toes. Finding his mother should have been a time of celebration. Instead, he'd loosed more menaces into the world. It didn't help that he wasn't in the full grandeur of a dragon, either. He was much weaker.

Selene found her way to his side. "Don't be hard on yourself, Nath. You couldn't have known."

"Your friend is right. Selene, is it?" Grahleyna said, fastening her eyes on Selene's.

"Yes, your majesty," Selene said, taking a knee.

"Oh, there is no need for that, my dear." She helped Selene up to her feet. "You have a great understanding of this darkness, don't you."

Frowning, Selene said, "More than I care to admit."

"Use that knowledge. You'll need it." Grahleyna turned back to Nath. "What led you here anyway?"

"Father gave us a hint: 'What you seek is in the peaks.'"

Grahleyna laughed. "Oh, and that was it. So like him. He gives you just enough information so it will only take one thousand years to find me. But here you are."

"So does father know that you have been here all along?" Nath said.

"Certainly."

Angry, Nath said, "Why wouldn't he tell me that? Why would he just leave you here like this? It's a terrible thing!"

"And boring, but it's mostly sleeping, so it's not so bad." She poked Nath's chest. "And don't you judge your father. It was my choice, not his. He didn't like it one bit. He had a fit like a one-hundred-year-old about it. He started stomping around and shooting up big puffs of fire. I was embarrassed for him."

"Father did that?" Nath said. He'd never seen anything like it from his father.

"Oh, don't be disenchanted. He's temperamental because he loves me." She checked her nails and pushed her hair up a little. "And that's probably why he endorsed your search."

"Couldn't he just come and see you?"

"By the Sultans, no! Balzurth would charge right through that wall and try to put an end to those titans. That's exactly what they want. Take down the Dragon King. End his reign. They were so eager to get out, they missed a golden opportunity. They overlooked you." Grahleyna turned her attention back to Azorath. "Now what do we do with you?"

"Me? I'm harmless. I just want to walk among men again." His eyes darted from face to face. "Just a man. One that can live and have a natural death."

"And a natural death you shall have." Grahleyna opened her mouth. Bright golden flames washed over Azorath. He turned to a pile of ash before he could even scream. "Never trust a shade, Son."

Nath convulsed. A river of life rushed through him. His blood coursed with a new spring of energy. "Thank you, Mother."

She patted him on the shoulder. "Evil—don't give it a chance. Now it's time for your first order from Mother. Find those titans. Bring them back or destroy them."

CHAPTER

37

GRAHLEYNA FLUNG HER HEAD BACK. "Ah! It's so good to be in the sun's light again. It warms me inside and out." She spread her arms wide and spun slowly around. The bright light enhanced her incredible beauty and elegance. "Come, walk with me, Nath, and bring your friends along, while I still have the time."

The Lost City of Borgash was still a barren place with strange and ugly vegetation. Nath carefully maneuvered through the thick vines. Brenwar's eyes remained fixed on the ground, Mortuun swinging at his side. Selene managed to find her own place over a dozen paces ahead on a broken path that led east and out of the forgotten city.

Grahleyna whisked them out of the catacombs. It was a confusing and winding path, but Nath could make it back and out again if he had to. He was sure of it. Walking stride for stride with his mother, he kept his chin up and chest out. The joy of having her by his side was incredible, but a frown started to crease his lips.

"You care for her much, don't you," his mother said to him, eyeing Selene.

"I care for you much, and now you are leaving?"

"Well, I'm going to leave you with good advice, and that will be much better than the advice I left you with the last time."

"Hah, well I suppose that is true." He laughed. "I don't want you to go, though. I want to stay with you. The titans can wait at least a decade, can't they?"

"Oh, a decade with our sweet mother. How flattering is that? You certainly get that side of you from me and not your father. Of course, he does have a dashing side."

"Father, dashing?"

She tousled his hair. "You are very handsome, like him, but more so."

Nath flashed a smile, "No doubt it's the part of you in me that shines."

"Tell me more about you and Selene. I want to know everything."

"Sh! Mother, she can hear everything."

"That's right," Selene said, waving her arm up over her head. "And I can't wait to hear what you have to say, Nath."

"Perhaps our time could be better spent talking about how you met Father, Mother?"

Grahleyna chuckled. "I'm not going there, but I will tell you this: we were in mortal forms when we met."

Nath's brows lifted and he said, "Like me. Like us now?"

"The same."

Nath's eyes glided toward Selene. She was staring back at him with a playful glint in her eyes.

His mother continued, "Balzurth roamed Nalzambor the same as you did. A hero among mankind with countless triumphs. He was so cocky." She sighed. "But I liked it. He picked the prettiest bouquets of flowers. And he could sing so soft the fairies would cry."

"My father?"

"Oh, think back, Nath. I'm sure you've seen a softer side of him."

There were plenty of lessons that Nath recalled, some harsh and others wise, but singing? He didn't remember any of that.

Grahleyna started humming.

Words formed in Nath's mind. He started singing.

"Ah praise the hills of daffodils, the kings, or run Tinny Lee. The dragons come, the fairies flee. Riding on the wings and scales came lightning from the clouds. Hondor the brave and ten thousand bannered warriors.

Run Tinny, run Tinny, run Tinny, run.

A thousand years, a thousand slumbers, comes the gentle crescent of night. Half for the light, half for the dark.

Run Tinny, run Tinny, run.

Home is there for the wayward son."

Nath came to a stop. "He did sing that to me, didn't he?"

"Yes, I'm sure of it. I never liked that song. It was sung by a drunken troubadour the day we met. The man's voice was awful as an ogre's, but your father made the song beautiful."

"What does it mean? Who is Hondor?"

"No idea," she said. "Just a silly song written by a sordid man who needed a button for his trousers. Not every song has to have a meaning. Sometimes it just needs to be fun to sing." She lifted her chin toward the sky. A flock of dragons streaked through the clouds. "What in the name of Morgdon were those?"

Not hiding the concern from his voice, Nath replied, "Wurmers."

Grahleyna's golden eyes became as big as saucers. "Please tell me my eyes deceived me? Those blasted things are an abomination." Fire sparked in her voice. "Oversized winged termites! Barnabus! They'll be perfect hosts for the titans!"

Selene rushed down toward them and said, "Your majesty, it is my error. A failure of my past!"

"Then I'd say you and Nath are made for each other. You let one terror out of the sack and he let out another." Grahleyna shook her head. "In the meantime, it looks like I'm going to have to deal with those wurmers myself. Stand back."

Nath and Selene stepped way back.

Wings sprouted on Grahleyna's back. Her body enlarged, and scales quickly covered her from head to toe. Within seconds, Nath gazed up at a most excellent gold dragon. "If I could only fly, I could go and destroy them with you."

"Hah, hah, hah," Grahleyna said, "if you could only fly. How silly you sound, Nath. I hope you figure that out soon, Dragon Prince." She spread her beautiful black-and-gold wings out. "Now, I must go. And you two need to figure out how to clean up your mess."

"But Mother, you can't leave. We just met!"

Grahleyna bent down and kissed Nath on the head. "I promise to see you again much sooner than the last time." Pushing off with her powerful legs, she launched herself into the air. Wings beating at a furious rhythm, she sliced through the air like a golden arrow and disappeared, pursuing the wurmers.

Shoulders slumped, Nath turned and faced his friends. "I can't believe she's gone already."

"Get yer chin up," Brenwar said, "I'm not of the impression that your mother would approve of you moping around."

"Me either." Holding her head, Selene said, "Gads, but now I feel even guiltier than before. We're going to have to finish off those monsters before it's too late."

Eyeing the sky and rubbing the back of his neck, Nath said, "You know, just once it would be nice if my parents gave me a little more information." He took a deep breath through his nose and pulled his shoulders back. "Well, I figured it out before, and together we'll figure it out again. Let's go."

"As long as there's a fight ahead, I'll always be ready." Brenwar swung Mortuun around with his wrist. "Where are we going?"

"It's time to visit one of Nalzambor's greatest historians."

"Aw, great! We're going to Morgdon," Brenwar looked elated and started marching away.

"I'm pretty sure Nath's not talking about Morgdon. I believe he's referring to Quintuklen."

Brenwar stopped and cocked an eyebrow. "Quintuklen? It's a pile of rubble. And that will be a long, wasted march, too. Morgdon is far closer." He eyed Nath and Selene up and down. "Not to mention the likelihood of danger. There isn't even a weapon between you."

"My wits are all that I need," Selene said, standing with her arms crossed over her chest.

Nath held his clawed hands out before him. Having battled the wurmers before in the body of a full dragon, his clawed fingers seemed wholly inadequate. He tapped his noggin and walked off with a shrug, saying, "I guess my wits will have to do as well."

But I'd feel much better if I still had Fang.

CHAPTER
38

IT TOOK OVER A WEEK on foot to find the tall hill grasses that surrounded Quintuklen. Nath stood shirtless, waist deep in a pond, with a long stick whittled down to a spear.

"What's the matter, can't you catch them with your hands anymore?" Brenwar said. The salty old dwarf stood on the bank running a rugged comb through his beard.

"You can always swim in here and fetch dinner yourself, you know," Nath said.

"You volunteered, not me. I said I could wait until we made it to Quintuklen anyway. It's you that has the growling tummy, not me. Pah." The dwarf picked up a smooth stone and skipped it over across the ponds and right by Nath's head.

"Watch it, Brenwar! My head isn't as hard as yours."

"It's gotten soft. I can attest to that."

Spying movement in the murky green waters, Nath jabbed his spear quicker than a striking snake. He pulled a fish bigger than his head out of the pond. Its big tail flapped back and forth and caught Nath in the face.

"Oh ho ho!" Brenwar laughed, holding his gut. "That fish has more fight in it than you!"

Nath waded out of the waters. "You keep holding that big gut of yours, because this fish is going to feed me and Selene."

"Gut!" Brenwar slapped the breastplate over his belly. "An iron gut, lad!"

"Lad!"

"Aye, lad! A big, scaly, flame-haired one. What are you going to do about it, strike me with that mighty fish?"

Nath swung the fish full into Brenwar's face. *Slap!*

Brenwar's eyes became big angry moons. "Never hit a dwarf with a fish!" He dropped his shoulder and charged.

Nath came off his feet and tumbled to the ground. "Blast it, Brenwar!"

Brenwar stuffed Nath's face into the soft bank. "Quit yer bellyaching, Nath Dragon!" He locked Nath's arm behind his back and pinned him half in the water and half in the sand.

"Have you gone mad? You'll pay for this!" Nath struggled against his friend's iron clutches. He didn't have any idea what had happened to Brenwar. They'd been bickering for days. Brenwar didn't have anything to be mad about, either; Nath did. He'd lost his power. Found his mother only to lose her again. Not to mention that he'd unintentionally turned a new menace loose on Nalzambor that he hadn't meant to. With a heave, he flung Brenwar over his shoulder and slammed him into the cattails and reeds. "Get off of me!"

Brenwar sprang to his feet and launched his head hard into Nath's chin.

His teeth clacked together and he saw stars exploding in his head. Staggering back, he felt his knees wobble, and he plopped on his butt into the water. While he sat shaking his head, his eyes became flame. "You're going to regret this, Bolderguild!"

Brenwar spat in the water. "Pah! I don't think you'll do anything with those tears in your eyes. Here, let me get a handkerchief. Maybe Selene will wipe them away for you."

Nath exploded into motion. His fists became striking hammers, fast and powerful.

Brenwar fought back, landing bone-jarring shots on Nath's ribs and chin.

Not holding back, Nath busted Brenwar hard in his breastplate, creating a dent. *Bang!*

Brenwar let out a wail. "Yer gonna fix that!" He rammed his elbow into Nath's groin.

Seeing red, Nath snatched Brenwar up high over his head and stuffed him head first into the waters. He held him down, ignoring Brenwar's flailing boots.

Zap!

Nath's hairs stood on end. His bones juttered from pure shock. His grip loosened on Brenwar.

Brenwar popped up out of the waters and dashed the water from his eyes with both hands. "What kind of trickery was that, Nath?"

"Have you two gone mad?" It was Selene. She stood on the bank. Her face was hot with confusion and rage. "Get ahold of yourself!"

Sitting in the water with his hands over his knees, Nath started laughing uncontrollably. He stopped abruptly and rubbed his jaw. "Oh!

Brenwar held out his forearm. "Feeling better?"

Rising to his feet, Nath said, "Thanks, Brenwar." It had been a long time since the pair romped. They'd done it plenty when Nath was younger. Brenwar had taught him all about fighting, clean and dirty. Nath's charging blood had him feeling better again. "I needed that."

"You both are mad," Selene said in astonishment. "But you are men, after all. What's next, hugging?"

"No thank you," Brenwar said, sloshing out of the water.

A dark shadow soared overhead and darted north toward Quintuklen.

"Shades!" Selene said. "You too buffoons distracted my intentions. I came to warn you: Quintuklen is under attack!"

CHAPTER
39

HOOFING IT OVER THE GRASSY knolls and hillsides, Nath sprinted as fast as he could, with Selene only a few strides behind him. Ahead, Quintuklen, at least what was left, was smoking. Dragons, flying above, were pelting it with fire.

"Those are wurmers!" Nath said, legs churning even faster.

Quintuklen had been all but destroyed in the last dragon war against the Clerics of Barnabus and Gorn Grattack. But now, from the distance, he could clearly see that it was being rebuilt. The stone walls that surrounded the town were almost entirely intact. Pulleys, bulwarks, and scaffolding had popped up all over the city. New stone buildings and wooden apartments. Fresh paint. The old roads were no longer mud and grass but filled with stone. And there were people. Throngs here and there, gathering stones and makeshift spears and hurling them at the dark-scaled dragons.

Fire came down on the valiant defenders.

Claws from the skies snatched people up and dropped them from high in the air.

"Noooooooooo!" Nath screamed.

He fought the helplessness that boiled inside him. If he could fly, he could rise into the air and battle the wurmers. Instead, he was stuck on the ground, racing over the expansive distance hoping he could get there in time and somehow help.

"Selene, have you any thoughts?"

"I was hoping you did!"

They made it to the first barrier wall that protected the city. It was more than ten feet tall. Rather than race down to the next gateway, Nath leapt clear over it. Five walls later, he was on the road that led straight into the city. A bright gleam of steel caught his eye. The midday sun shined off the breastplates of a squad of Legionnaires.

"What can I do to help?" Nath said, jogging up to the highest-ranking officer.

The commander had a long and wispy moustache that hung down past his chin. Stout and durable in his plate-mail armor, he looked Nath up and down and said, "Find some steel, and if one of those things lands, start swinging. Go for the wings. Their hides are as thick as, er," he looked at Nath's arms and said, "a dragon's."

"May I borrow a spear?" Nath said to the commander.

"Anything for you, Nath Dragon," the commander said. "Lieutenant, give this warrior your spear!"

Nath pulled back his shoulders and took the spear the soldier offered him. *They know me. They don't fear me. A good thing!* He scanned the faces of the Legionnaires. There was more duty than fear in their stern expressions. And there were less than twenty of them. All survivors who had returned to rebuild their city. Their determined looks filled Nath with greater courage. "Get those crossbows ready. We need to get their attention. Aim for the biggest one."

Counting the dragons, he noticed most of them were only about fifteen feet long. *Not too big, but still plenty deadly. If I can take the leader down, hopefully the rest will flee.* "Selene, can you bring some light? We need a distraction."

Selene's hands flared with bright purple light. "Like this?"

"It's pretty, but not exactly the attention getter I was looking for."

"Oh," she smirked, "you want something more like this." Lavender shards erupted from her fingertips and made bee lines toward a dragon latched onto one of the tower walls.

It let out a roar and crashed to the ground.

The legionnaires let out a triumphant cheer.

"Show-off," Nath said.

The dragon popped up off of its back. Snarling, it charged straight toward Nath and Selene. Nath lowered his spear and raced right into the face of the dragon. Finding a soft spot in its neck, he jammed the spear into its throat.

The dragon shrieked and thrashed. The spear shaft snapped in half. Its tail flicked out, catching Nath in the heel and pulling him off his feet. The fifteen-foot monster's head recoiled, and its chest filled with fiery breath. Nath started to roll.

Boom!

The wurmer exploded into scales and pieces.

Getting back to his feet, he found Selene and said, "Did you do that?"

"No. It wasn't me." She pointed toward one of Quintuklen's towers that was being rebuilt. "It was him."

Nath twisted his head around. A tall, rangy warrior stood at the top of a rebuilt staircase. Long brown hair with gray streaks flowing through it billowed in the wind. He took the arrow out of his mouth and fired again. The sound of the bowstring's snap was one of a kind. *Twang!*

The arrow caught a sky-cruising wurmer in the belly and turned it into dragon chunks with another thunderous *Boom!*

"Ben!" Nath screamed.

Holding the bow Akron high over his head, the old warrior saluted and cried out, "Dragon!"

Suddenly, a pack of three wurmers, wings beating, surrounded Ben. Their lungs filled with air, and fire gathered inside their jowls.

No, he'll be incinerated!

Nath looked for something to grab. Something to throw. There was nothing. "Let loose something, Selene! Soldiers, unleash those crossbows!"

"They might hit Ben," Selene warned.

Helpless and with bated breath, Nath watched Ben about to die. Without notice, the air crackled with new energy. From somewhere below, a streak of energy shot into the sky and struck the wurmers hovering over the tower. One beast turned to ash, and the other two let out startled cries. A fork of lightning rocked into both of them. They twitched, smoked, and plummeted hard into the earth. *Thud! Thud!*

With no more dragons in sight, the Legionnaires and city folk erupted into cheers. Coming down the street and heading straight toward Nath and Selene, two figures emerged. Ben, looking as tough and rugged as chewed leather, strolled, arms swinging, with a smaller person by his side. Bayzog was violet eyed, green robed, and looking calm and serious both at the same time.

With a broad smile on his scarred lips, Ben put Akron away. *Clatch. Snap. Clatch.* He gave Nath a hug. "Dragon, I never thought I'd see you like this again. Or at all again, for that matter. I can only imagine that something bad is going on."

"Thanks to you, nothing bad is going on at all here, Ben. You sure took it to those wurmers and saved my scales again."

"What did I miss? What did I miss?" It was Brenwar, rushing up to them, Mortuun ready, and huffing for breath. "Tell me I didn't miss all of the fighting."

"Of course you did," Bayzog said to him. "If we had to wait for you, we'd miss out on dinnertime."

"Watch it, part-elf."

Elderwood staff in hand, Bayzog patted Brenwar on the head. "I didn't miss you either, friend. Eh, nice hand. What happened, did you run out of hide jerky?" He gave a quick nod to Selene and then turned to Nath. "What have you done now?"

"Me?"

Selene interrupted the moment, pointing at the sky. "Look."

A white dragon, no horns, small legs, and with a very long body and tail soared high above.

"Strange," Nath said, "what would an ivory slider be doing here? They are messengers," Nath said

"Fascinating," Bayzog said. "It's quite a treat seeing a breed I have not seen before. It looks to be carrying something in its paws."

The ivory slider released something with a nice bright shine and disappeared in the backdrop of clouds in the sky.

"What was that?" Ben said. "Why did it drop it on the other side of the walls?"

"There's only one way to find out," Nath said. He took off at a trot.

"We don't have to run everywhere, you know," Brenwar said.

"Fine," Nath said. "We don't have to complain everywhere, either."

"You know, Brenwar, I could make you some boots that will make you walk faster," Bayzog offered.

"Why don't you make yourself some boots that will take you back to your homeland, part-elf."

"I love reunions," Ben said to Selene. "How about you?"

"I don't know. I've never had one before."

Eyes feeling a little misty, Nath started to round the gate at the outermost wall. There was no feeling quite like being around the friends that had fought for you again and again.

No feeling like it at all.

He came to a stop and gawked at the object sticking up out of the field. A beautiful sword pommel with dragon crossguards winked at him with gemstone eyes. "Fang!"

"I'll be," Brenwar said. "We really must be in for it."

Upon snatching the sword up, Nath began twirling it around in strokes that looked like lightning. New energy coursed through his veins. The handle was warm as an old friend's handshake. He kissed the grand and shiny blade.

"Looks like the pair of you have been reunited just in time," Bayzog said, eyeing the storm front coming from the south.

"Really, Bayzog, why do you say that?" Nath asked.

Everyone pointed where Bayzog was looking. Wurmers, wingless and big, were snaking through the tall grasses.

Nath raised Fang high, and with the fierce bellow of a dozen embattled warriors he yelled, "Dragon! Dragon!"

Epilogue

"**H**OW NICE IT IS TO see you again, Eckubahn. It's been too long," Lotuus said. The fairy empress hovered inside a portion of mountainside that looked to have recently been scooped out. Inside, three earth giants stood staring down on her with heavy eyes. The tallest, brawny and covered in coarse black-brown hair, petted the hairs on his forearms. He leered at her. "Does that body not please you, grand titan?"

Eckubahn scratched the scruff underneath his neck, wetted his thumb, and smoothed his eyebrows back. His voice was the sound of a rumbling volcano. "It will do, fairy."

Lotuus buzzed up and hung in the air right before his eyes. They couldn't have been more different. Her figure was grace and beauty that shimmered with seductive activity. His body was a raw-powered, stony-skinned abomination. She kissed him on the nose. "I've missed you, my lord. Have you missed me?"

"For centuries I've burned with vengeance. There was no time for pleasant memories."

She stood on his shoulder and spoke into his ear. "You are free now. Does that make you happy?"

"No, but soon it will." He formed a fist, cocked it back, and struck at the nearest earth giant with bone-shattering impact.

Boom!

The earth giant crumpled to the ground and lay dead. The other earth giant backed up a step, took a knee, and bowed.

Petting the giant's ear, Lotuus said with a thrill in her voice, "So powerful. So masterful. Oh, how I have missed you, Eckubahn. I must say, I was beginning to lose hope, but then Nath Dragon came along and I was freed. Hence, you were freed. I didn't hesitate to dupe him."

The titan's throat rumbled. "Make no mistake, you didn't dupe anyone. This was meant to be. Certain dragons want us gone." He punched his fist into his hand with a resounding smack. "I want them gone. And I pledge it will be done."

Lotuus clapped her hands. "Oh, how I can't wait to see you upend those arrogant lizards. I'd like to pluck the scales off of them one by one."

Eckubahn put his oversized finger under her chin. "I promise that you'll see it done." Feet shaking the ground, he headed out of the monstrous alcove. "This body hungers. Lead me to the nearest city so I can feast." He spread his arms out wide, tilted his chin up toward the sky, and yelled, "Then I will have my VENGEANCE!"

CLAWS

OF THE

DRAGON

-Book 2-

CRAIG HALLORAN

CHAPTER 1

WURMERS—DARK-SCALED DRAGON-LIKE CREATURES LARGER THAN men with an evil glimmer in their eyes—were coming by the dozens.

Ben loosed another arrow.

Twang!

The feathered shaft ripped through a wurmer's chest and dropped it to the ground.

"It's never a surprise when you show up."

"What's that supposed to mean?" Nath swung Fang into an oncoming enemy and shore clean through the next.

Back to back with Nath, Ben continued to stretch his bowstring and fire.

Twang! Twang!

"Trouble is your mistress."

Twang! Twang!

Stepping forward, Nath twirled Fang around his body and carved down two more jaw-snapping wurmers. "Are you being serious?"

A wurmer bit at Nath's leg.

He jumped high and away, turned, and clipped its hindquarters with Fang.

It whirled on him, its mouth heated up with energy.

Ben crept in behind it and let loose a point-blank shot in its skull.

Thwack!

The glow went out of the monster's eyes.

Ben readied another shaft. "Well Dragon, everything *was* peaceful and quiet until you showed up."

"Quit yer jawing and start fighting!" Brenwar brought Mortuun the war hammer down with all of his might and clobbered the scaly skull of a wurmer that was clamped down on the metal legging of his armor.

Krang!

A pair of wurmers popped up in the tall grass and pounced on the fearless dwarf's back and drove him into the ground.

"Brenwar!" Nath exclaimed. Sword high, he leapt into action.

"Get these lizards off me!" Brenwar whopped one in the head with the side of his hammer.

Its jaws locked over the thick muscles in his arm.

Nath stuck it in the side and sent it to the grave.

"Get off me!" Brenwar beat it in the head with savage force.

The monster's mouth glowed with life. Fire spilled out.

Thwack!

Ben shot it in the gut. "It's a good thing these are moorite arrows. Are you sure that's dwarven?"

Pushing himself off the ground, Brenwar made a skeleton fist and shook it at Ben. "You've been spending too much time with that part-elf. Shaddup."

Kar-Roooom!

The ground shook. Brenwar lost his footing. Nath caught his fall.

"Sultans of Sulfur! What was that?" Brenwar bellowed.

A powerful magic force blasted away the wurmers and blew down the grasses.

A handful of wurmers survived and attacked. Another half dozen lay dead, except one in particular that stood out as it rose up out of the tall grass. It towered over the rest, standing eight feet tall at the shoulder. Its long neck was scale and muscle. The seams between its scales glowed with inner fire.

A heavily armored knot of Legionnaires rushed it with long spears and lances.

"No, don't!" Dragon yelled, knowing the brave men would be incinerated.

They already knew their weapons couldn't hurt the wurmer. But they were fighters. Soldiers. They wouldn't turn from a fight. Not of any kind, no matter the odds. Not once their blood got flowing.

Nath took off at a sprint, waving his sword high. "Over here, you ugly lizard!"

The wurmer paid him no mind. Its eyes narrowed on the oncoming rush of man meat, its neck coiled back and mouth dropped open. A billow of fire exploded from its monster jaws.

"Noooo!" Nath yelled. He'd get there, just too late.

The lances and spears of the first Legionnaires in the charge were incinerated in a wash of flame. Bodies turned into smoldering piles of ash.

A mystic shield of radiant energy appeared over the rest of the soldiers and cut off the flames. Selene stood underneath it with her arms spread wide and shaking.

Nath's own face felt the searing heat as the wurmer's flames bounced off in all directions.

The grasses caught fire. Flames spread.

Nath closed in, Fang down and ready to plunge into the monster's side.

Out of nowhere, the wurmer's tail lashed out.

Whack!

Head over heels, Nath landed and bounced off the ground. He scrambled to his feet and found himself face to face with the lava-dripping jaws of the huge wurmer. He started back into his swing and gaffed. Fang wasn't there. The grand sword lay nearby. He jumped for it.

Whack!

The wurmer's tail drummed his back, flattening him on the ground.

Whack! Whack! Whack!

Taking a beating, Nath clawed toward Fang's pommel.

Come on, Fang! Help me!

Whack! Whack! Whack!

Fighting through the beating, Nath's fingertips nudged Fang's bottom pommel.

Just a little closer!

The one-ton dragon stepped on Nath's back and drove his face into the ground. Its claws sank into Nath's shoulders.

He let out a muffled scream. Dragon heart thundering in his chest, hand spread wide, Nath fought through the pain and grabbed Fang's pommel. He jerked Dragon Claw free.

The dagger inside of the great sword's hilt shined with blue light. Its energy coursed through Nath's veins.

"Get off me, Lizard!"

With tremendous effort, he ripped away from the wurmer's claws, twisted around, and plunged the blade into the armored scales that coated its chest.

Sckreeeet!

The giant wurmer reared up. Flames shot out of its mouth. Its scaly body crackled and popped. Inch by inch, scale by scale, its body iced up and crystalized. In seconds, the entire beast became a solid sheet of ice.

Bleeding, Nath tore himself out of its grip and grimaced with his hands on his knees, sweat dripping from his brow, and caught his breath. "That was close."

The rest of the wurmers were dead.

Selene, Bayzog, Brenwar, and Ben gathered around.

The old dwarven warrior marched forward with his war hammer raised high and prepared to strike the great wurmer.

"Brenwar, don't!" Nath ordered.

The dwarf stopped and looked at him. "May I ask why?" Brenwar huffed.

Nath didn't have a good reason why not, and several had died because of the monster already. "Never mind. Carry on."

Brenwar brought back the hammer and turned it around full swing.

Krang!

The giant wurmer exploded into thousands of icy pieces.

The Legionnaires erupted in a cheer.

Ben held his hand out and caught some of the drifting ice on his leather gauntlet. "Look. It's snowing."

CHAPTER 2

"**Y**OU NEED STITCHES," SELENE SAID to Nath in a motherly kind of way. "Be still."

Nath stayed her with his palm. "I don't need stitches. It's hardly a wound." He glanced at the claw marks in his shoulders. His stomach turned queasy. "Guzan, I miss my scales!"

Brenwar chuckled under his beard. He wasn't in much better shape than Nath was.

"Laugh all you want, Brenwar. But it's only your armor that holds you together."

"I don't need this armor. It's just a uniform showing dwarven pride," he grumbled. Ben was stitching up a gash over his bushy black eyebrow. "Careful with that needle. I don't want my eye poked out."

"Maybe you should start wearing a helmet," Ben said. "You aren't getting any younger, you know."

"He doesn't need a helmet," Bayzog said, leaning on the Elderwood Staff. His ivy-green robes with gold trim rustled in the wind. "Dwarven skulls get thicker the older they get."

"Well now, that explains a lot!" Ben laughed.

"One of these days I'm going to bust you in the mouth, part-elf." Brenwar got up, grabbed Mortuun, and stormed away.

The daylight was beginning to fade, and the Legionnaires had started moving their dead and wounded. The only ones sitting still were Nath and company and the dead bodies of the wurmers. Their scales rotted quickly.

Nath covered his nose. "Those things reek. How come they rot? I thought they had to be burned."

"They still need to be burned. Don't leave a trace of any of them," said Brenwar, turning away his nose. "And I thought orcs smelled bad."

"Commander," Nath said to a Legionnaire with a long moustache. "You heard him. Get oil and some torches."

"You're going to reek as well if you don't sit still," Selene said to him. She tried to poke his skin with a needle. He flinched away. "Don't do that again, Nath. I'm trying to take care of you."

"Take care of me?" He snatched the needle from her hand. "I'll take care of myself, thank you." Grinding his teeth, he turned away. He hated asking anyone for help, but even more, he hated feeling mortal. The wurmer's claws had burned like fire on his flesh where the scales from his arms stopped around the shoulder. He pinched the skin behind his neck but couldn't reach it with his free hand. "Great Dragons!"

"Will you set your pride aside for a moment?" Selene said, plucking the needle from his fingers. "You can't do everything, you know."

"Not anymore. That's for sure." He frowned and stared off at the sinking sun.

I have to get used to this. Nobody else is complaining.

"Fine, Selene. You win. Stitch me up."

"That's better. Try to have a better outlook on things. You just got Fang back. Doesn't that make you glad?"

Nath held up the beautiful blade before his golden eyes.

Fang's steel seemed to absorb every ray of sunlight. The magnificent blade's pommel sent shivers of power through his blood and into his bones. Fang was more than some precious object. He was a friend.

Nath let out a sigh and nodded. "Yes, having Fang back is good." He ran his scaled fingertips over the exquisite dragon-headed cross-guard. "Very good."

Bayzog stepped into view. The half-elf wizard had a curious look in his eyes. "I'm at a loss. Care to explain?"

"You're at a loss!" Brenwar yelled from a distant spot. "Hah!"

As Selene stitched up his back, Nath began to explain everything that had happened of late. He explained how he gave up his powers to save Selene. How the wurmers were a cursed carryover from Gorn Grattack. There was the issue of rescuing his mother, Grahleyna, and the fight behind the Great Dragon Wall.

"All in a good day's fun, right Bayzog? And now it seems we have these titans to deal with. My mother warned me. Eckubahn is one of their names. It seems they don't get along too well with dragons. Can you believe that?"

Selene bit off the thread and patted Nath on the back. "All better. Just don't swing that sword for a while."

"Now that we're all caught up, Bayzog, perhaps we can eat and drink." Nath saw that Bayzog's violet eyes were filled with concern. "Bayzog?"

"I know something of these histories." There was tightness in the half-elf's voice. "This is horrible, Nath." Covering his nose up with his long sleeve, he walked over to a wurmer's corpse. It fizzled and popped. The scales and bones were turning to goo. He looked at Selene. "How many more nests do you think are out there?"

"I destroyed several, but as soon as I found one, I'd come across another." Her brow creased. "I'm all for new solutions. I think that's why we're here."

"So what do you think, Bayzog?" Nath said.

"I think I'm going to have to check the histories. Over the centuries, so much has been lost, buried, or destroyed." His eyes landed on Nath. "But your kind might have a better solution to this than us. They've dealt with this problem before."

"I assume. My mother seemed to know something about it and the titans. And then, she was gone." He shook his head. "I swear, my parents are aloof."

Selene chuckled and patted him on the back.

"Sorry about that, Nath. I'm sure she had her reasons," Bayzog said. "We'll just have to wait and see how things turn out when you have children of your own."

"Can we just stick with the titans?"

"Nath!" Sasha rushed into his arms and gave him a great hug. She had aged little since the last time he'd seen her. Her soft eyes had little crow's feet, but she was still beautiful. "I've missed you. Come, sit down."

They were back inside Bayzog's tower. Somehow the magic abode of the wizard had survived. The grand table—round, elven crafted, and exquisite—that Bayzog studied from was still there. He sat on a stool with his nose buried in a great tome.

Nath sat down beside Sasha. "Is he still reading too much?"

"So it seems," she said, picking up a crystal carafe. "How about some wizard water?"

Nath shrugged his aching shoulder. It still burned. "Sure."

"And how about you, Selene?" Sasha said with a forced smile.

Nath felt a bit of a chill in the air. Selene had deceived Sasha, and he could sense Sasha's unease with the woman.

Oh my. I sort of forgot about that.

"Thank you, that would be nice," Selene said. She took a seat on Nath's other side and rested her hand on his knee, eyeing the surroundings. "This is a lovely place."

Sasha poured three glasses and handed them over. Her hand trembled a little.

"Are you alright?" Nath shifted toward Sasha.

For some reason he missed Brenwar.

His old friend hadn't wanted to come inside Bayzog's place, so Brenwar and Ben had decided to stay outside and inspect the rebuilding of the town. That left Nath all alone with the women, who he was pretty sure didn't like each other. And Bayzog wouldn't be much help at all. He'd have his nose in the books for hours.

Nath sipped from his glass. The enchanted water quickly refreshed his parched lips. Raising his glass, he said, "A toast, perhaps. To old friends and new adventures."

Sasha set her glass down on the table and sighed. With a frown on her lovely face, she said, "I'm sorry, Nath. I can't drink to that."

"What? Sasha, what is wrong? Have I done something to offend you?"

"It's not you, Nath," she said, fixing her eyes on Selene. "It's her. How in Nalzambor can you trust her?"

CHAPTER
3

BAYZOG'S HEAD SNAPPED UP FROM his book. "Sasha, please, these are our guests."

Sasha was on her feet with her fists balled up at her sides. She fired back. "No. I cannot be silent. I'm sorry, Nath, but have you forgotten how many lives were taken on account of her? Thousands died because of her bewitching. Not to mention Ben's family." She pointed at Selene. "She was behind their deaths. The same for my own friends and family. Just look at this city!"

"Sasha, please," Bayzog pleaded. He got up off his stool and made his way over to her and spoke in a stern voice. "You're embarrassing yourself."

Sasha's eyes flashed. "What! You of all people! Don't stand beside me." Her eyes watered up, and her lip started to tremble. "How could you?" She glared at Nath. "And how could you?"

Selene got up, set her glass down, and said, "I'll leave."

"Yes, yes, do leave, you schemer! You plotter! Go ahead and try to wash the blood from your hands!" Sasha's chest heaved, and her body shuddered. Bayzog tried to steady her, but she pushed right by him and ran out of the room crying.

Nath opened his mouth to speak but closed his jaw. He didn't know what to say. He'd never seen Sasha so angry. It shocked him like a jolt of lightning. He turned and watched Selene heading to the spot that led them out of the apartment. Her chin that was always up was down a little. He cleared his throat. "Selene—"

She cut him off with her hand. "No. She has a right to be angry and not to trust me. I can't expect everyone to forgive me." She showed him a dejected look, shook her head, and sighed. "Why would anyone forgive me?" She stepped on an arcane symbol on the floor, shimmered, faded, and disappeared.

"I've forgiven you," Nath muttered. He felt empty inside. Forgiveness didn't come easy for some people. He was a dragon and a lot more patient than most. He knew that in the world of men, where life was short and highly valued, taking one away from another hurt the most.

It hurt him, but he also understood that people are often deceived and misled. Evil was often taught and bred. Gorn Grattack had raised Selene. It was a wonder she had broken free of his spell.

"Apologies, Nath," Bayzog said. There was a look of disappointment in his eye. "Sasha should have more self-control than that."

Nath put his clawed hand on Bayzog's shoulder and gave it a gentle squeeze. "You can't expect her to keep her feelings bottled up all the time. She has a right to vent. Don't be so hard on her."

"A sorceress should have more discipline." He had a blank look on his elven face. "But the sad thing is I never knew she felt that way."

"Then I'd say you need to talk to her more often."

Bayzog glanced at the tome he'd been studying. "I need to research."

"No, you need to go to your wife, and the first words out of your mouth should probably be, 'I apologize.'"

The part-elf stiffened. "For what?"

"Who feeds you, Bayzog?"

"Why, she does."

"Well, you don't want to starve to death, do you?"

Bayzog lifted a brow. "Perhaps you are right. Thank you, Nath." He headed after Sasha.

Nath resumed his place on the sofa and gazed at the warm glow of the fireplace in the corner. He sipped on the wizard water.

I think a lot more happened in the twenty-five years I was gone than I realized.

Shuffling through the rubble-filled streets of Quintucklen, Nath found himself liking his isolation. He'd hung around Bayzog's place until the quietness made him uneasy. It had taken Bayzog more than two hours to return from his talk with Sasha, and when he did, the dark-haired part-elf wizard had little to say. If anything, his face was a little ashen when he stuck his nose back in his book and began flipping pages.

Time to go.

Nath thought there wasn't much sense in him hanging around with so much tension in the air. And in a surprising way, he felt a little foolish. Was Sasha right in her suspicions of Selene? Had he missed something? He was incredulous that she'd gotten so upset over it. It gave him much to think about. Things to ponder.

A long walk should do me good.

It was late in the night, and the streets were dark. The lanterns that used to light the fallen city were scarce. Instead, there were catwalks, planks, pulleys, and stacked stone blocks—some large, others small. A few buildings were almost complete, but so many had been demolished.

Nath stopped beside a wheelbarrow that was filled with broken blocks and sighed.

What a mess war makes.

But as he continued on through the dust and debris, his heart swelled with pity. There were tents set up all over the city. Camps full of people. Some faces sat around campfires and grumbled. He got a better idea of what Sasha was experiencing. This was her home, and so many had lost everything.

Sure, to a dragon it didn't seem so bad. After all, the people would rebuild. It might take a few years, but they'd bounce back. But some of them wouldn't bounce back. They didn't have enough time for that. They'd die homeless and poor.

This is horrible.

Nath crossed from street to street, picking his way through the city. He heard sobbing. Through a broken window he saw a woman's face in tears. Listening carefully from a place of concealment, he realized one of the fallen Legionnaires was her husband. They'd come to rebuild. They had children. Two of them. Twin girls. A woman friend was there to console the upset woman, who said, "Just when things settle, more of those dragons come and kill. I hate the dragons. They all bring trouble."

Nath's chest tightened, and he moved on. Her voice wasn't the only murmuring he heard. People all over were frustrated, and the truth be told, most of them couldn't tell one dragon from the other. And now, they were threatened again. After all of their work, the peace had vanished almost as soon as it had come.

Will this fighting ever end?

Edging deeper into town, he came across the shambled wooden porch of a tavern. There was a lot of commotion inside the walls of the torch-lit room. He ventured closer, with the porch creaking underneath his foot.

Seems pretty lively. At least not all spirits are broken.

Crash! Boom! Bang!

Inside, a booming dwarven voice yelled, "For Morgdon!"

CHAPTER 4

NATH DASHED THROUGH THE DOOR. A host of men armed with clubs and tankards encircled Brenwar. Some of them had chairs. Nath saw Ben out of the corner of his eyes. The older warrior stood in the corner, leaning against the wall with his arms folded over his chest. He shrugged at Nath.

"Take it back!" Brenwar said. He hiccupped. He smacked his fists together. "Take it back, or I'll slaughter every last one of you!"

Nath pushed through the throng of angry men.

One man shoved him in the back.

Nath shoved him back.

The man eyed his scales and faded back.

"Get out of here, Nath!" Brenwar growled. "This isn't your business. Go away. *Hic.*"

Nath spread his arms out and slowly spun around. "Easy, men. What's this about?"

"I'll tell you what this is all about!" Brenwar spat through his beard. "They say they'll rebuild this city better than Morgdon! Hah! And to think, I was trying to help them. Stupid men!"

"Is this true?" Nath said, gazing at all the men. "I've never known a dwarf to lie."

"Quintucklen is better!" one man said, holding a chair in two hands. "The dragons didn't ever attack their city! We are better. We are stronger!"

"I'm going to rip him apart!" Brenwar surged forward.

Nath held him back for a moment, just long enough to unload a warning to the men. "You had better take it back, or he's going to fight every last one of you. And you don't want that."

"Nay! Let him fight. No dwarf is going to tell us who and what we are in this city," said the man. "Let the bearded cur loose!"

Hometown pride.

Nath had to give the men of Quintuklen credit. They loved their city as much as the dwarves loved Morgdon. He released Brenwar. "Have at it, then."

The grizzled dwarf stormed into the man with the big mouth and chair. The chair came down and splintered on his head. Brenwar tackled the man, and all the other men piled on.

Nath stepped away from the fray and headed toward Ben.

Gaping, Ben said, "You're letting him fight all of them?"

"I don't think I could stop him. Do you?"

Ben ducked under a tankard that whizzed over his head. "I suppose not." He slapped Nath on the back. "Say, you look a little long in the face. How about I get you some ale?"

Brenwar squirted out of the pile, charged through the screaming voices and tables, and plucked a keg of ale up from the floor. Hoisting it overhead, he hurled it at the rush of men. Four men went down, and the keg of ale cracked open and started to spill. "And your ale is lousy!" Brenwar said. He climbed up on the bar and jumped into the throng.

"I think the price of ale just went up. Do you think you can afford it?" Nath asked.

"Come with me," Ben said, leading Nath by the arm. They picked their way through the broken chairs, tables, and pottery and slipped outside on the porch. Taking in a breath of fresh air, Ben said, "It's good to see you, Dragon, but you don't seem well."

"What makes you say so?"

A man flew through the glass window on the other side of the door. *Crash!* Another one came out and landed on top of him. *Whup!*

Nath and Ben shuffled away.

Ben continued. "I can tell when you have a lot on your mind. Sure, I'm not some seer or anything, but when I met you, way back when, you never worried. There's a crease between those brows of yours now."

The swinging doors burst open, and Brenwar stormed out. "*Hic!*" He grabbed both of the men by their collars. "I'm not finished with these two." He dragged them back inside, and another clamor arose. Wood clacked and shattered. Men howled in triumph and pain.

As if nothing were happening, Nath said, "That's disappointing. I haven't really aged so many years, but sometimes I feel as ancient as my father. Aw, Ben, I shouldn't complain. The truth is, I lost a great deal of my power."

"You can't fly anymore, can you?"

Nath shook his head no. "And that's not all. I'd say for the most part, I'm right back where I was when you met me. I know I sound vain, Ben, but with the power I had before, I could do almost anything. Now I'm a shadow of that, and I think, 'How am I supposed to protect so many people from such great evil?'"

Ben rubbed his beard. The stern-faced man had an iron jaw and weathered skin. He'd seen a hundred battles and survived. There was a steely wisdom in his eyes. "You'll do it just like you did it before, Dragon."

"Really, and how did I do it before?"

"With boldness. It didn't matter if we were facing giants or dragons. Wherever we went, there was never anyone bigger than you. Larger than life, you launched yourself into the threat without a sliver of fear in your eyes. You are Nath Dragon, The Dragon Prince. Maybe you're a little smaller than you'd like to be, but I know you. Your ego's bigger than all the mountains in the world."

Nath couldn't stop the smile on his face, and he didn't want to. It felt good. And Ben was right. Nothing had really changed. He was still faster and stronger than any man alive. And what did he have to be scared of? He had Fang. And, more importantly, he had friends who believed in him.

"You know, Ben," Nath said, throwing his arm over Ben's shoulder, "I always knew you were going to grow up to be one of the wisest men who ever lived."

Ben looked him in the eye. "You know you're always right, Dragon."

Crash!

"I think we had better get in there before someone really gets hurt." Nath bustled through the door and stopped just inside.

Brenwar sat on top of a pile of bodies. Beside him sat the man who had insulted him to begin with. Both of them had smiles on their bruised faces. The man, a thickset laborer with a bald head, had a pair of teeth missing that hadn't been missing before.

Nath said, "So I guess the argument is settled, then?"

"Aye!" Brenwar said, clawing at his beard. "These humans and I have come to an agreement."

Nath lifted his brows. "Oh, and what might that be?"

"Men love Quintuklen as much as the dwarves love Morgdon! And that's worth fighting for any day!"

"Aye!" said the men on the floor. They were slowly getting back to their feet and crawling up on unbroken chairs.

Ben looked at Nath and shrugged.

"And better yet. *Hic*," Brenwar continued, "They've agreed to let the dwarves come and help rebuild them!"

"Aye!" the men said.

"Now that the fighting's over," Brenwar bellowed, "let the singing begin! Aaaaaaah ... Home of the dwarves—Morgdon! Home of the dwarves—Morgdon!"

Ben sawed his elbow back and forth and joined in with a big smile behind his greying beard.

Nath was about to join in as well, when he felt a tingle on his neck. He backed up through the door and stepped out on the porch.

Selene stood in her purple robes alone in the moon's shadows.

"Selene?"

"Yes," she said, sounding dejected.

"Look, don't you worry about what Sasha said."

"No, it's fine, Nath. I understand her concerns. I just came to tell you I'm leaving."

CHAPTER 5

A HORNLESS WHITE DRAGON WITH GOLD flecks in its scales soared over the grasslands. It was an Ivory Slider more than fifteen feet long with beautiful wings and a very long tail. More graceful than an eagle, she glided from side to side in the air. Her long eyelashes blinked.

Ahead, a flock of wurmers dropped from the clouds and dove right for her.

Outnumbered and seeing the fire in their eyes, she turned and headed back in the direction she had come from.

"Oh no," she said in Dragonese.

Wurmers dropped from the clouds all over by the dozens.

Flapping her wings, she cut through the air, belly skimming the tall highland grasses.

Behind her, hungry shrieks howled out in pursuit.

She was fast, very fast. The Ivory Sliders were the messengers of Dragon Home. They cut through air like a knife through butter, and not many dragons could catch them other than the Blue Razors. Beating her streamlined body through the wind, she began to outdistance her pursuers.

Ahead, she saw a series of mountains with winding crevasses and ravines that would be the perfect place to lose them. Making a beeline for the rocky cliffs, she soared higher.

A spitball of fire whizzed by her ear. The wurmers were shooting balls of energy at her.

Head turned around, she barrel rolled and evaded.

Above her, another wave of wurmers dropped from the greying clouds and blanketed the sky. Balls of flame like tiny meteors showered her from above, singeing wing and scale.

Just as she turned to find a path of escape, a rock bigger than her head slammed into her chest. Spinning out of control, she crashed to the ground with balls of fire peppering her body, and she let out a tremendous roar that split the air.

The wurmers were scattered by the sonic wave of energy. They became disoriented and fell from the sky. Still more came.

The Ivory Slider let out another mystic roar, shattering the air. She shook off the flames and spread her wings once more.

One by one, wurmer after wurmer slammed into her and drove her to the ground. Jaws with sharp, jagged teeth bit into her legs.

She fought with all of her strength, thrashing and biting, but before long, her limbs gave out under the sheer weight of her growing foes. She let out a weak sonic sigh that flattened the grasses and stopped at a pair of massive feet. Pinned down, she still managed to lift her chin. Her eyes flashed.

A giant!

Dragons hated giants, and giants hated dragons. It always had been and always would be. But the wars between them had been quiet for centuries.

And here was one before her, almost twenty feet tall. A towering figure of brawn and muscle, covered in thick hair. But unlike the giants she'd known, this one was different. His entire head was covered in flame. In his mighty grip was a sling big enough to hurl a sheep.

Lizardmen appeared behind the giant with heavy robes in their hands.

She hissed at them.

They bound her up.

The flame giant's necklace of dragon bones shook when he spoke. "BRING HER," he said in a voice as deep as a canyon.

The Ivory Slider was dragged by the lizardmen over the grasses and into the belly of the mountain, where they marched until they stood on the edge of a small ravine. A pair of horned dragon skulls were on spikes that guarded the carved stone steps that led down.

"Take a long look," said the flame giant, pointing into the ravine.

Her nostrils flared. Her neck recoiled. The stench of death and decay was strong. But it was familiar too. Lifting her head, she peered down into the ravine. Her jaw dropped open. Her stomach turned to knots. *Nooooo!*

Down there, dragons lay dead in the brush and trees. Scales of many colors. Copper. Blue. Red. White. Yellow. Green. Their bodies were broken. Wings busted. Horns shattered. Even a massive Bull Dragon was down there.

She turned her fear-filled gaze toward the giant.

Head aflame, he said, "Fear not. You will be spared, messenger. What you have seen, report in every detail to Balzurth of Dragon Home. Tell him Eckubahn sent you."

Trembling, she nodded.

The giant wagged his finger in her face. "You will not fly." He slid out a dagger that was too small for his belt and dropped it point first in the ground. It was carved from a dragon's tooth, and it glimmered with enchantment. "You will walk. Lizards, cut off her wings."

CHAPTER 6

"**S**ELENE, YOU CAN'T GO." NATH laid his hands on her shoulders. She rested her palms on his hands, and with tear-filled eyes she looked deeply into his. "Sasha is right. I'm behind much of this. These people should kill me. I would if I were them."

"Don't say that, Selene. It's not true."

"It is true. Every last bit of it." She slipped out of his hands and stood on the edge of the porch beside the wooden post that held the ceiling. "I've been walking through the streets and listening to the conversations of men, women, children. You know, I never cared one lick for any of them before. They were rodents. No, not even that. They were bugs to be squished under my scales. Vermin to be chewed away at Gorn Grattack's order." She made a deep frown. "I hated them for their laughter. Happiness. I wanted to destroy it all. I still envy them."

"Selene," he said, looking at the sadness growing in her face. "Everyone can change. You proved that. Don't be so hard on yourself."

"What a jest, Nath. I'm sorry to be ugly, but I should be tried for my crimes."

Nath snuck up to her and tried to cover her mouth.

She slipped away.

He said in a harsh whisper, "Keep your voice down, will you? If someone were to hear you, it might just come true. There are tribunals, you know."

"I can't just wish my past away, Nath. What happens when people figure out who I am, hmmm? Do you think all of them will forgive me? Think of Sasha. She's a sweet and reasonable person, but she wants my head on a platter."

"No, she doesn't. Well, not on a platter anyway. Maybe mounted on the wall."

She glared at him.

"Er, it's a jest." He combed his hair out of his eyes and fell silent. As a stiff wind blew through the streets and stirred up tiny dust devils, his mind dove deeper into thought. Selene had made a good point. The world would not forgive her the same as he had. All over Nalzambor, grudges were still held that were centuries old. And now, it didn't seem fair that like him, she would have to walk the world as a human, knowing so many hated her. "Why don't we walk together?"

"No." She faced him. "Nath, I'm leaving."

A spark of anger flashed in his golden eyes. "I need you, Selene. We are in this together. To the end. You can't just go it alone!"

"Don't get testy. I'm not abandoning you or the cause, but I am getting out of this city. It makes me ashamed of all I have done. So many I have hurt. People I don't know. Family, friends, destroyed. Don't you see, Nath? Don't you see what I've done?" She pointed at some memory banners rustling in the wind that adorned many windows. "That's because of me. I really and truly wanted each and every one of these people dead! How and why," she said, exasperated, "could anyone ever trust me?"

"I trust you, Selene. You have to believe that. You saved me, and we stopped Gorn. If *you* hadn't done what you did, all of Nalzambor would have fallen." He stepped by her side. "You have to forgive yourself. And at least you care now."

"Yes, I do." She nodded. "And I'm not liking that so much either. Helping people is so … foreign to me."

"But it's rewarding."

"We'll see. I'm going north. To the high mountains. I think there might be a nest of wurmers there. I'll stay in touch. You find out what Bayzog suggests, and maybe we can rendezvous there, say, in a week or two. Goodbye, Nath." She kissed his cheek and disappeared into the dark streets.

Don't leave.

Nath's heart sank. Every time she left, he couldn't help but wonder if he would ever see her again.

Please.

A few moments later, Ben stepped out on the porch. He had a turkey leg in one hand. Looking into Nath's face, he said, "Now what? I thought I had you charged up. Now you look like Brenwar would look if someone shaved his beard off."

Nath made a sour face. "I sure wouldn't want to see that. No, Selene just swung by and departed."

Ben nodded his grizzled chin. "I see. And that upsets you because you are so fond of her."

"No."

"Aw, I know you better than that, Dragon." Ben tickled Nath's ribs. "You want her for a bride, don't you?"

"How much ale have you had?"

"Oh, I'm more of a cider man these days. The ale's too hard on my gut. So tell me, why did she leave?"

"Guilt."

Ben stroked the rim of his moustache. "I see."

"Can I ask you something, Ben?"

"Sure, you can ask me anything."

"Do you have any resentment toward her? After all, she did lead the war that killed an awful lot of people."

"Hmmm, you know, I really haven't given it that much thought. As a soldier I learned that life is full of losses, and you have to move on. It's full of many blessings too. I just keep marching forward. I can't let the past slow me down."

"But your family, Ben. You lost all of them because of Barnabus."

"True, and I miss them every day. But I don't blame the likes of Selene, but I do think ..." Ben's voice trailed off.

"Think what, Ben?"

He slapped his big hand on Nath's shoulder. "Nothing. If you've forgiven her, I've forgiven her too."

Nath eyed him. "No, you were going to say something else. What was it?"

Ben shrugged. "I do think, if justice is to be served, it will catch up with her."

CHAPTER

7

NATH STOOD FAR OUTSIDE OF Quintuklen's walls inside the valley full of stone markers. They were graves, thousands of them in rows as far as the non-dragon eye could see. Over the past couple of days he'd lain low, stayed out of the city, and begun noting each and every one of the markers.

He scraped some debris from one of the stones and revealed a familiar name. His eyes teared up. It was Ben's wife's marker, and beside it were two more, Ben's son and daughter. Nath's heart sank. Three names among thousands. He thought about all of the people who had suffered like Ben had. Men and women. Mothers and fathers. Not all of them could move on. Not when they had lost people they loved so much.

How many more must die for the sake of evil?

Clenching his fist, he rose up and walked a few miles, lost in thought. Eyes searching, he found something he was looking for. Wildflowers. He plucked some out of the ground and filled up his hands with three colorful bouquets. He marched back to the graveyard, set the flowers on the stones of Ben's family, then started the long walk back to the city.

It was mid-morning, and the laborers were hard at work under a hot sun. Hammers pecked and chiseled. Foremen shouted orders. Pulleys squeaked. Large loads of materials rolled down the main roads on huge wagons pulled by teams of horses. And there was a liveliness about the men. Some of them were whistling, even singing.

Nath pulled back his shoulders a little. Walked a little taller.

Their spirits aren't broken, so why are mine?

There was nothing like seeing men and women working together with such purpose. It kept their minds off the past. And that was a good thing.

They could look forward to the future, and Nath wanted to make sure that future was a bright one.

Making his way through the maze of walls that surrounded the fallen city, he spied a woman on top of one of the ways, waving her arms at him. It was Sasha. She was in a pale-yellow gown, trimmed in flowers. Her platinum hair was pinned up with a fine silver comb. He jogged toward her. She came rushing down the steps to greet him.

"Nath! Where have you been?" Sasha threw her arms around him and held him tight. "I've missed you."

"Uh, I've just been wandering and waiting for Bayzog to call on me." He lifted her off her feet in a hug. "You seem well."

"Well? Why wouldn't I be?" She slipped off of him, took his hand in hers, and led him back into the city like a little child. "Come on, let's get back home and see Bayzog."

He followed her lead, but it wasn't long before he felt long stares and eyes on him. Nath had done little to conceal his ebony-scaled arms. They were mostly bare under the tunic that he wore. And it didn't help that his great height and flame-red hair were far from ordinary. A small group of children slipped in behind him with giggles. He turned to look at them, and they scattered.

Oh no, here we go again.

"Come on. Come on," Sasha said, prodding him along.

Once again the children fell in step behind him. He ignored them. Focused on the others he passed who stared at him. One man, a burly fellow with a limp, nodded a greeting at him. So did the woman behind him, and she smiled. He nodded back.

"Hail Dragon Slayer, welcome!" said a bricklayer on top of a catwalk, waving a navy knit cap like a banner. "Hail!"

Nath waved.

That's odd, them calling me a dragon slayer. Of course, they probably don't know the difference between the wurmers and a real dragon.

"Dragon slayer!" another man cried out. It was followed by another and another, and before Nath knew what was going on, people were filling the streets and shouting encouraging words to him.

"See, Nath?" Sasha said, rubbing his arm. "They embrace you now. You are their hero. You are my hero as well."

Arm high, Nath waved and nodded in return to the folks who watched his small parade.

Now this is more like it.

The streets thickened with people, happy faces one and all. Children were on men's shoulders.

"This is almost embarrassing."

"Hah," she laughed. "Not for you. No, your name has spread, Nath. In the good spirit that it should."

But as the people chanted 'Dragon Slayer!' over and over again, a dark memory crossed through Nath's mind. Of his time in Narnum, when the people had crowned him the Champion after he defeated Selene's war cleric, Kryzak. A dark and shameful time.

He didn't like the association, not one bit. It was contradictory and perverted to him. And this parade he had unintentionally created was growing behind him. A few dozen people at least.

"We need to end this, Sasha."

She looked at him. "Why? It's delightful." She started waving her hand. "Enjoy the moment, Nath Dragon."

He played along for another block as he studied Sasha. There was something odd about her. She wasn't one to get caught up in moments like this. Though she wasn't quiet, she was reserved.

"So Sasha, you are no longer angry?"

"Angry?" she said, looking at him somewhat aghast. "What in the world are you talking about?"

"Last time I saw you, you were fighting with Bayzog."

"Bayzog and I never fight."

"Well, maybe I'm not putting this right. But you were very upset with Selene. Are you over that now? I can't imagine you would be."

Still walking and with a confused look on her face, Sasha said, "Where is Selene? I would like to see her."

"She left."

"Why would she do that? I'd love to see her."

"You would?"

"Of course I would," she said cheerfully.

Either I'm lost, or I really don't understand women.

Nath then said, "But you had some very choice words with her. Are you not still angry?"

Suddenly, Sasha whirled. Anger filled her eyes. "Nath Dragon, quit playing games! I don't know what you're talking about!"

CHAPTER
8

BACK INSIDE BAYZOG'S APARTMENT, NATH stood at the great table. Books were stacked up in neat piles. Some of them still floated open in the air. With a wave of his hand, Bayzog sent one book floating away and pulled over another.

"So you enjoy reading, don't you." Nath was just making conversation. His eyes were busy soaking in the grand oversized room that was much too big for the small building it was housed in.

"So you've noticed," said the wizard. His eyes darted over the wording of the ancient texts, and the pages flipped faster than Nath could attempt to read them. "Study creates the building blocks of knowledge."

Sasha wasn't in the room. She'd said she was heading out to the market so she could prepare food for them later. She'd only departed moments ago.

"There isn't a lot that escapes me," Nath said. "Something's amiss with Sasha, isn't it?"

Bayzog's face drew tight.

"Talk to me, friend," Nath said to him. He reached over and shoved the hovering book away. "Come on, Bayzog. I can't help if you clam up on me."

With a dejected voice, Bayzog said, "You can't help anyway, Nath. She has the Wizard's Dementia."

Nath leaned forward and patted his friend on the back. "I'm not sure what that is, but it sounds horrible."

Long-faced, Bayzog said, "Horrible is an understatement. There's no cure for it."

"There's a cure for everything," Nath said, "but it would help if you'd tell me what you were dealing with."

"Nath, this is my burden. Not yours. You have bigger tasks ahead that you need to remain focused on."

"If I can't be helpful with small matters, then how can I give aid to the large ones?" Nath replied. "Please, confide in me, old friend."

"For all the good it will do, why not?" Shoulders sagging, Bayzog made his way over to the couch, poured some wizard water, sat down, rubbed his eyes, and yawned.

Boy, he must be whipped. I've never seen him yawn before.

Nath took a seat. "So, what are you dealing with?"

Bayzog finished a long drink. "Wizard Dementia is caused by magic. It's very, very rare, but anyone—particularly a human—who calls on the powers of Nalzambor can be afflicted. You see, Nath, magic is not as natural to all as it is to dragons and to elves. We have a stronger nature for it, which I can't even explain. But with humans it's different. Even though Sasha is a fine sorceress and well disciplined, the magic she has used has taken a toll on her mind." His lip quivered, and a lump rolled up and down his throat. "Her mind is eroding—slowly, but still eroding."

"That's horrible, Bayzog. Certainly there is something to be done?"

"Nath, I've searched. I've tried. It's just so rare that there isn't much material on it."

"What about the Occular of Orray?" Nath suggested.

"I've sent word," Bayzog said, taking another sip of water. "But it's unlikely. The elves are more protective of it now than ever. Truth be told, they'd be very reluctant to use its powers on a human."

"I'll go down there and speak to them myself."

Bayzog held up his hand. "Nath, for some things in life there isn't an easy fix. Death takes us all, be it at twenty-five years or one thousand. I will quietly deal with this."

Nath didn't push. He knew it wouldn't do him any good. And now wasn't the time to argue with his friend. Bayzog had opened up, so it was time to listen. "Does she know, Bayzog?"

The wizard shook his head no. "That's the hardest part, Nath. I feel as if I am deceiving her. Sometimes she gets so confused."

"Do Rerry and Samaz know?"

"They do. Why do you think they are away?"

"Ah." Nath leaned back into the cushions. "I see."

So, someone is *looking for a cure. Good for them.*

"The worst part is her love for magic, Nath. She wants to practice and train. I keep having to distract her with something else. I tell her I'm too busy, or make up some petty lie. It's horrible. But if she uses magic, it could be disastrous. Fatal. Not to mention it would accelerate her condition. I can't risk that, and yet she loves magic so much. She was such a talented pupil. It sickens my heart, Nath. Every bit of it."

Nath swallowed the lump in his throat. This was one of the most devastating things he'd ever heard. And Bayzog, who hardly ever showed emotion, had deep creases in his brow.

All Nath could think to say was 'There's always hope.' But he didn't. Instead, he sat with his friend in front of the warm fire in silence.

Sometimes being there and saying nothing is the best comfort of all.

"It's stuffy in here," Brenwar said. He had his arms crossed over his barrel chest and was eyeing every detail of Bayzog's home. He stood with his back to the fireplace adjacent to the sofa. "Horrible construction. Looks like elves did it. I'm surprised it survived the war."

"I'm surprised *you* survived the war," Bayzog retorted.

"Watch yer mouth, part-elf."

Bayzog shook his head and faced Nath and Ben, who were both sitting at the table. Sasha was back sitting at the table too. She had a smile on her face as she hummed and prepared a tray of food. She brought each man a plate.

"Thanks, Sasha," Nath said.

"Yes, thanks," Ben added with a courteous nod.

Brenwar frowned at his plate full of fruit, pastries, and cheeses. "Haven't you any meat?"

Sasha giggled and patted him on his head. "Of course. Anything for you, Brenwar, but that comes later."

Bayzog cleared his throat. "Ahem. If you don't mind, I'd like to discuss the business at hand."

"I'm not stopping you." Brenwar sniffed a handful of purple grapes. His face soured, and he set the plate down. He walked over and climbed up on a stool at the study table and shoved away the floating books that blocked his face. "Go on."

With a studious look on his face, Bayzog said, "The good news is that I have found some history of the wurmers. And like many insects, it seems they all function on the order of a queen."

Nath nodded. Selene had already alluded to how the wurmers were more of an insect-like culture that built hives and had nests. "I've seen their nests first hand. And we've destroyed some of them. I would think we must have destroyed the queen that was in there too."

"Which brings me to the bad news," Bayzog said. "According to the histories, the last queen—their true queen—was never found and killed."

Leaning forward on the table, Ben asked, "So what does that mean?"

"It means there are wurmers we know of—Selene has discovered those—and then there are those we don't know of."

"You mean there are even more?" Ben asked. He looked at Dragon. "Those things are hard to kill."

Bayzog continued. "I'd say it's highly likely that the queen has been hiding. Possibly hibernating." His face turned grim. "And if I were to guess, she's been laying eggs for centuries. And if I were a titan, I'd be trying to find them, wake them up, and turn them loose."

"And what if that happens?" Sasha asked.

Bayzog's reply was devastating. "They'll blanket Nalzambor like a plague of enormous insects."

CHAPTER 9

THE ATMOSPHERE WAS SOLEMN IN the picturesque room. Everyone's face was long and silent. Again, Bayzog broke the silence. "This isn't all on our shoulders, Nath. The rest of the world will help out as well. This affects everyone's lives, not just our own."

"I know. Sometimes good allies are hard to come by, but I know I can always count on my friends." Nath stretched out his long-clawed hands and squeezed Ben and Brenwar's shoulders on either side of him. "Right?"

Ben was looking away and whistling.

"Ben?" Nath said again.

"Only joking, Dragon. You know that. I'm always with you. It's just that I'm heavily committed to rebuilding this city. I have people here counting on me. You know, I don't just sit around and wait for adventure to come and get me. I have responsibilities. And I need to be here to protect this city. I hope you understand."

Taken aback, Nath said, "Uh, Ben, I feel foolish. And I certainly didn't mean to make you feel that you were required to come along. None of you need to feel obligated. I only meant that I know I can always count on you."

"And we you, Nath," Sasha said. She slipped in behind him and gave him a hug. "That's why I'm coming with you."

Nath's gaze froze on Bayzog's widening eyes.

Oh my!

"Now, Sasha," Bayzog stammered. "We can't leave. Not now."

"Oh, you can stay. I'm going," she said, petting Nath's arm. "Nath needs me."

"I need you too," the wizard said. "I need you here. Our efforts to aid Nalzambor are best served here. I insist."

"I don't care." She made her way over to an open closet and draped herself in a fine grey traveling cloak. She also took the Elderwood Staff in hand. "Come, Nath. Let's go."

Tension filled the room as the staff's gem glowed with life.

Bayzog was on his feet, hand extended toward Sasha. His face was drawn tight. "Sasha, may I please have my staff?"

She hugged it. "I would like to use it on our journey."

Gently, the wizard replied, "I would also like to use it on our journey. May I please have it?"

"Only if you promise that you'll teach me to use it."

The part-elf crept closer.

Nath eased out of his seat. The fire growing inside the gem made the scales on his arms tingle.

Bayzog inched closer to her. "Sasha, do you want to walk or ride? Shall I gather us some horses?"

Her usually sweet eyes bore into Bayzog with frustration. "Promise me, Bayzog! Promise me!"

"Sasha, it is elven. You cannot use it," Bayzog said. "Please, release the staff to me. You could hurt yourself."

Her eyes shifted to the radiant power emanating from the gem. "It seems to like me. Its power courses through my veins. Teach me how to use it, Bayzog. Teach me now!"

The staff's green glow lit up the entire room. It reflected in Sasha's eyes. She began to radiate power. Something was about to erupt.

"Sasha," Bayzog pleaded with his worried face bathed in green light, "I will teach you what I can. But please, hand it over. You could hurt yourself. Or others."

"No. You won't let me use magic. You want it all for yourself." She lowered the staff at him.

Nath stooped, legs ready to spring.

This is getting bad! Dangerous.

Bayzog eased ever closer. "Sasha, you must trust me."

"No, it's mine." She tapped the bottom of the staff on the floor. The entire room shook, sending fine pottery crashing on the floor. Sasha's eyes widened. "Whoa." Wild eyed, she brought the staff up and down again.

Nath sprang. He arrived a split second before Bayzog and wrapped his hands around the staff before it hit the floor. A charge of energy went through him.

Zap!

His limbs went numb. As he fell, he saw the horrified look on Sasha's face. He landed hard. Forcing his eyes open, he saw Bayzog on the floor as well. The half-elf's eyes were closed. He wasn't breathing.

CHAPTER 10

"I'LL WAKE HIM UP," BRENWAR roared. He hopped over Nath and landed alongside Bayzog. Using his thick, stubby fingers, he pinched the half-elf's ginger arm.

"Ow!" Bayzog screamed. He sat up and found himself face to face with Brenwar. "What did you do *that* for?"

"I saved your life." Brenwar gave him two hard slaps on the back. He helped Bayzog to his feet. "And I'll never let you forget it."

Sasha rushed into Bayzog's arms. Tears were streaming down her face. Her body was trembling. "I'm sorry, Bayzog. I'm sorry! What is wrong with me? Please tell me what's wrong with me!"

"Shhhh." Bayzog hugged her and gently stroked her hair. "It's fine. I forgive you."

She sobbed. "Something's wrong. I know it is! Help me."

He kissed her cheek and said in her ear, "Let's rest on this. Accidents happen." He said something in Elven. Sasha passed out in his arms. Misty-eyed, he carried her off to the bedroom.

Ben reached down to where Nath lay and put a hand on his shoulder. "How are you feeling?"

"Shocked." Nath flicked the numbness from his fingers and stared at the staff. Its gemstone was now dim. Brenwar was reaching down for it. "I wouldn't do that. It's elven. No telling what it would do to a dwarf."

"How about I do everyone a favor and take my war hammer and break it?"

Allowing Ben to help him up to his feet, Nath shook his head. "That was interesting."

"That was strange," said Ben. "What has gotten into Sasha?"

Nath gave Ben and Brenwar a brief explanation. Just as he finished,

Bayzog re-entered the room with a very long look on his face. He picked up the Elderwood Staff. "That was too close."

"Too close to what?" Brenwar said.

"Our deaths."

"You *were* dead. I saved you."

"No, I was unconscious." Bayzog looked at his arm. "But thanks for the bruise." Holding the staff, he said, "Nath, you know that I can't take the journey with you."

"I never expected that you would."

"Listen, before you depart, we need to talk about the titans." Bayzog rubbed his head.

"Bayzog, you don't need to worry about this. You have enough to manage on your own."

"It is our burden to share, me and Sasha, husband and wife. We shall manage. And when she wakes up, we'll have a long and honest talk." Staff in hand, he took a seat on his stool. "Now, set us aside from your mind. We need to talk about the titans."

Nath wanted to press back and tell his friend 'Not now,' but he didn't. He knew Bayzog well enough to know that letting him talk about history would speed up his healing. He took his place at the table.

Silent, Brenwar and Ben did as well.

"It's interesting. There is no mention of the Great Dragon Wall in the histories. The dragons did very well concealing it." Bayzog scribbled some Elvish notes on some paper. With a bright look in his eye, he said, "I would have loved to have seen that. It's so fascinating. Perhaps you could draw or paint it for me one day."

"Perhaps," Nath said.

"Such a great secret, and in Borgash of all places," the wizard continued. "Well, according to the histories, the titans were worshipped by all. They'd attract throngs of men and women to them. Very charismatic. So, don't be surprised if it's not hard to find them. Or at least, find the bodies in which they host. They are arrogant. Proud. Deceitful. They love to boast and have no shame about them whatsoever. But they can take anyone's form. So, the goal is to trap that spirit. Return it behind the wall at Borgash and secure it. But killing the body is one thing. Trapping the spirit is quite another."

"Can the spirit be destroyed?" Nath asked. "I would think to find that casicr."

"If that were the case, the dragons would have done that already. Unless of course they just haven't figured out how. But for the time being, we want to trap them. In order to do that, you will need this." Bayzog flicked his fingers at a book's pages and said a mystic word. An image of a smooth stone with a pale-pink fire appeared over the table. "A spirit stone."

Looking around, Nath said, "Well, I hope you have one squirreled away in here."

"Ha!" Bayzog laughed. "No, like the titans, these stones haven't been seen for centuries. So either you have to find one, or I have to make one."

"You can do that?" Ben said.

Bayzog waved the image away. "I can at least try. But if you want to find one, my guess would be that if the Spirit Stones still exist, they are kept by the dragons." He looked at Nath. "That's where your influence comes in."

"Let me see if I have this straight. I need to kill all of the wurmers."

"Aye," Brenwar agreed.

"Seek the aid of my kin and get these Spirit Stones." He spoke a little more sarcastic as he went.

"Aye."

"Kill the titans' host bodies."

"Aye."

"And secure them behind the Great Dragon Wall once and for all."

Brenwar continued to agree, "Aye."

"Oh, and if I figure out how to kill the spirit, I'll execute it as well."

"Aye!" Brenwar hopped off his stool and was practically frothing at the mouth. "What are we waiting for?"

"Nath, remember you can't do it all by yourself," Bayzog said with a nod.

"Well, of course not," he replied. "That's what I have Brenwar for."

"Aye!"

CHAPTER 11

LEAVING BAYZOG AND SASHA WASN'T easy. It was one of the hardest things Nath had ever done. On foot, he led his horse, a fine dapple-grey steed, toward the exit through the outer walls to the north. Brenwar was with him, leading a small chestnut horse, and Ben walked beside him, sending him off. Facing the stiff winds and some spitting rain, Nath swiped the hair from his eyes and took relief in knowing that Bayzog, Sasha, and Ben would at least be safer in the city than with him.

Ben was seeing him off. "Don't be so quiet, Dragon. It's not like you."

"Aw, you're making me feel like an old man," Nath said, smiling at him.

The older warrior raised an eyebrow. "Man, you say?"

"You know what I mean. Sorry, Ben, I'm just worried about Bayzog and Sasha."

"I'll be looking after them as best I can."

They made it through the first line of exterior walls that surrounded the city. A group of workers were making repairs on a busted section of wall.

Brenwar grunted. "I've got to get word to Morgdon, keep those walls from being crooked." He handed Ben a scroll of wax-sealed paper. "This will take care of it."

"Oh, yes," Ben said, taking the scroll, "After all, nothing in this world is straight that isn't dwarven."

"You got that right."

Winding through the maze-like formation of walls, they finally emerged. The distant snow-capped mountains of the north lay ahead. Nath wondered if Selene was out there somewhere, and if she was safe.

"I guess this is it, Ben," Nath said to his friend. "I'd be lying if I said I was glad to leave you here, albeit in safety."

"I can't say that I blame you. Of course, even a stone is better company than Brenwar."

"Don't you mean a bearded stone?" Nath said.

"Ha ha!" Ben laughed. "Dragon, you know I'd come, and I wish I could, but I made a promise to someone that I wouldn't leave them."

"Someone who?"

"I have a new betrothed. Her name is Rebecca."

"Ben!" Nath said with excitement. "That's great. Why didn't you tell me? I'd like to meet her."

"She's in Narnum now, and her journey doesn't bring her back until next week."

Shaking Ben's hand, Nath said, "I'm happy for you, Ben. Very happy. It's not often that a man can find true love. It seems it has struck twice with you. I can tell."

"Thank you." Ben unslung his quiver full of arrows and unsnapped Akron from his back. "Here."

"No, Ben, you keep it. You'll need it to help defend the city."

"Dragon, I've a feeling that you'll need it more than me. Besides"—he stuffed the magic bow in Nath's hand—"it's always been yours. I was only protecting it while you were gone."

"It couldn't have been in better hands," Nath said, trying to pull it free of Ben's grip.

The older man held it tight. "Sorry, Dragon," Ben grimaced. He held the bow firm. "Boy, this just isn't very easy." He closed his eyes and with a gasp, he released the bow. Opening his eyes, he said, "That really was as hard as I thought it would be."

Nath pushed Akron and the quiver back into Ben's hands. "Farewell, Ben."

"I'm going to miss you, Dragon."

Nath climbed onto his horse, and Brenwar did the same.

The dwarf said to Ben, "Well, don't get all misty for my sake, Ben. Just deliver that letter."

Ben slapped Brenwar's horse on its hindquarters and sent it off in a lurch. "Goodbye, Brenwar!"

As Nath rode off, the last thing he heard was Ben's voice, shouting with cheer from the top of the outer wall. "Dragon! Dragon!"

It rained the entire day's ride north. The harder it rained, the louder Brenwar sang. Black beard soaked with water, he sang one ancient dwarven tune after the other. And the songs weren't too bad either. They lifted Nath's spirits.

"You like this, don't you," Nath said in a loud voice that carried through the heavy rain.

The dwarf kept on singing.

"You know," Nath started to say, but he stopped.

No one would hear them coming over the rain. Instead, as the horses clomped through the muddy hillside they climbed, he held his tongue.

Let Brenwar be happy. He deserves to be.

Brenwar stopped singing. "What? Did you say something?"

"I said, do you think you could sing something in Elvish?"

Brenwar wrung water out of his beard, shook his thick head, and started singing in Dwarven again.

Nath continued to lead the way over the sloppy hills that met with a forested mountainside. Ducking under heavy branches and weaving through the trees, he searched for shelter. Night would soon fall, and even though neither he nor Brenwar required much rest, getting out of the rain until it passed seemed like a good idea.

Half a mile up the mountain, he came across a large rocky overhang. Water poured off it like a waterfall. Nath ducked under it and took a breath. The space was big enough for four men and horses. Brenwar followed him in and shook the water from his rain-soaked face. Nath wrung out his long red hair.

"Why are we stopping?" Brenwar said. "It's not even dark yet."

Nath slid out of his saddle. "I need a moment."

"A moment? What's a moment?"

Nath flipped open a saddlebag, removed a pair of orange fruits with a stem, and tossed one to Brenwar. The other one he fed to his horse. He scratched behind the horse's ears. "You're a fine steed."

The dapple-grey horse shook his head and nickered.

Nath froze. His nostrils widened. Something foul lingered in the air. His hand fell on Fang.

Eyeing him, Brenwar started to speak.

Nath put a finger to his lips.

Brenwar readied his war hammer, Mortuun the Crusher.

Golden eyes peering into the deep black where the rock jutted from the ground, Nath spied a small cave opening.

Silvery eyes flashed within. Scales slithered over the wet earth, and the hooded head of a great snake slipped out. It was bigger than Nath, and it reared back to strike. Its black tongue flicked from its mouth.

"That's an awfully big snake," Brenwar grumbled.

Two more monstrous snakes slithered out and flanked them. Venom dripped from fangs as big and sharp as a dragon's.

"Pardon," Brenwar said, shifting in his saddle, "I meant snakes."

CHAPTER 12

A GREEN LILY DRAGON HALF FILLED a wooden cage big enough for a large dog. Its snout was bound shut with leather cords. Its torn wings were folded tight on its back. Its scales shined like green pearls in the moonlight.

"I say we eat it," said an orc. He was large, as most orcs are. A tangled mess of greasy hair covered his bare back down to the waist. He poked the dragon with the back of his spear. He licked his split and puffy lips. "I've never eaten dragon before. They smell delicious, like baby deer."

"Leave our treasure alone," another voice said. It was a gnoll. A huge wolf-faced man taller but slimmer than the orc. He wasn't alone. The party of poachers was made up of orcs, gnolls, and the much smaller yellow-eyed goblins. There were nine in all. "Once we sell it, you'll be able to eat all you want and more."

The orc at the dragon cage grumbled in his throat. Sounding a bit stupider than his gnoll counterpart, he scratched his head and added, "Are they worth more alive or dead?"

"Alive," the gnoll said, filing his long fingernails with a sharpening stone.

Unlike the others, the gnoll had more flare on him: shiny breastplate made for a large man, heavy axe on his hip. All of the others—gnoll, orc, and goblin alike—carried spears or smaller weapons.

"Now get away and don't pester it anymore." The gnoll walked over and eyed the dragon. "It may lie quietly, but don't let it fool you. It's thinking, not dreaming."

A goblin hopped over the campfire. "Dragons dream?" The filthy humanoid's necklace of animal bones rattled around his neck. He was feisty, even more so than his ornery kin. "How do you know they dream?"

"I know," the gnoll assured him. His chin was up in an attempt to be dignified.

"You don't know that," the goblin retorted. "You're just saying that. Think you're smart?"

The gnoll huffed on his fingernails and dusted them off on his bloodstained sleeve. "Of course I'm smart. That's why I'm the leader. And was it not my trap that caught the dragon?"

Fingers fidgeting at his side and glancing around, the goblin said, "It was luck. Strange fortune. You set no trap at all. The dragon was sleeping." He pounded his chest. "And I saw it first! Told you about it, I did."

The gnoll bared his canine teeth in a snarl. His blades whisked out of his sheaths and found a new home under the goblin's greasy chin. The leader then said to the wide-eyed goblin, "Perhaps you don't want to share in my good fortune, then. The less of you, the more for me and the rest."

Everyone in the poachers' camp's eyes were on the gnoll. The two goblins that remained drew the crude hand axes at their sides. Their feverish eyes had murder in them.

The gnoll pressed his superior blade harder into the goblin's neck. He marched the little monster backward. "You do realize that if I kill you, I have to kill all of your kind." He shrugged his shoulders. "I like the nine. Three gnolls. Three orcs. Three goblins. It's a fortunate number. But minus one goblin, we have eight. Unlucky. Minus two, we have seven. That's the luck of a human's number." He spat. "Bad luck for gnolls. So that means I need six. I like six, but nine is better. Twelve, too big to control."

Gaping, the goblin continued to back away until he stopped a couple feet from the hot coals of the fire. Sweat beaded and dropped over the creases of his brow. Stammering and flapping his hand, he said with a crooked smile, "Nine is good. Nine is good. You say dragons dream, I believe it. Dragons dream. Yes. Dragons definitely dream."

"Mmm, you know, now that I think about it," the gnoll said, rubbing his chin and glancing skyward, "I don't think dragons dream. So, it seems we are once again in disagreement."

The goblin's mouth fell open.

The gnoll cocked his sword arm back. "Six is my favorite number." He started to swing.

"Dragons do dream," said a voice out of nowhere.

The gnoll froze and turned.

A shadowy hooded figure emerged from the woodland.

Every poacher in the camp readied their weapon. Narrowing his wolfish eyes on the figure, the gnoll said, "We don't share our fire with strangers. We kill trespassers."

"Oh, I'm not here to share your fire. I'm here for the dragon." Selene revealed her face. "And zero is my favorite number."

CHAPTER 13

Sliding his sword out of his scabbard, Nath backed up his mount. "The horses, Brenwar. We need to ride out of here."

"I hear you," Brenwar replied. Imitating Nath's, his mount started backward.

The snake flanking it struck. The reptile buried its fangs into the horse's hindquarters.

Throwing the dwarf from the saddle, the horse bucked and instantly fell down dead.

The snake flanking Nath's dapple-grey steed slithered after him. It coiled its hooded head and struck.

Fang's blade flashed quicker than the blink of an eye and shore the snake's head clear off.

Nath hopped off the saddle and scared his horse away. "Get!"

The middle snake, bigger than the rest, reared up right before Nath's eyes. There was deep hypnotic power in the massive cobra's eyes. Deep and evil, its hooded face swayed back and forth. Drops of burning venom dripped from its mouth.

"You think you're faster than me, do you?" Nath said to the snake—whose body was thicker than his leg. "Belly crawler, beware. I'll cut you down like your dead brother over there."

"You need to cut them both down!" Brenwar mumbled. His entire body was encircled by the cobra that had killed his horse. His eyes bulged in their sockets, and his face purpled. He spat out his next words. "Quit trying to make friends with that lizard, and kill it!"

The great grey-black snake hissed. Its tongues flickered.

"You've given me no choice," Nath said, brandishing the glimmering blade of Fang. He spoke in the ancient Snake tongue, unknown to most. "Crawl back inside your hole or die, Snake."

Head reared up eye to eye with Nath, the giant snake struck lightning fast.

Nath banged the tip of its nose with the flat of his blade, driving the reptile back. "I told you I was fast," Nath said in an ancient warning. "My next blow will be fatal."

The snake's eyes bore into him like ancient black pearls of evil. Its head feinted with short strikes and then recoiled.

"Quit playing games with it!" Brenwar blurted out. His face was beet red, and he screamed. "Nothing crushes a dwarf!"

Nath's sure feet slipped on the wet rocks.

The cobra struck. Dripping fangs bore down on Nath's neck.

When Nath snapped his arm up, the cobra's jaws clamped down hard on it. The snake's teeth broke off on Nath's black scales. Toothless, the reptile struck again and held on, chomping down hard on Nath's arm like a vice.

Nath started laughing. "Look at this, Brenwar! It busted its teeth on my scales. I should have known."

"Grrrr!" Though Brenwar flexed with all his dwarven might, the snake that constricted him did not give. "Will you get this thing off me?"

"Certainly," Nath said. Dragging over the snake that was clamped down on his arm, he picked up Brenwar's war hammer and clobbered the lizard in the head.

Its diamond-scaled body eased its all-powerful grip.

Puffing for breath, Brenwar squirmed out of the scaly locks, plucked Mortuun from Nath's grip, and whacked the snake again.

"No! No!" cried out a scratchy voice.

A small shambling figure squeezed out of the snake hole. It was a dirty little man with a full head of scraggly brown hair and a partial beard. He wore strange robes made of snakeskin and had a belt made from snake skeletons. "Don't kill any more of my pets. Please."

Brenwar slammed the man into the ground. "Why? They tried to kill us, and they did kill my horse."

Blue eyes blinking, the odd wilderness man said with desperation, "They were only protecting me. Just as a dog protects his master."

"We posed no threat," Brenwar stated.

The snakeskin clad man let out an inhuman hiss. The cobra released Nath's arm and slithered away. "See! See! I control them."

Holding the little middle-aged man by the scruff of the neck, Brenwar shook him. "Can you bring back my horse from the dead too?"

"Er ... no," the little man said.

Nath sheathed his sword. "Who are you?"

"Ipsy the Snake Charmer." The scruffy man blinked a lot. "Ipsy the Hooded."

Brenwar toyed with the cobra-like hood hanging from Ipsy's strange robes. "He's a druid."

Fingers scratching at the air, Ipsy said, "I prefer woodland seer. Well, if one is being particular, I'm very keen on Ipsy the Hooded. Really draws the attention of the women in small villages." He winked at Brenwar. "What is your name, dwarf? Black Beard?"

Eyeing Nath, Brenwar shoved Ipsy to the ground and stepped on his back. "Druids can't be trusted, and I don't like the stink of this little man. Can I kill him?"

"Kill me?" Ipsy squeaked. "No, no, that would be fatal. It would bring a great curse upon you for the entirety of your days. Please." He eyed Nath's arms and changed his demeanor. "Er, how did you come across those scales? Are you cursed? A demon?"

Nath remembered a few other encounters with druids, in days gone by. They came in many shapes and forms. Men or women, they could be anyone from a halfling to a bugbear. They were loners, hunkered down in their territory, somewhat aloof to everything that was going on in the rest of the world. In a way, Nath envied them. But one and all, they were squirrely as a dryad or a fairy. "Let him up, Brenwar."

"This weird little man owes me a horse." Brenwar nudged his boot toe into the druid's ribs.

"Ow!" Ipsy whined. Gathering himself to his feet and eyeing Nath's arms with avid interest, he stretched out his eager fingers. "May I touch them?"

Flattered, Nath started to say yes.

But Brenwar cut in. "No."

"Let the flame-haired man speak for himself," Ipsy said to Brenwar. He pleaded. "Please? Please? You are so fast. I've never seen any man faster than a snake. And those scales. I marvel. They must be harder than steel."

Wary, Nath fanned out his yellow-gold fingernails on his clawed hand. "And sharper than steel as well."

With an awe-inspired gasp, Ipsy ran his grubby fingers over Nath's scales. "How is this possible? You are both man and dragon."

"It's a long story and one that you don't need to trouble yourself about." Nath watched the snake slither back into the hole. "You need to be more careful with your pets. And we are down a horse thanks to you. How do you propose to replace it?"

Ipsy's eyes enlarged beneath his unibrow. "Being a druid, I have no personal belongings. And if anything, that horse has been freed from a life of slavery." He sneered. "I should suggest that you free your mount as well."

"And let it starve to death? I think not." Nath closed in on the druid and glared down in his face. "Now, tell me, how will you compensate me and my friend?"

"I have nothing."

Brenwar hemmed the little man in from behind and growled, "Everybody has something." He slapped his hammer head in his hand. "Especially when their life depends on it."

Ipsy swallowed the lump in his throat, raised a finger, and replied, "I have knowledge."

CHAPTER
14

THE GNOLL LEADER LET OUT a rumbling chuckle from his throat. The others in his gang started to chuckle as well. Sliding out their weapons, they surrounded Selene on cat's feet. Stroking his chin, he eyed her up and down. "It seems that you are surrounded, traveler. But by the looks of you, I think more fortune has fallen into our hands. You might even fetch half the price of a dragon."

"Oh, you mean my dragon," she said, creeping closer to the dragon's cage.

The orc that stood closest blocked her view, looking down at her. "Perhaps I'll stuff you in that cage with it."

Selene's tail slithered from beneath her gown, coiled around the orc's neck, and jerked him up off his feet.

"Urk!" The orc clutched and clawed at her tail.

Effortlessly, she slung the orc far into the woods and out of sight.

Pointing his sword at her, the gnoll leader shouted a command to his ranks. "Kill her!"

The quicker goblins dove in with their weapons.

Selene's tail struck like the crack of a whip.

Whap! Whap! Whap!

She flattened the three little fiends, knocking two of them out cold.

Eyes filled with fear, the third's hands clawed at the dirt, trying to scramble away.

Selene's tail coiled around its ankles and lifted it off the ground. Using the goblin like a club, she swung the humanoid over her head and bashed the two charging orcs with it. *Whop! Whop!* Checking her nails, she pummeled them both some more. *Whop! Whop! Whop!* She tossed the goblin aside, sending him skittering across the ground in front of the gnoll's feet.

Canine snouts dropped open, the two remaining gnolls threw down their spears and ran. Looking from side to side, the gnoll leader said, "Cowards!" He narrowed his eyes on Selene and said with his sword raised high, "I'm going to cut that tail off and chop it into nine little pieces."

Without looking at him, and rubbing some smudge from one of her nails, she said, "There is zero chance of that happening."

Howling at the top of his lungs, heavy sword arcing high, he charged and struck.

Selene caught the blade in her dragon-scaled hand and jerked it free from the gnoll's grip. Her tail lashed out and knocked him clear off his feet. Holding the sword in both of her hands, she said, "I should kill you with your own sword."

"No, please. No!" the gnoll pleaded. "I'll do anything!"

"On your knees!" she demanded.

The gnoll did as she said.

"Hands on your head."

Shaking, he did as he was told and pleaded, "Please, don't kill me. I'll never touch a dragon again. I promise."

"Oh, after this, you're going to wish you were dead."

"Wh-what are you going to do?"

"Be silent!" Using both of her hands and squeezing the well-tempered blade, she bent it around his neck as easily as a man would bend a spoon. "Enjoy your new necklace. And when more of your filthy ilk ask why you have a sword wrapped around your neck, tell them the next poacher I find won't have a sword wrapped around their neck. It will be placed through their wicked heart instead."

Stammering, the gnoll tried to speak, but no words came out.

"Be gone."

The hairy, dog-faced brute quickly found his feet and, running full speed, vanished into the woods.

Pivoting on her heel, Selene headed for the dragon's cage.

The wooden crate was crude, but durable. The cage door-lock consisted of leather cords and a peg stuck through a latch. She plucked it out, opened the door, and with gentle hands she removed the lily dragon. Through her palm, she felt its heart racing. "There, there, little brother."

Using her nail, she slit the bindings that secured its wings and mouth.

The dragon slid from her grasp and strutted around the camp. It shook its head and hissed at her.

Taken aback, Selene said, "Excuse me?"

Spreading its grand wings, it pushed off with its rear legs and took flight. Seconds later it was gone.

Selene's eyes watered up, and she dropped to her knees, trembling. Her guilt and shame overwhelmed her. Tears streamed down her cheeks and dripped onto the ground. How many dragons, her own brethren, had lost their lives because of her? She had commanded the Clerics of Barnabus to have the dragons poached. She'd had them captured. Those who would not serve Gorn Grattack had been killed. Their parts sold.

Heart aching inside her chest, she started to pant and tremble. She was an abomination—both to mankind and to dragonkind. How could anyone forgive her? How could she replace all that she had taken? What about all the lives that were devastated? Families torn asunder. The innocent deceived.

Wiping the tears from her eyes, she glanced at the open cage. At least one dragon was free. It felt good, but it also reminded her of all her bad deeds. And that lily dragon knew who she was and what she had done. It had made that clear. No, she needed to pay for what she had done. She had to atone for it. If not, the past would catch up with her. She was certain of it.

Standing up, she dusted her knees off.

I need to turn myself in.

She resumed her trek to the north, chin down and heavy in thought.

I need to stop the wurmers too.

Using her powerful dragon senses, she looked for signs of the wurmers as she trekked through the changing terrain, scanning the misty night sky.

Does Nalzambor need me, or is it better off without me?

CHAPTER 15

"KNOWLEDGE, EH?" SAID BRENWAR. "WELL, it better be able to find me another horse. Nath, don't listen to what this fool has to say. We're better off going."

With the rain from the rocky overhang pounding at his back, Nath shook his head. "No, I'd be interested in hearing what this troublemaker has to offer."

"Excellent," said Ipsy, rubbing his hands together. "Excellent. Let me get us some food and some drink. You know, I don't have many people over. The snakes aren't too chatty, and the birds talk far too much." Eagerly, he turned toward the cave.

Brenwar barred his path. "We aren't hungry. I'm interested in hearing what you have to say that is worth more than a horse. Now talk."

The druid slid away from Brenwar and closer to Nath. His eyes kept attaching themselves to Nath's arms. "So fascinating."

Brenwar poked him. "Talk!"

"All right! No need to get testy. The world has shifted. The forest creatures' patterns change. Giants come down from their mountains and their massive caves. Though not one of long life, I'd not seen but one giant. Now, they pass and scatter the vermin constantly."

Brenwar's brows perched. "Giants, you say? Keep talking."

Ipsy rambled on.

Nath gave the druid his full attention, nodding and agreeing with what he said. There were giants roaming about more so than before, all right. Nath believed him. At the same time he wanted to test the druid. Catch a fib or lie—which their kind were known for.

But so far everything the druid said was at least half true. Of course, much of it was common knowledge. After all, it wasn't so long ago that Nath, then in the form of a dragon, had fought a handful of earth giants.

"So how many giants have you seen exactly?" Nath asked.

"A half dozen or so in the last few months."

"And where were they headed?"

"Oh, I can tell you that easy. You see, I followed them, I did. Heh-heh. They don't pay any attention to the likes of me. No, not at all. Too, too small." He grabbed some moss from a rock and rubbed it on his skin. "And my scent blends in. Giants are good smellers, you know. Like big hounds." He eyed Brenwar. "Smell your scruffy stink a mile away."

Brenwar drew his fist back. "Why you——"

Ipsy slid behind Nath and peeked around his waist.

"Let it go, Brenwar."

"I want my horse back," the dwarf said. He plucked a small spade from the dead horse's saddle. "And I'm not leaving until he buries this one."

Nath sighed. He understood Brenwar's point, but burying it? "We'll figure out something. Now, Ipsy, tell us, I haven't noticed any giants' tracks. Where did you follow them to?"

"Only a couple of leagues away they are, building in the Craggy Mountains. Dark and treacherous up there, it is. Nothing that giant slayers like yourselves can't handle. Are you going to kill them? I hope that you do. They attack dragons, you know. Kill them. Eat them. I saw some, dead, strung up like deer with purple scales. Two in all. Dead. Beautiful, but dead."

Nath's fingertips tingled. He grabbed Ipsy by the arm and squeezed it hard. "Don't toy with me, druid. Is this the truth?"

Holding up his hand, Ipsy said, "I swear it on my mother's mossy grave."

"Speaking of graves," Nath said, looking at the horse, "you need to get started."

"But it's raining!" Ipsy whined.

With little help from Brenwar or Nath Dragon, Ipsy carried rocks through rain and wind up and down the hill all night. One by one, he covered the dead horse with rocks. Many of them were bigger than his head.

Finally, the little druid had covered the horse's body in its entirety. Holding his back and stretching, he said to Brenwar, "Am I finished?"

The dwarf clawed at his black-grey beard. "A few more rocks would be better."

"I can't find any more. This is a hillside, not a quarry!"

"You should have thought of that before you killed my horse!"

Nath stepped in. "That will do, Ipsy. We'll be going now. I want to see if your story checks out."

With a sigh of relief, the druid said, "Thank you! Thank you! I did not deceive you!" He mopped the sweat mixed with rain from his eyes. "I promise."

Nath departed with a scowling Brenwar.

With a short maniacal laugh, Ipsy plopped down on the tomb of rocks and rubbed his aching fingers. "Guzan's feet, I thought they'd never leave. Hard men, the both of them. Love horses as much as a horse itself." He lay back on the pile of rocks and fell fast asleep.

While Ipsy lay snoring, a tingle at his feet awoke him.

He lurched up and faced a beautiful woman half the size of him, hovering over the ground. Long hair white as snow. Eyes dark as black pearls. Two violet wings beating gently behind her back. She was surrounded by a dozen dark and colorful hand-sized fairies. He dove to his knees and groveled. "Fairy Empress! Do with me what you please!"

"Arise, Ipsy the Hood," she said with a coy smile. "I see our little plan failed."

"I'm sorry, but my pets were not quick enough. And those two are quite formidable. I'm sorry. Punish me!"

She slapped his cheeks with her delicate hands and squeezed them. "Did you mention me?"

"No, they didn't ask. I just told them about the giants like you said. As a matter of fact, they walked right into it."

"And Nath Dragon didn't suspect a thing?"

"I wasn't lying, but his eyes were still wary." Holding his back, he grimaced. "They sure love horses. Ugh."

Her black eyes inspected the stone grave. "At least you killed a mount. That will slow them down and give me further time to plan."

Fingers fidgeting at his side, he asked, "So, I did well?"

"Of course, Ipsy." She caressed his cheek. "Of course. After all, you chose to follow me, the giants, and the titans. You'll be a part of our destiny to take down the dragons."

"What else can I do, Fairy Empress Lotuus?"

Glancing at the rocks, she said, "This pile of rubble is suspicious. You're going to need to remove it, and the horse with it."

His mouth fell open.

Lotuus waved her hand toward the small cave opening. The giant cobra with the busted fangs slithered out. "Come, come, sweet pet." The snake coiled up beneath her feet. She patted its head. "Ipsy, close your eyes."

"My eyes?"

Her face darkened. "Yes, your eyes."

"Uh, as you wish." He shut his eyes.

"You trust me, don't you, Ipsy?"

"Certainly."

"Good, now keep your eyes closed and don't move."

He swallowed and nodded. A new layer of sweat beaded on his brow. He felt his snake entwine itself around his body. The connection he had with it was gone, overpowered by a darker force.

"Now open your eyes," she said.

He did. He was wrapped from neck to ankle in the giant poisonous restrictor. Its muscles slowly started to squeeze the breath out of him.

"Fairy Empress, you said I did well."

"I lied," she said with a sneer. "You should have at least killed the dwarf."

"But—" he blurted out. Breathless, he could say no more. The snake began crushing his body.

Lotuus pinched his cheek and smiled. "Die knowing that your ultimate purpose was served." With the grace of the wind, she and her fairies departed.

All Ipsy could do was unleash a silent scream. "Noooooooo!"

CHAPTER 16

BRENWAR STOOD INSIDE A GIANT-SIZED footprint of pressed-down grass. Squeezing his war hammer, he said with a fierce grin, "There be giants."

Leagues away from where they had left Ipsy, Nath led his horse alongside his comrade. The footprints led straight toward the base of the Craggy Mountains. He hopped off the saddle and studied the prints in the grass. "I see three sets of them. Seems that the druid wasn't fibbing after all."

"He's not very good with distance. We're a good bit farther north than he suggested." Brenwar's eyes studied the mountains, whose peaks stretched up above the clouds. "And it's no surprise there'd be giants up in there. Probably be some mountain goats too. Har, he's fooling with us."

Scanning the ground, Nath said, "True." After all, he and Brenwar knew Nalzambor about as well as anybody.

Though he'd never ventured into them, the Craggy Mountains weren't so much of a mystery. Their high, jagged peaks were a coarse trek, and most men didn't go near, let alone bother to climb it. It was a great place to hide, for anyone, any size.

Nath took a knee and plucked up a handful of the flattened grasses. He sniffed it and made a sour face. "If it stinks like a giant, it must be a giant, right?"

"I thought it was obvious."

The sun gleamed through the grey clouds, but a light drizzling rain still fell. Nath's nose twitched. "How many days do you think, since they passed?"

"Three," Brenwar replied.

"Even with all this rain?"

"It's rained more south than north. I stick with three. Why?"

"Oh, that's my assessment as well." Nath eyed the mountain. "I say we go back."

"Back?"

"Let me rephrase that. Backtrack."

Brenwar clawed at his beard. "You mean, backtrack the giants?"

"Yes. I'm curious to see where they came from." Nath snapped off some grasses that were still standing high. Blood residue was on them. "I have a bad feeling about this."

"You should. It's giants."

Taking the horse by the reins, Nath followed the giants' trail over the rocky steppes.

For some strange reason, the land was quiet. Not a single bird crossed the sky. There was no rustle of vermin scurrying through the fallen leaves. Only the rattle and squeak of the horse's saddle accompanied them.

They'd made it about a league when Nath said, "I don't like where we are headed."

"Aye," Brenwar agreed.

"Why don't you get on the horse?" Nath suggested.

"Why?"

"So you can keep up."

Without hesitation, Brenwar climbed on the horse and took his place in the saddle. "You're that worried?"

"I feel trouble in my scales." Nath took off running, with Brenwar on the galloping horse behind him.

Based on the course they were following, he knew there was a large group of village communities only a few miles away. Good people, hardy and durable farmers and traders, and a mix of the races at that. They called the area Harvand, which was Elven for outcast. Nath never understood why it was called that. The people were like the rest of the world, but they did seem to prefer additional isolation and were quite accepting of people who were a little different.

Nath's long strides kept an even pace with the horse that ran behind him. His flame-red hair was a banner behind him. It felt good running at the speed of a horse. There weren't any two-legged creatures in the world that could outrun him. At least, he'd never known one that could. Not even the fastest elves were fleeter of foot. Charging up one hill and down another, blood pumping, he started to feel good. He might not be a full-sized dragon anymore, but his body and what it could do was still incredible.

It's not so bad, Dragon. Not so bad at all.

He bounded up a steep hillside and came to a stop at the top. The dapple-grey horse snorted when it caught up with him. Nath rubbed its neck. "You enjoyed that too, didn't you?"

"Harrumph. Running's overrated. A dwarf never rushes anywhere." Brenwar got off the horse and handed the reins to Nath. "He's always exactly where he needs to be."

With Brenwar at his side, Nath focused his attention on the valley of villages ahead. Tiny houses and barns were stretched out on the fertile land around Harvand almost as far as he could see. Aside from the barns and silos, no building was taller than two stories. He could see people milling about the streets. They looked small, but his keen eyes could make out some of the faces quite well. The people were long-faced, and many carried tools.

"What's that?" Brenwar pointed west of the village.

It was a pile of rubble. Wood and stone. People were dragging materials over on carts and wheelbarrows. Some carried it by hand. They pitched materials into the pile of scrap.

Scanning the buildings, Nath noticed that many of them weren't even standing. Several were crushed. A barn had a grain silo stuffed through its roof.

Nath's throat tightened. "We need a closer look."

The closer they got, the worse it looked.

Following the sloppy road, they crept into the nearest village. No one paid them any mind. The last time Nath was here, dozens of years ago, the people had been nothing short of accommodating. Of course, that had often been the case with him back then, and he had enjoyed it. Now, the people were grim-faced, and heads were downcast. They slogged through the torn streets carrying tools and scrap. Few words were spoken.

A woman with two small boys was trying to fix the door to a small home that didn't have a roof or a back wall. A group of children splashed through a puddle made by a giant's foot, chasing after loose chickens. There was hunger. Pain. Depression.

Finally, Nath approached a group of three sandy-headed men with scruffy faces and small points on their ears. They were sawing down a tree. One on one handle, one on the other, and the third measuring with a strip of cloth. "Might I ask what happened?"

"Giants," said the one who measured, without looking at him. "Best that you move on."

Nath pressed. "Did they take anything?"

The half-elves stopped sawing.

The taller one said, "Just our livelihood." His piercing eyes scanned Nath. "You best keep going. No room for heroes around here."

"Sssh," said the half-elf on the other side of the saw, glancing at Nath. He looked back at his counterpart. "Just cut, will you?"

"Come on, Brenwar."

That might have been the most impolite and brief conversation I ever had with an elf of any kind.

"Sorry to bother you."

Walking along Nath's side, Brenwar said, "Something's still amiss."

Nath headed toward the heart of the cluster of villages. "And we need to find out what that is."

CHAPTER 17

IN THE CENTER OF HARVAND was the grandest structure of all: a round stone building with a high cathedral-like ceiling. Smoke came out the chimney on the top. A pole stretched up taller than the chimney. On it, a checkered blue-and-orange flag bearing a wheat symbol flapped in the brisk wind. An archway covered by a sheepskin led inside.

Nath pushed through. "Hello?"

There wasn't much in the room. A rectangular table with long benches for chairs. Aside from the fire blazing, there was no life inside at all.

Nath spoke again. "Hello?"

The shuffle of sandals over the stone floor caught his ear. An old woman with long white hair and plain purple robes teetered out from behind the other side of the fireplace. She had a cane in one hand that clicked on the floor, and she held a horn to her ear. Her left eye was milky.

"Do my eyes and ears deceive me? Is that Nath Dragon I hear?"

"Marley?" He made his way over to her and took her wrinkled hands in his. "It's good to see you again."

"Oh, I can hear the disappointment in your voice." She rubbed his scales. "Oh my, that's fascinating." She coughed. "You've changed. But you're still the same."

"I could say the same of you."

She slapped his arm. "Oh, please. I've aged sixty years since you've been here last. I've more wrinkles than a prune. But it's good to know you're still a flatterer."

"Has it really been so long?"

"Oh, yes. The truth is, not a whole lot has happened since you left. Us old ladies still talk about the time you waltzed in here and dazzled us with your song and skills. And you got rid of the horrible bugbear, Mondoon.

Blecht." She clicked her cane on the floor. "And you danced with all the women and even saved the last dance for me. I swear, my feet didn't touch the floor."

Nath remembered. He remembered everything, even though time often slipped by him unnoticed.

Marley had been the most beautiful gal in Harvand. Chestnut-haired and dark-eyed, her natural beauty had rivaled that of the elves. She couldn't have been more than thirty years old then. A widow, for her husband was killed by the bugbear Mondoon. A terrible time for the whole village town. After a hard-fought battle, Nath had vanquished Mondoon.

"And you never remarried?"

"No point really, at least not after dancing with you." She sighed. "No man in the village could measure up to my tainted expectations." She poked him with her cane. "And they're still pretty high, you know. No, I raised the kids, worked until my back couldn't take it anymore, and let them place me in charge of this city. Things were quiet until now."

"Please, Marley, tell us what happened. We want to help."

Marley shuffled over to the bench and sat down, eyeing Brenwar. "And who is this hairy little fellow?"

"I was here the last time too, you know," Brenwar said with a grumble.

She cocked her ear toward Nath. "What did he say?"

Nath sat down by her side. "He said it's good to meet you, too."

"I did not. Oh, never mind." Mumbling under his beard, the dwarf proceeded to tour the small building while Nath and Marley talked.

Nath took her fragile hand in his. "Marley, tell us what happened."

She shivered. "They just came. Three of them. My, they were taller than those tall buildings in the cities. They were hairy, brawny, and had a smell about them. Started smashing things, toppling one home after the other. It was awful. They then gulped down our livestock, and we thought that might be the end of it. Maybe they were hungry. So we tried to plead with them, and they just laughed. They said in huge baritone voices, 'This is just the beginning.'"

Nath put his arm around her shoulder. "How many people were hurt?"

"Oh, well, that's the oddly fortunate part. There were some injuries, but not one person was killed."

"That *is* odd." Nath caught Brenwar looking at him. Giants didn't leave survivors. "But that makes me happy to hear it."

"Oh, don't be too happy. They said they would be back. They said they wanted people to come with them. Serve them and their new leader. They have built a mountain city in the Craggies. I don't understand it myself, but they made it clear that if they got enough, eh, volunteers, the village would be spared. But only to serve them. I think they want us to raise livestock to feed them. Oh, Nath," she sobbed, "we were peaceful, and that peace is gone."

Brenwar walked over and spoke. "How long until they come back?"

Startled, Marley said, "Where did *you* come from?"

"Morgdon."

She looked up at Nath. "Where?"

"It's not important. Marley, how long until they come back?"

"They didn't say. And though we are terrified, I think many believe they won't come back. But I know they will. Nath, I don't think anyone will go with the giants. I've tried to have meetings. We have no volunteers. We'll all be killed."

It rankled Nath's scales. Clenching his fist, he said, "No one will be killed. Not so long as I am here. But perhaps, Marley, you and your people should hide. I know a place. And when the giants come, Brenwar and I will take them on."

"Aye!" Brenwar injected.

Marley jumped. "Excuse me, who are you?"

"Brenwar!"

"Be easy," Nath said to his friend.

"Easy? She hears me just fine, just doesn't like dwarves. She didn't the last time either."

Nath recalled Brenwar and Marley getting into a spat. She'd told him to shave his beard, and he'd said he would shave her head first. But Nath couldn't tell if she was being selective with what she heard or if she was that feeble.

His thoughts drifted to Sasha.

I hope we can make her better.

"Is it warm out?" Marley asked. "I'd like to walk. The sun warms my cold bones."

"I think there's enough sun out there for you, and what *it* won't do, *I* will." Nath helped her up and led her out the door and kept his hand on her shoulder. Sunlight crept through the clouds. "Which way?" he asked.

"Eh, this way," she said.

She moved slowly, but that was fine with Nath. He wasn't in any kind of hurry. Instead, he took in all of the busy activity. The workers were far from robust, and only a few eyes found their way to him. There were some children who hid and giggled at him as he passed by the split-rail fences.

Scanning the distant fields, Nath noticed some odd structures. "What are those, Marley?"

She stopped and followed where he pointed. "Oh, those are just silos. I'll take you to see them if you like."

"It's just odd that all of them are still standing. Did you rebuild them?"

"I can't remember. I guess it must be good fortune. Come on, let's go and see what's going on."

Four silos stood in a perfect square. Made of stone, they were over thirty feet high, with round shingled roofs.

Brenwar stood in the midst of the four of them. "That's a strange design for silos. They're too wide." He rubbed his bearded chin and eyed the ground. "And I don't see any evidence of grain. And those stones. Awfully big. Did your people build those, or did someone else?"

Marley slipped out from under Nath's arm and looked at him with a painful expression. "Nath, I didn't have any choice." Her chin trembled. "They said they'd kill all of us. It's a trap, Nath. Run!"

CHAPTER 18

"**M**ARLEY! MARLEY! WHAT ARE YOU talking about?"

The old woman was suddenly more nimble than she appeared to be. She slipped away from Nath's outstretched grasp. "Run!"

Wary eyed, Brenwar growled. "I knew something wasn't right—with her or this hog hole—from the beginning. You should have listened to—"

Giant arms busted out of the silo walls.

Big, ugly bald heads popped out the tops of the silos.

"I knew it! I knew it!" Brenwar yelled. "They're stone giants, Nath! That's why I didn't smell them out!"

The stony makeup of the towering buildings crumbled away. Massive men stepped out of the debris and dust that rolled away from their feet. Four towering men almost thirty feet tall had them surrounded.

Marley ran screaming, but she was too slow.

The giant behind them lifted up his great foot and brought it down.

Nath screamed. "Nooooo!"

The ground shook.

Thoom!

Marley was gone, like a bug under a man's shoe.

Nath's heart sank. His jaw dropped. His hands were numb at his sides. So cruel and merciless it was, he didn't even notice the entire town scrambling in panic.

Evil. Such Evil.

"Fill your hands, Nath Dragon!" Brenwar roared. "Else you're going to be goo under their feet too." He raised his hammer high and banged it on the ground.

Krang!

The ground busted up underneath one giant's feet and knocked it to the ground.

"Woohoo!" Brenwar screamed.

Nath ripped Fang out of his scabbard and charged the stone giant who had smashed Marley.

The mountain of marble-like muscle sneered at him and laughed.

Summoning Fang's power, Nath struck the giant's ankle with all of his might. The blade bit deep.

Ice raced up the giant's leg and froze it fast to the ground.

The monster's eyes widened, and it screamed out in horror. Leg icing up, it lashed out. The monster's fingers clipped Nath's ducking head. The raw power of the massive man lifted Nath from his feet and sent him rolling through the dust.

Seeing stars, Nath lifted up his head at the sound of heavy footsteps.

The third giant charged right for him. Its huge fists came down together like a great anvil.

Nath sprang away.

The fists missed him by inches.

Boom!

Without hesitation, Nath whirled around and stabbed Fang through one of the giant's hands.

Its hand burst into flames. Slobbering from its jowls, the monster jerked its hand away, ripping Fang out of Nath's iron grip. The monster screamed at its burning hand with Fang still in it.

"Guzan! I need my sword back!"

"Take that, giant!" Brenwar climbed on top of the giant he'd knocked down and hammered away at it with Mortuun. The grand war hammer came down again and again with the sound of clapping thunder.

Boom! Boom! Boom!

The giant swatted at Brenwar with hands, forearms, and elbows.

Somehow, Brenwar slipped in and out of its efforts only to hammer it again and again with devastating effort.

Its ribs cracked. Its jaw and eye socket were broken.

"You'll regret the day you ever crossed me, giant!"

Boom! Boom! Boom!

Brenwar put everything he had into it. Stone giants were serious business. As their name suggested, they were stone and bone, not flesh and bone like most giants. Killing them was never easy, and plenty of dwarves had met the grave trying. He unleashed as much of Mortuun's power as he could.

"Come on, Mortuun! Come on!" Black-beardedly wild as a berserker, he unleashed all that his ancient dwarven bones had in him. "We've still got three to go!"

Boom! Boom! Boom!

Finally, the giant lay stretched out between the broken silos, dead.

Hammer in hand, chest heaving, and iron arms weary, Brenwar turned. "Whew, where's the next one?" He froze.

He was eye to eye with the next giant.

Bending down and clapping its hands together, it smashed Brenwar like a fly.

One giant fought the icy cords that tethered it to the ground. Another giant fought to put its flaming hand out.

Lucky for Nath, his sticky fingers had managed to snake Dragon Claw out of Fang's pommel. In a rush, Nath climbed up the distracted giant's back with Dragon Claw in hand and smote it in the temple.

The stone giant fell on its knees and collapsed face first in the muddy dirt.

Splat!

Nath surveyed the battleground.

The third giant was dead and sprawled out on the ground, but the fourth caught Nath's eyes.

"Oh, no!"

With Brenwar clasped inside the giant's hands like a little woodland creature, it leered down at Nath with a cold-blooded killer's gaze and said in long and loud words, "I'll take his life if you don't surrender, Nath Dragon."

Spitting through his beard with a great strain in his face, Brenwar said, "Don't surrender, Nath. Don't do it!"

CHAPTER

19

NATH RETRIEVED FANG AND STOOD before the stone giant. "Killing him will only bring you a swift death, giant. If you want to live, then put him down."

The giant shook his head and said in his long drawn-out voice, "And pass up killing this dwarf? No. I think not." He squeezed Brenwar harder.

Brenwar's eyes bulged. "Urk! Don't worry about me, Nath. Just kill him!"

With two giants down and only two remaining, Nath liked his chances.

Behind him, the one giant struggled and freed its frozen leg. Somehow, it managed to hobble forward toward Nath.

I can handle this. I have Fang, and Brenwar's plenty tough.

Brandishing the great sword, Nath said, "Just put him down, giant. Leave this village. It is under my protection."

"Oh ho ho," the giant said with a chill in its voice, "Nath Dragon, this trap was not sprung to fail. Be wise as a serpent and surrender, or the blood of every villager will be on your hands."

It was a trap, all right, but who had set it? And how had they known that Nath would be coming to this village?

I can't think of anything at all that led me here.

Uncertainty filled him. Someone somewhere was watching him. His thoughts raced back.

Ipsy!

Why had the druid set him up? He'd never met the druid before. He must have been working with somebody else, but who?

"I think you're bluffing," Nath said, creeping forward with his sword. "Now put the dwarf down so no one else gets hurt."

"You are a cocky little flea." The stone giant let out a strange hoot. "Howeet!"

Large stacks of hay that were scattered all over the villages came to life. Giant humanoids—ogres and bugbears—emerged from the hay and snatched up any screaming villager they could find. They wrapped them up in powerful arms and started to crush the life out of them.

The distraught people screamed and begged for mercy.

"Eeeeeeeee!"

"Oooowwwww!"

"Still feeling cocky, little dragon?" the stone giant said.

Aghast, Nath squeezed Fang's hilt so hard that his hand trembled.

How did I miss this trap?

It wasn't like him to overlook what should have been obvious details. But somehow his transgressors had deceived him. He'd missed the giants and dozens of burly humanoids. And the villagers of Harvand were so terrified, they'd played along as well. He should have listened to the half-elves.

Great Guzan! Those half-elves were trying to warn me.

"What is it you want, giant?"

"Just surrender, and all of them will live." He held Brenwar out in his long outstretched arms. "Including this bearded chipmunk."

"Am I to be your prisoner?"

"No, you are to be someone else's prisoner."

"Who might that someone be?"

"Surrender, and you will see."

That was a problem with the giants. They were liars. Their guaranteed word was no better than an angry orc's. For all Nath knew, he'd turn himself over, and they'd kill all of the villagers anyway. Which begged the question, how do you get a giant to keep his word? And this one wasn't even calling the shots.

"I need proof that no harm will come to anyone else, including the dwarf."

"Hmmm." The giant scratched its chin with Brenwar's head then showed a toothy smile. "You'll just have to trust me. You don't have any choice, little dragon."

Panicked cries of alarm and horror filled Nath's ears. The rough hands of the beasts that held the villagers were far from gentle. The message was clear. Nath could feel it. They wouldn't hesitate to kill anybody.

"Nath!" Brenwar said. "You are too important. Don't do it."

"If I think I'm more important than anybody else, then I'm truly not important at all." Nath stuck Fang in the ground and placed his scaly hands on his head. "So be it, giant. I surrender."

"Secure him," the stone giant ordered. A pair of bugbears marched forward. They were huge ugly men, somewhat bear faced, with huge muscles in their shoulders. They carried chains and shackles made from moorite. With rough hands they shackled Nath's wrists and ankles and put a collar on his neck. "That's good."

"I've submitted. Now put the dwarf down and leave these people alone."

The giant tossed Brenwar through the roof of a nearby home and wiped his hands on the muddy street. "Filthy little thing." He reached over and picked up Fang with the tips of his fingers. His stony skin started to sizzle. Grimacing, he ordered Nath, "Put it in a sheath."

Nath complied.

The stone giant picked up the sheathed sword and stuck it in his belt, which held up a roughhewn pair of trousers. "Let's go."

Escorted by the bugbears and the ogres, Nath followed the giant. Glancing behind him, he saw the village was left unmolested, but some of the people followed. Perhaps many of the people had already sworn a new allegiance to the giants or whomever the giants answered to.

A bugbear shoved him forward, almost knocking him down. "March," it growled.

Nath turned around and marched backward with the chains rattling around his ankles. "You mean like this?" he said.

It was a distraction. His eyes searched for Brenwar. Even though he didn't think the fall into the building would kill the dwarf, he could be seriously hurt.

He's fine, right? He always is, isn't he?

CHAPTER
20

SELENE STOOD ON THE NORTHERN shores of Nalzambor, less than a mile away from a small sea town called Dusky. The early-evening tide splashed over the rocks, creating pockets of sea-foam as the fishermen hauled in their nets and dragged them up the sandy banks. As the water chopped and smacked into the rocks, she finished braiding her long locks into a style more customary.

Perhaps I should go sailing.

For her entire life, she couldn't remember doing anything that she wanted to do. She'd been trained to fight, to conquer and deceive. But she was never taught to enjoy life.

Maybe there is peace for me somewhere out there.

"Peace. Hah. A child's tale."

Her tail snaked up under her robes, and she pulled down her sleeves. With sure footing, she traversed the rocks and headed down to the shore where the seafarers talked and joked. She envied them. Somehow, someway, they enjoyed the work they did, hauling in oily amounts of stinking fish.

"Ho there, Miss!" a man said, waving his cap at her. "What are you doing up there? You need to get down."

Stopping to survey her surroundings, she realized she stood on the jagged black rocks with strong waves smashing into the deep alcoves. Water was splashing up and soaking the hem of her robes. Clearly, for a mortal person this would be a dangerous position, standing on slick rocks where the slightest stumble would send a body into the cold water and dash it against the rocks.

Hand to her chest, she resumed her trek and navigated the dangerous path until she found herself in front of the wide-eyed sailor.

"Hello," Selene said.

The man wasn't old or young, and he wore standard attire of the seaworthy people: a white cotton shirt with long sleeves soaked to the elbow, brown trousers where the hem touched his bare feet. He had a mop of light-brown hair, thick side burns, and sea-green eyes. His features weren't handsome but fair.

He said, "Are you real, or do my eyes deceive me?"

She took his calloused hand in hers. "What do you think?"

"Real ... real beautiful," he explained.

She almost smiled. "Tell me, what is your name?"

"Gavlin."

"Gavlin, may I ask you a question?"

He shook his head yes. "You can ask me anything."

"Do you ever see dragons over the sea?"

"Oh, sure, we see them inside the waters as much as above. Do you want me to take you out in the morning? You never know when you might see them, but I know a place where many roost."

He said it as if the dragons weren't any more extraordinary than big birds. He didn't have any worries about dragons at all.

It surprised her. "I just might take you up on that sometime, but I'm looking for a different kind of dragon. Dark and rough scaled, not smooth and polished like mine." Still holding his hand, she lifted it up in front of his eyes. "See what I mean?"

He gasped and tried to pull away.

She held him fast. "Gavlin, you have nothing to fear from me. Why do you try to flee?"

"You're a demon!" His face was full of strain. "Please, let me go!"

"But you said you would tell me anything." She looked deep into his eyes and used a hypnotizing effect. "I want you to tell me, Gavlin. Have you seen these dragons I speak of?"

The rapid beating of his heart started to slow. "Yes, they fly in thirteens. Heh, I've never seen purple eyes before. I've never seen scales on a woman before."

"Gavlin," she said calmly, "where do those dragons go?"

"Well, I don't follow them. That's trouble. No, no, no. Here in Dusky we avoid trouble."

She rolled her eyes, breaking the connection. "You're an observant man. Just tell me where they fly."

"Where all the wretched go these days. Down into the Craggies." Wincing, he looked at their interlocked hands. "Are you going to kill me, demon?"

"I am not a demon, so no, I'm not going to kill you. I'm trying to befriend you." She released him. "I thought you said I was beautiful."

He backed away. "Just because you're beautiful doesn't mean you're not evil. My wife's told me about women like you. Stay away. Stay away from here, and stay away from Dusky." He turned and ran away, shouting to his fellow sailors. "Beware! A she-demon is in our midst."

Angered, Selene started after the man. Nath didn't have this problem. Even with his scales, people accepted him. What was so different about her? Anger turned to sadness. Maybe she hadn't changed. Maybe she was still evil.

Approaching the men with her arms spread wide, she said to them, "I am a friend."

The fishermen picked up their fish and started throwing them at her. "Go away, Demon!" they yelled. "Go, go back to the Craggy Mountains!"

"And what if I don't, you stupid fish-throwing people?"

They kept throwing the fish with deadly accuracy.

She swatted them away.

But one of the men said, "Then we'll summon Nath Dragon to kill you!"

"Agghhh!" she yelled. She snatched a fish out of the air and threw it back so hard, it hit one man in the face and knocked him over.

All of the fishermen dropped their fish and ran away, screaming toward their town, "Demon! Demon! Demon!"

Disgusted, Selene lifted up the hem of her robes and let her tail out. "No wonder I never liked people. They're stupid."

She climbed up the rocks onto the tall grass and marched back south, watching the skies for any wurmers going toward the Craggy Mountains.

Of course they don't like me. Why would they?

CHAPTER
21

THE MARCH TO THE CRAGGY Mountains wasn't so bad, but the march up the Craggy Mountains was. Nath, one to pride himself on knowing the terrain of so many places in Nalzambor, didn't find any familiarity with the cold mountains at all. Shackled at the ankles, he slipped and bumped into the rocks of the narrow pass that winded slowly up the mountain.

A bugbear whacked him in the back with the butt of its spear. "Keep moving, Scales."

Scales. That was what they were calling him. An unpleasant little nickname full of spite and mockery. It didn't take much for the big, cruel humanoid races to take their shots at him. They tripped him. Bumped him. Threw small stones at him. They pulled and clipped off strands of his hair. They did everything they could to provoke Nath to anger.

Jaw set and teeth grinding, Nath bore it all. One insult after another.

I'm glad Brenwar's not here. He wouldn't make it. How am I making it?

Getting back on his feet, he resumed his march. All in all, it wasn't so bad for him. His limbs didn't tire. His extremities didn't freeze despite the frost and snow thickening on the banks. No, he could take it. He was Nath Dragon, the Dragon Prince. He could take anything.

Walking up the frozen road with the real world he knew a mile or more below, they ventured through a sheet of low clouds. He momentarily lost sight of the bugbears that pulled him by the collar clamped around his neck. But he could hear the rattle of their armor. Smell their unpleasant sweat.

I've a feeling where I'm going will hold a far worse fragrance than Orcen Hold.

He shook his downcast head.

I hope Brenwar is fine. And I hope he doesn't come after me. He hates climbing these mountains. And if those giants get ahold of him, they'll bounce him down the hillside like a ball.

"Come on, Scales!" cried an unseen bugbear. The moorite chain connected to Nath's collar snapped taut and jerked him clean off his feet. "Get up!"

Nath's eyes turned into burning golden flames. From his knees, he coiled his hands around the chain and tugged it back.

The bugbear appeared in the mist, stumbling.

Furious, Nath rushed the bigger humanoid and tackled it to the ground. In a split second he had the chain around the bugbear's neck and was choking it.

The bugbear let out a croak.

Biceps bulging under his scales, red brows furrowed, Nath put his back into it. Why not kill his captor? Now was the perfect moment to make his escape into the cover of the mist. Sure, he was shackled, but if anyone could escape these moronic fools, he could.

Whack!

A spear shaft broke on the back of his skull. Out of nowhere, the ugly, greasy faces of the orcs, ogres, and gnolls crowded him. They smote him with clubs and big fists.

Nath held on to the chain. He'd had enough of his tormenters on this long, cold, miserable march. He was a dragon.

No one messes with a dragon!

The relentless assault of his captors hammered away at his face and body.

Whop! Crack! Smash! Whump! Whump! Whump!

Blood dripped into Nath's eyes. A sharp blade pierced his skin. He lost his grip on his chain.

The bugbear he had been choking to death crawled away. It clutched at its throat, coughing and hacking.

Somehow, from beneath the pack of bodies, Nath managed to kick and break its nose. "You'll think again before you jerk *me* around, stupid beast!"

Something hard smacked right into the side of Nath's temple. Bright spots erupted in his blood-filled eyes. Sagging underneath the greater weight and getting hit time after time, Nath's valiant strength gave out. They beat Nath without mercy and dragged what was left of him up the mountain.

Half-conscious, Nath was uncertain how much time passed before they stopped dragging him. Parched, he spat out the grit from his mouth and forced himself up to his hands and knees. Through his swollen eyes he could see that the mist had cleared, but it was night, a black, moonless sky with not a star in sight. Some of his captors carried flaming torches for light. Snowflakes fell from the sky, and he caught one on his tongue.

Pretty, but not filling.

Rising to his feet, he stumbled and winced. One of his captors had stabbed him in his calf. Taking another step, he was forced to limp.

"Huh huh huh!" one of the bugbears laughed.

But it wasn't the one Nath had nearly killed. No, that one looked at him and glanced away.

Good. At least one of these stupid beasts got the message.

One of his captors shoved him.

Nath hobbled forward, acting a little worse off than he was.

If you fool these morons once, you can fool them again. Smelly morons.

The pass was wide enough for a dozen men to squeeze through side by side, and the cliffs were steep and jagged on either side. It was a one way in, one way out kind of thing.

Nath saw movement in those rocks. A glint of metal from armor and weapons. Black faces were hidden in those roosted shadows, but he could make out their breathing. Dozens of soldiers manned the rocks. But why? Why would anyone want to live in such a harsh, cold, and unforgiving place?

Hmmm, probably the perfect place for harsh, cold, and unforgiving people. Yes, the giants and their smaller, fouler little cousins deserve a place such as this.

Twisting around another bend in the road, Nath finally saw the stone giants he'd lost sight of long ago. The towering monster men weren't so towering now. They stood side by side in front of a pair of great iron doors twice as tall as them. The ironwork was something like you would see in a dwarven city, only bigger, cruder, and unwelcoming.

Lifting his chin up at the ever-so-high doors, Nath gawked.

Sultans of Sulfur! Those are just as big as the ones inside Dragon Home. What in Nalzambor lives in there, a city of giants? Or worse.

CHAPTER 22

BALZURTH THE DRAGON KING LET out a roar that shook the Mountain of Doom. The great red dragon with gold glinting between his scales paced through the piles of gold and other treasure. His huge paws stomped the tiny coins and flung them aside. He shook the great horns on his head, and fire burst from his nose.

His voice was a rumble of thunder. "THEY WILL PAY!"

"Mind your temper," said Grahleyna the Dragon Queen. Her dragon body was covered in scales of old gold with traces of white. She was smooth and supine beside her bigger husband. She was a thing of beauty that outshone every bauble and trinket of treasure in the room. She brushed up against Balzurth. "You need to be statelier. You're setting a bad example for the rest."

Balzurth bumped up against her and said in his strong voice, "It's not going to be the end of the world because the king gets upset. Aw, that poor green lily. When I saw her, a she, with her wings shorn off..." His throat growled. "I don't know how I've been able to contain myself this long. Now is the time for action, Grahleyna. I need to strike now!"

She clocked her horns with his. "You need to stay here, Balzurth. This is where you belong. It's clear they are trying to draw you out so that they can kill you."

He stomped his clawed foot and rattled the coins. "Let them try! I welcome the challenge."

"Let me tell you something: I'm not letting you out of my sight, so don't try anything. Oh, and don't think I'm not still privy to your tricks. I know how you like to slide out of here, and just so you know, I have my eyes and ears everywhere. For now, we need to wait. Be patient."

"Grahleyna! You heard the lily's story. Those vile giants are decorating their chambers with dragon skulls! I can't sit back and allow that kind of mutilation. You know that!"

She curled her tail around his. "Yes, yes I do. And my heart aches as much as yours, but you have to have faith now. The word is out about the giants and the titans. I have seen to that. The dragons will be more cautious and careful from now on."

"Not all of them."

"No," she agreed. "But you can't be responsible for all of them."

He tightened his tail around hers and looked into her incredible eyes. "I'm glad you're back. Life's not the same without you by my side."

"You're sweet, Balzurth. And about that," she said, nuzzling him, "I find it very curious that our son, Nath, happened upon me. You wouldn't have had anything to do with that, would you?"

The grand dragon stammered. "The boy kept asking about his mother, so to keep him busy, I sent him on a quest. I only gave him one little hint."

"Balzurth!"

"I didn't think he would find you, though I hoped he would. Grahleyna, I missed you. A few hundred years without you was enough."

"A few hundred years is nothing to us, and don't try to play the romantic." She rustled her wings and shook her head. "You hate the Great Dragon Wall."

"No, I hate what is behind it. And WE SHOULD NOT HAVE TO SACRIFICE OUR LIVES CONTAINING AN EVIL THAT MUST BE DESTROYED! That wall cannot last forever, Love. You know that."

She uncoiled her tail from his. "Oh, so it wasn't really about me?"

Using his tail, he tried to grab hers again. "No, I didn't say that. You know how deeply I feel for you." His tail swiped through the treasure after hers, but she was quick, and he kept missing. "Grahleyna, don't be like this. I don't want to go decades without talking!"

"And you think I want to talk to someone who yells all the time?"

The massive chamber shook.

"I'M NOT YELLING!"

"Oh, really?"

Taken aback, Balzurth softened his tone. "Well, maybe a little. Grahleyna, please—"

She coiled her tail up with his again. "I forgive you. Honestly, Balzurth, you should know me better. I was only teasing you."

"I understand many things, but I have the hardest time with you."

"I know. But I like it that way. I find it … entertaining."

The closer she got, the more Balzurth's temper eased. He had plenty on his mind. Titans. Giants. Wurmers. His family was under attack again, and here he sat on his throne, feeling guilty. He wanted to take the fight to his foes. Vanquish the enemy once and for all. He glanced back at the Great Mural, where the images of the dragons moved at an impossibly slow pace. Time was so different on the other side.

"What are you thinking, Balzurth?" Grahleyna said, nuzzling him.

"Our son. It's so much to leave on his shoulders. It seems unfair."

"I know. I worry about Nath too. But I have faith he can do it."

"Yes, yes, I do too, but still ... I just want to help him. He's so young, and the world is so full of ancient evil."

CHAPTER

23

THE HUMONGOUS DOORS SWUNG OPEN with an ugly groan coming
from the hinges. Marching into the mountain, Nath noted a smaller
set of doors, man-sized, were built into the ones that had opened.
Interesting.

The two stone giants led him right through the mountain with their
great arms swinging at their sides. The road within was wide enough for a
dozen carriages, and it stretched as far as even Nath's eyes could see.

It looks like they've carved a canyon out of this mountain.

On either side of him, crude structures jutted toward the sky. They were
carved from rock and stone and merged with metal. Strange houses, open
faced, were tiered up several levels. There were wooden ladders and stone
staircases that all led higher and deeper into the strange new land.

Shuffling forward on his sore leg, Nath kept pace with his detainers.
They had some swagger to them now, a strut in their step. People from all of
the races were waving and greeting them, throwing dead branches and prickly
rose stems on the road at their feet and cheering them on.

*This is the oddest welcome I've ever seen. Men, orcs, halflings—ack! Is that a
gnome? Oh my, a human boy is riding on a gnoll's shoulders. It can't be!*

But it was. An eerie harmony pervaded these people. They were cheerful
almost, one and all. Many chiseled at rocks. Others hammered metal inside
the smithies Nath passed. The odd city seemed to have everything that a city
would need. People. Livestock. Store fronts and shanty-like homes. There
were coal-burning fire pits everywhere. And that wasn't all.

There were giants.

More than Nath had ever seen.

Brenwar's head would explode if he were here.

The giants, though outnumbered by the people, were monstrous men among them. Nath counted over two dozen of them. Hard bodied and bare chested, most of them stood between ten and twelve feet tall. They were the more common kind, unlike the stone and earth giants that towered around thirty feet high.

Nath stopped in his tracks.

Oh Guzan, I must be dreaming. No, it's a nightmare.

Four giant orcs strode down the street. Dark skinned and pig-nosed, with some canine teeth sticking out from their bottom lips.

Nath couldn't believe his eyes. He sniffed, and his eyes watered.

Oh, they are bigger and smell even fouler.

They walked right by Nath, flapping their jaws with chins held high, as if he weren't even there.

It was strange. Nath for a change was one of the smallest people there. He didn't like it.

What kind of an orc ignores me?

Nath stuck his foot out and tripped the one in the rear.

It stumbled into the others and knocked them all down.

"Ha ha! Stupid orcs. The bigger you are, the harder you fall!"

One of the bugbears turned around and took a swipe at Nath with his spear.

Ducking under it, Nath mocked him. "Nice try!"

One would think he'd learn his lesson from the last beating he took only hours ago, but the sight of the huge indifferent orcs infuriated him. He hated orcs.

I hate orcs! Certainly orc giants can be killed!

The giant orcs climbed back to their feet. Their dark eyes were hot with rage. Brows crumpled over their protruding foreheads. One of them yelled at Nath's guards. A bugbear started apologizing profusely over himself.

Huh, well if that isn't a twist. They're mad at my captors and not me. Maybe the bigger ones are smarter than the smaller ones.

A giant orc unhooked a metal hammer from its belt and launched a devastating swing. The blow crushed the pleading bugbear's face in and killed it.

Nath grimaced.

Bigger and meaner.

Every one of Nath's captors dropped to their knees, leaving him standing upright, front and center.

The orc giant faced him with its heaving hammer in its hands and glowered down at him with its nostrils flaring. It cocked the hammer back over its shoulder.

"Eh," Nath said, but he held his tongue. He wanted to say 'I didn't trip you.' He really did, but that would be a lie. And even though it was an orc, and his life was in peril, Nath just couldn't lie, so he said something else. Something positive. "Nice hammer. Can I hold it?"

The orc tossed it to him. Nath caught the massive thing with both hands. "Oof!" It was as heavy as an anchor. Straining, he lifted it over his head, teetered backward, and fell.

The orcs erupted in thunderous guffaws. Paying Nath no more mind, the one orc picked up the hammer, rejoined his group, and walked away.

"Whew!" Nath said, smiling. The hammer was heavy, but not so much as he'd led them to believe. He'd need to be more careful though. These giants were about as cruel as anyone he'd ever seen. They even killed their own kind.

Nath extended his hand to one of the bugbears on the ground.

It slapped his hand away.

For some strange reason, Nath almost said he was sorry. After all, it had been his actions that got the other bugbear killed. But the murder had revealed an awful lot to him.

These giants don't play around. They're stone-cold killers.

With him surrounded, his captors continued through the great but daunting city.

Nath, who had seen many things in his life, marveled.

This place was like the darker side of Narnum with all of its cultures, races, and sizes. Twenty-foot-tall ettins strolled the streets. Each giant traveled with a pack of smaller people that were enthralled by it. Huge slabs of meat cooked on monstrous grills and spits. There was the stink of sweat too. Filth and grime on every face. But the hard men and women worked with purpose and zeal. It was as if they wanted to help the giants. They enjoyed it. Hundreds of them. Maybe thousands. And they sang awful, ear jostling, horrible praises.

Bizarre. Yes. Bizarre.

Venturing into a great hall lit by great flaming urns bigger than ogres were tall, Nath stood before three empty thrones carved from black marble. Each one was about the same size as his father's. They chained Nath's links to the metal eyelets on the floor, and all of his detainers scurried away.

Skin crawling, Nath felt odd in his new isolation. There was an evil chill in the air that prickled the edges of his scales. Scanning the great vastness, his eyes glanced over the huge archways and columns where he found décor that was quite disturbing. Dragon skulls were mounted on the sides of the walls. Dragon skins hung like banners from poles.

Anger mixed with Nath's queasiness. The corded muscles in his arms strained against his chains. The moorite groaned, but it would not give.

Sweat burst on his brow. It was futile, and he gasped. The sound echoed throughout the massive chamber. That's when another sound caught his ear.

Something hard pecked and scraped at the floor and echoed everywhere.

I've a horrendous feeling about this.

An enclave of wurmers snaked out from behind the bone-covered marble thrones. Eyes glowing and mouths dripping acid that sizzled on the floor, they made a beeline for Nath.

Did I say horrendous? I meant extremely horrendous.

CHAPTER
24

WURMERS. THEY WERE DRAGON-LIKE, BUT not dragon at all. They had scales and were dark colored and rigid. They had wings, functional but not graceful. And their claws and teeth made their appearance even less desirable. It was like comparing a hummingbird to a hornet. There wasn't anything admirable about them at all, unless you liked killers.

Nath stood tall with his chest out as the wurmers eased closer with a deep-purple glow in their snake eyes. If he was going to go down, be devoured or torn apart, he'd do it with his head up.

He spoke to the mindless things. "Come on, then. I'm a better meal than you deserve, and the best meal you'll ever have. Kind of sad really. I probably won't even give you a stomachache."

One of the wurmers in the middle, standing a head taller than Nath, snapped at him.

Frankly, he was getting tired of being smaller than everything in this city.

And father says size doesn't matter. Hah. Wonder how he'd feel about that if he were in my shoes.

He recalled Balzurth's oft-quoted favorite saying.

It's the size of your heart that matters most.

Inside Nath's chest, it felt like his pounding heart was as big as his head.

Easy for him to say. He's as big as a hillside. I used to be as big as a hillside. Great Dragons!

Clap! Clap!

The wurmers recoiled and backed toward the foot of the thrones.

With his view no longer obstructed by the wurmers, Nath noticed a small figure sitting on the bone-clad throne on the left. "Lotuus!"

"Oh, you remember my name. How special I am." Lovely as a bee, she flew over and hovered eye to eye with him. She was a little under half his size. Her features were as beautiful and exquisite as ever. Her white hair looked soft as cotton, her skin smooth, and she had a radiant smile that could melt the snow. She reached out and touched his swollen face. "My, you look much worse than when I saw you last, Nath Dragon." She poked her finger in his cheekbone. "Do these bruises hurt when I touch them? I wouldn't know. I've never been bruised."

Nath didn't wince. "You have a funny way of thanking your liberator, Lotuus."

She started toying with his hair. "My, your mane is so feathery and divine."

"Well, that it is," he said, starting to brim. But then he remembered who she was. "Hold on, get your hands out of my hair!"

From behind him, she tangled her arms up deeper in his locks. "I could sleep in it."

"Keep dreaming."

"No, literally. I *could* sleep in it. Not with you attached of course. No, I'd shear it off, mend it with other gentle fibers, and sleep for a decade in it. My, if I'd had this in my prison, I might have stayed." She spoke with elation. "I love it!"

"Get out of my hair!"

She untangled her arms and floated around him, poised in thought. "You know, I could shave it. Imprison you. Let it grow. Ah, yes. Shave it. Let it grow." She rubbed his chin. "I bet you can grow the softest beard. I want you to grow that too. My, how rare it is. I mean …

Dragon scales are valuable and rare,

But how many dragons actually have hair?"

She twirled around. "My blanket shall be marvelous!"

Straining against the moorite chains, Nath yelled at her, "That's not going to happen!" He huffed. And then curiosity got the better of him. "Now tell me, Lotuus, what are your motives?"

She stared at him with her round black eyes. "It's not my motives that you need to worry about, Nath Dragon. It's the titans. You see, you might have thought Gorn Grattack was a threat to mankind, but he was still a dragon. He just wanted to convert them. I personally never liked dragon kind. So pure and arrogant. Even the ornery ones." She huffed on her lavender fingernails and dusted them off with Nath's hair. "Oh my, look at that shine. It's too bad there's only one of you."

Irritated, he asked, "As you were saying?"

"Oh, yes. You see, I like the titans. They almost took this world over before, but the dragons defeated them. At that time, I thought maybe I had picked the wrong side, hence my imprisonment. But I always figured I'd get a second chance, and now we do. Thanks to you."

Nath frowned. It seemed that everyone spoke in riddles that he didn't fully understand.

His father had sent him after his mother.

That had led him to freeing Lotuus.

Which had led to him inadvertently freeing the titans.

He still didn't fully comprehend his father's reasons, but there had to be good reasons for it. One thing was for sure, it seemed everyone knew more than he did. It frustrated him.

"So, what makes you so certain that'll you'll be victorious this time when you were soundly defeated the last time?"

Her brows perched. "Soundly defeated?"

"Certainly. After all, my father has never been defeated, and never will be. Why do you think this time the outcome will be any different?"

She touched his nose. "Because we have you, Nath Dragon, and not only that, we have the wurmers as well. And with leverage and greater numbers, I don't see how anything can stop us."

"Let me ask you something, Lotuus. What is it that you wish to gain from all this?"

"Control."

"Control. Is that what pleases you, control? In all of your years of life have you not figured out that you cannot take away free will? I'm far younger than you—and I might add, comelier too—and I've figured that out."

Lotuus frowned. "What we cannot control we will destroy."

"Then you will wind up with nothing. What will you control then when only misery and emptiness is your company? How will you control that growing pit in your stomach that devours you from the inside out?"

With defiant eyes she sneered. "We will see." She flew backward and stood on the left throne, which was so big, he barely even noticed her on it.

The floor in the great hall started to shake under the thunder of footsteps. Behind the thrones a flaming ball of light appeared. It was a giant with a husky and roughhewn frame wearing breastplate armor like a man with his head afire with blue flames. His mighty frame filled the middle throne.

He gazed down at Nath and said in a cavernous voice, "Son of my enemy, I am Eckubahn. Welcome to Urslay. It is Giantish for *torment,* and your time of torment has come."

CHAPTER
25

BRENWAR AWOKE ONLY TO FIND himself jailed in a stable. Hands and legs bound up, he rolled onto his belly, gathered his legs underneath him, and using the wall he pushed up to his feet.

A cow in a nearby stable mooed.

"Moo you," Brenwar replied. Legs and wrists tied up, he hopped on two legs and bumped into the stable gate. He peered in between the planks. The barn was typical. A ladder led into a loft full of hay, and about two dozen stables were inside.

Just outside of the barn's main doors, two of the villagers stood guard. One had a pitchfork. The other had a hand axe. They were talking to each other and not paying any mind to Brenwar at all.

He hopped backward, slipped in the straw, and tumbled down hard. He spat the straw from his mouth. "Great Morgdon."

Fortunately for him, his hands were bound in front of him, and it was a poor job at best. Clearly, the villagers didn't take many prisoners. Using his bony fingertips on his skinless hand, Brenwar started picking at the threads.

"Hmm, that's quite a trick."

The sensation was on in his bony hand. He could feel with it, but there wasn't any life to it. Still, he liked it and continued picking one tiny thread from another.

"No one but Brenwar has a hand like this. Ho ho!"

Though it was daytime, a few things escaped him. It wasn't often that anything had ever knocked him out before. As a matter of fact he didn't recall ever being knocked out before. He wondered how long he'd been out. Hopefully not more than a day. It couldn't have been that long.

"Certainly not."

Finally, the ropes on his wrists gave way. Using his dwarven strength, he snapped out of his bonds and undid the bindings on his legs. Wearing only his clothes from beneath his armor, he reached through the planks, unlatched the gate, and swung it open. He rolled his eyes as it groaned and the villager guards faced him with eyes filled with surprise.

"Where's my hammer?" He spat hay out of his mouth and started again, "Where's my armor?"

One of the villagers took off at a dead sprint.

The other one rushed up to him with a pitchfork and got dangerously close. It was a farmer, slack-jawed and slow-eyed, with some meat on his shoulders. He said, "Get back in that stable and tie yourself up again. You're going to stir up trouble."

Brenwar cocked an eyebrow at him. "Is that so, human? What are you going to do, poke me with that fork? Is that how you rump kissers feed those giants you're in league with?"

"We don't have a choice."

"Sure you do, you corn-shucking coward. It's called fighting, yellow belly."

"We can't even hurt them," the farmer said. He poked the pitchfork at Brenwar. "Now get back in there and be silent, before he gets here!"

When the pitchfork jabbed at him, Brenwar snatched it away. He broke it in half with his bare hands.

Snap!

"Now tell me where my gear is."

The villager swallowed. "The giant has it."

"There's just one giant?"

The man nodded his head.

Brenwar rubbed his beard. Sure, he could fight the giant, but they were tough to kill. He'd need the magic in his hammer or something bigger. He scanned the barn for a weapon of some sort. There was a horseshoeing station nearby with a large anvil in it. Brenwar marched over to the anvil.

The farmer eased in behind him. "What are you thinking? I can't help you pick that up."

"Did I ask fer your help?"

"No."

"Then shaddup. All I need you to do is lure the giant in here. Got it?"

The look on the farmer's face didn't give him any confidence. Shaking his head, Brenwar wrapped his arms around the anvil and lifted it off the pedestal. Then, in one quick cling and jerk motion he hefted it onto his shoulder.

The farmer marveled.

Brushing by the dumbfounded man, Brenwar made his way over to the ladder that led up into the loft. With his free hand he tugged on it and grunted. Rung by rung, he climbed the ladder like a bearded ape. Forehead bursting with sweat, he walked over the groaning planks.

Once he was in position, Brenwar glanced down at the farmer. "Did you build this barn?"

"No."

"No surprise there."

The barn tremored. Heavy footsteps approached from outside.

The lazy farmer started to shake.

"Just stand where you are and wait," Brenwar ordered him.

The man was frozen.

Through the barn's large doors appeared the figure of a giant. A full head taller than the opening, it stooped its head and stepped beneath the doorway. The giant was bald aside from a long ponytail that rested over its expansive back.

Mortuun was tucked between its bearskin loincloth and waist.

The giant eyed the villager with fearsome eyes.

The man glanced up and started pointing at the loft, screaming, "He's up there! The dwarf's up there!"

The giant's head snapped up.

"Hello, stupid!" Brenwar roared. Anvil hoisted over his head, he hurled the hunk of steel with wroth force. The huge missile smote the giant right between the eyes.

It stumbled around a few paces and fell flat on its back.

Boom!

Brenwar hopped down from the loft and landed on the dead giant's chest. After he retrieved Mortuun, he walked down the giant's chest and hopped off beside its head.

The farmer gawked. "What do we tell them when they come back and see his body?"

"Tell them Brenwar is coming—and Mortuun is coming with him."

CHAPTER

26

"**S**O I GUESS YOU WON'T be unshackling me." Nath rattled his chains. "Well, it's not so bad. At least it's moorite, so it doesn't chafe my scales. Well, what exactly is this torment going to consist of? As you can see, I've had a pretty rough day already."

Eckubahn's fingers dug into the wooden arms of his throne. He leaned forward. "I should devour you right now."

"No need to be hasty. I saw goats aplenty on my way in here." Nath searched for the titan's eyes.

His face could still be seen behind the flame-like aura that guarded it. The mystic flames flickered between deep-purple and bright-orange colors. Perhaps they revealed the mood the titan was in.

Still, Nath could make out enough to see that it was an earth giant by its big facial features. A flat, broad nose and long earlobes. It was just like the ones Nath had fought as a dragon months ago. The giant was still in there but was now possessed by the spirit of a titan. Nath didn't have a very good understanding of them still.

Aw, I wish Bayzog were here. Well, what he didn't tell me I guess I'll just have to find out for myself.

"I notice one of those thrones is empty. Did your wife leave you? Oh wait, I bet she caught on fire when she tried to kiss you."

Eckubahn slapped his hand down on the arm of his chair. "Silence!"

Nath held his tongue.

Fine, I'll let him do all the work, then. Keep talking, giant mouth.

The titan continued. "Torment is tearing someone apart a small piece at a time. That is what I am going to do to you. That is what I am going to do to your father. Just imagine the shock that will fill his eyes when a piece of you is delivered each week. Or each month. Perhaps once a year. So far as I am concerned, it might take forever. I'll start with something small at first. One of your precious scales. Maybe a fingernail. A lock of your hair."

"I think Lotuus has dibs on the great mane," Nath said, winking at her.

"Quiet, you fool!" Eckubahn said. His flames turned a deep red. "This is no place for your boasts or your jests. This is the place of your inevitable death."

Nath's shoulders sank. It was clear that the titan meant business. He could feel the deep hatred from where he stood. The titan's passion for destruction seeped into his bones. Eckubahn and his followers would execute their diabolical goals and would destroy anything that stood in their way. And Nath would be his pawn.

He wants to use me to draw my father out.

Tapping his fingertips together, Eckubahn said, "It is going to be a delicious time. Unlike the last time, this time we have the numbers, and Balzurth will come out and fight his final battle. But it won't matter. He won't stand a chance." He waved his hand.

The stone giant who had taken Nath into custody was coming down the hallway. It walked past Nath and took a knee in front of Eckubahn. Though little shorter than the titan, the stone giant seemed much smaller by comparison. It reached into its vest and handed over Fang.

The titan took the blade by the scabbard, studied it, put his fingers on the tiny pommel, and pulled out the sword. His fingertips sizzled and smoked. He eyed the glimmering blade, slid it back into the scabbard, and handed it over to the stone giant. "Interesting work. Take it to the Chamber of Contest. Let's see if I have a champion who can destroy it."

The stone giant slid the grand sword back into his belt and started to walk away.

On impulse, Nath stretched his hands and rushed toward the giant's feet. The chains snapped back his neck and held him fast. He squeezed his eyes shut and thought on instinct.

Fang! Come to me! Come!

The stone giant's hand fell to the sword on his belt and stopped. Glowering at Nath, he kicked him in the gut. After knocking Nath flat to the ground, the giant strode off.

Nath pushed himself up into a sitting position and clutched his gut. He started into a fit of coughing. Gathering his thoughts, he watched the giant's great form diminish down the hall. Subtly, he stretched his tingling fingers out again. He could feel Fang's presence.

The giant vanished from sight, and the sensation was lost.

Rubbing his fingers together, Nath pondered what had just happened.

Was that Fang I felt?

"Do not hope, Nath Dragon," Eckubahn stated. "There is no hope for you here."

Turning to face his captors, Nath said, "Yeah, I've had that feeling for some time now. So, what is next? What is to become of me now?" He patted his belly. "I'm a bit hungry."

"Interesting that you should mention it. The wurmers are hungry as well."

"I think you've made it clear you aren't going to dispatch of me anytime soon. So what are the wurmers to me?"

"Oh, I was not planning on letting them feast on you. Rather, I was planning on having you as my guest at their dinner. I think you will find it quite salivating."

Lotuus giggled.

Nath felt his scales start to crawl. Whatever they were implying, he had a gut feeling that he didn't want to see it.

Eckubahn motioned again.

Another figure emerged from the shadows behind the urns. It was the biggest lizard man he'd ever seen. It stood almost twice as tall as Nath.

The bigger they are, the more I hate them. What is going on in this place? Why is everyone so humongous but me!

The lizard man unhooked Nath from the rings on the floor and held the chain attached to his collar like a leash. With a powerful tug, he jerked Nath off his feet and onto the ground and started dragging Nath down the hall.

Nath, ever deft, fought to get back on his feet until he was finally walking again. He glanced over his shoulder.

Eckubahn still sat, but Lotuus was on the move. She floated after him with a ruthless smile on her lips.

How can someone so beautiful be so ugly within?

"I guess I'll be having the displeasure of your company?"

"You'll be having displeasure for certain," she said. "And this is only the beginning of your suffering."

"For the life of me I cannot grasp why people like you are so intent on harming people like me. And I've known plenty of fairies to be contrary. This spite that you share is a shame to your kind."

"You dragons are so arrogant. You think you are so much better than everyone. A little humility would suit you quite well."

"Do me a favor, Lotuus, please. Give me an example of a dragon wronging you."

Her pleasant features hardened with concentration.

"Funny, I didn't hear you say anything," Nath said. "Could you speak a little louder?"

I knew she didn't have anything. They never do!

Lotuus then blurted out, "You think you are so perfect!"

"I don't think I'm perfect. I mean, sure"—he flicked his mangled mane—"I look perfect on the outside, but I have flaws on the inside. I just keep them to myself. Unlike your kind, that lets all the ugly out."

"I embrace my passions. Why shouldn't I?"

"Because they are misdirected and harmful," he replied.

"Says your kind." She sneered at him. "My kind says, 'I'll do whatever I want, whenever I want, *to* whomever I want. If it is my heart's desire, so be it.'"

"You're a bitter little thing with a wicked little heart."

"Says you. Who cares?"

Nath sealed his lips shut as the giant-sized lizard man led them back into the streets. It was clear that arguing with Lotuus wouldn't get him anywhere. She was no doubt a petty and stiff-necked thing. It reminded him of how Selene used to be. He decided to change the subject. Watching the influx of over-sized people in his life, he asked, "Lotuus, honestly, where are all these giants coming from?"

She showed a smiling sliver of teeth. "Oh, you are a wonder, aren't you Nath Dragon? Noticed that all by yourself, did you? Well, I'll let you in on a little secret that just might ruin your trousers. Not only do the wurmers populate fast, but the giants are populating fast as well."

"You're joking."

"No, not at all."

Loud chanting came from inside a humongous archway where the lizard man stopped and tugged on Nath's neck chain. It led him to an indoor arena. The seats went downward and were carved from hard stone.

Nath's head sagged. He could smell it. The greasy skin and sweat build-up and foul moisture in the room.

Oh, surprise, another arena.

CHAPTER
27

THOUSANDS OF PEOPLE FILLED THE seats, with a minority of giants scattered all about. They all pounded on their chairs, chanted, and smacked their hands together.

Blood was in the air.

They wanted it.

Nath and company took a seat in a balcony that jutted out ten rows higher than the caged arena below. Nath got his first glimpse at the dragon inside. It was a red rock dragon, a big one too. It was bigger than a horse. He used to see them from time to time swimming in the streams of lava near Dragon Home's sulfurous springs. They were wingless and deep red with hard fireproof scales that covered their entire bodies.

"Good luck eating him," Nath said.

Lotuus scoffed. "It will be interesting."

Though the red rock dragon was a big one, it seemed small in this strange city of Urslay, where everything was bigger than it was supposed to be. The arena itself was a massive cage of steel big enough to hold many giants.

It was a setup that Nath had seen over and over during his years of rescuing the dragons. For reasons Nath could never comprehend, people had a zeal for tormenting dragons.

"Ah, I see the champions are arriving." Lotuus grabbed his chin and turned it. "Look."

A parade of four warriors rode down a runway toward the cage. They were heavily armored people—orc, gnoll, bugbear, and ogre—stuffed inside plate armor. They carried spears and halberds that gleamed with a mystic silvery energy. They rode on the backs of four wingless wurmers.

Nath's jaws clenched. His brow furrowed.

"What's the matter, Nath?" Lotuus said to him. "You seem a tad worried."

The warriors entered the cage, and the door was slammed shut behind them. An incredible roar burst forth from the crowd. Inside the cage, the fighters spaced themselves evenly around the red rock dragon and dismounted. The odds seemed to suddenly change from four against one to eight against one.

The red rock balled up into a heap of scale and muscle that resembled his name.

The warriors turned toward the crowd and raised their long weapons up in salute. The throng went wild. They stomped their feet and shouted like madmen.

Nath's frown deepened. Just when he thought he'd managed to lead his kind to safety by defeating Gorn Grattack, in no time another enemy had taken Gorn's place. It was one that seemed far deadlier than the first. Subtly, he tried to break his chains. The links had no give in them.

Still standing, Lotuus leaned on his shoulder. "Oh, you want to go and help your little dragon, don't you? Well, that is too bad. Instead, you must watch. But I'm sure you will get your chance."

"I never should have freed you," Nath said.

"I couldn't agree more." She stroked his cheek. "But I'm so happy you did."

A horn sounded that drowned out all of the shouting in the room. The crowd fell silent. Inside the cage the warriors turned, faced the dragon, and lowered their weapons.

The horn sounded again. The warriors charged. The excited audience jumped back to their feet and urged them on.

The deep-red ball of dragon mass burst into motion. Tail lashing out, it spun in a full circle. The warriors, weighted down in heavy armor, couldn't move out of the way in time. Each and every one fell and crashed in a pile of metal.

"Hah!" Nath cheered.

The wurmers, quicker than the men, pounced. Teeth and claws latched onto the red rock's body, covering it entirely. A burst of flame billowed out from under the pile, catching two of the four wurmers on fire. Rearing its thick neck, the red rock shook the other two off its back. Without hesitation, it plowed into a wurmer, pinned it down, and shot lava-like flames all over it.

The monster screamed and sizzled.

Back on its feet, a gnoll wielding a glowing halberd struck the red rock on the back of his scales.

The dragon let out a roar, spun, and slapped the gnoll with his tail from one side of the cage to the other.

Nath pumped his fist. "Ah-hah!"

The battle raged inside. The red rock was quicker and stronger. His speed belied his husky girth. He toppled the warriors. Pounded the wurmers.

The brood of insect-like dragons spat balls of bright fire at the dragon.

The red rock shrugged it off and spat scorching flames back.

The wurmers' hard scales crackled.

The dragon crushed their flesh.

The battle that had started with eight was down to three.

"Are you sure you want to side with the titans, Lotuus? To your folly, I fear that you underestimate the dragons."

Arms crossed over her chest, she said, "It's not over yet."

The ogre chucked a spear deep into the red rock's side.

The dragon let out a blast of fire, turning the ogre into burning flesh and melting metal. Spear buried in his side, he attacked the two wurmers. His jaws clamped down on one's neck, shook the life out of it, and slung it away. The last one he rendered into pieces with his claws.

All eight of the enemy were dead, and the battered and bloodied red rock dragon resumed his spot and balled up in the middle of the circle. He closed his eyes, paying no mind to the silenced crowd.

Brimming, Nath said to Lotuus, "Never underestimate a dragon."

She replied with, "And never underestimate evil."

A stir rose in the crowd. The cage doors were split open, and down the runway at least twenty wingless wurmers surged from the tunnel.

The red rock's eyes snapped open. Quickly, he was back on his feet.

The horde of charging wurmers consumed him.

Nath's gaze froze on the horror. The feverish crowd's cheers shook his very core. They chanted praise as the wondrous hard-fighting dragon was torn apart and devoured in pieces.

He shook his chains.

Unable to contain his anger, Nath whirled on Lotuus. 'You are depraved!"

"I know." She nodded to the giant lizard man. "Take him to the dungeon and triple the guards. Oh, and one more thing." A pair of scissors appeared in her hand. She cut off a lock of Nath's long red hair.

Snip!

"An heirloom for Balzurth." She started floating away. "Once we've conquered Nalzambor, I'll see you at your execution. Until then, enjoy the misery that is coming. Bind him!"

CHAPTER
28

AVOIDING THE ROAD THAT LED into the Craggy Mountains, Brenwar opted to make the climb with his own hands and feet. As much as he wanted to storm right up the path into the unknown hills and battle every monster he faced, the wisdom within let prudence intervene. Now, he hung by his meaty but strong fingers off the rim of a narrow ledge. Puffing through his beard, he hauled himself up on the ridge, staring up into the dark sky that seemed to seep into the mountainside.

"One hundred feet up, and only three thousand more to go. Now that's living. Hah. And that only took a couple of hours."

Brenwar sat up, spat on his calloused hands, then took out a pick he'd borrowed from the village and started the climb to the next bench. Though climbing wasn't his favorite thing, he and his kind weren't half-bad mountaineers with the right equipment.

Inside the caves and tunnels they carved out there were plenty of hazards to face. In Nalzambor there were just as many jagged cliffs to face inside the world as out. Some fascinating marvels to behold, too. Waterfalls, underground streams, and lakes. A magnificent world hidden in the darkness.

He climbed, walked, slipped, and fell a few more hours and managed a couple hundred more feet.

"The things I do for a dragon," he muttered.

Of course, he'd do anything for Nath, and not just because Balzurth had charged him with it either, but because he was his friend. And the truth was, things were always exciting with Nath around, even though Brenwar often bickered at him. Nath was fun to bicker with. It bothered the dragon prince. Bickering among dwarves didn't matter at all. It was their way. Pushing. Suggesting. Perfecting.

The aging dwarf took a seat on a narrow tier and mopped the sweat from his brow. He uncapped his canteen and drank.

Some white night owls bigger than hounds flew through the night. Wings stretched out like great fans, they glided through the night sky with ease.

This would be one of the rare times Brenwar would consider riding a dragon.

But only because time is pressing and I need to find my friend.

Out of the corner of his eye he noticed a shadow swooping down the mountainside in pursuit of the owls. Still as the stone, he only moved his ancient eyes enough to make out the sleek dragon forms of the wurmers cutting through the air. Three in all, they gave the agile owls chase until all of the flying parties vanished in the night's chill air.

"Morgdon's Toes," he said under his breath.

He reached over his shoulder and patted Mortuun the Crusher, who was secured to his back.

"As if this climb wasn't bad enough. This is why dwarves go *through* mountains, not up and around them. That's what the other knuckleheaded races do."

Frost covering his armor, Brenwar resumed his climb. His cold breath and iron will were his only company. He fought his way up the least likely path a dwarf would ever take, carefully keeping his ears pricked for any signs of wurmers that could be roosted in the rocks.

The night turned to day, and the day back to night as he clawed his way to the top.

It wasn't a straight climb either, but one where he might have to traverse a narrow ledge horizontally for a mile before he could find another way going back up again. The footing was slick, the effort hard and strained.

He ignored the gnawing in his gut. Finally, almost three days later he found himself on the top. He wanted to scream but held his tongue.

Bushed, he took a knee. The top of the mountain revealed little about the location that he wanted to find. At best, he was miles away from where the giant road led up into the mountains. With the cold wind biting at his frozen face, he closed his eyes and listened. There wasn't much to be heard aside from the wind howling through the icy mountains. No life stirred.

His nostrils widened. "Ah."

Something akin to nature drifted into his nose. Somewhere, meat cooked. There was no hiding that from a dwarf hungry enough to eat a boar. He untethered one of the strings on his pouches and pinched out a strip of jerky and chewed on it.

"Hmmm," he grunted. "Where there's meat there's ale."

He knocked the frost from his eyebrows and beard and unhitched Mortuun from his back. He was topside now. If there was life about, it lurked in the direction he was headed. Toward the warmth. Toward the food. Following the scent, he marched through boot-deep snow, between treacherous crevasses and ravines. There were some modest climbs too, and the pace was slow, but at the dawn of the next day he saw firelight in a distant tower.

"I'll be."

Through the bitter snow he spied a ring of tall stone towers spread out with at least a mile between them. It was clear that wasn't all of them either.

"Why in the world would there be towers all the way up here? No one can see them."

Brenwar made a climb to a higher elevation to get a better look above the towers. It took a few hours, but when he made it, his eyes filled with wonder. The towers overlooked a canyon, and inside that canyon was a city with giant-sized activity.

"By my beard."

He squeezed Mortuun's handle.

"There be too many giants in there."

He cocked his head. His eyes narrowed. Soft footsteps crunched down the snow behind him. He turned his shoulder and started to swing.

"No one sneaks up on a dwarf!"

Something knocked his feet out from under him.

As he rose up on his elbows, Brenwar's eyes widened. "You!"

CHAPTER 29

HEAD DOWN BETWEEN HIS LEGS, Nath sat with his eyes shut and tummy rumbling. He was a dragon, and dragons were patient, but at the moment, days into it, he was unsettled. Not that anyone would be comfortable in prison, but he wasn't used to misery being his only company. He was alone. Entirely. Forgotten. The giant lizard man had thrown him behind the metal bars and left him there. He hadn't seen anyone since.

He lifted his chin up and studied the same grey walls he'd been looking at for days. They were moldy. Ancient. Water and filth from the streets above dripped through the cracks.

He wondered what this strange city of Urslay really was. If anything, it was a city built on top of another city. And maybe this subterranean part of the city was built on another city. That was entirely believable. After all, the lost City of Borgash was mostly buried in the bowels of the earth, and in all of Nalzambor's thousands of years, empires of men, orcs, and dwarves must have fallen from time to time. Nath had found evidence of that everywhere.

His belly groaned so loud it echoed in the chamber. He laughed.

With my luck I'll go into a cocoon again. There's no telling what I'll be when I wake up next. Ah, those were the days. Sleep, wake up, get more scales. Sleep, wake up, get more scales.

He rubbed his eyes and yawned, though he wasn't really tired. There had been quite a few times, when Nath was younger, that he'd been in jail. He'd never really worried about it too much before. But now things were different. The world had ended up much bigger than he thought it was. And the giants, he'd never thought of dealing with more than a few of them at a time, but now it was clear there were hundreds, maybe thousands—and they were united against the dragons.

"Humph."

Keeping his ears open, he got up and put his hands on the steel bars. They were thick. Not moorite, but thick. A solid inch of spring steel.

"Hello?"

His voice echoed down the great hall that ran between his cell and all the rest. There weren't any replies. Not a shuffle. Not even a rat. At first, he had figured there would at least be some tormenters that would pester him. That maybe they'd put him on the rack and stretch his limbs as long as the giants'. But no. Nothing.

He gazed up and down the row again. Perhaps there was some other type of guard lurking in the cells. A monster or phantom of some sort. It seemed very strange that no one was there to keep an eye on him at all. The giants were often stupid and cocky. But careless? No.

Nath lowered his shoulder and rammed it into the cell door.

Wham!

A solid rock wall would have been softer.

So what if they hear me? I could use some company.

He hit it again, and again and again.

Wham! Wham! Wham!

Huffing for breath and shoulder aching, he pressed his face to the bars. "Come on now, somebody somewhere has to be listening. Someone? I'll even take an orc if you have one."

The silence was almost as annoying as his stomach aching. He was hungry. Very hungry. And it seemed to sap his strength and will.

Oh, don't start flailing like a fitful child, Nath Dragon. You're a prince. Stick with the plan. Bad as it must be, it's still a plan.

It was clear that his captors wanted to wear him down, and if that was the case, then so be it. He wanted to wear them down. Feign being weak and defeated. When he saw an opening, he would strike. The trick was getting out of his moorite chains. He was strong, but perhaps not that strong.

That led him to another plan. This city, Urslay, if it was built upon another city, perhaps there was another way out. Another place to hide and escape. There always was.

But after escaping, most important was the retrieval of Fang. Like any friend, he wouldn't want to abandon his blade. He could feel its presence. And he'd felt something else for a while now. A bond that was growing between them. Fang had a lot of power that Nath didn't yet understand. Perhaps he had taken it all for granted.

Instead of making the most of what I have, I've been making the most of what I've lost. That's no way to be a leader.

If anything, Nath's isolation had some benefits. It gave him time to think about how he dealt with things and how he could handle them better. He had so many advantages over others! But oft times he didn't plan, just winged it. His talents and skill prevailed in times of need. But now, with the stakes so high, he needed to be less reckless and more careful. A patient planner. One who paid attention to the details.

Certainly I have it in me to be wise?

As he tapped his fingernails on the bars, his mind picked away at what Eckubahn and Lotuus had said. Fang had been taken to the Chamber of Contest. There, the giants would try to destroy Fang. And Lotuus had hinted that Nath would battle inside that arena. It would be there, if anywhere, that he would make his escape.

No doubt they wanted to wear him down as much as they could before they turned him loose in the cage. And the goal wasn't to kill him. They'd made that clear. Or was it? Lotuus and Eckubahn were both liars. One could never trust a word that evil said.

Mind games. It's all mind games.

CHAPTER
30

"ARE YOU LOST, DWARF?" SELENE stared down at Nath's pet dwarf. At first she had thought he was drunk, the way he stumbled around in the snow so far away from everything. But no. The little bearded ape was just spying on the giant city. Like she was. Interesting.

Brenwar kicked at her tail. "Just when I thought it couldn't get any colder, you show up." He got up. "So, what brings you here?"

"Wurmers. You?"

"Nath."

Oh no! Does he know where Nath is?

Keeping her worry off her face, Selene just lifted her brows in what she meant to look like curiosity. "So, he's lost and so are you, it seems."

"No one is lost." He eyed her as he dusted the snow from his armor. "Let's hope anyway."

"What is that supposed to mean?"

"Nothing," he said.

"You don't trust me, do you Dwarf?"

"I didn't say that. But I will say this, I don't like you much."

"Perfect, I don't like you either."

"Good."

It was an awkward moment. Selene actually was happy to see Brenwar, but sad that Nath wasn't with him. "Tell me what happened."

Begrudgingly, Brenwar spilled out a disturbing story about giants tricking Nath in the nearby village cluster at the site of the old city of Harvand.

In this case, Selene agreed with Brenwar. She would have left the fate of the people in those villages to the giants in exchange for keeping Nath.

Why he fought so hard for people that were far inferior she didn't quite understand. "I see."

"So glad your eyes are open and that you can see, Selene." The annoying little dwarf glanced over his shoulder. "So, you've tracked the wurmers here?"

She relayed what she had encountered in the fishing villages. "Seems there is quite a nest here. So, should I wait here while you go in and rescue Nath?"

"You know, you're as funny as you look. But I'm doing just fine without you. Still, if you want to come along, I won't stop you."

"Oh, thank you for your generosity. A smallish escort is just what I need."

"Smallish?"

She gave him her best condescending smile.

Obviously choosing not to notice, Brenwar took the lead, making a wide trail through the snow, until they were less than a mile away from the first tower. "We need to be wary. There's no telling what kind of eyes are in those towers."

"Those are dragon towers," she said.

"How do you know that?"

"I know. This is Urslay, place of the giants, though it was fairly dormant during the time of Gorn Grattack. We sought their aid in the Great Dragon War, but they weren't interested. Giants aren't a race that wants to be unified with dragons ever. Those towers go back to the last battle the dragons fought against the titans and the giants. I know that much. They are there to watch the skies, not the ground. I don't think they'll be looking for us."

"Don't you think you should have mentioned this place before, back in Quintuklen?"

Uh, I didn't know it was active back then, stupid.

"No."

The little dwarf huffed, turned his eyes forward, and plowed through the snow.

Good, we've found a use for you: snowplow!

In the night, they could see silhouettes against the fires burning at the tops of the towers. Two people were within each hundred-foot-high tower, manning the ballistas that were mounted up there. To shoot at flying dragons.

Brenwar led them midway between the closest tower and the next tower. The wind blew his beard straight up in a very undignified way when he turned to speak to her. "Since you aren't very forthcoming, tell me, have you been inside Urslay before?"

Selene bit the insides of her cheeks so she wouldn't laugh at the funny picture he made.

No sense getting him all riled up. That will waste time that Nath may not have.

"Yes."

But the pesky little dwarf got all riled up anyway, running ahead of her as if he could leave her behind. He was such a child.

"You long-tailed giant-loving witch!"

"Oh, don't be so dramatic. I didn't have much of a choice then," she said, catching up to Brenwar, who was only a few steps from the canyon's edge. "And I only had a glimpse. Show some mirth. Who would have thought it would be something that could serve our cause now?"

Brenwar hurried, apparently thinking she couldn't pass him, came to a stop at the rocky edge, and leaned his head down. "That's quite the canyon."

Selene found her place by his side. "Yes, a very unique city."

The canyon was hundreds of feet deep and went on for miles. There was firelight coming from the small and large stone carved alcoves that made up the strange city. Tiny figures shuffled over the roads, and livestock in mass quantities were herded into pens.

Selene could smell everything. Hay, orcs, humans, halflings, cooked meat, coal, and wood smoke.

The last time she was there, it had only been giants, and not so many. For the most part, it had been abandoned, but now it was quite different. There were hundreds, maybe a thousand people, and they thrived. Their voices lifted up over the rocks with wild songs of praise.

"What are those people so happy for?" Brenwar asked.

"The titans have a uniting effect on weaker people." She started down the side. "Stay here. I'll take a look."

Brenwar seized her arm. "You'll do no such thing. I'm not going to sit here like a yeti while you go and reminisce with old friends."

She jerked out of his grip. "So you're coming, then."

"No."

"Then what do you propose we do, sit here and wait for Nath to greet us?" She searched Brenwar's hard eyes. "Brenwar, you will need to trust me."

His eyes pierced hers. "I don't."

She had tried to be nice. She had even called him by his name. Aggravated, she fired back, "And what was your plan? Did you think a dwarf could infiltrate the giants? They would sniff you out as soon as you set foot in there."

"I'm not worried about putting my life in peril."

"I'm not either, but you can't just go waltzing down there with me. It would be stupid."

"Are you calling me stupid?" he growled.

She shook her head. "No. I think you are well aware of your limitations already."

"I'm going to cut your tail off!"

"Try, and I'll strangle you with your own beard!"

Red-faced, Brenwar replied, "Leave my beard out of this." He drew Mortuun back. "Go ahead, say it one more time!"

"Will you keep your annoying voice down? The guards are distant, not deaf!" Finally, she sighed, leaned over, and kissed him on the forehead.

Brenwar shuffled in the snow, his temper cooled. "What was that for?"

She shrugged. "I just realized I'd do anything to shut you up."

"Ho ho ho!" Brenwar rumbled. "I don't like you, but I like your spite." He lifted his brows, reached into one of his pouches, and pulled out a colorful potion vial. "I have an idea that should satisfy us both."

CHAPTER
31

HOURS WERE USUALLY LIKE MINUTES to a dragon, except now. No, now the minutes felt like long, agonizing hours as Nath's insides gnawed at his outsides. He was hungry. He was angry. Typically, a dragon would sleep through a wait like this, hibernate like a bear. Instead, Nath paced and fought to keep his weary eyes open. Something had to give.

He yelled through the bars.

"Hello? Hello!"

His loud voice echoed down the hall.

Nothing replied.

He banged his fists on the bars and screamed at the top of his lungs.

"HELLO, I SAY!"

He followed it up with a roar so loud it rattled all the locks in the dungeon.

"RAWWWWRRRRrrrrrr!"

He shuffled backward and touched his throat.

Was that me?

He let out another cage-shaking roar.

"RrrrrrrAAAWWWWWRRRrrrrrrrr!"

Huh! It was *me! Seems I still have some dragon pipes in me.*

Suddenly he belched. "Urp."

A puff of grey smoke rolled out of his mouth. There was a charred taste on his tongue. His golden eyes lit up.

He blew smoke from his nostrils.

Can it be?

Stomach growling, he eyed the bars that caged him in. He rubbed his chin.

Hmmm, if I can summon my flame, then I can melt these bars. Hah! Wouldn't that be something?

He focused and concentrated on his fires within.

Come on, Dragon. You can do it.

His stomach burned like fire and surged up his throat. A blast of hot, smoky air spilled from his mouth. The plume of hot smoke filled his dungeon cell and the hall. Within seconds, the air was thicker than dwarven stew and he couldn't even see himself. He fanned away the vapors, coughing a few times.

"Well *that* was pointless!"

He coughed some more and screamed. His muscles ached, and weakness assailed him. Whatever he had done had sucked the life out of him. He sagged down onto his knees and stretched out on the floor. His heavy eyelids felt like they were filled with sand.

Maybe I should try and take a nap until the smoke clears. What a useless trick for a dragon. Who needs a dragon that blows smoke instead of fire? Such a joke.

Nath was drifting into slumber when the scuffle of soft feet caught his ear. He lifted his weary head, cocked his ear.

I must be dreaming that I have a visitor coming.

He lowered his head again and shut his eyes. Again, the scuffle came. Footsteps were making their way down the dungeon hallway. He sat up and peered through the dissipating smoke.

A man appeared in the smoke just outside the bars. The build of the man was very strange, thick, but with gingerly moves.

Am I dreaming?

"Where did all this smoke come from?" the man said in an irritated but friendly tone.

The sound of the man was very odd to Nath's ears, not rough and husky like most of the over-sized people.

"And what was that racket I heard? It sounded like a dog choking."

Nath made his way to his feet, rubbed his gold eyes, and sauntered over to the bars. There, he got a better look at the man, who was broad and round faced. Nath blinked his eyes and said to the unique man, "Are you a *halfling*?"

"What?" the man said really loud. He pushed his frosty locks from his eyes, fanned more of the smoke away, and stared at Nath. "Yer that dragon fella they talk about above, ain't you?"

"Are you a halfling?" Nath repeated with astonishment.

"You say that like you've never seen a halfling before." The giant halfling wore navy-blue trousers with a maroon shirt. He stuffed his long and slender fingers into a big pocket in the middle of his overall and withdrew a pouch. He loosened the strings and removed a pinch of snuff and snorted it. His eyes brightened. "Woo Wee! Now that is dandy!"

Gently shaking his head, Nath said, "Who are you?"

"What?"

Nath spoke louder. "I said, who are you?"

"You heard a moo?"

"No!"

The old halfling reached behind his back and brought forth a brass horn with a bend in the smaller portion of its neck. He held it to his ear and tilted it toward Nath. "Speak into my good ear."

"What is your name?" Nath asked.

"Pepper." His forehead crinkled, and his button nose sniffed. "Where'd all this smoke come from?"

Nath didn't want to lie, even though his first urge was to say, 'I don't know.' Instead, he changed the subject. If there was one thing he knew about people, especially halflings, they liked to talk about themselves. "How'd you get so big?"

"Speak up, flame mane."

Nath huffed and spoke directly into the earpiece. "Why are you so big?"

"Well, you don't have to yell! My name's Pepper."

"You told me that already. Sheesh. Pepper, why are you so big?"

"Oh, I see," Pepper said. "You want to know why I am so big. We are all big in my family. Well, most of us mostly." With soft eyes he stared down at Nath. "I just remembered. I can read lips. Go ahead and speak at your common loudness." He lowered his ear horn.

"Pepper, halflings are half as big as men. Why are you and so many others in this city so big?"

Rubbing his chin, Pepper studied Nath's lips and replied, "No, you can't marry my daughter."

"I didn't ask to marry your daughter!"

"Oh, so you are asking me—wait a minute, you're that dragon fella everyone is making a fuss about, aren't you?"

Unable to restrain himself, Nath slapped his forehead. He was dealing with an eight-foot-tall elderly halfling who was nearly deaf and enfeebled. Nath's claws dug into his long locks of hair and pulled on it.

Pepper cocked his head sideways. "What are you doing? Does your flame hair burn? Must you pull it out, eh? Oh, you want to put it out. Yes. Put the fire out. I'll fetch some water."

"No!" Nath said, trying to snatch Pepper through the bars.

Pepper scurried down the hall, weaving right, then left, then right again and out of sight.

Nath banged his head on the bars.

By the time he gets where he's going, he'll forget I'm here!

CHAPTER
32

"WILL YOU PUT THAT AWAY, Dwarf? What is it, anyway?"

"Don't you worry about that," Brenwar said as he put the potion to his lips.

Selene snatched it away and resealed it. "You're being hasty. I thought your kind were better planners than that. I think it will help if you at least tell me what this is going to do."

"Gimme my potion!" Brenwar leapt up for it.

Selene, much taller, dangled it over his head.

Ha ha! Dwarves are horrible jumpers.

"I'll bring you down to my level if I have to!"

"Potions don't last so long. We might be in there for days. Maybe longer." She shook the liquid in the vial. It swirled with a twinkle. "What are you hoping to accomplish?"

"It's a changer. I've taken it before. I'll blend in down there."

Fat chance, the way you stink! Ugh!

"Oh, and what were you going to change into?"

"Human, I suppose. And how exactly were you going to blend in with that tail and those scales?"

"I can control that." She held out her arms and concentrated, turning her scales to skin and making her tail vanish under her robes. "See?"

"And how long can you keep that up?"

"Long enough. Listen, you need to trust me, and I need to go it alone."

But the little dwarf just glowered at her. "No."

Such a little child! Even if I do leave without him, he'll just follow me on his own later. And get caught. And Nath won't leave here without him...

She dropped the potion.

Brenwar snatched it in his skeleton hand.

"Have it your way," she said, "but I'll be curious to see if it conceals that."

"Don't you worry about that. I have plenty of tricks up my sleeve."

She lifted a brow. "Really, so you have more magic at your disposal? That's odd for a dwarf."

"Well, I'm no lover of magic, but on occasion it's served me well."

"Oh, you like it, do you? How exhilarating."

He does like magic! He's trying to conceal it, but there's a glimmer in his eye! Ha! He needs magic to keep up.

She filed that information away for future use.

As Brenwar put the vial to his lips, she held up her hand to halt him.

He started to draw back his fist, but she rushed to explain.

"Why don't you hold off until we hit bottom and enter the city? We'll need every second of time that potion can last. I'm certain."

"Agreed."

CHAPTER
33

Sitting in the back of the cell, Nath watched a steady drip of murky water splatter on the floor. He'd counted five hundred and sixty two drops. Each just as annoying as the last. He focused on that water.

Splat. Splat. Splat. Splat.

Water. That was what Pepper had said he was going after hours ago. There hadn't been any sign of life in the dungeons since he left. There was only the drip of water. It wasn't just in Nath's cell either. It was all over the place. A steady, unrelenting, tormenting harmony.

Everything in his life was out of order. Everything he knew had been twisted upside down. Giant-sized orcs, lizard men, and halflings.

"Ugh, how can this be?"

Nath wanted to sleep. To wake up in a better time and place. Even Dragon Home perhaps.

The mountain home of the dragons wasn't really that bad. He just didn't fit in. The dragons didn't like him. That was supposed to have changed, which, to some degree it had, but other than Selene, he still hadn't really bonded with any of the dragons. He rubbed his nose and yawned.

Why is that?

He studied his scaly hands and long fingernails. Not so long ago he could have torn this entire dungeon apart. Not that he'd ever have been caught to begin with. In dragon form, he would have ripped those stone giants to pieces.

I have to have more power than just these clawed hands.

His stomach growled.

If only being hungry was a power! I could destroy anything!

He clutched his head.

Come on, Nath. Get it together and think. I have to have more powers. I have magic, because Selene has magic. I need to explore it. Let's see.

Twirling his finger in his hair, Nath made a mental list of things he could do.

I can grow gorgeous hair. Hah! Oh, am I not the envy of all dragons. Let's see, what else? I can yell really loud. And I can blow smoke. Yes, blow smoke. Such a terror I can become. Beware of the terrifying smoke-blowing dragon. I can complain. Be hungry. Oh, I'm useless without Fang!

He snapped his fingers.

Maybe I can summon the blade.

He closed his eyes and envisioned the magnificent blade. His stomach moaned. He slammed his fists on the ground.

Oh, this is useless! I can't even concentrate!

He stood up and eyed the metal bars that caged him in.

I can bend those. I know I can. I just have to believe that I can.

Stomach rumbling, he walked over to the bars and wrapped his fingers around the hard steel.

Clatch.

Somewhere, a door opened. Nath pressed his face against the bars.

Coming down the hall from the direction opposite where Pepper left, something rolled on squeaky wheels. It was coming straight for Nath. The loud, annoying sound would have woken up anything that slept. Wheels rattled and clanked over the cobblestone floor.

Nath's nostrils widened. His mouth watered.

Food!

Pepper the giant halfling came into full view. He was pushing a cart filled with huge amounts of food. Roast turkey. Baked hams. Hot rolls and steaming potatoes.

"Chow time," the halfling said to Nath. "You are lucky. There are no other prisoners to be fed. You can eat all of this."

Nath stretched his hand out through the bars.

Pepper slapped it. "A moment, please. Eh, put this on." He handed Nath a checkered bib that was the size of a small blanket. "Now, scoot back. Scoot. Scoot."

Staring at the food and licking his lips, Nath did as he was told. In the back of his mind he felt maybe it was a trick.

I don't care. I'm so hungry I could eat a giant's leg!

With a rattle of keys, Pepper unlocked the door and swung it open.

Nath fought the urge to make a dash for it. He was so hungry though.

Just see how this plays out.

The halfling shoved the cart inside and blocked the entrance. "Hold on.

I have to bless the meal." He closed his eyes and spoke some pleasant words in Halfling and reopened them. He closed the door back into place with a loud clank. "Enjoy."

Casting all the etiquette he'd ever known aside, Nath dove in.

Chomp. Chomp. Chomp.

The meal was a far cry from elven cuisine. There wasn't much flavor, but it was sustenance. Greasy, claw-licking, stomach-filling food. He tore off a turkey leg and gnawed it down to the bone. Huge chunks of ham were stuffed in his gullet. The bread was hard as a log, but Nath didn't care. He tore it in half and devoured it.

"Eh, Flame Hair, wash that down with that jug down there. And don't choke on the bones. You eat like a giant."

Nath grabbed the clay pitcher and gave it a sniff.

Honey mead!

He guzzled it down, wiped his elbow across his mouth, and said, "Ah!"

There was enough food to feed a dozen hungry dwarves. He must have eaten half of it before he was finished. He let out a long, loud belch. "Buuuurp!"

Fanning his huge button nose, Pepper said, "Oh, my. You might not be a giant, but you act like one. Sheesh. And I thought I was going to sit down and have a nice dinner with somebody for a change. How rude."

Nath wiped his mouth and fingers on his bib, walked over to the bars, looked up at Pepper, and said, "Thank you."

Pepper cupped his ear. "What?"

"Thank you!"

"You are welcome. So, is your belly full?"

Nath patted his bulged-out stomach. "I think I have some room left, but I'm not going to push it."

"You aren't feeling sleepy, are you?"

"No, why?"

"Oh, I always like a nap after a big meal. It settles the tummy, and the dreams are pleasant as a trickling stream." Pepper reached into his big pocket and retrieved his snuff pouch. "This here is what you need. It'll open up those heavy lids of yours."

"You don't say? No, I think I'll pass." Nath glanced at the door. "So, what now? Are you fattening me up for the giants?"

The halfling took a deep snort of the tobacco and shook like a wet dog. "Woo! I like that! Er, you said something?"

"What now?" Nath yelled at him.

"Oh, I think I need to get that cart out of there." He unlocked the door, reached inside, and dragged the wooden cart out. He eyeballed the wide-open door. "Well, aren't you going to run for it?"

Nath sidestepped over to the right, preventing the door from closing. "Are you helping me escape?"

"Oh no, I'd never do that. Ho ho, never. I mean, those giants would put me on a spit and eat me alive. No, never, never say such a thing." He got behind the cart and started pushing it down the hall toward where he came from. He stopped and looked back at Nath. "Are you coming?"

Nath trotted up to the big halfling, who led the way down the halls. He glanced in every cell that he passed by. There were bones. Tusks. Bodies mummified and petrified in armor. Chains hung from walls with hands and wrists still in them. The bodies were piled-up bones. There were no signs of life in any of them.

I sure am glad I'm getting out of here.

The food cart came to a squeaky halt. Pepper stood in front of a twenty-foot-high door. The wood was ancient and grey and the iron hinges tarnished. He grabbed the handle designed for a man even taller than him and pulled it open. To Nath's surprise, the hinges were silent.

Pepper put a finger to his lips, turned toward Nath, and said, "Wait here." He slipped inside the crack in the door.

I'm not waiting.

Like a shadow, Nath fell in step behind Pepper.

The halfling turned, saw him, and jumped back. "I told you to wait!" He pointed at something behind him. "Ssssh!"

Nath froze. Three giants were in the room. Each was more than ten feet tall, and they all had swords on their belts. They sat at a huge table fit for them, but small by their standards. Food was piled as high as their chins. One was leaned back, head dropped over his shoulder, snoring. It was a three-eyed cyclops. The other two's heads were resting on their arms.

"They ate too much," Pepper said with a little grin. "Come on now."

Nath scanned the room. It was a crude office, dining room, storage room, and barn. It smelled like sweat and stale ale. There were barrels and a pen filled with livestock. A huge goat bleated. Some oversized chickens clucked. With his dragon eyes, Nath searched the walls and the tall slime-coated ceiling above him.

Pepper came back and nudged him. "What are you waiting for?"

Nath held up his moorite chains. "I can't be hindered by these."

"What?"

Nath raised his voice. "I can't—" He shook his head.

Pepper scratched his eyebrow. "You'll make too much noise in those. Hmmm, moorite. My, you must be important." His slender fingers searched the soft curly locks of his grey hair and plucked out a sliver of steel as thin as one hair. "Stand still."

Nath didn't move.

The halfling's hands were as big as Nath's own head, but the fingers moved with the ease of a fairy in flight. The lock on his collar popped off. Seconds later his arms and legs were free.

Nath cocked his head from side to side and smiled.

Pepper patted him on the shoulder. "Feel better now, I figure."

"You have no idea."

"So, do you feel like running?"

Nath shrugged. "Not really, why?"

Gazing over Nath's head at the table full of guards, Pepper said, "'Cause I don't think I put enough sleeping lard in that cyclops's muffins."

Nath twisted around. The cyclops, the brute sitting in the middle, was wide awake. Soft footfalls caught his ear. He turned back. Pepper was off and running.

CHAPTER 34

S ELENE AND BRENWAR HAD MANAGED a slow trek down the canyon into the city undetected. Now, they stood in a quadrant filled with huge cattle and other oversized livestock. The animals stirred little, and not many people were around that she could see.

"Seems you found a good spot to drop into." Her nose crinkled. "I imagine it's just like your home in Morgdon."

"Hah hah." Surrounded by goats and lambs, Brenwar scooped up a handful of the dirt and rubbed it over his clothes and armor.

"This is no time for a bath, Dwarf."

"I'm covering my scent." He slapped some mud under his armpits. "And you aren't exactly looking inconspicuous either."

"I hope you don't think I'm going to mimic you."

"It would do you some good."

They were hemmed in by sheer canyon walls hundreds of feet tall. Animals were everywhere, but the people scarce. Not too far away were some barns and storehouses. They were bigger than what one would see in Nalzambor, but not exactly fit for the giants. Just big.

Selene wasn't surprised by any of it. The giants often kept throngs of people as willing servants. Those people handled the chores. Tended the herds and gardens. But the men and women had to be careful. If the giants got too hungry, they would eat them.

"Follow me," she said, making a beeline for the outer fence.

Pushing through the livestock, Brenwar followed.

"I'll be right back."

"No—" Brenwar objected, but it was too late.

Selene hopped the fence and scurried to the nearest barn and slipped inside.

A pair of long-faced country boys stood there in heavy cloaks, warming their hands over a crude stove.

She approached on soft feet.

One of them turned and faced her. "Who are you?" His eyes were filled with wonder.

"I'm new, and I was hoping I could borrow some cloaks for my family." She hugged her shoulders and shivered. "I'm not used to this mountain air."

The man stripped off his cloak. "Here, you can have mine."

"No," the other man said, removing his cloak. "Please, take mine. Much warmer than his. It's oxen wool. The best."

The first man shoved the second. "Don't listen to this pig farmer. Please, take mine."

Selene offered an enticing smile. "Oh, you men are so kind. It's such good fortune I have run into you." She grabbed both of the warm woolen cloaks. "May I bring my family in to warm by your fire?"

The second man smoothed back his hair, licked his lips, and said, "Are you spoken for, milady?"

"No, I am a lone widow traveling with my uncomely child. He's most comfortable among the animals. It puts him at ease. That's why we've ventured so far from the main city."

The first man stepped in front of the second, and with a toothy smile he said, "You'll find just as much hospitality here as you will in there. What duties will you be assigned?"

"I'll be a seamstress for the giants."

Both men scratched their heads. Finally, one spoke up and offered, "Please, bring the child in, and don't be ashamed." The man was poorly featured and built. "The child will be welcome here. I've got a daughter a bit long in the tooth as well." He winked. "She gets it from her mother. Yep, can't say what it is, but the men in my family don't marry well."

The second man shoved him. "Say, you're talking about my sister!" He drew back a fist and punched the first man in the face.

Selene spun on a heel and started walking away. "I'll be back, and when I return I'll grant a kiss to the winner."

The raw-boned country men let loose on one another.

As soon as Selene cleared the barn, she heard a gruff voice speaking from the shadows. "Uncomely child, huh?"

She tossed one of the cloaks to Brenwar and put the other one on. "I'm sorry, was that too much of an understatement?"

He covered up in the cloak and covered his head. The hem and sleeves were way too long. He grunted. "Worst disguise ever."

"Come on." Selene led the way.

As they walked, Brenwar said, "This is a big place. How do you suppose we track Nath down?"

"There's a chance that I'll catch his scent. And we can always ask. Well, I'll ask, anyway. I don't think too many people will be interested in talking to you. So for the time being, just be my uncomely mute boy and pray the giants don't get a good whiff of you."

Now dressed to blend in, the odd couple ventured forward toward the heart of the city.

Aside from the influx of people, not much had changed in Urslay. The alcove stone homes made the place look like an inverted honeycomb. People of all races and sizes worked along the streets and traversed the roadways above.

Brenwar brushed against her when an ugly giant walked by and leered at them and passed, and then the stupid little dwarf bustled in front of her with his long sleeves flapping.

She caught him by the sleeve.

He jerked away.

"What are you doing?" she hissed.

"I'm trying not to explode," he said. "In case you didn't notice, there are giants everywhere."

"I count three," she said, gazing up.

The towering men, ten to thirty feet tall, pranced throughout the city like overlords. Some carried whips, others swords and lance-sized spears.

She noticed a few more posted on the alcove terraces above. "We'd better look busy. Grab that wheelbarrow."

"You grab it." Brenwar scurried over to a stack of grain sacks and hefted one up on his shoulder. He grabbed another by the neck and tossed one after another into the wheelbarrow. He eyed the cart. "Well, put those hands to work. Push."

With a huff, Selene grabbed the handles, and with her head down she followed Brenwar. Shuffling through the streets, she said, "Where exactly do you think you're leading us? I was of the impression you'd never been here before."

"Just because I haven't been here don't mean that I don't know where I'm going." He cocked his head. "Hear that?"

Somewhere in the distance was a very loud hammering of metal striking metal. The banging was quite unique.

She nodded her head. "Yes. Iron strikes iron. So what?"

"That ain't iron, lady. That's someone trying to destroy Fang."

CHAPTER
35

NATH TOOK OFF AT A sprint after Pepper.

Halflings are fast, but giant halflings are even faster.

No longer shackled, Nath ran like a horse down the hallway before finally catching up with Pepper, who had ducked out of sight in an archway. Nath skidded to a stop. His toes hung over the edge of a bottomless pit. "Sultans of Sulfur!"

Pepper caught his arm and pulled him back. "Don't fret. It's not so bad as it looks. They say it's a hole from one side of the world to the other."

Gaping with his back pressed against the wall beside the doorway, Nath stared into the black expanse. There was nothing except a lone light more than two dozen yards away. It looked like a tiny doorway.

"I think I'll take my chances with the giant." Nath turned and found himself face to face with the cyclops stabbing at him with a sword. He sidestepped the blade's edge. "Gah! That was close."

"Oh my," Pepper said, sliding up behind the much taller cyclops. He tapped him on the shoulder. "Get away from my prisoner, one-eye!"

The cyclops grunted and unloaded a hard chop at the halfling.

Pepper skipped away and stopped with his heels on the edge of the crevice.

The cyclops spoke. "Your fun and games are over, Pepper."

The halfling cupped his ear. "What?"

The cyclops lunged.

With the ease of a dancer, Pepper back spun around the blade's edge. He fastened his hand on the cyclops's thick wrist and, using its momentum, flung him forward over the edge.

Shocked, Nath listened to the cyclops's outraged and fading scream. He studied Pepper. "Aren't you going to get into a lot of trouble?"

"Nah. I never liked that one-eye much. A big complainer, he was." Pepper dusted off his hands. "Besides, I'll just blame it all on you. Prisoner escaped, and that ugly feller died trying to catch him. Now, where to?"

"You're asking me?"

Scratching his head, Pepper said, "I see your point. Uh, where did you want to go?"

"I want to get out of Urslay, but I need to find my sword first."

"Sword, you say? What's so special about a blade? There are plenty of those around here."

"No, not like this one. This one is a friend." He recalled what Eckubahn said. "They took it to the Chamber of Contest."

Pepper made a leery face. "Ooh, you don't want to go there."

"I insist, Pepper. And you know what, you aren't having too much trouble hearing me now."

"What?"

Nath waited.

The halfling shook his head no. "I'm not helping you. I serve the giants. Yes. Yes. Serve the giants." He teetered back into the hall. "Come on, the coast is clear now. I'll show you to the Chamber of Contest, but I warn you, there are much safer paths out of here."

Nath caught him by the elbow and fixed his eyes up on the halfling's. "Pepper, why are you helping me?"

The giant halfling tried to pull away, but Nath held him fast. Finally, with a huff, Pepper said, "Everyone who knows good is obligated to do it."

In his heart, Nath knew that Pepper was good and truthful. "You couldn't be more right."

"What?"

"Just get me out of here."

With a confused look, Pepper shook his head. "Let's get you out of here."

On ginger feet, the giant halfling led him back into the stone carved corridor designed for giants as big as thirty feet tall.

They ran for minutes, and Nath marveled with every stride. There weren't many things that made Nath marvel, but this did. The world he'd known so well had become bigger and deadlier than he ever imagined. He'd taken too many things for granted. He was used to really tall trees, but he wasn't used to so many men bigger than he. It bothered him. Giants were rare, but apparently not as rare as he thought. Perhaps, long, long ago, the giants had dominated the world of Nalzambor.

"You know, we ought to be out of here by now," Nath said.

"Almost." Pepper stopped in front of a door and pushed it open. Inside was another storage room, abandoned and dusty, with a stairwell at the far end. "This will take us up into the city. Just below the Chamber of Contest that you seek. I don't recommend it though. The worst of the worst giants will be there proving themselves. It wouldn't surprise me a bit if they swallowed you whole. They eat a lot."

"I'll manage, somehow. Pepper, I have a question. Do you know where the hive of ugly dragons is, the wurmers?"

"What?"

"Dragons!"

Pepper's face turned sour. He shook his head no. "No, not taking you there. There is death."

"Tell me where, then."

"No, you just need to leave. Get your sword and go. You've caused a big enough stir already."

"Just a hint, please!"

"The eastern part of the city. There is a nest. But those things, brrr, are nasty. I'm nosey, but not that nosey. Beware. They will pick the flesh clean off of you."

Nath patted Pepper on the back. "Thanks. Every bit helps." He jogged for the stair and bounded up several steps then stopped and turned. "Aren't you coming?"

"By the giants, no. I have to round up a search party."

"A search party for what?"

"To find you." He saluted. "Got to go. Good luck, flame hair. I aim to not see you too soon. And if you make it, come back to where you came in to get out of here." He vanished through the doorway.

Where I came in? Strangest rescue ever.

While Nath was rushing up the steep flight of stone steps, an unseen force jolted him.

Bang!

Nath doubled over. His senses were jangled. Blinking, he searched all around him. It was just him inside the lonely stairwell.

What was that?

Clutching his chest, he resumed his climb and raced up the steps.

Bang!

He fell to his knees. Searching all around, he didn't see anything.

But he heard something.

It was the sound of metal hitting metal, but it wasn't any kind of metal. There was a unique sound to it. Almost like a tuning fork being struck. And the sound was echoing down the staircase from above.

For some reason Nath searched his feelings. Like a hard punch in the gut, he felt it again.

Bang!

His eyes widened. He realized what was happening.

Fang!

CHAPTER
36

"**D**RINK YOUR POTION," SELENE ORDERED Brenwar.

"What? Why?"

She pointed at the giants coming their way.

Shirtless heavy-eyed brutes were eyeballing and harassing the line of people trying to enter the chamber where the banging was coming from.

Reluctantly, Brenwar slipped into a storage alcove filled with cut stone. He took out the vial and drank the potion down. His stomach turned. His skin and bone stretched. The blocks of stone lowered in his sight. He slumped back against the wall and shook his head.

"Are you well?" Selene asked.

Brenwar steadied himself and looked at the slender hands that hung out of his once-too-long sleeves. "I've been better."

"You look much better, aside from the beard."

He looked down at her. "I wish I could say the same for you. Let's go." Brenwar made his way out of the alcove and merged with the crowd of people heading down the street toward the banging sounds that echoed throughout the city. Half a head taller than Selene, he led the way with a lengthy step and swagger to his gait. He kept his chin down as he approached the giants.

One of them, a ten footer with a fuzzy red unibrow, shoved him in the shoulder. It eyed him and said with a sniff, "You smell bad."

Head down with his fist balled up at his side, Brenwar replied, "Er, not everyone can smell as good as you."

The giant's head reared back, and a deep scowl formed on his ugly face. "You jest with me?"

Selene wedged herself between them. "Forgive him, master. My brother is addle-minded and not in the city much. He meant it as a compliment. He admires the giants. Pure admiration."

"I can speak for myself," Brenwar said.

Selene elbowed him in the chest. "Be silent."

The giant's hand went to a hammer at his side, started to remove it. "No, still don't like him. I think I'll crush him. It's been days since I've crushed anybody. And he smells funny."

"I'll crush—*umph!*" Brenwar's mouth was sealed by Selene's hand.

She then said to the giant, "My, you have such marvelous shoulders. I am a seamstress, and I could fit you in a most handsome cloak. You know, a little gold-and-silver trim. I have some leftover material that I could share with you if you spare my ignorant brother."

The giant stuck his face in hers. "I'll crush your brother, and you'll make it for me anyway."

"Sure, sure," she said, "go ahead and crush him, them. He's nothing but trouble." She winked at the giant. "I'll just need to explain to Eckubahn what happened to my assistant."

The giant swallowed and said with a stammer, "Go, go along. I will drop this matter."

"No, please, it's not a problem. Smash my brother. I'll make you a cloak so fine that everyone will notice."

"Go away!" The giant moved on down the street with the other one in tow. Neither looked back.

"My, you really want to get rid of me, don't you?" Brenwar asked.

"It's a risk I'm willing to take."

"Ha ha."

Following the throng, they finally entered through the archway that led into the massive chamber big enough for hundreds of giants.

Brenwar got his first eyeful of a ten-foot-tall orc and a nine-foot-tall goblin. He nudged Selene. "By the Sultans, what in their fiery flames is going on here?"

"Indeed, it is strange."

Brenwar knew all about the giants. There were cyclopes and ettins. Earth giants, stone giants. Those were the rare ones. Normally bigger than the rest. Then there were the others. They lived in clans. Brutish men, crude and hairy. The dwarves considered them pure bloods. The others were abominations of flesh and magic.

Now it seemed there were giant races too. Orcs, goblins, gnolls, bugbears, the biggest he'd ever seen. It didn't make sense. What could be causing this? He hated the idea of a world filled with giants. He relished the idea of killing them.

Bang!

The sound of metal on metal jolted Brenwar. He picked his way through the crowd toward the front.

Several giants stood inside a grand ring. Its flooring was a dark-red tile. In the middle was a huge anvil, bigger than a mule. Fang lay on top of it, like starlight in a night of grime. Hovering over the sword was a balding brute of a giant missing one eye. The twelve-foot pure blood held a blacksmith's hammer in two hands. Sweat dripped down his face. Packed with thick muscle, the barrel-chested monster brought the hammer down on Fang.

Bang!

The crowd cheered.

Bang!

Sparks flew. Face filling with red rage, the giant hammered away.

Bang! Bang! Bang! Bang!

Sweaty lips puffing and broad chest heaving, the giant dropped the huge hammer on the ground. Another giant, a little bigger, walked up with his arm swinging. He was chuckling under his grubby beard. With a sneer, the first giant drew back his fist and punched the second one in the face, knocking it down to the ground.

The people erupted with feverish excitement.

"I like it," Brenwar said in Selene's ear. "Let them kill each other."

As the pair of giants slugged and wrestled, a third giant took center stage. With one hand, he picked up Fang and eyeballed him.

Fang was a big sword, with a two handed pommel. He fit in the giant's huge hand like a glove.

Suddenly, the giant's pupils turned into huge pearls. His hand smoked. His skin sizzled and fried. He dropped the sword on the anvil with a clatter and let out a howling cry. He ran around holding his smoking hand, knees pumping and screaming.

The audience laughed.

Brenwar found himself caught up in it as well. There was nothing quite like watching a giant making of fool of itself. As stupid as they were, they could still be entertaining. He guffawed and guffawed and guffawed.

Over the next hour, the giants tussled back and forth in odd contests. They punched. Tugged. Head butted each other and the anvil. For the most part they beat themselves senseless and dizzy, all to the thrill of the crowd. But not a one of them could make a mark on the sword.

With a straight face, Selene said, "So glad you are amused. Need I remind you why we are here?"

"Of course not." Brenwar swiped his thumbs over his eyes. "We just need a distraction."

Someone jostled him.

Brenwar turned.

A pure bred giant stood behind him. It wasn't as stout as the one bragging and brawling front and center.

Not thinking, Brenwar blurted out, "Watch yerself, giant!"

The monster man looked down on him with an astonished look in his eye. Its nostrils flared. Muscles in its jaws clenched.

Astonished himself, Brenwar watched the angry giant get bigger and bigger. He looked up at Selene.

Her violet eyes filled with surprise. "Oh, no."

The giant screamed, "Dwarf!"

CHAPTER
37

NATH SAT AT THE TOP of the steps, clutching himself. Every hammer to Fang's steel was a blow to the gut. "Sultans of Sulfur," he muttered.

He had no idea why he had such an attachment to Fang. They'd been together for a long time, but they hadn't ever bonded like this before. It was very weird. So far as he knew, Fang still didn't obey him most of the time. The battering of metal came to an end, and he forced himself back to his feet.

A chained door made of barred metal stopped Nath on the top step.

Peering between the bars, he could see a room filled with oversized people with their backs to him. They were shouting and cheering. There were grunts and oomphs and the hard smack of fists on faces.

Sounds like the Chamber of Contest to me. How did that halfling expect me to get in there without a key?

But now that his belly was full, Nath discovered that his strength had returned. The bars and chains weren't as thick as the ones in his prison. They were aged and coated in green tarnish. He stuck his hands through the bars and grabbed the padlock on the other side. He gave it a hard tug.

Pop!

The lock and chain fell away.

"Huh, that was easy." Wary eyed, he pushed the door open and made his way into the chamber.

A well–built man staggered out of the crowd into Nath's path. His eyes filled with alarm.

With a quick punch, Nath knocked him out, and then he dragged him out into the hall, stripped off his heavy cloak, and put it on. He covered his head and ventured deeper into the chamber.

The giants inside the arena were brutes. Each was thick skinned and padded in heavy muscle. Nath shuddered at the thought of an army of them. On the humongous anvil lay Fang, like a twinkling gem.

This should be child's play. All I need is a distraction.

He closed his eyes and summoned the fire in his belly. It came surprisingly easily. He spat a small puff of smoke out of his mouth.

Ah, yes, a monumental plume of smoke should do.

He caught a pair of gap-toothed women staring at his lips. He thumped his chest with his fist, winked at them, and said, "All of this excitement gives me bad gas."

The women turned their backs, threw up their arms, and cheered with wild spirit.

Nath filled his lungs and focused on his goal.

Smoke. Snatch Fang. Vanish. Easy.

When he was ready to unleash his plan, a clamor arose from the crowd. A giant fell into the arena screaming and holding his leg. The startled crowd scrambled away and bustled one over the other to get out of the grand chamber.

The wounded giant kept saying the same thing over and over. "Dwarf!"

Two cloaked figures stood on the opposite side of the arena from Nath. One was Brenwar, the other Selene.

It can't be!

Before Nath could act, the chamber's main door dropped in place with the thunderous boom, crushing a handful of people and trapping others inside.

Nath made a quick count.

One, two, three ... fourteen giants!

"Dwarf! You got that right!" Brenwar yelled in a thunderous voice. He waved Mortuun over his head. "Come and kiss my hammer, giants!"

The entire chamber exploded into battle. The snarling giants charged with rage-filled eyes.

Selene slipped through the giants' clutches time after time. Giants fell and toppled hard. Frustration cried from their lips.

Brenwar's hammer swung and connected with bone-busting blows. The skittish dwarven fighter popped between legs, hammered feet, and broke bone after bone. But only a few suffered the wrath of Mortuun forged in Morgdon by Brenwar the dwarf.

The tide turned.

The hulking throng was overwhelming.

Within seconds, the giants—big, but still quick as men—had Brenwar and Selene in their clutches.

On instinct, Nath rushed to snatch up his sword and then stand atop the anvil.

Power surged up his arms and down his back.

He struck Fang's tip on the anvil.

Ting!

Nothing happened. Nath fully expected the sound to grow, fill the giants' ears, and drop them to their knees. He struck Fang on the anvil again.

Ting!

Nothing happened. Well, not entirely. Now, he had the attention of every last one of them, including the ones with their hands filled with the struggling forms of Selene and Brenwar.

"Is this the thanks I get for rescuing you?" Nath said to the sword. He looked at his friends. "What are you doing here?"

"Saving you!" Brenwar growled.

"Well, you're doing a fine job of it."

Kicking her feet and gasping for breath, Selene yelled, "Will you shut up and do something?"

A giant reached for Nath. He swung Fang and clipped off the tip of its finger.

The giant's bellow permeated his ears.

Still feeling a surge of power, Nath burst into action just as the giant blacksmith hammer came down and smote the anvil where he'd been standing before he leapt. Metal smote metal.

Clang!

Nath didn't hold anything back. The giants were cold-blooded killers. Any hesitation would leave him and his friends dead. He sprang at the giant who clutched Selene and chopped it through its wrists.

Selene landed like a cat and skirted away.

Ducking underneath the swing of a sword, Nath plunged Fang into the side of the giant who held Brenwar.

"RR-Rah!" the monster screamed.

"We need to get out of here!" Nath said, still chopping and hacking with intensity.

Brenwar was at his side, clubbing away.

Selene shot bright and tiny little missiles from her fingers. "There's a stairwell. Follow me there!"

"Lead the way!" Brenwar said.

To the tune of metal ringing against metal, they battled their way to the tunnel from whence Nath came.

"Great Guzan!"

The tunnel was filled with more giants. And there was a familiar face as well. Pepper.

The giant halfling was pointing at Nath. "There he is! There he is! I told you I'd find him. I told you so!"

"You rat!" Nath yelled at him.

Pepper shrugged at him. But the look in the halfling's eyes told it all. It hadn't been his choice to lead them to Nath. He was in over his head.

"What do we do now?" Selene said.

"Keep fighting!"

"Aye!" Brenwar replied.

They battled through the giants, downing one after the other, but it wasn't enough. Brenwar's iron endurance was puffing for breath. Selene's own fires had fled her fingertips.

Furious and relentless, the giants kept swinging. Their blows were taking a toll. All three friends were bruised and bleeding. Nath had no idea how he was going to get out of this. The doors were sealed. More giants filled the room from the tunnel.

Circling around the anvil, Nath said to his friends, "This is a horrible rescue."

"I told you not to give yourself up!" Brenwar replied.

"It's no one's fault," Selene added. With a whisk of her tail, she tripped a giant. "Just shut up and fight!"

They did. Nath cut one giant down only to face two others.

Where are they coming from?

Finally, after endless minutes of agonizing battle, the giants backed off.

Panting for breath and sword steady in his grip, Nath said, "What's happening?"

All of the giants took a knee and faced the gated entrance.

Eckubahn stood on the other side of the bars, his great head aflame with mystic green fire. Two ogres cranked the iron wheel that lifted the iron gate. Eckubahn stepped inside. Hundreds of wurmers flew inside with him. They covered the floor and attached themselves to the archways and rafters above.

Nath gazed up with wonder. "I hate those things." Out of nowhere he noticed Pepper was standing alongside him.

The giant halfling said, "You sure do fight a good fight."

Nath started to speak but didn't bother. He was too tired. Pepper wouldn't hear his last words anyway.

Finally, Eckubahn spoke. "Nath Dragon, you are too much trouble to keep around."

"I thought you wanted to keep me around to torment my father."

"No. I've decided I'll just send him your scales and draw out his vengeance. And what a delight it will be to have you watch me torment your friends before you go. I think we'll start with that dwarf. I see he needs more flesh taken from his bones."

Brenwar yelled at Eckubahn. "Come take it yourself, then!"

"No need for that. I'll let the giants handle it."

"Roast him like a sow, we will!" one true-blooded giant said.

Head downcast, Nath said to his friends, "I'm sorry."

"What?" Pepper replied.

A tingling sensation raced from Fang's grip up into Nath's arms. He didn't know why he did what he did and said what he said, but he tapped the tip of his blade on the anvil again and said, "Fang, get us out of here."

Ting!

The blade unleashed a gush of hidden power.

Zip!

Nath found himself standing in the middle of a flowered field with more colors than he could imagine. In an instant he knew exactly where he was. The Elven Field of Dreams. He wasn't alone either.

Brenwar and Selene were there with jaws dropped.

Filled with elation, Nath threw his sword up high in the air. "Ah-hah! Fang, you are wonderful!"

All of them burst out in sheer joyous laughter. Brenwar and Selene briefly hugged each other. Finally, with his emotions settling down, Nath noticed someone else was laughing. It was Pepper.

The giant halfling said, "Now that's my kind of rescue."

EPILOGUE

SITTING ON HIS THRONE, ECKUBAHN's head had a deep-crimson afterglow. His hands clutched the stone armrests and crumbled one of them to pieces.

There was blood on his hands.

Outraged, he had slaughtered half a dozen of his own giants. Two more he had hung by the neck in the streets. That didn't include the many that Nath Dragon and his company had killed. Now, the entire city of Urslay was silent. The howling wind was the only life in the abandoned streets.

Sitting on the throne beside his, Lotuus said, "Don't fret, Milord." She toyed with a tassel made from Nath's lock of hair that she'd had mended to a wand-like stick. "We won't have any trouble finding him. Shall I give the order?"

"Yes."

Wings coming to life, the tiny woman floated down to the floor, where dozens of wurmers lay. She fanned her tassel under the lead wurmer's nose.

Its deep-purple eyes filled with a hungry radiance.

She gave it two commands. "Seek. Destroy."

BATTLE

OF THE

DRAGON

-BOOK 3-

CRAIG HALLORAN

CHAPTER 1

THE ELVEN FIELD OF DREAMS. Nath lay face down in a pile of yellow and pink lilies, waving his arms and letting the fragrant flowers tickle his nose.

"Ah-hahahahaha!"

He rolled, hugging and kissing Fang. If there had ever been a time in his life when he had doubted his survival, it had been today. Surrounded by giants, wurmers, and the titan king Eckubahn, he'd cheated death once again.

That he was elated was an understatement. He rolled on his back and kicked his legs.

"Fang, you are amazing!"

"Tang is amazing!" said Pepper, the giant halfling. "What is Tang?"

"Fang," Nath said, sitting up and correcting the gray-headed halfling. "With an 'F'!"

Pepper cupped his hand to his ear. "Who's Jeff?"

"He said 'F' for Fang!" yelled Brenwar the dwarf, looking up at Pepper and then glancing at Nath. "Where in the world did you dig up this oversized mop top, Nath?"

Coming to his feet, Nath said, "The Urslay dungeons. He came to my aid, sort of."

With one eyebrow cocked and his nose twitching, Brenwar said, "Sure he did. Seems a bit shifty to me. Those beady eyes." His grip tightened on his war hammer's haft. "I don't like him."

Looking down at Brenwar, Pepper said, "I like you too." He wandered away, staring at all the lush greenery.

Brenwar yelled after him, "I said I didn't like you!"

"You don't like anybody," Selene added, rolling her eyes. She sauntered over to Nath and ran her thumb over a bloody scratch on his cheek. "You look terrible."

The nearness of Selene's beautiful face revealed a swollen eye and a bruise on her chin. Nath took her hand in his. "And you've never looked better. Didn't I tell you two not to come after me?"

"Yes," Selene and Brenwar said together.

"I just wanted to make sure you were each just as hardheaded as the other." Nath stuck Fang tip first in the ground and marveled. "Sultans of Sulfur! I don't know what made me do that. I didn't know he was capable of such a feat. My scales are still tingling." He turned his head.

The Elven Field of Dreams was a place of wonder and marvel. Every imaginable flower and bush of beauty was there. Lavender and sage splashed the tree line in the distance. Pink-, blue-, and white-spotted roses and knee-high daffodils spread as far as the eye could see. The fragrant aroma was intoxicating, energizing, and soothing. "I wonder why he brought us here."

"Morgdon would have been far better." Brenwar flicked Fang with his finger. "Take me to an ale house."

"Don't do that," Nath said, shielding the blade.

"Oh, pardon me." Brenwar patted the blade on the pommel. "Apparently everyone else can have a sense of humor, but I can't."

"Oh, the dwarf made a jest." Selene had bent over to pick some flowers. "How unfunny."

"You're one to talk, frostbite queen," said the dwarf.

"None of this bickering will make our wounds any better," Nath replied.

"Maybe not you, but I'm feeling better already." Brenwar rolled his burly shoulders and grimaced. "Ooh!"

Selene chuckled.

"No, but seriously, why did Fang bring us here?" Nath cocked his head. Nearby was the sound of cascading water. He pulled the great blade out of the ground and started heading in that direction.

Alongside him, Selene said, "Isn't that blade of elven craftsmanship? Perhaps that's why."

"Pah!" Brenwar scoffed.

"Perhaps the elves had a part in it, but Father was always clear that he made Fang for me himself."

"Pah!" Brenwar said again.

Nath turned around and walked backward so he could face his friends. "What are your thoughts, Brenwar?"

"Only a dwarven forge could have sired that blade. Your father used the fires of Morgdon to temper it."

"And you know that for a fact? Didn't Laedorn say he was there for its making?"

"I know what I know!" Brenwar stormed forward right by the both of them. "Now get out of my way. I'm thirsty. And if I can't get any ale, I guess I'll have to make do with this elven pond water."

The three of them approached a pond so clear you could see to the bottom. Bright fish darted back and forth underneath. There was plant life too, like mushrooms with a soft radiant glow to them. On the other side, water cascaded over rocky falls, plunging into the pond to create foaming bubbles. It didn't make any ripples.

Seeing the looks on his friends' faces, Nath turned to look. "That's odd."

Selene lifted her brows. "That's magic."

"Hi-Hoooo!" Pepper yelled from out of nowhere. He was standing on some rocks to Nath's left, gazing at the waters. He was waving his arms and only wearing his trousers. "Watcha waiting for? Get in!"

"No, Pepper, wait!" Nath cried.

Knees up and jumping high, Pepper cannonballed into the pond.

Splash!

On his knees, scooping a mouthful of water into his bearded face, Brenwar glowered. "Dirty halflings aren't good for anything. Now the entire pond is ruined."

Floating on his back and paddling with his feet, Pepper waved his hand in the air. "Get in. This water is unlike anything I've ever felt before. So exhilarating!"

Nath lifted up his foot, tried to tug his boot off, and fell down. "Perhaps I'm a little wearier than I expected." He rubbed the scales on his shoulder. He was aching all over. More so than he'd realized. With a grunt, he tugged at his boot again, but it didn't come off. "I'm going to have to cut them off."

Selene approached. "Maybe your feet grew." Her tail snaked over and coiled around Nath's ankle. She grabbed his boot by the heel and pulled it off. She did the same with the other. "You just needed a woman's touch."

"Apparently so." Nath removed his chest plate and the tunic underneath. He moved toward the water and said to Selene, "Coming?"

"Perhaps."

Nath waded in. The cool water cleansed every pore and filled his body with a tantalizing sensation. The throbbing in his sore muscles and bones subsided. Elated, he submerged himself. A school of fish swam past his eyes. They were a brilliant lime-yellow with green stripes. One of them winked at him. He gaped, choked on some water, and resurfaced, coughing and laughing. Finally, he said, "This feels great! Get in, Brenwar!"

Arms crossed over his barrel chest and sporting visible cuts on his arms and legs, the black-bearded dwarf said, "No."

Nath splashed him.

Backing away, Brenwar said, "Cut that out!"

"You really need to get in. There's nothing to fear here. It's the Elven Field of Dreams. A place of sanctuary." He eyed Selene. "Join me?"

Eyeing the surroundings and settling her gaze on an arm of the pond that jutted into a grove of trees, she picked up the hem of her robe. "I could use privacy."

Nath nodded. "As you wish."

Selene disappeared into the trees.

Nath shrugged and splashed through the waters. He swallowed a mouthful and smiled. He'd been to the Elven Field of Dreams before, long ago when he was much younger. There was no other place like it in Nalzambor. The creatures were friendly, not one bit shy. Two stags with black coats and white horns drank from the waters on a nearby bank. Blue birds with red wings skimmed the surface. A family of pink-feathered swans swam nearby. As he lay floating, all of Nath's worries faded away.

This is how life should be—for every creature in the world.

"Ho! Fighting Dragon, come and feel this!" Pepper sat beneath the small waterfall that ran over the rocks and fell into the pond. Its foaming bed now formed around him. "It makes me ticklish. I'd forgotten what it was like to be tickled. It's funny."

Nath found a spot near the giant halfling and soaked up the refreshment. He couldn't remember the last time he'd felt so good. At least, not in the form of a man. Being in dragon form was different, oh so different.

"I want to thank you for coming to my rescue," Pepper said.

"To be clear, saving you wasn't part of the plan."

"You never know what the true plan is until it plays out." Pepper rinsed his puffy face off. The giant halfling's bulk still dwarfed the gilded frame of Nath. "You can count on that."

"It seems the waters have improved your hearing, Pepper."

The halfling cupped his ear and said, "What?"

"Uh-huh."

Nath soaked up the cool waters and enjoyed the warm sunlight.

I could sit here forever.

But out of the corner of his eye, he noticed some movement cutting through the cove Selene had vanished into.

Maybe I should check on her. Just to be safe.

He scooted out from under the falls.

"Where are you going?"

"Uh, just checking things out."

Pepper pointed his huge finger toward the cove and winked. "Checking things out that way, I reckon."

Nath's throat tightened. "No, just…"

Pepper leaned behind the falls and disappeared from sight.

Shaking his head, Nath paddled toward the grove. The waters were a little mistier below the surface once he crossed beyond the jetty of trees. Neck deep, he slipped through the coolness, but he saw no sign of Selene. The pond didn't extend any farther, it just ended. Other than a distinct lack of wildlife, there weren't any signs of Selene at all. He headed for shore with his heart racing. He spun around in a full circle.

She'd better not have abandoned me again.

"Brenwar," Nath called out. "Brenwar!"

His gruff friend wasn't anywhere to be heard from. He hurried up the bank, hoping to find a sign of her tracks.

Something seized his leg and pulled him under.

He started choking.

Ulp!

CHAPTER 2

LEGS BOUND BY AN UNSEEN force, Nath was pulled deeper into the pond. Thrashing and flailing his arms, he swam for the surface to no avail. A strong arm locked around his neck and squeezed his throat. He clutched at it. Without the use of his legs, his desperate maneuvering was futile. A strong supine figure had latched onto him, pressing its body into his and with angry force, dragging him up above the waters. He gasped and choked from his constricted throat.

A familiar voice with a sharp and biting tone spoke harsh words into his ear. "What kind of Dragon are you that spies on a bathing woman? Do you not know the meaning of privacy? Discretion?" She tightened her lock on his neck. "Hmmm, Dragon Prince?"

Coughing, he forced out his words. "Sorry. I was worried."

"Worried? About the likes of me, in this place of refuge? The safest spot in all the world? Don't toy with me, Little Dragon."

"I thought you might have departed. That's all."

Her strong grip eased. "And why would I do that?" Her voice became more of a purr. "Especially after all we've been through."

Nath swallowed. The mood had changed. The taut muscles of Selene's majestic figure had softened into something else. His throat turned dry. He turned his body into hers. Her long arms no longer held him in her grip. Instead, they draped over his shoulders.

His eyes searched her face. He'd never seen Selene look like this before. Her hard features had softened. A playful smile was on her maroon lips. Her dark wet hair lay on the waters like black lily pads. The violet in her eyes sparkled. She was glowing. Happy.

His heart started pounding in his chest.

"What?" she said to him.

"Nothing, it's just that you look so … beautiful. A hundred ballads from Helflim wouldn't do your radiance justice. I'm at a loss for words."

Her tail came up out of the waters, pushed the hair from his eyes, and touched his cheek. "How flattering." She eased into him, chest to chest. "I can feel your heart, Nath. Tell me more."

Nath's hands found her waist. He'd never felt like this before in Selene's presence. He was excited and uneasy. Maybe it was the waters or the sanctuary, but she was different, in a very good yet confusing way. "Uh—"

She put her fingertip on his lips and said with dreamy eyes, "No, let me speak. Nath, I don't think I ever properly thanked you for all you've done for me. Nath, will you kiss me?"

Nath could barely remember the last time he kissed a woman of any kind, but it must have been at least thirty years, aside from Sasha kissing him on the cheek. He closed his eyes and leaned in.

Someone interrupted. "Ahem."

CHAPTER 3

NATH'S EYES POPPED OPEN. SELENE'S were still closed. Slowly, they fluttered open.

"Ahem." A voice repeated.

It was Brenwar. Nath was certain of that.

Go figure.

Wrapped up with Selene, Nath turned. "You always have to spoil every—"

Brenwar wasn't alone. He was surrounded by a host of elven soldiers clad in light but ornate black-and-green armor. Each had a tall spear. The slender-faced elves looked even taller alongside the bulk of Brenwar. They didn't wear helmets. Instead, their handsome facial features were distinguished by their long, wispy moustaches.

"See what happens when you fool around?" Brenwar said. "These lanky predators show up."

A pair of elves lowered their spears on Brenwar's ribs.

Another who was a half head taller than the others, with silvery hair, stepped forward. "You are trespassing on elven land, strangers. You taint our waters. There is a high price to pay for that."

"Get those toothpicks away from me," Brenwar growled. "Don't point things if you don't aim to use them."

"Oh, we will use them," the commander said to Brenwar, but he was looking at Nath. "On all of you."

Selene slipped out of Nath's arms. "Strange, but I think they mean it." She whispered to Nath, "Something doesn't seem right." She eyed the commander. "I hope the elves haven't lost all of their manners to the point where a woman would be deprived of the chance to clothe herself upon getting out of the water. A moment of privacy, if you please."

With the distinguished haughtiness of an elven commander, the leader said, "As soon as the red hair steps out of the waters and into our custody, you can dress yourself." He let out a whistle. Another pack of soldiers came forward, shorter. They were hard-eyed elven ladies with blue meshed into the black of their armor instead of green. "Don't let her out of your sight."

Nath sloshed out of the waters. Trousers soaked and dripping wet, he said to the commander, "You wouldn't happen to have a towel on you, would you? I'd hate to catch cold from this sudden frost."

The elven commander looked around but zeroed in on Nath's scales. "Oh, you jest. You can rely on your jokes to keep you warm, then. Bind them."

"Now, now. Hold on." Brenwar backed away. "Wait until I get ahold—"

"Do as they say," Nath ordered Brenwar, "and please, keep your thoughts to yourself. We don't want any trouble."

Brenwar looked like his beard was going to explode, but he fell silent.

The elves marched them to the other side of the pond, where Nath gathered his tunic. His breastplate was seized, along with Fang and his scabbard. Brenwar's war hammer, Mortuun, had been gathered up as well.

Nath scanned the pond and the surrounding area, but Pepper was nowhere to be found. He felt Brenwar's eyes on him. It was clear that the dwarf was at a loss too.

How does the biggest one of all of us evade the elves? Halflings never cease to surprise me.

"You know," Nath lifted his bound wrists before him, "I can't put my shirt on with my hands tied like this, and I just don't feel right strutting around half naked." He pulled his shoulders back, flung back his long, wet red hair, and smiled. "I fear I might distract the elven ladies from their duties."

The commander gave a nod to one of the guards. The wiry elven warrior rammed his spear butt into Nath's gut. It dropped him to one knee.

Nath's golden eyes burned like flames when he said to that elf, "I wouldn't ever do that again if I were you."

"Then you had better mind your comments," said the commander.

Nath took a stand. The waters had completely refreshed him, healing up his wounds, but now he had a throbbing in his gut and was surrounded by elves with bad attitudes.

Can't win for losing.

"Point taken."

"Let's go," the commander said. "Onward."

"Er, I can see by the insignia on your armor that you are a high commander, but I don't recognize your crest. Do you care to identify yourself? Or selves, rather."

"We are the guardians of the Elven Field of Dreams. Wilder elves. I am

Slavan Fonjich, the leader." He stepped up alongside Nath with his hand on the pommel of his elven-crafted sword. "I'm curious how you came here undetected. No one, especially a dwarf, has crossed into the fields for a decade—and hopefully not another stubby foot ever will."

Brenwar puffed hot air out of his beard. "Nath."

Selene and the female warriors met up with them. Her playful gaze was still there. She winked at him.

"Uh," Nath stammered to Slavan, "if my memory serves, the fields have never been guarded. Anyone who could find them was welcome to them. They were the reward at the end of the long journey for those who dared to seek them. Of course, that always made me curious. Why would travelers who came here ever leave?"

"Not that many travelers make it in the first place," Slavan said, ducking under some branches. "And the fields have a way of sending one off with a renewed purpose. It's not so remarkable to the elves. We already maintain the loftiest of standards."

"Pah!" Brenwar clawed at his beard with his skeleton hand. "The problem with you elves is you think you're better than everyone. But you're not. Every good thing you ever did, you learned from us."

"It's beneath me to argue about it with your kind," Slavan said. "I'd be better served talking with hogs in pens."

"Why, that impudent, scrawny, pointy-eared jackal!" Brenwar strained at his bonds. "I'm not putting up with this, Nath, and why are we captives anyway? Pah! There's treachery afoot!"

Slavan let out a command. "Gag him!"

"What!" Brenwar said.

"Slavan," Nath said, standing a full head taller than the commander, "this treatment is below your kind, and you can't be foolish enough to believe we are enemies of the elves. We are well known among your kind. Just send word to the High Council, to Laedorn himself. He will certainly vouch for Nath Dragon and Brenwar Bolderguild."

Slavan stayed his elves with his hand, faced Nath, and looked him in the eye. "It grieves me to inform you, but Laedorn is dead."

Nath's chest felt like it was collapsing within itself. Elves could die of old age, certainly, but that would take centuries, and Laedorn was far too young for that. He could still see Laedorn, noble and friendly, an exemplary example of the proud elven heritage.

With dread, Nath asked, "What happened? Was it a battle? Please don't tell me it was the titans."

"He was murdered," Slavan said.

CHAPTER 4

"**M**URDERED!" BRENWAR SAID WITH ALARM. He grumbled. "Where did such a crime take place?"

"In Elohim, in the very heart of the city, right in front of everybody. His heart was pierced by an arrow, straight and true. It happened while he spoke to the people, warning them of the dangers to come, the power of the titan Eckubahn. He was telling us how Evil can turn one elf against another. To be wary. Hold fast and stick together."

Still marching through the meadow of flowers, the troupe veered down a steep hillside that led into a valley. "His words couldn't have been more true. Since his death, the elves have been divided. Without his leadership, many seem lost."

"Who killed him?" Nath said.

"No one was ever captured. The assassin escaped." Slavan motioned to one of his guardsmen, pointed deep into the ravine where the meadows merged with a dark forest, and said, "Take us in."

"What do you mean you never caught the assassin? How is that possible? There must have been thousands of elves present," Brenwar said. "I tell you what, no dwarf has ever been assassinated in Morgdon."

"What do you mean?" Ginger footed, Slavan skipped over the rocky steppes that led into the ravine. "Uurluuk was killed just the same."

"You're a liar! Uurluuk Mountainstone is not dead!" Brenwar blustered through his beard. "It's not possible! No single arrow could kill our top general."

"He died by the same means: an arrow, straight through the heart." Slavan's face was a mask of confusion. "The entire dwarven realm, much like the elves, mourned for months. All of Nalzambor knew of it."

Brenwar looked at Nath. "He's talking madness."

"Agreed," Nath said, eyeing Slavan. Everything the elf was telling him was bizarre. Out of place. Still, Nath felt deep sorrow inside his heart. Slavan's words rang true, even while none of what he was saying made any sense. If Laedorn and Uurluuk were dead, Nath certainly would have known about it. "You say the elves and dwarves mourned for months, Slavan, so how long ago did all this happen?"

"It's been all of a year and a month since Uurluuk was slain. Almost a year to the day for Laedorn," the elf replied.

The elves were leading them along a creek bed in a ravine that was thick in green foliage and shadows. It was a place where the day felt more like night. An odd still quiet prevailed. No vermin rustled over the ground they passed.

"Ever since," Slavan went on, "a host of guards has been stationed at every corner of Elven lands. It is the same for the dwarves. Everyone is on guard—including the humans and even the orcs."

"Have there been other assassinations?" Nath asked.

"No. That was the end of it, for security has become tight."

Brenwar forced his way to Nath's side and puffed under his beard, "These elves are quite mad. I've been to Morgdon since then. Crossed the dwarves. There's been no mention of any of this over the past year. It's not possible. Maybe within weeks, but months, a year? Preposterous."

"I assure you my words are true, Dwarf. I don't know what mountain you crawled out from under the past year, but you've clearly missed out on the madness that is upon us. Upon all of Nalzambor. The titans have a presence in almost every known city. They now rule from the center of Narnum."

"Narnum!" Nath gasped. "That's not possible. They barely had a presence in the world just a day ago. They hold up in Urslay of the craggy mountains. Everything you're saying is preposterous."

"Agreed!" Brenwar said.

Nath found Selene's eyes. She didn't seem alarmed. Instead, there was a cattish playfulness in her eyes. He tore his gaze away, wondering what in Nalzambor was going on. It seemed his entire world had been turned upside down. Again. "Slavan, where are you taking us?"

"I'm taking you where we have arrived," the elven commander said. He stroked the fine long hairs of his moustache with the leather gauntlet on his hand. "The Inner Sanctum of Lheme."

They stood before a wall of overhanging vines coated in white and yellow flowers. With a word—an enchanted Elven word from Slavan—the vines parted with life of their own, revealing an archway of rune-carved stone. The elves marched into the dark passageway. The lady elves went next, along with Selene. The guards behind Nath and Brenwar pushed them forward.

"I'm going!" Brenwar said. "Humph, at least it's underground. A little cold dirt will do my bones some good."

In the front, middle, and back of the ranks, elven warriors lit and carried small torches. The tunnel was nothing more than packed earth held up by wooden beams, much like the miners used. It didn't slope up or down, but had hairpin bends left and right, and it split off in many places.

They walked for an hour, then two, before winding up in a cavernous chamber. Its floor was checkered tiles in different shades of jade. The walls were sandstone, and archways that supported the roof and ceiling were made from blocks of marble. The elves with torches lit the iron lanterns that hung on the walls. The room filled with a soft glow.

"Hah!" Brenwar lifted a brow. "I should have known. This place is dwarven crafted."

"And elven crafted as well," Slavan added.

"So you say," Brenwar grumbled. "And what is the point of bringing us into these catacombs? Did you want to ask me how we built it?"

"Subdue your bickering, Brenwar." Nath pushed his now dry hair out of his eyes, briefly enjoying how clean and silky the waters had made it. "But why *are* we here, Slavan? And why are we bound? You must know we are no threat to the elves, nor to any of Nalzambor's people. What is the meaning of this?"

Slavan pointed at his chest and said with an angry voice, "Because you are a suspect, Nath Dragon!" His voice echoed.

"Suspected of what?"

"Killing Laedorn and Uurluuk!"

"Madness, I say! Impossible!" Brenwar said. "I'm a witness to that!"

"I'm my own witness," Nath replied, "and so is Selene. I haven't been anywhere close to Morgdon or Elohim. Surely you jest."

"I wish that I did, but I do not. Witnesses place you at both spots." Slavan walked over to a large, round stone pedestal that was waist high. "It happened at the four hundred and tenth Festival of Raye. That is where Laedorn addressed his kinsmen, only to be shot down in cold blood. Witnesses recall a red-haired man with scales on his arms. When they gave chase, the assassin left his weapon behind." He waved his hand over the pedestal and muttered some words. An image appeared hovering above the stone. He turned to Nath and said, "Does this look familiar?"

Nath's face turned white as ash. The image he beheld was of Akron.

CHAPTER

5

N ATH GAZED AT THE EXQUISITE bow. It was of the finest craftsmanship he'd ever seen. A glorious weapon indeed. "Where is the bow now?"

"It is safely kept in Elome now." Slavan shook his head. "Such treachery, Nath Dragon. That bow was a gift to you and your father. Laedorn carved it with his own hands, and now your betrayal has slain him."

Nath felt Selene's eyes on him. There was confusion in them. Worry.

The elves who surrounded them were not vengeful people, but they would want retribution. They would need answers. Like the dwarves, they would have justice, find the murderer.

Nodding his head, Nath said to the commander, "You say it was the four hundred and tenth Festival of Raye. I'm not crazy. I know the four hundred and ninth festival has not even occurred yet. Judging by the stars in the sky, it will occur this year, and soon at that."

"You are confused, Nath Dragon. Perhaps an illness has taken your thoughts. Maybe that can be your case when you stand trial."

"Trial!" Nath said.

"Lock them up!" Slavan ordered.

"No elf is about to lock me up!" Brenwar stormed into a pair of elves, bowling them over.

Quick as serpents, the elven guard pinned him in with spear tips at his throat. "Go ahead, try and kill me!"

"Stand down, Brenwar!" Nath said. "We can't be found guilty of something we didn't do."

"You'd better hope for your sake you speak the truth." Slavan pointed to the other side of the chamber, where iron doors led deeper into the cavern.

"Of course, death would be a better recourse than what the elves have in store for you if you are found guilty."

"And what about my friends? What are they being accused of? Let them go."

"Aiding and abetting, allegedly. And we can't risk someone trying to break you out. Think about it this way, Nath Dragon. You are safer with us than you are outside. The elves and dwarves have not stopped their search for you since the incidents occurred. If you cross any of those armies or militias … you will be killed." He lifted his chin. "You should thank me."

"Sure," Nath said. "Thanks. In the meantime, with me in here—who is fighting the wurmers and the titans? I'm warning you, a plague is about to happen out there."

Slavan scoffed. "That has already happened. Take them away."

The elves marched Nath, Selene, and Brenwar through the iron gates and locked each of them in their own cell. The dungeon was small, with a thick iron door and barred high portals. Cramped inside a stone cell that just had bars above his waist in the front—with a solid iron door—his head brushed against the rock ceiling. Brenwar was across the way. Selene he could not see. Nath crouched and sat down, staring at the heavy steel bars that closed him in.

Great Guzan, what's going on?

"Out of the fryer's pan and into the pyre, eh Nath?" Brenwar's voice boomed inside the small space. Their only company aside from one another was the glow of the torches they had passed when they entered. There was a rattle of bars. "We need to get out of here, you know. These elves, they are shifty ones."

Arms clasped over his knees, Nath said, "We need to get a handle on what's going on. How can anybody think I would ever kill Laedorn or Uurluuk? That's insanity. Selene. Selene? It's quiet over there. Are you all right?"

"I'll be fine so long as I am always near you, but I would be far better if you were in my cell with me," she said, not shielding the desire in her voice.

Nath's neck hairs stood on end. His scales tingled. Selene wasn't anything like her normal self. The allure in her voice was almost opposing. "Er, they didn't hit you in the head or anything, did they?"

"Quite the contrary, my love. My head only aches because I'm away from you."

It sounded like Brenwar smacked his hand into his head. The dwarf said, "What is wrong with you, Dragoness? You're all daffy in the head. Did you swallow too much of that pond water?"

But Selene's words stirred Nath. He crawled to the cell wall and reached his hands through the bars, stretching his fingers out. "Can you reach me?"

"No, no, Nath my love, I cannot."

"Will you two get ahold of yourselves?" Brenwar said through the bars that held him in. "She's one cell over, looking like a dragon about to eat a herd of lambs. I think you're in more trouble than you bargained for!"

Nath's chest tightened. In a good way. He'd never felt so bonded with Selene before. A closeness was growing within his heart like a fire spreading. He'd felt love and passion with women before, but never anything quite like this. He grasped the bars and tried to bend them. The biceps underneath his scales bulged. The cords in his forearms knotted.

Across the way, Brenwar's eyes widened. "You can do it, Nath."

The metal, thick elven steel, would not give. Nath gasped. He wiped the sweat from his brow. "Not this time, I can't." His passion for Selene eased. "We need to figure out what has happened. I'm worried. Really worried. Ben had Akron. Something might have happened to him. To Bayzog and Sasha. And the elves say they and the dwarves have been searching me out for over a year! How is that possible? Where did the time go?"

Brenwar started banging his head into the bars of his cell.

Bang. Bang. Bang.

"What in Nalzambor are you doing?" Nath asked.

"It helps me think," the old warrior replied.

Bang. Bang. Bang.

Sounding a little bit more like her normal self, Selene commented, "Perhaps your sword did it."

Nath lurched up. His golden eyes widened. The scales on his back shivered. Had Fang teleported them through time and space? "It can't be possible."

CHAPTER 6

"ANYTHING IS POSSIBLE," SELENE SAID. "And it would explain why I'm feeling how I'm feeling. I've never been so out of sorts with things. A female dragon's life cycles differently than a male's. Perhaps that's why I'm so—"

"Spare my ears from it," Brenwar barked. "I don't need to know." He pillowed up a handful of beard in front of his eyes and grunted. "Seems I have a tad more gray than what was there yesterday. By the Sultans, Nath! You managed to age us all a year in a day."

"It looks more like ten years in your case," Selene remarked.

"Great Dragons, we have been gone a year." It was Nath's turn to bang his head on the cell bars. "Why did Fang do that?"

Selene calmly said, "He saved us, remember? Assuming this is the truth, he took us all as far away from titan town as possible. I don't blame him. I doubt we would have lasted a moment longer, surrounded by all those giants and wurmers. The funny thing is, Eckubahn has probably been looking for you all this time, and finding no sign of us at all. That must have been frustrating. It's troublesome too. Just think of the power Fang must be able to unleash."

Nath clutched at his skull. "And I don't have Fang anymore! The elves do!" He staggered back, feeling all clammy inside. His greatest treasure was gone. It was unsettling. And being cooperative seemed to have only made things worse. If nothing else, he needed to secure his sword. A sinking feeling crept into his stomach. "Guards!"

Brenwar yelled too. "Guards!" And then he turned to Nath. "What are we yelling for?"

"Something about Slavan and this particular pack of elves bothers me. Does he not bother you? He was truthful in his words, but I sensed he wasn't telling it all." Nath grabbed onto the bars. "There was a shiftiness about him that made me very wary. Am I the only one who sensed it?"

"All elves bother me!" Brenwar threw up his arms. "I told you they couldn't be trusted. A dwarf, now, a dwarf you can trust. We don't lie about anything. We'd die first."

"This isn't about lies, this is about half-truths," Selene said, "And not about your blind loyalties to yourselves. You're a proud and stumpy little fool, no less corrupt than the high-and-mighty elves themselves."

"You watch your tongue. You're the last one who should talk about honesty!" Hands clutching the bars, Brenwar pulled himself up to see out and banged his head again. "Guards! Get me away from this scaly woman!"

Nath ran through his thoughts. Everything Slavan Fonjich had said rang true, but there were things Nath deduced from what the elf had avoided discussing. The elves fought among themselves. There was discord. A divide. The titans' presence filled the cities abroad, and people had flocked to them.

Hah! Eckubahn is no fool. He hasn't just been searching for me, but me and the sword. He sent the word out to every bounty hunter, cutthroat, and murderer all around, trying to manage my capture. I bet he's promised them the world.

A pit formed in Nath's gut. He hit the bars. "Guards!"

There was no response. Only the gentle flicker of the torches answered. The three of them were all alone, sealed away in the twist of the catacombs where no one would ever find them if they weren't wanted to be found.

"They'll be back. I'm sure they'll be back. No elf can do without taking a jab at a dwarf. Well, I've got some words for them. Plenty." Brenwar mumbled insults in Dwarven.

Fang had done his thing, had gotten Nath and his friends as far away as possible, but the plan had backfired. The Elven Field of Dreams should have been safe. It wasn't. The world had changed, and in his heart Nath knew Slavan and the elven guard had changed with it.

"Guards!" Brenwar said. "We need some food and fresh air! It smells like dirty elf down here."

Nath broke out his conclusion. "There aren't any guards, Brenwar. They took Fang, and they're gone."

"Gone! What about Mortuun!"

Nath closed his eyes and concentrated. He and Fang had become closer, and he didn't have to worry about the blade operating in the wrong hands. It could protect itself, but without the blade, he was almost defenseless against the giants and wurmers. That was hardly the problem now. He needed a way out of this cell.

Brenwar started ramming his shoulder into his iron door.

Wham! Wham! Wham!

"Will you stop doing that, Dwarf?" Selene said. "All you do is make noise."

"Perhaps Pepper will come for us," Nath said with a sigh.

Brenwar stopped his charge. "Pepper? He's too big to stuff his chubby behind through those holes. No chance that he will find us." He lowered his shoulder and started ramming again.

Wham! Wham! Wham!

"Selene," Nath said over the loud noise, "can you cast a spell to get us out?"

"I'll try." She muttered an incantation.

Zzzz-pap!

Pressing his face to the bars, Nath said, "Selene?" He looked at Brenwar. "Can you see her?"

"It's all smoky."

Nath bent his ear. He couldn't hear anything. A green smoke rolled by his eyes. "Selene, say something!"

"Something," she replied in a little bit of a moan.

Nath exhaled. "What happened?"

"I shot a charge into the bars, but they're too thick. Other than that, I'm all out of ideas. I'm sorry."

Squeezing the metal rods in his clawed hands, Nath said, "Yes, they are pretty thick. Perhaps..."

"Perhaps what?" Brenwar coughed and fanned the smoke from his face.

"I might be able to melt them."

"With your breath?" Selene said. "Can you do that now?"

"I can at least try. I know I've melted metal thicker than this before. But it was different then."

Not so long ago, he'd had dragon breath like a thousand infernos. He'd been a flying volcano. All-powerful. Capable of anything. Bars like this had been nothing. But he'd given all of that up. Given it up to save Selene. It was worth it, yet it still made him angry. He wanted to fly again. Have the dragon breath back.

Something stirred behind his breast. He took in a lungful of air, closed his eyes, channeled his energy, and envisioned turning the bars into liquid metal with a single huff. His lungs warmed.

Here goes!

He exhaled. Grey smoke rolled out of his mouth, filling his cell, filling the dungeon. In seconds, they all were covered in smoke so thick they couldn't see a hand in front of their face.

Everyone was coughing. Nath groaned and struck the bars. It hadn't worked. There was no way to escape, and it felt like time was running out.

CHAPTER
7

I T WAS QUIET. STARK. LONELY. The minutes were long, the hours like eons. Nath, being a dragon, wasn't bothered by the passing of time so much, except now. Now, he and his friends were trapped and left for dead. His stomach rumbled.

"Don't do that, Nath," Brenwar said from his cell. "I'm trying not to think of food. I'm a bit hungry, you know. A little parched. That battle with the giants expended my reserves."

"Sorry," Nath said, holding his stomach. Being hungry was hardly the immediate problem. He, Brenwar, and Selene could last for weeks like this, he figured. Being a dragon, chances were he'd hibernate.

Perhaps if I sleep, I'll wake up and have more dragon powers. It's happened before.

He couldn't bear the thought of anything happening to Brenwar, though. He'd have to think of something.

"Don't blame yourself, Nath." Brenwar's voice echoed in the chamber. "You need to focus. Think of a way out."

"We aren't all sitting here twiddling our thumbs, you know," Selene said with irritation in her voice. "Not that you could bring anything useful to the table."

"I can argue you to death anytime if that's the way you want to go! Have at it, then, you sorceress from the gates of the under realm!"

While Selene and Brenwar bickered back and forth, Nath closed his eyes and went into deep thought. His concern for his friends was heavy on his mind. The whereabouts of Bayzog, Ben, and Sasha worried him. And what of Sasha's condition? She wasn't well. Unstable. And then there was his father, Balzurth. Eckubahn was trying to bait the Dragon King. Draw him into a huge fight. Finish their rivalry once and for all. Without a doubt, all of them were in danger. Nath dipped his head into his hands.

And to think a year has passed! Eckubahn is the host in Narnum. People have started to worship him. So quickly? It's inconceivable.

Those were only a few of the items weighing on his mind. If he had to guess, Slavan and the rogue wilder elves had fallen in league with the enemy. Why else would they abandon him here? Would they come back and kill him and his friends? No, not even a fallen elf would have such blood on his hands. Instead, Nath and company were left to their own fate. And there was yet the major issue at hand. He'd been accused of murder! But Laedorn and Uurluuk's assassin was still out there. The dwarves and elves were hunting for him. But who had posed as him? There was only one creature on Nalzambor whom he knew for certain could do such a thing.

Gorlee!

The changeling knew about the bow, Akron. He was familiar with Ben and Bayzog. That was whom he had to find for answers. But Gorlee had been working with his father, Balzurth. Nath rubbed his temples.

See what a fine mess this world gets into if I'm not around? Maybe I'm useful after all.

He sulked in the darkness. Selene and Brenwar's bickering subsided. Nath counted down the hours that became a day. On and off, Brenwar would sing dwarven chants.

With an axe in one hand and a hammer in the other,
Uurluuk slew the giants.
With a brown beard filled with a jaw made of iron,
Uurluuk slew the giants.
With a tankard of ale and chest plate armor,
Uurluuk slew the giants.
He slew them, he slew them, and made a mighty stew of them!
He slew them, he slew them, and it wasn't hard to chew them.
With a missing eye and a belly full of ham,
Uurluuk slew the giants.
With a host of dwarves clad in nothing but muscle,
Uurluuk slew the giants.
With the sun in his eyes and the ogres at his back,
Uurluuk slew the giants.
He slew them, he slew them, and made a mighty stew of them!
He slew them, he slew them, and it wasn't hard to chew them.

The chant went on like that for half a day. Nath had his own songs that he could sing too, but he wasn't in the mood. It wouldn't do his mood a lot of good right now anyway. Back against the wall, facing his cell door, his eyes would open and close as he caught small naps between blinks.

A child-sized head appeared in the portal, between one blink and the other.

"Huh?" Nath leaned forward. There was nothing there.

I must be seeing things.

He leaned back against the wall, eyes open. A soft scuffle caught his ear. Two childlike hands grabbed one bar, and that small head came into view. A pair of little eyes was squinting, peering into the darkness of Nath's cell.

"Pepper?"

The figure dropped from sight.

Nath rushed for the door and grabbed the bars. "Pepper!"

"What's going on?" Brenwar's face was pressed to the bars. "That halfling wouldn't fit in here. Are you seeing things?"

"I see everything," Nath said with excitement, "and I saw Pepper. He was smaller."

"You dream, perhaps."

"I don't dream, at least not like that. No, it was him. Pepper! Pepper!" Nath's nostrils flared. He could smell the halfling now. Sense his warmth. "Where are you? Reveal yourself. Selene, can you see him?"

There was no answer.

"Selene?"

"At least she's quiet," Brenwar said.

Nath sniffed. "Pepper, I know you're in here. Please, reveal yourself."

"I'm here," said a little voice. It came from right outside Nath's cell door. "But how do I know that's you in there?"

"Pepper, it is me." Nath tried to peer downward. The halfling must have been right up against his door and out of his line of sight. "I'm the one who brought you to the Field of Dreams, by my sword, no less."

Brenwar managed to pull his face up to the bars. "I see him! I see him! Get us out of here, you walking mushroom!"

Backing up, Pepper stepped into Nath's view. He was barely three feet tall, if that. Just a little man with a mop of salt-colored hair and long, fuzzy sideburns. "I can see your eyes now. It is you." He reached over to the latch on the iron door and pulled the pin out of it. "Eh, there's still a lock on it. I'll go and find the key."

"No, wait!" Nath could see the fearfulness in Pepper's eyes. There was danger out there. He didn't like the thought of Pepper going beyond the threshold. He might not see Pepper again. He couldn't risk it. "Don't go just yet."

"But you need to get out. I need you to get out so I can get out. I'm lost."

Pepper vanished from sight. Nath's jaw tightened.

Please come back. Please come back.

CHAPTER 8

"WHERE DID HE GO?" BRENWAR asked. "Stupid halfling, where did you go?"

A strange groan of the living came from deep within the caverns. Dark and disturbing.

"What was that?" Brenwar said.

"I don't want to know."

Moments later, Pepper reappeared. "I can't find a key, and we ... we need to get out of here."

"What's out there?" Nath asked.

"I don't know, but I think it wants to eat me." The halfling eyeballed the lock, rubbed his chin, and tapped his foot. "You know, I used to be a locksmith. I think I can pick this." He reached into his trousers and produced a leather satchel. Gingerly, he unfolded the flap, revealing some metal utensils. He eyed a long, sharp, slender rod with key-like teeth on the end. "That should do it."

Nath heard the tool fishing around inside the lock.

Pop.

The door swung open.

"Well done, Pepper!"

The deep moan from the tunnels started again.

"Hurry, get the others out."

"Start with me," Brenwar demanded.

As Pepper worked the lock, Nath asked questions. "Pepper, why are you so small? What happened?"

"I don't know. One moment I'm sitting in the pond, big as a boulder, and the next thing I know I'm buried underneath a bunch of lily pads. That's when those elves showed up. They had a look about them, so I hid and watched them march you off. Huh, I don't think I can pick this lock open. It's stubborn." He looked up at Brenwar's face through the bars. "Go figure. Perhaps I should try the other."

The moaning came again, louder this time.

"You will open this one now!" Brenwar said with wide eyes.

Pepper started picking at the lock again. "Be silent. You're making me nervous. Anyway, I followed those elves to this place. Saw them depart and everything. Thirteen in and thirteen out, ladies included. My, they are something pretty. I snuck in to look for you, fell in a pit, climbed out, fell in a pit again, climbed out, got lost, and somehow found myself here." The lock popped open, and he let Brenwar out. "Whew, what a relief. Come on out, Grumpy."

Nath made his way over to Selene's cell and peered inside the barred portal. "Selene. Selene." He could see her body huddled in the corner, as if she was sleeping. "Selene, wake up."

She didn't stir.

"Pick it. Pick it now, Pepper."

A howling moan tore through the tunnels.

Pepper dropped his pick and snatched it up again. "I don't like the sound of that."

"Me neither," said Nath.

Working the lock, Pepper added, "It sounds big. Really big. But the tunnels are small. Maybe it's not that big at all." He twisted his tool in the keyhole. A click followed. "Got it. Three for three, not bad for an elder rogue, er, I mean an elder halfling."

Nath flung the door open and rushed inside. Selene wasn't moving, but she was breathing. He gave her a firm shake. "Selene. Selene. Wake up."

"She must be really, really tired." Pepper put his tools away. "And she looks heavy."

Nath scooped her up in his arms and tossed her over his shoulder. "Let's get out of here. Brenwar, lead the way."

"That's the best advice you've given in months." The dwarf marched them straight through the grand chamber of the Inner Sanctum of Lheme. The gorgeous room was far from threatening. If anything, it was peaceful, and a pair of torches still flickered. He cut right through the middle of it and made a beeline straight for the archway that they came through to begin with. "This way."

From down the dark corridor, a loud moan hit Nath right in the face, jangling his nerves.

Pepper covered his ears.

Spinning on his heel, Brenwar pointed to another exit on the right side of the chamber. "That way sounds better."

With Selene over his shoulders, Nath followed the dwarf. "We don't know where that goes."

"It's got to go somewhere, and if I can't find it, by my beard, I'm not dwarven."

Nath snatched a torch off the wall and handed it to Pepper. He had plenty of faith in Brenwar. None knew their way underground better. Facing whatever guardian roamed the tunnels was a different matter entirely. Aside from his claws and his tail, they didn't have any weapons to defend themselves.

Selene was out of commission. Out in a strange way.

Ahead, Brenwar marched through every twist and turn, choosing the way at forks instantly. "This way. This way." The only time he came to a stop was at a triple fork in the corridor, and even then he only scratched the back of his head with his skeleton hand before he headed into the one in the middle. "This way."

They were moving along at a brisk pace when Pepper, looking side to side and back and forth, gave a warning. "There are pits. Be wary. You move too quickly."

"If there's a pit, I'll find it before it finds me." Brenwar argued. "Come on, then, I sense a twinge of fresh air this *gaaaaaaaah*!"

The floor opened up underneath them, and the company plummeted down. Nath hit the bottom hard, with Selene landing on him and knocking the wind from him.

Pepper lay on Brenwar's broad chest. "I *told* you about the pits. But you didn't listen. I knew it. I knew it." He glanced up. "My, this is a deep one. Really deep. I'd say fifty feet at least."

Pushing himself up onto his elbows, Brenwar replied, "More like thirty."

"Heh, look at this." Pepper held up a skeleton's head. "It matches your hand."

Nath propped Selene against the wall and stood up. The pit floor crunched beneath his toes. Bones were everywhere. The walls were sheer and high. He stuck his claws into the rough-hewn stone. "I can't jump to that ledge, but I think I can climb out. No worries. Hauling Selene out will be the difficulty."

The howl returned. It was right on them, a thunderous moaning that brought out the goosebumps on every inch of Nath's skin.

Pepper's lips peeled back in a horrified smile. He covered his ears once more.

Brenwar stood up with a grunt. "I've never heard a sound like that before. It's as awful as an elven accordion."

The death moan continued. Louder. Closer. Debris and dirt from the rafters high above rained down into the pit. The vile and horrible sound cut to the bone.

Nath balled up his fists. Whatever it was, spirit or beast, he'd fight it with everything he had left. "Pepper, get behind me."

"I already am."

CHAPTER 9

T HE EAR-SPLITTING MOAN CAME AGAIN. It was right on them. Nath feared nothing, but that sound made his skin crawl and his stomach churn. Whatever it was should've woken the dead, but Selene didn't stir.

Pepper clamped onto Nath's leg with his eyes squeezed shut. "Save me, save me!"

Head tilted toward the clamor above, Brenwar picked up a thighbone and walked backward.

Two huge sets of claws appeared on the lip of the pit's edge. They dug into the stone. A frightening howl started up again, shaking the very earth, weakening Nath in the knees. He set his jaw and prepared himself for an epic battle against the monster that waited above.

The horrifying sound came to a stop. Over the ledge, a head on a long neck revealed itself. It had four long horns stretching along its neck. A beard of skin and scales started underneath the monster's jowls and ran down its neck. It cocked its head and looked at Nath with bright-green eyes, opened its mouth, and said, "Urp?"

The pounding in Nath's chest slowed. He said in Dragonese, "Hello, thunder beard."

The dragon's tongue flicked out of his mouth. His head was small, compared to his claws. He hissed at Nath, lowered his head into the pit, and said again, "Urp?"

"Come, come down," Nath said in Dragonese. "Come, friend, please."

The dragon shook himself, flapping his beard.

"What *is* that thing?" asked Brenwar.

"A dragon. A thunder beard. They make excellent guardians. Not too big or violent, but their roar can scare a hundred bull dragons away." Nath extended his clawed hand upward. "Come, come down, little brother."

The dragon slithered over the edge and stuck to the wall of the pit like a great lizard. His body was long and lean, his feet very big and awkward. He had no wings, but a very long tail. His scales were green and blue with some pink mixed in. He climbed down the wall and crept by Brenwar, flicking his tongue at the dwarf.

Nath kneeled down and petted the dragon's head. "You had us terrified, little brother."

The small dragon batted his snake eyes. "Urp."

Stretching his small hand out, Pepper said, "Will he bite?"

"No, not now at least. We're in good company. As a matter of fact," Nath said, picking Pepper up, "I think you're just small enough to ride him, if he'll let you."

"Hey, wait," Pepper objected, "I'm too old to start riding dragons!"

"Just hang on to his horns," Nath said, "and have a go at it."

Pepper clenched his teeth and hung onto the horns of the dragon. The beast lurched forward and then, smooth as spider silk, it raced up the pit wall and vanished.

"Harrumph," Brenwar said. "You don't see *that* every day, but the rest of us are still stuck in here."

"I'll be back. Just keep an eye on Selene." Nath dug his claws into the stone wall and made his ascent.

"It's not like she's going anywhere. Just make it fast. I don't want to be stuck down here when she wakes up."

Nath pushed up over the lip of the pit and found Pepper still on the back of the dragon. The old halfling had a smile on his face. "Aw, you like it, don't you?"

"As long as it keeps its mouth shut, I think I could get used to it."

Nath started to yell down into the pit just as Brenwar flung the torch up. Smiling, he called down to his oldest friend, "You read my mind." He found another torch in the tunnel and lit it along with a couple more. "We need some rope, or a ladder or something."

"Do you think he can help?" Pepper said of the bearded dragon.

"Perhaps." Nath spoke in Dragonese some more, asking the dragon where the materials he could use might be. The dragon made a rattle in his throat and took off with Pepper.

"Eeee! Where is he taking me?"

Nath didn't answer, just watched Pepper's torchlight disappear around the bend. And then he dropped one of his torches down into the pit. "Heads up."

Brenwar snatched it out of the air. "What do you want me to do with this?"

"Stay cozy."

"Pah."

It was more than an hour before Pepper and the dragon returned. The halfling held a coil of rope—and Nath noticed a shiny new ring on his hand. He took the rope from Pepper. "Where did you get that?"

Pepper covered his ring with his free hand. "The rope?"

"No, the ring."

Cupping his ear, Pepper said, "Huh?"

Lowering one end of the rope into the pit, Nath said a little louder, "I said where did you get the *ring*?"

"Pardon?" Pepper said.

From down inside the hole, Brenwar yelled, "What ring are you talking about?"

"I'm not talking to you," Nath said down to Brenwar. "I'm talking to Pepper."

"Oh."

Holding the rope tight in one hand, Nath grabbed Pepper's ring hand with the other. "Where did that come from?"

"Oh, *that* ring. Well, the dragon led me to the most marvelous place... Actually, it's not anything you should worry yourself about, but that's where the rope came from. We really need to get out of here." Pepper rubbed his narrow shoulders. "It's chilly."

Nath noticed a bulging leather pouch tied to the back of Pepper's trousers. He snatched it.

Pepper objected. "Hey!"

Nath emptied the pouch on the ground. Gold coins and gemstones spilled out. "Did this dragon take you to its trove?"

Pepper scooped up the treasure and shrugged.

Brenwar emerged from the pit, sniffing the air. "I smell gold."

Nath looked down at his friend. "Aren't you forgetting something?"

"No."

"Selene. You were supposed to tether up Selene."

Brenwar leaned over the hole. "I didn't see the point in it. I say leave her here. Let her sleep."

"Guzan!" Nath stuffed the rope into Brenwar's hands, glared at him, and hopped into the pit. He loaded Selene over his shoulder, and hand over hand, he climbed back out of the pit. When he got to the top, he said to Brenwar, "You really should know better by now."

Brenwar grumbled and turned away.

Nath then said to Pepper, "Were there any weapons where you went?"

Looking up and seeming to see far away, Pepper said, "Yes, I believe so."

"Good, because we're going to need them."

CHAPTER
10

THE SMALL BEARDED DRAGON LED them to a cave full of supplies. Everything from weapons and armor to dried rations and kegs of wine. Brenwar sat on a bench at a table, helping himself to some jerky and remarking at the horrible taste of the elven wine as he guzzled one goblet after the other.

"We are most fortunate," Nath said, strapping on a belt and scabbard. He had an elven longsword in his hand. He cut the air. It was well balanced. Finely crafted. He tried to find some clothing in some chests, but everything was too small for him. He grabbed an oblong shield. "Why not?"

Finishing his food, Brenwar came across some dwarven arms. He hefted a battle-axe with a handle carved from black wood. "Not bad."

Nearby, standing atop a table, Pepper managed to make a fitting shirt from an elven jerkin. He cut the sleeves down and stitched up the neck. Spinning on the table, he said, "How do I look?"

"Old and stupid," Brenwar said.

Pepper shook his head. "It's a good thing I don't understand Dwarven."

"I didn't say it in Dwarven." Brenwar turned to Nath. "Now what?"

"I'd be lying if I didn't admit I was a tad fearful of what we might face out there. One year gone, and now it sounds like the entire world hunts me again." Nath sighed. "We need to get our weapons back. But even more, we need to clear my name."

"The dwarves won't stop until they find you. That's for sure." Brenwar rubbed his beard. "And I don't think those rogue elves are angling to turn you in, either. No, they have something else up their sleeves."

"I'm of the impression they're trying to appease the titans." Nath pushed the hair out of the pretty closed eyes of Selene, who was lying on a bear rug on the floor. "I do wish you would wake up. I could use some of those thoughts of yours."

"I know you don't like it, but she might be safest here. She'll just slow us down." Brenwar swung his axe around his head. "Let your dragon friend keep an eye on her."

"That's what you did for me, isn't it?" Nath was referring to what had happened to him. He had slept more than twenty-five years—the longest slumber of his life, but not the only long one. What if this was a long sleep for Selene? He placed his hand on her cheek. The skin was smooth and warm. It stirred him. "I just can't do that. Not here anyway. Perhaps somewhere else."

"The Mountain of Doom, perhaps?"

"They'll be watching, that much is for sure." Nath picked Selene back up and placed her over his shoulder. "Let's get out of here."

"Where are we going?"

Nath had to make a decision. It wasn't easy. He was worried about his friends Ben and Bayzog. His father, Balzurth. But the other mystery bothered him most in the moment. It fluttered in his guts. Slavan and the rogue elves. They'd taken his sword, and wherever they had gone with Fang, that was where he would find answers. "We're going after the weapons."

Brenwar slapped his hands together. "That's what I like to hear. They're no more than a day off. We can catch them."

"Only if they don't catch us first. And remember, we're deep in elven territory. I'm sure we'll be noticed if we're not careful."

Brenwar dug some traveling cloaks out of a chest.

"I don't think that's going to work," Pepper said. "They're too small for him."

Brenwar tossed one to Nath. "Just try it on."

Nath slipped it on. The elves were skinny, so it was snug, but it fit. He wrapped Selene in one against the cold and put her gently back over his shoulders. "Let's give it a go, shall we?"

Getting out of the Inner Sanctum didn't prove to be too difficult, and to Nath's surprise, the bearded dragon agreed to come with them. Pepper never even left his back. Before long, they found the trail of Slavan and the rogue elves. It led them right out of the Elven Field of Dreams.

That's where the trouble started. Less than a league west of the fields and having avoided any scouting eyes, the rogue elves' trail took a new form.

"That's just great," Brenwar said. He was kneeling down with his hand in the impression of a hoof print. "They took up on horseback."

It was another one of those times that Nath regretted giving up the ability to fly. But not really. Saving Selene had been worth it.

No, that would make things all too easy.

Standing among the small bushes that popped up like mushrooms in the rolling greenery of the elven lands, he scanned the horizon. It shouldn't be too hard to follow them. So he walked. They all trotted all day long and through the night with no sleep, until the next morning. They were still a day's journey from escaping the territory of the vigilante eyes of the elves. Cutting through the tall grasses, they kept their distance from the villages and farmlands. Though peaceful, the elves didn't take in strangers. It was uncommon for anyone without elven blood to pass through without elven company.

"I can't wait to get out of this place," Brenwar said, looking from side to side. "Every step is dreaded. I feel like an elf is about to pop out of the grasses at any moment."

"Agreed," Nath said, but he was confident that his keen sight and hearing would pick up any sign of trouble. He'd noticed very little so far. "Huh."

"Huh, what?" Brenwar asked.

Ahead a few hundred yards was a stretch of farmland. The cornfields should have had a golden hue among the green this time of harvest, but what Nath spied was dingy and gray. He headed in that direction. The closer they got, the more the fields were in decay, and the rot continued as far as the eye could see. The aqueducts that watered the fields were dried up as well. The storehouses and sheds were disheveled and in disorder.

A morbid feeling crept between Nath's shoulders. "It's no wonder we haven't seen any elves about. Their lands have been poisoned. They've fortified closer to Elome, if not within. This is dreadful."

Brenwar picked up a husk of corn and chucked it away. "I hate to admit the same, but I agree." He raised his battle-axe with a white-knuckled grip on the haft. "Do you hear that?"

"I hate to admit that I do," Nath said. He could feel the ground moving under his feet.

Pepper stood on the back of the bearded dragon, cupping his ear. "Hear what?"

"Hooves. Dozens of them, but I don't see anything coming," Nath said. "I can only feel ... oh." Coming from the north, a cloud of dust stirred up like a storm. A row of horsemen came, the likes of which Nath had never seen before. He uttered a command. "Hide!"

CHAPTER
11

NATH AND COMPANY DUCKED INTO a storage shed. Through the cracks between the planks of wood, he watched the horde that thundered their way. It was massive men on massive beasts. Orcs by the looks of them, on horse-like creatures the size of two stallions with curved tusks on the sides of their heads.

"Barnum's beard! Those orcs only have one eye!" Brenwar exclaimed. "And I've never seen horses like that before. I guess you'd have to be awfully ugly to allow an orc to ride on you."

The knot of brutes approached at rapid speed, over a dozen in all. The orcen cyclopes were powerfully built and ugly, carrying lances and spears. Armored from head to toe in heavy gear and approaching the fields Nath and his friends hid within, they slowed to a trot less than one hundred yards away.

"What are orcs doing on elven land?" Nath said. "One eyed or not, they should be cut down."

"Aye. Those hounds would normally be cut down if they came so far as an inch over the borders," Brenwar said, clawing at his beard.

"It explains why we haven't seen any elves this far out, I guess."

"What do we do?" Pepper asked. "I'm not much of a fighter, but I'm a good hider."

"If we get into a scrap, you ride on that thunder beard and get out of here, Pepper," Nath said. "That dragon can't fly, but he's fast. Really fast. Just be sure to hang on tight."

"I wouldn't feel right, leaving you fellas behind."

Nath patted the old halfling's shoulder. "Don't worry about it. I'm sure you have a family or village you should seek out."

"No," Pepper replied. "I'm a loner. Have been a long, long time."

"Well, you aren't anymore, so worst case scenario, run and get help."

Pepper objected, "But—"

With his eye to a hole in the wall, Brenwar hissed, "Keep it down. They're upon us."

The horse-like beasts' heads were down to the ground, sniffing the earth like hound dogs. A rattle of metal sounded from the weapons harnessed to their large saddles. The orc cyclopes, burly and battered, towered in the saddle. They studied the land before them with hard beady eyes. They were hunters. Killers. One looked as dangerous as the other.

"Oh my," Pepper said in a hushed voice. He was trembling. "They seem much more intimidating now that I'm so much smaller."

"Be silent. It doesn't matter how big they are—they're orcs," Brenwar reminded them. "I'll take every last one of them if I have to. You'll see."

"Now's not the time to be stirred up." Nath's hand fell on his sword. "Lie low. Pray they don't notice us."

It couldn't have been a worse situation. There wasn't anywhere to run or hide. They only had the cover of the old storehouses and barns, and that was little. No, they were surrounded by endless farmlands and meadows without a better place to hide in sight. No river or stream to hide their trail. No mountains to lose the cyclopes in.

Nath was more than ready to fight. And even carrying Selene, he and Pepper and the bearded dragon could run. They would be fleet enough. But not Brenwar. The dwarf couldn't outrun a one-legged elf on his best day. And Nath feared Brenwar's loud protests if he offered to carry the dwarf or suggested he ride with Pepper on the bearded dragon.

Eyes on Nath, Brenwar said, "Take her and go. I can handle them."

"No, whatever happens, you and I stay together." Nath extended his hand. "To the end."

Brenwar clasped his hand. "Aye, I like it."

One of the beasts snorted. The monster mounts were right next to the shed they were in. Nath's heart raced. Once again, he was small among a new world of bigger men. He didn't like it, but sometimes the small can be overlooked.

Breathless, Nath watched the heavy-hooved beasts stomp toward them. One shook itself and let out an awful nicker.

"HrAAAAA huh huh huh huh huh."

"Grah! Grah!" the orcen cyclops rider said, tugging at the reins. The troupe of ghastly riders was only a few steps away. Alongside the shack, the rider brought its mount to a stop. It sniffed the air. "I smell. I smell foulness in the air."

Looking at Pepper, Nath put his finger to his lips.

The halfling nodded.

The cyclops poked the shack with its lance. *Tap! Tap! Tap!* It grunted. Its beast snorted. It pulled the lance up. "Onward."

The orcen cyclopes were moving on. Ten yards away. Twenty. The tightness in Nath's chest started to ease. He smiled at Brenwar.

"Hold!" the huge orc suddenly yelled. It snorted the air again with big, wide nostrils. Its horse did the same. It turned its mount back toward the shed. "I smell. I smell a dwarf in there! My nose does not fail me! Surround it! Dwarf, I say, come out!"

Gripping his axe in two hands, Brenwar said under his beard, "I'll come out, gladly."

"Just a moment," Nath said, pulling Brenwar back. He looked at Selene. "We can't just dive into this. Pepper, don't hesitate to run. Just go. We'll offer you a distraction for getting away. And don't look back either."

"I'm no coward," Pepper said.

"Dwarf! I smell you! Come out! Your bearded face will adorn my lance!" yelled the giant one-eyed orc.

Shrugging, Pepper added, "Well, not a full-blooded coward, that is."

"You stay here, both of you," Nath said, getting up. "Perhaps I can talk us out of this."

"Are you mad? Why don't you just let me cut off your head and throw it to them?" Brenwar said.

"Because that would defeat the purpose of me talking to them." Nath plucked away Pepper's purse. Hands and head concealed within his cloak, Nath stepped out into view. The entire shack was surrounded by the extra huge orcs on their enormous beasts.

I must look like a child to them.

"We are weary travelers, just passing through. We don't want any trouble."

The cyclops with its face adorned with small chains and a bone through its nose said, "Your travels are at an end."

"I plead for mercy. We are of no consequence. Just migrating from one safe hovel to another." He held out the purse. "I can pay for safe passage."

The orc leaned forward in his saddle. "I smell a dwarf. I hate dwarves."

"I can't say I blame you," Nath agreed. "They are irritating people, but he is our guide in these treacherous times."

"Send him out, and we shall relieve you of him and your gold. Then, I shall consider whether or not I let you live."

Under his cloak, Nath sneered. He hated the orcs as much as Brenwar did.

Stupid. Arrogant. Smelly and difficult. There was nothing noble about a single one of them. Despite the one eye, these weren't different than the average orc in demeanor, just bigger and more amplified. They were eight feet tall, solid in build, and hardened by raids and battle. Their strange beasts were something different altogether—flat headed, hard skulled, and deadly. A single one of them could trample an entire halfling village.

Nath shook his head no. "Take the gold. I offer you no more and no less."

The orc's canine teeth jutted up from its bottom jaw in a cruel smile. "I'm going to enjoy this." It barked an order to the other orcs. "File in. We're gonna run these trespassers through!"

CHAPTER 12

"AW, FINE THEN!" BRENWAR EMERGED from the shack. "You want to fight me? I'll fight every last one of you spangbockers!"

The orcen cyclopes turned and rode away a little ways on pounding hooves. One hundred paces away, they turned and paused. The wind pushed down the high grasses, and their black-and-silver streaked flag waved like a banner of death.

Brenwar set his feet.

Nath took his hood down and drew his elven sword. "Guard the shack."

"To the death," Brenwar replied.

Nath had been in plenty of scrapes with orcs before, but this was different. He didn't have Fang, nor most of his powers. The orcs had been more manageable back then. Nath had been quicker, smarter, and able to outwit them most of the time. But this battle? It was going to be brute force against brute force. He didn't have any more dragon fire or extra scales to save him. And to top it off, these giant one-eyed versions were an abomination.

Raising his lance high, the orcen cyclops leader bellowed a command. The entire row of riders lowered their spears and lances. All at once, they charged.

The ground quaked. The boards of the shack rattled. Nath braced himself for the oncoming wave of terror. Fifty horse lengths. Forty horse lengths. Thirty lengths. Twenty.

"Nobody tramples a dwarf!" Brenwar yelled.

Pepper squeezed between Nath and Brenwar on the back of the thunder beard.

"I told you to run, Pepper. Run! Get out of here!" Nath said.

"It's not me, it's him," Pepper said.

CRAIG HALLORAN

The thunder beard eased in front of all of them, coiled back his head, and opened his jaws wide. He let out a ground-shaking roar that filled the valley.

"RRRRRRRAAWWRRRRRRRRR!"

The demonic horses reared up. Some halted dead in their tracks. Others skidded. The giant one-eyed orc riders were tossed and toppled. Several of the strange horses bolted, dragging their riders by the stirrups. The terrifying squad of blood-mad soldiers had been turned to chaos.

Sword high, Nath charged and cried out, "Dragon! Dragon!"

"For Morgdon!"

It's me against them! There's no other way!

He had to strike, and strike fast. Nath swatted a jabbing spear aside and ran a giant orc through. Other cyclopes were scrambling for their gear. Using what quickness he still had in him, Nath attacked. He caught one orc in the backside and sent it howling. Another he stuck in the chest.

Wham!

Something heavy clobbered Nath in the back. Shooting stars blinded his sight. A boot stomping in the ground caught his ear. The sound of a heavy weapon descending on him urged his desperate movement. He rolled to the left, evading the huge hammer that bit into the ground. He hopped to his feet and swung. Metal bit into metal, and a monstrous voice wailed. A giant orc fell. Regaining his sight, Nath waded into an angry knot of fighters that had surrounded Brenwar.

The husky dwarf was bleeding and yelling, "Come, you smelly two-legged trees!"

Nath propelled himself into the back of one giant orc and stabbed the arm of another. The orcs fought back with fury. Obstinate and angry, they were born fighters. Even if they were overly matched, they'd fight to the end, most of the time. That wasn't the case this day. Big and strong, they had numbers. The clash of steel on steel and flesh and bone shifted back and forth.

Back to back, Nath and Brenwar kept the horde at bay.

Clang! Bash! Glitch! Slice!

Nath and Brenwar were holding up just fine, out-quickening the lesser-skilled orcen fighters. Together, they had just brought one down with a pair of heavy chops when a pair of riders burst through their own ranks and plowed right over the both of them.

Flat on his back, Nath fought to rise again. One of the demon beasts pinned him down with its hooves. The orcen cyclops leader lorded over him with a crude sword in one hand and Selene's limp form hanging by the hair in the other.

The cyclops orc rumbled a wicked laugh. "Scales, scales, scales. Tsk, tsk, I know someone who will give a kingdom for the people that walk with scales. The question is, are you worth more dead, or alive?" He kicked Nath's elven sword away, pulled down his hood, and rolled up his sleeve. "My, my, it's the one and only Nath Dragon. Har! The titans will be pleased!" He slugged Nath in the jaw. "Very pleased."

CHAPTER
13

NATH AND BRENWAR WERE BOUND up with chains and marched toward the orcen city of Thraag. Selene was still in her deep sleep, slung over one of the demon horses' saddle. Pepper and the thunder beard were gone. Long gone, Nath hoped.

At least he was finally smart enough to listen.

"Orc," Nath said to the leader, "what do you call your beasts? And yourself. I like to have some familiarity with my captors. The rapport can be soothing on both sides."

Jaw jutted out, the orc glanced back at Nath. "I am Gaak. One of the nuurg. The steeds are wrathhorns. We orcs now breed them."

Brenwar stared up into the cyclops orc's one eye. "Breed with them, is more like it."

"Go ahead and delight, dwarf. We'll see how much you have to say after we shave your beard and make you eat it."

"What's a nuurg?" Nath asked.

"We are the nuurg. The new giants. The usurpers of lands. Servants of the great titans." The huge one-eyed orc spat. "Conquerors we are. Invincible."

"No one is invincible. You've certainly heard of Gorn Grattack and the Clerics of Barnabus?" Nath inquired. "He was quite mighty, I assure you."

The orc growled in his throat. "Not mighty enough to win. The titans will never lose. They will defeat Balzurth. We will inherit all the treasure in the Mountain of Doom. You'll see soon enough."

"I'll never understand why orcs are so overconfident," Brenwar whispered to Nath. "They've never won a major battle in all my centuries."

It was true. The orcs, though many, fought among themselves as much as with the various races. They had never been fully united. But Nath knew that strong leadership could change all that. It had just been a long, long time since they had any. Under the guidance of the titans, the orcs could be galvanized and turned into a great weapon of destruction.

It started to rain. The dirt road became sloppy, and before long they were trudging through the mud into a land where the trees had more bark than leaves. The orcen land that surrounded Thraag was mostly briars and stone. The brush was thick, and hungry vermin cawed and hissed as they passed by. Nath wasn't so much worried about himself as he was his friend. Brenwar would be killed. He was certain of it. And it wouldn't be quick. The orcs would torment and humiliate him. *I can't think of a much worse scenario than this. I have to find a way to save Brenwar and Selene.*

Tethered to the wrathhorns, their march was hard. Yanked by one of the beasts, Brenwar stumbled and was dragged. With a face filled with mud, he climbed up on his feet again and jerked back. It was futile to fight against the pull of the powerful beasts. They were thrice as strong and just as ugly as the orcs that rode on their backs.

Nath had a natural affection for all living creatures, but the wrathhorns were something else entirely. An evil breed. Bone-crushing war rides. There were bloodstains on their tremendous spiked hooves. He made a count. There were just eight riders left, but it wasn't likely he could take them all while tethered like this. Not and protect his friends too. The only option was to find a narrow break in the terrain where the huge mounts and orcs couldn't go—and hide. The problem was Selene.

How am I going to get her?

Selene's body was draped over the front of the leader's saddle.

Don't lose hope, Nath. Just think of something.

Doubt crept into his mind, and the pounding rain seemed to weaken his limbs. He didn't have the power he'd had before. In the form of a dragon, he could level mountains, cities. Now, he felt like an insect. He still hadn't adjusted to it. He thought he had, but had not. When he was young, there had been giants running around everywhere, but life had been more manageable. Now, it had all changed. He was the little fish in the big pond. He ground his teeth.

This stinks.

The nuurg leader raised his hand up and came to a stop. "Ho." He eyed the sky and all around.

"Problem?" Nath said, walking up alongside the giant orc leader's saddle.

Rain running down his furrowed brow, the nuurg leader said, "Something stinks."

"Yes," Nath said, looking at him and his dirt-marred skin, "I'd think you'd be used to that by now. These rains present an excellent opportunity to wash yourself."

The orc cyclops leered at him. "Quiet." He pointed at two of his followers. "Ride up. I sense an ambush near."

The riders on the wrathhorns thundered by Nath, splashing him with mud and bumping him down to one knee.

It was Nath's turn to look around. With all the heavy rain it was difficult to see anything, but nothing seemed out of the ordinary. It was strange. Why would the orc cyclopes be worried about an ambush on their own land?

It doesn't make any sense. Perhaps even these monsters are divided against one another. Interesting.

Minutes passed.

"So are we going to stand here all day?" Brenwar said.

"You're safer here than where we're going," Nath said, wiping the rain from his eyes. "And it's not like you to be in a hurry."

"Hanging around you makes me rush things." Brenwar looked at the huge cyclopes on the backs of the beasts and shook his head. "It's not right."

A few minutes later, one of the riders reappeared and said to the leader, "It's clear. Holorf still scouts ahead. He'll await us at the next fortress. Send up fire if there is trouble."

The leader, Gaak, nodded. "Let's go, then. We have great treasure. Ale and females shall meet us at the gates!" He snapped his reins. The beast lurched forward. Gaak slung forth his hand. "Howhaho!"

"Well," Nath said to Brenwar, "at least you're going to get a closer look at a city you've never seen before. They say it's not half bad once you get used to the smell."

Brenwar shook his head no.

Out of nowhere, an arrow rocketed through the rain and impaled Gaak's sleeve.

He roared and cried out, "Ambush! Ride hard for the city!"

Nath ran apace.

Brenwar was jerked off his feet and dragged by the wrathhorns. With a mouthful of mud, he yelled, "No one drags a dwarf!"

Arrows whistled through the air.

Zing! Zing! Zing! Zing!

A cyclops toppled from his mount with an arrow in his side. An arrow struck another rider in the skull, but that nuurg fighter kept riding.

Still tethered, Nath kept running.

It was a crossfire. Beasts and riders went down. Three arrows feathered an orc in the chest. Another arrow struck a beast in the hide of its hindquarters, rearing it up and toppling its rider.

Nath hopped on the chest of a cyclops that was being dragged by one of its feet, which was caught in the stirrup. He found his elven sword harnessed to the beast's saddle, drew it out, and cut his bonds, yelling, "Brenwar! Brenwar!"

Being dragged behind a wrathhorn, the dwarf managed to sit up. "What?"

Nath flung the sword end over end. It sliced through the taut rope that secured Brenwar.

The dwarf diminished in the distance but was up and running after him.

Nath hauled himself up into the beast's saddle and took the reins. With the beast still dragging the dead cyclops, he dug his heel into the mount's ribs. "Yah! Yah!"

The wrathhorn reared up, clawed the air with its hooves, landed back on its front hooves, and stopped. Its head swung around and bit into Nath's arm.

"Sultans of Sulfur!" Nath cried out. Ahead, Gaak and the surviving riders were getting away in long, fast strides. "Release me, beast! I have to get Selene."

A heavy fog rolled in. Selene and the riders were gone.

CHAPTER 14

THE WRATHHORN BUCKED, TURNED ITS head, and slung Nath out of the saddle by the arm with its teeth. Wrist deep in the mud, Nath got up. The beast lowered its head with the curved horns out and charged. Spiked hooves splatted through the mud and water and bore down on Nath.

At the last moment, Nath jumped high, sailing over its head.

The wrathhorn kept going, making a startling whine and not looking back.

Puffing for breath, Brenwar caught up with Nath. "There goes your ride."

Nath scoffed. "They still have Selene. You stay here. I'm going after them on foot." He started to run. A huge winged creature dropped out of the sky and onto the road, cutting off his path. "Sansla Libor!" Nath said.

Half a dozen roamer elves emerged from the rough woodland and encircled them. They were tall and hardy, long haired, with swords strapped beneath their round bellies. The tallest of them all was Shum, and his brother Hoven was there too. Their piercing eyes bore into Nath and Brenwar. "Hail and well met, old friend."

"Hail nothing, Shum," Nath said. "I don't have time for chatter. The nuurg have Selene! I must rescue her."

Shum and Hoven blocked his path. Hoven spoke. "You must come with us immediately."

Nath busted right between them.

Head to toe in mud, Brenwar was right on his heels. "Out of the way, elven bellies!"

Nath found himself face to face with the great white winged ape, Sansla Libor the King of the Roamers. The cursed elf was as big as ever, layered with bulging muscles under his fur. His chest was broader than those of three strong men. His eyes were sky blue, but with a savageness behind them. He held out his oversized hands, and towering over Nath, he said, "Stop, Nath Dragon."

Not hiding the urgency brewing within him, Nath said, "I'll do no such thing. Now get out of my way."

"Aye!" Brenwar agreed.

"I cannot. You must come now."

"No, I must *go* now." Nath got a run and jumped over the great ape.

Sansla, quick as a big cat, sprang into the air and dragged Nath down by the ankles.

Floundering in the mud, Nath kicked the gorilla-like beast in the chest. Sansla slammed him to the ground. Nath flipped Sansla off his back, drew back his scaled fist, and hit Sansla square in the face.

A savage snarl erupted from Sansla's black lips. He attacked Nath with savage fury. Fists the size of hams hammered into his body with bone-jarring ferocity.

Nath's temper ignited. He'd been holding back—against the rogue elves, the nuurg, and the wrathhorns. Selene was being taken. He'd hold back no more. He cocked back his fist and hit Sansla as hard as he could.

"Oof!" The mighty ape doubled over, clutching his belly.

Nath whaled on him, blow after blow after blow. "Stay out of my way!"

Sansla balled up and covered his face with his fists. He got peppered with lightning-quick jabs. Harder and faster they came.

Wham! Wham! Pap! Pap! Pap!

With fire in his eyes, chest heaving, Nath backed off. "Leave me be!"

Standing in the pouring rain, nose bleeding, Sansla rose to full height and spread his wings out and back in, and with seriousness he said, "I cannot." His head ticked left. He tensed up, visibly fighting the growing rage within. "You must listen."

Nath wanted to fight. To finish it. He could not tell if Sansla was being truthful or just a thorn in his side. He pointed at the winged ape. "You'd be wise to leave me be." He turned and ran. The elves closed in and piled on him.

"You must listen to us," Shum said, grappling Nath by the arms. "It is urgent!"

Covered in elves as big as he, Nath slung them off one at a time.

They kept coming.

Brenwar dove into the fray. "Foolish elves! I'll snap your bones like twigs."

In a brutal moment, Nath and Brenwar were swinging hard in a tangled knot of bodies. The elves, skilled and quick, wrapped up Nath, time after time. He slung them off again. Brenwar busted faces and bruised bones with powerful punches. The roamers would not give. Limping and bleeding, they pulled both fighters down into the slippery mud, time and time again. Nath's restless energy fueled his might. Quicker and faster, he wore them down. Brenwar, a battle-tested iron tree stump, fought with the fury of a dozen storms. A loyal hound, fighting to the death.

Pinned down in Nath's grip, Hoven choked out, "Nath, you must listen."

Nath shoved him face first into the mud. "I'm done listening!"

Brenwar slammed his shoulder into another one of the elves, freeing up a path.

Hair streaming like a banner behind him, Nath dashed down the muddy road, leaving the elves to battle the angry dwarf for themselves. Moving with the speed of a great antelope, he traversed the sloppy trail ahead of him, determined to track Selene down and finish off her captors.

Sansla Libor swooped down through the rain and plucked him up off the ground and soared back up into the air. "You must not resist, Dragon Prince! A moment, listen, please, listen!"

"There's no time!" Nath screamed from a hundred feet in the air. He could make out Gaak and the other nuurg fighters charging toward the great stone outposts of the city of Thraag. They were much closer than he realized. The fortress was heavily fortified and guarded. "Sansla, do as I say and let me save Selene!"

"I cannot. I have my orders," Sansla said. He started flying away from Thraag. "You are coming with me."

Fighting to free himself, Nath kicked and yelled, "Whose orders?"

"Your mother, Grahleyna, sent me with the utmost urgency."

Nath was so worried about Selene that his mother's name almost didn't register, but he asked, "Why?"

"It's your father. Balzurth has gone missing."

Wind and rain tearing at his face, Nath said, "It will have to wait."

"It cannot," Sansla argued. "You must come, and come now. Time is precious. We cannot lose it."

"I cannot lose *her*!" Nath pulled his legs up and walloped Sansla right in the face.

The great winged ape's grip loosened.

Nath twisted away and plummeted to the ground. He smashed into a pile of heavy brush. Charged with desperate energy, he sprang back to his feet. Knees jarred, he nevertheless bulldozed through the brush and down the road after Selene. He gained ground, just enough to see Gaak and the riders vanish into the sanctuary of the fortress's ominous gates. From the twenty-foot-high parapets, the orcen cyclops soldiers on the wall unleashed a volley of heavy crossbow bolts at him.

Zip! Zip! Zip!

A new squad of pure-blooded orcen riders, at least twenty, charged. They were accompanied by three of the one-eyed orcen nuurgs riding on the backs of wrathhorns galloping out of the fortress.

Nath sank to his knees. Selene was gone. His eyes lit up like molten lava. He charged the overwhelming oncoming horde of riders. "Nooooooo!"

CHAPTER 15

CHARGING UP THE RAIN-SOAKED ROAD, the riders lowered their lances and spears. The terrifying gigantic beasts and their over-sized riders would have frozen a hardened soldier's limbs.

Not Nath's. Defying reason, ignoring logic, and with bolts soaring past his head, he rushed toward the oncoming horde. "Have at me, then!"

The wrathhorns snarled. The orcs roared. "Kill him!"

Ten feet from certain impalement, Nath sprang into the air, snatching a bolt midflight and burying the bolt into the lead orcen cyclops.

The nuurg rider gawped and clutched at his chest.

Standing on the saddle, Nath snatched the reins and jerked them back.

The wrathhorn reared up. The ranks of riders behind it crashed into its haunches and one another. A rending of flesh, bone, and metal filled the air with a chaotic sound of confusion and butchery.

Nath sprang from the back of one beast to another, punching the orc cyclopes in their faces and toppling them from their mounts. He was an angry hornet, stinging the ravenous bears. His claws raked across their faces. His iron-strong limbs broke jawbones. His clawed hand filled with heavy steel and took on a life of its own. One towering long-limbed monster after another fell under his wrath, but the brawl was far from over. It was just beginning.

Nath was locked up with a cyclops when a hammerhead of steel clipped the back of his head, shuddering his scales and drooping his eyelids. Dazed and bloody, Nath staggered into the path of a spike-hooved beast. It plowed over him as if he were dirt. Elbow deep in the mud, he fought his way to his feet and set himself for the oncoming charge. He was busted up bad. Bright spots were in his eyes. "Come on, dogs! Come *at* me!"

Sansla Libor darted out of the sky and locked his steel-strong fingers around Nath's wrist. He pulled Nath up into the air and out of the dangerous path. With crossbow bolts still ripping through the air, Sansla shielded the stunned dragon-armed man.

"No, Sansla, no!" Nath's lip was busted, and his head was throbbing. Below his feet and vanishing in the rain was the impenetrable fortress that held Selene captive. His rescue had failed. He struggled with his captor. "Take me back, Sansla. You must take me back!"

"I cannot." Sansla continued his flight into the misty gray clouds above. The world below was lost from sight. "I cannot."

It was futile. Nath's heart sank. Selene was lost. Alone. Imprisoned.

Someone will pay for this!

Clouded by anger, it took his thoughts quite some time to subside into sense.

Meanwhile, Sansla flew with Nath for hours, staying above the meadow of dark clouds below them. The day turned to night and the night to day. Finally, a break came in the field of storms below, and the winged ape soared down through the gap.

Below were lakes of fire and sulfur. A torched landscape. Sweltering heat rose with the steam. It was Dragon Home—not the mountain itself, but the lands just west of it, a bitter stretch of land that stretched for leagues around the great mountain in all directions. Landing, Sansla set him down on the ground.

"Why did you bring me here?" Nath said.

"It is where I was ordered to bring you." Sansla said, grimacing. He peeked over his shoulder and spun around. A crossbow bolt was stuck in his back between his wings. "Be a friend, will you?"

"Guzan, Sansla! You flew all this way with this in your back?" Nath grabbed the bolt. "Hold on." He yanked it out.

Groaning, Sansla dropped to a knee and sighed. "Thank you."

Nath pitched the bolt into a nearby pool of lava. The bolt sizzled and sank. "I'm still angry with you."

Turning to face Nath, the great winged ape said, "I would be too. I'm sorry Nath, but I had my orders."

"Yes," Nath nodded. "I know you did. From my mother. Since when do you work for my mother?"

"Since you disappeared."

The Mountain of Doom stretched into the clouds leagues away. Nath and Sansla were on the outer edge of its natural barriers of protection, where the hot streams slipped into the earth again.

"Why here? Doesn't my mother want to meet me inside?"

"She did not say."

"You know Brenwar is not going to be too happy being left behind with the roamer elves. Was it so necessary that we leave them all behind?"

"They'll be safe."

"They are in orcen land!" Nath said. "How safe can they be?"

"I'll go back, if I can. We'll see." Sansla's wings collapsed behind his back. He sat on a pile of stones. "This place makes me thirsty."

Nath brushed his sweaty hair from his eyes. His face was dripping with sweat. "It's better than frost that freezes the bones. You seem to be doing quite well. No issues with your temperament."

"The curse is what it is. As long as I stay focused on what is right, I can control it."

A bright light appeared out of nowhere. Nath shielded his eyes. The light faded, and a mystic doorway appeared. A woman stepped out. She was as beautiful and radiant as the morning sun. Hair of golden light. Eyes the color of honey. She wore powder-white robes trimmed in silver.

"Mother," Nath said.

"Yes, my dear son, it is me," Grahleyna said.

Sansla took a knee.

"Please stand, Roamer King," she said, beckoning at the shimmering door. "Now come within. It is not safe out in the open like this."

Sansla went through the door.

Nath followed. Immediately, he knew he was back inside Dragon Home, but the room he was in was an entirely different one than the throne room. Amazing and wonderful carvings filled it with colorful pictures—people, dragons, and landscapes. The chamber wasn't large, but it was tall, and big enough for a pair of large dragons. Humongous pillows covered most of the floor. Every detail in the room, though simple, was exquisite, but with no furnishings other than the pillows at all.

"This is my spot," Grahleyna said, offering a pretty smile and a healing potion to each of them, "a place where I hide from your father."

"I'm sure this isn't your only option." Nath drank down his potion, recalling many memories. Dragon Home was an enormous city within the great mountain. Not even the work of the dwarves could rival it. There were thousands of rooms and caverns as well as roads, wide and narrow, that twisted and turned. Some of the places were very small, made for the little dragons, and the others were quite huge, big enough for a sky raider to squeeze through. All in all, it was a marvel. Amazing. When Nath was young, he had made it a goal to search out every place there was. He never found the half of it. The room he was in now was new to him.

"Selene, Mother," he said to her. Chin high, fists clenched, he stepped forward. "She's been captured by the nuurg. I was attempting to rescue her when Sansla arrived and fouled everything up!"

"Watch your tone," she said softly. She took his hand. "It is unfortunate about Selene, but she can take care of herself. You know that as well as I."

"She's in a deep slumber."

Squeezing Nath's hand hard, she said, "You cannot wake her?"

"No, Mother. She's defenseless. I was in the middle of saving her when I was rushed back here against my will. What is so urgent and pressing that I had to appear here this instant?"

She held his cheeks and said with great sympathy, "I am so sorry, Nath. Forgive Sansla. He was merely following my direct order as he should have been. I did not suspect it would be in such a moment of peril. Forgive me."

He hesitated, then said, "I do. But I must save Selene—among other things. Fang is stolen, and the elves and dwarves think I killed Laedorn and Uurluuk. How can all this be? And Father, what of him? He's gone?"

Grahleyna guided him to a seat on an orange-pink pillow. "He was angry. The titans had sent rather cruel messages. The bones and skins of dragons. They taunted him. Realizing that you were missing, Balzurth went after you."

"Me?" Nath pointed to his chest. "He's like a flying city in the sky. The giants and wurmers will be all over him. Please tell me he took an enclave of dragons for protection?"

Shaking her head with a face filled with worry, she said, "He is alone."

Nath jumped up. "Alone? That's insane!"

CHAPTER

16

"**Y**OU ARE SO MUCH LIKE your father," Grahleyna said. "You, like him, always want to solve Nalzambor's problems on your own. Things would be so much easier if you learned to trust others."

"I don't like putting others in harm's way," said Nath, looking in the direction where he thought Selene lay, helpless and surrounded by monsters. "Not on my account. But Mother—"

Grahleyna held up her hand for him to listen. "People do what they want to do. If they want to help, let them. It's their lives, and they have to live them. How would you feel if I tried to protect you all the time? Never let you leave here, not even to help in times of dire need?"

What! No! She can't mean that! I have to go rescue Selene! Better not make Mother angry.

"I suppose I wouldn't like it."

"No, you wouldn't. So you left here with Brenwar—and left a good bit early. I don't think you were ready, but I think you are the better for it now." She poked his noggin. "Just a little hardheaded. There is so much you can still do. You just haven't learned how."

So tell me, already! Enough with the hints! Tell me how to fly again so I can go back this instant and rescue Selene!

But Nath couldn't speak to his mother that way, especially not when she had just threatened to ground him. She had the power to enforce that. If she ordered it, he really would not be leaving Dragon Home.

Shaking his head in frustration, Nath chose his words carefully. "Is there something I should know that you could tell me? Wouldn't that be helpful?"

"It's best that you learn these things for yourself. Your own trials and tribulations will purify your golden spirit. Just keep doing the right thing,

Nath, no matter how hard it might be." His mother gave him a sad smile that made her years show in her face, and the look in her eyes was faraway.

Guzan, she's more worried about him than I thought.

Nath took his mother's hands. "So how long has Father been gone?"

"In secret, he managed to storm out of here weeks ago. He was insistent that no one go with him or after him. I pleaded with him," she said, squeezing his hands tight. "I fear I may not see him again. When I got word that you had been spotted and Sansla was already searching, I sent him after you immediately. Nath, you have to find your father. You have to find him now. If Eckubahn comes across him, captures him, kills him, the entire Great Wall of Dragons will come down. Every evil spirit will be unleashed. And the races will fall. The dragons with them."

"With all the dragons at our disposal, can none of them find Father?"

"Since you've been gone, the wurmers have grown to outnumber the dragons at least five to one. The dragons are maintaining a low profile, to say the least."

"We can't hide forever. At some point we will all have to fight." Nath turned, dropping his mother's hands to push his hair back. He wanted to hit something. "If only I were still a dragon."

"You still *are* a dragon," she reminded him.

"But I've lost so much power. Everything's bigger than me. The giants. The wurmers. Now even the orcs out-size me. They were big enough and obnoxious enough already."

"Don't lose your composure, Nath. Now is the time to plan and think."

"Ugh!" He flung his hands to his sides. "It makes my head hurt."

"Yes, you are your father's son." She let out a small chuckle.

Still, Nath could tell she was sad. He didn't know his mother well. He'd hardly spent any time with her at all. He needed to be strong and console her. "What do you think I should do?"

"What is best for the future of Nalzambor?"

"Your question comes across as a riddle," he said. "I've a feeling you know the answer."

"No, I have an opinion, but I'm not going to share that." She smoothed out the ruffles in her robes. "I shouldn't influence your decision. I can offer you this." She held out a knuckle-sized gemstone that shined like a blue star. "This will help you find your father. It will only work in your hands."

Nath took the stone. In his palm it pulsated with a life of its own. "What is it?"

"A searcher. It bonds mystically with the one it touches. It is tied to us— me, you, and your father. See how it gleams when I am near? It knows me. In my hands it will know you. Near your father, it will come to life again." She reached out and closed his hand over it. "Its magic is limited. You'll need to be close, but if you are close enough you will know he is near."

"How near?"

"It's difficult to say. A few feet? A hundred yards?"

"What will Father look like?"

"It's quite possible he looks like us. Or an elf. Maybe a dwarf," she said, rising to her feet.

"He can do that? Like a changeling?"

"His powers are mighty."

Nath's thoughts went to Gorlee. "They say someone who looked like me killed Laedorn and Uurluuk with Akron. It must have been a changeling."

"I know about the horrible demise of our allies, Nath, but are you assuming everything you hear is true?"

Nath certainly had his doubts about the rogue elf, Slavan Fonjich. After all, he had imprisoned him and left him for dead. "Do the elves and dwarves not hunt for me?"

"They do, but that doesn't mean what they heard was true. Perhaps witnesses lied about what they had seen."

"But they have my bow. Ben had my bow, and I need to know if he lives." Nath wanted to pull out his hair. "Everything's upside down since Fang took me away! And he's gone too. I don't know where to start."

"You need to realize you can't be everywhere at once, Nath. You need to remember you aren't a man. You are a dragon. The Dragon Prince. You have power at your command. You just haven't figured out how to use it." She hugged him tight. "Think like a dragon, not like a man."

"You're leaving me again, aren't you?"

"No, I'm staying here. I have to keep everyone convinced that your brazen father is brooding in the throne room. You're the one who's leaving." She snapped her fingers. A new mystic door appeared and opened. "Where do you want to start, Nath? The door will take you there. Just think of it. I have faith in your journey."

He looked at the gem in his hand. Where would his father be? He had no idea. He kissed Grahleyna on the cheek. "Goodbye, Mother."

CHAPTER 17

BLACK EYED AND WHITE HAIRED, she was beautiful and small, standing just over three feet tall and fluttering her black-and-pink wings. She stood on a tree stump, surrounded by dozens of fairies. They were all black eyed and covered in leaves, like the surrounding forest. One fairy was just as adorable and deadly as another. Encircled by her mystic people, Lotuus had a twinkle in her dark eyes.

"I have brought you gifts, Fairy Empress," said an elf. He took a knee and bowed. It was Slavan of the rogue wilder elves. A long object was wrapped up in cloth. A sword with a sharp tip that pointed out. He stuck it tip first in the ground and tore away the cloth.

Eyes wide, Lotuus gazed at the magnificent blade.

"Does this please the empress?" Slavan held his palm out. The skin was red and blistered. "I paid quite the price when I grabbed it. Be careful of its steel."

Wings coming to life, she floated around the sword. "I'm well aware of its powers."

"I have another present, though lesser than the blade," Slavan said. He outstretched his hand behind him. Another rogue elf handed him Brenwar's hammer. "I've not only disarmed your enemies, I've captured them too."

"Where?" she demanded. Her small hands locked around Slavan's collar. "Where is Nath Dragon?" she yelled in his face.

"He is secured," Slavan calmly said, "Empress."

Up in his face, she said, "Why did you not bring him here?"

"And risk his escape? No, the farther I separate him from his weapons, the better. I was not going to chance it. He is quite secure, I assure you."

"You had better be right," she said. Her eyes glowed with bright-green light. "Or I will kill you."

"You know I aim to please you, Empress. I would rather die than let you down." He reached for her.

Lotuus slapped his hand. "Don't you dare, Elf. Now tell me, where is he?"

"The labyrinth in the Elven Field of Dreams. The Inner Sanctum of Lheme. He's quite secure. No one knows he's there. And there's no escape for him—or for his friends. Are you pleased?"

"So he lives?"

"I wouldn't call it living, but he breathes quite well. As a matter of fact, he gave up quite easily."

Lotuus picked up a wand from her tree stump throne. It had a lock of Nath's hair on it. He had disappeared without a trace more than a year ago. Even the wurmers hadn't been able to find his scent. Now, she had him right where she wanted him. She sniffed the clipping of Nath's flame-red hair.

"Are you going to share my achievement with Eckubahn?" Slavan asked. "I want audience with him myself. I believe I have earned it."

"Now is not the time," she said.

"I disagree." Slavan poked at his black chest plate. "I didn't have to bring this gift to you. I could have taken it straight to Narnum. Sought the audience with Eckubahn myself. What I have done is worthy of my desires. I want full authority over Elome once it falls. I deserve it. I demand it!"

Tapping the tassel of Nath's hair in her hand, she said in a sweet voice, "And you will have it."

"Really, well, uh, that's much better." He adjusted his composure. "Me and my elves are ready for the journey."

Lotuus's eyes flashed. Green bolts of power shot from her eyes and cut a hole in Slavan. "Your journey is over." She twirled the wand over her head. Concealed wurmers, at least a dozen, appeared in the woodland. She pointed at the remaining rogue elves—who had drawn their swords. "Kill them."

The Elven Field of Dreams was not easily accessed by just anyone. The wilder elves were the guardians of it. And there were more of them, many, many more. The sanctuary was known by very few, including the elves. Lotuus and an entourage of fairies made their way through the lands of the elves, but they looked different. Using their dark magic, they had transformed themselves to appear as the wilder elves the wurmers had slain.

Posing as Slavan, Lotuus led the way. They came across more rogue elves—who were easily convinced—headed deeper into the Elven Field of

Dreams, and slunk through the ravine into the Inner Sanctum of Lheme. It took hours to traverse the labyrinth.

Finally, they found the open cells.

Lotuus shook her head and screamed. "Aaaaaaaeeeeeehhhh!" Leaving the sanctum, she said, "Now I'm truly glad I killed that failure."

Outside the elven lands, she headed back into her forest sanctuary. Sitting on her tree stump throne, she toyed with the wand and tassel. Nath Dragon was alive and well.

Should I send the wurmers after him now?

She snapped her fingers. A wurmer glided over. It was the size of an ox and had deep-grey scales. A purple fire was in its eyes. She waved the wand under its snout. "Find out where Nath Dragon is, and report back to me."

The dragon spread its wings and departed.

She stared at the sword, Fang. Its steel shimmered with silvery life. "Humph, what Eckubahn doesn't know won't hurt him right now. My secret's safe with me."

CHAPTER 18

"Y OU'RE CERTAIN NO ONE HAS left?" Nath said to Hoven. He had made his choice and departed from his mother. He was rescuing Selene. He arrived a mile from the fortress on the path to the city of Thraag. It was his choice. His father would have to wait. He couldn't leave Selene helpless like that. "You've had eyes on it the entire time?"

Hoven pushed his braided hair back over his shoulders. "The dwarf insisted on it. It was our desire to depart, but he managed to convince us otherwise." He glanced down at Brenwar. "It would have been easier to pull a tree stump out of the ground with my bare hands than move him."

"Well now," Nath said to Brenwar, "it seems someone has taken a shine to Selene. I knew you liked her."

"Pah." Chin up, head turning, Brenwar crossed his arms over his chest. "I like her as much as I like the porridge of bugbears. I stayed only because I knew you'd be back."

"Sure, sure," Nath said. Concealed in a high spot among the heavy brush and thickets, he gazed at the fortress beyond. It was square, twenty feet high, and made of heavy stone. It had a tower at each corner like a castle. The red-and-black banner of Thraag waved from the highest tower. Soldiers guarded the wall on every side. "How many do you think are inside?"

"At least a hundred," Hoven said. "That would include the nuurg. Of course, you did manage to whittle them down."

"*We* managed to whittle them down," Brenwar reminded them.

"Oh, but of course," Hoven said.

Standing among the present company of Hoven, Sansla, and Brenwar, Nath said, "I don't suppose anyone has ever been inside an orcen cyclops stronghold before?"

No one replied.

"That's what I thought. Well, I'm going to need to get in there," Nath said.

"You can't be serious?" Brenwar said, puffing through his beard. "They'll be waiting for you in there. It's what they want."

"It's what they expect," Sansla added.

"I suggest we wait them out," Hoven said. "It's possible they'll move her. They were heading toward Thraag, were they not?"

Nath was torn up inside. He knew in his mind that caution was the best option.

I want action! I cannot just leave her in there.

"I need to go in, and go in soon. I can't just stand here while she's helpless in there. I cannot."

Putting his hand on Nath's shoulder, Sansla said, "Give the orcs time to reveal their hand. After all, they are quite stupid. It won't be long before they squirm around in there."

"True." Nath rubbed his chest. It had been healed by the potion his mother had given him, but he still remembered what it had felt like, being trampled by a wrathhorn. "Let's keep our eyes open, then, shall we? I'm going to get a closer look."

Brenwar bumped up against him. "Not without me, you won't. I know what you're thinking."

"I won't rush in," Nath said.

Not in the daylight.

"I know better. Where you go, I go." Brenwar pointed at Hoven. "And if I don't have an eye on him, then you'd better have one."

Hoven nodded. "We will."

Consumed, Nath watched the fortress like a clock, day and night. Brenwar hung close to his side. Quiet. Alert. Nothing came or went out of the fortress, which was odd. The orcs should routinely send patrols out, surely, like the nuurg Nath had encountered. The fact that they weren't moving told him something. The orcs suspected he was out here. Watching. Waiting.

It was dusk. Sitting in a grove of large stones, with a full view of the fortress, Brenwar said to Nath, "So what did your mother have to say?"

Nath gave him most of the details and went on. "The sad thing is that the elves and dwarves truly are after me. They think I'm a murderer. Or a madman."

"Do you think doing this is wiser than looking for your father?" Brenwar said.

Nath shrugged. "I don't even know where to start with him. I can't say for sure if I'm doing right, but in this case, I do at least know where Selene is. I can do something." He picked up a stick and doodled in the ground with it. "And at the last moment before I departed, I got to thinking on going after him, but then I thought, 'What would Father do if Mother was in the same situation?' Then it was easy."

Brenwar nodded. "Aye. Even I can't disagree with that logic, but then again, Selene is not your mother."

"Brenwar..."

"Fair is fair," the dwarf said, taking a bite of some elven jerky. "She has quite a past."

"You need to move on."

"Tell that to the families of the dead she left in her wake."

Nath tried not to think about it and didn't very often. To some, everything Selene had done was unforgivable, but he'd been taught that on the higher road, everything could be forgiven if there was a true change of heart. He believed that. He pitched the stick. "I think she's trying really hard to make up for it. Many more would have been lost without her."

"Aye."

"Brenwar," Nath said, "you've spent time with my father. Where do you think he's looking for me?"

Rubbing his beard and gazing at the sky, Brenwar said, "Good question. I know your father likes to fly. Explore. He likes to be alone. I honestly think he would walk the world as a man and do good things. It's just a theory, though. What about you? You were close when you were young. He took you all over, did he not?"

Nath showed a smile. "Yes, he did. They were grand times too. Riding on his mighty back and soaring the air like a bird. It was the greatest feeling in the world. Me and him felt like one. He told me I could always fly, but look at me now." He lifted his boot and laughed. "I'm a landlubber."

Brenwar stomped his foot. "I like it. There ain't no worse feeling than nothing underneath you."

"You never know. One day bearded dwarves might fly—" Nath sat up in his perch. A flicker of movement had caught his eye. A violent act in the brush erupted in a patch where a roamer elf once stood. Nath took off running.

Brenwar yelled after him, "Where are you going?"

Crashing through the thickets, Nath burst into a clearing.

Down on the ground, Hoven fought the wurmer tearing into him.

CHAPTER 19

HOVEN THE ROAMER ELF FOUGHT for his life. A huge gash was on his chest. His hands pushed up against the wurmer's snapping jaws.

Nath collided with the scaly beast, pushing it off Hoven.

Brenwar grabbed the elf's arm and dragged him out of the way.

The wurmer's tail whipped around, caught Nath in the chest, and knocked him off his feet. He sprang back up and braced himself for attack.

The scaly beast squared off on Nath. It sniffed the air. Its purple eyes narrowed in recognition.

Nath advanced with his elven blade. "What are you waiting for, insect?"

The wurmer darted forward and spun around, flicking out its tail.

Nath jumped backward.

The wurmer ran into the brush, cleared a path, and spread its wings.

"He's running," Nath said, sprinting after it.

The wurmer took to the air.

Nath dove for its tail. His fingers stretched out at full length, grasping for the flying monster. He whiffed and crashed into the ground.

The wurmer ascended toward the setting sun.

Nath slammed his fist in the dirt. "Guzan!"

Sansla landed beside him. "What happened?"

Gazing at Sansla's great wings, Nath yelled at him, "That thing's a scout. It knows me. Get after it, Sansla." He pointed at the sky. "You must stop it now!"

Without hesitation, Sansla leapt into the air and took off like a giant bat, making a straight line for the wurmer. Within seconds they were both gone.

On his feet again, Nath trotted back to Brenwar and Hoven. More roamers had formed a circle around the fallen roamer. Brenwar had Hoven's head in his lap. The long-limbed elf's chest was bloody and still bleeding. His complexion was turning a deep purple. He coughed and spat blood.

Taking a knee, Shum said, "I must get him out of here if he is to live."

"Where will you take him?" Nath asked. "The Elven Field of Dreams?"

Shum picked his brother up in his arms. "That's an option." He let out a sharp whistle. Two of the magnificent horses bred by the roamers showed up. One of them lay down. Shum climbed on with Hoven in his arms. The horse rose up. Checking the sky, Shum shook his head and said to one of the roamers, "Liam, you have my charge."

"Dragon speed," Liam said.

Shum nodded, nudged his heels into the horse's ribs, and galloped away.

"Well, that was awful," Brenwar said.

"Awful indeed," Nath replied. His eyes remained fixed on the sky.

Liam came alongside him. "I'm ready to go in if you are."

"Huh?" Nath said, lowering his gaze on the roamer elf. Liam was much younger than Shum and Hoven. His potbelly was not so pronounced, his long bones not quite as heavy as those of his elders. As another sign of his youth, his gray eyes were eager and energetic. "What are you suggesting?"

"We go in and rescue your friend Selene. Time is wasting."

Nath smirked at the long-haired rangy elf. "Let's see what Sansla has to say when he returns."

Bouncing up and down on his toes, Liam said, "And if he doesn't?"

"Have some faith in your king," Nath said with surprise.

"I do, but he can be inconsistent. You know, when he gets all excited, the curse, it will run away with him."

The other roamers crowded in.

Quick to order, Liam said, "Resume your posts."

Like apparitions, the roamers vanished into the falling darkness, leaving Liam, Nath, and Brenwar all alone.

Chin high, Liam said, "We can speak freely now."

"You were speaking freely," Brenwar said. "Quite clearly."

"Yes, you do seem quite eager to take charge of things," Nath added.

"But I *am* in charge of things. You heard Shum. He trusts me. I say we get moving. Strike in the night. The time is right." He rubbed his hands together. "I'm ready for some action."

Lifting a brow, Brenwar said to Nath, "Remind you of anybody?"

"I believe so," Nath said. "So Liam, tell me, what is your plan?"

"Oh, it's simple." Liam kneeled down and motioned them in. With his finger, he drew in the dirt. "This is the fortress. I noticed on the western wall there is a small entrance. We sneak inside, kill all the orcs and cyclopes, and rescue your friend." He dusted his hands off. "See? Easy."

Nodding, Brenwar said, "I like it. I like it a lot."

Nath rubbed his temples. "Oh my."

"What's wrong?" Liam asked.

"I sense the world ending," Nath replied.

Brenwar stood up with his battle-axe, looking all around. "Why's that? I don't see anything. Why is the world ending?"

"Because you're agreeing with an elf."

Brenwar shrugged his shoulders. "Even elves have their moments."

Sansla Libor dropped out of the sky. His fur was torn and bleeding. He huffed for breath. "I'm sorry. The wurmer escaped me."

"Do you think it was a scout?" Nath asked.

"Aye." Sansla shook his jaw. "I came back to warn you. They'll be coming. Soon, they'll be coming."

CHAPTER
20

"**H**OW MANY?" ASKED LIAM. HE pulled his quiver off his shoulder and started counting the arrows. "I can take at least two dozen."

"I don't know," Sansla said, keeping his attention on Nath. "In the case of the wurmers, they often come by the dozens. In some cases we've seen them in the hundreds. Valcatrine was wiped out by a horde of them."

"Valcatrine?" Nath said with surprise. It was a small elven city where a few thousand farmers and tradespeople lived. "When did this happen?"

"Months ago," Sansla replied. "Nath, I'm sorry. It might be best to abandon this mission if we want to get out alive. If there's too many, well, we aren't capable of handling too many."

"I've fought wurmers before. We can handle them," Nath said, gripping his sword tight in his hand. "I'm not abandoning Selene."

"I'm all for going in and getting her," Liam said. He tested the string on his bow. "Every moment is precious."

"Yer a good bit more eager than your kin," Brenwar commented.

"Yes, much unlike his father, but his father trusts him. So do I," Sansla said.

Looking at Liam, Nath asked, "Who's his father?"

"Shum. He's a bit too cautious, if you ask me. Says I need more wisdom." Liam drew both of his swords, twirled them around his fingers, and slid them back into his sheaths. "But he also admits my skill and instincts more than make up for it. So, are we doing this?"

Nath weighed his options. He could possibly shake the wurmers from his trail and come back. But they were after him. Perhaps he should leave Selene's rescue to someone else. If anyone could pull it off, it was the roamers. They were the most-skilled fighters and rangers in the lands. He knew this. He'd fought alongside them often enough. They could handle the orcs, even the big ones. They, like the dwarves and so many other rangers, were giant killers.

Staring at the fortress, Nath remarked, "There must be a hundred soldiers in there, not to mention their beasts."

"I can take half on my own," Liam said.

"Aye, and I'll take the other half," Brenwar agreed. "You just focus on getting Selene out."

Sansla rubbed his fist in his palm. "I'm up for a good scrap as much as any."

With the evening breeze rustling his red hair, Nath nodded. "By Guzan, let's do this."

As everyone else readied themselves for the rescue, Nath stood alongside Brenwar, eyeing the fortress. They were less than fifty yards away. Torches cast flickers on the top wall. The orcen banner in the top tower waved in the stiff winds. Nath counted ten orcs with heavy crossbows guarding the walls. They wore full metal helmets and chest plates of iron.

Battle-axe over his shoulder, Brenwar said, "Any day you fight orcs is a good day. Let's take them."

Nath agreed, but he wasn't in it for the bloodshed; he was in it for Selene. However, he'd do everything in his power to get her. If orcs went down, so be it. "This assault will be considered an act of war, you know."

"There's a war already."

Liam appeared from the brush. "We're ready."

"Go, then," Nath said. "I'll await your signal."

With a smile, Liam vanished into the woodland.

"You know, it would be better if there were dwarves instead of elves," Brenwar said.

"Sometimes you have to make do."

"Humph."

"Let's go." Nath crept through the brush until he got close enough to the entrance at the bottom of the western wall that Liam had mentioned. It was a solid iron door with a narrow road that led out onto another roadway.

Nath climbed up into a tree. He could see the walls now and had a closer look at the orcen faces of the guards. Even at night, he could see the yellow of their eyes.

At least I still have my dragon vision.

Brenwar whispered up at him. "What's happening?"

"Nothing yet," Nath said. "Be silent."

Looking up at the fortress from down on the ground, Brenwar popped up on his toes. "Something should be happening already. The elves are slow."

"Give it a moment."

"I've got enough gray in my beard already."

Nath sat perched like an owl amid the sounds of wind whistling through the tree limbs. Cocking his head, he closed his eyes. A faint unnatural sound caught his keen ears, coming from the other side of the eastern wall.

Ah, the sweet sound of a stretching bowstring.

An orcen soldier fell over with an arrow stuck in his chest. Another volley cut into the ranks. Orcs clutched their chests or necks, teetered, and fell.

Inside one of the towers a bell rang.

In Orcen, one of the defending soldiers yelled, "Attack! Attack!"

"So it's finally started," Brenwar said with excitement. "It's about time."

The orcs abandoned this section of the wall, running to defend the eastern side.

"Perfect." Nath hopped out of the tree, landing on cat's feet by Brenwar. "Wait for me to get that door open."

"Make it quick. Can't let the elves have all the fun." The dwarf's eyes were fixed on the orcs that had deserted their posts. "They're so stupid. A dwarf never abandons his station."

"Wait for my signal," Nath reminded him. He darted for the wall.

The plan was simple. With the orcs' attention turned, he'd climb the wall and open the fortress's service door from the inside to let in Brenwar and the roamers. They would infiltrate with him, battle their way to Selene if needed. Though stealth was ideal, battle might be the only option.

Bursting through the brush, Nath made his way to the wall.

A giant orc cyclops, a nuurg, rushed out of the tower onto the western wall.

Nath hunkered down behind some long-abandoned quarry stone and peeked up.

The nuurg had spoiled his plan. There was no way he could sneak in there now.

Great Guzan!

CHAPTER
21

"**T**HERE!" THE NUURG FASTENED HIS eyes on Nath and pointed with his sword.

Flying at full speed, Sansla appeared from around one of the towers and blindsided the nuurg. The powerful impact sent the brutish giant falling over the wall and crashing hard, armor and all, onto the ground.

Brenwar stormed out of the brush and said to Nath, "You go! I'll handle this!"

The one-eyed orcen eight-footer climbed to his feet and straightened his helm.

Brenwar took a whack into its knee.

Howling, the orc collapsed.

Brenwar didn't stop there.

Without looking back, Nath leapt high up on the wall. His hard claws dug in, and he ascended like a squirrel. Reaching the top, he slid onto the landing. A battle raged on the other side, in the fortress courtyard. The orcs fired crossbows. The roamers fired into their ranks with deadly accuracy. Reinforcements came storming from the ground level up the stairs. At least a dozen held the eastern wall, launching crossbow bolts from behind the stones that protected them.

Nath looked at the ground level.

Orcs had gathered weapons and were feeding more crossbow bolts to the upper wall. The nuurg were shouting orders. Nothing was right below him. Assured that no one saw him, he jumped down into the courtyard and turned toward the outer wall, searching for the service door. It was there, but it wasn't alone. A nuurg stood tall, swinging a long-handled stone-headed mace. It was Gaak.

Nath caught the hammering blow in his shoulder and fell to the ground. "Gah!"

In an instant, the giant orc was upon Nath, stepping on his foot and bringing down another swing.

Nath rolled to one side, evaded the first blow, and dodged another.

"Be still, scaly one." With two hands, the orc cyclops brought down the oversized mace with wroth force.

Nath captured the handle with both hands.

The pair wrestled over the hard ground, rolling back and forth.

The orc was bigger and heavier, his strength impressive, his leverage an advantage. He pinned Nath on his back again. "I'm no fool. I knew you would come here. You fell into my trap. This is where you die and I scale you like a fish."

Nath's nose crinkled. "Your breath is awful. Just awful. Is manure part of your diet?"

Brows buckling and face in a vicious snarl, Gaak put all of his crushing weight on Nath. He got the mace handle over Nath's neck, pinned him down good, and leaned into it. "Heavy, aren't I?"

Choking under the orc's weight, Nath pushed back with all of his might. With his face red as a beet, he managed to choke out, "Your mother must be proud. Did you know her?"

"You're a dead man!"

"Dragon, actually."

Hands on the handle, jaw clenched, Nath pushed back. A vein popped out in his forehead. His dragon blood surged. "Get off of me!" he growled.

"When you're dead!"

Slowly, with shaking arms, Nath started to lift the handle, watching Gaak's eyes widen. Sweat dripped from the nuurg's brow into Nath's face. "Yech!"

Gaak put his full chest over the weapon's haft and forced his weight with more effort.

Nath's arms locked in place. Then, he started pushing the huge orc off of his chest again.

"Impossible!" Gaak shouted.

With a heave, Nath shoved Gaak off, ripped the mace from his hands, and lorded over him. "Nothing's impossible when you're a dragon."

Laboring for breath, Gaak said, "Is that so?" He launched his foot into Nath's groin.

"Oof!" Nath sank to his knees.

Gaak gathered his powerful legs under himself and pounced.

Striking quick, Nath smote Gaak in the jaw with the head of the mace.

Krang!

The hardheaded giant stood dazed.

With the mace, Nath walloped him in the belly and crowned him in the head. "You'll never hit me there again."

Gaak was out. Dead maybe.

Nath didn't try to find out. His skirmish had caught the attention of the other soldiers. With angry cries and barking orders, they charged across the courtyard toward Nath. He found the door. Two steel crossbars sealed it shut. One by one, he shoved them out. He flung open the door.

Brenwar stood just outside. "Duck."

"Why?"

"Just duck!"

Nath squatted down. From outside the door, arrows zinged over his head.

Twack! Twack! Twack! Twack!

Behind him, Nath heard the thuds of four orc soldiers dropping dead on the spot.

Five roamer elves rushed in, led by Liam. He was shooting one arrow right after the other. "Find your friend. We'll keep these brutes off your back. Go!" He pointed at the tower and said to his men, "Take it."

"Don't order me around," Brenwar said, swinging his axe into an orc that charged from the side. "I like the ground level. That's where battles are won!"

Liam tossed his bow aside and drew his swords. "I couldn't agree more."

Together, Brenwar and Liam waded into the fray, with Brenwar screaming, "For Morgdon!"

CHAPTER
22

AVOIDING THE BATTLING TROOPS, NATH snaked through the chaos. The fortress had a simple layout, with the barracks, stalls, storehouses, and other needed areas built out of wood underneath the wooden catwalks between the stone outer walls where the orcs were posted. There was plenty to search. He ducked into a room where the orcs ate. The wooden tables were covered in stacked-up dirty plates. He covered his nose.

"Awful here. Awful everywhere."

He moved out to the next building. It was the barracks. There weren't any beds, just blankets piled up on the ground. Some loose weapons were left behind. Bones from leftover foods stank. The orcs didn't have much discipline, and the word "tidy" wasn't part of their vocabulary. The barracks butted up against and used the stone fortress wall.

Brenwar would have a laugh if he saw this. It's a wonder they built this fortress at all.

Nath could make a case for the orcs to some degree. They didn't care for comfort like many races. The hard ground and dirt were just fine with them. Also, to them, the more they stank, the better. It wasn't uncommon that the leader was the smelliest and ugliest of all of them.

It was part of the reason Nath hated them. They relished filth. Their hard hearts were filled with destruction. They were impossible to get along with. Always.

He abandoned the barracks. A battle raged outside. The roamers and Brenwar cut into the ranks of orcs but vanished in the knot of pig-nosed men. He wanted to help, desperately he did, but a voice in his head said, *Have faith.*

Blocking the clamor out, Nath snuck into the stables.

Immediately, something beastly snorted.

Liam was young for an elf. Barely a hundred years old, he fought like a ranger with five hundred seasons. His elven steel flashed in the night, cutting down one orc after the other. His two swords struck like lightning. Both blade tips bit deep into an orc's chest, sending it to the grave.

A broad machete-like blade cut at Liam's head.

He ducked.

Swish!

The young roamer cut away, removing the attacking orc's machete hand at the wrist.

Slice!

More orcs fell. More orcs came.

"I can do this all day!" Brenwar roared. In one hard swing, he brought two orcs down at once. "All day!"

From the tower above, the feathered shafts of the elves dropped the orcs one by one. The roamers on the ground fought hard and struck fast. Their skill and speed overwhelmed the heavily armored inferior orcen fighters.

A crossbow bolt clipped Liam's shoulder. He cried out, "Zauass!" Bleeding, he noticed the orc crossbowmen up on the catwalks. They shot at everyone, even their own kind.

Ducking and dodging dozens of arrows, Liam ran up the steps and stormed the catwalk, swinging his sword left and right. Orcs pitched over the catwalk rail and bounced off the ground. The orcs tossed their crossbows aside in order to draw their bladed weapons, but before they could pull them out, Liam engaged.

Slice! Slice! Hack!

In a matter of seconds, the bloodied orcs were fighting for their lives. Cut, slashed, busted, and bleeding, the orcs that survived Liam's onslaught fought on. They weren't brave nor valiant, just angry, stubborn, and stupid. Orcs hated to lose—and even worse, they hated elves. In a knot of blood and sweat, they poured it on.

Their anger was their downfall. Taking advantage of their rage and confusion, Liam carved them to bits. Out of breath, skinned, scratched up, and bloody, he peered over the wall and shouted out to the remaining roamers in the woods.

"To me!"

Suddenly, the catwalk shook.

On both sides of the catwalk, the monstrous one-eyed nuurg fighters appeared. Each carried a halberd—an axe head on a spear shaft. The single eye in the middle of each of their heads was intent on murder.

Roamers in the tower tops fired at the huge orcen cyclopes. Arrows stuck into their backs like the spines on a porcupine. The nuurgs didn't even grunt. Their skin was leathery. It took special magic to cut them. Liam made a signal to the tower. The volley of arrows was redirected.

Liam flipped his sword and beckoned the cyclopes into battle. "What are you waiting for, an invitation?"

The cyclopes charged.

Chopping the orcs down like saplings, Brenwar caught up to Liam on the catwalk, hemmed in by two giant cyclopes. He buried his axe in one's belly, pushed off, and shouted up at Liam, "Wait for me! Wait for me!"

A cyclops swinging a chain with spiked heads stepped into view. The chain whistled over his head.

"What kind of silly weapon is that?"

The chain licked out and wrapped around Brenwar. He looked down at his constricted legs. "Nobody tangles a dwarf!"

Putting his shoulders into it, the cyclops gave the chain a heave that jerked Brenwar off his feet onto his back. Hand over hand, the cyclops pulled the dwarf forward.

Chopping at the chain, Brenwar said, "Nobody drags a dwarf!"

The surrounding orcs swarmed him and piled on.

CHAPTER
23

WRATHHORNS. THEIR NICKERING WHINE COULD freeze a man's blood. One reared up as soon as Nath walked into the stable. Its hooves clawed at the iron gate that penned it in. It was just one of many—all of which were growling. Two of them butted their gates with the horns on their heads.

Nath forged ahead. There were plenty of stalls, and many of them were empty. He peeked in each one. There was nothing but hay, straw and stubble, and water troughs. Clothing was in one of the barrels, grain and burning oil in others. Casks of ale filled the entirety of one stall all by themselves. Moving quickly, he didn't find any sign of Selene.

He hit the back wall. "Sultans of Sulfur!"

There wasn't much to the fortress at all. Nothing mysterious. A simple layout. There were supplies and soldiers. It being a fortress of orcs, there wasn't any place for discipline or detention. If there was a problem in the ranks, they'd just fight it out. Maybe to the death. Hence, no dungeon cells nor any sort of brig. He kicked the hay piled at his feet.

"Come on Selene, where are you?"

The wrathhorns continued to buck, claw at their iron bars, and whine.

"Oh shut up!"

Starting to depart and scanning his surroundings, he slipped on the straw floor and caught his balance. Kicking the loose straw away, he said, "What's this?"

A flat piece of metal lay under the hay. He dusted it off with his feet, discovering the outline of a trapdoor. Kneeling, he found an iron ring and pulled on it. A stiff breath of stale air caught his cheeks. A stone staircase led down into the darkness.

Hemmed in by giants and halberds, Liam danced in and out of the jabbing blades. The cyclopes were cunning. They poked and stabbed. Liam ducked and shifted from side to side.

"Stand still!" roared one of the nuurg fighters.

Ducking under a slicing blade, Liam popped up again. "And let you skewer me like a pig on a stick? No way!" Swords up, he batted another lethal strike aside. "How about you hold that sticker of yours still?"

Working as a team, one cyclops struck high and the other low.

Twisting in midair, Liam dove between the blades and landed on his feet.

One cyclops counterattacked with a powerful chop Liam hadn't anticipated. The head of the ogre's halberd caught him flush in the chest and slammed him back into the wall. Liam lost his wind.

The halberd's blade came in with a decapitating blow.

Liam parried.

Clang!

The savage blow knocked his arms and swords back so hard that one of Liam's sword pommels clipped him in the head. Another heavy chop followed. Liam rolled aside. The halberd's axe head bit deep into the planks of wood inches from his cheek. Eyeing the blade with blood dripping in his eyes, Liam said, "This is getting serious."

The one cyclops tried to pull his halberd out of the catwalk. The other drew back to take another swing.

Liam jumped up and landed on the stuck halberd's handle.

Tugging at the handle with both arms, the cyclops said, "Get off of there!"

In a single bound, Liam landed on one monster's shoulders and waved at the other one coming his way. "Come and get me!"

The second cyclops zeroed in on Liam, charged, and unleashed an over-the-head chop.

"No! No!" yelled the first cyclops.

Liam back flipped off the one cyclops's shoulders just as the other's halberd cracked its skull. The cyclops's eye widened to the size of a moon. "No! Sorry! No!"

The dead cyclops fell over, crashing through the catwalk's rail and onto the ground below.

Liam was face to face with the shocked cyclops. "You really should work on your aim."

The cyclops's ugly face turned into a mask of rage. "I'm going to kill you!"

Twirling his swords, Liam said, "No, you aren't. You're dead already."

Halberd pointed at Liam's chest, the orcen cyclops charged. "Raaaaah!"

Liam shifted to one side and stuck the cyclops in the chest and belly with his swords.

The huge orc moaned, "Urk!"

Liam shoved the brute off the catwalk. "And that's how you kill a giant."

Brenwar punched, but he couldn't kick. His feet were still tangled, and the orcs were trying to pummel him to death. He socked orc after orc in the nose, ribs, and face. All the while, the nuurg fighter drew him in closer, hand over hand, link by link.

"I smell a dwarf!" the nuurg would say. "A dead dwarf! Save his beard for me!"

Brenwar bent an orc's arm and twisted until it snapped. The orc let out a howl, startling its fighting kindred. It gave Brenwar some breathing room. He snaked a dagger out of an orc's belt and poked over and over. The deadly jabs sent them away—dying and screaming. Still being dragged, Brenwar sat up again and chucked the dagger at the cyclops. It bounced off the cyclops's chest.

The cyclops smiled. "It takes a sharper blade than that to harm my flesh." The cyclops hauled Brenwar up by his tangled feet, leaving the dwarf suspended upside down. The cyclops leered at Brenwar. "This will be fun."

"Fun!" Brenwar spat back. "I'll show you fun." He took a swing that wasn't even close.

Still holding the chain that held Brenwar up, the cyclops spun around. The momentum lifted Brenwar's head higher off the ground.

"What?" he said. "What in Morgdon are you doing?"

The cyclops spun faster and faster. "I'm going to sling you like a rock into that wall."

Brenwar objected. "Nobody slings a dwarf! Nobody!"

The cyclops let him fly.

Brenwar sailed through the air, bunched himself like a cannonball, and smacked hard into the wall. The stones loosened under his stout weight and popped out on the other side. Shaking it off, he marched out from under the catwalk.

The cyclops gawped.

Brenwar lifted his arm up. "Liam!"

On the catwalk standing above Brenwar, the elf replied, "Yes?"

"Lend me your steel!"

Liam dropped it right into the dwarf's open mitt.

Sword in hand, Brenwar stormed toward the cyclops. "I've had my fill of you!"

The giant orc tossed aside his chain and rushed right for Brenwar. "I'm going to fill my pots with your hide!"

With hundreds of years' experience to his favor, Brenwar cut the cyclops to ribbons. The monster was dead in seconds.

"Well done!" Liam yelled to him.

"Aye." Brenwar marched back into the fray. The rout was on. The orcs were dropping like flies, second after second.

CHAPTER
24

COLD, DAMP, AND DARK WOULD describe the dungeon cellar Nath
crept into. At the bottom of the steps under the hatch was a high
and wide tunnel dug out of the dirt. Wooden beams held the earth
in place, and oil lanterns hung on the posts, giving off a dim light. Nath
sniffed the moldy air. A familiar scent wafted into his nose.

Selene!

He hurried down the tunnel and came to a stop at an iron door that
barred his path. It was solid and without a portal for him to see through.
He put his ear to the door. Something scraped on the other side. It was like
the sound of a varmint clawing on a stone floor. He tugged on the handle,
but there wasn't any give. That's when he noticed a set of keys hung on a peg
nearby.

The first key he tried turned the lock, and with a tug, the heavy creaking
door swung open. A moth bigger than his head flew out. A strange raccoon-
like critter bolted out of the room and vanished down the tunnel. Nath
pulled the door open wide and went in. Steel bars and doors decorated both
sides of the tunnel.

Venturing into the dungeon, he noted some of the cells were empty,
but not all. Locked up in one cell, a pair of halflings huddled in the corner.
They were small, young, and shivering like leaves. A brown-haired male and
female. Their round eyes fixed on Nath then looked away.

"It's going to be fine. Come on," he said, unlocking the door and opening
it up. "You're free now."

The male halfling stirred and came his way. The female tried to tug the
male back by his tattered clothing. Without looking at Nath, he grabbed the
door and shut himself back inside. "Go away. You bring certain death upon
us."

"The orcs will be defeated. You are free. The nuurg have fallen."

The halfling huddled back with his female and said as he tucked his head away, "They are not what we fear. Go, go away."

"There is nothing to fear here," Nath said. "The path is clear."

The halfling said nothing.

Nath unlocked the cell again and proceeded to the next. There was a skeleton with the bones picked clean. It was empty, and so was the next, but for more skeletons. The only living things he saw were the halflings. Otherwise the entire place was abandoned. At least it looked to be. There were still a few cells left at the end.

Selene, you must be here. I can smell you. My nose doesn't lie.

Debris fell from above.

Nath glanced up. The dirt in the ceiling was moving. At first he thought it was from the battle above, perhaps the giants shaking the ground.

No, it's not that.

His hand fell to his elven sword.

A mouth full of teeth burst through the dirt ceiling, swallowing Nath's arm up to the elbow.

"Gah!" Nath tried to shake the creature off. It was a ghastly huge centipede thing. Its sharp teeth chomped down on his scales. It continued to inch up his swallowed arm, farther and farther. "Sultans of Sulfur! Get off me!"

The monster's tail looked and shook like a snake's rattle. It was one of the weirdest creatures Nath had ever seen.

He started banging the creature into the metal bars.

Bang! Bang! Bang!

"Get off of me!"

The insect held on. Nath kept on hitting it. Like with a tick, the harder he hit it, the deeper it bit. The only thing saving his arm was his scales. He grabbed it by the tail and started pulling it off. "Argh!"

The insect wouldn't give.

"That's it!" Nath said. On his free hand, he bared his claws. "Two can play at this game!" He plunged his fingers into the crunchy armor of the insect and ripped it off him, hunk by hunk. Finally, the insect's jaws gave way, and Nath slung it down the corridor. Slinging the insect's remaining muck off his arm, he said, "That was gross."

Eyeing the ceiling, he backed toward the last two cells at the end of the row. The one on the left was empty. The one on the right had a body. He grabbed the bars. "Selene!"

Selene lay on the cell floor, huddled up but breathing. She was still in the deep sleep and otherwise unharmed.

Nath tried the keys in the lock. There were several. None of them worked.

"What's going on?" Again, he stuck in key after key after key. Nothing worked. "Great!"

The steel bars were thick. "If I could just breathe fire on them, I could melt them." He clasped his hands around the bars. "I guess I'm going to have to try and get you out of there the hard way." He tried to pull the vertical bars apart. Muscles bulged in his arms. Sweat dripped down the side of his cheek. "Come on!"

The metal started to bend. It began to groan under his power. Nath took a breath, held it, and pulled with raw power. The steel stretched. The bars parted wide.

"Yes!"

He squeezed through the metal and picked Selene up in his arms. After brushing her hair from her eyes with his nose, he whispered in her ear, "Selene? Wake up, Selene."

Lips parted, she said nothing.

Nath noticed that other than being scraped up a little, she was in good condition. He slipped himself and her out of the cell and headed back toward the main tunnel. The halflings were still in their cell. Nath kicked the insect monster's teeth toward them. "Are you coming? I don't think there's anything to fear now."

Eyes fixed on the teeth, the halflings squeaked. They looked at Nath, and the little halfling man said, "There are no more?"

"No more."

The male halfling took the female halfling's hand. "Lead the way."

Seconds later, they emerged topside of the tunnel and were back inside the stables. The wrathhorns were quiet. Perfectly still. Nath headed toward the exit. No sounds of battle were heard on the other side. He set Selene down, drew his sword, and—fearing the worst—he headed outside.

Brenwar stood in the center of the courtyard along with Liam, Sansla, and the rest of the roamer elves. The orcs and nuurg had been defeated. The survivors were bound up and had surrendered.

Crossing the courtyard, Nath called out, "Brenwar, where's the celebration?"

The dwarf's bearded frown didn't change. He pointed at the high walls and towers.

Like a giant flock of scaled pigeons on the walls, parapets, and tower tops, wurmers perched side by side with each other by the dozens.

CHAPTER
25

HOVERING ABOVE THE MIDDLE OF the courtyard for all to see was Lotuus the Fairy Empress. Her black eyes landed on Nath. "Hello, Nath Dragon. We meet again."

Nath sheathed his elven sword. "The pleasure is all yours."

"Hah-hah-hah-hah-hah. My, you have such a charming wit. Too bad it hasn't done you any good." She glided down in front of his eyes, bouncing the wand with his tassel of hair off her cheek. "You really should be more careful with that lovely hair of yours. This led me right to you. Well, it led the wurmers, anyway. They make excellent bloodhounds."

"If they're so good, then why did it take you a year to find me?"

"I think your little sword had something to do with that. Oh, that escape you pulled off at Urslay was really something. Eckubahn is still furious. Poof. You were gone." She rapped him on the head with her wand. "But that will never happen again, now that your sword is in my possession."

Nath nodded in agreement, but his mind was racing. It was good news that Lotuus had Fang. That solved one of the mysteries. "You know, I don't think you have it. It's not possible. Fang doesn't play well with fluttering foul ilk."

"Fluttering foul ilk?" She touched her chest. "Me? How unflattering for you to say."

"There's more to come. It's sad, though, you being such a beautiful fairy. One that I alone freed. Only to have you turn on me."

She flipped him in the head with her tassel again. "You are such a pawn."

Fastening his eyes on hers, he spoke in a sweet and gentle voice. "Lotuus, you are far too marvelous to be so evil. Why not side with the dragons? Why the wicked spirits of the titans? You are a creature of magic and dignity. You know that, yet you defy it. Why?"

Long-faced, she said, "Because."

"That is not an answer. How about you and I talk? Just talk. I sense the hurt inside you. I want to help take it away."

"No!" Wings buzzing, she drifted backward. "I like my anger. It makes me strong. It reminds me that the fairies don't have to rely on anybody—not you, not your father, nor even the titans. But at least they will destroy everything I hate."

"Like the living?"

"Especially the living. They're the ones ruining everything! They fight. They steal. They lie. Who needs them?"

"It's not the races stirring the pot this time, Lotuus. It's the titans, and you know that. Now more people die because of it."

"No, the dragons caused this long ago. They imprisoned me and the titans. Wrongly. It is your kind that causes the problem, not mine."

"The titans destroy. The dragons preserve. Even an orc knows that." Palms up and out by his sides, he pleaded with her. "Your kind are not evil. At least not all of them. They follow your lead. You can change their path."

Hovering around Nath, she replied, "You say your dragons preserve life? Then where are they? Hmmm? People fall prey to the titans every day by the hundreds, and not a single dragon has shown up to stop them. They don't care, and I'm curious. Why do you?"

"They care," Nath said under his breath.

Lotuus made a good point, though. Her captivating eyes and voice made her argument quite convincing. If the dragons cared about the people so much, then why didn't they help them more?

"The dragons did help the people. And the people turned on them," Brenwar blurted out. "That's why!"

"That's not how I recall it," she said.

"While you live, it's never too late for redemption, Lotuus," Nath said, offering his hand. He had to try to win her over. Be sincere. There wasn't any other way out of the situation they were in. On a single word from her, the wurmers would strike and kill them all. "Why not change?"

"I tried it the other way before, and it just didn't suit me. I'm more suited for what I do now."

In a warning tone, Nath said, "You'll lose. And this time you won't be locked up again. This time you'll be destroyed by dragon fire."

"What dragon fire? Yours? You don't have any, Nath Dragon. And you don't have that sword to get you out of this bind. No. You're coming with me. We're going to see Eckubahn."

Nath nodded at his friends. "And what about them?"

"You and I are going to watch the wurmers kill them."

CHAPTER
26

A SHADOW COVERED THE FORTRESS AS if a cloud had rolled in above. Looking up, Nath said, "You might want to rethink that!" He pointed at the sky.

Staying the wurmers with her hands, Lotuus peered above. Her lips curled into a sneer. "No, no, no!"

Circling above them was a mountain of scales with wings. A flying fortress with claws and teeth. A dragon. And not just any dragon, a sky raider with horns on its skull the size of twisted oaks.

"I'm guessing he's here to help *me*, not you," Nath said. "And judging by the look in his eye, well, he won't be taking any prisoners. So what will it be, Lotuus? Do you want to surrender?" Nath hitched his leg up on a barrel of grain. "I tell you what, give me back my sword—"

"And my war hammer!" Brenwar blurted out.

"Yes, and that," Nath continued, "and I'll let you go free. See, I'm reasonable. No bloodshed. No violence." He cleared his throat. Nath was buying time.

Where in the world did that sky raider come from? His timing couldn't have been better. Good thing she doesn't know that. I'd better pour it on.

"I know what you're thinking, Lotuus. Certainly a dozen of your wurmers can take down the raider. But that would divide your forces. I don't mean to brag, but more dragons are on the way. He just happened to be the closest one in the area."

Fists balled up at her sides, Lotuus replied, "You're a horrible liar, Nath Dragon."

He shrugged and glanced up. "Am I?"

A second shadow fell over the crowd of onlookers below. Another sky raider had appeared. Saliva dripped from the jaws of the wurmers. Their throats rumbled like rattles. Death filled their bright eyes. Their sharp teeth chomped and grinded together. They wanted to fight. They wanted to kill. It was their only purpose.

"Impossible," she said through her teeth.

"Am I not the Dragon Prince? You shouldn't be surprised." He stretched his hand toward her and clasped his fingers in and out. "Return my sword."

Eyeing the sky, Lotuus chewed her lip. Her eyes glided between Nath and the sky raider dragons. She swallowed a lump in her throat. "I don't have your sword."

"Now who's the rotten liar?"

"Well, not on me," she said, displaying her lovely figure and spinning in the air. "Do I look like someone who would adorn myself so heavily?"

"Where is it?" Nath demanded.

"Oh, you'll find it." She pointed. "It's in the woods, over there somewhere."

The two sky raiders started to descend.

"I think you need to be more specific."

"Do I need to draw you a map?" she yelled.

"Yes," he replied. "And I want my lock of hair back."

Hugging it, she said, "But I'm so fond of it."

"Hand it over."

"Fine." She threw it down on the ground. "Your sword is with the dead wilder elves a league that way. Just follow the stench." She motioned to the wurmers. "Come."

She darted off into the sky, looking over her shoulder, heading north and away from Thraag. The wurmers took right in behind her.

The sky raiders' roars were louder than thunder. Their voices shook the walls like great brass horns. "MAAAAAOO-OOOOOOOO! MAAAAAOOOOOOOO!" The pair of great dragons gave chase after the wurmers.

"They're going after them!" Nath ran for the steps that led up the catwalk and watched from the walls. "Look!"

The huge sky raiders tore through the sky and descended on the wurmers. The wurmers turned and attacked. Flames gushed out of a sky raider's mouth, enveloping the wurmers in a great ball of fire. They screeched and burned. Tumbled from the sky. The second sky raider smashed through the wurmer ranks. The wurmers pinned themselves to its body, scratching, clawing, and biting. The sky raider took the dragon insectoids to the ground and ripped them to pieces with its claws. It gored them with its horns and tore them apart with its tail.

The wurmers fought in a knot of fury. They spat balls of fiery energy. They dug in with claws and teeth. The sky raiders, mighty and strong, brought the heat. The entire valley turned into dragon flames. Pillars of black smoke went up in a huge plume.

Nath lost sight of the battle in the all-consuming smoke and fire. Only the angry roars were heard, so loud that they seemed to shake the entire world. He could feel the searing heat on his face. He smiled.

A minute later, the sky raiders burst out of the flames and let out a roar of victory.

"MAAAAOOOOOOO! MAAAAAOOOOOOO!"

The grand dragons circled once, and upward they went, vanishing into the clouds.

Standing beside Nath, Liam said, "That was awesome."

"Where did they come from?" Brenwar said to Nath. "Did you summon them?"

"I wish I had, but no." He shook his head and shrugged. "I guess today just happens to be my day. Selene!"

"What about her?" Brenwar said. "Did you not find her?"

"No, I did." Nath's eyes searched out Sansla. He saw him on a tower and motioned for him to come down. The great ape glided down and landed by Nath's feet. "Sansla, I need you to take Selene somewhere safe. Can you take her to Dragon Home for me?"

"I will," Sansla agreed.

Nath went into the barn. Selene and the halflings were gone.

CHAPTER
27

"**S**ELENE! AW, WHAT AM I yelling for? She wouldn't hear me anyway." Nath kicked up some hay. "She sleeps like the dead." He raced from stall to stall and searched high and low. He looked in every spot he could find.

Oddly, the wrathhorns were silent within their stalls. Not a single one of them nickered. Nath spun around. There wasn't anywhere for Selene or the halflings to go, and the halflings certainly couldn't have carried her off.

"Everyone search," Nath said to Liam.

Brenwar marched in and said, "What are we looking for?"

Aggravated, Nath said, "Selene!"

"Oh," Brenwar muttered.

"They couldn't have gotten far." Nath stormed out of the stables. Eyeing the towers, he said, "Search them too!"

A pair of roamers sprinted up to each tower. It was absurd to think the halflings could have taken Selene into the towers. Even in human form, she was twice as heavy as them. They wouldn't have been able to carry her away. And the battle hadn't lasted that long, so they couldn't have gotten that far anyway.

What if they weren't halflings? What if they were something else?

"Sansla!" Nath yelled to the great white ape who was perched on the catwalks looking over the walls. "Will you check from the sky?"

In a single bound, Sansla leapt into the air with his wings beating and took off into the sky. Nath sighed.

Brenwar stepped into view. "You need to settle yourself down. You're going about this all wrong."

"Am I?"

Fists on his hips, Brenwar gave a matter-of-fact, "Yes."

"And what would you do differently?"

Rubbing his bearded chin, the dwarf replied, "First, I'd go and secure my hammer, but I guess we can try to find your long-tailed woman."

"Brenwar, don't start—"

"You're a tracker, aren't you?"

"The best."

"Then track! You've got me and the roamers, all of the best trackers in the world, and all you are doing is running around and screaming."

Nath's boiling blood started to cool. Taking a breath he said, "You know, you're right."

"Of course I am. I'm a dwarf."

"That's clear." Nath headed back into the stables where he left Selene. He took a long draw through his nose. Among the straw and manure and other things, Selene's scent still lingered. There was an impression in the ground where he had left her. There were signs of her body being dragged over the dirt and straw.

"The trail seems pretty clear to me," Brenwar said. "I'm not sure how you missed it."

"You missed it too."

"I did not. I wasn't looking."

The trail came to a stop in front of one of the wrathhorns' stables. The huge beast eyed Nath from the other side with intent eyes. Nath had to get up on his toes to gaze within. The wrathhorn shuffled into his path, blocking his view.

"Will you get out of the way?" Nath argued.

The beast-like horse snorted all over him.

"Hah!" Brenwar laughed, slapping his knee.

Wiping the monster snot off him, Nath glared at Brenwar.

"Well, that was funny. 'Humor is good in sour times.' The great dwarven philosopher Puukiin said that."

Nath grabbed the stall's latch handle and pulled it back.

"What are you doing?" Brenwar said, dropping back with his elven battle-axe. "Pardon me for not wanting to get stomped on again."

"Are you telling me you can't take it?"

"I'm telling you I've been trampled enough for one day and I'm not keen on it ever happening again."

Metal scraped against metal, and the latch was pulled back. Slowly, Nath pulled the door open.

On the other side, the wrathhorn's spiked hooves clawed at the dirt. It nickered and shook its great head.

"Stay here and secure the door behind me," Nath said, glancing back at Brenwar.

"Somebody must have hit you in the head today, but I'll do it."

When he stood face to face with the wrathhorn, the gate clanked shut behind Nath.

"Are you still breathing in there?" Brenwar said.

"Yes."

Nath reached out and softly placed his hand on the bridge above the horse creature's nose. He traced around the curves of its horn. The wrathhorn stood a full head taller than a normal horse. It was built stronger too. Though it lacked the grace and refinement of its smaller, less formidable counterpart, there was still something remarkable and beautiful about it. Staring into its eyes, Nath saw a deep horse-like intelligence lurking within. He petted the shag under its chin and wondered if it had indeed been just a regular horse once or if it had always been something else entirely.

"Excuse me," said a soft little voice. It was the female halfling whom Nath had rescued. She stood right underneath the belly of the dangerous monster stallion. "Are you looking for your friend?"

Squatting down, Nath said to the pie-faced, toe-headed little halfling, "You shouldn't be under there. It's dangerous. This beast will trample you. Turn your bones to meat."

The halfling giggled. "No, it won't." She had a coarse horse brush in her hand and started stroking its belly. "We take care of the beasts. We feed them. Brush them. Train them. They won't hurt us because they know we wouldn't hurt them. Boy, you sure had them stirred up earlier. It's a good thing we arrived in time to calm them down. They can smell those gates. One charge. One kick. I've seen it happen before." She grinned. "It killed two orcs. That was funny. Orcs are stupid."

"Can you tell me where my friend Selene is?"

Out of nowhere, another voice chimed in. "She's in the back." The male halfling was sitting backward on the wrathhorn's neck. His eyes were brown, but bright. There was more life in them than there had been before. "Safe, thanks to us. Are all the orcs dead?"

Squeezing by the beast and toward the back, Nath said, "Yes."

"All of them?" asked the female.

"We're double-checking." Nath ventured to the very back of the stall. In the back was a trough, and on the other side lay Selene, fast asleep. He rushed to her side.

"Why is she sleeping?" asked the female halfling, standing on the lip of the trough to look over Nath's shoulder.

"Yes, how can anyone sleep in the middle of all this excitement?" asked the male halfling on the other side of Nath.

Picking Selene up in his arms, Nath said, "I wish I had an answer to that."

"She has a tail," said the female. "Do you have an answer to that?"

Rubbing Nath's arms, the man said, "And why are your arms so scaly? Are you a demon?"

"No!"

The halflings scuttled underneath the wrathhorn, clinging together and eyeing Nath. "Don't smite us, demon."

"I'm not a demon. No one is going to smite anybody, not anybody non-orcen at least."

"Oh." Resuming their friendly and curious demeanor, both halflings asked, "So why does she have a tail?"

"Nath!" Brenwar yelled from the other side of the gate.

"What?"

"Get out here! We've got a problem!"

CHAPTER 28

WITH SELENE IN HIS ARMS once more, Nath followed Brenwar into the courtyard, where Sansla and Liam were talking. "What's going on? As you can see, I found her."

"More company is coming," Sansla said. Liam nodded beside him and added, "Yes, come see for yourself." He led them up the catwalks to where they could gaze over the western wall.

"Oof," Brenwar remarked.

Well over a mile out on the open plains that led to Thraag, an Orcen army marched. It wasn't a small army. Orcs by the thousands. From the long distance, Nath's keen eyes watched the orc banners wave. There were heavily armored foot soldiers along with riders in the dozens.

"Excellent," Liam said. "I like a challenge."

"I don't imagine they know we're here, but they will know, soon enough," Nath said. "We need to move on."

"But this is a victory," Liam said. "This fortress is our prize. I see no reason to give it up."

"We didn't come here to take the fortress. We came to get Selene. Now that we have her, we must go."

"I want to stay. We have the wall, the towers. We'll pick them apart," Liam said. He wasn't being argumentative, just passionate.

"And what will you do when you run out of arrows?" Brenwar said, poking Liam's quiver. "Will you play the lute for them until they go away?"

"There are plenty of crossbow bolts in that armory. As I said," Liam replied, "we can hold them off for days."

"Liam, our mission here is accomplished," Sansla said. "It's time to depart."

"I need a favor, Sansla," said Nath.

"What do you wish, Dragon Prince?"

He handed the winged ape Selene. "Take her somewhere safe. Dragon Home would be best. I cannot continue to carry her with the journey ahead."

"In case I cannot make it to Dragon Home, I know another place of safety to secure her." Sansla eyed the roamers. "We shall guard her with our lives. Roamers, it's time to depart."

Liam took a knee. "My King, perhaps I could render aid to Nath Dragon on his journey."

"That is up to him." With Selene cradled in his arms, Sansla took off into the sky with a powerful leap.

"Liam," said Nath, "I need you to lead the orcs off our trail. Surely they will be in pursuit, and Brenwar and I need to make haste to find our weapons."

"The roamers will handle that chore just fine without me," Liam said.

"I don't think your father would be pleased if you left your men. Especially with your uncle Hoven in such peril." Nath put his hand on Liam's shoulder. "I appreciate the offer, but what's the right thing to do?"

"Stay behind and kill the orcs?"

"No."

"Fine." Liam made a hand signal and let out a sharp whistle. The roamers lowered the front gate, and their horses came in. Liam's horse stopped just below the catwalk. Liam patted Brenwar on the shoulder. "You're not a bad fighter, for a dwarf." He jumped onto the horse's back. "Soon again, Nath dragon. Soon again." He galloped off after the roamers.

"Stupid elf," Brenwar grumbled. "He's got spirit, though."

Eyeing the oncoming army, Nath noted a cloud of dust that had come up. The orc riders were galloping their way. "Guzan!"

"What?" Brenwar asked.

"If I were to guess, I'd say the orcs were waiting for a signal and hadn't received one. We'd better get moving."

"I'll never outrun those horses on these short little legs." Brenwar leaned his axe against the parapet wall, spat in his hands, rubbed them together, picked the battle-axe back up, and said, "No. I guess we'll have to stay and fight. I'll go close the gate."

"Don't be silly. We can ease out of here and be on our way just fine."

"You know those orcs can smell me from a mile away."

"Excuse me!" the halfling man called up to Nath from below the catwalk. He was riding on the back of a wrathhorn. Two more wrathhorns were being towed behind him. "If you want to outdistance the orcs, you should ride on one of these."

"I'm not getting on one of those things!" Brenwar yelled.

"I don't think you have a choice."

"I do."

"No, you don't," Nath said. "I'm getting on. You're getting on." He hopped off the catwalk, eased up to the middle beast, put his foot in the oversized stirrup, and climbed on. He looked up at Brenwar on the catwalk. "Come on. Those orcs are closing in fast. Can't you hear them?"

"I hear them, I hear them, already!" Eyeing the beast with wary eyes, Brenwar jumped down into the saddle and grabbed the reins. He stared at the female halfling, who was smiling at him. "What are you looking at?"

"Why is your hand so bony?"

Brenwar glowered at her. "Why is your pie hole so big?"

"What's a pie hole?" she asked.

"Let's go," Nath dug his heels into the beast's ribs. It took off at a thunderous trot toward the gate that led out of the fortress. A soft clicking sound caught his ears. In the saddle he turned. The orc cyclops Gaak stood underneath the bottom of the catwalk where they had fought. He was taking aim with a heavy crossbow in his arms. "Nooooo!"

Clatch-Zip!

The bolt rocketed through the air and plunged into Brenwar's back.

The dwarf pitched forward in the saddle. "Aargh!"

"Hang on, Brenwar!" Nath turned his mount and rode back for his friend.

Gaak was running right for him with a sword in his hand. "I will kill you, Nath Dragon. I will have your head!"

Nath scooped Brenwar out of the other saddle onto his. He shouted at the halflings, "Ride! Ride! Ride!"

CHAPTER
29

IN TREMENDOUS STRIDES, THE WRATHHORNS thundered down the road faster than any horse could run. "Where are we going?" the halfling yelled back at Nath.

Snapping the reins, Nath rode up alongside him. "West, toward the forest."

At least, that was the impression he'd been given by Lotuus. She could have been lying, but he had sensed she was defeated. "Brenwar! Can you hear me?"

The dwarf didn't reply. The bolt still protruded from his back, and it was buried deep, right near the spine.

"Brenwar!"

Even with a bad wound it wasn't often that a dwarf stopped fighting. Perhaps there was something worse in that bolt. Poison maybe. Nath wouldn't put anything past the orcs. Especially one that had been turned into a nuurg.

Suddenly, the female halfling started screaming from behind them. "He's coming. Gaak's coming!"

The cyclops rode hard and right after them. He was on the back of a wrathhorn with a hungry look in his eye.

I should have finished him.

Brenwar shifted. His head popped up. "What's going on? Ow! What did you stick in my back?"

"It's a bolt. A cyclops shot you," Nath replied.

"What cyclops?"

On the back of the galloping wrathhorn, Nath spoke above the rushing wind, "The big one with one eye. The nuurg called Gaak!"

"A slimy orcen one-eyed coward shot me in the back?" Brenwar puffed through his beard. "I'll kill him!"

"Just hang on. I told you to wear armor that covered your back."

"Why would I do that? Dwarves advance, they don't retreat. Back armor is for cowards!"

"And so is shooting people in the back," Nath reminded him.

Brenwar squirmed in the saddle.

"Be still!" Nath said.

The dwarf twisted away, fell off the saddle, and bounced off the ground.

Nath wheeled the monster horse around. "Are you mad?"

Brenwar popped up on his feet and with the bolt still sticking out of his back was off and running toward the oncoming nuurg.

Seeing his dwarven prey, the nuurg bore down on Brenwar. The wrathhorn's thundering hooves kicked up the dirt. "Hahahaha!" the cyclops bellowed from his saddle. "The dwarf and the dragon both will die!"

Still barreling forward, eyes up and lowering his shoulders, Brenwar shouted, "For Morgdon!" He tackled the wrathhorn in the legs.

The beast pitched forward with a frightening whine and crashed to the ground.

The cyclops Gaak tumbled head over heels over the beast's head, popped up on a knee with a mouthful of grass, and wiped the mud from his eye.

Brenwar plowed into him. His powerful arms, like balls of muscle, punched away.

Whop! Whop! Whop!

The cyclops recoiled. His arms were flailing. "Get off of me!"

Brenwar didn't let up. There was blood in his eyes. A deep, angry hatred. Every punch he threw was as fanatical as the next. He climbed up on the dazed giant's back and locked his arms around his neck. The small grizzly of a dwarf squeezed.

"Urk!" The cyclops clawed at the air. His eyes popped open wide.

"This is what you get for shooting me in my back!" Brenwar yelled. He squeezed the life out of the cyclops Gaak.

The orc breathed no more. His giant body lay limp on the earthen floor.

The dwarf shoved the body to the side and rose back up on his feet. "For Morgdon."

Not hiding his amazement and excitement, Nath said, "Aye, for Morgdon. I've never seen anyone tackle a horse before. A giant horned one at that."

"And you probably never will again." Brenwar marched forward and teetered. "I feel odd." His eyes fluttered in his head, and he fell face first in the grass.

"Brenwar!"

CHAPTER
30

NATH, THE HALFLINGS, AND THE wrathhorns rode about a league to the general area where he thought Lotuus meant. They had dismounted and were resting in the deep woods. Nath sat on a fallen tree, and Brenwar lay at his feet on his belly. The bolt was still in his back. The halflings were on either side of him.

"Is he dead?" asked the female halfling.

"No, he's not dead. See how his back rises and falls? He's quite alive," Nath said.

The male halfling poked Brenwar with a stick.

Nath snatched the stick away. "Don't do that."

The female halfling hopped off the log. "How come your friends sleep so much? Why does he have a hand made from bone? Where is the skin? And you never told us about your scales. Or her scales."

"Yes," the male halfling agreed, "tell us about the scales. Are they fish scales? Do you come from the water? Are you a merman? I've heard of mermen in the sea. They have scales and fins." He inspected Nath with his eyes. "I see no fins on you."

The female halfling crawled back on the log. "Look for gills. He should have gills like a fish." She piled up his locks of long hair in her tiny hands and lifted them up and tilted her head. "I don't see any gills either."

"I'm not a fish!" he said. "I'm Nath Dragon!"

"I thought Nath Dragon was a dragon," said the female halfling.

"Yes, bigger than the biggest clouds, he is," the male halfling said, nodding his head eagerly.

Nath stuck his face in his palms.

Halflings. How did I get stuck with halflings?

Nath sighed and asked, "What are your names?"

"I am Zoose," the male halfling said, coming to his feet and sticking his chest out. "And my sister is called Goose."

"Zoose, huh? You seem awfully small to be called Zoose." Nath glanced at Goose. "And you're named after a bird?"

"No, my greatest grandmother Goose." She ran her hand over the scales on his arm. "So, you aren't a dragon, you're a fish."

"No, I am a dragon."

"But you don't have any wings or any tail," Zoose said.

"Not all dragons have wings or tails. Most dragons do have tails, except for the tailless dragons. But they are mean. Very mean. They'll swallow the both of you in one bite."

Face drawn up tight, Goose said, "That would be horrible. Do all dragons eat people?"

"It depends." Nath kneeled down by Brenwar and wrapped his hand around the bolt in the dwarf's back.

"Ooh, are you going to pull that out?" Goose said. "Won't that be painful?"

"He could bleed to death," Zoose added. "But I've heard that dwarves have sand for blood. Is that true?"

"No," Nath said, "can't you see the blood on his back? It's his, not someone else's."

Together the halflings said, "Eeeeew."

The wound in Brenwar's back looked bad, but he had been through worse, Nath was certain. Brenwar's last effort when he let loose against Gaak had been something else—a demonstration that proved his friend's will outweighed the dwarf's powerful constitution. Brenwar had tapped out all of his reserves. The dwarf was exhausted.

"Uh, Zoose and Goose, can you fetch me some deckle leaves and pine needles? A few handfuls of dirt would help too. And some water if you can find it."

They nodded eagerly. "Sure, sure," Zoose said. He and she darted into the brush and out of sight.

"That's better," Nath said. He let go of the bolt and leaned back against the fallen tree. His limbs were achy, and he was weary himself. He tilted his head back far enough to where the sun crept through the trees and warmed his face. "Ah."

There was plenty on his mind. Number one, the orcs would be hunting after him. He could only hope the roamers had managed to lead them away from his trail. Number two, Selene was rescued and in safe hands now. At least he hoped so. He'd gotten off to a rough start with Sansla Libor years ago, but he knew the Roamer King could be trusted now. It gave him some relief. And three, his best friend, Brenwar, was down. He wasn't used to seeing the dwarf laid out. It was easier to knock out a tree than a dwarf.

"I hope you aren't going to be out for years, like I was."

Nath felt guilty recalling all those years he'd been in a dragon coma. Twenty-five years at one time, even. Brenwar and the dwarves had guarded him that entire time in the snow-filled banks, high in the mountains. His eyes popped open.

"Sultans of Sulfur. Selene!"

What would it be like if she was going through such a change like he did? He might not see her for decades. And at the rate the titans were going, there wouldn't be anything left of Nalzambor in another decade. He sat up.

"I have to stop them."

"Stop who?" Goose said. She was standing right behind him with her hands full of deckle leaves and her pockets full of pine needles. "Oh, and Zoose is bringing the dirt. Or mud. Or water, was it? What is all of this for?"

"It's to stanch the bleeding."

"Oh." She cocked her head. "Who's bleeding?"

"Bleeding?" Zoose had arrived. He had made two bowls out of green leaves and twigs. One was filled with mud and the other water. "Who's bleeding?"

"Brenwar," Nath said.

Scratching his brown locks, Zoose replied, "Who is Brenwar?"

"Just bring over what you have."

The halflings laid out their supplies by Nath's side.

Nath rubbed his hands together, grabbed the bolt in Brenwar's back, and said, "You might want to get back, in case he kicks."

Neither of the halflings moved. Their eyes were filled with anticipation.

Nath yanked the bolt out.

Brenwar jumped up and cried, "Yeouch! What in Morgdon are you doing? It felt like you just ripped my spine out!"

Staring at the crossbow bolt, Nath noticed tiny barbs on it. It was meant to go in but never come out. "Sorry, Brenwar."

Brenwar snatched the bolt out of his hand and huffed through his beard. "I hate those dirty orcs." He turned his back to Nath. "All right, all right. Stick some dirt in that pothole you just put in me."

"Just lie down again," Nath said, looking at the wound in Brenwar's back and grimacing.

"I don't like lying down." Brenwar said, stretching out flat on the grass. "Sleeping is for the weak."

CHAPTER
31

"T HIS IS HORRIBLE," GOOSE SAID. The little female halfling was
aghast and covering her nose with her shirt.

Nath had found the area that Lotuus had mentioned. The
rogue elves lay dead. Slaughtered. The claws and the teeth of the wurmers
had torn them to bits, but not without a fight. A couple of wurmers were
withered husks. Their decaying bodies wilted like acid had eaten them.

Nath took a knee where one body had been destroyed by an unknown
energy. He plucked a metal pin from the ashes. It was the mark of the rogue
elf leader, Slavan. He clenched it in his fist. "Lotuus."

Brenwar lumbered through the nearby woodland, a little gimpy and
grumbling. "She's a liar. All fairies are liars. It wouldn't surprise me one bit if
my hammer was sunk in the sea."

"I don't think it's made it that far," Nath said. Rising up to full height, he
scratched his head. It didn't really make a lot of sense that Lotuus would leave
the weapons out in the open. They were too big for the fairies to carry, and
the wurmers didn't have the means, but she would have hidden them with
magic, and they could be anywhere. Inside a rock or a stone. Maybe inside a
tree—or just invisible. He put his foot up on a stump that looked a little like
a throne. "Where are you, Fang?"

"Who is Fang?" Zoose asked.

"That's the sword we're looking for, you fluffy-headed little iggit!"
Brenwar yelled.

Appearing at Brenwar's side, Goose asked, "What's an iggit?"

"Nath, can't you dismiss them?" Brenwar said.

"I suppose I could. Zoose and Goose, you are both dismissed. Free to go
home. Wander. Roam." Nath shooed them away. "It's been nice to meet you.
Now move along."

Standing with each other, Goose said, "Go where?"

"To your home."

"Oh," Zoose said, "and where might that be?"

"You don't know where you're from?" Nath asked.

"We were born inside the orc fortress," Goose said, picking a wildflower and stuffing it in her mouth. "But we like it out here. It's pretty."

"Brenwar, I think you're stuck with them for the moment."

"Great," the dwarf grumbled. "Now I've got a pain in my back and two more pains in my behind."

"Brenwar!" Nath tossed his head back and laughed. But something caught his eyes. There was a faint trail of blood leading away from the scene. Taking to his feet again, he said, "I think we just might have a witness."

"What's a witness?" Goose asked.

"I tell you what. You two stay with the wrathhorns and wait here until I come back. I shouldn't be gone too long." He patted their little heads. In a comforting way, the halflings made Nath feel bigger again.

If they can survive in this world at such a wee little size, then certainly I can.

"So, will you do that for me?"

The halflings gave excited nods.

"Let's go, Brenwar."

"Gladly."

It appeared that one of the rogue elves had survived by crawling away and then jogging off into the woods. The footprints were staggered and small.

"A female elf," Brenwar said, eyeing the ground.

Nath noted a smear of blood on a tree branch. "It seems a remnant always survives, no matter how bad the devastation is."

Brenwar pointed his thumb over the patched-up wound in his back. "Case in point."

They followed the blood trail over a mile. The rogue elf had done a decent job covering her tracks, but not good enough to avoid Nath's keen eye. Traversing the woodland another two miles, the tracks led them up a hill with a fairly steep incline.

"Whoever it is will run out of blood at some point," Brenwar said, puffing up the hill. He pointed at the ground. "Look."

A bloody handprint was on a sliver of stone that jutted up out of the ground. The rogue elf had started to crawl, gotten up, and fallen down.

Nath caught Brenwar's eye and put his finger to his lips.

The dwarf nodded.

On cat's feet, Nath proceeded forward. His scales tingled from his fingertips to his elbow. Someone was close. He could hear ragged breathing in the brush ahead. He pushed through.

Clatch-zip!

He jerked his head down. A crossbow bolt zipped over his head and lodged itself in a nearby tree. Before him, a wounded lady elf tried to load the crossbow again. Nath closed in and took the crossbow away.

She jerked a dagger from her belt and took a jab. The blade skipped off the scales on his arm. She moaned.

Nath took the blade away. "Enough of that now. You've got enough trouble already." Her wounds were severe. There were gashes in her abdomen, arms, and legs—clear through the black-and-green armor that she wore. Her fine elven features were exhausted, her breathing rough, and her limbs trembling. "Find her some water, Brenwar."

The lady elf's dark eyes found his. "S-Sorry, Nath Dragon. We betrayed you."

He took her in his arms and propped her up.

She coughed and grimaced in pain. "Slavan was not himself. He was deceived." She reached behind her and stuck her hand in the brush. "I secured it."

There was a glint of metal in the brush.

He dusted the woodland debris away. "Fang! And Mortuun!"

"Again, I am sorry. I only followed orders. It was my obligation."

Zoose and Goose popped into the clearing with large leaves filled with water. "Is somebody thirsty?"

"Have you been following us all this time?" Nath asked as he took a leaf and put it to the lady elf's lips.

"Certainly," Goose said.

"What about the wrathhorns?"

"We let them go," Zoose said.

"Let them *go*? There is an army of orcs in pursuit of us. Why would you do that?"

In a cheerful voice, Goose said, "It just seemed like the right thing to do."

"Sure, it was, just the wrong time to do it." Nath grabbed Fang in one hand and picked up the lady elf with the other, laying her over his shoulders as he had done with Selene. "We have to go."

Brenwar appeared. "Did someone say Mortuun?" He noticed the halflings. "And where did you two iggits come from?"

"Don't ask," Nath said. "Grab your hammer."

Brenwar picked his hammer up and gave it a hug. "Mortuun."

CHAPTER
32

"I AM LAYLANA," SAID THE LADY rogue elf. "I'm new to the order that protects the Elven Field of Dreams. Less than five years."

Nath had managed to patch her up good enough that she could walk. Still, their pace was slow. He'd offered to carry her, but once she was able, she refused. She ambled along using a cut branch as a staff to lean on. The lady elf was tough and yet very pretty. Chestnut-brown hair and light-green eyes, trim and captivating.

"You really should rest as much as possible," he said to her. "Everything will mend better."

Eyes forward, she replied, "I'm getting stronger with every step."

"Well, the orcs aren't getting any slower," Brenwar remarked. "I can tell you that." The burly dwarf marched past them both. "We'll be up to my beard if we don't move any faster."

"Pay him no mind," Nath said to Laylana.

"I don't," she replied.

Nath was taking them far north of Narnum into Quintuklen. The hills and dales were easy to travel, and there were plenty of villages where they could get food and rest. Possibly some horses to continue their travels. It was far out of the way of the dwarves and elves that were hunting after them. Nath was curious about that. The deaths of Laedorn and Uurluuk still seemed so unlikely.

"Do you think me guilty of the crime of which I'm accused?" Nath asked Laylana in Elven.

"No," she said.

"Why not?"

"There was no motive. Why would you assault the elves? Of course, it's not my place to question my orders. I am bound by my duty. I'm not a fool, but some of my brethren are. How quickly they've forgotten that you saved the lands from the hordes of Barnabus."

Nath smiled. It felt good to hear someone say something nice for a change. After all, Nath had put a lot of work into saving the land. "Yes, it's awfully strange that the races forget things so quickly."

"That's how it is. People are forgetful, and they seem to always blame someone else for their problems."

"You are awfully wise for such a young elf. Where does that come from?"

"My mother says I get it from my grandfather."

"And who might that be?"

"Laedorn."

Nath stopped in his tracks. His heart sank. It hurt, even. Though he'd had nothing to do with Laedorn's death, he felt guilty for some reason. "Laylana, I'm so sorry. We will find the murderer."

She came to a stop a little bit ahead of him and turned around. "You don't need to apologize, Nath. My grandfather and I were quite close, and he told me a great many things. He knew much about the dragons and told me I could trust them more than the races. Just that I shouldn't poke around in their business."

"There are bad dragons too."

"But you'll know them by their scales, won't you?"

He stuck out his arm. "And what do you know of black-scaled dragons?"

"Nothing, but you're far too handsome to be bad." There was a playful look in her eye. "I've never before seen a person more attractive than an elf."

"Yes, well, don't be deceived. There are many forces that can change the color of scales." Concentrating, he turned his scales from black to white with gold stripes. "Don't judge a dragon by their color. We know what they are by what they do." His scales reverted back to black.

Resuming her trek forward, Laylana said, "Can you change into anything?"

"No." He frowned.

I use to be able to turn into a dragon that could blot out the sun in the sky.

"Just my scales right now."

"But you have other powers, don't you?"

"I can blow smoke." He puffed out a few rings.

She giggled. "That's it?"

Zoose and Goose came rushing out of nowhere, yelling, "Do it again! Do it again!"

"No," he said.

Bouncing up and down like children, they said, "Please! Please! Please!"

Brenwar came storming down the bank. "Don't give in to them. Go away, you silly little things."

Seeing that Laylana was entertained, Nath puffed out some more smoke that covered the halflings.

The halflings started rolling around on the grass, coughing and holding their throats. "No more! No more!"

"That ought to do it," Nath said, tapping his chest with his fist. "I use to be able to puff out fire."

"What happened?" Laylana asked.

"It's a long story."

"Well, I'm sure you have a lot more power within. Be patient. You'll find it again."

"Time will tell." Nath believed it, though.

They walked through the tall grasses for a few more hours. The sun was setting behind the distant mountains. From their high point, the hills rolled down into the river valley.

Brenwar pointed far up ahead. "Village."

Gathering around the dwarf, everyone looked at the village in the valley below. It was a network of small wooden buildings surrounded by split-rail fences where countless livestock grazed. Gardens stretched as far as the eye could see.

"Holbrook," Nath said.

There weren't many places he didn't know from his travels. Holbrook was on the edge, just far enough away from where the orcs travelled. But that might have changed. Holbrook was a place of men with but a smattering of the other races. If anything, it was an extension of Narnum's multicultural environment. "We should be able to find some supplies there."

"I'm not so sure about that." Brenwar swung Mortuun over his shoulder and pointed at some movement just outside the city. Huge men walked among the people, who looked like ants in comparison. "There be giants."

Laylana swooned and collapsed.

CHAPTER 33

N ATH BRUSHED THE HAIR OUT of Laylana's face. Her skin was burning hot. "She's got a fever. That's not good."

Some of the wurmer bites were poisonous. Their claws could burn. Laylana seemed to have avoided the worst effects, but now it had caught up with her.

"We need a healer, Brenwar."

Clawing at his beard with his bone hand, the dwarf said, "Of course we do."

"We'll need supplies from that village. I'm certain they have what I need. Or we can at least find somebody."

"We can go," Zoose suggested.

"You've never been outside the fortress, you said," Nath replied. "I think it's best that you stay here with Brenwar."

"I'm not staying back here with them," Brenwar said.

"Yes, you are. You know you can't get within wind of those giants." Nath spied the colossal figures in the small town. They stood at least twenty feet tall. Three in all. He needed to slip in and slip out quietly. "You'll wait, won't you?"

"Aye, but you better make it quick." Brenwar looked at the halflings. "And I won't be answering any questions from you two chatterboxes."

"Where is the skin from your hand?" Goose asked of Brenwar.

Brenwar glared at Nath. "Just hurry."

Nath tossed Fang on the ground.

"What are you thinking? If those giants find you unarmed, it's all over."

"I won't fit in so well with a giant sword on my back. It'll be hard enough to get around anyway."

"Well, don't be so careless." Brenwar stooped over and pulled Dragon

Claw from out of Fang's hilt. He tossed it to Nath. "Something is better than nothing."

"Good thinking." He tucked the dagger in his belt. "Thanks."

Nath took off running. He made it into the valley in no time and used the cover of the outlying buildings to stay out of the giants' line of sight.

Night had fallen, and very few people were milling through the streets. With the weather being warm, there were plenty of people that sat and talked on porch fronts. By the sound of their voices, it was men and women, maybe some half-orcs and part-elves. Some halflings skittered through the streets carrying buckets. Back pressed to the wall in one of the alleys, Nath peered farther down the street.

Villages of a few thousand people were always quick to spot a stranger. Though not a giant, Nath would stick out like a sore thumb. He noticed something else that was different from before. There were armored patrols walking around in twos. They wore steel caps and carried long wooden clubs.

Great.

Finding a healing ward wouldn't be difficult, but getting inside one without being seen would be a problem. If he was caught, someone would ask questions. If the giants were called, there wouldn't be a place to run, and he had to get some potions or ointment to take care of Laylana. If only Brenwar still had his chest, but that had been left in the care of Bayzog.

Something tugged at his cloak. He snatched a tiny hand in his iron grip and drew the small body that was attached to the hand off the ground. It was Zoose. "What do you think you're doing?"

"I wanted to see the city. I've never been to a city before. It's marvelous."

"You need to go back."

"But I want to help."

"Then go back," Nath said, setting the halfling down.

Rubbing his wrist, Zoose replied, "That doesn't sound much like helping. Please, let me do something. I owe you."

Time was pressing, and discretion was needed. Glancing down the street at all the people on the porch fronts and the patrolling guards, Nath knew he would be noticed. He had a few acquaintances here, but from a long time ago. Things had changed. For all he knew, the people in Holbrook village were under the influence of the titans. It was safer to assume they were.

Nath kneeled down and said to Zoose, "So you want to help?"

Little hands clamped together, and nodding, the halfling said, "Desperately."

"Listen to me, then, and do exactly as I say. Do you know what a sage is?"

Zoose shook his head no.

"A sage is someone who helps the sick. They have potions, balms, ointments, salves, many things like that. Well, every town has a sage of sorts. There is one in this town, as I recall. There is a yellow lantern that burns a green flame from his porch. You will smell incense."

Zoose held up his hand.

Aggravated, Nath said, "Yes?"

"What is incense?"

"It's a pleasant smell, like perfume."

"What is perfume?"

"You've been with the orcs too long," Nath said. "Look, the building will smell different than the rest. A nice smell. The place you seek is several buildings down and across the street." He turned Zoose toward where he wanted him to go. Nath then turned him in another direction, pointed at a barn, and said, "I will wait for you there. Do you understand?"

"What do I tell them?"

"Tell them you have a friend who has a fever, but you'll have to pay them later. If he doesn't help, tell him it's for a man called Nath and that a wurmer got his friend."

Zoose saluted. "I'll see you soon." He skittered into the street and hustled right down the middle. A pair of soldiers stopped him.

"Oh no." Nath dug his nails into his palms. "They're going to skewer him."

One of the soldiers kicked Zoose in the back of the pants. The other shooed Zoose away and started laughing. Zoose hustled down the street rubbing his backside and vanished onto one of the porches.

Talking to himself, Nath said, "I hope this works."

CHAPTER
34

THE BARN NATH OCCUPIED WAS empty of life. No stable hands or farmers. No livestock. Just piles of hay and other farming supplies. Plows. Harnesses. Pitchforks, picks, and shovels. It was dark too. Quiet. Nath climbed up into the loft. There was a window overlooking the village where he could keep an eye out. The soldiers slowly walked the streets. The villagers talked quietly in the shadows of their porches. There were a couple of small taverns where fires burned within, sending smoke up through the chimneys. The people weren't lively like Nath remembered them, but oppressed. He could feel it.

People shouldn't be so miserable. They should be free to think and do as they please.

Spread out among the fields just outside the village were the giants. They stood as statues. They were ugly brutes, bald headed and hairy chested. They wore animal skins for clothes. They had no weapons, just hands that looked like they could crush boulders.

And I thought I got rid of all this treachery.

Nath pulled up a hay bale and took a seat. He figured it would only take a few minutes at most for Zoose to fetch the supplies he needed. It was a risk. Perhaps the help he sought would not come. A sage would help just about anyone. They were like that, finding the good in even the worst of people. They were curious that way. Many long minutes passed into the next hour. Nath got up and started to pace.

I should have gone after it myself. It's taking too much time.

He was worried about Laylana. The sooner they treated her, the better. Wurmer strikes could not only be lethal, but toxic to others in some cases. The lady elf was strong, from a great family. With Laedorn dead, Nath couldn't bear the thought of anything happening to his granddaughter.

I can't wait any longer.

A commotion occurred down the street. Zoose was talking to one of the soldiers. He had with him someone in robes. A wizardly figure, older, with a crown of white hair around the bald top of his head. The older man started talking as well. The soldiers nodded and departed the other way down the street. Zoose and the man Nath assumed to be a sage skittered down the street and into the barn. Nath remained in his spot.

"Nath. Nath," said the soft voice of Zoose. "I've come and brought help."

Nath didn't reveal himself. He waited. Something prickled his scales.

"He said he would be in here," Zoose said to the sage. The halfling rattled a sack of goods the sage had in his hand. He spoke louder. "I have treatments for the lady elf. We need to hurry."

Nath eased his way through the loft, stood on its edge, and said from the darkness, "Who is this with you?"

"I am Leander." The old man spoke with his hands. "A sage, as you requested. I've only come to help and to warn you."

"Warn me of what?"

Leander threw the bag of goods up to Nath. "This halfling has betrayed you. Run, Nath Dragon. Run!"

A knife appeared in Zoose's hand. He stabbed Leander in the side.

Glitch!

"No!" Nath yelled. "Zoose, what have you done?"

The halfling's eyes narrowed, and he waved his knife high. "Praise Eckubahn! Hail the death of Nath Dragon!" He ran out of the barn, sounding the alarm. "He's in there! He's in there!"

Nath peeked through the loft's opening. Soldiers were storming toward the barn. Two of the giants were moving in. One was heading up into the hills where Brenwar and Laylana hid. Nath hopped down, closed the barn door, and barred it shut.

The old sage was coughing and bleeding. He beckoned for Nath.

Nath embraced the man in his arms. "Hang on."

"The halfling came," Leander said, coughing and wincing in pain. "I knew he would deceive you. He told me. Wanted to turn you in. I played along. That's why I came. To warn you. Long ago you saved my father. My mother. I was a boy. I remember. I owe you my life." He patted the sack of goods gripped in Nath's hands. "The magic is good in this. Use it." He looked up into Nath's eyes with one last gaze. "I had a good life, Nath Dragon. I owe you my thanks."

Leander the sage died in his arms. Nath's eyes watered up. He didn't know this man at all, yet the sage had given his life for something Nath had done long ago. With his palm, he closed the man's eyes.

Something whacked the barn door. Axes were chopping into it from the other side.

Chop! Chop! Chop!

Nath carried Leander to a spot in the barn that had a thick bed of hay to lay him in. He set him down. "Thank you, friend." He wiped the tear from his eye. He was still stunned at what Zoose had done. The little halfling had murdered the man in cold blood. How had the halfling deceived him so easily? He hadn't detected anything evil from Zoose or Goose at all. It made him angry inside. He drew his dagger, Dragon Claw, and faced the barn door.

I've got to get to Brenwar!

The chopping stopped. A silence fell. Suddenly, the ceiling groaned and popped. A giant ripped part of the roof off and glared at Nath.

Great Guzan!

CHAPTER
35

FINGERS OUTSTRETCHED AND HUGE FACE snarling, the giant reached for Nath.

Dragon Claw poised to strike, Nath plunged the mystic dagger into the giant's hand.

The monstrous man jerked his hand back and let out a pain-filled bellow. He gaped at his hand. It was disintegrating right before his eyes. "No! Nooooo!"

Nath watched in awe. The disintegration spread up the giant's arm to the shoulder and then across his chest. Through the gaping hole in the roof, Nath watched the giant's screaming face turn to dust and take flight with the wind. He gazed at Dragon Claw. The blade had a violet gleam in the metal. It pulsated in his hand. Nath jerked the bar off the barn door and swung the door open. Holding the dagger out for all of the wide-eyed soldiers to see, he said, "Who else wants to taste my blade's fury?"

The soldiers backed away.

Behind them on horseback was a soldier wearing a full helmet of iron, with a red plume on top that billowed in the evening breeze. He had the insignia of an officer on his chest. "He is only one. We are many!" he said. "Kill him."

"Easier said than done!" Nath tucked Dragon Claw away. He didn't want to kill anybody, but he couldn't waste any time. Surrounded by the advancing club-wielding soldiers, he exploded into action, disarming two men at the same time and using their clubs against them. He sent them to the ground cradling their ribs.

Crack! Crack!

One bludgeoning blow came right after the other. Nath sidestepped and ducked. He parried and twisted. Wood clocked off wood with a crisp resounding effect. He busted knees with hammering blows. Soldiers wailed as he popped their elbows. In less than a minute, all ten soldiers were down on the ground grimacing in pain. One gazed at his broken and swollen hand. Another held his bleeding mouth.

Nath spun the clubs around. "What about you? You on the horse. You started this. Now finish it."

"I'd be happy to!" The commander drew a sword from a scabbard on the saddle. Its blade shimmered like blue lightning.

Nath took a step back and drew his dagger.

Maybe I should have brought Fang.

The commander in the iron helm cracked his reins. "Yah!" The horse charged straight for Nath. The long, bright sword was cocked back, ready to strike.

Eyeing the razor-sharp blade and the galloping horse snorting with fury, Nath gathered his legs underneath him, ready to spring in an instant. The horse closed the gap. Nath hunkered down and sprang away from the cutting blade.

Slice!

"Argh!" Nath yelled. The commander hit him. Right across the back. It burned like fire.

The commander turned the horse around and prepared for another run. He held the sword high. The blade was longer than it had been before. It seemed to stretch like fire toward the dark sky. "You look surprised, Nath Dragon. You should be!"

The man had spoken with vague familiarity. Behind the horse and rider, Nath could see a giant still climbing the hill. He'd lost track of the third one. He eyed the mystic blade again.

And I thought I only had the giants to worry about.

He pulled his shoulders back. "You'll miss."

"With this blade," the rider said, "I never miss!" He dug his heels into the horse. "Yah!"

With thoughts faster than movement, Nath had to consider the possibility that the soldier wasn't lying. The blade he carried must have had a special power that made the man so sure of himself. Nath had Dragon Claw, but like Fang, its powers were unpredictable. And its length was much too short. As the oncoming horse and rider came closer and got larger, Nath made an instantaneous decision that he hadn't considered before.

Run!

He ran back into the barn and bolted the door behind him.

Whew! That should buy me some time.

Outside the barn door, the horse nickered.

Nath started for the other side of the barn. He could cut through there and make a run for the hills and find Brenwar. He jogged to the other side and swung the big door open. He was greeted by a pair of giant legs and was eye level with the knees. He backed up. "Not a good idea."

Slice!

He turned. The man in the iron helmet had sliced through the secured barn door. He kicked it open and marched inside. "Going somewhere?" he said with a confident voice.

"No, but I was hoping you were." Nath studied the man. There was something familiar in his walk. It had a slight hitch in it. The iron helmet was different. It had two metal horns that pointed down on the sides. The eyes were rectangular slits. The mouth was small bars of metal. "Who are you?"

"You would like to know that, wouldn't you?"

"Actually, no, I was just buying time." Nath backed up into one of the stalls. "And I'm certain there's a really good reason why you hide your face so well."

"So brazen. So bold!" Twenty feet away from Nath, the warrior cranked the sword back and swung. An arc of energy cut through the barn and knocked Nath Dragon from his feet.

Nath clutched at his chest. The force had sheared through his clothes and seared the material.

Guzan, what kind of sword is that?

He rose to his feet with wary eyes.

The warrior sliced the blade back and forth over the ground. It made a strange humming sound with each ground-dusting swipe. "I never imagined a day when you walked right into my hands. But you did. How delightful. Revenge is such a tasty, tasty dish."

Now Nath really was curious who the man was, but he wasn't going to ask. He shuffled back. There was a stir behind him. The giant. Caught up in the moment, he'd forgotten about the other giant. His head whipped around too late. The giant caught Nath in its massive steel-strong grip. "Gah!"

"You killed my brother," the giant said, bringing Nath up into his face. "I will feast on your bones one at a time."

CHAPTER
36

Gripped inside the monstrous hand of the giant, Nath squirmed and gulped for air. The giant's fingers were crushing his ribs. Arms still free, he held out his glowing dagger and said to the monster's face, "You saw what happened to your brother. Do you want to suffer the same fate?"

"I just want to kill you," the giant said. His jaw dropped open, and he brought Nath toward his mouth.

"I warned you!" Nath stabbed the giant in the hand. The blade sank deep and drew blood.

The giant's hairy eyebrows buckled. A sneer curled on his lips. He said, "Ow."

Nath stabbed the giant in the hand again and again. The blade bit deep and drew blood.

The giant's grip tightened.

Nath's eyes bulged. "Thanks for nothing, Dragon Claw," he spat. "You're just like your brother."

Using both hands, the giant tried to stuff Nath in its mouth.

Nath braced his free hand against the upper row of the giant's teeth. "I am not a meal!" He gagged. "And your breath is horrible!"

The giant jerked his head back and brought it right back forward, head-butting Nath.

Blurry-bright stars exploded behind Nath's eyes. His limbs loosened from head to toe. Dragon Claw started to slip from his fingertips. Head rolling on his shoulders, he watched the giant's gaping maw open up once more. It had a second row of teeth in its huge mouth. Its red tongue was like a spongy rug beneath his feet.

Nath's inner fire ignited.

He caught his breath and unleashed it.

A stream of gray smoke poured out of his mouth and filled the entire barn in seconds. The giant started coughing and choking. Nath's grip refastened on the dagger. He plunged it into the giant's wrist again, but this time with all his dragon might.

The monstrosity screeched in pain. "AAAAIIIIEEEEEEEEEE!" Its grip loosened.

Nath twisted free and landed flat on his feet. He fumbled through the barn and snatched up the sack of goods Leander had brought him, now glad he had set it down before the giant grabbed him. He dashed through the blinding smoke and out of the barn. More soldiers approached, shouting and yelling. Nath raced up the hill, making a beeline for Brenwar and Laylana. He glanced over his shoulder.

The man in the iron mask staggered out of the barn and fell to his knees. His chest heaved. He gave a sharp whistle. His horse trotted to his side. The man pulled himself up into the saddle, snapped the reins, and galloped after Nath.

Ribs aching, Nath sprinted at full speed. He could run faster than most four legged animals, including horses. Aside from the roamer steeds that were much faster than most, he could outrace almost anything.

I might not be able to fly, but at least I can run like I have wings on my feet.

Brenwar stood over Laylana. The elven princess's breathing had become ragged. She trembled. He put his calloused hand on her head. It was hot. "You'll have to forgive me. I'm not much good at helping elves."

She reached up and grabbed his hand. Her eyes were open, but she wasn't there. She squeezed tight and let go again.

Brenwar's throat tightened. Seeing the lady elf hurting hurt him. Even though he had little love for the elves, he did have love for life. "Goose," he said. He hadn't seen the female halfling in a while. He'd told her to keep a lookout over the village. "Goose?"

He and the elf were surrounded by the cover of trees, tucked away out of sight. He clawed at his beard. Sniffed. Something somewhere was burning. Wood. Brenwar headed out of his hiding spot in search of the halfling. On the nearby hilltop overlooking Holbrook, the orange glow of a fire caught his eyes. He spied Goose dropping branches on it. The small blaze was catching fast in the wind. "By Morgdon, what the gallows is going on?" he yelled at her.

Startled, she dropped the wood she held in the fire.

"Put that out, you little fool!" he said.

"No," she replied. There was a devious glimmer in her eye. "If I do that, the giant will have a hard time finding you. And he might need the fire to cook you on."

"Are you mad?"

"No, I'm Goose. Long live Eckubahn! May the giants feast on you!" She fished something out of a little pouch and tossed it on the fire. The blaze shot up toward the sky, lighting up the hillside like day.

Brenwar shielded his eyes behind his forearm. Once the bright blaze went down, he rushed up the hill toward it. Goose was nowhere to be found. "Halflings! I knew they'd do something stupid."

The ground shook.

The town below was alive with activity. Soldiers charged down the dirt roads in a clamor. A hundred yards away and storming up the hill was a bigger problem. A giant was on its way with a hammer the size of a man in each hand. At least a dozen soldiers were behind him.

Brenwar's face scrunched up. His grip tightened on Mortuun. He butted the war hammer with his head and yelled down the hill, "You want to dance? Then let's dance! For Morgdon!"

CHAPTER
37

A BLINDING FLASH FROM THE HILLTOP smote Nath's eyes. His pace slowed. A horse nickered way behind him.

What was that?

He forged ahead. Behind, the man in the iron helm had lost control of his mount. A fire blazed ahead. A giant was charging up the hillside a ways away with a knot of well-armed soldiers following behind him.

That's when Nath heard Brenwar's battle cry. Against the night sky, the dwarf's silhouette appeared in front of the blazing fire. Brenwar was winding up the hammer like a windmill. A second later he let it fly.

A thunderclap rocked the summit.

Kraa-Booooom!

The charging giant's head snapped back. He teetered backward and stumbled on two soldiers, smashing them into the grass. His oversized limbs were still moving. He shook his head, stuck his hand in the earth, rubbed his chin, and rose again. The soldiers surged by and stormed Brenwar.

Nath cut through the grasses like a knife through butter. He blindsided three soldiers, knocking through them like a stampeding bull. Still running, he snatched Mortuun off the ground and tossed it over to Brenwar, saying, "Fang?"

Snatching the hammer from the air, Brenwar said, "Right where you left him." He started winding up again.

"I'll be right back. Hold them off until then."

"They'll be dead by then," Brenwar replied.

Nath dashed into the deep woods. The rider in the helm had almost crested the hill. Nath weaved through the trees into the hidden clearing. Fang was stuck in the dirt several feet from where Laylana rested. He carefully dumped the sage's gifts onto the ground next to her. Not sure what was what, he popped off the lid to a jar of salve. It was cool and soothing to the touch. He rubbed it on her forehead.

The horse and iron-helmed rider erupted from the brush. The rider hopped off the horse and slapped its hindquarters, sending it charging into the woods. He cracked his neck from side to side and flexed his powerful arms with the incredible blade gripped tight in his fingers. He tipped his chin at Fang.

Nath glided over to his magnificent blade, took the hilt in both hands, and pulled it free of the ground. "I take it you want a duel with me?"

The rider nodded. His build was powerful and familiar. The height of the man matched Nath's own. His shoulders were that of a bull, and the muscles in his arms were hammered iron. The blade glimmered with angry energy.

"It's seems you know who I am, but I don't know who you are," Nath said while he stuck Dragon Claw back inside Fang's pommel. "Care to share?" He rested the sword on his shoulder.

With one hand, the man removed his iron helmet and dropped it on the ground.

Nath lost his breath. "Kryzak!"

Brenwar's next swing sent two men flying back down the hill. "That's what we call a dwarven kiss!" Mortuun busted, dented, or popped the rivets of every armored soldier that crossed his path. Soldier after soldier fell. Brenwar battered a path of bodies to the giant, who had finally regained his feet and secured his grip on his hammers. Gazing up at the huge man, Brenwar said, "Now it's just you and me, big belly!"

Striking as fast as a normal man, the giant's hammer came down.

Brenwar spun aside.

The giant's hammer left a huge divot in the ground. The second hammer did too. Moved by arms like pistons, the heavy hammerheads dropped like drumsticks off a plate, tearing and shaking the ground.

Bam! Bam! Bam! Bam! Bam!

Brenwar slipped away like a bearded mouse scurrying from the falling keys of a piano. He snuck between the hammer strikes and busted the giant in the shin. The head of Mortuun, forged in the great fires of Morgdon and enchanted by the dwarven Mystics of the Mountainside, splintered the bone like it was dry-rotted kindling.

Letting out a tremendous moan, the giant dropped to a knee. Its eyebrows buckled. Its face hardened with rage. Giants were cocky. Not so smart, but when wounded they fought like wild animals. A wild swing took Brenwar from his feet and skipped him down the hill.

He rolled to a stop and charged up the hill again.

The giant chucked one of his hammers at Brenwar.

The dwarf flattened on his belly.

Two men piled on him and hammered away with fists and elbows. Something sharp bit into his leg.

Brenwar popped one in the forehead with the head of his war hammer. He kicked but couldn't free his legs.

The giant was coming.

The dwarf was tangled up in a knot of flesh.

The giant scooped the three of them up off the ground and started stuffing them into its oversized mouth.

Struggling frantically, Brenwar yelled, "Nobody eats a dwarf!" He shoved one soldier forward.

The giant's jaws clamped down on the screaming man.

Crunch!

Arms free, Brenwar unloaded on the giant and busted out a row of teeth.

The giant dropped him and growled.

Brenwar wound up and turned loose a mighty swing that collided with the giant's other knee.

The giant fell to the ground.

Without hesitation, Brenwar unloaded the wrath of Mortuun.

Whop! Whack! Boom!

The giant died from the final divot Brenwar put in its head.

Puffing for breath, the dwarf looked down the hill. More soldiers were coming, and giants too. "I don't suppose they're coming to congratulate me. Humph."

CHAPTER
38

NATH STOOD IN DISBELIEF AT seeing the Barnabus cleric, Kryzak, who had tormented him. He had defeated the man—put him to death—in the Contest of Champions. Now, one of Selene's greatest servants had come back from the dead. Yet something was different. This man was not marred with tattoos.

"Your keen eyes do not deceive you, Nath Dragon, at least not how you think they would." The hard-faced warrior circled. "Yes, my face is familiar, the same as my brother Kryzak's, but I am not he. I am Rybek."

"Your brother was an evil fool, and I take it you're just the same."

"Worse. My brother let his love for Selene blind him from his mission. It made him weak." Rybek sliced clean through a small tree with his sword. "Though he was a fool, I still feel compelled to avenge him. You see, I was there the day you took him down in your monstrous form at the Contest of Champions." His voice became angry. Deadly. "I saw your woman, Selene, turn him inside out and made a pawn. A sacrifice. I vowed revenge not only on you, but on her. And her execution, if it has not already happened, will happen soon enough."

Eyes narrowing, Nath demanded, "What do you mean?"

"The eyes of the titans are everywhere. Surely, you have encountered the betrayal of the halflings. There is nowhere you can go where we will not see. We know that Sansla Libor has taken her. The wurmers, I'm certain, have hunted them down. Hah, one winged ape versus a hundred wurmers? She's dead by now."

"Who is we?"

"It doesn't matter. All that matters is that you die!" Rybek swang. An arc of energy sliced through the air, wiping out everything in its path.

Nath brought Fang around in front of him. The great blade collided with the great energy, jarring his arms and knocking him back. Fang's metal let out a moan. The grip filled with wild energy that coursed through Nath's veins. Nath's eyes flashed like golden lightning. "You say you're a warrior! Then let's fight, steel on steel!"

"Gladly!"

Man and dragon charged one another. Nath turned loose a devastating swing.

Rybek parried.

Clang!

The surrounding branches on the trees bent. The mystic blades danced an angry dance. Mystic sparks sizzled off the metal.

Nath brought his blade forward, blow after blow.

Rybek ducked, dodged, and dived. He countered with surprising speed. Struck with the strength of many men. He matched every move Nath had— and snuck in some moves of his own.

The blades sang out songs of clashing steel. Back and forth the fighters went, toe to toe, blade to blade, pushing back and forth against one another.

When the two of them were locked up by the cross guards, Rybek said in Nath's face, "I will kill you. I will kill your woman! The titans will slaughter the dragons!"

The cold-hearted words from the killer jarred something loose in Nath. He was tired. Tired of the evil that wanted to kill him and wipe out his friends. He was tired of it all, and he wasn't going to hold back anymore, waiting for people to have a change of heart. He shoved the powerful Rybek back so hard that the man's back smashed into a tree. Nath rushed him and let loose his speed and power. He and Fang became one. He swung with wroth force.

Rybek brought his sword up to block.

Steel collided with steel. Metal snapped. A mystical explosion knocked Nath backward onto the ground.

Still charged up, he sprang to his feet.

A section of the forest was missing. Leaves were falling.

Rybek lay on the ground, unmoving. His sword was broken in half.

Fang still burned with exhilarating fire in Nath's hand.

On instinct, Nath found Laylana, half-covered in leaves. Her eyes were open. He slung Fang over his back and picked her up in his arms. "How are you?"

"What happened?" she said.

"Nath!" Brenwar yelled.

With the lady elf in his arms, Nath rushed out of the devastated woodland onto the hilltop. Brenwar was surrounded by soldiers and a dozen giants.

That wasn't all. Wingless wurmers the size of small horses snaked through the grass.

"Are you going to swing that sword or that elf?" Brenwar said, backpedaling toward Nath.

"Hello!" said a voice from the shoulders of one of the giants. "Up here, Nath. It's me, Zoose!"

I wish I had Akron. I'd blow a hole clear through him.

"I can see that, Zoose."

"Yes, you do have awfully keen eyes, don't you?" Zoose said. Goose popped up on the other shoulder and smiled a smug little smile. "Too bad your sense of character is not as good as your eyes."

Nath wanted to kick himself. He couldn't understand how the halflings had fooled him.

I can't let that happen again. Ever.

Zoose continued. "This is the part where you surrender. And that would be wise. No one can hide from the titans. They have eyes everywhere."

"I know. I've heard that before. It's getting old."

"We can take them, Nath," Brenwar said.

"No, we can't, but I'm not surrendering." Nath held his sword in front of his eyes. "Fang, get us out of here." He tapped the blade on the ground.

Ting.

Nothing happened.

Brenwar let out a breath. "Thank goodness. I didn't want to wind up in the next century."

"Enough games." Goose pointed at Nath and company. "Just kill them."

Not knowing what to do, Nath let out a cry for help in Dragonese that sounded like a great roar that sent shockwaves through the valley.

"HAAAaaaaAAAAaaaaght!"

The advance of the giants stopped. Zoose and Goose covered their ears. The massive men looked at one another dumbfoundedly, but then on Zoose's new order they advanced once more.

Nath set Laylana down. "Stay close."

"I will, but I'm going to fight." She drew her sword. "It will be a great honor to make my last stand with Nath Dragon."

"Well, let's hope it's not our last stand, but it sure looks like it."

CHAPTER 39

A BUZZ IN THE AIR CAUGHT Nath's ears. His head snapped up. A dozen blue streak dragons the size of big dogs darted out of the sky and surrounded Nath and his friends. Their blue wings shook like rattles and glowed with energy. Their mouths dropped open, and lightning shot out.

Sssrazz! Sssraaa! Sssrazzz!

The bolts of energy shot into the wurmers. One by one, their scaly hides lit up like the day, sizzling and exploding. Rocked by the moment of surprise, the giants completely overlooked another terror. Four bull dragons, red as brick and as big as the towering giants, dropped out of the sky.

Whump! Whump! Whump! Whump!

Horns lowered, the bull dragons charged into the first wave of giants. They pinned the huge men down, and fiery infernos exploded from their mouths.

Filled with shock and elation, Nath let out a cheer. "Yes!" In all his life, he'd never expected such a rally. The dragons, even after the battle against Gorn Grattack, still seemed to shy away from him. Perhaps after all these centuries, that had changed. He certainly felt something, a new attachment, deep in his bones.

A giant hammered away at a bull dragon with thunderous blows.

A second giant pinned its wings.

Nath charged in and sliced one of the giants in the backside.

The dragon ripped into the other giants with his claws. His tail lashed out and knocked the huge man down. The dragon pounced and unleashed more fire.

The giant's skin turned to ash. Only the smoking bones remained.

The blue streak tore into the wurmers.

Bull dragons slugged it out with the giants, but the battle was far from won. It was a savage battle of teeth and scales, claws and fire. The iron and steel of men striking and howls of pain filled the air. The giants and wurmers, hardened, mindless and savage, recovered fast. They still had the superior numbers.

A dragon of golden-bronze scales slipped out of the darkness of the sky and landed on two wurmers the size of Nath Dragon.

Nath whirled around to face him.

His head was huge, and he had a magnificent set of horns. Golden eyes boring into Nath's own, he said in Dragonese in Nath's mind, "This isn't a battle. It's a rescue. Get on!" His tail cracked out and struck a giant instantly dead.

Nath called out to his friend, "Brenwar, quit swinging that hammer and get over here. Right now!"

The dwarf clobbered a wurmer's skull and froze in his tracks. He eyeballed the huge dragon. "Balzurth?"

"Father?" Nath said with shock. He gestured to Laylana, and together they climbed onto the great dragon's back.

Brenwar's stumpy legs powered over. It was one of the few times Nath had ever seen the dwarf do anything without arguing.

He helped Brenwar up. "You never cooperate so easily with me."

The dwarf grunted.

The monster bronze-gold dragon's wings beat and lifted them into the air. Balzurth let out a roar.

The bull and blue streak dragons broke off their attacks and took to the air.

Nath felt his father's lungs fill and the scales beneath him heat up.

A gush of fire exploded from Balzurth's mouth.

The giants and wurmers turned to ash. The hillside burned with fire. As they rose higher into the air, the burning hillside was a bonfire below them.

In astonishment, Nath said, "Father, I can't believe it was you who came!"

"Lucky for you I was in the area."

EPILOGUE

ZOOSE AND GOOSE STOOD FAR away from the burning hillside. The flames crackled and shot up into the sky. All of the giants and wurmers, along with what was left of Holbrook's soldiers, were nothing but burning pyres that would one day fertilize the scorched soil.

Goose stared into his sister's eyes. They were black pearls that shined with the orange blaze that reflected in them. She was no longer who she once was. Neither was he. Now, they were spies controlled by the spirits of the titans.

"Are you well?" he said to her.

She nodded.

Zoose saw a struggle within her. The dragon that came. Its fire had not only been destructive, but also cleansing. Those flames had destroyed the giants and wurmers and all of the evil within. He saw his future in those flames. He trembled. He stared at his bloodstained fingers.

I killed that man. Why?

A huge man marched out of the smoke and flames. It was Rybek. He carried his helmet in his hands. He stopped in front of Zoose. "Did I hear correctly? They called that dragon Balzurth?"

Zoose didn't want to nod, but the evil that prodded him did it anyway.

"Good, then we have succeeded." Rybek put his helmet back on. "It's time to let the titans know that Balzurth is out in the world, just as they planned. Let the hunt for him begin."

EYES

OF THE

DRAGON

-Book 4-

CRAIG HALLORAN

CHAPTER
1

THE MOUNTAINTOP WAS A BEAUTIFUL vision of tall grasses and bright, long-stemmed wildflowers. The massive rocks were covered in soft blue-green mosses. The swirling winds bent the branches and rustled the leaves in the trees, giving them an animated life of their own. It was one of the most picturesque places Nath had ever seen in Nalzambor and one of the many places he'd never ventured to before, a high precipice overlooking the distant Pool of the Dragons.

"It's always so peaceful so far away from everything," Nath said, gazing at his father, Balzurth.

The titan-sized dragon's armored scales of bronze and gold gleamed in the sun. His monstrous body crushed the vegetation beneath him. Balzurth scratched his great dragon horn on the rock as if he was sharpening its tip. His jaw, with teeth as big as men, opened up into a yawn that let out a hot burst of steam. He eyeballed Nath and replied, "The farther away from men, the better. I've been trying to teach you that."

"Me too." Brenwar's arms were crossed over his barrel chest. He looked like a bearded chipmunk beside Balzurth. He clawed at his beard. "He won't listen to me."

"The youth never do." Balzurth stretched his long neck around and faced the elven woman on his back. It was Laylana, the dark-headed, green-eyed elven daughter of the murdered Laedorn. "You seem to be enjoying yourself up there, pretty princess. Do you find my scales divine?"

Traipsing over Balzurth's back as if it were a bridge, she nodded with wide-eyed excitement. "Yes. Fascinating. Can we fly again? Soon?"

"Certainly, young lady. Certainly," Balzurth said in his powerful and reassuring voice. "I have a bit of an itch between my scales. Do you think you could scratch it for me?"

Clasping her hands together, she replied, "Oh, could I?"

"Of course." Balzurth wriggled his neck and added, "Over here where the horn meets the scale. That would be wonderful."

Without hesitation, Laylana climbed over to the back of Balzurth's head, dropped to her knees, and started scratching where he'd said. "Is this good?"

"Perfect." Balzurth turned his attention back to Nath. "You look disappointed. What's on your mind, Son?"

Nath should have been elated, but his father was right, he was disappointed. He didn't understand why. At least, not that he wanted to admit, but seeing his father in full dragon form bothered him. His father had wiped out a mountain full of giants in a single breath, but as much as Nath had enjoyed seeing it, he wished it had been him. Finally, he responded, "You've abandoned Dragon Home, Father. Why?"

Checking his claws, Balzurth said, "I can do as I wish."

"Oh, so you can do as you wish, but I can't?" Nath approached Balzurth and stood in his face, looking up at him. "Mother is worried, and you're placing yourself in danger. You're playing into the titans' hands. It's only a matter of time before they find us."

"I highly doubt your mother is as worried as she makes herself out to be. If anything, she's elated that I'm gone for a spell. You know how she loves decorating."

"Actually, no, I don't," Nath replied. "I only met my mother a short time ago, remember? She was imprisoned in the Great Dragon Wall all my life before that."

"Of course I remember," Balzurth scoffed. He poked a claw into Nath's chest. "I remember everything. And don't you dare get on your high horse and worry about me. I don't need to be worried about. I'm the King of the Dragons, am I not?"

"Aye!" Brenwar shouted while hoisting his war hammer Mortuun up in the air. "Aye! Aye!"

Seeing the dwarf's enthusiasm, Nath felt a little bit foolish. His father could clearly take care of himself. Still, he sputtered out, "Well, you should still be more careful. It's been awhile since you last trekked through the world of men."

"Careful? Pah." Balzurth let out a puff of smoke. "I've handled the titans before, and I can handle them again. And I won't let them survive at all this time. No. There won't be any banishment." His voice filled the mountaintop with thunder. He stomped his paw and shook the ground. "It will be obliteration!"

Nath stepped backward. The power in Balzurth's voice shook the marrow in his bones. Laylana froze on Balzurth's back, and Brenwar stood stiff as a board. Nath found his breath again and said, "Father, thanks."

The furnace in Balzurth's eyes cooled, and he asked, "Thanks for what?"

"Saving us."

"Yes, well, you are my son and my friends." Voice softening, Balzurth scanned the three of them. "And as wretched as people can be, they are all still worth saving. Son, I've sat on my throne doing nothing long enough. I cannot stand it any longer. They take the dragons, they slaughter their own, and it's time for action. Do I think it will be easy? No, it never is. But it must be done." He sighed.

Looking deep into his father's eyes, Nath could see a hint of regret. Something was eating at Balzurth. He approached his father and laid his hand on his snout. "What is it, Father?"

"My selfish actions have led to all this, I fear," Balzurth said, not hiding his regret. "I sent you to find your mother. Alas, I did miss her, and I knew if you freed her, there would be consequences. Letting out the spirits of the titans had a much more rapid effect than I expected. Their anger and hatred made their evil spread faster than I imagined. I thought they could be contained, but I underestimated them. Yet I knew it would have to come to this eventually. I could not let our kin hold the Dragon Wall intact forever. It just wasn't fair."

"Don't be so hard on yourself, Father," Nath said, patting his father's huge snout. "I'm sure I would have done the same thing for Mother that you did."

"No doubt you will do the same for those you love, Son." Balzurth nudged him with his nose. "Besides, I feel that you are ready. Actually, I know it. You are ready to take down the titans."

Nath's eyes enlarged. He swallowed and said, "Me? What about you?"

CHAPTER 2

I T WAS ZOOSE THE HALFLING's first trip to the City of Narnum. He walked stride for stride with his sister Goose behind the powerful armored build of Rybek the war cleric. The towering warrior walked with huge steps that made it difficult to keep up on his much shorter legs, but he and Goose pressed on. He nudged Goose with his finger and pointed up.

"Stop doing that," she said, slapping his hand away. Her once-amiable face was pinched into a grimace of evil. She tugged at the long brown ponytail that hung over her shoulder. "I've seen plenty of wurmers already, and the colorful tile tops too. Get control of yourself and act like you've been here before."

That wasn't easy to do. Instead, his eyes searched over everything at once. The wurmers, dark and scaly with their purple eyes aglow, hung in the nooks and crannies of every building. Their eyes seemed to scan for any suspicious move. The people fought and haggled over food, weapons, and clothing. A burly roughneck shoved an elderly woman down, and not a single person helped her up. Heavy boots trampled by her instead. Zoose gravitated toward the fallen woman.

Goose grabbed him by the elbow and jerked him back into step. Under her breath, she said, "What are you doing, fool?"

Zoose's nostrils flared as he took in a deep draw of air. The scent of meat cooking filled his nose. Patting his belly, he said, "I'm hungry."

Goose punched him in the arm. "Be silent."

Rubbing his shoulder, he hunched down and kept the pace but continued to survey his surroundings. There was a festival in the market square they were passing through. Men and women frolicked with wickedness. Shouted and screamed with shameless glee. They'd made giant masks painted in vibrant colors that covered their faces. The images were wicked and evil. Dark and disturbing. Drums pounded. Songs were sung, strings were plucked, and horns blared. It shook Zoose to the core. Evil members of all the races had gathered, including many elves. He'd never seen or imagined such a thing. The grand City of Narnum was deteriorating into a depot of ruin. He hugged his shoulders, rubbed the cold seeping into his limbs, and cast down his eyes.

Goose gave him a firm shove. "Buck up, Zoose. We have arrived, and arrived on the right side."

I don't know about that.

Something had stirred inside him when he saw Balzurth's flames consuming an entire hillside and everything living on it turned to ash. The wickedness inside him that allowed him to commit crimes against his nature had fled. His rationale and humble halfling consciousness had returned. The distorted world he was now living in had been revealed to his once-tainted eyes. With his little heart pumping in his chest, he decided to play along.

There's nowhere to run anyway.

Marching through the cobblestone street, Rybek led them straight toward the tallest building in the city. It stretched a thousand feet into the air. A walkway wrapped around its massive column like a snake, level after level.

Zoose had never imagined anything so huge and vast in his life, but there it was in the heart of the city, a marvel of architecture. Head tilted back and eyes up, he said, "Are we going up there?"

His sister shushed him.

Rybek's head turned over his armored shoulder. He lifted his massive arm and pointed at a stone temple being built around the base of the tower. The stones were huge. The people who moved them were monstrous. Giants, dozens of them, men and orcs, shoved stones over logs and stacked them up on top of each other to form a temple with a huge thirty-foot archway that was near completion. "Eckubahn awaits. Come with me."

On each side of the archway that formed the temple's entrance, a giant sentry stood. Bare-chested and hairless, their alabaster skin blended in with the stonework of the black-eyed brutes. Each sentry held a leaf-tipped spear that rested on the ground and stood up to his neck.

One of the expressionless titans glanced down at Rybek and waved him in.

Staying close, Zoose and Goose followed after.

Inside the confines of the temple, the stone archways crisscrossed more than fifty feet above. Flocks of worshippers were stuffed inside. They wore masks and plumes full of feathers and black flowers. Among them were giants dressed in clothes like men, who towered over all of them. They lounged in great stone chairs chiseled by the hands of giant masons. The people laid trays of food and ornate gifts at their massive feet.

Zoose had never felt so small and insignificant as he did now.

This is twisted. I want to go home.

Unable to see beyond the hordes of jaded people, he heard a voice cut through the room like a crack of thunder. "People, go. Rybek and company, come."

The enchanted people departed in a stream. Seconds later they were all gone, leaving Zoose and his sister alone with Rybek among the giants.

"Come," the loud, canyon-like voice said, "and tell me what you know, Rybek."

Sweating from his brow, Zoose managed to peek around Rybek's legs at the source of the voice. A titan sat on a throne made of stone. His enormous hands squeezed the stone arms of his seat, and his head burned like an urn of flame. Zoose squinted and dashed the sweat from his eyes. He wanted to run, but he dared not. He was in the presence of the most powerful of all titans, Eckubahn.

Rybek took a knee and bowed.

Without hesitation, Zoose and Goose did the same, but unlike his counterparts, Zoose shivered and dripped with sweat. It took the life right out of him when Eckubahn said, "Why does that tiny one shake?"

CHAPTER 3

Inside the gardens of Quintuklen, Bayzog sat on a bench alongside his wife Sasha. The beautiful human woman was dressed in a fine white-linen gown. Her stare was blank but fixed on the arrangement of flowers blooming behind the pathway. The half-elf wizard waved his hand in front of her eyes. "Sasha, it's time to go."

The gentle woman didn't stir.

Bayzog's heart sank. He'd been bringing her to the gardens every day in hopes that she could regain some of her memory and return to her normal self, but the magic within her was eroding her mind. He'd hoped watching others rebuild the war-ravaged gardens might rejuvenate her. It had not. There were only glimpses of her former self that surfaced from time to time. Now his hope rested in their sons, Samaz and Rerry. The young but formidable pair had set out on their own to find a cure for their mother, and he'd not heard from them since they left.

He took her warm hand in his. "It's lonely without you, Sasha. If I never appreciated you as much as I should have, I hope you'll know how much I appreciate you now." He reached behind him and plucked a purple flower and held it under her nose. "One of your favorites."

Sasha's chin shifted and her gaze changed. Wurmers streaked through the sky in flocks like birds. With effort she lifted her hand and pointed, saying, "Birdie. Birdie. Ugly birdie." Her hand dropped, and she became listless again.

Bayzog's chin sank into his chest. It was agony watching her deteriorate. Her beautiful life was withering away like a flower that blooms in the day and dies in the night. It was even worse with him being part elven. To him, her life was already fleeting, and now that process had accelerated. It was heartbreaking. At one time in his life, he'd felt himself free of such burdens, but now with a family, it was different. He had even caught himself wondering, *Will I even outlive my own sons?*

Night began to fall as the sun sank behind the buildings. The shade started to cool his bones, and Sasha's teeth began to chatter. He picked up his cloak, which was lying at his side. It was a rich forest green with golden leaves that traced over the hem and sleeves. Sasha had woven it for him when they met long ago. He covered her shoulders with it. "Sweetest Sasha, it is time to go."

Her stare remained deep and spacey.

He took her hands and tried to pull her up.

She stiffened and pulled free of his grip.

This was the hard part. People were walking about, staring. The last thing Bayzog wanted to do was draw attention to himself. Attention was dangerous. If the leadership of the city had any concerns about the state your family was in, they wouldn't hesitate to throw you out. He tugged at her again. "Please, Sasha. Come."

She rose to her feet without looking into his face. Instead, it seemed as if her stare was in a world beyond. Bayzog hoped that if she saw anything at all, it was pleasant. He wrapped his arm around her waist and guided her down the path beneath the archways of tree branches and leaves. The night birds started to sing the last song of the day, darting back and forth through the branches before they settled in.

A tear formed in the corner of Bayzog's violet eye. He wiped it away with his sleeve, remembering how the night birds' songs had so often made Sasha giggle for no reason. He'd never understood why the little speckled birds made her laugh. All she would say was, "It's joy, pure joy that they sing, and it gives me the tickles."

Oh, what I wouldn't do to hear that laughter again. I'd do anything.

Exiting the garden through the gates of iron, Sasha pulled him back. He whirled around in disbelief and found her eyes on his. She was blinking. His heart started racing inside his chest. "Sasha, can you hear me?"

"Of course, husband. Why wouldn't I?" She twisted around on her feet, glancing up, down, and over all of her surroundings. When she stopped, she said, "Where have Samaz and Rerry gone? They were just here. They must be hiding from the danger." She called out, "Rerry! Samaz! Come to the voice of your mother. I'll protect you!"

"Easy, Sasha. The boys are fine," Bayzog assured her. He pulled her into his arms. "Let's go home. Soon we will see them there."

She tore out of his grip. "No, Bayzog! They are in danger. I saw it with my own eyes. Those horrible birds in the sky will devour them if we don't help them!" Dashing into the gardens, she continued to call out for them. "Samaz! Rerry!"

Chasing after her, Bayzog broke out in a cold sweat. What Sasha had said was so convincing that it all seemed real. He'd known the hallucinations from the wizard's dementia would be powerful, but this bout she had shared tightened around the heart in his chest. A deep nagging feeling bore its way into the recesses of his mind. Somewhere, something was wrong.

"Aaaiiieeeeee!" Sasha screamed.

Fighting his way through the now flourishing garden, Bayzog found Sasha on her hands and knees. She faced two oversized stones the size of men that lay silent on the soft ground. Tears started to stream down her face and she said with riveting meaning, "They're dead. My sons are dead!"

CHAPTER
4

"Y OU KNOW, FATHER," NATH SAID to Balzurth, "you said that as if you weren't planning on helping me with it."

"Oh, so are you telling me the Dragon Prince isn't up to it?" Balzurth chuckled in his throat. "And I thought my son was up for anything."

Backpedaling, Nath swatted at some leaves in a nearby tree. "And I certainly would be, if I were in your condition. But alas," he said with a shrug of his shoulders, "I'm just this."

"Oh, I see. You're pouting because you can't turn into a dragon like me." Balzurth leaned his head toward Brenwar. "What do you think, old friend?"

"He's pouting for certain. If I've seen that lip stuck out once I've seen it stuck out a hundred times." Brenwar shook his head. "It's the redheaded ones that always seem so fragile."

"I'm not fragile," Nath objected. "And the both of you know I'm in no condition to take down the titans. We'd be dead ten times over if not for Fang bailing us out. I can't always count on Fang, though. Sometimes he's on it, and sometimes he's not."

"Oh, don't bellyache, Dragon Prince," Balzurth replied. "You're only upset that you haven't turned into a dragon yet."

Nath perked up and approached his father. He grabbed one of the long claws on his father's feet and held him fast. "You said *yet*? Does that mean I'll get my powers back?"

"Not if you hide up here on this mountain, you won't." Balzurth tried to pull his foot away from Nath's grip without hurting Nath. "Will you let go of me before I boil you like a fish?"

"Tell me how to get my powers back. I want to be a dragon again."

"Don't be so antsy. You made a sacrifice for Selene, and you should respect that. In the meantime, make the most of what you do have." Balzurth looked up over his back at Laylana. "That will do, Princess. Thank you."

She climbed down off the grand dragon's back onto the ground and said, "My pleasure."

Nath kicked at the dirt. One of the things that bothered him so much about his father being back was having to see a reflection of what he could be but no longer was. He didn't have any regrets for saving Selene, but my, how he missed his powers. If he had them back, he'd take it straight to the titans in a heartbeat. He took a breath, pulled his shoulders back, and faced his father. "So what is it I need to do?"

"Stay the course, Son."

"So you want me to go back to doing what I was doing before you arrived, which was essentially dying. Perhaps I should just turn myself over to the titans." Nath shook his head. "Great Guzan."

"Son, you called for aid and it came. Me and the dragons. Victory was snatched from the jaws of death, and you should be happy." Balzurth lowered his head. "I know I am."

"So what are you going to do while I'm doing what I'm going to do? I thought you were ready to take down the titans now." Nath said.

"I'm not going to rush in there without a plan. I still need to gather one. While I do that, you and your friends can do what you need to do. Just think about it." Using his tail, Balzurth uprooted a tree from the ground and started eating its leaves from the branches. "Mmmmmmm. It's not cattle, but it will do."

Nath tried to recollect where he'd been before his last adventure. What was going on in the wide world of Nalzambor?

Hm.

The giants were filling the cities and poisoning the minds of the people. Selene was comatose and hopefully safe with Sansla Libor. She should be in Dragon Home. There was the other item of issue too. The elves and dwarves were trying to hunt him down. They thought he'd murdered Laylana's father Laedorn and the hero of the dwarven people, Uurluuk Mountainstone. He needed to bring the real menace to justice and clear his own name. He needed to find out how the assassin got his hands on his bow Akron. He needed to visit Bayzog and Ben to see what happened. Who stole Akron?

Crunching on the branches, Balzurth peered down at Nath. "Have you decided what you want to do yet?"

Aggravated, Nath said, "I guess we'll just hustle off this mountain, leagues from where we need to be, and visit our old friend Bayzog. Of course, you could give us a ride and move our destiny along a little bit quicker."

"No, the walk will be good for you, won't it, Brenwar."

"The only thing I like better than walking is fighting." Brenwar was beaming. "Well, drinking and brewing ale aside, of course."

"Of course," Balzurth said.

Dumbfounded, Nath looked at his father and friend and said, "I suppose we should go then. It's been good seeing you, Father, if brief." He started to walk away. There was nothing quite like being in the presence of his father. Despite some understandable jealousy, Nath's best times were with Balzurth, even though on occasion they could be boring. There was something different about his father now, though. That liveliness he'd known as a boy was back. He liked it. He wanted to bask in it. Boots marching over the ground and without looking back, he carried on.

"Oh, I can't stand it," Balzurth blurted out just as Nath and Brenwar headed over the mountain's crest and down the bank. "Hold on."

There was a rattle and snapping of branches. Nath whirled around.

The tree was there, but the dragon was gone. Only a rustle remained under the branches. Suddenly the tree moved and Laylana gasped. A man appeared under the thirty-foot oak tree, pushed it up over his head, and tossed it aside like a log for a fire. He dusted his hands off. "I need to be more careful next time I shape change. It's been awhile."

Gaping, Nath watched as Balzurth changed.

No longer a dragon, a broad-shouldered statue came to life. His eyes were as golden as the sun, with long red hair that flowed over his shoulders like the ripples in a river. He tugged at the fiery locks cascading under his chin.

Brenwar nodded and said, "That's a fine beard. You wear it like any dwarven king I ever saw."

Putting his arm around the dwarf's shoulders, bearded man Balzurth said, "That's a fine compliment coming from you, Brenwar." Balzurth draped his other arm over Nath's shoulders. A hair taller, he said to Nath, "Any objections to me coming along?"

With a smile as broad as a river, Nath said, "No sir!"

Balzurth smiled in return. "We're off to see the wizard then."

CHAPTER

5

H EAD AFLAME, ECKUBAHN THE TITAN said, "It seems we have a deceiver among us. I do not sense the spirit of evil within this flea of a halfling." He pointed at Zoose. "Come to me, insignificant one."

With every one of his limbs shaking, Zoose tried to rise and shuffle forward but could not move. His shoeless feet were stuck to the floor.

Rybek reached around and grabbed him by the scruff of his shirt collar and pulled him forward. The warrior gave him a hard shove straight into the foot of the stone dais that held up the titan's throne. Zoose jammed his knee on the step's edge, sending a sharp pain through his limbs to his eyes.

"I sense this one's fear. It is great." Eckubahn reached down with an arm the size of a tree and scooped up Zoose into his palm. He lifted the halfling into the air, holding him like a wingless bird. "Who do you serve, half-a-man?"

Soaked with perspiration and drenched in fear, Zoose pulled his knees into his chest and balled up like a clam. The searing heat from Eckubahn's burning face made steam rise up from Zoose's sweat-drenched clothes.

I want to go home. I want to go home. I want to go home.

"This halfling is not one of us. He has defiled the temple." Eckubahn's fingers closed around Zoose. His huge hand was slowly crushing Zoose's little body like a walnut shell. "Do not allow such vermin into my temple again, Rybek."

The warrior nodded.

"As for this tiny defiler, let his life become an example of what happens to those who do not succumb to my power. I am Eckubahn. I will reign over all Nalzambor. Those who resist me shall be destroyed." His hand continued to slowly, agonizingly close.

Zoose felt immense pressure building around him. Squeezed fiercely in the titan's palm, he couldn't even peep. And then a warm light pierced through the veil of his eyelids. It became brighter and hotter until he finally let out a horrible scream.

Goose watched in astonishment as her brother Zoose was enveloped in the titan's hand. The giant's hand glowed with a fiery light, and a muffled scream from within pierced the center of her heart. Eckubahn opened up his fingers, tilted his hand over, and the fire-charred remains of Zoose spilled out onto the temple floor. Her throat tightened, but there were no tears. All she could think was, "What a shame, what a shame."

Eckubahn turned his attention to her. "Clean this up, half-woman. And be hasty about it. I don't care for the dust of fleas."

Scrambling forward, she dropped to her hands and knees and started scooping the cremated remains up into the lower length of her dress. The dust of her brother filled her nose, and the smell was awful. She sneezed, scattering halfling dust everywhere. Wide eyed, she glanced up at Eckubahn just in time to see his foot lift up and stomp right back down on her head.

Squish!

Rybek watched Eckubahn stretch out his hand over the remains of the halflings. An orange glow emanated from his fingertips and scorched the steps with a cleansing effect. No sign was left of the halflings. They were gone.

"Rise," Eckubahn said to him. "What do you have to report?"

Rybek stood, keeping his chin down. "Balzurth roams the land again. I have seen him with my own eyes."

"And you are certain of this?"

"Aye," Rybek said. "Our enemies confirmed it in our very presence. You have drawn him out, my lord. Your plan bears the fruit of everything you have wanted."

Eckubahn leaned forward. "Tell me what happened. What did you see?"

Rybek's gauntleted fingers twitched. He lifted his head to face the titan's fiery gaze. "We had Nath Dragon trapped by giants and wurmers with no chance of escape when Nath Dragon called out for his brethren. Within moments, dragons dropped out of the sky—and one of them was Balzurth.

He turned the giants and wurmers into fire with one hot blast that set the mountain ablaze. Not a single giant or wurmer survived."

Eckubahn pointed at Rybek. "But you did. How is that?"

Throat tightening, Rybek replied, "Nath Dragon had defeated me earlier, shattered my blade, and I lay woozy in the forest. By the time I came out of my fog, the battle was over and the hilltop aflame." He glanced at the spot where the halflings once were. "I beg for another chance, milord."

Eckubahn lowered his hand. "Let me see this shattered blade."

Rybek took the scabbard out of a sack he carried, slid the broken sword blade out of the scabbard, placed it in the titan's palm, and stepped back.

"With evidence comes truth," the titan said, closing his grip around the weapon. "I hate the truth." He opened his hand again, revealing the sword fully intact. "But I appreciate loyalty. You, Rybek, will be given the chance to redeem yourself, but not without superior help."

Rybek took the sword. "It will be my pleasure to accept any assistance you offer."

From behind the throne, an ominous figure emerged. Standing over twelve feet tall, a pasty green-skinned humanoid stood beside the throne. He was a ghastly giant, ugly from head to toe, covered with knots on this arms and legs that looked like boils. His arms and legs were long. He was broad chested but appeared out of shape. The wild hair on his head was shoulder length and his nose long. He wore a brown tunic with a huge brass-buckled belt wrapped around it. Deep, spacey black eyes resonated with evil.

Eckubahn made the introduction. "This is Bletver, a triant. He is going to aid you."

Rybek nodded. He was used to seeing giants, but he'd never seen anything quite like Bletver before. The oversized hands and long nails at the end looked like they would tear a grizzly to pieces. There was something disturbing about how the triant carried himself. He stood with cunning in his eye and his own air of dignity.

Bletver said to Rybek, "A pleasure."

Anticipating a little more company, Rybek said, "Who else will accompany me?" A sliver of ice raced down his spine as a shadow fell over his shoulder, and he turned.

A black shadow with a glow for eyes hovered right behind him.

Unlike his twin brother Kryzak, Rybek was more fighter than cleric. He wasn't as accustomed to the supernatural, but he knew a phantom when he saw it.

"The phantom and the triant will accompany you as you seek out Balzurth and his son, Nath Dragon. Separate them. Destroy their allies. Their friends. Trap them. Hunt them. You will need this." Eckubahn stretched out his hand to reveal a silver amulet on a wrought iron chain. A purple gem sparkled in the center of the amulet with the fire of a moody star. "Place this around the dragon's neck, and you will be finished."

Rybek took the amulet in his hand and tucked it away. "Anything else, milord?"

"All of my resources will be at your disposal. Make good use of what you have, and do not fail me again," Eckubahn warned. "Remember the halflings. Your fate will be far worse than theirs, which was merciful."

CHAPTER 6

BAYZOG WAS BACK IN HIS tower, eyes scouring his texts at his center table. Books floated all around as he shoved one book aside and replaced it with another. He hadn't slept since he'd returned with Sasha. She'd spaced out just after she wailed over her hallucinations of the deaths of Samaz and Rerry. Now, his problems were twofold. Perhaps his sons had died—and his wife still needed a cure for the wizard's dementia. He needed help and answers, and he had only one place to go.

"Umph!" a voice cried out. A man appeared inside the living room on a pile of pillows. The rangy, bearded man shoved the pillows aside and rose to his feet, shaking his head. "There has to be a better way to make an entrance in here."

"Thanks for coming, Ben," said Bayzog. It had been less than a year since the last time he saw Ben, but the man looked like he'd aged a decade. Brow perched, Bayzog asked, "Are you well?"

Checking the buckle on his sword belt and straightening himself, Ben approached with a little wobble in his legs, holding his stomach. "I will be once my tummy turns right side up again. Really, Bayzog, get another entrance. It's no wonder you don't have many visitors." He headed toward the nearest sofa and flopped down, facing the fireplace. "It's cold as the peaks in here, too."

With a twitch of Bayzog's fingers, the fireplace burst into flame, and ambient warmth filled the room.

The old rugged warrior clasped his hands behind his head and leaned back into the sofa. "Ah, that's better." Peering around, he asked, "How's Sasha?"

"Asleep, but not well." Bayzog grabbed a pitcher of wizard water and a pair of fine glasses and took a seat in a padded chair. He poured two glasses and said to Ben, "Again, are you ill?"

"Why, do I look ill?" Ben took the glass of wizard water and drank. "Perhaps this will make me feel better."

Ben tended to be as refreshed as any human could be, positive and engaging, but now the creases in his forehead and the sacks under his eyes were a cause for concern. Ben's eyes were avoiding his, too. "What's happened, Ben?"

The man tensed up and closed his eyes. "Nothing."

"Ben?"

Finished with his drink, Ben set the glass down. "You sent for me, I didn't send for you. I came, so what do you want, Bayzog?"

Bayzog took a sip of the wizard water. It wasn't like Ben to be so defensive. Something was bothering the man. Deeply. "Fine. I need you to go track down my sons."

"You know I'd love to help, but I'm too old to do that." Ben rubbed his hands on the thighs of his pants. "And I've started another family of my own, you know."

"Ben, this is serious. I need you. Your family can stay with me. I can't leave Sasha. You know that."

"It's too dangerous out there for me. Giants roam the world like common men, and wurmers flock like fleas. It's taking all we have to hold this city."

Trying to sound reassuring, Bayzog said, "You'll be fine. You have Akron."

For the first time, Ben's eyes found his. The man's face filled with strain. With a heavy sigh, he said, "I lost it."

Scooting to the edge of his seat, Bayzog asked, "You lost what?"

"Akron. I lost Akron."

Bayzog scooted back into the cushions of his chair and sat quiet for a moment as if he was frozen in time. He'd come to expect the unexpected in his life, but the loss of Akron was disheartening—especially coming from Ben, who was as responsible an individual as you could get. Softening his tone, he asked, "What happened?"

Ben lifted his shoulder and shook his head again. "I hadn't used it for quite some time, so I locked it up. This was years ago, and I hadn't even thought of the bow in a long time. Then, a few weeks back, there was talk in the streets. You probably heard it."

"Forgive me, but I haven't heard anything of late. I've been very distracted. Go on."

"Word came to the Legionnaires that Laedorn had been assassinated. A moorite arrow right through the heart." Ben's gaze landed right on Bayzog's. "Witnesses say that a man fitting Nath Dragon's description fired it."

"Impossible!" Bayzog exclaimed. His fingers dug into the soft cushions of the padded chair. He glanced toward the hallway that led to Sasha's room. "Sorry, but this news actually startled me." He grabbed his glass and took a long drink. "My heart beats in my chest like a galloping horse. How did I miss this news?" He drank again. "Please continue."

Resting his calloused hands on his knees and sitting up straight, Ben added, "It was elves that came, and they didn't want to make anything public about it. It's been very quiet, but they asked for me. I told them what I knew and everything about the last time I saw Dragon, er, Nath. They caught me completely off guard, but when they departed, they seemed convinced of everything I knew. And why shouldn't they be? After all, I told them the truth."

"Of course you did," Bayzog said, pouring Ben another glass of wizard water.

Ben drank again and set the glass down with a throaty "Ah!" He shook his head. "This seems inappropriate. That brew makes me feel better for telling the horrible news I had. I shouldn't feel good, but I do. Is that bad?"

"Ben, don't worry about it." Bayzog reached over and patted him on the back. "You carried this guilt too long and needed to get it off your chest."

"That's a true statement if I ever heard one." Ben let out another heavy sigh. "So as soon as the elves left, I rushed back home and opened the chest where I'd stored Akron. It and the quiver were gone. I swear I felt my heart sink straight into the very heart of Nalzambor. I was sick. Mortally sick. I wanted to tell you, Bayzog, I did, but I was so ashamed." He sank his face into his hands and sobbed. "I've been a wreck ever since."

"I hate to ask, but was the chest locked?"

Ben nodded. "And it was still locked when I opened it. I don't understand how this could happen. My wife and children…none of them saw anything. And the lock is dwarven, and I always keep the key on me. There are but a very few who can pick such a lock." He sat back up and leaned into the sofa. "It's my fault. All my fault, and now they're hunting for Dragon. Can you believe that?"

Rubbing his finger under his chin, the half-elf wizard said, "There isn't much I don't believe can happen these days. I don't suppose you've heard from Nath, have you?"

"Nothing. I wanted to search him out myself, but I won't leave my family—and if anyone can take care of himself, it's Dragon. But deep in my bones, I feel like something is greatly wrong. Do you ever get that feeling?" Ben asked.

"All too often." Bayzog rose to his feet and started over toward his large, round study table. "You are aware that plenty of eyes have seen you use that bow. It's far from a secret, and you are one of Quintuklen's heroes. Have you noted anything suspicious? Perhaps someone is avoiding you who didn't before?"

"No. Everyone's too worried about the giants, and I haven't been fool enough to speak about it. Even my wife doesn't know." Ben punched a pillow. "I'm a fool!"

"Easy now." Bayzog wanted to say whatever he could to bring Ben relief, but these troubles were even worse than he'd suspected. The elves would avenge Laedorn. Certainly they would try to capture Nath and bring him to justice—and they would have it one way or another. That was one problem, but the other was finding out who had taken Akron. There were two possibilities. In one, Nath was possessed, and he took it. Or in the second possibility, an imposter was setting Nath up—which was more likely. But there were very few who could pull off such a feat, and the only one they knew personally capable of such a crime was Gorlee.

So little is known about the changelings. Perhaps they have sided with the titans. After all, they're a neutral breed.

Ben got up and started pacing around the sofa while tapping the glass in his hand with his finger. He made a few rounds before stopping at Bayzog's table, looking right at him, and saying, "Bayzog, you have the power. You need to go after them."

"Go after who?" he said with mild astonishment.

"After your sons and Dragon. Can't you see it has to be you? You can get word out and warn him. Find your sons and bring them back before things get even worse."

"I can't leave Sasha."

"We can take care of her, me and my family. It would be our honor." Ben took Bayzog by the shoulders and squeezed them. "You know it has to be you."

"No," said another voice that had entered the room. It was Sasha. "It has to be us."

CHAPTER

7

BALZURTH WALKED WITH HIS ELBOWS swinging and a grand smile on his face. His strides were long through the tall grass, making it tough for Brenwar to keep up. The grim dwarf was like a child around Balzurth, having to rush forward to keep up from time to time, only to fall to the rear again. "It's good to walk. My feet on the earth have meaning," said the Dragon King. And then he turned around to yell, "How are you doing back there, Brenwar?"

"Never better," the dwarf yelled back. "I like stretching my stumpy legs."

In step with Balzurth, Nath beamed with admiration. There was nothing like being in the presence of his father, especially when he was showing his lighter side. The Dragon King wore a tunic crafted from leather that was a dull shade of emerald. He'd created the dye from the bark of trees combined with the local grasses. There were boots on Balzurth's feet formed from the skins of lizards and snakes and the hide of a boar. Though he was human in shape and form, there was an uncanny quality about him. An air. It lifted the spirits of them all.

"It's good to be with you, Father." Nath stretched out his clawed hands and compared them to the bare arms of his father. "No scales?"

"There should be," Balzurth said, glancing at the black scales on Nath's arms. "But you picked an interesting color. Why is that?"

"I like it, but I can change it," Nath replied.

"No, that won't be necessary. I know your heart is as red as mine, and that's what counts. Besides, the black looks good on you." Balzurth clamped his hand over Nath's wrist. "But be reminded, Son, that there is more to your scales than meets the eye. They do more than protect you like armor from piercing weapons, and they aren't for show or decoration."

Nath felt his father's strength coursing up his arm. It was as if the strength of an entire dragon was in the palm of a man's mighty grip. It was the power he'd once had and ever longed for. "What else do the scales do?" he asked, trying to distract himself from his oppressive feeling of loss.

"They're stronger than flesh in more ways than one. They protect you from many of the temptations men suffer. Have you not noticed that?"

Nath had never thought about that before. Thinking back, he realized the ways of men weren't as appealing as they had been before. He had better control over his emotions and urges. "I suppose I have been different since I got my scales."

"Yes, you are, and that's why dragons don't get caught up in the affairs of men. They have no desire for all the drama." Balzurth reached down and scooped up some wildflowers from the ground and handed them back to Laylana. "For you."

She sniffed the flowers with a thrill in her light-green eyes. "Thank you, Balzurth."

"The pleasure is mine, elven lady." He turned his attention back to Nath. "You were about to say something, Son?"

"Aren't you at risk without your scales?"

"I'd be lying if I denied I was tingling all over. It makes me think of the times when I was free like you, adventuring from town to town and freeing one damsel in distress after the other." Balzurth smacked his lips with a gleam in his eyes. "Those were adventurous times. One does silly things when he thinks his life is only mortal. But the greater treasures are rewarded through patience and discipline. You're doing good things, Son, and I'm proud of you. You wear those scales quite well."

"Not as well as you, apparently."

"In time it will come, so long as you do the right thing." Balzurth reached his hand into the air, and a blue bird landed on his finger and began singing. He hummed along.

"You know, Father, I've been trying to do the right thing, but the world is still a mess."

"Yes, and we journey to remedy that. For now. I'm not saying it will be easy. It never is, and it never lasts. But we must do it. Besides, we want to."

The four of them marched for hours toward the setting sun like an invincible army. On their journey, Balzurth revealed many things about his youth that were similar to Nath's. It seemed his father had had his own pitfalls. Nath felt a closeness between them begin to build, and the stories Balzurth told weren't as long and boring as they used to seem.

These stories are fantastic. Was I really so impatient?

They were still days away from Quintuklen when the skies began to darken. Night fell, and as they walked on, the sound of war drums caught Nath's ear.

Balzurth stopped and said, "That sounds interesting." He tilted his head. "Sounds like orcs are in our midst and having a party without me." He slapped Nath on the shoulder and looked back at Brenwar with a broad grin. "Let's go give them a greeting they'll never forget."

"Aye!" Brenwar replied.

With his long red locks waving in the wind, Balzurth made a beeline for the thumping sounds that stirred the menace of the night. The drums were a warning that orcs would often beat. It was their deranged custom to instill fear in their enemies and to let the weaker people in the world know they were coming. Nath always thought it was stupid to make so much noise where stealth should be applied, but they were orcs. Everything they did was offensive and brash.

The drumbeats were joined by howls and cries after they'd walked a mile to the drumbeats. Soon, they were overlooking a band of orcs that had formed a camp nestled in the woodland. Hidden among the trees, they watched the orcs beat their armored chests and guzzle wine from flasks. A huge campfire blazed, and beyond its flames were two husky orcs pounding on their drums as the celebration and clamor rose among them.

"Hmmm," Balzurth said. "They seem happy. Happy orcs mean trouble. I'd better see what's going on. All of you stay here and watch."

"No, Father, wait," Nath said.

But Balzurth slipped free of his grasp and cut for the camp with the ease of a leopard.

Brenwar, war hammer in hand, rushed to Nath's side. "What's he doing?"

Laylana pressed into Nath from his other side and added, "He's going to fight them all, isn't he."

"I have no idea what he's doing. I never have any idea what he's doing." Nath crept forward from one tree to another, with Brenwar and Laylana on his hips but with his eyes never leaving his father. Balzurth was moments away from wading into the middle of the orc camp. Nath knew in his head it wasn't anything he needed to be worried about. After all, they were orcs, and they were about to face Balzurth. Still, his scales tingled.

"Nath," Brenwar said, nudging him in the back. He pointed in another direction. "Look."

Beyond the fire and back against the clearing tree line were cages. Long necks lifted up with serpentine heads, and bright eyes locked on Balzurth, who had just waded into the middle of the orc camp.

The pounding on the drums stopped. The orcs, at least ten that Nath could see, stopped in the middle of their celebration. Discovering Balzurth standing among them, they dropped their drinks and drew their knives and swords and advanced.

Balzurth froze them in their tracks when he said in a dangerous voice, "How dare you cage my dragons? You'll pay for that!"

CHAPTER 8

"SASHA, PLEASE, YOU NEED REST," Bayzog said, taking her hands in his and trying to sit her down. "Let me get you something to drink."

"No!" She jerked away from him. "I heard everything, Bayzog. I know I have the dementia now, or at least I've put it together when I'm in my right mind. But I know what I saw. Our sons are dead if not in horrible danger. I can feel it in the marrow of my bones!" She walked over to an open closet and grabbed a backpack and threw it at Bayzog. "Let's go!"

"As you wish." Bayzog glanced at Ben, turned, and headed to a wooden chest that sat on the floor and opened up the lid. He began placing items inside the pack that she'd given him, one by one.

"Hello, Sasha," Ben said, approaching with open arms. "It's good to see you again."

Sasha burst into tears and rushed into Ben's arms. She clutched him, and with heavy sobs, she said, "Oh Ben, you must help Bayzog and me find my sons. I can't bear to not see them again while I rot away." Her body shuddered. "I know I need help. Bayzog needs help. The evil in me is destroying me."

"I will help," Ben promised. "I will help." He gave Bayzog a feeble glance. "You know you can count on me and Bayzog. And I know Rerry and Samaz can take care of themselves until we find them." He separated himself from her a little. "It wouldn't surprise me one bit if they were on their way back with a cure right now. Sasha?"

The woman stood staring back at him as if he weren't there. Her vibrancy was gone, and the tears began to dry on her face.

"She's gone," Bayzog said with a sigh. He wiped his eyes on his sleeve. "Every time that happens, I fear it will be the last I ever see of her again. I swear my heart is imploding in my chest."

Dumbfounded, all Ben could say was, "I can't imagine."

Bayzog carefully emptied the contents of the rucksack back into the chest and closed the lid. He hung the pack back up in the closet. "Did you believe her when she said our sons were dead?"

"I know a mother's instinct is far greater than a father's. So yes, I'm convinced they are in great peril." Ben put his arm around Sasha's slender waist and led her to the sofa. "Do you have any way of finding them?"

"I can attempt to find them with my resources, but I've tried that and haven't had any success as of yet." Bayzog grabbed the books that floated over his desk, closed them up, and stacked them on the edge. He made his way back over to the closet and grabbed the Elderwood Staff, which leaned back in the corner. "Ben, I'm going to have to take you up on your offer. Is it still available?"

"Of course it is, Bayzog," Ben said. "But I can't let you go it alone. I must come with you. You're no tracker. You'll need me."

"Who will take care of Sasha? I can only trust you."

"My wife, Margo, can handle it." Ben showed a confident smile. "Trust me, she and the girls can handle anything. They'll thrive at this. They're wonderful caregivers. The best. Just ask the Legionnaires. My family's stitched up more men than dragons have scales. I promise, Sasha couldn't be in better hands. Besides, I promised her."

Bayzog got on his knees in front of Sasha. Her face was so thin, and her eyes were listless and weak. He couldn't stay put and do nothing any longer. It was time he took matters into his own hands, and he'd have to trust some friends to do it. He kissed her hands and said, "I'll find a cure for you, my love. And I will find our sons and bring them back. I promise."

CHAPTER 9

A N ORC WITH A BIG body and a little head stepped into Balzurth's path. The ugly humanoid was half covered in iron armor that rattled and squeaked. He had a horrible underbite, and two canine teeth popped up on both sides of his nose that gave him a menacing look. "Fool! What are you doing in my camp? Have you come to be slaughtered?"

The snickering orcs formed a tight circle around Balzurth.

Nath's grip tightened on Fang's hilt. His father had told him to wait and he was obeying, but it didn't seem natural. It was uncomfortable, and it didn't help that his blood was rising. He eased forward.

Brenwar caught him by the elbow and tugged him back. "I'm as ready as you are, but we have our orders."

Balzurth stood face to face with the orc. "You have my dragons. I suggest you let them go, but if you'll allow me, I'd be glad to do it myself."

"No dragons will be freed, old man," the orc said with a sneer. Spittle dripped down his chin. "If anything, you'll be joining then in your own cage." He gave Balzurth the once over and stared hard into his eyes. "Your eyes are like gold. Perhaps we should cut them out, orcs. What do you say? Seize him!"

Surrounded by weapons, Balzurth watched with muted interest as the orcs bound his wrists up in heavy ropes.

"Put this fool in a cage," said the leader of the orcs, and then he leaned into Balzurth and added, "Keep quiet, too, or we'll have you for dinner."

Nath watched the rough-handed orcs shove Balzurth into a steel cage barely big enough to fit him in, and they padlocked it.

Laylana pushed Nath in the small of his back. "We need to free him. Oh, I'd like to show those orcs a thing or two."

"Great Guzan, what is my father doing? Is this what he wanted us to see, him getting captured?"

"He doesn't seem to be in any danger," Brenwar said. He had a stern look on his face. "Just give it a moment."

Concealed in the forest, they held their position for several long minutes. The drums started to beat again, and the orcs renewed their celebration, drinking and singing horrible songs that would make the deaf cringe.

Taken up in the scene of orcen frivolity, Nath momentarily forgot his father, so that when he looked back, his father's cage door was open.

Balzurth's mighty man frame was twisting the padlocks off the dragon cages and letting a small orange blaze and a green lily dragon go free. Both of them nuzzled into Balzurth as he stroked their long necks and the tiny horns on their heads.

"Hold there!" an orc yelled at Balzurth. The drums came to a stop again. The orc snatched up a spear and hurled it at Balzurth. The drunken throw sailed high and vanished into the forest.

The small cat-sized dragons' wings beat, and they took to the air and were out of sight through the tree branches that hung over the camp.

The orcen leader gaped and screamed. "Who let him out of there? I'll have your head!"

In a voice that rose over all of the weapon-drawing scuffles, Balzurth said, "No one let me out, you fool. I let myself out." He stepped back and opened up the door of his cage once again and said to the leader. "Now you get in there! Come on. I don't want to be standing here all night. I have better things to do than teach orcs a lesson."

With narrowed eyes, the orcen leader stepped over toward a stump that was in the ground with a battle axe stuck in it. He ripped it out and stormed toward Balzurth. Chest heaving, he said, "You're going to die for that, human."

"First, I'm not human. And second, well, there is no second, but if you want to try and kill me, then try and kill me." Balzurth spread his arms out wide. "Come on, you can have the first shot."

The orc lifted his battle axe over his head and brought it down with wroth force.

Balzurth sidestepped.

Swish!

The axe bit into the ground.

Using the orc's forward motion against him, Balzurth grabbed the orc by the scruff of the neck and shoved him into the awaiting cage. He slammed the door shut with authority and latched the lock. He said to the orc leader,

"You are as slow as you are stupid." He faced the others. "Now, how about the rest of you?"

The dumbfounded orcs looked back and forth at each other.

With his lower jaw jutting outside of the bars, the orc leader yelled, "What are you idiots waiting for? Kill him and get me out of here."

The nearest orc took a stab at Balzurth with his sword.

The Dragon King snatched him by the wrist and pulled him around and swung him with ram-like force into two of his comrades.

The next orc jumped on Balzurth's legs.

Two more piled on.

Balzurth was half laughing and half struggling to keep his feet. "Same old orcs, same old tactics." He wrapped his arms around one of their waists and flipped the orc back over his head, sending the husky body smashing into the trees.

At the same time, the leader of the orcs was yelling, "Get me out of here! Get me out of here!"

An orc warrior shoved his dagger into Balzurth's chest, puncturing the tunic.

The Dragon King replied, "Your orcen steel cannot harm me." He slapped the orc in the face so hard his canine teeth fell out. "Don't ever try to scathe me again."

The drunken orcs turned into a knot of clumsy ferocity. Teeth and weapons bared, they piled onto the big man in a frenzy.

"We need to get in there!" Laylana urged Nath.

He couldn't even see his father now. It was just a pile of orcs swinging and punching with wild-eyed ferocity.

"I agree," Brenwar said, nodding his head. "Let's go."

"You're the one who's so eager to follow orders," Nath argued.

"I know, but this is killing me," Brenwar replied. "I can't stand it anymore. He's having all the fun."

"Look!" Laylana said.

A pair of big hands popped out of the angry knot of orcs and grabbed two of them by their heads of mangy hair. The heads were yanked back and the faces slammed together. The same hands made fists and started punching the orcs in the jaw and hammering them on the head. As the orcs sagged into the dirt, Balzurth's handsome face appeared unscathed, saying, "They stink. My, they stink so bad. Dragon fodder smells far better than them."

An orc snuck up behind Balzurth and whacked him in the back of the head with a hammer, rocking his head downward.

The Dragon King's head snapped up, and his gold eyes were ablaze. He twisted around with the speed of a striking viper and ripped the hammer free from the orc's hand.

"Guzan," Nath muttered. He'd seen that look in his father's eyes before. The fires in the center of a volcano were nothing compared to it. The orcs had aggravated Balzurth. "He's going to kill that orc."

"Good," Brenwar nodded. "Take out those spangbockers!"

"Aye," said Laylana. "Let's help him."

Slinging off the disheveled orcs that lay scattered at his feet, Balzurth snatched up by the neck the one that had hit him with the hammer. He lifted it from the ground. Instantly, eyes bulging from the sockets, the orc started to choke, flail, and gasp.

Nath burst into action. Crossing from the forest into the camp in three quick strides, he rammed his shoulder into his father, jarring the orc loose from his grip.

Hot eyed like a god gone mad, Balzurth glared at Nath. "You dare!"

"We're not supposed to kill them!" Nath replied.

An orc rushed him with a spear.

With ease, Nath sidestepped and drove his boot into the orc's belly, dropping it on the ground and gasping. "We just beat the stupid out of them."

"They're orcs, they don't matter," Balzurth said. Fierce as a charging bull, he lifted a woozy orc over his head and shoulders and hurled him like a stump of wood into the upper branches of a tree. "Now get out of my way!"

Nath shoved him back and said, "So you lied to me?"

"I don't lie," Balzurth said.

"So I can kill orcs then?" Nath fired back.

Balzurth hesitated. The hot glare in his eyes cooled. Clenching his fists, he shook them and said, "My flesh lusts for battle! But no, Son. You are right. I should not be slaying these impudent things, regardless of how stupid they may be. Unless of course my life is in peril." He took a glance at his surroundings. "Which it clearly is not."

A banging of metal resounded on the cage the orc leader was trapped in. One of his brethren knocked the lock off, and in a wide-eyed hustle they scurried away.

"Aren't you going after them?" Nath said to his father. "After all, it *is* pretty fun throttling them from time to time. And I must admit it was a delight seeing you in action. I've never seen you like this before."

"Aye, but I got carried away." A long look formed on Balzurth's bearded face. He raised his fingers and studied the specks of orcen blood on them. "This flesh is weak. Son, it's been so long that I've forgotten how hard it must be for you to be you. It's exhilarating but dangerous. Perhaps this form I've taken is not for me." He scanned the fallen orcs with a sneer. "So many are soaked in evil that it's impossible to avoid it. A shame."

"What do you want us to do with these orcs, King Balzurth?" Brenwar had an orc locked up with the war hammer handle under the orc's chin. "I'd be glad to vanquish these poachers on your command."

Nath awaited his father's answer. There had been a time in Nalzambor when poaching dragons was a crime, but those days were gone. How were they supposed to deal with orcs that committed crimes against his kind? There wasn't any way to enforce those laws nowadays without killing. There was no longer anywhere to imprison simple poachers.

"Destroy their weapons and belongings. That's going to have to be punishment enough for now. We have our own mission." Balzurth picked up the orc leader's axe and spun it around with a twist between his fingers and said to the orcs, "Just because you receive mercy today does not mean you will receive mercy tomorrow."

Deep in the bowels of the forest, a horn blared.

A tremor shook the ground under Nath's feet, and the branches shook though there was no wind.

Rising up with Laylana at his side, Brenwar said, "What in Mortuun's beard is that?"

The sound of branches snapping could be heard in the distance. It came closer and closer. A lone orc, the one Balzurth had hurled, fell out of the trees, hit the ground hard, and scurried away. Nath knew the sound. It was footsteps. Giant footsteps that shook the ground. And it wasn't just one set but many.

Balzurth looked at Nath and said, "It seems the fight is just beginning." He lifted the orcen axe in front of his face and with a single breath he turned the twin blades to flame. "I hope Fang is ready. We're going to need him."

CHAPTER

10

A STEADY DRIP OF WATER BOUNCED off Rerry's head. The icy water ran down his back under his clothes and plopped into a puddle. The pool of liquid made its way down the rocky cavern floor like a tiny river that winded around the cave wall into the black out of his sight. It had been going on like this for hours while the limbs of the part-elven son of Bayzog burned with agony.

"Ugh…I don't know which is worse, the water or the stretch," he said in a gravelly voice. Licking his cracked lips, Rerry wriggled against his bonds. His wrists were bound over his head by chains, just barely allowing his toes to touch the floor.

"The water wouldn't be so bad if I could only taste a drop. Ugh!"

In the corner opposite his was Samaz. The stouter brother of the two hung the same way as Rerry: upright and uncomfortable. But Samaz's hair hung over his eyes. His bare chest had bruises and red marks all over it. A nasty cough revealed the taut muscles of his abdomen.

Rerry let out a light laugh. "This is fitting for you, Samaz. You have lost some of that baby fat that guarded your ample belly. Just think, a few more days and you'll be as skinny as me."

Samaz coughed and convulsed. It was a sick cough, not some annoyance that comes with a dry throat. Something worse.

Rerry squinted. A single torch just outside the cavern of their prison was the only source of light they had, and it was very little. Just enough to make out his brother's body but not enough to provide any kind of warmth. "Samaz. Samaz? Are you sick?"

Samaz shivered in his shackles, and the wet cough came back again.

"Great Guzan, you are sick." Rerry tugged against the steel links of his bonds. The fire inside him had far from dimmed, but his wiry strength was lacking. His hands bled from trying to squeeze them through the steel cuffs that held them. The bonds were secure. "My captors are clever. They know better than to take a chance with a brilliant swordsman like me, eh Samaz? Rerry the Ravager. No, Rerry the Rage." He blew his sweaty blond locks from his eyes. "If only I had red hair, I could be Rerry the Red."

"Rerry the Rooster," Samaz sputtered out in a raspy voice.

"You speak!" Rerry beamed and then frowned. "Uh, why rooster?"

"Because you're clucking all the time." Samaz broke into another fit of coughing.

Rerry grimaced and said, "I need to get you help. You are very ill with hallucinations. Do I look like a chicken to you?"

Samaz shivered so hard that his teeth clacked. Gulping for air, he said, "It's a fever. It will break."

"You will break if you don't have nourishment." Rerry let out a sharp whistle. "Guards! Guards!" His voice echoed down the tunnels and came to a stop. He shouted again. "Guards! Guards!"

It was as if they were the only ones in the caves. Rerry wasn't even certain where they were, because they'd been hooded when they were brought in. And now, after days in the dark, the grim, damp cave was taking a toll on Samaz. And Rerry feared it might take a toll on him as well before long. He glanced down at the skeleton that lay on the floor with its mouth hanging open. It had long, wispy black hair, and its clothes were finely woven. Judging by the hair and the narrow features of the skull, Rerry was certain it was elven.

How long did that elf live in this cavern before he died?

A scuffle of soft steps splatting over the damp waters that ran through the cave caught his ear. Whoever was coming moved with the gentleness of the falling night. Gazing at the tunnel, Rerry waited for his captor to emerge. Limbs still burning, he struggled in his shackles. He blinked away the sweat that dripped into his eyes, and when he looked up again, an elf was there blocking the torchlight and casting an ominous shadow over him.

"It's high time you stopped disturbing the gloom," the newcomer said. Tall and slender, the elf was handsome in his features, but his brown hair was shorter than that of most of their kind, cut neatly just above the shoulders. An eye patch covered his left eye, and a white scar split the dimple in his chin. He wore a leather tunic dyed black over a white shirt the covered him from the knees up over his trousers. The feathered insignia of an elven officer was on his collar, and he carried himself with a sinister air. "So I take it you are needing something?"

"I don't, but my brother needs care, Scar," Rerry said. "He's sick."

"It makes no difference to me. Suffering is part of your punishment,"

Scar said. "It goes hand in hand with your imprisonment." He glanced at the skeleton on the floor. "Just ask him."

"I did. He's not answering."

"Your tongue is awfully sharp, little Rerry. You sound strong. I need to remedy that." Scar grabbed the chains that hung over Rerry's head and gave them a yank. Rerry let out a groan. Scar added, "Perhaps they need to be a little tighter."

"This is not right. Where is our counsel, Scar? We are entitled to counsel. I might not be a full-blooded elf, but I know the elven rules. You cannot hold us like this against our will. It's not the elven way!" He stretched out toward Scar. "Help my brother!"

"Oh, your brother will be fine." Scar made his way over to Samaz, took him by the hair, and pulled his head up. Samaz's face was pasty and white. His eyes were sunken into their sockets. "He looks fine to me, for a human that is."

Voice straining, Rerry said, "We might be part human, but we are still entitled to our elven heritage. I demand our counsel now, Scar!"

Scar slipped his well-honed rapier out of his sheath in the blink of an eye and held the blade against Rerry's throat. "It's Captain Scar, and you bastards are entitled to nothing. Your kind is poison to the elven world. Your father is an embarrassment, and it's no surprise that his atrocious sons are nothing but common thieves. I should cut you both open right now and be done with it."

Showing his teeth, Rerry replied, "Then what is stopping you, Captain Scar?"

"Unlike you, I have orders that I follow. Otherwise, I would have finished the both of you off the moment we met."

Staring down Scar—who looked middle aged for an elf—Rerry replied, "Why don't you give me a blade so we can see who'll finish who off fairly?"

Scar smacked him on the cheek with the flat of his sword and said, "You whelp. Do you have so little value for your life that you'd let me cut you down in a moment? I'd carve you to ribbons. Pah. I bet you've never even killed in battle."

"I doubt you have. Cut me down, Scar. Let our swords dance, and we will see what happens."

"You'll never get the pleasure. You're dead already." Scar slid his sword into his scabbard and walked away.

CHAPTER 11

THE FIRST GIANT SHOVED TWO smaller trees aside, snapping them both at their bases. It ripped another tree out of the ground and lifted it high over its head like a club. Standing at fifteen feet tall, the ugly brute was nothing but thick layers of fat over muscle. Its neck was as wide as its head, and it opened up a mouthful of teeth that numbered more than the hairs on its head.

Covering his nose, Balzurth said, "And I thought the orcs were smelly."

Two more giants emerged from the startled black of the forest. Like the other giant, they were bestial men with hides and furs for clothes.

Flipping his flaming axe around his wrist, Balzurth said, "I'll take the one in the middle." To Nath he said, "There will be no mercy to these unnatural beasts."

Without hesitation, Nath rushed in with Fang arcing high. He swung the great blade into the giant's leg with authority.

The giant let out an angry bellow, and its fingers clutched for the locks of hair on Nath's head.

Nath stepped under the giant's legs and cut deep into the back of its knee, sending it sprawling to the ground.

Wham!

There was a clap of thunder, followed by the moaning of a giant that Mortuun the war hammer sent staggering into the trees. Brenwar was yelling, "For Morgdon!"

Balzurth's flaming battle axe sliced off the fingers of the outstretched giant's hand.

Letting out an ear-splitting howl of anger and anguish, it brought the tree it carried like a club down at Balzurth's head.

In human form, the Dragon King knocked the tree club aside with his blazing axe, bursting the branches into flames.

The trio of warriors pressed the giants back into the forest, hacking, stabbing, and chopping the bewildered giants down. The battle raged, and the forest turned to flame. Smoke stung Nath's eyes as he gave chase to the giant he'd toppled, which had gotten up and was running for its life through the branches. Nath clipped it right behind the heel, and it crashed headlong into a tree. Dazed, the giant turned, just as Nath ran Fang straight through its heart, ending its life. Surrounded by smoke and the burning haze of the orange fire, he heard Laylana's voice calling out.

"Nath! Nath!"

Rushing straight for the sound of the elven woman's voice, Nath picked up a rattling sound in the woods that sent shivers down his spine. The giants were not alone. Wurmers snaked through the smoky murk.

When he caught sight of Laylana, she was surrounded by wurmers. The rogue elven fighter chopped with the ferocity of an attacking lion, keeping the wurmers at bay, but then a tail lashed out and struck her square in the back of the head, taking her down.

"Laylana!" Nath screamed. Charging with amazing speed, he attacked the slithering knot of wurmers. His great sword Fang cut off a wurmer's head at the neck. With a stamp, he punctured another wurmer in the chest, turning the purple gleam in its eye cold.

Jaws clamped down on his free arm, and he drove Fang's pommel into an eye, jarring the creature loose.

Claws slashed into him.

Jaws snapped at his knees.

Nath fought on, tearing through the wurmers one by one, trying to reach Laylana. His powerful sword strokes swept the wurmers aside until he found himself standing over the elven princess. She was on her hands and knees, bleeding. "Laylana! Can you fight?"

Clutching her sword and rising to her feet, she said, "Do I have a choice?"

Back to back, they fought off the wurmers. The man-sized lizards moved in, one right after the other, swarming them from all directions. Fang bit through scale and bone.

"There are so many!" Laylana coughed, and tears from the smoke were streaming down her pretty face.

Nath sensed her strength was beginning to wane. Blood pumping, he redoubled his efforts and chopped deeper into one wurmer after the other, killing them instantly. Like an angry flock of hissing birds, the wurmers kept appearing. It was only a matter of time before the monsters consumed them. "Guzan! Where are they all coming from?"

All around him, the forest was blazing. Crashes and cries of alarm erupted from the haze. Brenwar was letting out battle cries, and Balzurth blurted out boasts. Giants growled and howled. A huge hunk of rock soared through the air and crashed into the branches behind Nath's head.

Nath screamed out, "Father, you're setting the entire forest on fire!"

Out of nowhere, a giant backpedaled through the smoke and smashed into the trees. A flaming axe burned in its forehead.

Balzurth spurted out of the chaos with havoc in his eyes. He stormed toward Nath and grabbed two wurmers by their tails. With a tremendous heave, he slung them into the smoke and out of sight. "These nasty insects are many!"

Revved up in the presence of his father, Nath unleashed everything he had left. Fang splintered scales and skulls. The nasty, inky blood of the wurmers burned through his scales into his flesh, but his battle-raged mind didn't care. With one sweeping swat after another, he poured it on until all of the wurmers were dead. Finally, chest heaving and fighting for breath, Nath caught Laylana by the wrist and dragged her out of the forest.

Brenwar stood several dozen yards outside of the forest's edge, patting out the flame that was burning a hole in his beard. "Blasted giants!"

Nath heard a gusty laugh coming from behind him, outside of the flames.

"My, that was fun! Was it not, Son? We need to seek these giants out and do that again."

Coughing, Laylana replied, "I'm ready."

"You were a bit careless, Father. The smoke could have suffocated us in there," Nath said, watching the flames rise into the night sky. He stuck Fang in the ground. "Not everyone is accustomed to smoke for breath."

"Noted," Balzurth said. The glow in his eyes started to dim. "I suppose I did get carried away, but this body wants to work without the mind. It's so lively." He approached Laylana and took her by the hand. "Are you all right, my sweet elven lady?"

"I'll be fine."

Balzurth patted her hand. "I'm sorry for my carelessness. I hope you'll forgive me."

"Most certainly," she said. "No regrets on my end. You men certainly know how to show an elf a good time."

"You mean dragons," Balzurth said.

"And dwarves," Brenwar added.

"Of course," she said, wiping her hair from her eyes.

"Well, if someone is looking for us, they shouldn't have much trouble finding us now," Nath said. "And it would not surprise me one little bit if there were many enemies nearby beyond that blaze. I don't suppose the fire will burn itself out anytime soon. It's a bit of a shame."

"Oh, I can take care of that." Balzurth reached over and grabbed Fang by the hilt, pulling him free of the ground. The wondrous blade twinkled with bluish light. Balzurth marched into the flaming forest and stabbed a tree.

Nath's jaw dropped.

Ice spread from the tip of Fang's blade. With crackling movement, the veil of ice covered the ground and raced up the trunks and limbs of the trees. A sizzling hiss followed as the flames were extinguished one by one, leaving a twinkling, white-blue ice tree city shimmering in the moonlight.

"Whoa," Laylana said, "I am without words."

Hefting Fang over his shoulder, Balzurth walked over and offered the sword to Nath. "Fang is quite something, isn't he?"

Taking the sword in hand, Nath replied, "How did you get him to do that?"

"I just asked Fang to do what I created him to do, and he did it. Next time there's a fire, you might want to give it a try."

Nath stood there gawping while Balzurth pivoted around on his foot and faced north toward Quintuklen, saying to Brenwar, "Is it time to resume our walk again?"

Slinging Mortuun over his shoulder, Brenwar said, "After you."

Nath and Laylana tagged along behind through the chill wind of the night, silent for several miles.

Crossing over the rocks that made a path over a babbling brook, she eyed Nath and said, "You look troubled. It's disturbing. What's wrong?"

"So many things are going on that I don't know where to start. Those giants came out of nowhere, not to mention the wurmers. I don't know that we can travel a day without fighting something." He reached out his hand to help Laylana over a fallen tree. "It's depressing, really. I can't help but wonder how this few of us can defeat so many."

"Oh, I don't think that's the only thing bothering you. You have no fear of these hordes of dangers. I think it's your father who's getting to you." She twisted her hair around her finger. "He's so confident and wily. And the things he does are so amazing."

"Yes, and I should be able to do those things too, but I can't. It's frustrating."

"Give it time," she said, "I'm sure you'll figure it out."

"That's the problem. I don't think there is much time left to figure it out. I just hope Quintuklen still stands by the time we get there. I swear I feel as if all of Nalzambor has gone mad." Sidestepping a rock, he bumped into her shoulder, almost knocking her over. "Sorry."

She ran her fingers down his arm and replied, "It's quite all right, Nath."

The twinkle in her eye made him think of Selene.

Sultans of Sulfur. I wonder how she's doing.

Nath picked up the pace, catching up with Brenwar and Balzurth. "You two are doing a good job steering clear of any trouble."

"We hope not," Balzurth said. "This is the most fun I've had in centuries."

"I don't recall saving Nalzambor being very fun the last time," Nath said.

"Oh, it's all about making the most of the journey, Nath," said Balzurth. "Being in the company of your friends when the stakes are so high that you can barely sleep at night. Ah... Nothing worth fighting for is ever easy. Eh, Brenwar?"

Combing his fingers through his beard, Brenwar replied, "I've never had fun doing anything easy."

"Well said, well said, my stumpy little comrade." Turning around to walk backward, Balzurth said to Nath, "I'm glad you joined us. Now put a smile on that grim face of yours. There's no apparent danger at the moment, and we live, we breathe, we'll fight again."

Nath didn't get caught up in the high spirits of the others. He wasn't used to seeing his father this way—jolly, laughing, or even smiling. Sure, there had been some frivolous times when he was younger, but for at least the past hundred years, Balzurth had been ... serious. Downright stern, even. And now the dragon-turned-man had become something else. If Nath didn't know better, he'd swear that some dangerous spirit had entered his father.

He couldn't possibly be this happy.

Finally, Nath gave in. "Fine, Father, but will you please be more mindful of the mortal company we are in?"

"Certainly, Son, certainly, but I heard you clearly the first time. No, I think Laylana will do just fine."

Onward they went, laughing, joking, and carrying on as if nothing could stop them.

CHAPTER 12

BEN SAT ATOP HIS HORSE, looking back at Quintuklen. The men worked day and night fortifying the mighty human city that had been turned to rubble by the Clerics of Barnabus not so long ago. Now new fortifications and buildings began to rise toward the sky again, thanks to the help of the dwarves. In each high tower were soldiers manning a ballista to fend off any flying terrors.

He filled his chest with air, sucking in the morning mist that covered the grasses and daisies. He was proud of these people. Even in the face of such adversity, they never gave up. He was proud to be among them. In the distance, stout men carried stones up ladders and set them down on scaffolding. They'd learned much from the dwarves and the dwarves some things from them. It was a joy to see them working together. It reminded him of Dragon and Brenwar. It seemed so long since he'd heard from them.

Considering the journey ahead, Ben thought to himself, *I wonder what they're doing now.* Noting the rising sun warming his face, another thought came to mind.

Bayzog ought to be out here by now.

The part-elven wizard had said he'd need ample time to prepare himself for the journey ahead. The violet-eyed scholar had seemed a bit rattled when Ben left him last night to be by himself. Leaving Sasha wouldn't be easy, but it was the right thing.

Come on, wizard. I'm itching to get going.

Ben unslung his bow from his back. He ran his fingers up and down the string. It was a fine bow, but nothing like Akron. His quiver of arrows rattled when he shifted in the saddle. There was a distinct sound to the arrows he shot. They were made from ash wood and tipped with tempered steel. He slipped an arrow out and nocked it on the bowstring. The thick callouses between the joints of his fingers were as hard as ever. He pulled the string back, aimed for a distant dogwood tree, and let the arrow fly. The arrow sailed high in the air and missed the mark by ten feet.

A little late to practice now.

He slung the bow back over his shoulder, longing for the *snap-clatch-snap* sound of Akron. There was already sweat forming on his brow, and his butt felt a little sore in the saddle.

Please don't tell me I'm too old for this, but I've barely made it out of the city.

Finally, Ben saw Bayzog come out through the outermost of the city's rebuilt white catacomb walls.

The half-elf wizard's expression was grim, but it perked up a bit upon seeing Ben. Riding up to the veteran warrior, he said, "Sorry for the delay, but I have something for you." He patted the bulging blanket behind his paint horse's saddle. "Take it. We will need it."

Ben lifted the blanket, and his eyes popped wide open. With astonishment, he said to Bayzog, "This is Brenwar's chest!"

"Indeed."

"Can we even open it?"

"See for yourself. I don't think it cares for elves. If you can't open it, I'm leaving it."

"No, no, no." Ben couldn't hide the thrill in his voice. He loved magic. It fascinated him, and he regretted not having an opportunity to experiment with the chest before. He took the strongbox by the outer handles and lifted it into his lap. "My, it's a lot lighter than it looks."

"Dwarves make everything appear stronger than it is," Bayzog said.

Ben's fingers searched the whole chest for a latch of some kind, but the area around the lid was almost seamless. "Bayzog, I can't open this up."

Bayzog stuck his staff out and poked the front of the box with the end.

Ben took a second look and discovered the face of a dwarf gilded in iron, flush on the front of the chest. It looked vaguely like Brenwar.

Raising his chin and wrinkling his brow, Bayzog said, "Stick your finger in the dwarf's mouth, and hope it doesn't bite."

Studying the gilded face and looking at his finger, Ben said, "You'd think there would be latches or something."

"Get on with it," Bayzog said with an arched brow.

Heart pumping in his ears, Ben poked the dwarf in the mouth.

Clatch.

The chest's lid popped up a hair, and a golden light peeked out.

"It opens!" With both hands, Ben started to lift the lid.

Bayzog reached over and closed it back. "It works. Good. Now let's get moving."

"No offense, Bayzog, but I'm going to take a look."

"Now is not the place or the time." Bayzog pointed the Elderwood Staff south. "Onward."

"Am I leading, or are you?"

"You're the one trained by the best tracker in the land. I trust your instincts."

Securing the strongbox on his horse, Ben tied it down and said, "Fine, but the next time we stop, I'm taking a longer look in this chest."

CHAPTER
13

BLETVER THE TRIANT TORE THE roof off a shed. A man shielded a woman inside. In a grisly but polite voice, Bletver said to them, "Have you seen a man with flame-red hair?"

The woman screamed, and the man fought to cover her mouth with his hands. He kept saying, "No, no, no, we haven't seen anyone like that!"

"Are you certain of that?" Bletver said, showing off his rows of teeth.

"I wouldn't lie! I wouldn't lie!" the man yelled back.

"Well, there's no reason to yell at me. It's impolite. After all, I am a guest in your quaint little farm town." Bletver licked his lips. "The smell of livestock is simply delightful. You know, I've been a thousand feet deep in a hole. I'd completely forgotten how salivating this world can be." He dipped his monstrous head deeper into the shed.

The man covered his face and gagged.

"Uh, are you absolutely, positively certain you have not seen a man with golden eyes and flame-red hair?"

"No, no, no," the man said. "I swear it on my life."

Bletver gave them a nod. "And I believe you. Thank you." He pushed the shed, collapsing it under his power and crushing the people within. He stepped on top of it and hopped on it a few times. The wood planks snapped under his weight, and that wasn't all that gave. The man's hand jutted between the boards and went still. Bletver dusted his hands off and eyed the goats that were crying behind the distant fence. "Ah, it's time to dine."

Taking his time to cross through the small farm village, he noted the withered husks of the once-vibrant bodies of people who had once nourished their surroundings for a hard but simple living. Faces of men, women, and children were frozen in horror. Their fragile lives had been sucked from the very marrow of their bones.

Nearby, the phantom swallowed up a man in the black shadows of his being. The blood quickly drained from the choking man's face. He dropped to his knees, frozen and lich-like, and then finally dead. The phantom's glowing eyes grazed over Bletver, then it passed through the stone walls of a well and moved toward the hidden voices that sobbed in terror.

"Bletver!" said a stern voice.

The triant turned.

Rybek had two well-knit men by their arms and was dragging them face first over the dirt roads like children. The men were busted up, and their spirits were broken. They didn't even cry out when they saw Bletver.

"What do you want me to do with them?" the triant said. "Crush them? Eat them?" He hitched his head over toward the fence that wrapped around the barn. "I'm thinking those sheep would be more succulent. These people tend to be a bit chewy."

One of the men gulped. His feet dug into the ground as he tried to pull free of Rybek's iron grip.

Rybek kicked the man in the ribs. "Be still." Drawing his dagger, he looked up at Bletver. "If you don't want to eat them, I'll kill them myself."

Lifting up his foot, Bletver stomped the life out of the nearest one. "Just because I don't want to eat them doesn't mean I don't want to kill them. They're humans. I can't stand them."

Rybek stabbed the second man in the heart, cleaned the steel on the man's shirt, and eased the blade back into its scabbard.

With a disapproving look, Bletver said, "Are we keeping score on the dead? Because I just added two other bodies over there. That gives me a count of ten—no, eleven, counting this one."

"Well, I'm not chasing down everyone that fled just to catch up. Besides, the phantom has doubled up on the both of us." Rybek picked up a stone from the ground. He chucked it at a husk of a woman on her knees clutching a bucket. His aim was true. The rock smote her in the face, and her body crumbled into a billow of smoke and a pile of ash.

"Humph, that was mildly amusing." Bletver sauntered over to a nearby fence post and yanked it one-handed out of the ground. He hurled it into a pair of phantom-struck bodies and turned them into a puff of smoke. "Not as thrilling as it looked. So you don't want to kill them all? I can smell their fear-filled sweat, you know."

"No," Rybek said. "Let them spread the news of our terror. It should draw out heroes like Nath Dragon. Eventually someone will show up. Someone that knows something will come. They always do, and we'll be waiting."

"Seems like an odd way to get results." Bletver gave a nod and headed for the barn. "If you'll excuse me, dinner is calling."

Rybek watched Bletver step over the barnyard fence, scoop up a whining goat, and devour it down in crunching chomps.

With a bitter expression on his face, Bletver tapped his chest with his fist and let out a disturbing belch.

Bllaaat!

"My, pardon me." Winking at Rybek, Bletver reached down and scooped up a sheep. Jaws wide, he stuffed the sheep into his mouth like a pillow into a case and swallowed it whole. "Mmmm...that's better."

Rybek's stomach gurgled. The thought of eating live flesh and bones wasn't something that sat well with him. He was human, after all, just evil to the core. Still, he wondered why the goat had cried out and the sheep hadn't. He'd noted that before in his conquests, where in some cases even people didn't have the slightest fear of their eminent death. Much like the sheep, they faced their fate with dumbfounded innocence. With life being so fragile, he wouldn't have thought they'd be so silent when it was about to end.

Venturing out of the town, he noted the crows circling overhead. The dead in the dusty streets were ripe for plucking. Grim faced, he set his sights on another conquest. Eventually, someone would stand up and face him, and his hope was that it would be Nath Dragon. He fingered the pouch that held the amulet he'd been given to capture Nath Dragon. The soft leather was cold and stiff to the touch. Rolling his stiffening fingers, he lowered them to the pommel of his sword. The blade's metal offered another reassuring feeling.

Eckubahn wants him alive, but I'll take his head. I'll have that betrayer Selene, too!

Rybek recalled the defeat Nath had given his brother, and a raging fire burned within him. Selene had taken full advantage of Kryzak's worship for her and turned him into an abomination. His brother had become a monster. The very essence of the man had been lost and was gone forever.

Rybek whipped out his sword and cut through the husk of a withered corpse.

I almost had her!

Indeed, he had tracked her as far as the seashore cities of the Pool of the Dragon, but he had lost her when she disappeared into the giant home of Uurluuk. No one had seen a trace of her for more than a year—not until what he'd discovered recently. She would surface again, along with Nath Dragon, and when they did, this time, now that he'd tested Nath's mettle, he'd be ready.

No mercy.

CHAPTER
14

Aftertraveling a day and a night without incident, Nath found himself on a hilltop with his father and their friends, gazing down at the City of Quintuklen. The humans had made grand progress since the last time he'd been here, which seemed like only weeks ago. He still hadn't adjusted to the year they'd lost when Fang had teleported him and Selene and Brenwar, but it could have been worse.

"There's an awful lot of soldiers," Brenwar said, shielding his eyes with his hand. "That outer wall has been rebuilt. No doubt there were many dwarves working on that. I imagine word has spread regarding Uurluuk's treachery. Perhaps I should go in by myself and see Bayzog."

"I can go," Balzurth offered. "No one's looking for me."

"No, but you and I look so much alike, I doubt you'll avoid suspicion," Nath said. And it was true. If it weren't for all of Balzurth's hair and long beard, he could almost pass for Nath. "As for you, Brenwar," Nath continued, "they know how close you are to me. You'll be interrogated instantly."

With a grumble, Brenwar agreed, saying, "Perhaps."

"I can try," Laylana offered. "So far as I know, no one's looking for me."

"Judging by the soldiers," said Nath, "I have a feeling they aren't going to let any outsiders within. I'm still surprised they're working with the dwarves."

"Oh, this is silly," said Balzurth. "I can get us all in. We just need to be quick about it." He pushed up the sleeves on his arms. "Come closer, everyone."

They formed a tight circle.

With a twinkle in his eyes, Balzurth said, "Now hold hands."

"Dwarves don't hold hands."

"Brenwar, if you please," Balzurth replied.

Standing between Nath and Laylana, the dwarf took their hands, but he said, "Don't get used to it."

Standing before them like a priest, Balzurth laid his hands on their shoulders and muttered words in Dragonese. A prickle of energy shot through Nath's shoulder into his hand.

Laylana giggled.

Brenwar blurted out a stifled grunt.

"That should do it," Balzurth said with a nod. "Let's go."

Nath lifted his hands. All of his glistening scales were intact. Balzurth looked the same, and so did Brenwar and Laylana. He had fully expected some sort of transformation, but the only thing he'd gotten from it was a tickle. "Father, I hardly see how whatever you did is going to help."

"That's because I didn't change you. My spell will change the others' perception of us. We know what we look like, so we cannot fool ourselves, but we can fool the ones who don't know us," Balzurth assured him. "Now lead the way, Son. I'm excited to meet your friends who you've spoken so highly of."

Rolling with the odd sensation that was rolling underneath the skin of his body, Nath gave a shrug to his friends, who did the same. He wasn't sure what his father had done, but he felt confident that it would work. He'd have to trust him.

The soldiers met them on their approach just outside of the first gap in the wall. Dressed in full suits of chain mail and wearing skullcaps, the formidable men let out a giggle when they saw Nath. There were broad smiles on all their faces. One of them, a stern-looking man with bushy eyebrows bursting out from under his helm's metal frame, asked, "What is your business in Quintuklen?"

"We are meeting with my sister," Nath replied in a voice that wasn't his. He looked down at Brenwar. The brows on his comrade had lifted into his hairline. Laylana's lips were parted in an O. Nath cleared his throat and added, "It will just be a short stay."

Great Guzan! I sound like a woman!

"Oh," the soldier said. The broad-faced man took off his helmet and offered a generous smile and looked Nath up and down. "Is she as fair as you? And so tall?"

"Uh... oh sir, it's difficult for me to say," Nath stammered. He broke out in a cold sweat.

What did Father do to me?

"I'd be honored to give you and your family a personal escort," the soldier said.

With all of the soldiers' eyes fixed on him, Nath replied in his woman's voice, "Er, that won't be necessary. I know the way." He swallowed. "But, perhaps you could share a meal with my other sister later. She's a fine lady and has a penchant for ale."

"Oh really?" said the soldier. "I'd be quite eager to meet her."

"She's right here." Nath walked over and put his hands on Brenwar's shoulders. "Please, dear sister, introduce yourself."

The soldier's face soured, and the other soldiers blanched. Noticing Brenwar for the first time, each of them looked as if he had swallowed a frog. Sputtering for words, the soldier said, "Perhaps the next time you visit." He waved his arm at the men guarding the gates. "Let them in. Quickly."

The iron gates split open.

Nath bowed his head slightly and said, "Thank you."

Passing through the gates, Brenwar smiled and waved at all the soldiers. Each of them looked away, and one of them laughed.

Cheeks warmed, Nath said to his father, "They think we're women?"

"Yes," Balzurth replied.

"Why don't you sound like a woman?"

"I wasn't planning on speaking."

"Change me back," Nath demanded. His voice was that of an angry woman. "Oh, I can't take this. I sound ridiculous!"

Laylana burst out laughing like a man. Her guffaws were as baritone as Brenwar's. Wiping the tears from her eyes, she said, "Oh, I hope I don't look hideous."

"Clearly, I do," Brenwar said proudly. He took the lead and marched straight for the next break in the second outer wall.

The wall that encircled Quintuklen was made up of five rings with a break in each at different points. Designed like a simple maze, it made travelers walk a mile before they made it into the city.

They passed by several sets of secure gates before making it to the next open break in the wall. Lips sealed tight, Nath overtook Brenwar and led them through the next two walls. His breathing eased as they approached the final pass, but unlike at the three rings inside the circle, here more soldiers were gathered.

Nath stopped, turned, and faced his friends. "I suppose I'll do all the talking again?"

Balzurth's face twisted up. Laylana cocked her head.

"What now?" Nath said.

"Your voice," Laylana said in her own voice, which had returned. "It's back."

Nath clutched his throat. Incredulous, he said, "No, it can't be back so soon?"

CHAPTER 15

"**F**ATHER, ARE YOU TELLING ME the spell has worn off already?" Nath rubbed his throat. Indeed, his voice had returned.

"I'm afraid so, Son," Balzurth replied. "But you have to admit it was fun while it lasted."

Flicking his fingers out, Nath said, "Fun? Pardon me, Father, but you have used that word far too many times."

"Entertaining," Balzurth offered.

"Same difference."

Brenwar chimed in with, "Merry. Dwarves like the 'word merry.'"

"And the elves consider such moments convivial," Laylana said. "Or witty."

Nath locked his hands behind his head and took a breath. "It's annoying. But please, allow me to take a moment to refresh everyone's memory on where we stand. I am being hunted by the elves and dwarves of Nalzambor."

"Yes, you're a fugitive."

"That's not helping, Father!" Nath threw his hands up. "If I were to guess, half of this city knows what I look like. Brenwar too, probably. We need to get inside undetected. Without trouble. I can't just go waltzing in there, and now I don't have anywhere else to go."

"Perhaps we should have traversed the wall in the dark of the night? Blended in with the shadows and avoided the light?" Balzurth said. "Now that would have been lively."

"You said you could get us through this, Father. That's why I did what I did. I like the night plan. That would have been easy." He held his head down and squeezed his eyes shut. "That would have been much easier than doing this in broad daylight. Sultans of Sulfur!"

As assuring as Balzurth seemed, it was complicating things with Nath.

He was used to being in charge and doing what he could with what he had. Now, Balzurth had changed all that. Following his father's lead was not easy. If anything, it was the opposite.

Balzurth threw his arm around Nath's shoulder. "Son, let me do the talking. We've made it through the first gate, so I doubt they'll be worried about us passing the last. The goal is near. Just keep it in sight." He took Nath by the arm and rubbed his scales. "Besides, you have magic. Use it."

"Fine, Father, fine. I guess I can try it."

"You can do it, Son."

It had been a while since Nath had tried to use any of the magic in him at all. He'd come to rely on the skills he'd been used to having before, but back when he and Brenwar set out to find his mother, he'd changed the color of his scaled arms to all black with no white in between. Now, if he could, he'd like to conceal his scales with flesh. Closing his eyes, he envisioned his arms turning to skin. Something caterpillar-like crawled over his arms. On opening his eyes, he beheld the diamond-shaped scales rolling over to become flesh. The naked splendor of his forearm caught the light of the sun. "Huh, I did it!"

"Of course you did," Balzurth reassured him.

"Here," Laylana said, stepping behind him. Her ginger fingers tied his long red hair behind his head and tucked it in behind his shirt. "Now you look human."

In return, Nath took the tiara off her head. He adjusted her silky locks with his fingers to make her hair cover her pointed ears. "Now you do too, and a very beautiful one at that."

She blushed.

"Come on then," Balzurth said. Arms swinging at his sides, the grandly built man with his red hair flowing over his great shoulders sauntered right up to the soldiers. "Hello."

Hanging back a little with Brenwar and Laylana, Nath observed his father striking up a wonderful conversation with the soldiers. Two of the armor-clad men leaned on their spears, and the third one was laughing. For more than ten minutes, Balzurth spoke to the men as if he'd known them all his life.

Brenwar nudged Nath in the back and under his beard he whispered, "Don't just stand there waiting to sink."

Nath took Laylana by the hand and dragged her over to Balzurth and the soldiers. "Excuse me, but without sounding rude, we have an urgent matter that needs attending to. It seems our water has built to the top of the dam, and it seeks relief."

The soldiers gave Nath and Laylana a quick look then waved them inside, saying, "Stop in the Highside Tavern. Tell them Josh sent you, and they'll take care of you."

Giving Laylana's hand a squeeze, Nath scuttled into the busy streets of Quintuklen with her and Brenwar. The people milled about so quickly that they didn't even pay them a glance of notice. He stepped onto a boardwalk that ran along an unending row of marketplace stores, finding shade beneath the colorful awnings.

"Whew!" Nath said. He gave Brenwar a gentle shove. "We did it."

"My heart is still racing," Laylana said. With avid interest, her eyes searched her unfamiliar surroundings. "A busy place. Very intriguing. Do your friends live very far?"

"No." Nath could still see his father talking to the soldiers. "Oh no. He's going to talk to them until their ears fall off. Poor men. Humans would die of old age before he finished one of his stories."

Giggling, Laylana ran her hand over Nath's back and said, "I've heard you're quite the storyteller too."

"I've been known to spin a yarn or two." Laylana's caressing hand on his back sent a delightful shiver up his spine. He backed into her, allowing her hand to glide further up his back and massage the steely muscles underneath. The mild attraction he'd felt before had turned into something exhilarating. "Perhaps I'll tell you one later."

"Perhaps we can stop standing around and swooning over one another!" Brenwar said.

Catching his breath, Nath turned toward Laylana and backed away. Her eyes had a desirous sparkle in them. It was a growing temptation.

What's going on?

"Nath, is something wrong?" Laylana said, coming closer. She rose on her toes and touched his cheek. "You're sweating. I've never seen a dragon sweat before."

Unable to control his desire, he swept Laylana into his arms and kissed her.

CHAPTER 16

EN'S HORSE'S HOOVES CAME TO a stop inches from the stream. He swung his leg over and hopped to the ground. Putting his hands on the backs of his hips, he stretched and said, "Great dragons, my back aches. I can't be this old and this stiff. How are you doing, Bayzog?"

"I've never been very comfortable in the saddle, but it's not any worse than it's ever been." Planting the Elderwood Staff on the ground, he climbed off the horse onto the grass. "And I always chafe."

Both horses nickered and shook their heads, flipping their tails and drinking from the water. It was a little past midday, and the skies were cloudy. "Looks like there's a heavy rain coming, but we should make it to Quinley by then."

"If you're too weary, I can make other arrangements for us to sleep comfortably." Bayzog lifted the hem of his robes and dipped a canteen in the water. "I don't want you to overdo it."

With both hands, Ben guzzled down the remaining water in his canteen. "Ah! Glad we're right near a fill-up. You know, I'd like to take you up on whatever magic quarters you're offering, I really would, but I need to get on another layer of dirt to thicken my skin." He scratched his chin and swatted at a buzzing insect. "I can turn old, but I can't let it turn me soft. I need to rugged up."

"You aren't that old, Ben. You're not even Sasha's age." Bayzog tossed Ben a canteen. "Drink more. Heartily. Perhaps these streams will return your youth."

Ben hung the canteen on his saddle and said, "I envy you."

"Why is that?"

"You elves live so long, and you can even use magic. But the long living part is the hard thing. I know life can be hard, but I still enjoy the challenge I have when I wake up every day."

Bayzog corked the second canteen and hung it over his shoulder. Standing at full height but still several inches shorter than Ben, he said to him, "And that's why I envy you. You in particular, and many humans, are never complacent. I envy how you live every day to the fullest. It's why I was so attracted to Sasha. There was so much life in her."

The pair of them stood silent, watching the stream flow over the shallow rocks.

"We're going to find a cure for Sasha and find your sons, Bayzog. It won't be easy, it never is, but we can do it." Ben gave Bayzog a soft pat on the back. "Have faith."

"Perhaps it's time you took a look inside Brenwar's chest. Balzurth set him up with many wondrous gifts. I'm certain there's something that will make you feel younger."

Ben felt several years fall away. "Really? No, don't answer that." He untied the chest from his horse and set it down. On his knees with his fists on his hips, he said, "I haven't stopped thinking about this for two days."

Standing behind him with a soft breeze rustling his black hair, Bayzog said, "Me neither."

Ben popped the lid and pushed it wide open. Vials filled with a mosaic of colors were lined up in neat little rows. The entire tray of potions was on a single rack that he lifted back over the lid. It hung suspended on the folding arms that held it like some jewelry boxes he'd seen before. Underneath the tray of potions were several items. What caught Ben's eye was a pair of leather gauntlets woven with metal chain and a folded sheet of black cloth. He picked up the cloth and handed it to Bayzog. "What's this?"

Bayzog unfolded it and tossed it over the chest. The chest vanished.

"Great Dragons!" Ben said. "What did you do?"

Bending over, Bayzog seemed to pick at something out of thin air. He lifted something that reflected everything around and behind it, and before Ben's eyes the black cloth reappeared. "I believe it is called a Cloth of Concealment."

Touching the fabric as if it was an apparition, Ben said, "I like it!" Placing the Cloth of Concealment back inside the chest, he started taking count of the potion bottles with his finger. "There are so many. How do you know what they do?"

"Good question." Bayzog plucked a vial out with orange liquid that had sparkles swirling through it. There was tiny lettering on the bottle.

"What does it say?" Ben was squinting at the vial. "And what language is that?"

"It's called Scrollhewn, mystic lettering that magic users like myself often use. It certainly does take a discerning eye to read it, but it deters foolish abuse of what is within. This potion I think is one you'll like." He handed it to Ben. "It's dragon fire."

With both eyebrows arched, Ben said, "You mean if I drink this, I can breathe fire like Dragon?"

"Assuming it works."

Ben felt like a child again. When Bayzog looked away, he shoved it into his pouch.

Without looking at him, the wizard said, "Ben, it's fine if you take it. I'd tuck away some of those yellow ones too. They're for healing."

Ben picked out a few more vials, filling his pouch and buckling it up. The stiffness from the long ride began to ease, and he didn't feel so bad about the long journey now. Spying the gauntlets in the chest, he couldn't help himself and put them on. He stood up straight as an arrow. "Whoa!"

Clenching his hands, he said, "Bayzog! I feel like ten men in one." He strolled over to his horse that was still drinking from the stream and stroked its mane. "Be still. Be still." He bent down, braced his shoulders under the horse's belly, and heaved it up over his head. "Haha! Bayzog, look!

One of the corners of the part-elf's mouth turned up. "Perhaps the horse should be riding you?"

Ben set the horse down. Excited, he said, "Oh my, oh my!" He fetched his bow and quiver and loaded an arrow. He took aim at a distant tree farther away than his customary targets. He pulled the bowstring back along his cheek in one smooth motion. His arm didn't quaver. He released the bowstring.

Twang!

The arrow sliced through the wind, sailing true to the mark and burying itself in the distant tree.

Thunk!

"I never could have made that shot before!" Ben exclaimed. He nocked another arrow and pulled the string back.

Snap!

"Oops."

"It looks like someone got a little carried away," Bayzog said. "Be careful, Ben. Power like that is something you don't want to get used to."

Ben slipped off the gauntlets, walked over, and dropped them back into the chest. "I know. I think that's why I feel so horrible for losing Akron." He closed the lid on the chest and loaded it back onto his horse. "Come on. Let's hurry up and get over to Quinley. All this fooling around made me hungry. And besides, they make the best fish and biscuits in Nalzambor."

With a nod, Bayzog said, "I look forward to it."

While they crossed the stream on horseback, the wind picked up, and the rain-clouded sky started to darken on the horizon.

"The rain's coming sooner than I expected," Ben said. "But don't worry, Bayzog. A little water never hurt anybody. Try not to slip out of your saddle."

Eyes cast upward, Bayzog said with a grim look on his face, "It's not the rain I'm worried about."

Following Bayzog's line of sight, Ben lifted his chin to the heavens. High in the sky, a formation of birds soared toward them beneath the clouds. His chest tightened. "You don't think those are birds."

"No, I think they're wurmers."

CHAPTER 17

BRENWAR STROKED THE WHISKERS ON the corner of his mouth. Minutes ago, he'd grabbed Nath—who'd been lip-locked with Laylana—by the belt of his pants and pulled him free and into an alley.

Nath paced back and forth in a narrow passage between the storefronts. "I don't know what got into me. I've never acted so impulsively before."

"Hah. Your memory can't be that bad." Brenwar gave Nath the eye. "I recall plenty of times in your earlier days when you sucked face with ladies who were little more than strangers."

Nath pulled up a wooden crate and sat down. "I did, but that was so long ago. Another time. Was I that bad?"

"I hardly ever saw you pass up a pretty woman who batted an eye at you. It's not any of my business, but you've come too far along to go back down that path." Brenwar showed the calloused knuckles on his fist. "I'd hate to have to throttle you if it happened again."

"It was just a kiss."

"It looked like more than a kiss to me. Even I haven't forgotten about Selene. Imagine if she saw that. She'd tear those golden eyes out of your head." Brenwar gave a huff, flipping some of the hair of his moustache up. "Don't just sit on your hind end sulking. We have things to do. Important things. Now straighten this out with Laylana. I don't want to be around any awkwardness. It's bad enough being a dwarf in a human city."

Nath leaned over, peering around Brenwar. He didn't see Laylana at the end of the alley. If he could, he'd rather avoid the apology. Not that she didn't deserve one, but rather because he was embarrassed.

How could I do such a stupid thing?

Laylana was a beautiful elf with fine features. It was quite natural that any man who saw her would desire her. But he wasn't a man, he was a dragon. And she hadn't had such a profound effect on him when he'd first met her. What happened had come on so suddenly.

With a sigh, Nath said, "Why don't you give me a few minutes, Brenwar?"

"A few. No more." The dwarf turned and started down the alley, but when he neared its end, Balzurth emerged, blocking his path. "Pardon, sire."

Balzurth stepped aside and Brenwar was gone, leaving him alone with his father. With bright eyes, his father said, "So, I understand you had yourself a little kissy-kissy."

"She told you!" Nath exclaimed. His head fell back between his shoulders. "I can't believe that."

Pulling up a crate, Balzurth sat down in front of Nath. "She doesn't have anyone else to talk to, and most women like talking. Particularly about their feelings. Speaking of which, how are you feeling, Son?"

Gaping at his father, Nath replied, "We aren't really going to do this, are we?"

Balzurth's heavy stare didn't change.

Nath knew when his father meant business. They weren't going to move an inch until he opened up about it. He didn't want to sit in this smelly alley for a decade. He remembered the last time that had happened. "Guilty and embarrassed."

"Good." Balzurth gave him a little pat on the knee. "You should feel that way. But you aren't the only one feeling embarrassed. You left Laylana standing on the porch all alone. Poor girl looked like a frightened rabbit."

"Brenwar dragged me back here. Father, I was going to apologize." He gave his father's crate a little kick. "What happened? I just lost control."

"You let your guard down."

"What guard?"

Balzurth took him by the skin of his arms. "Your scales are gone. I told you they protected you in more ways than one. You're all flesh now. When that happens, it doesn't take long for your carnal instincts to surface."

Nath rubbed the fine hairs on his arms. "Flesh is awfully weak, isn't it?"

His father nodded.

"But you don't have scales at the moment," Nath said. "How are you coping with it?"

"I've got thousands of years of coping under my belt, so to speak. Come on." Balzurth stood. "Like the fifer gnomes say, let's nip this in the blossom's bud."

Nath found Laylana sitting on the porch, leaning against a post, and took a seat beside her. Her chin was down when he opened his mouth to speak.

At the same time, they both said, "I'm sorry."

"Please, me first," Nath insisted. He took a little breath. "I apologize for kissing you. It was very forward of me to do that, and it shouldn't have happened."

Showing a faint little smile, she replied, "It was a grand kiss, and I have no complaint. I've never kissed a dragon before, but I understand, Nath Dragon. The fault is not all your own. I did welcome it."

He swallowed. Her warming way with words was enticing him anew. Taking control of his impulses, he said, "Let's just shake hands and move on from it."

She extended her hand. "Certainly."

"I'm relieved." He saw the disappointment in her eyes. "Laylana, you are a magnificent woman, but I need to stay focused—and I can't forget about Selene."

Clasping his hands in both of hers, she said, "I'm a fighter, Nath. I'll be fine." She rose. "Let's go see these other friends of yours."

CHAPTER 18

DRIPPING WET, BAYZOG STOOD BY a stone fireplace inside a small home in the village of Quinley. As the logs crackled and popped, he wrung out the sleeves of his robes, splattering drops of water on the floor. He and Ben had been half a mile from Quinley when the rainstorm hit, the downpour so bad he could barely see ten feet in front of him. If it weren't for Ben, he'd have been lost.

"Bayzog, take off those robes," said Ben. "It will take you too long to dry if you stand there in wet clothes." He sat at a candlelit table nibbling at a plate of food with one arm hitched over the back of his chair. His brother Jad—much older but similar in demeanor—was at the table with his wife beside him. They were thrilled to see Ben and hadn't stopped talking and feeding him since they'd arrived. "Make yourself comfortable and join us."

The quaint home offered very little in terms of privacy. It was one big room, with a window on every wall. The wind whistled through the planks of the boarded walls. A bucket caught a steady drip of water that streamed down from the rafters.

Not having a change of clothes with him, Bayzog smiled and said, "I'll be fine."

"He'll be fine," Ben reassured his family. "Just a little waterlogged."

Laughing, Ben's family resumed their talking. Ben had been quick to ask if they'd come across Rerry and Samaz, but they hadn't. The older couple were concerned about some of the other rumors that had spread, about the giants and the wurmers. That's when Ben had started making his case. "I wish you would both come to Quintuklen. You'll be safer there."

"And abandon my sheep and cattle?" Jad rapped his knuckles on the table. "Why, they'd never forgive me for it."

"They wouldn't miss you one lick," Ben said, joking.

"Oh yes they would," Jad said.

His wife nodded, saying, "He spoils them. How can a man spoil a cow? Yet he does. He walks out into the field and they come mooing. Silliest thing I ever saw."

"It's not silly," Jad said. "They like the attention."

"I'd like some attention too, you know," she said. "I shouldn't have to play second fiddle to the cows."

The light conversation went back and forth, creating a grand atmosphere of simple comfort. Bayzog cast a small spell that dried his robes, leaned his staff by the front door, and finally took a seat at the table.

Jad's wife filled him a clay cup of water. She stared at Bayzog and said, "I've never seen eyes like that before. I have that violet in my garden. It's beautiful."

"Thank you."

After a couple of hours of talking without ceasing, Bayzog made himself comfortable in the corner of the cabin. He pulled his legs into his chest, closed his eyes, and listened to the rain that continued to pitter-pat on the roof. The long ride had finally caught up with him, and he drifted off to sleep.

A startling crack woke him. Blinking, he noted the room was almost pitch black aside from the faint glow of some of the embers in the fireplace. There was a rustle of movement on the floor. Ben was under a blanket, starting to stand. His brother crept along Ben's side.

"What was that?" Ben said. He was up on his feet and slipping his trousers on. "Do you think a tree has fallen?"

"That wasn't a tree." Jad buckled his pants and grabbed his boots from beside the door. "And the rain and wind have stopped. It sounded like a beam cracked."

Outside, horses had started to whinny. Some of the livestock were crying out, too. Bayzog's ears prickled. Eyes now alert, he stood up and reached for his staff.

Whoom.

The small home shook. The clay goblets on the table rattled.

Whoom.

Bayzog noted the whites of Ben's eyes were huge. Ben whispered to him, "What in Nalzambor is that?"

Jad's wife slipped through the cabin, hugged him, and said with a tremble in her voice, "I'm scared."

"Don't be," Jad reassured her, "It's probably just some wolves or something."

A woman's cry screeched through the night. An agonized man cried out and fell silent. Buckling on his sword belt, Ben donned his leather armor and pushed his brother back. "Stay here."

Elderwood Staff in hand, Bayzog followed Ben out the door. In the center of the courtyard two foreboding figures stood, as out of place as an orc at a dwarven Festival of Iron. At fifteen feet tall with a back as wide as a stream, an abomination stood with his great hands hanging down well past his knees. He held up a length of fence post in one hand and snapped it in half.

Beside the giant was a man with a powerful build, wearing an iron helmet. His arms were bigger than most men's legs, and in the sinking moonlight they bulged with muscle. There was a dead body beside him. Blood was on the ground. He spoke with thunder in his voice and said, "Wake up, village. Your time to die is at hand."

CHAPTER 19

IT TOOK A LONG CONVERSATION, but finally Nath convinced Ben's wife Margo to let them into Bayzog and Sasha's apartment. The wizard's place was as neat as ever, but the mood was somewhat dark. Sasha sat on the sofa, staring into the corner firelight. Her sunken eyes were distant, but her natural beauty was hanging in there.

"Ben's going to be so disappointed he missed you, Dragon," Margo said. She was a pleasure of a woman to be around. Her hair was strawberry blond and short. She had the sunny personality of a country girl, simple in her clothing and a smile of beautiful white teeth. "But I never imagined you'd be even more handsome than he spoke of. And your father, too. It's uncanny." She rubbed her eyes with her finger and thumb. "Yes, you're real. I hope the food I prepare is worthy."

"Please, Margo, you flatter us. I'm certain that whatever you prepare will be more than sufficient."

"Without a doubt," Balzurth said, taking a seat on the sofa beside Sasha. There were two young dimple-cheeked girls hiding behind Bayzog's circular table and staring at Balzurth with eyes as big as the moon. They were very little. One favored Margo and the other Ben. He caught them looking. "Who are these two little delights? Come over here. I have something for you."

With a nod from their mother, the girls hopped up into Balzurth's lap.

"That's Trista and this is Justine. They're Ben's pride and joy."

"You have a handsome family, Margo. I say Ben did well to come by you," Nath replied.

"I'm just glad I found him. Things were very hard before he came." Her eyes watered up a little. "I'm not used to being without him. He never leaves my side for long, and I'm just not used to it. I didn't think it would be so hard after only a couple of days."

Nath felt that guilty nagging in his gut again. Ben had lost his first family during the war, so it only made sense that he would stay close so that it didn't happen again. Nath had never even gotten to meet Ben's first family. He'd been in his decades-long dragon sleep when they were around. Rubbing Margo's shoulder, he said, "We shall catch up with them soon, and I'll send him right back."

"No, no, I understand. You have to do what you have to do, and I feel horrible for Bayzog. Sasha is a sweet woman. Though I don't know her, I can feel it. She needs her family close. Ben is doing the right thing. He's a brave man. You taught him well."

"He was born brave," Nath said.

"These young little things are adorable," Balzurth said.

Laylana walked over to the dragon of a man and picked up one of Ben's little girls in her arms. She tickled Trista under the chin, bringing forth some giggles. "I've never held a baby human before. They are heavy."

"If you think *they're* heavy, you should try holding a baby dwarf," Nath joked.

"We're built to last," Brenwar said.

"If you'll excuse me," Margo said, "I'll finish preparing something to eat. Come, Trista and Justine. I need someone to sample the pudding before I serve it."

The little girls squirted out of Laylana and Balzurth's grasps.

The Dragon King started laughing. "If only people could remain childlike in their worries, Nalzambor would stay a better place." He turned his attention to Sasha. "This is a sad predicament. What did you say happened to her?"

"Bayzog calls it the wizard's dementia. It's rare, but it affects humans who use magic. She was a fine sorceress at one time."

Brow furrowed, Balzurth placed his hands on Sasha's face. He pulled the skin under her eyes down. "Hmmm. And you say they're on a quest to heal this? This is deep. Dark. There is no cure for this that man can find—that I know of."

Nath's heart sank. He knew there wasn't a cure for every ailment in the world. Life was hard. People were mortal. Old age and tragedy weren't the only ways people died. There was sickness, too. The flesh was weak, and it didn't hold up forever. "We hoped the Ocular of Orray might help, but it's closely guarded by the elves."

In a serious tone, Balzurth said, "I believe you experimented with that before, Son. How did it turn out?"

"It didn't." Nath reflected on the time in the elven city of Elome when he'd tried to rid himself of the black scales. It wasn't favorable. "That doesn't mean it won't work for her."

"No, this woman doesn't have long, I fear." Balzurth's big hands covered her shoulders. "Buried deep inside is a love for family that has let her hold on this long, but her attachment to life is hanging by a thread. Her hope and her very essence are fading. It's a good thing we arrived when we did."

"What do you mean?" Laylana took a seat on the other side of Sasha. "So we can comfort her?"

"Why no, so she can be cured."

"Father, I thought you said she couldn't be cured."

"Not by any human means." Balzurth rubbed his hands together. "But I'm not human."

The room filled with new warmth. The hairs stood up on Nath's arms, and as a soft golden glow formed around his father, he closed his eyes. The entire room was bathed in new light. Brenwar and Laylana were transfixed. Deep inside Nath's belly, he was uneasy.

Should Father be doing this, whatever it is?

But Nath's feet were glued to the floor, and all he could do was watch.

The heavy lids over Sasha's eyes lifted. New life gleamed in her eyes. Raising her wrinkled hands, she rested them on Balzurth's forearms. Her head tossed back, and she gasped for air. Head still back, her mouth was hanging wide open. Something dark began to seep from her pores, like tiny black droplets of rain. It gathered above her like a small cyclone in the air and floated over Balzurth.

No!

Nath wanted to stop whatever was happening. His raw instincts told him something was horribly wrong. He shifted his gaze from his father back to Sasha. She was refreshed and rejuvenated. Decades of life had returned. Her eyes watered like a new rain.

Just then, Balzurth lifted his hand into the dingy swirl. Like a hive of angry bees, it attacked and burrowed into his skin. The golden light faded to nothing, and the warmth was gone.

Following a long moment of silence, Sasha said in a voice like honey, "Nath, is that you?"

He rushed over to her and clasped her hands. "Yes, yes, Sasha, it's me."

She did a double take between him and his father. "Then who's this?"

The gold in Balzurth's eyes had turned to black, and he sat still as a stone.

"It's my father," Nath replied, but the cold expression on Balzurth's face sent spiders crawling down his legs.

CHAPTER
20

"**B**EN," BAYZOG SAID UNDER HIS breath. "Get to the chest. Now." He watched as Ben darted for the stables.

The door to the small house cracked open, and Jad peeked out.

Bayzog pushed his head inside and said, "Please. Stay quiet and stay in there." The door creaked to a close. As he turned away from the house, the man and the hideous troll-like giant turned and faced him.

"What do we have here, an elf?" It was a humongous giant who spoke in a polite, measured tone contrary to his face. "Strange place for an elf."

"Strange indeed," said the warrior wearing the iron helmet. He slid his sword out of the scabbard. The blade had a living shimmer swirling in the metal. "What brings you to these parts, elf?"

"I'm just passing through," Bayzog replied. He moved away from the house, positioning himself between the aggressors and the open fields behind him. He ran his fingers down this staff and added, "Perhaps you monsters should do the same."

Placing his fingers—which were unnaturally long even for his size—on his chest, the monster said, "I was only stopping in for a bite. I get very hungry moving from town to town. And my ears are still ringing from all the screaming."

"There will be no more screaming here," Bayzog said.

"Oh?" The giant troll lifted a brow. "Are you sure about that?" He hurled the fence post across a field into one of the nearest neighbors' homes. The beam crashed right through the window. Startled voices cried out. Cupping his ear, the monster said, "That sounds like a scream to me."

"What do you want with these people?" Bayzog said. "They're no threat to you."

The warrior came forward. "Perhaps they should be. The weak deserve the slaughter."

"They're not weak," Bayzog defended. "However, it *is* weak to take advantage of hardworking people."

"Oh, we have a *politician* among us." The giant clapped his hands together and bowed a little. "Tell us your name and your platform. Maybe we'll vote for you."

All Bayzog was trying to do was buy time in hopes that the people of the town had enough sense to slip out and find safety. The man and monster before him were killers. He could see it in their black eyes. He could smell it on the giant's rancid breath. They had no guilt. They sought devastation. But why? Even the giants that were taking over the towns weren't slaughtering people en masse. They were just controlling the masses with fear. Now this. "Why don't you tell me your names? After all, you're our guests."

"There's no point in that," the warrior said.

Taking a long step forward, the giant said, "I am Bletver, a triant. This is my boss, Rybek the Devastator. We are servants of Eckubahn, here to spread his blessing throughout Nalzambor."

"By killing people?" Bayzog said.

"We like to consider them mercy killings," Bletver said.

"Be silent, triant." Rybek blocked Bletver with his arm and stretched out his sword. "Elf, if you're going to attempt to stop us, I suggest you get on with it. But I'll show you mercy if you hand over that staff of yours."

Bayzog planted the staff in the ground. The wind picked up, blowing strands of his hair in his face. "The only way you get this staff is if you pry it from my part-elven hands."

"I'd be delighted." Rybek started his advance.

Bayzog pointed the staff at the triant Bletver. The gemstone centered inside the nest of wood that cradled it flared with amber light. A bolt of energy shot from the Elderwood Staff and smote Bletver in the chest with a clap of thunder.

The triant toppled over and fell hard to the ground. His chest was smoking, and he lay still.

Bayzog pointed the staff at Rybek. "Don't take another step."

Resting his sword on his shoulder, Rybek said, "And if I do?"

"I will turn you to dust."

"And here I was planning on turning this entire village to dust." Rybek lifted his shoulders. "Well, plenty of things will be dust once this is over."

Bletver rose to his elbows. Looking down the length of his nose, he saw his smoking chest and said, "What in a bearded wart hit me?"

"Stay down, triant," Bayzog warned. He pointed the staff between the two of his enemies. "Stay down or just crawl away."

"It's going to take more than your little stick to stop me," Bletver said. "Now the fight becomes interesting." With speed that belied his grotesque girth, the triant sprinted away, making a beeline for a nearby house and calmly announcing, "Incoming."

Rybek attacked.

Bayzog pointed the staff at the armored warrior and turned loose its power. A bright beam of energy struck the fighter's striking blade, which turned aside the blast.

Rybek shuffled back several steps, regained his balance, lowered his head, and charged.

Without hesitation, Bayzog loosed the staff's firepower again.

Sword swinging, Rybek knocked the bolt aside, kept churning, and powered his body into Bayzog's. The jarring impact knocked the staff loose from the half elf's fingers.

Bayzog moaned under the weight of Rybek's crushing body. The warrior was a big man, and with the armor, he felt like he weighed a ton. Fighting, wrestling, and punching weren't Bayzog's ways.

In an instant, Rybek had him pinned down on the muddy ground with the blade at his throat. "It seems I didn't have to pry the staff away from you after all, now did I?" Rybek clamped an iron grip over Bayzog's throat and squeezed. "Now tell me, bastard elf. Who are you?"

A crash of wood followed by screams caught Bayzog's ears. The triant's reign of terror had begun. The horrified cries multiplied. Choking out the words, Bayzog replied, "You are not worthy of my name, you murdering monsters."

Applying more pressure to Bayzog's neck, Rybek replied, "You are right about two things. We are murderers and we are monsters. Prepare to die, nameless bastard that you are."

CHAPTER
21

"**H**OW ARE YOU FEELING, FATHER?" Nath asked.

Balzurth didn't reply at first.

Instead, Sasha embraced him. He patted her back without speaking as she thanked him several times. Her body was shaking against his, and finally she broke off her embrace.

That's when Balzurth said, "Eh, I'm quite well, Son."

Nath watched as the gold in Balzurth's eyes overtook the black, driving away the inky murk that had been there. "Are you certain?"

Hands on his knees, Balzurth said, "I think I would know if there was something wrong with me." The richness returned to his voice. "But what's important here is for nothing to be wrong with this young lady. How do you feel?"

"Exquisite." Sasha hugged Balzurth again.

Nath didn't think his father had been all there the first time Sasha hugged him. No, while what his father had done for her was wonderful, he couldn't help but think a price had been paid. His father, though vibrant in appearance, sat hunched over a little bit.

He'd better be fine.

Margo entered the room with a tray filled with food. "What's all the commotion about? Why is everyone so excited?"

"Margo!" Sasha said. "What are you doing here?"

Staring over Sasha's shoulder, Margo said, "Is this another episode?"

Smiling, Nath shook his head and said, "No, my father has healed her."

Brenwar made a skeleton fist and pushed it up in the air, saying, "We need to celebrate!"

For the next couple of hours, the friends gathered around the table, talking and enjoying themselves. Everyone was thrilled for Sasha, and she couldn't stop thanking Nath and Balzurth.

Now refreshed and with the color back in her cheeks and her pretty eyes as bright as the moon, Sasha became serious. "I remember terrifying dreams about my sons. You know I have to go find them."

"Ben and Bayzog are only a couple of days away from us. We'll catch up with them in no time and continue our search for Rerry and Samaz from there," Nath said to her. "I'm confident we will find them."

"When you catch up with them," Margo said, "will you please send Ben back home? I'm sorry, Sasha, but I miss my man. And the girls are sick without him."

"I insist on it," Sasha replied. "Don't you fret. Families need to be together during these dark times." She placed her hand on one of the spell books stacked on the table. "Now, if you'll excuse me, I have some preparation to do."

"Sasha, are you certain you're ready to venture out so soon?" Nath asked as he stood up from the table with the other men. "You might need more time and rest."

"I'll never rest until my family is back."

Getting back out of the city proved easier than getting inside had been. Sasha merely read a scroll, and they popped over the wall to the outside. It was early morning, and the dew was heavy on the grass. Balzurth was ahead, but he wasn't leading. Nath was. His father had been quiet since they'd begun the next leg of their journey. The weird thing was that Balzurth was talking to himself in Dragonese. His words were faint, and Nath couldn't quite catch them enough to understand.

Marching alongside Nath, Brenwar said, "What's wrong with your father?"

"You're asking me? You know him better than I do."

Brenwar had a more serious than normal look on his face.

"I'm joking," Nath reassured him. "But no, I do have a strange feeling about him."

Pawing his black-and-gray–streaked beard, the dwarf replied, "I've got that tickling the hairs on my toes feeling, too. He's off. The ever slightest, but enough."

Nath adjusted the strap that held Fang between his shoulders on his back. "I can only imagine he's adjusting." He scratched his arm with his golden-yellow claws. His black scales were back. True enough, they seemed to have restored the air of purity he'd earlier lacked. Taking a look behind him, he noted Sasha and Laylana chatting away. The fire that had burned inside him for Laylana was now gone.

Perhaps I should suggest that Father restore his scales.

"Take the lead while I have a moment with you know who?"

"Aye."

He glided back past his father.

Balzurth's stare didn't change its course. It was half in the trees and half in the sky, searching for something. His arms were swinging like he was in a grand parade.

Nath snapped his fingers before his father's eyes.

Balzurth swatted at Nath's hand, came to a stop, and said, "Huh?" He gave Nath a spacy look. "Oh, yes, Son. What is it I can do for you?"

"That was really incredible what you did for Sasha."

"I know, I know. It had to be done."

"I'm feeling better, myself," Nath added.

Staring at the clouds that drifted overhead, the Dragon King said, "What was wrong?"

"My scales. I have them back."

Balzurth nodded.

Nath took his father by the elbow and pulled him to a stop.

Balzurth jerked away, saying, "Unhand me, boy!"

Pheasants that had been hunkered in the tall grasses scattered into the air. Standing with the distant woodland at their backs, everyone in their party came to a stop. They stared right at Balzurth.

Balzurth's face became angry. His frown deepened. Casting a glance at all of them, he took a deep breath and let it out again. His stern features eased, and the slightest smile formed when he said, "Apologies. I am deeply distracted with our situation. It troubles me." He lifted his hands in a gesture of surrender. "Lead on. I'll follow. Please, it will do my heart good."

With a nod, Brenwar resumed his trek, pushing through the waist-high grass. The women followed.

"Son, what is it that you were trying to say to me?"

"I was trying to suggest that you might need your scales back in case this world is getting too deep for you. And I say that with the utmost respect." Nath patted his father's wrist. "My scales certainly made a change in me. I'm glad you shared that with me. Otherwise, I might not have known."

"You know, Son, sometimes even I can forget myself. You help remind me of the mistakes I once made, and that's not a bad thing. As a matter of fact, you remind me of a mistake that I'm making now."

"You, a mistake? Give me a moment while I have Brenwar hammer it out on a tablet." Nath was a little astonished. "I really don't know what to say, but what do you mean?"

"My power is not a frivolity. Even I can get carried away with it. I'm a dragon, not a man. I need to act like it."

"So, when you healed Sasha...did you harm yourself?"

"No regrets, Son." Balzurth changed the subject. "So where are we off to, exactly?"

"Quinley is the first stop. It's where I met my dear friend Ben."

CHAPTER
22

INSIDE THE STABLES, BEN OPENED the creaking lid of a wooden storage box. He hustled out Brenwar's strongbox and laid it on the ground. He was dripping with sweat. It had been a long time since he faced men and monsters the likes of those he'd just seen. The ugly one was bone chilling. The iron helmet on the other sent a wave of terror straight through him. Depressing the dwarven medallion on the box, he popped the lid open.

Sssray-Boom!

An explosion outside shook the hay from the loft, dropping filaments over his clothes.

"Gut up, Ben. Gut up!" he said, encouraging himself. The phrase was something they'd said in the Legionnaires during their rigid training. "Oh, I wish I had Akron."

All around Quinley, his people started to shriek and yelp.

He grabbed the gauntlets and slipped one on. His sweaty hands were sticking to the leather. Using his teeth, he pulled on the second one. Power filled his limbs. He found his bow hanging on a wall, snatched it up, and grabbed his quiver. In two long strides he was back outside, surveying the chaos.

Bayzog was down on the ground, with the iron warrior holding him down by the throat. Ben nocked an arrow, pulled back the string, and let the missile sing. The arrow struck the warrior in the helmet's temple, knocking his head. Bayzog's hands charged up with white light and knocked his assailant aside.

Scrambling to his feet, Bayzog yelled at Ben, "Help them! Help them! Get them away from Bletver!"

"What's a Bletver?"

The wizard pointed at the triant that was running roughshod through the houses and crushing Ben's frightened people.

"Noooooo!" Ben cried. He fired arrow after arrow into the monster's bulk. The arrows stuck like cactus needles.

But Bletver paid them no mind at all. He continued on the warpath.

Ben took off at a dead sprint right at the horrible monster that was yards away from tearing another innocent home apart. With the force of a charging steed, he tackled the monster by the leg and drove it to the ground.

"Ugh!" Bletver said. "What in the deep well hit me?"

Ben planted his feet on the ground, tangled Bletver's greasy hair around his wrist, and with his free fist started punching the triant in the face.

"Leave"

Whack!

"my"

Whack!

"people"

Whack!

"alone!"

Whack!

Bletver's skull was as hard as a rock, but Ben kept on hitting it anyway.

"Quit hitting me!" Bletver said. The triant flailed on the ground like a spoiled child. "It stings something ghastly!"

Ben punched the face that was almost as big as him in the neck and nose. He drove his fists in hard with the gauntlets of power. Jumping onto Bletver's body, he smote him in the belly, sending up ripples of fat that shook Bletver's sagging chin.

"Ooooof!" the triant cried. And then in a speech more formal than his face, Bletver said, "This is getting out of control, little man!"

Ben punched like a mule kicks.

Bletver sat up. "I don't know what's gotten into you, but I'm going to make you pay for it!" He scooped Ben into his hands and gave him a squeeze. "I'm going to make you pop!"

"Never!" Ben said, flexing his iron-powered muscles. Veins bulging in his neck, he began to wriggle free. "And by the way, your breath stinks!"

"Impossible!" Bletver hoisted Ben over his head and tossed him away.

After sailing through the air for what felt like a long time, Ben crashed head first through his brother's roof and landed on the table at which they were just talking earlier. He pounced onto the floor. His eyes rolled up. Rods of pain lanced through his eyes, neck, and shoulders. He blinked, and his brother and sister-in-law were there. He tried to move but couldn't. Hearing the terror erupting all around him, he said, "Quick, find everyone and get them out of here!"

Ben's crack shot couldn't have come at a better time. The arrow glancing off the iron helmet was the perfect distraction Bayzog needed. With a quick-lipped incantation, the half elf turned loose his mystic juice and stood every one of the warrior's hairs on end.

"Gagh!" Clutching his helmet, the fighter practically jumped out of his boots before dropping to his knees on the ground.

Bayzog wiped the blood from his split lip. He didn't know what had gotten him, but he summoned more of his power into his legs and marched right at the warrior—who was trying to stand up—and kicked him square in the gut.

The tremendous impact sent Iron Helmet Man skipping through the mud in a splatter.

Rain started to come down in heavy drops.

Bayzog reached down for the Elderwood Staff and picked it up. Its gem-light rekindled. The wizard's eyes flashed. He began spinning the staff's head in a tiny circle.

The warrior's body spun and flopped in the mud.

Soaked in the muck, Bayzog used telekinetic power to fling the fighter hard into a stone well in the center of the farm town.

Mud oozed down the iron helmet and plopped in a puddle. The man hitched his arm over the well's wall and with a groan got back to his feet. His sword dangled in his grip, tip first in the mud. "Who are you?" he demanded in an angry voice.

"It's not a matter of concern," Bayzog replied. "Drop your weapon."

Slowly, the warrior lifted his hands above his head with the sword still firm in his grip.

"I said, drop it," Bayzog repeated.

"I'm not keen on taking orders from half-breeds. If you want it, come and take it."

Another round of melee was out of the question. Bayzog knew he'd been a moment from getting pummeled the last time.

I need to end this standoff, quick.

He absorbed more power from the staff. Deep inside, he knew he needed to destroy this man, that mercy would be too good. But the man needed to be held accountable, too.

Try something different.

He began casting a spell. As soon as he muttered the lengthy words of the incantation, the warrior burst into action.

Twisting his hips and shoulders with a fierce sword swing, he sent an arc of energy ripping through the village. It tore two homes apart. He swung again, unleashing more of the lethal force, turning more homes into rubble. "This is just the beginning! Nothing will be left standing when I'm finished."

Bayzog finished the last syllable of his spell.

The ground beneath the warrior came to life. The mud oozed up to his waist. He yelled at Bayzog, "What cowardly witchery is this?"

"Elven," Bayzog replied.

The mud and dirt gobbled the man into a sinkhole until he was shoulder deep in the earth. The sword vanished into the mud. The warrior looked like an iron statue covered in a mudslide. Spitting grit from his teeth, he said, "You have won. Now tell me, who are you?"

Squatting down in front of his foe, the wizard said, "If you insist, I'm Bayzog. And I'm no half-breed. I'm part elven."

"Bayzog…" The whites of the man's eyes behind the eyelets of the helmet showed recognition. He grunted a laugh. "Nath Dragon's ally. Perfect. And I am Rybek, the brother of the man Nath Dragon murdered."

Rising, Bayzog put his staff in Rybek's face. The staff's jewel was hot with dangerous light. All of Bayzog's senses screamed in warning that something even more sinister was afoot. "You know me how? Speak!"

"Heh heh," Rybek said. "I'm tired of talking, but maybe the phantom will speak."

An unseen force fell from the wet night sky, covering Bayzog in darkness from head to toe. His skin tightened, and all of his sinew seized up like a man struck by lightning. The Elderwood Staff went dark.

Something was sucking the life out of him, and he couldn't even scream.

CHAPTER
23

Q UINLEY WAS A DISASTER WHEN Nath and company arrived late in the day. Half of the small houses built from wood and stone had been torn asunder. The barns had holes in one side and out the other. A carriage was turned upside down. A cow lay on the other side of a broken fence, crushed as if it had been squeezed to death.

Nath kneeled down and placed his hand on a footprint in the ground. It was humongous, the size of four men. He sniffed his fingers. "This doesn't smell like any kind of giant I've smelled before."

Brenwar took a whiff. "Triant."

"A what?" Laylana asked.

"Their mothers are trolls and their fathers are giants. Filthy things, even for giants." Brenwar scooped up a handful of dirt and rubbed it between his hands. "The vile creature won't be so hard to find now. The strange thing is, they usually stay underground."

"Way underground," Nath said. He recalled Gorlee recounting his imprisonment in the city of Narnum and how he was held in a place called the Deep by a similar creature named Bletver. He'd shared it with Brenwar.

It has to be a coincidence.

"Where are all the people?" Sasha asked.

Glancing around, Nath said, "I'm not sure that I want to know." The sound of voices softly singing caught his ear, and he turned. Facing the rolling hills just beyond the village, he recalled a graveyard he'd passed through when he'd met Ben long ago. Balzurth was already heading in that direction. He and the others followed.

A ceremony was taking place inside a cemetery that was hundreds of years old. Most of the tombstones were covered in moss and overcome by grass. A pair of stonemasons chiseled on a new flat rock while people held hands and sang. There was a black wagon pulled up to the cemetery entrance, which was marked by a modest iron archway. Bodies wrapped up in burlap bags lay in the back of the wagon, and two men loaded one body off and carried it to a grave in the ground and lowered it inside.

Keeping their distance, Nath felt Sasha wrap her arms around his and hang on as if she was about to fall. "I'm so sick of all this death. Innocent people die for nothing. My blood boils."

Her words brought Nath some comfort. The woman had much passion within, and it was good to see it back. The warmth of her body was comforting too. He hated to imagine the day that would come when Sasha's body turned cold. Thanks to his father, she had much life to live yet.

The citizens of Quinley had a humble ceremony. They prayed over the graves. They sang as the shovels dug in the dirt and buried their loved ones in Nalzambor's soft earth. Once the last grave was covered, each person lit a candle. One by one, they placed the candles on a stand made from stone until they all burned as one. There were many, too many.

Nath wondered if two of those candles were for Ben and Bayzog. It just didn't seem possible.

The long-faced people of Quinley dispersed back toward their fallen town. Women clung tight to their children. Men wore slings and other bloody bandages. One fellow was being pushed uphill in a cart. His legs were missing. Hardly any of the people gave Nath or his friends a single glance when they walked by. They'd seen the worst. Now they feared nothing.

One of the last people up the hill was a man in trousers and a woven canvas shirt. He was tall and lanky and looked like Ben but older. Tears had long dried on his cheeks that had cleaned some of the dirt from his face. He said to Nath, "They said you would come. I just didn't think it would be so soon."

Nath's chest tightened. "Pardon," he said. Taking the moment into consideration, he didn't want to just jump in and ask about Ben and Bayzog. "Er...I'm sorry for your losses, I'm—"

"I know. You're Nath Dragon. My little brother Ben has talked my ears off about you." He extended his hand. "I'm Jad. It's good to meet you. All of you. I just wish it was under better circumstances." The man's eyes welled up with water. Wet sobs and tremors shook his body. "I'm sorry. My wife is gone. Crushed." He glanced back down the hill at the cemetery. "Those aren't even all the bodies we need to bury."

Nath caught the sagging man by the waist. Sasha assisted. Together, they walked Jad back into town and sat him down on some busted boards and stones that had been set up like a bench.

Hands on his knees and still crying, Jad said, "Ben and the elf, Bayzog—

they took them. Said if you came around to let you know they have them."
He blew his nose in a rag. "I don't have any other family left. Just Ben."

Sasha intervened. She took the man's hand and said, "Who took them,
Jad?"

"Their names were Rybek and Bletver." He looked up at Nath. "The
one, Rybek, said you'd know him. He said to *come alone* if you want Ben and
Bayzog to live."

"That won't happen," Sasha said. She took Nath by the wrist. "You aren't
going anywhere without me."

"Or me," Brenwar added.

Even though Nath felt that Jad was being truthful, he wasn't certain
about his story. "How could Rybek possibly know I would come here? What
did he say?"

Sniffling, Jad said, "He said you'd probably ask that because you aren't as
stupid as you are arrogant. But he wanted me to let you know that it was a
hunch is all. He figured you'd come across his handiwork at some point. He
said that seeing how he has your friends, he'll have plenty of time to play with
them. If he didn't get word of you coming, or when his patience ran out, he'd
just kill them and move on. He doesn't seem like the patient kind."

Sasha's fists balled up at her sides. "I'm not the patient kind, either. I'm
going to find this scoundrel and put an end to him. All of them!"

Jad's eyes widened.

Nath laid a soft hand on her shoulder and nudged her back. "That's what
we all want, but I've crossed Rybek before. He's truly dangerous, as you can
see. What else did he say, Jad?"

Jab blew his nose again. "He said he'd be at the Temple of Spirals. I've
never heard of it."

"If they've only been gone a couple of days, I'd say they just made it there
by now," Nath said to Brenwar.

"Where is this Temple of Spirals?" Laylana asked.

"It's south of here, nuzzled between the Shale Hills and the Ruins of
Barnabus." Nath noticed that Balzurth was no longer there. He'd forgotten
that his father actually had been Barnabus to begin with, the one who as a
man had slain black dragons. Perhaps the ruins had been named after him
before his name had been corrupted by the foul acolytes and clerics that
twisted it into a dragon-hating abomination. "Where's my father?"

Everyone looked. It didn't take long to find him. Balzurth was carrying
two heavy wooden beams on his shoulders. He was following a pair of
villagers, who were carrying one of the support beams together. Balzurth
yelled back at Nath, "I heard you. Work now. Plan later."

"I'm not waiting," Sasha insisted. "If you know where it is, we go now." She turned her attention back to Jad. "What condition was Bayzog in?"

"I only got a glimpse, but his skin was shriveled and his hair white. It was as if he'd aged decades in moments. He barely moved, but he breathed." Jad let out a ragged sigh. "That giant thing carried them off on its shoulder. A nasty thing. It's what killed my wife." His head lowered.

Sasha pressed him. "Know how sorry my heart is for all this tragedy, but I must ask. Did they leave anything behind? A staff, perhaps?"

Jad shook his head, "No, it was taken." He perked up, shoulders back. "Ben told me to take these. He said if you came, you'd know what to do with them." He reached behind his back and produced the leather-and-chain gauntlets. "I fashioned it as a keepsake of him. There is a chest back in the stables too." He glanced at Brenwar. "It has a face that looks like you."

Nath handed the gauntlets to Brenwar.

Brenwar slid them onto his meaty hand and his skeleton hand and punched the first into the latter with a loud smack. "Let's go find that triant."

Nath held his tongue. Rybek had made it clear that Nath was to come alone. The last thing Nath wanted to do was jeopardize Ben and Bayzog. "Like my father says, we need a plan. At least we know what we're up against."

"A triant and a man you defeated before," Brenwar said. He twirled Mortuun around like a stick. A gleam was in his eyes. "I can handle the triant. You know that. This Rybek, I'm sure you'll see to it he has another bad day. Perhaps his last day."

"I wish I could come with you to help," Jad said. He stood up. "But I'm a farmer, not a fighter. My village needs me now, but please, bring Ben back like you always do, Dragon. Alive and as talkative about you as ever."

"I will."

"Oh, and one more thing I forgot to mention. Come, you must see."

They all followed Jad over to one of the barnyards, where no more animals were alive. Inside the barn was a figure of a man with his clothes hanging off of him. He was nothing but flakes and withered skin layering his bones. His fingers were outstretched, and his mouth hung open in agony.

"I don't know what did this, and he wasn't the only one. The others perished in the wind."

When Nath gave the figure a light touch fingertip to fingertip, the dead man's hand crumbled.

"But I can tell you this," said Jad. "He used to be the fattest man in the village."

CHAPTER

24

RERRY HAD COMPLETELY LOST TRACK of time, but hanging by his arms was more agonizing by the minute. Spikes of pain lanced through his back, waking him up from what mild slumber he was able to steal between gasps of suffering. He stretched out his tongue, straining to turn and sate his horrible thirst with the water that trickled down the wall. The corners of his mouth burned from the dehydration that had set in.

If I feel this bad, I can't imagine how my brother feels.

He had been calling to his brother, Samaz, with no response for what had seemed to be days. His brother quavered and coughed. It was the only sign of life in him. As hard as it had been for Rerry to get along with his brother in the past, he'd now come to regret every bit of their bickering. His brother had been good to him, but Rerry had been nothing but ornery toward him. Samaz was an odd and quite deep thinker. He didn't act out, and he talked very little. There was no reason to punish him for it. He and Samaz were just different.

"Samaz, if we ever make it out of this, I hope you'll forgive me. You're a good brother. I should have treated you better."

Samaz shivered in his shackles.

"Lords of Knollwood, don't die on me, Samaz. Don't die."

Something brushed under Rerry's bare toes. Feet dancing in his chains, he said, "Eep! What was that?" Straining, he tried to get a look at what was under him. Chin buried in his chest, he got a gander at something that shimmered like the scales of a fish and disappeared. "Samaz! Samaz! Wake up! Something's in here with us!" Head pounding, Rerry jerked at his chains.

Something was crawling up his leg.

"Scar! Scar! Where are you, Scar?" Rerry hollered for the jailer.

Rerry had once prided himself on not being scared of anything, but with the unknown, that had changed. He'd heard tales about what huge bugs had done to people. There were some that could poison or paralyze. They'd come in the thousands, devouring man and elf tiny bit by tiny bit.

"Samaz, do something!"

Tiny prongs dug into his legs and inched toward his body.

"Oh, I don't want to die like this. I'm a sword fighter. I deserve a better death." Rerry flailed his arms and legs against the chains. "Get off me, you cowardly vermin! Get off!"

Something that felt like sharp, tiny fingers dug into his toes and crept up his other leg.

"No! No! No!" Rerry cast his gaze from side to side, straining to see the unseen enemy.

A fierce prick stabbed into his knee.

"Aaaah!"

Samaz sputtered. His head lifted and turned toward Rerry. In a weak voice, he said, "Will you quit screaming? You're giving me a headache."

Voice echoing in the prison chamber, Rerry shouted, "Samaz! Samaz! You wake!"

"The dead have wakened. Put a pipe in it, won't you?"

"What?" Rerry exclaimed. "Can't you see I'm being devoured?"

Samaz's face barely showed in the weakening torchlight. He squinted at Rerry. "I can barely see anything—it's too dark—but I can assure you I hear everything."

"Ow!" Rerry cried out. Moisture his dehydrated self would have sworn moments ago that he couldn't possibly contain beaded his forehead and started to drip. Rattling his chains, he tried to lick the sweat from the tip of his nose. "Clearly not! I've been trying to wake you for days."

"I heard what you said. You said you were sorry," Samaz replied.

"You're delusional!"

"You're the one who thinks something's crawling up his body," Samaz retorted. "I don't see any—oh!"

"What?" Rerry's cracked voice was shrill. "What is it?"

"You seem to have something crawling up your pants leg."

"I know that! Do something!"

Samaz replied in his usual matter-of-fact tone. "I can't. My hands are tied."

Rerry jerked at the chains. "And you wonder why you drive me out of my skull, you emotionless sack of human parts and elven bones."

"I never wonder."

Veins bulging in his neck, Rerry retorted, "I'm not sorry for anything, and I hope you never forgive me for anything I've done. Ow!" He started to whine. "Oh, ho ho, will you do something, brother of mine?"

Samaz's head sank back into his chest. He started snoring.

Tiny claws, more than Rerry could count, dug into his body.

"Noooooooooooo!"

CHAPTER

25

NATH'S COMPANY RODE ON HORSEBACK without stopping except to rest the horses. He'd been trying to sort out a few things in his mind on the trip. According to some of the people they encountered, Rybek and Bletver had been wreaking havoc everywhere. It didn't take long for Nath to put it together. They wanted him. It wasn't a surprise.

Ahead, Balzurth brought his horse to a gallop just outside the ravine that cut through the mountains. It seemed so unnatural to see his father riding a horse. It just wasn't anything he'd ever imagined he'd see. "What is it, Father?"

Balzurth dismounted. "My horse tires. Let's all rest a spell, shall we?"

They made a camp with no fire. Brenwar whittled on a piece of wood with a buck knife. Balzurth dropped a pile of rocks on the ground. When he placed his hands on them, the rocks glowed, and the immediate area filled with new warmth. Sasha and Laylana cozied up to it. Nath sat down just as Balzurth started to speak.

"Son, I'd care to know what your plan is."

"And I was curious to know yours, Father."

Balzurth squatted, warming his own hands. "I'm fully prepared to eradicate them all, but my concern is our friends in peril. Those who hold them hostage do not value life. They are controllers. They use the flesh of others to manipulate people. We must be careful."

"And that's my concern, Father." Nath swallowed. "If we all go in at once, we might not see Bayzog and Ben alive again. I'm willing to go in and take my chances on my own."

"We can't let you do that, Nath," Sasha said, staring at the orange glow of the rocks and twirling her hair on her finger. "It would be unfair."

"They want me. They're using Ben and Bayzog to get to me," Nath said.

"And they only want you in order to get to me." Balzurth pushed the sleeves up over the cords of muscle in his forearms. He was a king if there ever was any. "You're bait. Your friends are bait. It's one of evil's oldest and best-working tricks. I can foil it. I can put an end to this once and for all." He plucked a stone from the pile. "I'm angry. The suffering must end."

"I've seen you angry before," Nath said.

"No, you've seen me pretend to be angry." Balzurth dusted the debris from his hands. "That was nothing."

"Oh, it was something. Your voice shook everything in the mountain when you raised it." Nath nudged Brenwar. "You heard it."

"Aye." Brenwar held a carved wooden figurine in his hand and walked it over to Sasha. "For you."

She took it and said, "It's Bayzog."

"It's the best I could do. I've never done an elf before, let alone a wizard."

She gave him a hug. "Thank you, Brenwar."

"All right, all right now, nobody hugs a…oh, never mind." Brenwar hugged Sasha back.

Nath continued talking with his father. "So you're telling me you weren't ever mad at me?"

"Disappointed, yes. Mad, no."

"But the yelling?"

"Raising my voice isn't the same as yelling. If I had ever yelled, you'd still be crying on the golden floor."

Laylana let loose a giggle.

Nath picked up one of the stones. It was warm to the touch but far from scalding. "I don't know. You were quite stern with me."

"Stern? That's because I was trying to scare the human out of you. There's nothing wrong with a stern talking-to. Wait until fatherhood happens to *you*."

Nath caught Laylana looking at him. She covered her mouth but still laughed.

"Quit that," said Nath to the elven princess. "I'm sure motherhood won't be any better for you. It's easier to keep up with jackrabbits than baby elves."

Balzurth looked up into the stars. "Why don't we all just sit and listen for a moment? Enjoy the world that surrounds us. Ease your mind, and don't worry so much about the journey ahead. Let nature run its magic through you."

The harmony of the woodland comforted Nath. The scuffles in the branches were soothing. The insects sang their songs. Not far away, beavers chewed into the wood to build their dams. Balzurth started to hum a tune in dragon song.

Nath wanted to enjoy the moment, swim in the peace, but he couldn't. So much was on the line, and his father had something up his sleeve. He envisioned Balzurth storming into the Temple of Spires and wiping Rybek and his brood of fiends out. He'd seen his father turn a small army of giants into a smoking graveyard. He wanted to see Balzurth turn loose the cleansing flame again—against all the giants—but more than anything, Nath wanted to do the same. Be a dragon who controlled the great flame that destroyed the evil that it burned.

At least Father seems to be back to normal, for now.

Laylana stretched out her arms and yawned. "What's this song he's singing?"

Nath knew it, but it had been so long since he'd heard it that he wasn't certain.

Sasha curled up on the ground and cuddled with her figurine of Bayzog. "It's wondrous, whatever it is."

Standing on his feet, Brenwar's eyes blinked open and closed. He started to sway, caught himself, and said, "Aye."

Nath's eyelids became heavy. He yawned.

I'm not supposed to yawn. What is this song that father sings? I usually don't forget such things.

He watched his father's lips. A sparkling swirl gathered around the Dragon King's body and twinkled to the rhythm of his words. Some phrases in Dragonese briefly pricked Nath's ears.

Sleep, little dragon, sleep.
The fairies come,
The giants run,
The wings of the goldlings beat.
Sleep, little dragon sleep,
For on the morrow a new world is at hand...

Nath's eyelids became impossibly heavy. He sank to the ground.

Great Guzan, he's singing my lullaby. Why?

Balzurth took on the form of Nath Dragon, black scales and all. He kneeled, brushed Nath's hair aside, and kissed him on the cheek. Rising with a black fire deep in his golden eyes, he whispered, "Sorry, Son, but I'm going to handle this."

CHAPTER
26

C LAWS DUG INTO RERRY'S SKIN and climbed over his belly. That's when he saw them, two lizards with a soft illumination in their green eyes flicked out their tongues and licked his chin. "Gah! What are you things?"

The lizards raced up to his shoulders, and their eyes bored into his. Their heads swiveled from side to side, slowly winking one lizard eye after the other. One of the lizards had eyelashes. It licked Rerry's nose. The other one revealed rows of teeth that looked too big for its mouth. It climbed up his arm, claws digging in until Rerry bled, and started nibbling on the chains.

Frozen in horror, Rerry watched a lizard the size of a kitten chew through the metal like it was bark on a tree.

These lizards won't have any problem devouring me! Sultans of Sulfur! Must I die like this?

The other lizard, the one with the eyelashes, climbed onto the top of Rerry's head and slammed him in the mouth with its scaly tail.

"Watch it, will you!"

The tail cracked him over the eye.

"Ow!"

The lizard on his head stretched out for the chain on his other arm, grasped it with its claws, and started chewing through the metal. The grinding and crunching sounds hurt Rerry's ears and bored into his brain. There was nothing he could do to fend off this new torture. Pushed to the limits of his stamina and beyond, he had almost no strength left.

In defiance of his fate, Rerry said, "I knew that some lizards were stupid, but I didn't think they were so stupid they would miss a fresh meal. You're supposed to eat me, not the chains. What happened, did orcs train you?"

The lizard without the eyelashes stopped chewing. Swiveling its head, it glared at Rerry and spat a tiny ball of metal into his eye.

"Ow!" With his eye closed, Rerry said, "Spit all you want, but if you keep this up, all you are going to do is free me, and when that happens, I'm going to stomp you under my heels."

A tail whipped out and cracked him across the mouth.

Fwap!

"Ow!" Rerry winced. "It even hurts to say 'Ow.' I swear, if I didn't know any better, I'd say you lizards could understand me, but I know better. You're just a couple of hungry—"

He got struck in the face by both tails this time.

Fwap! Fwap!

Somewhere in the tormented recesses of his mind, an uncanny thought registered as he watched them continue to nibble at the chains, little hunks at a time.

Maybe they do understand me?

In the dim light, he couldn't see too much color or detail on the lizards, but he took note of their scales, which were more rigid than those of most lizards. Like small suits of armor. And lizards didn't have eyelashes, but one of these creatures did. Rerry's head toggled between the two. He gasped with elation.

"You're not lizards. You're dragons, aren't you!"

The tiny gray metal dragon with the eyelashes turned her head around on her long neck and winked at him.

"Hah! You're freeing me?" He was incredulous, then he blurted out, "But you don't have dragon wings."

Their tails swatted his face again.

Fwap! Fwap!

"Oh, that's right. Not all dragons have wings. Father told me that. He's an expert, you know. Oh! And we are friends of Nath Dragon."

The dragons—little bigger than his feet—continued to gnaw at the chains.

The first link popped through.

Rerry's arm dropped to his side.

"Oh," he moaned. "That feels wonderful."

The second chain link gave, and both of his arms were free. Blood rushed there, bringing forth a stinging pain. He rubbed his sore arms and shoulders, hugging himself.

The dragons crawled down the wall and went to work on the shackles on his feet.

"Oh, thank you, thank you, thank you, you mighty little dragons!"

The dragons smiled up at him.

He leaned back. "With incredibly large but delightful teeth." Feeling a new lift surge through his sore limbs, Rerry shook his fingers and wriggled his toes.

I'm so thankful.

The dragons finished off the links on his feet, and the one without the eyelashes let out a burp. Rerry assumed that was a male, based off what he knew.

I wonder what kind of dragons they are.

He reached down and patted the tiny horns on their heads and stroked their chain mail–like skin.

They scurried away to his brother Samaz and began chewing on his shackles.

Rerry touched his brother's forehead with the back of his palm. Samaz's body was hotter than a biscuit that had just come out of the oven.

"How were you even talking to me earlier?"

After a few more minutes, the chains gave way to the iron-eater dragons.

On shaky limbs, Rerry managed to hoist his brother over his shoulder. "At least you're lighter now." He glanced down at the dragons at his feet. "I really hope you'll lead me out of wherever I am."

The dragons lifted their chins, and then, with their tails sliding behind their bodies, they led him through the dark caves until he found himself face to face with an arched wooden door, strapped in metal, that was sealed shut.

To the dragons, Rerry said, "I don't suppose you have a key, do you?"

The iron eaters blinked at him and left through a crack in the stone wall.

CHAPTER 27

ISGUISED AS NATH, BALZURTH SPROUTED wings and quickened the journey to the Temple of Spires. He landed little more than a mile north of the rigid peaks that jutted toward the sky. The black wings on his back collapsed and disappeared into his body until he was in the human form of his son Nath once more.

Brow furrowed, he marched over the rocky landscape where the edge of the Shale Hills ended in a nearby stream. He splashed through the waters knee deep and continued on from the other side. He pushed through the branches and cut through the rough. Nothing slowed his pace.

Guiltless, he'd made his decision to leave Nath and his friends behind. He needed to take matters into his own hands and get to the bottom of this himself. Eckubahn and his servants had to pay, and it was time for Balzurth to get to the heart of the matter and put an end to the evil spirits once and for all.

Walking at a brisk pace, the Dragon King ducked under the woodland branches and stepped out into a clearing.

The Temple of Spires waited.

Stark like a black monolith against the dawn of a purple sky, the temple sat with the wind howling through its peaks. The entire temple, vast in size, had once been just a hill made of stone. It had been crudely carved out from top to bottom, leaving the peaks like a crown on a small castle's forehead, unique in design. A narrow roadway curved toward the mouth of the long-abandoned temple. An arched bridge crossed over a foggy, bottomless canyon that was the only way in or out. The urns that adorned the high walls and edges were cold, but inside the temple's yawning entrance was light.

Balzurth headed toward it.

Heading down the long path toward the temple, he came to a stop.

Two stone giants, twenty-footers, stepped out onto the road from their concealment behind some boulders. The long-faced humanoids were skin headed, with heavy brows that shadowed their eyes. They wore nothing but loincloths around their waists and carried no weapons. They peered behind Balzurth, glancing from side to side, searching.

Continuing his walk, Balzurth said in a voice the same as Nath's, "I'm alone."

One giant stepped behind him and the other in front. The humongous escort crushed the ground beneath their heels, footstep after footstep, flattening the overgrowth.

Balzurth's fingers twitched. He wanted to set their heads on fire and send them running for the lakes. He hated giants. He'd put an end to the lot of them right now if he could. But there was more movement against the rocks that made up the temple. Wurmers had nuzzled into the stony nooks.

The giants separated and stood to the sides of the temple's entrance.

Without looking at them, Balzurth said, "I'll be back for both of you later."

He entered a rough-cut hallway hewn from the rock big enough for giants to stroll through. Torches flickered beyond the hall's end, which opened up into a grand ceremonial chamber. Support columns were not as they seemed. They had been cut out by working hands and chisels, with warring images of the races carved in them. There were eight, merging with the temple ceiling that seamlessly merged with rock beams the shape of snakes. The entirety of the chamber was cold, and the shadows of the torchlight gave the engraved images a life of their own.

Balzurth walked between the columns and came to a stop.

A huge slab of stone lay on a massive pedestal in the center of the chamber, big enough for one of the stone giants to stretch out on. Ben and Bayzog were shackled there, on the bloodletting stone. They lay silent. Unmoving.

Lording over them was Rybek, the man in the iron helmet. His sword was sheathed, and he rubbed his hand on the pommel. Behind him, all smiles, was the triant Bletver, who fondled the grimy whiskers on his shaggy chin.

"You have arrived much sooner than expected." Rybek slid his sword out and lowered the tip onto Ben's cheek. "Your promptness suggests trickery."

Balzurth, in the form of Nath, said, "As you can see, I am unarmed."

"You might be unarmed, but I am certain your allies are near." Rybek flicked the sword tip over Ben's cheek, drawing a spot of fresh blood. He smeared it on his fingertip. "Do not toy with me, Nath Dragon. The only way they will live is with your full cooperation."

"And if they die, you won't get any cooperation. I am here. Let them go."

Bletver stepped around the sacrificial slab to the front and leaned against it. He had a cleanly picked skull that he was rolling through his fingers like magicians did with coins. "I suggest that Nath Dragon needs to have a go at me before we release his friends. If he loses, I get to eat him."

Balzurth balled up his fists. "I promise you this: I'll give you a sore jaw and a sore belly if you come one foot closer to me."

The triant pushed his flabby back off the slab, leaned closer, and stuck his chin out. "Oh? Try me, little dragon. Nothing can knock out a triant."

"I'm not nothing," replied the disguised Dragon King.

"You're like a fish." Bletver licked his lips. "A meal with scales."

Balzurth sprang forward, launching himself at the triant. Arm cocked back, he slugged Bletver in the jaw. The blow snapped the monster's head back.

Stumbling on his short legs, the triant staggered into one of the columns head first and sank to his knees on the cold stone floor.

Rybek raised his sword. "I warned you, Nath Dragon." The sword started to fall.

"You expect me to put up with that?" Balzurth said. "We are here for an exchange. Me for them. The blot of foulness over there does not factor into it, Rybek." He slapped his chest two times. "You are so close to what you want. Don't miss out on it now. I'm here. I've surrendered. Shackle me if you have to."

"It's too simple." Rybek glanced from side to side and let out a strange whistle.

"You have the advantage, Rybek. Your plan has worked. You have won." Still disguised as Nath, Balzurth shook his black-scaled arms. "You can see there is nothing up my sleeves, and you know I pride myself on honesty."

A shadow entered the ceremonial chamber and hovered beside Rybek. A phantom. Its head and eyes conversed silently with Rybek. On Rybek's nod, the phantom lifted off and disappeared through the cathedral ceiling.

"It's confirmed that you're alone. Interesting." Rybek unshackled Nath's friends and gave them each a firm kick. The man and part-elf were disordered, and mud covered their clothes. They looked like they'd been dragged the entire way. Bayzog looked old enough for his death bed. Ben was hunched over. "Get out of here." Rybek shoved both of them off the altar.

Ben supported Bayzog. They hobbled over to Balzurth, thinking he was Nath.

Bayzog said, in a gravelly voice, "I need my staff."

"Keep going," Rybek shouted. "The staff is mine to keep. Any tricks Nath, and your friends will be slaughtered out there by the phantom or the wurmers. I've seen to it there won't be anyone to save them no matter what."

Balzurth gave Ben and Bayzog one last look over his shoulder.

Ben nodded and said, "You don't have to do this, Dragon. Our lives are ours to give."

"Go," Balzurth commanded in a voice that sounded like Nath's. "I'll see you soon."

CHAPTER

28

O N THE PATH OUT OF the Temple of Spires, Bayzog collapsed, dashing his knees on the stones. Ben scooped him up in his arms and continued, glancing back from time to time, eyeballing the stone giants that guarded the entrance.

"Stay with me, Bayzog."

He shuffled down the path, grimacing. His legs were wobbling and his arms shook. The journey to the temple had been nothing short of harrowing. Bletver had carried the both of them over his shoulder at first, but then for fun he'd dragged them through the mud, laughing and saying he liked his food with a little muddy seasoning on it.

Despite the jostling trek, Ben had been relieved.

Bletver had thrown him against a wall so hard, Ben had thought he shattered his back. The stunning shock had faded barely in time for him to gather his senses just enough to tell his brother Jad about the gauntlets and the chest. He'd been urging Jad to find safety just when Bletver tore back through the house and scooped Ben up. Lucky for him, the paralysis had been only temporary, and he now felt his limbs again.

"Let me walk. Let me walk," Bayzog said. The hollow eyes of the half elf burned with life, but his body was as feeble as a newborn baby's. His skin was wrinkled, and the long strands of hair were ghost white. "I live. I live. I need my staff, but I live."

"We aren't going back for the staff. I'm getting you to safety."

"Need to help Nath," Bayzog rasped.

"I know, but there isn't much we can do to help him right now. We're just going to have to hope he can take care of himself."

"Not right," Bayzog said, shaking his head. "Not right."

"I know it's not right, but I can't go back and fight all those wurmers and giants by myself now, can I? We need help." He stumbled on a loose rock and fell to his knees.

Bayzog fell out of his arms.

Gasping, Ben said, "I'm turning out to be a fine help, aren't I?"

From the ground, Bayzog pointed at something crawling behind Ben.

Head low, a wurmer came, moving slow but chomping its teeth.

Ben broke out in a cold sweat. "So much for Rybek keeping his word. That doesn't look like an escort." He crawled backward like a land crab until he bumped into Bayzog.

The feeble mage's bony fingers plucked at his belt pouch.

Ben had forgotten about the potions. He fumbled through his own mud-coated pouch and produced two vials of yellow liquid. He popped the cork from one and handed it to Bayzog, then drank the other. The tantalizing nectarine flavor coursed new life through his body, washing away the aches and pains in his bones. "That's more like it!"

Head lowered, eyes slit, and jaws slavering, the wurmer came.

CHAPTER
29

ATER SPLASHED ON NATH'S EYELIDS. A storm cloud drizzled cold drops over his face. He sat up with a gasp. "Balzurth!"

Brenwar, Sasha, and Laylana lay fast asleep.

Going from one to the other, Nath shook them all. "Wake up! Wake up!"

First to his feet, Brenwar smacked his lips and with woozy eyes said, "I feel like I've woken from the dead."

Rubbing her eyes, Laylana added, "My head aches." She peeled off a leaf that had stuck to her face.

Yawning, Sasha asked Nath, "What happened? Where's Balzurth?"

"He's gone."

"Gone?" Brenwar clawed his skeleton hand through his beard. "And where do you think he's gone to?"

Judging by the sun's position in the sky, it looked like they'd been asleep for the better part of a day. Balzurth had a long head start on them. He'd wanted it that way.

The horses whinnied.

"He didn't take the horses," Sasha said. "Can't we track him down and catch up with him?"

Using his keen sight, Nath searched for footsteps or any other signs of his father's passing. He circled the camp. There were only signs of his coming, but not his going. "It seems he's abandoned us." He kicked up the dirt. "How could he do that do us?"

"Now we know where you get it from," Brenwar grumbled. He strapped his war hammer over his back. Looking above, he said, "Do you think he turned back into a dragon? Did he fly to the Temple of Spires?"

Nath's nostrils flared. Certainly his father wouldn't have risked the lives of his friends. No, Nath had to figure out what he would have done if he was in Balzurth's place. While he thought, everyone else mounted up.

Brenwar opened his strongbox. "I'd say he got to the Temple of Spires hours ago." He arched a brow. "Of course, that's assuming we only slept through the night. If we want to catch up, these horses have some hard work to do. They're going to need something." He flicked a vial over to Nath. "Give each one of them a little bit of that."

Nath poured a little bit in his hand and administered the potion to the horses one by one. They nickered and reared up.

"Whoa! What does it do?" Laylana asked.

"They'll run hard and fast all the day long, so you'd better hang on tight. They won't be stopping," Brenwar said. There were only three horses though. Brenwar turned to Nath. "I'm assuming you can keep up?"

"No, you need to hope the horses can keep up with me. Let's go." Nath took off for the temple with fast and lengthy strides. His mind was racing. What had gotten into his father?

What's his plan? If I were Balzurth, what would I do?

The answer smote him like the clapper striking a bell.

I'd do what I always do, show up as me.

Darting through the grasses, he sped up his pace.

CHAPTER 30

"It's down to just the two of us now, Rybek, speaking from a general point of view of course. I'm not counting the flock of wurmers and giants at your disposal." There were more stone giants backed into the shadows standing as statues against the walls. Wurmers snaked through holes in the ceiling, positioning themselves in the rafters. "What's your end game? Or should I say Eckubahn's end game?"

Rybek jumped off the end of the slab. "Certainly you know you're the bait for taking down Balzurth. Eckubahn wants you alive, but I want you dead." He swung his sword, and an arc of energy knocked Balzurth from his feet and skipped him over the stones into one of the pillars. "But if I can't have you dead, I'll turn you over to him severely damaged."

Balzurth didn't even try to stand. He said to Rybek, "Oh, you're giving Eckubahn the glory. Why not the glory for yourself? You don't need him. Go ahead, take me down all on your own."

"Humph. You fight back with words and not fists. I'm surprised." Rybek sheathed his blade. "It seems the cocky dragon is humbled."

"Humility comes with age."

"I'm no spring fairy. I don't feel humble in the slightest, but I do enjoy humbling people. And by humbling I mean killing."

"Get on with it, then," Balzurth replied.

"As much as I hate you for destroying my brother, you and Selene both, I'm still a faithful servant of the new ruler of this world. I can wait for my reward."

"Your reward, if you don't change, will be fire when the end comes, one way or the other." Balzurth took a look at his surroundings. The giants and wurmers began to stir. Something was happening or about to happen. "You stall, Rybek. Why?"

"I don't need to stall. I'm being wise with my time. Turn around."

Balzurth did so.

Rybek bound his wrists behind his back with a silk rope that tightened with the power of a great snake. "You're making this entirely too easy. I expected a fight, not such cooperation." He spun Balzurth back around. "Still…" He punched him in the face. "Ah, that feels better."

Balzurth spat a tooth out. "Well, at least one of us isn't disappointed."

"Tell me, Nath, before I turn you over, where is your father Balzurth?"

Balzurth wouldn't lie, so he said, "My father is where my father wants to be."

Rybek tossed his head back and let out a little laugh. "And Selene?"

"I can't say, because I don't know." Both of the statements were true. It was important to Balzurth that even in the worst of circumstances, he still was honest. He just didn't want Rybek to catch on.

The warrior head butted Balzurth, helm first, in the chin.

Disguised as Nath, the Dragon King staggered back and gave his head a hard shake. "Are you quite done with that? You won't ignite my ire, if that's what you're attempting."

From a pouch strapped to his side, Rybek produced and amulet on an iron chain. Its yellow stone was the eye of a cloudy storm.

"Jewelry for me? You're vastly more thoughtful than you look. Vastly." Balzurth tilted his head. "What does it do?"

Dangling the amulet by the chain and swinging it gently from side to side, Rybek said, "It teleports you to Eckubahn."

Balzurth's heart raced. His eyes fixed on the amulet. "Why hesitate? Give Eckubahn the prize he wants. Receive your glory."

Rybek pulled the amulet back from Balzurth's burning eyes. "No, something's wrong. I sense it. There is no reason you should be so eager. What kind of fool rushes into certain death?"

"I'm bait. Eckubahn won't kill me."

"You don't know that. I don't know that." Rybek swung the chain around his wrist and back. "What are you up to, Nath Dragon?" His boot kicked something white over the granite floor. He went over and picked up a tooth as big as his hand. It was Balzurth's, the one he'd spat out. No longer a part of his body, it had resumed its normal dragon tooth size and shape. "What's this?"

"Perhaps I knocked that tooth out when I walloped Bletver. You really shouldn't let the little things distract you in the midst of a moment. Focus. The moment might slip away."

Rybek glanced between Balzurth and the tooth. He bent his head down.

"I don't see the tooth you spat out." He scraped his foot over the ground. "What treachery is this, Nath Dragon?"

Eyes transfixed on the amulet of teleportation, Balzurth said, "You certainly should be the one to lecture about treachery, but no one lectures me." Balzurth snapped the cords that bound his arms behind his back. He lunged for the amulet.

Rybek jerked the amulet away and cradled it with his whole body. "This is madness. Why do you want the amulet?"

Balzurth wrestled the fighter to the ground.

Rybek, strong as a man can get and a seasoned fighter but no match for Balzurth in strength, squirted out of his grip.

"Give me that amulet!"

Rybek scrambled over the floor.

Balzurth snatched the man's ankle and dragged him back. He punched Rybek in the chest, denting the plate armor.

With the amulet tucked tightly in his muscular arm, Rybek groaned, "No."

Balzurth-Nath pinned Rybek's face down by the helmet, holding him tight while using his free hand to fish out the amulet. A shadow fell over his shoulder. "Huh?"

Bletver had walloped Balzurth with an uppercut that practically lifted him out of his shoes. It sent him colliding into the legs of another giant. "That's payback, Nath Dragon."

Shaking off the blow, Balzurth lifted his eyes to the triant, who stood as tall as a tree behind him. The wurmers climbed down the walls. More giants stepped into full view. It was him versus an army. He snorted. "I've got bad news for you. All of you. I'm not Nath." His hands and feet sprouted into dragon claws. "I'm Balzurth, and I'll be having that amulet."

CHAPTER
31

BEN PICKED UP A ROCK and chucked it at the wurmer. The stone skipped off its snout. "Just run if you can, Bayzog. Run. I'll hold it off as long as I can."

The giant lizard streaked toward him on all fours. Its claws scraped over the stones, flicking up the dirt and moss between the path of flat rocks.

Energized, Ben braced himself to make his last stand. Man with hardly a stick of clothing on versus a monster fully covered in natural armor.

Jaws wide, the wurmer scuttled in and bit.

Ben bounded up over the beast, clearing its snapping jaws and landing on its back. He wrapped his arms around the creature—which was just as big as him—and held tight. "Run, Bayzog! Run!"

Man and twisting scales wrestled in the dirt.

The creature let out bestial hisses. It stretched its neck to bring its head around, snapping at Ben's ears but missing.

Ben tucked his head down and held on for the ride of his life.

The wurmer's tail flogged every bit of Ben's body that it could hit.

Each lick brought the pain of a leather whip. Fighting the odds and the pain, Ben wouldn't let go of the tireless monster. No, this was his last stand. He might lose his life, but he could save another.

Whap! Whap! Whap!

The tail beat him without mercy. The wurmer would twist one way and Ben, feet digging in the dirt, would twist the other. Pushing himself to the limit, hand locked over his wrist, he cranked up the pressure. "I'm going to squeeze you to death, wurmer!"

The monster spun in a version of an alligator roll on land.

Ben's head cracked against a stone. His grip broke. The next thing he knew he was flat on his back with the wurmer's claws at his throat. His strength was gone. He thought of Margo and his girls. He said to anyone that could hear, "Tell them I'll miss them."

Ssssrazzzzz!

A jolt of light struck the wurmer, sending shivers through its scales. Smoke came from its eyes, and it wriggled and jerked and collapsed on top of Ben, dead.

With a grunt, Ben shoved it off. Huffing for breath, he said, "I don't know how I did that, but I knew I had it in me. I beat the smoke right out of it." But then he noticed Bayzog leaning back against the rocks. The wizard's withered skin had thickened after he drank the healing potion, and streaks of black were now layered into his greying hair. "So you did that?"

"I might have had the elf beaten out of me, but I still have my spells." Bayzog closed his eyes and shook his head. "Oh, that wasn't easy."

Ben got up with a grimace. "Well, thanks." His body stung all over. "I have a feeling I look as bad as you."

"You do." Bayzog opened his eyes. The violet fire had returned. Scanning the area, he said, "Odd."

Following his gaze back toward the temple, Ben said, "What's odd?"

"When we fight wurmers, we usually fight them all."

Holding his hip, Ben said, "Well, I'm not disappointed."

Loud noises came from inside the temple. Heavy booms and thuds. Angry howls so loud only a giant could be making them. "We're going in there, aren't we?"

"I need my staff," Bayzog said.

"We need Nath Dragon," Ben replied. He started forward. "Nath can't handle all of them at once."

"No, he can't. But that's not Nath Dragon in there," Bayzog replied.

"Sure it is. I saw him for myself."

"No, it's someone else. That's why I wasn't so worried."

The rocks shook at the top of the temple's spires, and a piece of rock broke off. It bounced off the temple roof and slid, spinning, into the canyon.

"So if that wasn't Nath, then who was it? Gorlee?"

Making his way to the bridge, Bayzog replied, "I don't know, but I'm going to find out."

Ben was relieved to hear it wasn't Nath in there, but he didn't want to go back inside. The temple was filled with giants and wurmers. He and Bayzog didn't stand a chance. And whoever was posing as Nath had made a great effort to save them in the first place. He held his hands up in front of his face and made two fists. "I guess these are going to have to do."

Robes dragging the ground, Bayzog didn't stop his trek back to the temple. "I have spells. I can handle this myself. You should wait."

The word "spell" triggered a thought. Ben reached into his pouch and produced a vial filled with a sparkling orange liquid.

A raucous, painful sound echoed out from the temple's entrance.

Ben said to the vial, "Bottoms up, 'cause they're going down."

CHAPTER
32

SLUMPED AGAINST THE WALL, SAMAZ'S head rested on Rerry's shoulders. They'd been sitting in the same spot for hours. Feeling his brother's forehead, Rerry said, "I don't know how a person can be so hot and live. Of course, I don't know anyone as stubborn as you. In this case, it's a good thing."

He eased his brother to the floor. Still weak and dying of thirst even after drinking some sour cave water, he pressed his eye to the keyhole of the door.

If only those iron eaters would have gnawed out this lock, we could be out of here by now. Look at those hinges. There's plenty of good metal right there.

He slapped his forehead. "Aw, the hinges."

His fingers worked at the pins. He cracked his nails with the effort, but none of the pins would budge. He needed a tool, but even after searching all the chambers in the strange prison, he didn't find anything of use at all.

Rubbing his wrists, he sat back down and said, "Someone will come. Someone." With the cool rock against his back, he relaxed. He'd been so uncomfortable in his shackles that he'd barely caught any sleep. Leaning a little on his brother, he drifted off into a deep sleep.

A ring of keys jingled. Rerry's mind started to awaken, but he didn't register what was happening. His eyes peeked open, and as if he was in a dream, the door swung open, concealing them behind it.

Is this really happening? I can't move. I don't want to move. I want to sleep.

Two elven guards appeared in the crack between the door and the cave. With swords on their hips and wearing the cloth tunics of soldier's uniforms, they ventured forth with a bucket of water and a tray of food.

Rerry's nose twitched. The smell of food aroused his senses.

I smell meat on the plate.

His stomach groaned.

The elven guardsmen set the food and water down and turned.

In Elven, one said, "What's that?"

At the same time, the other elven guard said, "Who's there?"

Finding new strength, Rerry burst out of his corner. Just as the nearest elf went for his sword, Rerry hit him in the jaw and knocked him out.

Whap!

Desperate for freedom, Rerry used his bigger body to overpower the second, smaller elf. Using a move taught to him by his brother, he locked the elf up by the neck and silenced him in a sleeper hold. The elf's kicks subsided, and he too went out. Chest heaving, Rerry shoved the elf aside, grabbed the bucket of water, and guzzled it down.

"Ah!"

He scarfed down some of the hard bread and dried fruit. After taking care of himself, he did what he could for Samaz. Surprisingly, his brother—asleep with fever for all intents and purposes—nibbled down the food. Rerry poured some water down his brother's throat, too.

Sputtering and coughing, Samaz sat up.

"I thought that might wake you from your nap," Rerry said.

"Yes, a dream of drowning usually does." Samaz grabbed the bucket and guzzled between gasps. "Thank you. How did we escape here?"

"Don't you remember the dragons?"

"I hardly remember anything."

"Figures." Rerry made his way over to one of the guards and buckled on the sword belt. He slid the sword from the sheath and cut it through the air in a few intricate patterns. Eyeing the blade, he said, "At least it's elven."

Samaz crawled up the wall to his feet. He looked through the open door and back at the guards lying on the stone floor. "You didn't kill them, did you?"

"Yes."

"Rerry!"

"Will you keep your voice down?" Rerry put on one of the guards' uniforms, but the cloth tunic was very tight on him. The almond-shaped steel skullcap fit fine. "No, they're only out cold—and just so you know, I used one of your moves."

Donning the other tunic, barely, Samaz said, "Ah, you used the sleeper."

"Begrudgingly. So are you fit for the journey?"

"No." Samaz coughed. "But I'm not going to let feeling like ogre stew warmed over stop me."

Rerry tried to hand his brother the other elf guard's sword.

"No."

"Just strap it on. We'll need to blend in at some point, I imagine." Rerry planted the other elven helmet on Samaz's head. With effort, he got it down to his brother's ears, but it still looked too small. "You and that melon head. If I didn't know our parents for certain, I'd swear you were part orc. You're built like a chimney. What kind of elf is built like that?"

"A durable one." Samaz stepped aside. "Lead the way, Rerry."

"And am I to assume we're going back after the Ocular of Orray?"

"Do ducks have feathers?"

"It was your wild idea that got us captured in the first place."

"Oh, you like it."

"Well, I do, but only because it actually sounded like something I would do, not you," Rerry said. "So, shall we attempt to defy all odds again?"

"Anything for Mother," Samaz replied.

CHAPTER
33

BALZURTH CAUGHT THE STONE GIANT'S fist coming down at him
like a hammer. He had popped his dragon claws out of his human
fingers, and now he dug them into the giant's hard flesh and yanked
the giant face first into the stone slab.

BLAM!

"Don't you run, Rybek! Don't you run!" Balzurth ducked under a metal
urn that whizzed over his head.

Bletver was throwing everything he could get his hands on at him.

"You stay out of my way, triant! I'll turn you into cinders." Balzurth
caught Rybek creeping behind the stone slab with his sword out. "Surrender
and find mercy, Rybek. This is your last chance."

Wurmers dropped from the ceiling. Fierce and nasty, the mindless things
clawed and slashed.

Chest-high in wurmers, Balzurth poured it on. Now transfigured into
part dragon and part man, Balzurth had covered himself in red and gold
scales from head to toe. He busted the wurmers in their snouts and slung
them away by their tails. Nothing was going to stop him from getting Rybek
and the amulet. No, he wasn't going to let his plan fail. He was so close, he
couldn't let this chance slip away.

A stone giant closed in, lifting its man-sized foot to stomp Balzurth into
the floor.

The Dragon King pulled a wurmer by the tail under the giant's foot in
his stead.

The wurmer's scales crunched and squished. Black ooze squirted out.

Hopping on one foot, the giant wailed. His skin sizzled and crackled
from the acidic blood of the wurmer.

A wurmer pounced on Balzurth. Claws raked his scaled chest.

He laughed. "You mindless thing." He threw his arm around the wurmer's neck and snapped it like a twig. He caught Rybek running for one of the temple's many exits. He plowed through the sea of wurmers, shoving and throwing them aside.

But when Balzurth veered for the tunnel, the entrance was blocked off by Bletver's surprisingly agile bulk.

"Let's have a go at it again," Bletver sneered. He beckoned with his finger. "I'd love a trophy from the King of the Dragons. My, those scales and claws will look fantastic about my neck."

"You had your chance, triant. Now your doom is at hand." Balzurth filled his lungs with air, stoking the furnace inside his belly. Smoke puffed out of his nose, and Bletver's narrowed eyes widened. "Goodbye, Bletver. So long, evil one!"

But just then, the phantom dropped onto Balzurth, clouding his eyes and dousing his flames.

He dropped to his hands and knees, clutching at his throat and fighting for breath. The essence of the phantom's power attacked his mind and spirit. Probed his weaknesses. Exposed his failures. A flicker of doubt entered Balzurth's mind, and the phantom drove its poison deep into his heart. He saw his plan slipping through his fingers. He wanted to use the amulet to appear right in front of Eckubahn, turn his full powers loose, and destroy the unsuspecting titan once and for all. He let out a roar!

CHAPTER
34

A LOUD ROAR ERUPTED FROM INSIDE the temple, shaking the bridge. Bayzog stumbled.

At his side, Ben helped him up to his feet. "What was that?"

"Pain," Bayzog replied. "Anguish." He found new strength in his legs after hearing the desperate cry.

Ben had him by the arm, and stride for stride they were racing up the bridge. Carefully, they hugged the entryway wall and slipped unnoticed into the chamber.

A fierce battle was on. Wurmers agitated together in an angry hive. Two stone giants slammed huge clubs down over and over with wroth force. Perhaps most ominous of all, a cloud of blackness lingered in the air.

Ben inched forward.

Bayzog grabbed him by the arm. "Too dangerous. That phantom has him. I need my staff."

Puffing out smoke, Ben said, "I can't hold whatever's in me much longer. I'm about to explode."

"What did you drink?'

"That fire-breathing potion." Ben's eyes glowed with the fires of a volcano. "I have to do something."

"True, you cannot hold that fire in for long, or it will incinerate you from the inside. Hold it for just a moment." Bayzog closed his eyes and narrowed his focus, blocking out the clamor of battle that filled the chamber like the inside of a ringing bell. He sensed his staff. It was within the temple, but the temple had many chambers. Several paths. He opened his eyes and touched Ben. "You should come with me."

"No, I have a feeling I need to help whoever that is in there." Ben clasped Bayzog on the arm, shook it, and said, "You're just going to have to go your way and I'll go mine. Best to you, Bayzog."

"Best to you, Ben."

CHAPTER
35

A ROAR OF ANGUISH ECHOED THROUGH the valley. Flocks of birds scattered out of the branches. The horses came to a stop and reared up. Brenwar and the women were staring at Nath, who said, "Father!"

Dragon heart pumping, Nath doubled his pace, racing through the valley toward the Temple of Spires at full speed. He had heard plenty of sounds from his father, but never any of pain. It didn't seem possible. He veered off the path and cut into the forest, bursting through the low-hanging branches and leaving the others far behind him.

I might not be able to fly, but I can certainly run like the fastest gazelle. Hang in there, Father. Hang on!

It was surreal, his father being in peril. The Dragon King was invincible. Wasn't he?

Nath hit the bottom of the hill and was back on the overgrown path to the Temple of Spires. He could see the temple's jagged peaks stabbing at the clouds. That wasn't all. Nath wasn't the only one who had been attracted by Balzurth's roar.

A gigantic wurmer as big as Nath ever saw circled above. It landed on the other side of the temple's bridge. Its eyes glowed with red fire that bored into him. Behind the ancient archway it waited, opening its mouth to roar every so often.

Nath slid out Fang, shouting, "Dragon! Dragon!" Shoulders set, he charged.

CHAPTER 36

ILLED WITH THE SAME FEAR every warrior gets before battle, Ben
hurried across the chamber toward the sacrificial slab. His body was so
hot he felt as if he might burst into fire at any moment.

I can't hold this in.

Stepping out from beyond the phantom's blackness and the battling
throng of wurmers, Bletver emerged. The triant's face was filled with a bestial
delight. "You again? Mmm, another morsel for my belly. And the timing
couldn't be better. All of this fighting makes me very hungry."

Swallowing down the flaming butterflies that stirred in his stomach,
Ben pulled himself up onto the stone slab and faced Bletver. Forcing down
the stammer in his throat, he said, "If you're so hungry, then what are you
waiting for?" He did a little jig, feet tapping and elbows swinging. "Come
and eat me, ugly!"

Bletver's brows buckled. He bared his teeth, chomped them, and said,
"I've had all I can stand of you idiotic people. I don't know what trick you're
up to, but I'm not taking any chances with delay." He reached for Ben.

Ben huffed a big breath and blew it, but no fire came out.

Bletver seized him in his powerful grip and jerked him up off the slab.
"This time I'm going to ensure you are dead." He smashed Ben down onto
the stone table.

A whoosh of fire came out of Ben's mouth.

It spread up the triant's arms, and he let go. "Agh! What have you done
to me?"

Gulping in another lungful of air, Ben let out another flaming burst,
covering Bletver's bulging body in flames.

The triant flailed and screamed wildly, but somehow, he caught sight of

Ben and came right back after him again, shouting in rage at the flames that sizzled the skin on his body, "I'm going to kill you!"

Ben let out another gust.

A stream of fire covered the giant's face.

"Nooooooo!" Bletver yelled.

How that bloodthirsty giant saw him through the flames on his face, Ben didn't know, but somehow it came right at him. Ben dove off the sacrificial stone slab.

Bletver caught Ben's leg and held him fast. "I might die, but you will die with me." Drawing him in with Ben's pants catching fire, Bletver let out another phrase. "Let's burn together!"

With all of the commotion, Bayzog pressed his advantage. He muttered a spell he'd not used in a long time. It wasn't an aggressive one, rather something passive but helpful. Feeling endowed with new powers, his vision sharpened and refocused. His keen senses were all enhanced. Moving quickly, robes dusting the ground, he followed the beacon of magic he sensed into one of the corridors that branched off from the main chamber.

There it is.

A slightly translucent trail lingered in the hall like a dying will o' the wisp. Careful not to be followed, he chased after it. The corridor led him into another passage cut from the stones and ended in a chamber that spread out into many alcoves. The mystic vapor trail came to a stop inside the blackness of a small cavern.

Breathing softly, Bayzog advanced into the darkness. If not for his elven vision and the help of the spell, he'd have been as blind as a bat and not nearly as effective. Shoulder grazing the wall, he followed the trail. His toe clipped something that rattled on the floor.

I'm as good at sneaking as I am at hand-to-hand fighting.

It was a skeleton, one of many that were strewn over the chamber floor. At first, the wizard thought they'd been dead for centuries, but the tang of blood and the stench of rotting flesh lingered in the air. He covered his nose with his hand and ambled on. Inside the alcove, the Staff of Elderwood leaned back against the wall. Ghost white from the spell, he saw it and not much of anything else to note.

Inching forward, testing the hard floor with his toes, he thought, "It can't be this easy."

Arms outstretched, he reached for it. His fingertips stroked the smooth elder wood. He wrapped his fingers around the long shaft, and his old friend felt alive in his hand. He shuddered. He had never hugged his staff before, but he wanted to now.

Scraping caught his ears, and he turned back.

Wurmers slithered out of the other alcoves. Their purple eyes were a burning haze as their talon-covered paws scratched toward him. Heads low and teeth clacking, they converged on him in a frenzy.

CHAPTER 37

WIND WHISTLING THROUGH HIS EARS, hair waving in a banner of flame, Nath's legs churned like a chariot's wheels, thundering into battle. Nothing was going to get between him and his father no matter how big or strong it was. Nothing!

The monstrous wurmer's long neck coiled back. Black smoke spilled from its nostrils. Its horned head shot forward and turned loose a radiating pulse of energy. The scale-searing blast took Nath's feet out from under his body and sent him sailing over the railing and into the mouth of the bottomless canyon.

In midair, he clutched at anything he could get his hand on and caught himself on a beam that dangled beneath the bridge. Squeezing, his fingertips dug in. With one arm he hoisted himself up and managed to crawl up the beam with Fang still secure in his other hand. Taking a glimpse below, he saw nothing but a black abyss.

I've never wanted my wings back more.

He shimmied up the beam and into the arch under the bridge. Wedging himself into the stonework, he caught his breath.

Whew.

The wurmer's head lowered from above, twisting from side to side. Its nostrils snorted and flared.

Nestled in his spot between the beams, Nath pressed as deep into the crevice as he could. All he could do was hide. Without any footing underneath, he couldn't risk taking a swing. He would fall into the abyss.

What a predicament.

He started to ease Fang into his back scabbard.

Just then, the wurmer slipped off the bridge with a roar and vanished into the fog that spiraled like a tornado, its growls echoing deep in the canyon.

Nath made his move. Feet dangling over a certain death, arm over arm he climbed from beam to beam, making his way to the top.

Hurry, Nath, hurry. You're faster than this.

A wild ape couldn't have climbed any faster. His hands gripped the stones, and he began pulling himself up onto the bridge.

The wurmer exploded from under the mist with its jaws wide open, a huge fish chomping at the bait.

Fastened to the rail of the bridge, there was nowhere for Nath to go as the wurmer's maw closed in. He flung himself off the bridge and into the dragon's mouth.

Chomp!

CHAPTER
38

CLASPING THE ELDERWOOD STAFF WHERE it stood in front of him, Bayzog stretched out his fingers. Tendrils of lightning exploded from his fingertips into the nearest wurmer. The white-hot bolt of energy shot right through its scales and spread from wurmer to wurmer in an expanding chain of light.

The monsters screeched and howled. Their scales smoked. The first one exploded, and the others dried up and crumbled to the floor.

Head sagging, the half elf panted. His own magic was gone for now. And all he had was the staff. He slogged forward, brushing by one of the wurmers.

There was life in its eye, and its tail twitched. Its neck stretched out and its mouth opened. The bottom of its jaw fell off.

He poked it in the nose with his staff.

Its body quavered and fell into a pile of scale and bones that finally turned to dust.

I hate those things.

Bayzog trudged back to the chamber with heavy shoulders and legs that felt like lead. He felt old. The phantom's drain had cost him, yet he lived. Staff in one hand, braced against the wall, he peeked into the chamber. The blackness still lingered in the back end, yet there were fire and screaming near the slab.

Ben!

His friend was in the fight of his life. Half underneath the sacrificial altar, he kicked and screamed at the flaming giant. "Get off me! Get off me!"

Summoning his strength, Bayzog shot across the room like a wild berserker. With the tip of his staff lowered like a lance, he drove into the back of the burning Bletver.

Crack!

The triant's back arched, and his arms flung wide. Dripping hunks of flaming flesh, he teetered, swayed, and fell backward.

Wham!

In a moan of defeat, the triant's flesh boiled its last and died.

Ben rolled over and over on the floor, yelling, "Get it out! Get it out!"

Springing to his friend, Bayzog covered the man with his robes and patted him out. Ben had boils and burns all over him. His face was a mask of pain.

"Will you die?" Bayzog asked.

"And miss all this suffering?" Ben coughed and grimaced. "I'll live."

On the other side of the slab, the battle in the phantom's blackness yet raged. The wurmers dove in, only to be tossed out again. A stone giant hammered at something with its fists. Another giant turned, and its gaze fell on Bayzog. It came.

CHAPTER 39

INSIDE THE WURMER'S JAWS, NATH took matters into his own hands. He braced himself between the clenching jaws and shoved back. "Yuuurgh!"

The beast shook its head. Its throat muscles swallowed, and its tongue rolled under Nath's feet.

"You can't swallow me unless you kill me!" Nath buried his claws deep in the soft flesh of the wurmer's mouth. He pushed harder.

The creature gagged and spat Nath out.

Cahack!

Free falling through the air, all he could see was the wurmer's face. "Oof!"

He was back on the bridge, covered in slime and with the wind knocked out of him.

Above, the wurmer's wings flapped, and it barreled through the sky, letting loose a mighty shriek. "Reeeeeeek!"

Nath sprang to his feet and dashed toward the temple entrance.

The wurmer swooped, landing in front of the gateway to cut him off.

Not slowing, Nath drew Fang and churned forward, giving the blade a single command. "Fang, destroy!"

A radiant burst of energy exploded from the wurmer's mouth.

Nath plowed straight through the searing heat and buried Fang hilt deep in the wurmer's body.

The wurmer exploded.

Boom!

Scales, flesh, and claws scattered through the air and rained down on the bridge.

No longer on his feet, Nath brushed a hunk of wurmer flesh from his shoulder and wiped some soft grit from his eyes. He studied the shimmering blade and felt the throbbing in his hand. He and Fang were one at last.

A clamor filled his ears. Springing to his feet, Nath rushed through the smoldering wurmer lumps into the temple.

Bayzog was standing over Ben with his staff raised over his head. A citrine dome of energy covered them in a sizzling glaze. Lording over the dome, a stone giant hammered at it two fists at a time. Bayzog was staggering on his feet, and the shield was blinking in and out.

Waving his arms, Nath yelled, "Over here, giant!"

But the monstrous man continued his focused assault on the dome. *Wham! Wham! Wham!*

Closing the gap between him and the giant, Nath angled for its leg and chopped high. "Destroy, Fang! Destroy!" The great blade bit deep into the giant's knee, drawing forth an angry cry. But there was no explosion. No boom. Just a giant that wanted to kill him.

The raging humanoid clutched at Nath and screamed, "Die!"

Nath turned his hips into the swing of his sword and sheared the giant's hand off at the wrist.

It let out an awful howl so loud that Nath's teeth tickled.

"EEEEAAAAAAUUUGHHHHHH!"

Not backing off, Nath seized the moment and pressed his attack on the bewildered giant.

Slice! Slice! Slice!

Clutching at its wounds, the giant collapsed on its knees and died. Still upright, its limbs transformed into stone with a fast then slowing crackle. It was a statue now, a memory of a monster that lost its final battle.

Nath rushed over to his friends. Ben was a horrible sight, and Bayzog's face looked sickly. "Are you well?"

"Dragon, it's you!" Ben exclaimed. He hitched his chin over his shoulder at the blackness that still whirled around the room, fighting someone else. "Then who's that?"

Giving Ben a hand up, Nath said, "My father, Balzurth." He started forward, eager to rip his father out of the raging darkness and enemies that surrounded him.

But Bayzog held Nath fast. "Wait. That phantom will steal your powers. It's absorbing your father's powers now." The Elderwood Staff's gem winked with new fire. "I can stop it, but not if I'm interrupted."

"But Bayzog," Ben said, "the phantom almost killed you before."

"I wasn't ready for it then. Now that I have the staff and know what I'm up against, I am."

"What do you need?" Nath said, glancing over at the fracas.

"Just stay close and don't let anything interrupt me." Gripping the staff in both hands, the wizard planted one end of it firmly on the stone floor and raised his face to the ceiling.

Nath slipped Dragon Claw out of the bottom of Fang's hilt and handed it over to Ben. The silvery blade swirled with a mix of red and purple within.

Marveling, Ben said, "It lives."

The Elderwood Staff flared up in a white wash of light. Its brilliance lit up the entire chamber, driving the shadows and darkness away as the rising sun does to the night. Bayzog's white-knuckled hands were glued to the shaft. His eyes were white as snow. His mouth hung open, but somehow his voice was calling in a deep Elvish form of ancient song.

Above them in a swirling storm, the white gathered and took form. A white phantom-like creature grew with a distinct head and hulking shoulders. It pulsed and drifted toward the blackness. Then, like a snapping bowstring, it attacked.

A shrill whine shattered the clamor of battle. The night and the day had collided. The phantoms went at it with a howl.

The flock of wingless wurmers was quick to find new prey. The mindless creatures fixed their eyes on new blood: Nath and Ben. Slithering over the floor, they advanced with startling speed.

"Have at them, Ben!" Nath decapitated the first wurmer that came into his path.

Ben buried Dragon Claw in another's skull.

Pushed to the limit, Nath struck as hard and fast as he could. Anticipating every mindless move, he hacked the swarm of wurmers one by one, but it wouldn't be enough to stop them from clawing down Bayzog—who controlled the fighting white phantom above.

And Dragon Claw or not, Ben was overwhelmed.

"Get behind me, Ben! Just guard Bayzog!"

Splintering bone, teeth, and scales with his own might added to Fang's, Nath battled down the horde. Desperate for another plan, he gave Fang another order. "Repel, Fang! Repel!" He hoped a sonic wave would toss the slithering legions away. Between scale-rending swings, he banged the tip of the blade on the floor.

Ting.

Nothing.

A wurmer burst through the opening in Nath's defense and bit into his leg.

"Argh!" Nath cried. He beat the thing in the head with Fang's pommel, but its jaws were locked on his leg. He was practically immobile.

"Dragon!" Ben called. "I can't hold them off any longer! And look!"

Another storm giant was coming up from the recesses of the temple, headed right for them. Its coal-black eyes were intent on smashing Bayzog. The bestial man with skin of stone did something clever and unexpected. It picked up a wurmer and slung it straight at Bayzog.

Locked to the stone by the jaws of the wurmer, all Nath could do was watch the scaly missile soar.

CHAPTER 40

INSTINCT. SURVIVAL. NATH DIDN'T KNOW what, but for some reason Ben flicked Dragon Claw at the flying wurmer.

On impact, the scaly creature exploded into shards of ice.

"Ben!" Nath yelled, just as two wurmers tore into his defenseless friend. "No!"

The giant reached down to scoop Nath up.

Nath cocked Fang back to swing. "You'll pay, giant!"

A huge projectile smote the giant in the skull with a thunderclap.

Kraaang!

The enormous man's knees buckled under its body, and it fell face first on the slab.

"Brenwar!" Nath shouted.

Storming into the temple on horseback came Brenwar, with Sasha and Laylana close behind. "Don't be fighting giants without me! You owe me!"

The three warriors ran roughshod into the wurmers. Fiery missiles streaked from Sasha's fingers, puncturing one wurmer after another. Laylana's elven steel cleaved wurmer after wurmer in twain. Brenwar, powered by the gauntlets, punched with bone-snapping effect.

Nath locked his fingers into the jaws of the wurmer locked on his leg and began pulling them apart. Face reddening, arms bulging, he freed his leg and shoved the now dead but formerly vise-like clamp aside. Limping, he made his way over to Ben and hacked through the two wurmers attached to him.

"No, Ben, no," Nath sobbed, cradling his friend in his arms. Ben's face was marred in blood and burns. He'd never seen a man in such sad shape before. "Stay with me, Ben. Stay with me."

"I've been through worse," Ben said. He pawed at his side with a broken wrist. "Give me, give me the magic." His eyes rolled up in his head.

Nath fumbled through the belt pouch, found a restoration potion, and poured it into Ben's mouth. "Ben. Listen to me, Ben. You aren't dying on me."

Brenwar found his way to Nath's side. "I think that's the last of them."

Above, the phantoms continued their battle of darkness and light. Howling and shrieking back and forth in a knot of mystic sheets, the ghosts raged.

Bayzog's body trembled. His feeble frame seemed to be crushed under some unseen weight. The blackness of the phantom began to absorb the luminous white light.

Nath's chest tightened. He could barely breathe. Ben was dying and Bayzog was fading. He felt helpless.

From the heap of dead wurmers piled up all around, Sasha appeared. As lovely as ever despite the dirt on her face and robes, she gracefully made her way over to her husband. With the gentleness of a dove, she locked her arms around his waist and whispered in his ear, "I'm here for you, my love."

Bayzog straightened. The yellow in his eyes turned whiter than the snow on the peaks. The phantom he had summoned snaked out of the darkness. In an odd hand-over-hand movement, the white phantom reeled the black phantom in as if to swallow it whole. The black thing wailed and stretched. Its essence clawed at the air. Pawed for life. In two more tremendous gulps, the black phantom was gone and only a warm white ghostly light remained.

Bayzog collapsed into Sasha's arms and the Elderwood Staff's light went cold. The white phantom disappeared, and only the wavering torchlight illuminated the temple.

Weakly, Bayzog said, "Sasha, you're well?"

Brushing his sweat-drenched locks from his eyes, she said, "Aye."

"Dragon," Ben said, still cradled in Nath's arms. His color began to return and his heartbeat steadied. "I want to tell you something."

"Absolutely, Ben. Anything."

"I'm retiring."

"Oh? Ha ha! It looks like you're going to be fine after all." Nath brought Ben up to a sitting position. "Wait here."

Ben fell back down again, but Nath was on the move. He had to find his father. Brenwar followed right behind him, and as soon as they rounded the massive slab, they came across a startling sight.

CHAPTER
41

RYBEK STOOD BEHIND BALZURTH, WHO was sitting on the temple floor. The Dragon King's head was down on his chest. Haggard and drained, he breathed short, raspy breaths. Rybek had a chain wrapped around Balzurth's neck, with his sword poised to pierce the dragon man's heart through the back.

"Ah," Rybek said. "It seems the true Nath Dragon has arrived. Such a joy. I've had no fun dealing with this imposter. Oh, it's not what I want. It's what Eckubahn wants, but I feel that today, we can both have what we want." He tugged on the chain, choking Balzurth. "You see, Eckubahn wants him, and I want you. Your father, so clever and wise, hoped for me to send him to Eckubahn at full strength and give him a deadly surprise. He nearly pulled it off."

"And how was that to happen without Eckubahn knowing?" Nath asked, buying his father time while he desperately looked for a way to free him.

Rybek dangled the amulet before them. "This will take you right to Eckubahn. Oh, he would be more than ready for the likes of you, but not Balzurth. No, I have a feeling Balzurth would destroy him. But now, with Balzurth in such a weakened condition, he'll be ripe for the picking. A veritable sheep for the slaughter."

"If you do that," Nath warned, "there will be no escape for you. Look around. You'd be smart to use that amulet on yourself." He stepped forward.

Rybek pushed his sword into Balzurth's back, drawing forth a moan. "Nah ah ah. Stay right where you are. If anything smells like a trick, I'll end him myself."

Nath took a half step back. "You won't win this if you stay, Rybek. Let my father go, or I'll end you."

"No, you won't end me, Nath. The dwarf might, but you won't. I know that about you."

"You'll die for all the innocent blood you've spilled one way or the other," Nath said. "Let go of my father and live to fight another day."

"That's out of the question. Eckubahn would kill me," Rybek said.

"Eckubahn won't know what happened here," Nath remarked.

Everyone in Nath's party had flanked Rybek. There was nowhere for him to go. And it was quite possible that Brenwar would kill him. The way the dwarf's hands twisted on Mortuun's handle suggested he wouldn't hold back.

"So you can take your chances with us," Nath said, "or with your leader. If you are so cherished, then I'm certain he'll need you later. Just do what your kind does: lie and curry his favor. You'll find no favor with us."

Rybek scanned all of their faces. He stepped back but kept the sword needling into Balzurth's back. "Perhaps you're right." He gave his helmet an angry shake. "You played well today, Nath Dragon. It won't happen again. Now back away."

The party spread out.

Easing his sword away from Balzurth's back, Rybek stepped away.

The tightness in Nath's chest subsided. He'd won. His father was safe. There wasn't anything Rybek could do to harm any of them now.

Sultans of Sulfur, that was close.

In the blink of an eye, Balzurth came to life. In a blur of motion, he twisted around and smacked the blade from Rybek's grip with one hand and snatched the amulet with the other. Standing up at full height in a body of restored strength, the Dragon King said to an awestricken Rybek in a voice filled with raw power, "Justice for you. Vengeance for me." He shoved the man to the floor.

"Father!" Nath cried out. "What are you doing?"

Balzurth turned. He'd transformed into a mirror image of Nath. "Playing possum." He dropped the amulet over his neck and said, "I'm sorry, Son, but what must be done must be done." He vanished.

FLIGHT

OF THE

DRAGON

-BOOK 5-

CRAIG HALLORAN

CHAPTER 1

"LET ME BUST HIM UP." Brenwar had Mortuun shoved in Rybek's face. The evil warrior was bound up with his hands behind his back and sitting on the stone floor. There was a victorious sneer on his face. "I'll remove the snide look from his jaw forever!"

Rybek's broad shoulders heaved with his chuckles. His dark eyes moved back and forth between Nath and his company with nothing but a taunting look in them. His voice was a dark rumble when he spoke. "Look at you. Look at all of you! You've fought so hard and lost. Now your father is lost. What a fool! Eckubahn will have been ready for his ploy, and it wouldn't surprise me one bit if Balzurth was dead already." His nostrils flared. "Victory. I smell victory. The world of dragons falls."

Brenwar cocked back his elbow and made a fist. The leather of his gauntlet squeaked. "I'll show you victory!"

"Enough, Brenwar. You'll get your chance to question him later." Nath was standing by the sacrificial slab of stone, tending to Ben and Bayzog. Both man and part-elf looked about as bad as he'd ever seen them. Ben's face was burned. Laylana, Laedorn's elven daughter and a fine warrior, was treating the red blisters on Ben's cheeks with nimble fingers. Sasha and Bayzog were reunited. Bayzog lay in his wife's arms, eyes closed, with a wheeze behind his breaths. His hair was almost all white, but some of the color had returned to his face. Nath watched Sasha stroke her husband's cheek and looked into her soft eyes. "I don't think I've ever seen him sleep before."

"It takes much to get him to rest," Sasha replied with a faint smile. "Don't feel responsible, Nath. He's going to make it. He just needs his rest."

Nath nodded back. Moving away, he picked Rybek's sword up off the cold stone floor. It was a magnificent weapon. The steel was smooth and polished so fine that he could see his reflection in it. The leather on the handle made for a fine grip, and the weight was near perfect in balance. He thumbed the edge. There wasn't even a notch in it. He cast his eyes down at Rybek. "I bet you could chop down a stone tree with this."

Broad jaws clenching in his hard-featured face, Rybek nodded sideways at Brenwar and said to Nath, "No doubt it could chop down this stump of a man." He leered. "In time, I'll chop you down as well."

Brenwar popped Rybek in the forehead with his knuckles. The back of the man's head smacked hard into the column of stone with a *crack*.

Eyes squeezed shut, Rybek shook his head and spat.

Nath said to Brenwar, "What did I say?"

Puffing through his beard, Brenwar said, "I can't help that. It's instinct. Nobody threatens a dwarf." He swung his war hammer from side to side. "Just let me knock his head off. We don't need him to find your father."

Nath held his left hand up, palm out, and flipped Rybek's sword around with his right wrist. He shuffle stepped and jabbed. Parried. Twirled.

Rybek's eyes followed every precise and quick move.

Nath swished the blade through the air in a masterful display of the swordsman's craft. "It's an amazing blade, no doubt." He chopped into the stone column just above Rybek's head. Hunks of stone and dust fell on the man's tattoo-covered head. "It really can hew through stone."

"Just imagine what it could do to a skull," Brenwar added. "Heh-heh."

"You need to leave my blade alone, Nath Dragon." There was an edge in Rybek's voice. "Put it down."

Nath started banging the flat of the blade hard against the pillar. The sound echoed through the Temple of Spires. "Why, do you fear I might break it again?" With two hands, he smacked the blade hard into the stone.

Bang!

Rybek winced.

Nath struck the stone again.

Bang!

"Stop that!" Rybek shouted.

"Oh, I see someone is very fond of his blade." Nath squatted down and said in Rybek's ear, "Do you fear I might warp it?" He held it out for Rybek to see and turned the blade from side to side with his wrist. "It's still straight, for now, but I notice an imperfection."

"There is none."

"I disagree." Nath ran his fingernail over a hairline fracture just above the middle of the blade. "See that? It's where I broke it before. It's where I'll break it again."

"If you break that blade, you'll kill us all," Rybek said.

"I'm curious, Rybek. How did you manage to mend this sword so well?"

"You fool. Eckubahn did it with his bare hands. Such power he has, it's unrivaled. There might be a crack in the steel, but believe me, it's stronger than ever." Rybek's dark, hollow eyes caressed the blade with a passion only a warrior could understand. "You and that cleaver of yours could never break it again."

"Is that so?" Nath asked with an unbelieving tone. He rose back up to full height. "I really find it hard to believe." He waved Rybek's sword back and forth like a conductor's baton. "It's out of balance."

"It was made for my hand, not yours."

"I see." Nath rested it on his shoulder. "Why don't you tell me where my father is, Rybek? It would be the right thing to do."

"I'll tell you when you are dead." Rybek glanced at each person in the room. "And that goes for the rest of you as well. Including the women."

Brenwar launched another punch.

But Nath caught the dwarf by the meat of his upper arm. He changed places with Brenwar and turned loose a punch of his own. His fist connected with Rybek's jaw, snapping his head to the side. "You overestimate my capacity to show mercy."

Rybek's tongue fished through his mouth. He spat a bloody tooth out. "Perhaps I do. But mercy is your weakness. It's your father's, too. Eckubahn preys on it even as we speak."

Nath had to have some measure of faith in his father for knowing what he was doing, but the risk was so great, and his mother had warned him about his father taking those risks. He couldn't just stand around and hope his father's plan would work out. Deep down in his gut, he knew his father needed help.

Strength comes in numbers.

He stuck the sword tip first into the stone between Rybek's legs. "As evil as you may be, you still fight by the warrior's code of honor. How about one last fight, metal against metal? I win, you tell me where my father is. You win, I die."

Rybek lifted his head, sneering. "I'll take it."

CHAPTER 2

BALZURTH ARRIVED IN ANOTHER PART of Nalzambor on his knees, trembling. The amulet had done more than just transport him. It had drained him, somehow. His stomach gurgled and moaned. His limbs were heavy.

Chains rattled on his ankles, wrist, and neck.

How did those get there? Clever.

Balzurth lifted his hands up to his face. His scales were still midnight black, his clawed fingernails still sharp and golden yellow. He tossed his head. The flame-red hair cascaded over his shoulders.

At least my disguise is intact.

He surveyed his surroundings. He was outside in a misty smoke that covered jagged rocks. Colossal stones surrounded him in what looked to be the cold, dead mouth of a volcano. Somehow, sunlight illuminated the vast gap through the dimming gray mist. He rose to his feet and walked.

The heavy chains scraped over the stone. The iron of the chains was dense, the kind fashioned by men with a heavy ore mined by the dwarves in Morgdon.

It seems Eckubahn isn't going to take any chances with me. Or Nath, rather.

Balzurth walked outward until the chains brought him to a stop. He stretched them to their limit, about twenty feet, where they hung suspended, secured by the other end to a metal ring big enough to go around a horse's neck. It was mounted to a huge slab of square-cut stone at least ten feet tall and just as wide. He strained his arms and legs against his metal bonds. They held fast, like extensions of the world itself. He backed up, letting the links go slack. "Huh."

Accompanied by the wind whistling through the cracks in the stone mountain that was now his prison, he sat down. Crossing his legs, he lowered his chin onto his fist and waited. Balzurth's plan hadn't turned out the way he had hoped. He'd figured on landing right before the king of the titans, Eckubahn himself. From there he'd meant to take it right to him. A full onslaught. One swift stroke. He wanted to end it quick in a final stand. One last battle. But it hadn't happened the way he'd envisioned it. And that was a problem.

Now time has become my enemy.

With his clawed finger, he etched some patterns in the dirt and began to hum. His rich sound filled the expansive chamber. His thoughts landed on his son Nath. He was proud of Nath, what he'd done, how he'd overcome his trials and stayed faithful to the right cause. It hadn't worked out that way with his other children. But Nath was special, and no doubt his youngest son would be trying to find him. Balzurth just hoped to end this war before his son arrived in the thick of it. Now was the time to save lives and put a stop to Eckubahn and his mad reign.

I should have destroyed that titan when I had the chance. Let evil live and all it does is thrive.

He eyed his claws.

Next time I'll put it out of our misery forever.

Balzurth was still humming when a scuffle stirred the rocks. His keen dragon sight pierced the wavering mist. As he scanned the rock walls, the shapes of men formed in his eyes. These weren't average men but the larger sort: giants. Their huge frames eased between the rocks as they moved. Given the mist, the average person wouldn't detect them, but Balzurth could see all sorts. Mighty limbs came to life on legs of iron. They were fifteen feet tall and shaggy headed. Their noses were broad and flat.

And then their moans and huffs echoed through the strange canyon. On giant feet, they came forward, shaking the ground and surrounding Balzurth.

"I was wondering where the smell came from," said Balzurth in the guise and style of Nath as he counted their faces. There were fifteen of the monstrous men. They were bestial and savage, yet there was cunning in their beady eyes. Cruelty. "You know, Nalzambor is full of lakes you could bathe in. The fish might not like it—actually, they wouldn't like it—but the deep waters are said to take the stench out of anything. I know a great place I'd be happy to show you. It's just below—"

A powerful, echoing voice split the air.

"SILENCE!"

A giant emerged from the ranks. He was a head taller than the rest, more man than monster, with a green fire in his eyes. He was adorned in dragon skins hung like armor over his brawny shoulders and part of his chest. Bones rattled on his neck. Dragon bones and teeth. A belt fashioned from the same white bones hung from his waist. His head was mostly bald, and what hair he did have formed a long ponytail.

Balzurth rose with fire in his eyes. His heart thundered behind his breast. The atrocity enraged him. Many dragons had died to make this arrangement. Good ones. Blues, greens, and even a gold. It was just like the horrifying message the giants had sent to Dragon Home. A dragon's corpse. Broken. Mangled. Balzurth strained against the chains. "Who are you that defiles my kindred?"

"I am the spirit Isobahn, brethren of Eckubahn, the king." He stomped the ground.

Thoom!

Balzurth lost his footing and dropped to his knees.

"You will bow in my presence."

As much as he abhorred to do so, Balzurth fought back his commanding voice, popped up again, and continued in Nath's voice with a defiant tone. "I will not!"

Isobahn nodded his tremendous square-cut chin.

The other giants converged on Balzurth. Taking turns, they swatted, punched, stomped, and shoved him between their ranks. The blows were hard and heavy. The giants giggled like maniacal children. They tugged at his chains. Jerked him off his feet, dangled him, and patted at him like cats playing with a ball of string.

It was futile, but he fought back as best he could in Nath's form and chained. "You'll pay for this!" Balzurth yelled. Shaking his fist, he yelled even louder. "You'll all pay!"

By the chains, a giant swung him hard into the stone to which he was tethered.

Wham!

Balzurth absorbed all of the punishment he could endure. He couldn't break his cover. He just hoped his body could hold up, but his magic hadn't ever been drained before, so he didn't know how long he would need to rest before enough magic came back for him to change into his dragon form.

It could take years. Years of sleep! Let's hope not.

He took several more lumps.

Now I know how Nath must feel.

The beating continued until all of his physical strength faded. It stopped when he was face down and bleeding in the dirt. Two of the giants unhooked his chains from the stone pillar. By the chains still linked to his body, they dragged him over the hard ground through a slit in the rocks into the darkness.

Scraping along, he regained his feet—only to be jerked down again. It was futile. Miserable. They strung him along, and he had no idea where he was going.

CHAPTER 3

"**C**AN YOU MOVE ANY FASTER?" Rerry said, looking over his shoulder at his brother. "A one-legged orc could pass you!"

Samaz hobbled up the path. They'd managed to make their escape from the dungeon hours ago, but his legs were like noodles. "I'm pacing myself."

"Ah, pacing yourself. Makes perfect sense for a pair of men trying to escape." Rerry pushed some low-hanging branches aside and waited for his brother.

Samaz ambled up the incline.

Rerry let loose the branch, which slapped his brother in the face. "And let's hope our pursuers are pacing themselves as well."

Samaz slunk under the branches. "You have such an annoying way with things." He laughed.

"What's so funny?"

"I don't know, you just look funny with a metal almond on your head." Samaz peeled off his own elven helmet and chucked it aside. "I can only imagine how silly I must look."

"You always look silly." Rerry picked Samaz's helmet up. "Now put this back on. We need to blend in, just in case we run into anybody. Now you blend, you bulging misfit."

With a huff, Samaz took the helmet, but he didn't put it back on. "I'll carry it for now."

Mocking him, Rerry said, "I'll carry it for now."

For some reason, the banter that had gone on and on between them since birth lightened Samaz's spirits. Some strength returned, and he pressed on, keeping pace while his brother navigated the woodland like one of the forest's own creatures.

Ahead, Rerry was a strapping figure of grace and warriorhood. Adorned in the elven armor with his light hair spilling out from under his helmet, Rerry carried the look of a soldier quite well. Light footed, he moved on top of the stumps, fallen trees, and flat rocks, careful to avoid leaving any kind of trail.

In truth, neither of them had much experience in the woodland, but it came naturally to them, unlike it did to their father, Bayzog. And they had less elf in them than their father did, which was odd.

"What do you make of Captain Scar imprisoning us? Or any of the elves doing so? They swarmed us. They threw us in a dungeon." Rerry adjusted his helmet. "It's so hard to get used to this thing. As I was saying, what do you make of that? Elves aren't supposed to imprison elves."

Samaz hopped from one rotting log to another. "I don't think they took us in because we're elves but because we are part-elves. But I was sick when you did most of the parlaying, remember?"

Rerry led them down into a ravine, where a stream trickled by. He scooped up a handful of water and slurped it down. He wetted his face. "Everything was fine until you mentioned Father's name," he said.

"Me?" Samaz straddled the stream and sloshed some water on his own face then drank. "You're the one who said 'Bayzog,' not me. I tugged the back of your shirt, but you didn't listen. Those gums kept flapping."

"They asked. What was I supposed to say? I thought it would be a good thing, seeing how Father is known as a hero in this realm. Instead, we received a throttling and days in the clink. What kind of elves treat other elves so poorly?" He plucked a stone out of the water and chucked it down the stream. It skipped once and splashed to a stop. "It was as if they were looking for him."

"We aren't full bloods. That's problem one. Father lives outside the elven lands. That's number two. Nalzambor is under duress. That's number three."

"Oh, enough with your numbers. The world's a mess. I get it." Rerry unsheathed his sword and cut through some of the reeds growing along the bank. "But as long as I have a fine piece of steel, I can handle it." He eyed Samaz. "Seriously, when are you going to master some sort of weapon?"

Samaz poked his temple. "As long as I have a sound mind matched by my quick feet and hands, I'm never defenseless."

Rerry rolled his eyes. "That's so encouraging."

At the top of the ravine rim came a sound of branches cracking, followed by heavy footsteps. Something or someone was up there. It was big and not ordinary big but beyond. It dragged something through the brush.

Rerry's eyes met Samaz's. Both of his thin blond eyebrows perched. With a nod, he darted after the sound.

Samaz ran after him, bounding from one side of the stream to the other and racing up the hillside. Rerry was climbing over the rocks, still focused on not leaving a trail. One thing was certain: the trail of whatever was up there couldn't be missed. He crested the top alongside his brother. The soft-footed brothers edged into the foliage until they came across a path of crushed and snapped saplings.

Rerry kneeled down inside a footprint as big as him. He crinkled his nose. In a whisper, he said, "It smells awful." He flashed a row of white teeth. "I bet it's a giant."

"There's no need to pursue it," Samaz warned. He bent over and picked up some animal hair grafted to the bark of a tree. "It feeds, whatever it is. Leave it be. Pursuit will only draw its attention."

"I won't bother it." Rerry crept forward.

Samaz followed. There wasn't much of a choice in the matter. Rerry wouldn't listen. They'd just have to resume their quest to find the Ocular of Orray and help their mother later.

Rerry came to a stop. He turned to face Samaz with his blue eyes the size of the moon. He pointed.

Samaz came alongside his brother and stared along the path Rerry indicated.

There it was sitting on the ground, a giant. Sitting, it was still much taller than them. The expanse of its back was just as wide too. Coarse brown hairs like fur covered the giant up to its neck. The head was bald, knotted, and scarred. It was eating. Samaz moved closer and watched from another angle. It was eating a bear. Its jaw moved up and down, making a horrible crunching sound that threatened to turn Samaz's bones to jelly. "Let's get out of here," he mouthed to his brother.

Rerry nodded and backed away.

But the giant took in a deep draw of air through its nostrils. It sounded as if it was going to inhale the entire forest. Its bullish neck snapped around. Mouth still full of bear, the giant locked its eyes on them. Nostrils flaring, it licked its lips and got to its feet.

"Samaz, it's got horns. Horns on its head. I didn't think giants had horns. Why would they need horns on their heads?" Rerry finished with his jaw hanging.

Samaz watched the giant rise to its full height. It did have horns, like a ram's, on either side of its forehead. Its face was ugly, almost like a beast's, but more like a wild man's.

The giant smacked its lips and, with a bellow, filled the forest as it came right at them.

CHAPTER
4

"**H**AVE YOU GONE MAD?" BRENWAR was blowing the layers of moustache that had become one with his beard. "This vermin doesn't deserve the opportunity."

Nath eyed Brenwar. "Mind yourself."

"But..." Brenwar's heavy shoulders slumped. Head down, he backed away.

Without any notification, Nath brought Rybek up to his feet and cut his bonds.

The powerful warrior, as tall as Nath, stretched his limbs and rubbed his wrists. With wary eyes, he said to Nath, "A straight fight then?"

Still holding Rybek's sword, Nath picked up the man's iron helmet. It was crudely crafted—not from a lack of skill but by intent. It was designed for intimidation more than protection. He tossed it to Rybek and said, "You'll need this."

Laylana appeared at his side. "Nath, this crude man will not fight fair. His word cannot be taken. In this instance, I concur with Brenwar. Let me beat the information out of him."

"He'll die first," Nath said. He faced off with Rybek. The cold look of a murderer was in the man's eyes. Vengeance was behind them too. Rybek blamed Nath for his brother's death. He blamed Selene as well. He would never stop until they were both dead. Nothing Nath could say would change the man's mind, but he spoke anyway. "Your brother had choices in life, Rybek. You do too. You don't have to race down the same path of destruction your brother was on. He cannot witness your accolades in the grave, no matter how large."

"Oh, he might not see it, but from the grave he will feel your blood when I spill it into the ground." Rybek stretched out his hand. "I accept your offer.

Your head against my information on the whereabouts of your father. I swear it on my sword in front of witnesses and fellow warriors—a bond in blood from the blood we've shed from battle. If I lie, take my hands, take my skill, forever."

A thunderclap boomed in the skies above. A heavy rain came down. The Temple of Spires was an ancient place, and its dome was filled with cracks. Water wetted the floor.

Rybek stepped into the rain and spread his arms wide. He was a hulking man layered in bulging muscles. "Eckubahn, aid me! Grant my revenge!"

Ben made his way to Nath's side and handed him Dragon Claw. "Just finish him."

Nath locked Dragon Claw back inside Fang's pommel. He moved away from his friend and into the litter of dead surrounding them: slaughtered wurmers from the earlier battle, chopped up into bits. Giants who had fallen and turned into stone, parts of them already busted up into rubble. Then there was Bletver, the triant. His huge body was still a smelly mound of burning flesh on account of the potion of fire breathing Ben had drunk. Rain drops sizzled on his dead hide.

Nath motioned with his sword. "Come, Rybek. Let the battle commence."

Rybek pulled his sword from the stone floor and wiped the water from his face. "It will rain your blood today."

Nath readied into his stance. Rybek was as good a swordsman as he'd ever faced. He'd about gotten him the last time, but perhaps he was underestimating the man, so he wasn't going to take any chances. He set his feet and lifted his sword. "Come then, make it rain."

Rybek kicked the head of a wurmer out of his path and moved in. He stood tall, sword at the ready, with his free hand fanned out. Raindrops bounced off the steel. The sword he carried was an exquisite blade with a grip made for two hands. Its length was shorter than the long blade of Fang, but it was just as broad. Rybek waded in and unleashed the first swing.

Both fine blades appeared to be otherworldly when they met. They collided in a clash of steel. Mystic sparks flew.

Clang!

Fang's energy flowed into Nath's hand with an angry hum.

Back and forth the warriors went, each fighting one handed.

Rybek jabbed his blade at Nath's eyes and legs.

Nath slid his head aside and swatted the blade away.

Rybek broke off and backed away, saying, "What's the problem, scared to attack me?"

"Not at all." Nath jumped right at him and let loose a chop at Rybek's side.

Rybek caught the swing on his sword and countered by spinning back into Nath, cracking him in the jaw with his elbow.

Nath stumbled back with spots in his eyes. A flash of metal came down. He brought Fang up, parrying the blow before it could cleave into his shoulder. He backpedaled. He defended himself against Rybek's assault of steel. The taste of his own blood was in his mouth.

Clang! Bang! Clang! Ting!

Mystic sparks flew.

Nath shook his mane of red hair. He parried one blow after the other.

Rybek assaulted—quick, deadly, and unrelenting. The warrior's blows weren't trying to cut him in half and overpower him. No, Rybek was a true master swordsman. He was determined to wear Nath down with skill as opposed to strength.

One thing is for certain. He's an excellent fighter.

Nath got the hang of the man's routine. Within moments he timed every blow, every stroke. He played along. Let his footing slip, only to desperately catch one fatal blow after the other.

"What's the matter, Nath Dragon? Why don't you attack? Do you feel my arm will tire and you shall vanquish me then?" Rybek stepped and jabbed. "I don't tire. My will of steel won't allow it."

"No, Rybek, you're a fine swordsman, one of the best I've ever encountered. Just not better than me." With that, Nath smacked Rybek's sword aside in a vicious counter rather than a parry. The warrior's arm was flung wide, exposing his chest. Nath back swung at the mark in a strike sure to end it, but at the last moment he held back, aiming to wound rather than kill by slowing the strike of his sword.

Rybek dropped beneath the swing in an uncanny move with surprising speed.

Nath missed.

Swish!

Overextended, Nath glanced down at the man lying beneath him.

Rybek swept Nath's legs out from under him with his booted foot.

Nath fell onto his back. Before he even realized what was happening, Rybek's blade was on a collision course with his face. In a fragment of thought, he knew he could not bring Fang around to stop the blow in time. His free clawed hand lashed out, trying to stop Rybek's attack at the wrist. The effort didn't match the goal. Rybek's blade cut through scales and bone.

Rybek let out a triumphant bellow.

"YYYyeeeeaaaaahhhhhhhhhhhh!"

Nath looked for his fingers. Half of his hand was gone.

CHAPTER
5

RERRY SHOVED HIS BROTHER SAMAZ back down the path. Fueled by fear, the pair of part-elves careened over the embankment and down the ravine they'd just climbed up. He was yelling to his brother, "I always wanted to see a giant, but not like this!"

"I told you we needed to go around!" Samaz said, but his foot became tangled, and he tumbled over and down the hill.

Rerry rushed after his brother, stretching his arms out, fingers clutching for his brother's clothing.

But Samaz balled up, probably to protect himself. Rolling like a boulder, he hit the rock bottom and splashed into the ravine creek.

Rerry scooped his brother up by his underarms. "You're so clumsy!"

"I beat you down the hill, didn't I?"

"ELVEN MEAT! I SMELL ELVEN MEAT!"

Both of the brothers glanced up the hillside. The giant's tree-trunk legs pumped down the hill. Its yellow eyes were still locked on the both of them. Humongous and hideous, it came like a rampaging one man herd.

Gaping for a moment, Rerry said, "That stupid thing can talk."

"It's startling," Samaz replied.

Side by side, the brothers took off at a dead sprint, ankle deep in the water.

Behind them, the giant's feet shook the ground in heated pursuit.

"What's your plan, Samaz?"

"Run!"

Rerry bounded over the water cascading over the stones. "Run where?"

"Until we lose the giant!" Samaz leaped over a fallen log and landed in the shallows. "Just keep moving. Surely he can't keep up with us."

"Not me, maybe." Rerry took a quick glance over his shoulder.

The giant moved through the pass like a charging bull. Head lowered, it picked up steam. Using one of its massive hands, it scooped up a handful of stream stones and dirt and flung it at them.

"Duck, Samaz!"

The rocks, some as big as a man's hand, pelted both of them in the back.

"Augh!" Rerry cried out. One stone clonked off of his helmet, knocking him sideways. He caught himself, hand out, on the trunk of a tree, retaining his balance. His legs churned. He'd always been confident he could outrun anything, but the giant's legs were longer than he was tall.

It was gaining, and gaining fast.

"I FEED!" the giant said. "I FEED ON FLESH AND BONES!" It flung another handful of dirt and rocks at them.

The heavy debris pelted Rerry's back, sending lancing pain from his shoulders into his eyes.

Samaz dropped to a knee, dashing it on a jagged rock and tearing his clothes at the knee. His brows buckled between his eyes. Jaw clenched, he forced himself up and resumed his run.

Sword in hand, Rerry said, "You run! I'll stay and slow the beast until you get to safety. Who knows, maybe I'll get lucky."

"Most likely you'll get dead, and I'm not ready to part with you yet." Samaz snatched up a smooth stone from the water and closed his fist around it. "I need you to steal me a few moments."

"For what?" Rerry turned his chin over his shoulder.

The horned giant filled both of its hands with more gravel from the creek. Its arms cocked back. It flung the debris like a sea of sling stones.

"Duck, Samaz!"

The gravel ripped through the air. The hard pellets of rock pelted both of the brothers. Rerry had been hit with rocks before in some strange games he and his brother used to play, but never dozens of stones at once. They struck like a hive of hornets stinging all at once.

"Now I know why so many prefer to wear armor. Thank Guzan I have at least one coating on," he said, flapping his arms. "Dear mother, it hurts!"

Samaz didn't reply. His eyes were closed, but his feet still navigated the path over the stream of water. Both of his hands were clutched over the stone he held, and a mystic light seeped out from within it. His pace slowed. "Buy us some time, Rerry." He halted in the middle of the stream.

"Have you gone mad?"

Samaz stood with the waters rushing around his ankles. His eyes were up in his head. "Hold the giant off a few moments longer."

With his lip curled up under his nose, Rerry said to his brother, "You're so weird." He faced the oncoming giant and started waving his sword high over his head. He yelled out loud. "Halt, giant! I am Rerry, and this is my mystic sword…Giant Killer! One strike from its keen edge and you'll be instantly slain!"

Hands filled with mud and rock, the giant came to a stop. Its massive head tilted to the side as it squinted and eyed the blade held by Rerry. Its throat growled in a strange but giant-like thoughtful manner. It chewed something in its mouth and swallowed.

Rerry guessed it was part of the bear it had been dining on. He swallowed and said, "I see you are as wise as you are big, giant. You fear my blade, and you should." He poked the sword in the air. The giant eased back, eyes narrowed. "Be gone, giant. There is no meal for you to have here. Be gone and finish the bear."

With its eyes still fixed on Rerry's blade, the giant replied, "The entire world shall be mine to devour." It snorted. "Man and part-elf alike. I shall suck the marrow from your bones, you little liar."

And I thought giants were big and stupid. This one is certainly not.

Rerry took a quick look at his brother.

Samaz hadn't moved.

Facing the giant again, Rerry stuck out his chest. "Only a fool would dare trifle with Rerry the Great. I offered mercy. You passed up my offer. Now I can only offer death." He advanced.

The giant took a huge step back.

Speaking as loud as he could, Rerry said, "Having second thoughts, are we?"

The fifteen-foot-tall giant blinked its immense eyes. Thoughts were being processed somewhere behind the horns of its brutish skull. It was like an animal, a smart one, fighting against its instincts. Its belly moaned and gurgled. Its monumental jaws widened. Saliva dripped from its huge teeth.

"Elven meat's the best kind of meat. Tender are the bones." It leaned down. "I smell no danger in your steel. Like a flea, you cannot harm my thick hide. No mortal blade can."

"Uh," Rerry said, easing back a little, "you sound very sure of yourself. If I were you, I wouldn't take a chance."

"If you could kill me, I'd be dead. But you can't. Now, no more chatting. I hunger. It's time to dine." It allowed the rock and sludge to spill from its hands. Its arms slowly closed in on Rerry. "Make it simple, little flea. Get inside my belly."

The rancid breath of the giant soured Rerry's stomach. He covered his nose and tried not to gag. He wanted to move, but his legs seemed frozen into the water.

Dear Mother, this thing really is going to eat me! I-I-I can't move!

CHAPTER 6

NATH'S THOUGHTS RACED THROUGH A suspended time. He gazed at the part of his hand that lay in a puddle on the stone floor. What had happened? He'd been careful, testing Rybek's skill. He'd had a chance to end it. Finish the man. He'd held back. Why?

Now his enemy was on the verge of finishing him.

Jaw hanging on the ground, Nath caught the flash of Rybek's blade.

With two hands clutching the handle, Rybek brought the blade down with wroth force.

Nath rolled out of harm's way.

Rybek's blade bit into the stone floor and stuck.

Brenwar started forward with his war hammer ready to go. His bearded face was a mask of worry. Laylana was right beside him with her sword poised to strike at Rybek.

Sword out before him, Nath said, "No! I can handle this." There wasn't a mortal in the world who had undone Nath in a long time. There'd been close calls when he was much younger, testing his skills in the world of men, but he'd always overcome the odds.

This was different.

The feeling in Nath's gut now was not the same. He bled. He was maimed. Rybek, somehow, had shown more skill and outwitted Nath.

Don't let him get in your head, Dragon. There's too much riding on this. Your own scales, for example.

Rybek yanked his sword free of the stone floor. With the rain dripping over his body, he said, "Oh, what a glorious day for victory."

Nath could have sworn the evil man's ugly iron helmet was smiling. Nath pulled his wounded hand to the side. It dripped blood. It burned as if it was a torch on fire. His jaws clenched. "I'll grant you a small victory, but that's it."

Rybek swiped his sword back and forth, scattering the rainwater that was filling up the floor. "I can see the anguish in those golden eyes. The doubt. The pain. Your cocky voice trembles. You are lost, Nath Dragon."

Nath planted his feet and readied his stance. "No, I know exactly where I am." He beckoned Rybek over with the stump of his hand. "What are you waiting for? Come on, then."

Ben's heart pounded in his chest. It took everything he had in him to not rush out and try to battle alongside Dragon. Ben himself gasped for breath. The healing potion had restored him, but he wasn't getting any younger. He was beyond tired, yet his fingers were wrapped around the pommel of his sword, gripping it tight. He slid the blade a little into the scabbard and out again, snapping it in and out of place.

Click. Click. Click.

Eyeing the fight, he made himself breathe deeply and stop gasping.

If I had Akron, I'd blow Rybek away. One shot. Boom! Dragon would forgive me. Eventually.

The battle between Dragon and Rybek raged on. Rybek was a gorilla of a man with hard muscles bulging in his arms. Two handed, he swung his sword in tremendous swings meant to cut a man in half. Nath backed away. Ducked. Dodged. Parried. He climbed over the dead wurmers and fallen giants, changing the ground where the men battled.

Clever, Dragon. Clever.

Ben had never seen two men fight so hard. Rybek was a force. His sword skills were nothing short of a marvel. Tirelessly, he took it to Dragon. Every strike was powerful, determined, and precise. Even for a man his size, it seemed impossible he could keep up the pace at which he attacked. Deep creases formed in Dragon's perfect face. He'd parry one blow only to defend against another. Rybek's sword licked out like a striking snake. Its point grazed the outermost skin of Dragon's forehead.

Laylana gasped. Brenwar stirred.

Ben's heart jumped.

That was close!

He ground his teeth.

Too close!

Blood trickled over the bridge of Dragon's nose, washed away by the pouring rain that came down in sheets through the cracks above.

Rybek continued to taunt Dragon. "I'm going to take you down one piece at a time. Fingers, toes, legs. Once I'm finished, I'll feed you to the wurmers." He struck. Swords collided with jarring impact, sending anguish through Dragon's face. "You're losing precious dragon blood. You weaken. Your fall will come fast."

Dragon's grim face remained silent. Normally, he'd have something to say even in the worst of situations, but not this time. No, his eyes were fastened on Rybek's, and his face was a mask of agony and concentration.

Come on, Dragon! I know you have something up your sleeve. Use it!

Ben watched in helpless fascination. Two monumental swordsmen seemed equally matched in power, skill, and strength. Ben never thought any mortal could stand a chance in a one-on-one fight with Dragon. He was too strong. Too fast. Yet Rybek impossibly did. The warrior's iron helmet had a living glow to it. The eyelets in the helmet pulsed with a life of their own. As the sparks flew between the wondrous swords, Ben got a sense Rybek's power was not going to fade, but Dragon's was.

"Keep those elbows up, Dragon!" Ben yelled.

Brenwar looked up at Ben and snorted. Then the dwarf yelled, "Quit fooling around, Nath, and just kill him!"

Dragon kept his wounded arm pinned to his side. His broad shoulders sagged. His jaw hung open. He swatted at Rybek's strikes desperately.

Clang! Clang! Clang!

Ben clutched at his chest. Dragon continued to retreat, now at a faster rate. He moved toward the temple exit, outside, and into the pouring rain. Ben and his companions followed the battling men outside. They stood at the top of the steps watching the two fight on the bridge.

The sheets of rain pounded the fighting men, but even the pouring rain couldn't drown out the sound of colliding steel.

Rybek's voice cut through the torrent of nature, saying, "Did you come out here to drown before you die by my blade?"

Lightning flashed. Thunder clapped. The bridge shook.

Rybek pounced. Swinging his sword in windmill-like circles, he beat Dragon and Fang down in strikes coming one stronger than another.

How Dragon managed to hold onto Fang Ben did not know, but he did. Dragon was down on a knee. His arm juttered beneath every bone-jarring blow. It rang out so loud it tickled Ben's teeth.

Do something, Dragon! Do something!

Clang! Clang! Clang! Clang! Clang!

CHAPTER 7

T HE HORNED GIANT'S HANDS CLOSED in.

Rerry's locked-up joints came to life. He stuck his sword in the giant's eye.

It lurched back, clutching at its face, and let out a tremendous bellow. "YOWOOOOOO!" It stood with its shoulders heaving up and down. The sword protruded from its eye. It said, "I was just going to eat you. Now I tear you apart, bit by bit!" It stomped the ground.

Rerry fell.

The giant came right at him.

A blue ball of energy streaked by Rerry's head and smote the giant in the chest with a mighty explosion.

Ka-BOOooooooooM!

The ram-horned giant teetered backward. Its arms flailed wildly at its sides. It stumbled backward, groaning and clutching at its chest ... and fell.

Boom!

The giant lay on its back. Smoke rose from its expansive chest.

Rerry looked back at Samaz. "What did you do?"

Eyes no longer rolled up inside his head, Samaz dusted off his hands. "Just a spell Mother showed me. I've had it mastered for quite some time, but I've never had the chance to use it."

"You could have used it sooner!" Rerry crept closer to the giant. Standing beside its massive foot, he said, "Did you kill it?"

Samaz shrugged. "I don't think we should wait around to find out. Let's just get going."

With bright eyes, Rerry said, "Samaz, do you know what this means?"

Staring at the foul monster that lay strewn out on the creek bed, Samaz replied, "No."

"We killed a giant!"

"You mean *I* killed a giant."

"No, if I hadn't stalled it—extremely bravely, I might add—you never would have gotten around to casting that sorcery." Rerry lifted his chin. "It was a team effort we can both take the glory in, even though I did the hard part."

"Do you have any idea how hard it is to cast a spell while running through a forest? No, of course you don't. You don't have the ability in you." Samaz pulled his helmet off and dropped it on the ground. "With this ugly helmet on, no less. But it's not a competition, Rerry. We live. That's what matters, so let's get moving again."

Rerry crinkled his nose. Eyeing the body of the giant, he said, "I need a souvenir, a trophy or something."

"Don't be foolish."

Rerry bent over the giant's crusty hand. It was almost big enough to pick him up with. He spied a ring on its finger. "I'll be!" Using both hands, he wiggled it loose and tugged it off. With his back to Samaz, he held it up over his head. "Looky looky what I found. I think it's gold." He spat on it and rubbed the grit off with his sleeve. The metal twinkled in what sunlight cut through the trees. "Yes, it is gold. Hah, what do you think of that, Samaz?" He stuck his entire arm through the hoop. "Now that's a trophy we can be proud of. Right, Samaz? Right?"

The forest was oddly quiet.

Rerry turned, eyes searching for his brother.

Samaz was nearby, but he wasn't alone. He was surrounded by fully armed elves. His hands were above his head. Rerry didn't recognize any of the elves—except for one, Captain Scar. The edge of his rapier was at Samaz's throat.

Wearing the standard black tunic of the elven guard, left eye covered in a patch, the fit, brown-haired elven soldier said to Rerry, "That is a fine trophy. It will look great hanging from my wife's neck."

Rerry made a move.

More elves emerged from the woodland with bows nocked with arrows pointed at him.

Captain Scar motioned to him. "Please, toss the bauble over. Finders keepers, eh?"

"I tell you what, Scar. How about this? I keep the ring. You keep my brother."

Samaz's eyes widened.

Scar showed a cocky smile. "Why settle for one when I can have both?"

With a shrug, Rerry said, "I see your point." He rubbed the ring, shining it up a bit, caressing it with his eyes. "How about I fence you for it?"

"No."

Holding the ring in both of his hands, Rerry looked at the golden object and said, "I promise I will see you again."

Birds scattered from the trees. Many of the elven soldiers clad in black tunics trimmed in silver glanced up.

Without warning, the horned giant's hand came to life and smote one of the elves dead with a single strike. With an angry groan, it sat up, saying, "Ah! A feast of elven meat is upon me! I'll relish all of your bones!"

Every elven warrior sprang into action. Bowstrings were pulled back. Arrows were let loose.

Twang! Twang! Twang! Thwack! Thwack! Thwack!

The arrows skipped off the giant's horns. Some of them pricked its skin. Their efforts were futile. The giant brushed the missiles aside and attacked. It snatched an elf in each of its hands and snapped their spines, making a horrible sound.

The elven ranks ripped out their swords and swarmed the giant. They chopped and hacked. Their blades hacked at the giant's fingers. They climbed up its body like stinging ants and smote it in the face.

But one by one, the giant slung them off. It grabbed one elf and tossed it into the trees. It rammed its horns into two elves, grinding them into the ground.

Scar shouted out, "Take the legs! Take the legs!"

A pair of elves worked a coil of rope and entwined the giant's legs.

The giant's foot snagged. It stumbled. Its angry eyes found the rope. It snatched up the coil.

The elves hung onto the rope just long enough for the giant to dangle one of them toward its mouth. It bit into one of the elves' legs, making a loud crunching *chomp*.

The elven soldier screamed. "Aaaaaugh!"

"Enough of this!" With his blade still under Samaz's chin, Scar said, "Don't you go anywhere, because if you do, I'll track you down and kill you!"

Rerry, who had concealed himself away from the fray, saw Samaz nod. Instantly, Scar's eyes somehow found his. "And don't you try to run either, prisoner!"

With a wild look in his elven eyes, Scar charged the giant at full speed.

The giant took a swipe at him.

Scar slipped beneath the swing, jumped onto the giant's chest, locked one hand in the scruff of its facial hair, and said, "You've brought enough death! Now it ends!" He pierced the giant's chest with his rapier. The blade sank deep, right where the heart should beat.

The giant's eyes enlarged. Its great limbs drooped.

The surviving elves, two of them, chopped into the heel of the giant.

The horned monster fell like a great tree and splashed into the creek. Giant blood mixed with the waters.

Still standing on the giant's chest, Scar yanked his sword free. Without a drop of sweat in his eyes or stain on his uniform, he said, "That's how you kill a giant. No dwarf could do any better." He wiped his sword on the giant, checked its clean edge, and slid it back into his sheath.

Rerry approached from the brush. He couldn't believe Scar had killed the giant with a single strike. "You have my admiration, imprisoner or not. That was—impressive."

Hand out, Scar said, "I'll be taking the giant's ring now."

Without a word, Rerry tossed the ring to Scar. The elven fighter had earned it.

"Hands up," Scar said.

Rerry and Samaz both surrendered their hands.

Only two elves out of the small band remained alive. The rest were dead, their bodies scattered and broken. One hung in a tree, and the others were smashed into the ground. Even though Rerry wasn't a full-blooded elf, he still felt great loss. He said, "You could use our help caring for the dead. It would be our honor."

Rolling the giant's ring like a bracelet around his wrist, Scar said in a nasty tone, "If you hadn't run away, none of them would be dead, now would they?" He shook his head. "I'll think about it."

But in the wink of an eye, the giant smashed Scar between its hands so hard his helmet popped off his head.

CHAPTER 8

THE BATTLE WITH RYBEK WAS the longest sword fight Nath had ever been in. Regardless of the outcome, the unrelenting warrior had gained his respect. Rybek's mighty blows would have burst the elbows of a lesser man. The jarring impact felt as if it could shatter bone.

Where does he get his strength?

Nath deflected another devastating blow.

Clang!

And yet another.

Bang!

No one of any race but dragonkind had ever before matched Nath's speed and strength, not even when he was young. He was a dragon, with a dragon heart the size of four men's. Nath suspected Rybek possessed supernatural powers like his brother Kryzak had, probably from the sword but possibly from that helmet. He already knew Rybek's sword had magic within. He'd seen its power level the trees in the forest when they'd first clashed.

He's got to have a weakness. Find it before his sword finds your neck!

Rybek cocked back to uncoil another bone-shattering swing.

Nath rolled backward, pushed off the ground with his powerful legs, sprang high in the air, and did a back flip. He landed on his feet a dozen yards away.

"Buying time, Nath Dragon?" Rybek scraped the edge of his sword over the bridge. "I can't blame you. Your death is inevitable, for I am invincible."

"You sound too sure of yourself, Rybek." Nath gulped down some air. "You should know nothing in Nalzambor is certain. Not even death." He glanced at his missing hand. The bleeding had stopped. His hand was a stump of ebony scales, but his thumb remained. He wiped the gash on his forehead. The wound Rybek had cut open had healed up.

Thank Guzan!

Pointing his sword at Nath, Rybek said, "Stand your ground! No more dancing! It's time to finish this!" He stormed forward, feet splashing in the puddles on the bridge. "Now it ends!"

Fang pulsated in the palm of Nath's good hand. He pulled his shoulders back. His blood churned. He'd bought enough time. Saved his energy. The bleeding had stopped. The loss of his hand had frightened him. Shaken his confidence. Now the fighter within was coming back. Confident. Certain.

I am Nath Dragon. I am the Dragon Prince. I could beat this man without any hands. Well, maybe I do need one.

He set his sight on Rybek. Locked his jaw. Narrowed his golden eyes. "Dragon! Dragon!" He charged.

Rybek laughed. He lowered his sword and shoulders and rushed at Nath in giant strides. "You're a dead dragon!"

The great blades collided. Thunder clapped.

Boom!

Rybek poured it on. His eyes behind the helmet were ever intent to kill. Metal scraped against metal. The men battled back and forth with lightning-fast strokes that were the stuff of legends.

Nath parried.

Rybek counterattacked. The warrior's magical blade came dangerously close to Nath's vitals.

Nath fought back. The strength in his arm renewed. His power seemed everlasting. The weakness from the loss of blood was gone. One handed, stroke after stroke, he pressed back against Rybek's fierce attacks.

"You might have a second wind, but it will still be your last."

"Will it?" Nath brought Fang down on Rybek's awaiting blade. In an impossible move, he shifted his swing. Fang slipped by Rybek's guard and slapped the man upside his iron helmet.

Krang!

Rybek staggered backward. His head wobbled on his shoulders. He shook off the blow.

Nath hit him in the head again.

Rybek fought to parry Nath's striking edge. His parries were too slow.

Nath weaved around Rybek's defense, Fang striking like a metal snake. He skewered the man in the meat of his shoulder. He jabbed him in the thigh. He punched Rybek in the helmet again, knocking him backward.

Rybek fought back more slowly.

Nath attacked faster. "Give it up, Rybek."

Hobbled, Rybek said, "Never!" He swung.

Nath sidestepped with ease, and with the tip of his sword, he flicked

Rybek's helmet off his head. The helmet sailed over the bridge and into the canyon.

"Noooooooooooooooooooooooooooooooooooooooo!" Rybek screamed. He bull rushed Nath, sword arching high. It came down like a bolt shot from the sky.

Nath's instincts saved him. He twisted out of harm's way at the last moment.

The blow would have split him in half. Instead, it dug into the bridge. The sword's magic powers were unleashed. The rock of the bridge exploded. A gaping hole formed, and the heavy stones of the bridge fell through.

Nath backpedaled away.

More of the bridge collapsed. The distance between him and Rybek expanded. The bridge cracked and buckled.

Nath yelled to Rybek, "Get away from there!"

The warrior stared down into the abyss between them then held his sword up to his head in a salute. "Remember this, Nath Dragon. You did not beat me." The bridge floor gave way right underneath the huge warrior. He plummeted through the gap into the abyss.

"Nooooooo!" Nath screamed.

The bridged trembled a few moments longer before it finally stopped crumbling. Numb and one handed, Nath stood empty in the midst of the storm's pouring rain, gazing down into the gaping hole.

CHAPTER 9

SCAR WOKE UP WITH AN aching head and a burning shoulder. He was sitting on the ground with his feet bound up together at the ankles, leaning against a tree. His sword arm—not on the broken side—was tied down to his waist. The last thing he remembered was talking to Rerry, then blinding pain, followed by blackness.

"Oh ho ho, look who has awakened." It was the sprightful voice of Rerry. The part-elven swordsman stood between the shallow stream and the fallen giant. He had Scar's rapier in one hand and the giant's ring in the other. He was tossing the ring in the air and stabbing the sword in and out of the hole. Rerry looked at Scar. "This is the finest steel I've ever held. Enchanted, isn't it?"

Scar let out a muffled groan. A strip of cloth sealed his mouth shut. The cloth tasted awful. He wanted to spit but couldn't.

"Oh, you can't speak just yet," Rerry said, twirling the giant's ring on the blade of the sword with acrobatic ease. "But we'll get to that when you're ready to cooperate."

Scar's eyes beheld the other two elven soldiers from his unit. Both of them were bound up tight and sitting on the ground on the other side of the stream. It was clear they weren't going anywhere. A rustle caught his ear. Samaz emerged from the woodland bank of the stream with a dead soldier in his arms. The husky part-elf gently lowered the corpse to the ground, setting the soldier beside the others. All of the fallen elves were there. All seven of them. Scar's throat tightened. Those were his soldiers. He was responsible for their lives. Though he wasn't close to any of them and he never showed it, he cared.

Rerry squatted before him, sword over his shoulder. "It seems the giant had one last effort in it. Squished you like a fly, it did. A last-ditch effort from the grave." He glanced at the massive humanoid. "It died after that. We overtook your soldiers. Now this is where we stand, Scar. We bury the dead. Then we talk. But we'll need the help of your two remaining soldiers to get it done quickly. My brother and I will need to move on. Without pursuit."

Rerry might have been young, but Scar knew that at the moment, Rerry had the upper hand on him. He nodded.

Removing the gag from his mouth, Rerry said, "Give me your word in Elven."

"On the leaves from the limbs of Elome, I swear it," Scar said. He spat the foul taste from his mouth. "Where did you get this cloth from?"

"It was something I found on the giant."

"Blech!" Scar spat again. "You're no swordsman. You're a trickster." He surveyed their surroundings. "How do you propose we bury them? We did not pursue you with shovels."

"No, but soldiers should always bring a spade, now shouldn't they?"

Scar frowned. Rerry was right about that, but Scar liked to move quick and light, unencumbered. "What do you know about an elven burial? You're barely an elf. Neither is your father. A family of abominations."

"I am what I was intended to be and proud of it. The human blood in me makes me all the person your elven blood makes you. And it doesn't come with all the snobbery. I like the strength and passion it lends." Rerry stood. "Besides, my father Bayzog—the most powerful mage in the world who was gifted the Elderwood Staff from Elome's council of full-blooded elves—has taught us all about the claims and customs of elven kind. The stones of these waters will make for honorable graves."

Rerry had made a good point about his father Bayzog. Still, Scar's orders came from a higher authority, and, being a good soldier, he did not question them. But for the time being, he caved in. "Agreed."

Rerry cut him loose. "Let's get to work then."

Seven graves made from thousands of stones, large and small, were stacked neatly over the fallen elven bodies. The graves lay several yards up from the stream, nestled at the top of the bank where it leveled off in a small, flat spot of wildflowers. Helmets off, the three elven soldiers stood with their heads down, eyes closed. Rerry did the same.

Samaz sang. It was an elven hymn—sad, dreary, and long, but not without hope in it.

They say the winds can speak.

They say the waters play
And trifle in the hearts who love the fallen.
Oh lands of Nalzambor, take them home from whence they came.
*Oh, Rivlenray of Escalay, lead the fallen down the path of the next rising
sun, and beyond.*

Samaz sang verse after verse, and several minutes later, it was over.

"Well done, Samaz." Rerry thumbed a tear from the corner of his eye.
"Well done." He faced Scar. "I think it's high time you told us what's going
on. You imprisoned us, and we hadn't even committed a crime. What's going
on, Scar?"

"I don't answer to you," Scar replied. His shoulders drooped. He shifted
his wounded arm in his sling and grimaced. "I answer to my superiors. I
follow orders."

Standing taller than Scar, Rerry said, "Even when they have broken away
from protocol? No justice. No representatives. Surely in your heart you had
to question that."

"Don't pretend to bluff me, child."

"I'm no child. And what do you mean by bluff? What do I have to bluff
about?"

Fingering the white scar on his chin, Scar replied, "You can't be that
stupid."

Rerry looked at Samaz and found Samaz looking at him with an expression
just as perplexed as he must have been making. He opened his hands up and
said, "What in Nalzambor are you talking about?"

"Laedorn of the High Council is dead. Assassinated, months ago. Nath
Dragon is the killer! All who have ever been connected with him are to be
captured and detained."

"Are you mad?" Rerry said, rising up on his toes. His cheeks warmed.

Even Samaz's jaw dropped. "Nath Dragon didn't kill anybody! Least of
all Laedorn. Only a madman would accuse him of something as ridiculous
as that!"

"There were witnesses," Scar fired back, neck straining. "Dozens. He
shot him with the bow the elves gave him, Akron. And that's not all. He's
accused of killing Uurluuk Mountainstone of the Dwarves as well. Two entire
races are hunting for him. You should consider yourselves lucky the elves
found you before the dwarves did. They'd put you in the belly of a mountain
so deep the world would forget about you."

Rerry shrank away. Scar seemed convinced whatever he was told truly
had happened. Holding his head, he said, "What is going on? This truly is
madness. Samaz?"

Expressionless, his brother shrugged.

"We have not seen Nath Dragon since the end of the war, Scar." Rerry poked the soldier in the chest. "You need to leave us be."

"Then what are you running from?" Scar said.

"Running? We're not running from anything. We seek a cure for our mother, Sasha. She has fallen under the power of the wizard's dementia. It's our quest to find a cure."

Scar's taciturn face softened. "I've heard that's a terrible thing. The elven council will have her brought in too. The same goes for your father. Any allies of Nath Dragon are considered with suspicion."

"Nath has hundreds of allies, if not thousands," Rerry argued. "Are they going to bring them all in?"

"Just those closest to him. You'd be wise to surrender and wait until this all clears up, or..."

"Or what?"

"Or until Nath Dragon is dead."

CHAPTER 10

"THAT WAS SOME FIGHT," BEN said, hours later. The storm had passed and the entire party had moved on from the Temple of Spires. They were all back on the woodland path that had brought them there to begin with. Boots covered in mud, they trudged on.

Chin up, Nath said, "It was, wasn't it?"

Brenwar glanced at his hand and said, "Costly. Mmmm, I've never seen a man fight like that. Not on his own merit. Rybek cheated." He scratched his beard with his skeleton hand. "Evil's never truthful. I think he would have lied to you anyway if you beat him."

"I did beat him," Nath said to Brenwar. "You don't think I won?"

"He was more intact than you when I last saw him," the dwarf said.

"Don't listen to him, Nath," Ben said. The older warrior hobbled along, using a stick for a cane. "You had him. I saw it with my own eyes. I've never seen a sword move so fast. I just wish when you flicked his helmet off, his head was with it."

"Well, he's gone now." Nath shook his head. "And the whereabouts of my father with him."

"I'm sure we'll be able to find your father, Nath," Sasha said to him. Her pretty, bright eyes had a sparkle in them.

Bayzog walked with the aid of his staff in one hand and the fingers of the other locked with hers. With most of his black hair now gray from the battle with the phantom, he looked as old as her. "There's always more than one way to accomplish anything. You'll find him."

"With friends like you, no doubt I will," he said. Sasha's face became sympathetic and distant. "What?"

In a raspy voice, Bayzog said, "Our sons, Nath. They search for a cure for

Sasha. We need to find them. Given the nature of what I've seen and heard, these times are perilous. We must go to them."

"Aye," Brenwar agreed. "You aren't getting any younger. The dirt you tread on has more youth to it than you do."

Violet eyes still filled with endless strength, Bayzog replied, "Well, at least it's not smarter."

"What? Why you rigid little elven trickster. I'm as smart as any elf, particularly in all things dwarven."

"That hardly matters in the grand scheme of things," Bayzog replied.

As everyone bickered back and forth, Nath's thoughts went elsewhere. To his father's whereabouts, and to Selene. It seemed like forever since he'd seen her, and he had no idea about her condition. She'd fallen into a slumber, and there was no telling when she might awaken. And if could happen to her, then it could happen to him. Again.

Nath thumbed the stump of his missing hand.

I want my hand back, but I can't let it happen at such a critical time. I have to find ... I have to help Father.

He turned his attention back to his friends. "I don't think the two of you are equipped to go it alone. With all the wurmers and giants scouring the countryside, it's too big a risk. We should stay together."

Sasha walked over to him, rested her forearms on his shoulders, looked deep into his eyes, and said, "When you have children one day, you'll understand. My sons lost me once, but now they need to know I'm back again." She kissed his cheek. "I have faith in you, Nath. I always have. And I'm oh so grateful to your father for lifting the curse from me. I think I'm doing right by him in going after my sons. Family. It's the most important thing of all."

"I know." He clasped her hands and watched her and Bayzog go. All the wizard did was wave.

"Dragon." Ben the durable warrior stood beside him now. "I'll go with them."

"Ben, you can hardly walk."

Ben opened up his hands, revealing several clear but colorful potion vials. With a devilish grin, he said, "I'll make it." He squeezed Nath's shoulder. "Margo, Tristin, and Justine will kill me if I don't."

Brenwar pushed the chest over to Ben with his boot. "Take this."

"No, I couldn't."

"You'll need it," Brenwar argued.

"Perhaps, perhaps not." Ben's eyes were wide on the chest full of magic. "I'm certain you'll need it as much as we will."

"Nath?" Brenwar said with a perched brow. "Help him make a decision."

Rubbing his chin, Nath gave it more thought. His father had given the chest to Brenwar to help them. But it was to give aid to anyone, not just them. He opened it up and removed several items. He gathered them up into a small sack hidden within his clothes. "There, we have something, that's better than nothing." He closed the lid and handed the chest to Ben. "You and those sorcerers need to make the most of it. And take the horses too."

Ben smiled, then burped a puff of smoke. "Sultans of Sulfur! Did you see that?"

"Yeah, I did. Don't overdo it on the fire-breath potions," Nath said. "They stick with you."

"Will do, Dragon," Ben moved on, horses in tow, after Bayzog and Sasha, who had veered down a steep split in the path. It left Nath, Brenwar, and Laylana with only one another's company.

The dark-haired, green-eyed elven woman dressed in the leather garb of an elven warrior said to him, "If you like, I'll go with them, too."

"You would?"

"Yes. As much as I've enjoyed your company, I find my questions have been answered. You're a good man—dragon—Nath. It's been nothing short of an honor to fight by your side." She gave him a warm embrace and a kiss on the cheek. "I know you were a true friend of my grandfather Laedorn, and that like your eyes, you have a heart of gold. But now my instincts beckon me to return home. And it wouldn't surprise me in the slightest if the elves were still in pursuit of you, Nath. They won't rest until Laedorn's slayer is found. It's best I get some sense of what's going on. There must be clues to who did this. You don't need any other distractions while you look for your father. The world's dangerous enough as it is."

Nath wrapped her up in his arms and lifted her off her feet. He liked Laylana very much and found it difficult to let go. "I'll miss you. Be well." He let her slip out of his arms.

Arms still draped around his neck, her eyes held his with a deeper passion. Slowly, she looked away. "Farewell, Nath." She waved. "Farewell, Brenwar."

With a grunt, Brenwar said, "Uh, goodbye, elf lady."

Moving with the grace of a swan and the strength of a lion in her strides, Laylana vanished down the path the others had taken.

"I guess it's just the two of us versus the world again," Brenwar said.

Nath looked at his missing hand. "What's left of us, anyway."

"Har!" Brenwar showed a fierce smile. "By the time it's over, nothing will be left of us but my beard and those flaming locks of yours."

Nath lowered his satchel over his shoulder. "True, but you know what?"

"What?"

"We're still going to win."

"Now you're talking like a dwarf."

CHAPTER 11

NATH AND BRENWAR MOVED NORTH at a brisk pace.

"I don't think your father should be hard to find."

"Why do you say that?"

"He's too big to hide. Someone or something will have seen him." Brenwar grumbled, "Besides, Balzurth would never get himself into a situation he couldn't handle."

"No, but he's not himself. Not since he cured Sasha. I saw darkness in his eyes when it happened."

"Your father will be fine." Brenwar stroked his beard. "I'm certain of it."

"Of course you are," Nath replied.

There wasn't much else for him to say. Part of him didn't want to help—not because he didn't love his father. He did. But in the back of his mind, Nath kept thinking maybe he should be working on something else. For one thing, he needed to find out who Laedorn and Uurluuk's assassin was. Every elf and dwarf, aside from his friends, thought it was him. There were the titans to worry about, too. He needed to stop them. They and the giants had taken over every town they had passed. The world was a disaster. Evil had it by the throat again.

"Brenwar, what do you think I should do? I'm not even sure I should be looking for him at the moment. You said it yourself: he knows what he's doing. But ... I don't fully believe that in this case."

"We'll find him. Besides, wherever he is, we'll find the heart of the trouble. You're kind of like him in that manner." A pair of deer bounded through the woods right in front of them and vanished into the brush. "See, a good sign."

"Deer crossing one's path is not a good sign. It's just deer crossing a path." Nath took his scabbard filled with Fang from his back and lay it on the ground. He sat down.

Brenwar came to a stop and looked down at him. The dwarf had plenty of recent scuffs and scars to show for himself. A gash in his leg. New dents peppering his breastplate. A wurmer's claw marks in the leather of his tunic arms. "What are you doing on your backside? We need to go."

"Go where?"

Shaking his war hammer, the dwarf said, "To the heart of the fight!"

Nath huffed. "That's a fine idea, except we don't know where the heart of the fight is." He grabbed a pine cone and slung it hard into the woods. "It's hard to fight an enemy we can't find."

"What are you talking about? They're giants. Huge! They aren't hiding. They're out in the wide open. We're the best trackers in the world. How can we not find them?"

"I'm not as much of a tracker as I used to be. Guzan!" Nath held up his missing hand." What am I supposed to do with half of my hand missing? The enemy gets stronger. I get whittled away a hunk at a time."

"You'll get used to it." Brenwar scratched his nose with his skeleton fingers. "Besides, you should be tired of looking like you've never been in a fight before. Heavy scars put the fear in people."

"I know." With a stick, Nath stirred patterns in the ground. His thoughts were heavy. Something inside of him just didn't feel right. "Brenwar, do you ever feel like sometimes I go about things the wrong way?"

"Like how?"

"Well, like fighting. I feel like maybe I'm always doing it the hard way."

"Fighting's not supposed to be easy." Brenwar huffed. "If it was easy, it wouldn't be any fun."

"I just feel like I'm working harder and not smarter. I mean, is the fate of the world only up to a few of us? Shouldn't we have more help? We can't count on the elves and dwarves, because they're hunting us. Leaves us with the humans and halflings. Maybe some gnomes."

"Har!"

"Why just us? There has to be a smarter way to go about things. I like to fight. I love to fight. Not only do I want to fight harder than ever before, but I feel like I need to fight smarter as well. What am I doing wrong?"

Eyeing Mortuun, Brenwar spun the great hammer in his hands. "I've been fighting and feuding in one way or another for hundreds of years, Nath. I've never fought with anybody like you. You have instincts only a few who ever lived had. Trust your instincts. What do they tell you?"

Nath brushed his hair from his eyes. "They tell me I need more help than you and me." He looked at what was left of his missing hand. "Clearly."

"If you need help, then ask for it."

"I can't drag Bayzog and Ben back into this. Did you see them? They looked like a bull dragon chewed them up and spat them out. No, I've asked plenty from them. I've asked plenty from you. I'm tired of seeing my friends hurt."

"You can't protect them always, Nath. They're in this fight too. But they aren't the only friends you have. And you have family, too." Brenwar took a quick look up into the sky. "Lots of family."

Nath lifted his chin. Puffy white clouds with gray at the bottom drifted through the rich blue sky. Flocks of birds crossed his line of sight and disappeared into the great beyond.

I sure miss flying.

"Are you saying I should call for the dragons?"

"No, I was thinking you should call out for the dwarves." Brenwar puffed his moustache out. "Of course I mean the dragons!"

Nath eyed him.

The dwarf's chin dipped. "Sorry, Your Highness."

"It's fine. Any other suggestions?"

"Maybe Fang has some answers. He's a friend as well, is he not?"

Nath ran his fingers over the finely crafted scabbard. The leather over the wood was weathered and soft. He partially drew the weapon. The dragon-headed crossguards were exquisite. Each of the dragon's eyes had perfect little gemstones in them, ruby and emerald. There was a living sparkle on both of them. Only recently had Nath been able to figure out how to call upon the sword's abilities. He'd summoned vibrations, fire, ice, and even teleported Nath forward in time. Sometimes Fang even did as Nath asked, but most of the time he still didn't.

Sword crossed over his lap, Nath held the handle firmly. "What other mysterious powers do you think Fang has?"

Combing his skeleton fingers through his beard, Brenwar suggested, "Why don't you ask him?"

If any friend of Nath's had been neglected, it was Fang. His sword had bailed him out as much as anybody. He slid the magnificent blade all the way from its sheath. The brilliant steel showed like silver. He could see the sky above in the metal. Nath felt a little guilty. Perhaps he should have taken more time getting to know Fang. Training, talking, or something. He said to the blade, "Fang, I'm sorry for any neglect, and I hope you'll forgive me, friend." He gave Brenwar a quick glance and continued. "Fang, will you help me find Father?"

CHAPTER 12

SELENE'S EYES CRACKED OPEN. SHE was in a glorious domed room with wondrous murals of dragons and the lands of Nalzambor filling the walls. Every scene looked real, as if she were standing right there. Stiff limbed, she rolled off the bed of satin pillows in which she lay. She swung her feet onto the floor. The bed was so soft and deep she could barely get out of it.

Where am I?

It was a question she asked herself, but she was certain she knew the answer. She was in Dragon Home—or, to its enemies, the Mountain of Doom. The dizzying display of surrounding artistry left her head a little woozy.

How did I get here?

The last thing she remembered was fighting alongside Nath. For some reason, it felt like a dream or something that had happened ages ago. She pushed herself up to her feet and traversed the mosaic floor. Each tiny tile was painted a different color, but overall it looked like a meadow filled with splendorous wildflowers in a multitude of colors. A breeze came from somewhere, and a gentle melody of music hummed in her ears. The environment was comfortable and soothing. It was clear she had been well cared for. But what had happened? She rubbed her head.

Perhaps something smote me from behind. I must have been blindsided, but I feel fine.

She moved about the room, violet eyes straining to see where the exit might be. It only made sense that whoever had brought her to the chamber would not know of her awakening. Certainly someone would check on her at some point, but she didn't want to wait. She moved toward the nearest painting on heavy feet. Her limbs seemed more cumbersome than normal. She stretched her back and rolled her shoulders.

I feel like I gained two hundred pounds.

She stood in front of one of the murals with her arms outstretched but not touching the wall. It was a painted green forest, with tall trees and a path splitting the middle, leading to a mountain range she recognized from the northeastern part of Nalzambor. She couldn't see one single flaw in the painting. It appeared as real as if it were a window.

Whatever creature painted this is a marvel.

A little uncertain if the mural was real or not, she leaned forward to touch the wall with her fingertip.

It can't be real. Selene, something's missing.

Her breath quickened.

She touched the surface and let out a sigh. She felt the stone under the paint. "Ah, that's better. For a moment I thought I was going to have to pinch myself." Marveling at the extraordinary painting, she continued to run her hands over the surface of painted trees, leaves, and even the dirt path. But something in the scene wasn't right or was missing.

Her gut twisted.

What is out of place here?

She ran her black-scaled fingers over the smooth stone once more. The golden claw of her index finger pecked on the face of a brown squirrel nestled in the branches of one of the trees. It winked at her. Her brow furrowed.

"What in Nalzambor is going..." Her voice trailed out.

Her eyes became big as saucers, fixed on her scaly fingers.

She rotated her palm back and forth.

Her jaw hung.

She lifted her arms and gazed.

Coal-black scales covered her from her fingertips to her elbows and beyond. "Great Guzan!"

She'd transformed, like Nath had. Her arms were sleek and marvelous. There was power in them too. She brought her tail around and draped it over her shoulder. She stroked it with a caressing hand and smiled. "I'm glad you remain. I wonder what else has changed." Her fingers found her face, touching around the eyes, cheeks, and chin. The soft flesh of a human was underneath, but she still wasn't sure. She lifted up her lavender-and-white lace gown, revealing her legs. They had scales on them. Even her abdomen did. Not all over, but mostly. She jumped up. Her feet propelled her so high her head almost hit the sky-painted ceiling.

"Oh, Nalzambor, is this right? Have I become a dragon again?" She tossed her head from side to side. Her jet-black hair was still there. "I need a mirror." She searched the room, but there were only the bed and the murals. On the floor she noted a pond of clear water. It looked so real she swore she would be able to see her reflection in it, but that was impossible. It was just a mosaic. On a hunch, she took a knee and gazed. Her reflection appeared on the surface of the water. She gasped, "Huh!"

Her face was what it had always been as a human. Her high cheeks and pale skin contrasted well with her maroon lips. She was filled with relief—and disappointment. This was nothing quite like having the full power of a dragon, but at least she had more scales—and they were exquisite.

She caught another image appearing behind her in the reflection. She twisted around and gasped. It was Grahleyna, Nath's mother. She was beautiful on beautiful, and in the form of a woman. But scales, gold and white with hints of red, adorned her limbs where they weren't covered in silky robes, like jewelry.

"How do you feel, Selene?"

"Grahleyna," she answered, taking a bow. "I-I don't know exactly. Why am I here?"

Brushing the honey locks of wavy hair aside from her shoulder, Nath's mother replied, "You fell into a dragon's slumber quite some time ago. Do you feel rested?"

"Dragon slumber?" Selene took a seat on the bed and put her face in her hands. "How long have I been asleep? Please don't tell me the world has turned upside down again." She recalled moving forward in time on account of Fang's transportation, and she was aware of the many long slumbers Nath had fallen into in his lifetime. Looking up at the dragon queen, she said, "Please don't say a century, please."

Grahleyna let out a delightful laugh and sat down beside Selene. "No, nothing like that. Weeks, I believe. Months, perhaps. Barely a nap."

Selene let out a sigh. "So, what happened? Why am I here?"

"Nath had Sansla Libor bring you here for your protection. He went through an awful lot to have you rescued."

"Rescued?"

"From the nuurg, a strange sort of giant breed which now plagues the lands." Grahleyna studied her gold fingernails, which Selene now saw were peppered with flecks as white as snow. Nothing was out of place with the dragon queen. She was perfect. "They've run amok, the giants have. How do you like your new scales?"

"So I was kidnapped? Where?"

"Oh, you'll have to have Sansla explain to you. I've been rather busy in the absence of Balzurth. The males of our kind," Grahleyna nudged Selene's shoulder with her shoulder. "They're drawn to danger, and nothing makes them more happy—or miserable—than carrying the world on their shoulders."

"So where is Nath?" Selene asked with a frown. She was concerned about the answer.

"I can't say, Selene. He, like his father, could be anywhere. No doubt they are trying to take down Eckubahn before Eckubahn takes down them." Grahleyna took Selene by the hand and squeezed it. "I'm worried about both of them. Right now, it's taking everything I have to stay here and keep Dragon Home safe. Our kind are restless without Balzurth in his home. And as much as I hate to admit it, they don't mind me the same as they mind him." Her beautiful face, which had a dragon-like quality about it, frowned. "And I feel there is something very, very wrong."

Selene patted Grahleyna's hand. "I can help, can't I?"

With a nod, the dragon queen said, "You couldn't have woken up at a better time. Come." Grahleyna led her to a mural shaped like a stone tunnel going into a mountain. They passed right through the opening and walked up a spiraling walkway illuminated by the torches painted on the cavern walls. They walked for miles, maybe leagues, until they arrived at the top of Dragon Home. A stiff wind tore through both women's long locks as they stood just beneath the clouds.

"It's quite a view, isn't it?"

The top of Dragon Home was the highest point in all of Nalzambor. The view was crystal clear, and whether it was from her own power or something radiating from the rock on which she stood, Selene could see for miles, leagues even. Her eyes were more open then they'd ever been before.

Grahleyna pointed north. "What do you see?"

Over a league away were giants by the hundreds. With huge axes, they chopped down trees. There was fire. Great fires in the middle of a camp made up of the giants. Huge rocks made for the bellowing of forges and furnaces. There, they made tremendous weapons of iron and steel. And there were men, like toddlers among them, following their every command. Giants by the hundreds, orcs and men by the thousands. In the distant hilltops she could see more were coming. An army building like Selene had never seen.

"What are they doing?" she asked.

"They are preparing for an invasion," Grahleyna replied.

"Where?"

"Here."

CHAPTER 13

BRENWAR'S HEAD COCKED FROM SIDE to side like an old hawk's. "Well, is Fang coming to our aid or not?"

Nath shrugged. He'd run through an entire list of commands with Fang. He'd barked out orders, and then he'd asked politely.

"Fang, take me to Balzurth."

"Fang, please take me to Balzurth."

Nath tried many other phrases.

"Fang, bring fire. Summon rain. Lightning. Ice!"

Holding the sword over his head, he said, "By the power of Balzurth!"

The blade did not charge up in his hand. Its metal and pommel remained lukewarm to his commands and promptings.

Leaning on his hammer, Brenwar said, "You know, when I command the thunder of Mortuun, I never have any trouble." He patted the war hammer's fat head. "He does exactly as I say."

Nath held his great blade in his arms and flipped it around. "Well, I guess those powers only unleash when they are needed. Truly needed. In the meantime, Fang is still the finest sword ever made." He flashed a smile. "And you know what, he's always been there for me whenever I've really needed him. Maybe he doesn't turn it loose until the danger is truly imminent. Perhaps he's wiser than I and preserves his power."

"Perhaps." Brenwar hefted Mortuun over both of his shoulders and rested his hands on the ends. "Can we start walking now? All of this standing around feels a little silly. We need to move, whether it's an inch or a mile. That's progress."

"I suppose so." Nath took the lead. "North it is, then. We'll just have to do what we normally do and find more clues along the way."

"Aye. That's the way I like it."

They walked for the better part of the day. Storm clouds rumbled overhead. Light drops of rain splatted off Nath's scales. He carried Fang in his arms like a small child, talking to the blade from time to time, trying to connect. Fang was like a brother in some ways. Not a servant but family. His father had often said, "Take care of the little things, and then you can be trusted with true riches." Perhaps Nath hadn't cared for the blade as he should.

"We are nearing some towns. We might need to get some supplies and horses," Brenwar said. "What do you say?"

"One horse should do. I don't mind running." He took out a cloth he had and started rubbing it over the blade. "I don't know if this feels good or not, Fang, but I hope you like it. I never saw the need to clean a blade which always shines and never nicks, but that's no reason not to give you the care any other fine sword would get."

Brenwar held Mortuun out before himself and said to it, "You like the dirt, don't you. Heh-heh." He head butted the flat of his hammer. "I like the dirt, and busted-up orcs and giants, too."

A couple of miles later, they crested a hill and surveyed the town resting on a flat plain between the steep hillsides. Night was falling on the small wood-framed homes and stone buildings. Men and women were finishing up their day and gathering the children inside. Firelight could be seen through the windows.

On one knee, Brenwar said, "I can't help but be suspicious." He took a deep draw through his nose. "Should I go, or should you go?"

Nath gave a little shrug. He never would have had the slightest trepidation going into any town of any kind before. That had changed. Now, he couldn't go anywhere without some sort of suspicion. He had enemies of all sorts, and no one could be trusted. It was a sad time. A dark time. "Probably not the best time to go in there. Not in the dark of night. We could wait it out until morning... or just keep moving."

"Eh, I'm fine walking. I wouldn't mind a bite to eat though. Can't remember the last time I ate as a matter of fact." Brenwar pounded his armor over his stomach. "It's hard to admit that."

"You must be hungry then. I've never heard you mention it before."

"All the fighting works up the ol' dwarven appetite. I miss the feasts that used to come at the end of the battle." Brenwar peeled a piece of bark from a tree and chewed on the end. "Not bad. Could use some salt and pepper."

Nath couldn't help but chuckle. "You'd eat dirt if it would fill you."

"I'll have plenty of dirt to eat in the grave."

"Brenwar, I'm pretty sure I can rustle up some game. We can cook it on an open fire. We're pretty far away, so I don't think anyone will take notice."

He tipped his chin at the town down in the valley. "Or I can scurry down there and get some eggs from the chickens. Just like a weasel. It'd be stealing, but we are pretty hungry."

"Dwarves don't steal. Dragons shouldn't either."

"True, but I could leave some coin. More than enough."

Brenwar's dark eyes were fixed on the village. His lips twitched. With an eyebrow perched, he said, "Nath, I'm tired of hiding. Let's just go down there and ask. They can't all be bad." He sniffed. "Besides, something good is cooking."

Nath got up on his feet, patted his belly, and said with a smile, "Well, I have to admit, I like your direct approach. Let's follow your nose."

Brenwar led. He ambled down the hill right into the very heart of the small town. No more than a couple hundred people could have lived there. The barns were small and the livestock few. Smoke puffed out several of the small chimneys, and the smell of baked bread and hot stew lingered in the air.

Nath's mouth watered. He didn't admit it, but he was just as hungry as Brenwar. He wasn't going to mention it. He still couldn't believe Brenwar had.

He had better not be going soft on me.

Many of the small, gabled houses had empty porch fronts, aside from one, where three men were standing outside, talking and smoking their pipes. The talking came to a stop as soon as Nath and Brenwar crossed their line of sight. Nath's keen ears picked up one man's whisper to another, "Fetch the magistrate."

A lanky figure scurried across the street and vanished into the shadows. It left the remaining two men on the porch all alone to face Nath and Brenwar.

"Let me do the talking," Nath said softly to Brenwar.

"Aye."

CHAPTER
14

RERRY AND SAMAZ WERE FACED with a difficult decision. What to do with Scar and his men? The choice was simple: knock them out and leave them or bring them along. Bringing them along would only slow their pace. Letting them go would bring more elves in pursuit. It was a no-win situation, but in the end, Rerry and Samaz took the elves as their captives.

Once his hands and his soldiers' hands were secured behind their backs, Scar said, "You two don't know what you're doing, do you. Have you even taken anyone prisoner before? I venture to say no."

"Just because you haven't done something before doesn't mean you aren't any good at it." Rerry kept Scar's own sword lowered on the elf's back. "Just keep walking and stop talking."

"It might help if you mentioned where we were going," Scar fired back. "And remember, you're going to need to feed us."

"Feed you!" Rerry said. "You left us to starve to death in that dungeon back there."

"Orders are orders."

"I've got an order for you." Rerry sliced the rapier through a branch, cutting the limb clean. "Mind your tongue or lose it."

Scar started laughing. "You're a child. You wouldn't hurt anybody."

Rerry lifted his arm to strike the elf in the back of the head.

"Rerry!" Samaz said.

"What?"

"Are you planning on dragging him through the woods? Leave him be. He's just trying to be annoying." Samaz had the other two elven soldiers at sword point.

"He doesn't have to try," Rerry replied. "He just is."

Scar let out another chuckle. His voice wasn't as elegant as those of most elves. He was gruff. "Fine, boys. I'll cooperate. But it wouldn't hurt to mention where we're going." He eyed the sky. "South is good. South is Elome in the furthest, but I can't imagine why you'd be going there."

"It's not your concern where we're going." Rerry shoved the soldier forward.

Scar stumbled onto a knee. Slowly, he got back up again.

A pair of hummingbirds with bright green feathers zipped by Rerry's face and into the trees. "That was strange."

"That's a bad sign," Scar said.

"You're a bad sign." Rerry shoved the man in the back again. "And quit buying time by falling down. You're an elf. Elves don't trip, especially not in the woods. A deer would trip before we did."

"As you say." Scar moved on, head down, stepping up his pace.

Rerry didn't mind the faster pace. Behind him, Samaz and the other soldiers weren't having any trouble keeping up. They weaved their way through the forest, dodging the trees and ducking the branches. In all truth, Rerry wasn't entirely sure what he was doing. He wasn't equipped to handle this situation. It was encumbering. Beyond encumbering.

What have I gotten us into?

He got a closer look at Scar's backside. The man's hands were tied behind his back with elven twine. The soldier's palms were showing swordsman's callouses thicker than Rerry's. He felt his own. His callouses were small bumps by comparison. Scar's hands were rough as cowhide, his muscles thick in the arms and shoulders, a bit more so than a typical elf's. Scar moved with purpose and determination, but there was still the graceful ease of a fencer in his step. Rerry couldn't help but feel he wasn't in control. Scar still was, somehow.

I need to be careful. An enemy never shows his true intent until it's too late.

They made it a few more miles, but then as they crossed through a thicket-filled gulch, the briars jabbed into their knees.

Scar spoke up again. "You know, it would be best if you remembered the farther south we go, the more likely it is we'll run into elves. If they come upon us as your prisoners, it won't go well for you." Scar's neck craned. His eyes were fixed in the trees. "It'll be too late once you run into them. It's best you turn yourselves over. As a matter of fact, I'll even take you to Elome rather than back to the dungeon." He walked around a low-hanging branch and turned around so he was walking backward, facing them. "I'll be truthful. You'll get better treatment there in Elome than you did back in the hole where I had you."

"I'll be making the decisions, thank you."

Scar stopped, shaking his head slowly from side to side. "Boy, you don't know what you're doing."

"Keep moving." Rerry still had the rapier out, keeping Scar an arm and sword length away. Something crawled up his spine. He kept his eyes fixed on the elf. "I'm not playing games with you, Scar. Move."

"You aren't going to harm me. You aren't going to harm my soldiers, either. You're incapable." Scar pursed his lips and let out a sharp whistle.

The two elven soldiers exploded into motion. Hands still tied behind their backs, they hopped up, bringing their knees to their chests and slipping their hands under their feet so that they were in front of them. Heads low, they bolted into the woods.

"Samaz!" Rerry's head twisted back and forth between his brother and Scar. "Go after them!"

Samaz gave chase, but it was clear to Rerry his brother would never catch the leaner and quicker elves. Samaz wasn't slow for a man, but he was for an elf.

"Ha ha ha!" Scar belted out a wicked laugh. "You'll never catch them. At least not your brother. They're gone. Long gone. It's only a matter of time before they bring more after you, foolish boys."

"Well, we still have you." Rerry's confident voice was now shaken.

"You don't sound so sure of yourself, Rerry." Scar walked right up to him and stared him in the eye with the sword right on his chest. "Make me march somewhere now, child."

"Don't tempt me, Scar. I might not kill you, but I won't hesitate to maim you if you try to escape."

Brows high, Scar said, "Really? Like your brother did? Do it."

Rerry swallowed. Sweat rolled from his hairline into his eyes. The salty sweat stung. He blinked.

Scar struck. A leg sweep took Rerry from his feet and landed him flat on the ground. Before he could bounce back up, Scar's boot collided with his ribs—once, twice, three times.

He curled up and groaned.

That did not just happen!

Rerry sat up just in time to see Scar standing a bit away under a tree with his rapier back in his hand. How Scar had slipped his bonds Rerry would never know.

With a grunt, the rugged elven soldier banged his shoulder into the tree, making a nasty *pop*. Pain filled his eyes, but it was quickly replaced with victory. "My shoulder was out of joint, not broken. Your bindings were weak. Your mind is as slow as a human's." Scar walked up and lorded over Rerry with his rapier. "Tell me, Rerry, who's in command now?"

CHAPTER
15

A MAN STEPPED OFF THE PORCH with a curled wooden pipe in his hand. He was a rangy fellow, tall, with the broad shoulders of a farmer or a smith. He gave Nath a double take, looking up a little in his eyes and stepped back on the porch, meeting him at eye level again.

"Good evening, travelers." Broad faced and fish eyed, he broke out in a sweat. "Pardon my directness, but what do you seek?"

"I apologize for the late intrusion, but we only seek to purchase some food and maybe a horse, and we'll be on our way." Nath smiled. "It certainly wasn't our intention to cause a stir, and we hope we don't."

The rocking chair groaned as the other man on the porch shrank back in his seat. His fingers fidgeted with the chair's arms, and he kept looking up at his friend and Nath's sword.

The man with the pipe then said, "We don't have much means these days." He let out a stream of smoke and sucked on the end of his pipe. "It's hard enough to feed ourselves. The crops aren't what they used to be." Sweat dripped down the side of the man's cheek. "And truly, as much as we'd like to help out, we have a standard here where we take care of our own."

Brenwar shifted on his feet. His mouth opened and shut twice before he finally spoke. "You're telling me you can't use any coin? Coin can buy you more food. Our offer will be generous."

Looking down at Brenwar, the man said, "We can't spare it."

Brenwar stiffened. His fists balled up.

Nath wedged himself between the dwarf and the man with a polite nod. "We'll be moving on then."

With an air about him, the man said, "I think that's for the better. As you say, you don't want to create a stir. And folks are pretty jumpy around here." He let out another stream of smoke. "We bid you safe travels." He pointed at a pair of buildings, the rising moon visible between the two and added, "That avenue makes for the most discreet exit."

Nath nodded, and with Brenwar at his side, headed down the alley.

"People aren't very friendly these days," Brenwar said under his breath.

"Or honest either," Nath replied. "They do have food to spare, and I've never seen small places like this turn away anyone in need. Something's going on."

"We, I might be hungry enough to eat a four-tusked boar, but I'll live."

"Me too." Nath took a look over his shoulder. The men from the porch had gathered around another figure who was little different than the rest of them—aside from a broadsword hung from his hip. He assumed it was the magistrate they'd sent for. All of their eyes followed him and Brenwar as the men argued in hushed voices. "It seems we caused a stir after all, didn't we."

"Aye."

He and Brenwar passed between the buildings into where the open fields awaited. Nath pulled Brenwar aside, and the pair of them paused with their backs to one of the buildings. Under his breath, Nath said, "Let's give it a moment and see what happens."

Brenwar nodded.

Nath had a couple of concerns. As harmless as the simpler people of the country could often be, it didn't always take much for them to get riled up and do something stupid. Second, given the nature of Nath's enemies, there was no telling whether or not his enemies were among them. It wouldn't surprise him a bit of a giant, a nuurg, or a flock of wurmers exploded out of one of the storehouses at any moment. It wouldn't be the first time.

A drizzling rain began, dulling the sounds around them. Head tilted, Nath tried to make out what the men were saying. It wasn't easy, given the vast distance between them and their use of lowered voices, but he could tell they were still arguing. It must have gone on for at least ten minutes before it came to a stop. There were some murmurings and the scrape of boots on the wooden porch and the faint creaking sound of a door opening and closing.

Nath peeked around the corner. The men on the porch were gone.

"Seems they've had enough excitement for one night," Nath said under his breath. He eased away from the wall. "No eggs and biscuits tonight. I guess we're going to have to head back to the woods and rustle up some possum."

Shoulders slumped, Brenwar started his trek back into the woods. "Eating from a table is soft, anyway."

A scuffle of dirt caught Nath's ear. He grabbed Brenwar by the elbow and pulled him back into the shadows.

Someone on light feet was making his way down the alley. A man emerged from the alley and into the open plain. His eyes were forward, scanning the outline of the forest. He wore a cloak over his shoulders and held a broadsword at the ready. He moved well, with the technical craft of a seasoned soldier. He turned from side to side. Something dangled from his neck. It was metal, a whistle or something.

That must be the magistrate.

Staying low, ready to spring, the magistrate started toward the forest on soft feet.

Out of nowhere, Brenwar's stomach rumbled like rolling thunder.

The magistrate whipped around. His eyes locked on Nath and Brenwar. He grabbed the whistle and put it to his mouth.

CHAPTER 16

RERRY, *GET UP!*

But Scar said, "Stay put, fledgling."

Rerry rested back on his elbows. "I underestimated you."

"Oh, that's an understatement." Scar tossed the elven rope to Rerry. "Now we get to see how well you fare on an ever-so-long march back to Elome. No food. No water. Just one long stiff march with a needle at your back."

Rerry's chin fell to his chest. After all that hard work, he was right back where he'd started. A captive. A failure. He wanted to scream. He picked up the rope and said, "So what do you want me to do, bind myself?"

"No, save it for when your brother returns at the hands of my men. They'll have him wrapped up in no time, I'm certain." Scar admired his sword. "It really is a fine piece of weaponry, and yes, it is enchanted. All of the captains of the guard receive blessed weapons when they survive the test and make the rank. I even helped to forge it myself. Me, the smith, and a pair of lovely elven enchantresses." His fingers caressed the blade's edge. "I don't think I could live with myself if I ever lost it. And the thought of your kind even touching it makes me want to wash it." His face soured.

"What is your problem with me? I may not be a full-bred elf, but you act like I'm an orc!"

Without looking at Rerry, Scar cut the blade through the air a few times. "You might be."

Rerry's lips tightened. He glared at Scar. The elves were possibly the most sophisticated race in Nalzambor, but their snobbery was often overbearing. He and Samaz hadn't done anything wrong, and his parents hadn't either, aside from love each other. His eyes found the sword Samaz had been carrying. His brother had dropped it before he went to pursue the other elves.

Every little bit makes him faster, and he doesn't know how to use a sword anyway.

Scar caught him looking at the sword and said with a confident air, "Go ahead. You say you're a swordsman, pick it up."

"Why, so you can try to kill me?"

"Oh, there won't be any 'try' in it. If I want to kill you, I will. But that's not my plan. I was just planning to teach you a few lessons." Scar flexed the rapier behind his shoulders. The steel bent a little between his hands. "This blade won't break. It's like a living thing in my hands."

Rerry crawled over to the sword on the ground but didn't pick it up. He considered himself a fine swordsman, but the truth was he was self-instructed for the most part, though he had spent some time with the legionnaires. "You sound like someone who relies on his sword more than he does his own skill."

"Oh, it took ample skill and the sword to kill a giant with one blow. Just imagine what I could do to you."

Rerry picked the elven longsword up and stood.

Scar's green eye brightened. The patch over his left eye darkened. "You really do have the fire of a fool in you, don't you."

Eyeing the man's patch, Rerry said, "And you have a blind spot."

Scar lifted up his eye patch, revealing a solid milky white eye. "Do you know what blinded me, boy?"

"I couldn't care less." Rerry tested the heft of the longsword. The fine elven steel was well balanced, but it was still heavier than the rapier Scar carried. "So, are we going to spar or not?"

Scar flipped his eye patch away. It left his appearance unsettling. Menacing. "A blade caught me, in a sparring match such as this. They told me my career as a soldier was over. They washed me out of the ranks. But I practiced and practiced and practiced until I overcame my disadvantage. I climbed back up the ranks." He flicked the blade around in a twirl of blinking light. "I defeated my own master."

Rerry swallowed. There was truth in Scar's words. He didn't doubt a single syllable. Rerry was the bigger of the two, looking down at the smaller elven man whose presence yet seemed as big as his own. A sparring match seemed impractical, but his pride wanted to take a shot at the cocky elven captain.

Just one mark. I'll give him a scar he'll remember.

"I tell you what, Scar, let's fight for blood. If I nick you three times, you have to leave us be."

Scar huffed. "I can't do that. An elf releasing a prisoner? Shame myself? If I lose you, I have to suffer the fate they had in store for you, and I'd rather not know what it is."

"You sound like you fear you might lose."

"Hardly. I'm just giving you an education. I should have known it wouldn't have been a custom you were aware of, seeing how horrible a captor you are."

"Well, if I win, you can be my indentured servant. At least then you could be on the right side of things."

"I'm on the right side when I follow orders." Scar eyed his sword's keen edge. "And what are you offering me when you lose? Oh, that's right, you have nothing to offer. But maybe, just maybe, you could give me one of those eyes of yours."

"That's just sick."

"That's life with an edge. So, do you want to spar, surrender, or just fight? The truth is, Rerry, your only chance to escape and help your mother is to beat me. What are you willing to lose to save your mother?"

Rerry readied his sword. "Everything."

"It sounds like we have a fight then." Scar's feet twisted in the dirt. He lowered himself into a swordsman's stance and waved Rerry over. "Let the steel dance."

Rerry rushed in swinging. He delivered hard, fast blows.

Scar parried and shifted. Metal smacked on metal. Scar batted Rerry's sword from his hand and cut his forearm open.

Rerry jumped away, holding his bleeding arm.

"It was a fine attack. Fast. Powerful." Scar took out a cloth and wiped the blood from his sword. "But you lack refinement. Finesse." With the tip of his rapier, he flipped the fallen longsword up into Rerry's hands by its crossguard. "This time, don't try to kill me. Just use what you know and fight."

Grimacing and with a flutter in his ear, Rerry poised his sword. Staring Scar right in the elf's bad eye, he said, "So be it then."

CHAPTER 17

"T HAT'S AN AWFUL LOT OF giants," Selene said to Grahleyna. "And the wurmers. Their numbers will only grow. You need to strike fast if you're going to strike at all. Scatter those forces before their numbers become even stronger."

"No army has ever penetrated Dragon Home. No army ever will."

"I don't mean any disrespect," Selene said. "But have the dragons ever had to fend off an army so big?"

"Selene, we'll stay on the defensive and seal all the entrances. But I'm not going to send the dragons out to attack. Not without Balzurth or Nath." Grahleyna stood out on the very edge of the mountain. The wind tore at her elegant robes. Hair streaming in the wind, she said, "I'm not willing to risk the dragons in a fight right now. Not if I don't have to. Balzurth is King. Nath is the prince. The battle is up to them. But in their stead, I'll certainly do what must be done in defense. Between now and then, I need you to find them."

"I'd be glad to track them down, but the search would go quicker with wings beneath me."

"Getting out of here will be easier without them." Grahleyna's eyes scanned the horizon.

Wurmers flocked through the air like birds. Selene couldn't count them by the hundreds. The insect-like dragons made an evil humming sound, swarming like locusts. They weren't the biggest dragons—only the size of large dogs or small horses—but there were so many it didn't matter.

"Couldn't you send dragons out to search?"

"I could send a flight of dragons out and hope some of them squeezed through the ranks of those foul things, but I've made my decision. No dragons are going out. There are some in Dragon Home, Selene, but not many. I have to wait things out. It won't be easy."

Selene found it hard to breathe. A dreadful feeling overcame her. Her failures haunted her. She was part of the reason the wurmers thrived, and she hadn't yet figured out how to stop them. A strong part of her wanted to resume that quest. "If the dragons can't leave, how am I supposed to get out of here?"

"There are other methods." Grahleyna turned.

Something caught Selene's eye: a flock of small dragons whose wings beat with rapid fury. "Oh my!"

They were young crimson dynamos, cinnamon scaled and very deadly. The three of them formed a wedge. The one in the rear fought to keep up, with its damaged wing. The dragons must have slipped through the wurmer ranks undetected.

But the wurmers caught the burst of wings and scales beating through the sky. A sea of the evil creatures let out a shrill sound, splitting the air. They gave pursuit. And closed in fast.

Crimson dynamo dragons were not known for their speed. They were a breed strong in power. And this group was young.

"Come to me, brothers and sisters, come to me!" Grahleyna cried out. Her body shimmered. She was transforming into her dragon self.

Selene caught her by the arm. "No, you can't go out there. It's just what they want. We can't lose you, Grahleyna."

In a voice wroth with anger, Grahleyna yelled at Selene, "Unhand me!" With eyes like fire, she jerked her arm away. Wings sprouted from her back.

But Selene knew it was too late. Just as she lifted her gaze into the distance, the wurmers caught up with the young crimson dragons. Swarmed the three of them. Claws and teeth flashed. Fire exploded in the sky. Wurmers crackled and sizzled, but not enough of them. The fires of the young dynamos faded. The wurmers latched onto them and tore them to shreds.

Grahleyna screamed, "Noooooooooooooooooooo!"

Selene held her back by the waist. It was difficult.

Suddenly the sky darkened. Wurmers were everywhere, blanketing the sky like clouds.

"We must get back inside!" Selene felt Grahleyna sag in her arms.

The three young dynamos' broken bodies hung from the jaws of the wurmers, which flew away in triumph and dropped the dead dragons into the waiting arms of the giants.

Above, the wurmers circled in a taunting formation, hundreds of them all at once. The hum they made was deafening.

"We must go inside, Grahleyna, we must!" Selene urged. "Come. They need you inside."

Wurmers landed on the peaks of Dragon Home.

Selene's own blood stirred. An enemy dragon landing on the peaks of Dragon Home was like an orc planting an orcen flag in Morgdon. She was appalled. Finally leading the reluctant Grahleyna back inside, she said, "We're going to end them, my queen. We're going to end them!"

But how?

CHAPTER 18

NATH SMACKED THE WHISTLE AWAY from the man's lips before he had time to blow. The metal whistle spun around the man's neck and whacked him in the side of the head.

"Ow!" The man reached up to rub his temple.

Brenwar knocked the man down to his knees and put him in a chokehold. "Urk!"

Nath peeled the man's sword from his fingers. Seeing the man's eyes bulge from their sockets, Nath said to Brenwar, "Ease off a bit. Let's at least question the assassin."

Brenwar let off just enough so the magistrate could manage to speak.

He sucked for air and said, "I'm not an assassin. I'm here to help."

Holding the man's own sword up, Nath flicked the metal with his claw.

Ting.

"With this?"

"I'm a legionnaire. What did you expect? I'm not going out into the dark unable to defend myself." The magistrate coughed. His sagging jaws shook from the effort. "Please, let me breathe some more. At my age, breathing's hard enough as it is."

Nath took a careful look at the man. His wavy hair was grey, his muscles were softer than a legionnaire's, and his wrinkly skin had age spots all over. He must have been sixty, maybe older. But Nath could tell he used to be iron strong. He gave Brenwar a nod.

The dwarf released the magistrate.

He fell onto his hands and knees, wheezing. "Sorry, I'm trying to keep it quiet. I guess I should have known better than to try and sneak up on the likes of you two." He looked up into Nath's face. "My, it really is you."

"Pardon me?"

The man's focus shifted between Nath and Brenwar. Hands up, he said, "Nath Dragon and Brenwar Bolderguild. In my town." His voice rose. He covered his mouth. "Sorry, I need to keep it down. Too many light sleepers around here." He extended his hand. "It's an honor."

Nath shook the man's hand.

Many of the man's fingers were missing, but he still had a strong grip and shook vigorously.

Nath asked, "You know us?"

"Well, we've never met before, but you'd be hard to miss given the description. The hair and eyes alone are a dead giveaway, even in the dimness. Both of you. The rest wouldn't know it so much, but I do. I've been around."

"You say you're a legionnaire?" Nath said.

"I am." He pointed at his sword.

Nath noted the eagle image crafted into the pommel. He handed it to the man. "A fine piece of steel."

"It served me well against the throngs of Barnabus, but my steel's not as quick as it used to be. And my joints burn like fire if I move too fast—and when it rains." He wiped the rain from his face. "I'm Timothy. Call me Tim." He shook hands with Brenwar. "Gah! What happened to your fingers?"

"I got hungry."

Tim looked at Nath with bewilderment.

Nath said, "It's a long story, Tim. Now, you say you came to warn us about something."

Tearing his glance from Brenwar's skeleton hand, Tim said, "That fellow you talked to on the porch, that's Malden. He's a rat. I tried to talk him out of doing what he's about to do, but it won't stick."

"What's he going to do?" Brenwar grumbled.

"The nuurg oversee this town and many like it. They have quarters a few miles away. It's a sad situation, but we survive by feeding them." Tim sheathed his sword with a click. "Well, a fair part of this town worships them. They turn my stomach. It's as if people's minds are turned inside out. Well, the nuurg demand that if any stranger passes through, we let them know about it. I tried to convince Malden to let you be. We have plenty of people pass who are hungry. He agreed, but he's a liar. He'll slip out of here at first light, if not tonight."

Tim peeked down the alley between the plank wood buildings. "He doesn't like me much. He was magistrate before I was, until the people spoke. You can bet your boots he'll have those giant fiends on their giant horses riding after you in no time." He rubbed his eyes. "And I thought I'd seen all there was to see in the war on Barnabus. Now we have giant orcs. Giant trolls. Giant ogres. Giant everything."

"Thanks, Tim," said Nath. It was good to know the good people could still conquer their fears and do the right thing. Tim, an old soldier, was bound by that. Whether he was still a soldier or not, he had a sense of duty, the duty to take care of his people. It was clear Tim was ever willing to risk his life to do that. "Tim, have you heard the saying 'Sometimes the greatest battles are won from the smallest victories'?"

"Wars are won one battle at a time." Tim's eyes gleamed. "What are you getting at?"

"I think it's time for the nuurg to have a little surprise."

"Really? There's an awful lot of them."

"How many?" Brenwar asked.

"Ten nearby. They scour the towns in pairs." Tim took a breath. "Boy, my blood's churning. I'm ready to stick it to them."

"I don't want your departure to rouse suspicion. Just tell us where they are." Nath patted Tim's shoulder. "We'll do the rest."

"But I can help."

"You could really help by grabbing us some food," Brenwar said. "I can't sneak through the woods with my belly growling."

"That wasn't a growl I heard, more like a roar." Tim shrugged. "I'll do it."

Somewhere in the town, a horse whinnied.

"Did you hear that?" said Nath.

"I did. Come on." Tim led them toward the eastern face of the town and huddled behind the split fence of a barn. The man, Malden, led a horse out of one of the stables and outside. Once he got out of earshot, he mounted the horse and trotted away. "Yep. Malden the overgrown rattle snake is going to report to the nuurg."

"How long will it take them to get here?"

"As fast as those big monsters move? They'll be here in an hour, and you'll hear them coming a mile away."

"Good," Brenwar said, "That gives us plenty of time to eat then." He patted his belly and said to Tim. "Now go fetch food."

CHAPTER 19

I T WAS A HEATED SPAR. Rerry attacked, blocked, shifted, and foot
shuffled. Sweat dripped down his face and stung his eyes. He labored
for breath.

"Chin up! Shoulders back! Eyes on me!" Scar the master swordsman
picked his way through Rerry's defense and tore the longsword from the
part-elf's hands. He put his blade right at Rerry's throat. "I thought you said
you were good."

With the blade nicking his skin, Rerry lifted his chin high. "I'm just
getting warmed up."

"I can't help but say I'm shocked you made it this far in your journey."
Scar backed away. "You aren't horrible. You have the same skill level as many
of my students. Given a hundred years of practice, you might be half as good
as me. Oh, but you won't live that long, will you. As a matter of fact, you
might not even live through the day. You're bleeding everywhere."

Rerry touched his neck. Blood smeared his fingers, making things look
worse than they were. But his forearm was pretty bad and needed treatment.
Shoulders drooping, he bent over and picked up his sword.

Everyone has a weakness, Rerry. Find his.

"Oh, so you don't want to surrender. I almost admire that." Scar twisted
his torso from side to side and made a couple of thigh lunges. "I think I'm
now warmed up. Let's let the new lesson begin."

I'm not bad. I'm not bad.

Rerry had always been confident that he was a fine swordsman. He'd been
practicing since he was old enough to hold a blade. But Scar was hundreds
of years old. His sword arm was like a living piece of iron. Rerry had never
encountered anyone so masterful.

But he had to beat the master or be imprisoned, and deep inside him there was fear. He might not see his mother again. He might not see anyone again. He pulled his shoulders back, set his stance, and caught his breath. "This time, you attack me."

Scar almost smiled. A deadly delight showed in his good eye. "So, you want to test your defense. So be it then." Scar shuffle stepped but then stopped.

Samaz appeared out of the woods. He had both of the elven guards who had escaped slung over his brawny shoulders. The elves were out cold.

"What is this?" Scar was gaping. He shifted his focus onto Samaz.

Rerry couldn't believe his eyes. Somehow, his weak brother had impossibly managed to roust out two formidable elves on his own. He made a silly smile. "By the trees, Samaz, how did you pull that off?"

Samaz set the unconscious elves down. "I have skills."

"Clearly you have more than your brother." Scar's eyes slid back and forth between the two. "Don't get any clever ideas. Both of you are still my prisoners. Alive, barely alive, or dead, I'll have you both." He gave Samaz a once over. "Back away, rotund one. Your brother and I have business."

Hands on his knees, Samaz asked, "What sort of business?"

"Assuming he doesn't bleed to death first, after I beat him into submission, he's going to surrender."

Samaz wrinkled his brow and looked to Rerry, "Is this true?"

With a little shrug, Rerry said, "I don't have much of a choice."

Watching the blood drip from Rerry's arm, Samaz said, "You can beat him." He sat down on the ground and crossed his legs. With a nod at Scar, he said, "Do it, Rerry."

"Your brother believes in you. Both of you are lacking in judgment. So, shall we resume the bout?"

With a nod, Rerry readied his stance again. "Come on, Scar. Attack me."

Scar didn't hesitate. He jabbed right at Rerry. The tip of his blade was on a course to impale Rerry's eyeball.

Rerry's instinct, more than skill, deflected the blow. For the next several seconds, he fought for his life.

Scar came at him, hard and fast.

If the elven guard was holding back, Rerry couldn't tell. Every blow he parried was a finger's breadth from cutting him open. He must have beaten ten solid whacks off with his own blade. His arm was like lead.

Though in actuality smaller, Scar's tireless arm was as strong as a warrior's twice his own size, and the elf's rapier struck quickly but heavily.

Rerry's lungs soon burned again.

"I admit, your defense is much better than your offense. Good for you."

Scar broke off his attack and took a breath. "Whew. I'm actually enjoying this. It's been a while since I had a half-decent workout."

Rerry wanted to reply but didn't have the breath in him. He actually did feel a little good about himself. He was learning from Scar. He could now anticipate the elven guard's attacks. A dip in the shoulder. A shuffle to the side. A twist in the neck. All of them were signs of the next attack. The problem was, he didn't have any energy left to keep up. He looked at his forearm. His sleeve was blood soaked and still dripping. Nearby, his brother sat on the ground with his eyes closed, head lifted toward the sky. He looked so peaceful.

Samaz, you are so strange!

"So, are you going to surrender now, or do you want to see if you have a few decent strokes left in you?" Scar swished his rapier through the air. "I can do this until the rooster crows."

The wind picked up, rustling the leaves and cooling Rerry's body. It somehow rejuvenated him. He received a charge of power he didn't understand. His heavy breathing eased. Strength returned to his weary arms. His blood coursed through his body.

I feel wonderful!

Rerry's thoughts were clear. He focused on Scar, and with a wave of his fingers, he beckoned the soldier forward.

"It seems someone has gotten a second wind. Well, it won't last long." Scar attacked.

Steel collided with steel. The fine elven blades danced like metal snakes.

Scar attacked. Rerry parried. The exchanges went back and forth for a few more seconds.

And then without warning, Rerry counterattacked. He deflected Scar's attack and twisted his sword down and under Scar's defenses and cut through the chest of the soldier's black leather armor.

Scar gasped.

Rerry pressed the attack.

Now Scar was on the defensive. His face became a mask of concentration. Brows buckled, Scar said, "Impossible!"

Rerry used his heavier sword and bigger body to his advantage. He beat Scar's sword down.

Bang! Bang! Bang!

Scar counterattacked.

Rerry swatted it aside. He attacked.

Scar retreated.

Rerry wasn't sure what was going on. He could anticipate Scar's moves before they happened. And his strength and skill had increased. It was as if something else, something vaguely familiar, had become a part of him. A presence. He went with it. Seeing an opening, he cut Scar across the shoulder, drawing blood. "That's one!"

Scar let out a howl.

Rerry cut the elf's thigh. "That's two!"

Scar took his sword in two hands and said, "You are not going to beat me!" He attacked in an unorthodox style, chopping at Rerry like a woodsman cuts a tree—only with ferocity. "I'm going to kill you!"

Rerry saw blood in Scar's eye. The elven soldier meant it, but Rerry caught every stinging blow on his blade, shrugging aside the jarring impact.

Scar didn't let up.

Clang! Clang! Clang!

Anticipating the next move, Rerry jumped aside.

Scar's sword bit into the ground.

With Scar overextended, Rerry smacked him hard with the flat of his sword.

Sprawled out on the ground, Scar twisted around only to find Rerry's sword at his throat.

Rerry nicked the elf's neck. "That's three."

Chest heaving and with an eye of contempt, Scar said in a voice full of denial, "I don't know how you did what you did, but this is not over."

"You gave your word," Rerry said, poking Scar in the chest with his sword. "Are you taking it back?"

With a sneer, Scar said, "No."

"Good." Rerry's boundless strength fled his body. The world spun. He was falling without control, and the day turned into night.

CHAPTER
20

THEY CAME, STARK AGAINST THE night. The nuurg. The pair of monstrous humanoids rode on the backs of the colossal horses called wrath horns. Rain splashed off of them, splattering the muddy streets. Their spiked hooves made huge puddles. They trotted into town, stopping in the middle of the main road. Behind them was Malden. The man seemed insignificant among the towering ten-foot-tall monsters. Malden spoke, gestured, and pointed.

Nath could hear door bolts sliding shut. Shutters closing. The light of oil lamps dimmed, and many were extinguished. Fear was in the air, heavy as the rain. The mood of the tiny town was brooding.

The presence of evil had taken over.

The nuurg resumed their advance. They were covered from head to toe in heavy armor. One carried a spear longer than a man was tall. The other nuurg had a spiked flail far too big for an ordinary man to wield. Their faces were ugly, like those of orcs or ogres. One was a cyclops, and the other, with the flail, seemed more man than orc.

Malden led them down the street and pointed down the alley where he'd sent Nath and Brenwar earlier.

The nuurg paid him no mind. With awful nickers, the wrath horns, shaking the tusks on their faces, snorted and veered toward the alley.

Nath's blood stirred. He stepped from the shadows into the rain-soaked street and called out, "Pardon me! But I think I can save you some time. I'm the one you're looking for!"

Malden's jaw hit the saddle. Visibly gathering his thoughts, he pointed, saying, "That's him! That's him! That's the stranger I told you about!"

The nuurg pulled back on their reins and backed up. Facing Nath, they spread apart and continued their advance.

Out of the night from the backside of the nuurg, Brenwar bellowed out, "And don't forget me. I'm the one you're looking for as well!"

The nuurg with one eye, the cyclops, slowly turned his horse around to face Brenwar. He lowered his massive spear. The wrath horn snorted. Its front hoof clawed at the muddy ground.

"You know, you might not want to do that," Nath said in a loud voice. "Dwarves don't like to be poked or trampled."

From the far end of the street, Brenwar said, "I can speak for myself!" The dwarf didn't even have Mortuun in hand. He was nothing but soaking-wet beard and breastplate. "Come on, one eye, what are you waiting for?"

The wrath horn reared up and charged. Its great hooves thundered down the road on a path to overrun Brenwar.

All eyes were on the event.

What in Nalzambor is that crazy dwarf doing?

The naked end of the spear's metal tip was right on course to skewer Brenwar like meat on a stick when Brenwar slipped to the side. His powerful fingers grabbed hold of the spear and yanked the nuurg right out of the saddle. Strengthened by the bracers of power that he wore, Brenwar pummeled the giant of a man into the mud with his skeleton hand.

Wham! Wham! Wham!

Covered in grit, Brenwar stood up and waved. "He's finished."

The nuurg with two eyes turned his attention to Nath. He drew his flail. His head swiveled on his shoulders. His dark eyes pierced Nath.

"Looking for me?" Nath said from behind the nuurg, in its blind spot. And smacked the horse hard on its backside.

It reared up.

The nuurg rider, no longer having its hand on the reins, toppled. It hit hard with a splash and a thud. The big humanoid scrambled up to his feet and came out swinging. The flail ripped over Nath's ducking head.

Without hesitation, Nath ran the nuurg through with Fang.

The monster died in the rain.

Nath shook his head. Killing wasn't what he wanted to do.

Brenwar came along and said, "Don't doubt yourself. You can't keep evil in prison. It will get out. You did what had to be done. This is war."

"What have you done?" Malden yelled, clutching his head and hair as if the world was crumbling down. "You've doomed us all. The other nuurg, they'll kill us. They'll kill us all!"

Brenwar walloped the man in the gut with a quick punch.

Malden sank to his knees. He groaned.

"Listen to me, farmer! The only ones dying are them! But if you side with them, you'll die with them. Tonight we turn the tables."

Tim rushed over, feet splashing through the water. He carried Mortuun in his arms. He handed it over to Brenwar. Catching his breath, he said, "That thing's heavier than it looks."

"It's supposed to be," Brenwar replied.

"I-I couldn't believe my eyes. The two of you made such quick work of those giant beasts. You both truly are what the songs say you are." Tim shook his head. "I never would have believed it if I hadn't seen it for myself."

"That was nothing," Brenwar remarked.

Nath had one of the wrath horns by the reins and said to Tim, "Do you think you can handle one of these things?"

Staring up at the huge beast with wide eyes, Tim said, "Are you joking?"

"They aren't as mean as they are ugly. You just have to take command." Nath handed the man the reins. "Just imagine if the legionnaires had horses like these back when."

Tim petted the horse between the forehead and muzzle. It snorted. Stamped its hooves. With a nod, he said, "I think I can manage." He climbed into the saddle. Looking down at Nath, he said, "Whew, this is different. So where are we going?"

"You say you know where the other nuurg reside. Brenwar and I want to pay them a visit." Nath put his fingers to his lips and whistled. The other wrath horn walked over with its head down. Nath mounted the creature and held down his hand. Brenwar took it and climbed up behind him. "It's going to be our first and final visit."

Knees deep in the mud, Malden said, "You'll doom us. You'll doom us all. Tim, don't be a fool."

Tall in the saddle, Tim said, "If I weren't so darn set on being a good guy, I'd trample you into a mud hole."

Malden smirked.

Tim dug his heels into the wrath horn. It reared up.

Malden cringed.

The hooves crashed down right in front of the country man.

Up on his feet, Malden took off running.

With the look of a hardened soldier firing in his eyes, Tim said, "Let's go get them."

CHAPTER
21

RERRY AWOKE. HE WAS LEANED against a rock, head spinning. Something tugged at his arm. Eyelids flickering, he slowly made the image of Samaz form in his vision. His brother had him by the forearm. There were at least twenty stitches in the wound. Samaz was wrapping it up. "What happened?" Rerry asked.

"You passed out."

Rerry's heart fired. He lurched up. "Where's Scar?"

"He'll be back. He and the other two are out scouting for food. It's been a busy day. Everyone is hungry."

"What are you talking about, Samaz? Are we their prisoners again?"

"No, they're our prisoners." Samaz finished up the wrap. "Keep it clean." He tried to get up.

But Rerry held him down. "Samaz, I don't see any prisoners. You must mean they're our escaped prisoners."

"You beat him, Rerry. Scar is honoring his debt. He's in your service, and his men are in his." Samaz traced his finger along the cut in Rerry's neck. "That might scar. I'll see if I can find some of nature's loam for it."

Scratching his head, Rerry looked around and said in a whisper, "I did beat him, didn't I. For the life of me, I don't know how. Something just ... overcame me. I felt like two men in one. It was strange, very strange."

Making sure no one else was around, Samaz said, "It was me."

"What do you mean, it was you?"

"We became one. I was merged with you. I can't explain it. It just sort of happened."

"You don't know anything about fighting with a sword." Rerry leaned back against the boulder and closed his eyes. "But something happened, for certain. What do you mean, you merged with me?"

"I've always felt something, a connection. I've talked to Mother about it before. She says that, being brothers born with magic in our veins, we might bear special powers. She says that if we do, one day these powers will reveal themselves." He sat down shoulder to shoulder with Rerry. "That revelation came today. I don't know what happened, but you were fighting, and I felt it. I tingled from head to toe right before I said you could beat him. Besides, I dreamed it."

"Dreamed it? When?"

Samaz caught a colorful butterfly on his finger. "At least ten years ago."

"I'd have trouble believing you if you weren't so strange." Rerry sighed. There wasn't any reason for his brother to lie, and he'd indeed felt something. There wasn't any better explanation. Scar should have cut him to ribbons, but he hadn't. He hated to say it, but he did. "Let's not let Scar know about this. He'll want a rematch."

"Don't worry, I won't."

"So, how did you catch those elves? Did you use some kind of spell on them?"

"I'm faster than you think."

They helped each other to their feet.

"Well, I'd hope so."

Scar and the soldiers returned. They had some dead rabbits and a sack of small green apples. The captain had a hard time looking at Rerry when he said, "We'll get the meat cooked. These apples are sour as an elven elder, but they'll fill your gut and quench your thirst."

"I'm famished," Rerry replied.

Scar tossed him a pair of apples.

He caught them both with one hand. "Thanks." His lips puckered as soon as he bit into one. He pitched it away. "No thanks. I'd rather eat a rock."

Scar took a big bite out of his own apple. "I'll gather you all the rocks you want to eat. Mmmm, that's good."

What's he up to?

Rerry was far from comfortable having Scar as his indentured servant. He wasn't even certain to what extent he could order the elf around.

Time to push.

"Let me see your sword, Scar."

Scar unbuckled his sword belt. "It's yours to have. All I have to offer is yours. Even my life. The same goes for my men. We'll keep our word." He handed Rerry the sword—belt, scabbard, and all.

Rerry examined it.

The working of the scabbard was of the finest craft. The leather of the belt was worn and soft but well maintained by the natural oils of the lands.

Countless hours must have gone into crafting the sword. It had been forged by the finest blacksmiths.

"Put it back on. It's yours to keep for a lifetime. I have to be honest with you, Scar, I'm not comfortable having henchmen."

"Then you're releasing me from my word?"

"No, you are not released. As soon as I do that, you'll be right back after me again. Instead, you and your men shall accompany us on our quest. I didn't say I wouldn't get used to it." He gave a nod to Samaz. His brother was making a fire while the soldiers skinned the rabbits. "And it might just last forever."

Scar adjusted his eyepatch. "I couldn't have cared less before, but seeing how your quest involves me now, enlighten me some more."

Rerry filled him in on his mother's problem with the wizard's dementia and went even further back to the final battle of the Great Dragon War when the elves and dwarves teamed up and turned loose the Apparatus of Ruune on the Floating City.

Scar and his men hung on every word.

Without realizing it, Rerry captivated himself. He just kept going on and on until the sun dipped behind the trees and the darkness came. When he finished, the campfire crackled and all the rabbit meat was gone. He wiped his fingers on the grasses. "It was something."

"I must admit, I'm envious." Scar stirred a stick in the ground. "I wasn't doing anything when all that went on. As for your mother, I sympathize. But going into Elome to acquire the Ocular of Orray? Hah! You look more human than elf. You'll never acquire the gem. I don't think you can even find it. It offers no guarantees it can heal her anyway." He broke the stick in half and tossed it into the fire. "'There's more than one way to do anything,' they say. But some things can't be undone, Rerry. Listen to me. You too, Samaz. I don't think your mother would want you to die on her account. Go home. Abandon this quest."

Rerry stiffened. "That won't happen! You just want to be free."

"You aren't going to slip through the elves' and dwarves' clutches forever. You should turn yourselves in. See what happens. If Nath Dragon truly is who you say he is, his name will be cleared."

"Not if they kill him."

"That's easier said than done, based off what you've told me. For the love of Elome, he's a dragon. I've never heard of a dragon being put on trial before. But they'll make it happen."

"Nalzambor has enough evil in it. Nath Dragon is the least of their worries. He's the one fighting the danger lurking out there."

Scar rubbed his hands over the fire. "The greatest danger is what lurks within the hearts of all. We're all quick to judge one another, Rerry. We always want a scapegoat. I hate to admit it, but your friend's enemies will only pile up."

"Why do you say that? It doesn't make any sense."

"There's a flaw in all of us. If there weren't, we'd all get along." Scar lay down with his hands behind his head. "You're young. You've much to figure out yet. Now, get some sleep. Your human side needs it. I can see the blackness under your eyes where if you were an elf, they'd still be bright as day."

"I don't need any sleep. I need to help my mother."

"Things will be clearer once you get some shuteye. Be a soldier. Take a moment. You never know when you'll get another chance to rest." Scar closed his eye. He breathed easy and slept. The other elves did the same.

The glow of the dying fire showed on Samaz's face. He looked wide awake. He always looked wide awake. "I never sleep," he said. "Take some rest."

"What do you think we should do?" Rerry asked.

"I might abandon Elome, but I won't abandon Mother."

"I'm glad we agree." Rerry lay down, but he couldn't sleep.

There has to be another way to help her, but I don't know where to start.

CHAPTER 22

T HE NUURG. THEY MADE NATH'S skin crawl. He could see one of
them standing outside a small fortress made from logs and rock. It
had heavy orcen features and only one eye. It chewed meat from the
bone of a stag near where a metal urn filled with burning firewood blazed.
The animal's rack of antlers lay nearby. The nuurg stuck the meat in the fire,
cooked it, then pulled it out of the flame and ate some more.

Concealed in a spot of higher ground fifty yards above Nath overlooking
the distant open plain where the nuurg's fortress stood sentry, Tim fidgeted.

The rain had stopped, but the humidity was up. Everything outside was
quiet.

In a low voice, Tim asked, "What are the nuurg? I understand giants, but
these are bigger, are they not? These monsters are something else."

Nath couldn't really explain it himself. There were plenty of creatures in
this world he hadn't seen before. He hadn't even seen most of the dragons.
But one thing was certain: the nuurg were a twisted abomination brought
about by the titans. He rubbed the neck of his wrath horn. "I believe they are
a mix of orc and giant blood. Maybe there's dark magic behind it. We were in
Urslay, the giant home in the mountains, not so long ago. There were faces
from all of the races as big as them. Somehow, the titans are building an army
of giant races."

"Are you telling me there's going to be a lot more of them?" Tim thumbed
the sweat off his brow.

"They war with the dragons, not men."

"I say it's man's fight as much as any. We're slaves to those beasts." Tim's
grip tightened on his reins, making a squeaking sound. "So what's the plan?"

"We ride in and take them out, but you don't need to come," Nath said.
"You've done enough by leading us here. I thank you."

"I might not be as young as I used to be, but there's still plenty of fight left in me. I can't just stand here, watch, and do nothing." He pulled out his sword. "I want to fight."

Nath nodded. "I know you do. So, you said there were ten that patrolled the towns?"

"Yes. And you've killed two, so now there'll be eight. They stay in at night and make plenty of noise in the morning. But they aren't alone in there. They keep our people, who need to be freed."

"Oh." Nath noticed Brenwar's eyes on him. "That changes things."

"Aye," Brenwar said. His eyes were intent on the nuurg fortress. "We can't just storm in there and bust their bones up. We'll have to be more careful. I don't like being careful."

The nuurg sentry crunched through the bone, chewed it up, and swallowed it down.

"I suppose the nuurg expect company before long." Nath readied the satchel he'd put the contents from Brenwar's chest in. "We should just give them what they expect then." He took out a potion vial. A tangerine-colored fluid swirled within.

Tim's eyes enlarged. "Is that magic? What are you going to do with it?"

"I'm going to make Brenwar drink it."

"No you are not!" the dwarf objected.

"Well, I'm not drinking it, and I'm in charge, so there you go."

"What does it do?" Tim asked.

"It's a polymorph potion. It will turn you into whatever you want to be, for a short time." Nath held the vial up against the sky. Mystic fragments twinkled within. "The idea is Brenwar drinks it and turns himself into one of the nuurg. As a disguise. He waltzes me in there as his—"

"I'll drink it! Let me drink it!" Tim's fingers grasped at the air.

"Aye, let him drink it. He's volunteering for it. Let the soldier have at it." Brenwar pumped his skeleton fist. "It's a good idea."

"But they'll be expecting two nuurg, not one," Nath said.

"You didn't say that."

"We have to do it right if we want to pull this off."

"What do I do?" Tim asked.

"Think of the nuurg that come into your town. The one I slew. Can you picture it?"

Tim nodded.

Nath handed the legionnaire the vial. "Then drink half of this and concentrate on its image."

Without hesitation, Tim took the vial and slurped half of it down then handed the vial back to Nath. "I tingle."

"Oh, you'll tingle," Nath said. He gave the vial to Brenwar and sat behind him. "Your turn, faithful friend."

"Hah." Brenwar frowned, closed his eyes, and swallowed the remainder of the potion. "Happy?"

"Delighted." Nath dismounted.

"Oh my stars," Tim said. His hands were outstretched. He gaped at them. The man's body contorted and grew. His face became mean and ugly. His body filled the saddle. In mere moments he'd gone from man to man-monster. His one eye blinked. "Did it work?"

"Perfectly." Nath turned to Brenwar. The dwarf was now a nuurg like the one he'd slain, but something wasn't right. "We might have a problem."

"You can say that again. I look like an orc again. A giant one at that."

"That's not it. The problem is you still have more beard than face."

CHAPTER
23

TRANSFORMED INTO NUURG, BRENWAR AND Tim rode on the wrath horns. They took a road that led straight to the fortress with Nath in tow behind them, hands bound up by a rope.

Brenwar grumbled under his beard, "I even smell as bad as they do." He caught Tim smiling and glowered at the man-turned-giant. "The nuurg don't smile."

"I can't help it. I still tingle."

"Nath, what do I do if they say something about my beard? Can I bash them then?" asked Brenwar.

"I don't know. Let's hope it doesn't come up." It wasn't that the nuurg didn't have facial hair. Many of them had plenty, but not to the extent it looked like a black bush beneath their faces.

"I can do the talking," Tim suggested. "I've communicated with them plenty of times before. I have a feel for them."

Brenwar drifted back and said, "That's fine by me."

Closing in on the fortress, Nath caught a glimpse of the nuurg sentry. It tossed the stag's antlers aside and picked up its spear, barring the gate that led into the fortress with its body.

Tim and his wrath horn came to a stop several feet away from the sentry. He didn't say a word. The sentry didn't say a word either. Its single eye bore into Tim. Spear ready, it moved by Tim and gave Brenwar a longer look. Brenwar glared right back. With a grunt, the heavy-footed cyclops made it over to Nath. A bunch of men's skulls made up its belt.

Here we go.

The cyclops stood a full three feet of muscle taller than Nath. It leaned down, nostrils flaring, and sniffed him. With its finger, it poked Nath in the chest, knocking him down.

Nath got up but kept his eyes down and didn't say a word.

The nuurg poked him harder.

Nath shuffled back without falling.

Someone's going to lose a finger!

"Quit fooling around with the prisoner! Let us in. I hunger," Tim said.

The nuurg sentry touched Nath's cheek with its fingers and said, "He's pretty like a bauble. I want his head. Humph. That hair would look fine on my belt."

"We'll cast bones to see who gets what. Now open the door," Brenwar interjected.

The sentry waggled the spear in front of Nath's eyes. "I bet those eyes would make a fine seasoning for people stew." He breathed on Nath.

Nath coughed.

Sultans of Sulfur, that's awful.

The cyclops walked away. A pair of twelve-foot-high doors still barred the entrance to the fortress. The brute put its back into it and shoved both doors open wide. With a quick look back at Nath, Tim the nuurg led them inside.

The fortress wasn't very big. Square and straight on all sides, it would house about fifty men in close quarters—or ten nuurg. The middle was an open courtyard, and the rest of the establishment was nothing but barracks and stables.

The nuurg sentry made its way over to one of the barracks. It was taller than the doorframe. The nuurg pounded on it with its fist, saying, "Bruke! Bruke! Wake! A meal awaits!" The sentry stepped back.

A loud moan stirred within the confines of the wooden barracks. The door swung open, smacking against the frame of the building with a loud *whack*. A big body filled the doorway, ducked down, and squeezed beneath the frame. It was a nuurg, a huge one-eyed orc with small knuckle-like horns on its head. Bare chested, but furs and hides covered it below the waist. "Why did you disturb me? What is it?"

At least they speak Common.

"What do you mean?" the sentry said, irritated. It pointed with its spear. "See for yourself."

Bruke rubbed his eye and yawned. He peered beyond Tim and Brenwar. Spying Nath, he blinked. Warily, he leaned over and grabbed a halberd that was leaned against the barracks. "That one is too fast to be fooled." He gave Tim and Brenwar a look. "How did you catch that one?"

"Caught him hiding. Hemmed him in and overpowered him." Tim shifted in his saddle. "He's slippery. Not slippery enough. Heh heh."

In a fierce voice, Bruke said, "There was mention of a dwarf. Where's the dwarf?"

Brenwar the nuurg held up Mortuun the war hammer. "Dead by his own hammer."

Studying Brenwar and the weapon, Bruke said, "Something smells about your story."

More of the nuurg emerged from their barracks. Each carried a heavy weapon crafted from iron and steel. In a few long strides, they had encircled Nath and his companions.

Nath counted heads.

...Six, seven, eight. The full welcoming party has arrived. Unless Tim's count is wrong.

He noted the faces of people crowded back in the shadows of the barracks. He felt their hearts racing.

These people are terrified.

"I don't remember you having a beard," Bruke said to Brenwar the nuurg. "And where's your weapon?"

"It got lost in a mud hole, but this one is fine." He held the hammer in front of Bruke's face. "Just fine."

Bruke's nostrils widened. His shoulders tensed. "You don't talk like yourself. You don't smell like yourself. You smell...dwarven."

Nath caught a look from Brenwar. He gave a quick nod.

"Do you want to know why I smell like a dwarf?" Brenwar said.

The nuurg sentry said with confidence, "Because you killed one."

"No," Brenwar replied. "Because I am one!" Powered by his bracers of strength, the dwarf-turned-nuurg cranked Mortuun back and dotted Bruke smack dab in the middle of the forehead.

Crack-Boom!

The entire fortress shook.

Bruke dropped to his knees. Knuckles dragging on the ground, the nuurg collapsed backward, dead as a stone.

Timothy wheeled his wrath horn around and snapped the reins. The bestial mount charged over the nuurg nearest him, horns down with ram-like force.

The flat-footed nuurg recovered their senses. Two of them focused their efforts on Nath. They rushed him.

"Brenwar!" Nath yelled. "I need Fang!"

The dwarven warrior in nuurg form had another nuurg pinned down to the ground by the neck. He bellowed, "Get him yourself."

The nuurg collided right on top of Nath and drove him into the ground. *This is not part of the plan!*

CHAPTER
24

WHILE TIM WAS TURNING THE wrath horn around for another charge, a huge body collided into him, knocking him from the saddle. He barrel rolled back up to his feet, sword poised to strike or defend against his attacker. His sword, a fine broad blade, didn't fit in his hand as it usually did. It was awkward but light as a stick. He slashed back and forth.

I can make this work.

He took in a deep breath. His body was alive, more so than it had been in decades. His muscles were strong and powerful.

"Oh, what a body!"

A nuurg fighter wheeled into his path. It held a flail with both its hands and swung it over its head. The steel-spiked ball whistled through the air in wide circles. The nuurg rushed in, bringing the flail head down with wroth force.

Tim caught the chain of the flail around the length of his sword.

The pair of giants stood chest to chest, shoving one another back, snarling and growling.

The nuurg enemy puffed and spun.

Struggling for balance, feet sliding through the dirt, Tim held on for dear life. The monster was strong. Fierce. Its force unrelenting. He'd never faced such power before.

Come on, soldier. You're as big as him. Act like it.

Hard knuckles punched Tim in the ribs.

He groaned. His body might have been as big or as strong, but he wasn't used to it. The size was awkward.

The nuurg bent him backward. Its shovel-sized hand fell to a knife inside its belt. It snaked it out and tried to stab Tim.

With combat experience coming back to him, Tim locked his fingers over the monster's wrist.

The blade edge nicked his flesh.

The old fires of battle within Tim ignited. He rammed his forehead into the nuurg's nose.

The cartilage gave way.

Crunch.

The nuurg bellowed. Its grip released its flail. It held its nose.

Big mistake.

Tim slung the flail from his sword and closed in, piercing the nuurg right through its heart.

It dropped dead.

He hoisted the sword high. "Victory!"

A nuurg with two eyes close set together rushed into his path with a machete matched to its size and body.

Flashing his sword, Tim said, "Have at me then! I've got a body as big as yours, and now I'm used to it!"

His stomach churned.

He belched.

His body collapsed to its normal size.

With two colossal bodies piled on top of him, no sword in hand, Nath fought back with the only available weapon he could think of. He bit the one-eyed nuurg in the leg.

With an angry howl, it punched him in the side of the head.

Stars burst forth.

Nath's teeth clattered.

The one-eyed nuurg grabbed a handful of Nath's long red hair and jerked Nath up off his feet—and practically out of his boots.

"Now you've done it!" Nath said, kicking and flailing. "Nobody touches my hair!" He dug his golden-yellow claws into the flesh of the giant's hand and raked them down.

One-eye moaned and released him, but Two-eye stabbed at him with a knife made from a solid piece of iron.

Nath sprang from the strike. He jumped at the giant orc and punched it hard in the throat.

Two-eye choked and gurgled, but One-eye charged from behind, swinging its anvil-like fist.

Nath ducked.

The fist collided with the choking nuurg, flopping it to the ground.

Nath unleashed a flurry of punches in One-eye's heavy gut, hard and fast. The nuurg might have been bigger and heavier than him, but they weren't any stronger. He was a dragon who just looked like a man. Well, and had to walk like a man rather than fly. He hit as fast as his heart beat.

One-eye crumbled under the assault.

Nath wrenched its arm behind its back and called out, "Brenwar, I need Fang!"

"Hold yer horses! I'm coming!" Brenwar had resumed his normal form.

"Don't you mean hold your wrath horns?"

Brenwar dashed his war hammer against the head of the nuurg.

Nath punched it in the throat.

Whop!

Brenwar marched over and said, "Hold him still, will you?"

"Are you serious?"

"No." The dwarf cocked back and smote the wriggling giant in the skull.

Neither giant moved again. The nuurg lay scattered in heaps all over the courtyard.

"Where's Tim?" Nath said. A scuffle caught his ear.

Tim was pushing himself out from under a nuurg's big body. With his legs still pinned beneath the giant, he held up his sword and said breathlessly, "Victory."

Regaining his feet, Nath rolled his sore jaw and combed his fingers through his hair.

Four, five, six, seven …

"We're missing a nuurg, the sentry with the skulls for a belt."

Outside the fortress, the shrill sound of a metal whistle ripped through the sky.

Nath rushed out the front gate.

The sentry stood there blowing an iron whistle the size of a curled ram's horn.

"I'll stop him!" Brenwar slung Mortuun head first into the nuurg's chest. Bone cracked. It hit the ground. He ran over and tore the whistle from the wheezing nuurg's hands. "What is this for?"

With a smile on its crooked lips, the nuurg said, "They come."

Against the deep blue sky with their black wings, the wurmers came like great bats of the night.

CHAPTER 25

"INCOMING, EH? WELL, I'M STILL itching to fight. Let them come. Let them all come." Brenwar moved away from Nath, twirling Mortuun around his body and yelling into the sky, "I'm right here, insects!"

Timothy lumbered over, shoulders sagging. He had his shoulder in one hand and Fang in the other. Blinking, he looked up in the sky. "It's like my old soldiering days. Never enough time to catch your breath between the battles." He took a deep breath. "I can still do this."

Nath took Fang. "Not with ordinary steel you won't. They have hides hard as iron, Tim. Get inside with the others and take cover."

Tim nodded. "If it weren't coming from you, Dragon Prince, my pride wouldn't let me retreat, but I'll follow your order." He took another look above. The wurmers dove like black lances in the night sky. "Yes sir, I'll follow your orders."

Fang warmed in the palm of Nath's hand. The blade hummed with angry life.

Me and you, Fang. Me and you.

The swarming wurmers closed in. There looked to be ten of them, a hundred yards away. Fifty yards.

Nath and Brenwar cocked back.

Something whistled overhead. With blinding speed, streaks of silver slammed into the oncoming wurmers. It was a collision of scales followed by roars of fury. Dragon fury.

Nath's heart wanted to burst from his chest.

Silver dragons. Man sized, quick, and powerful. Their claws shredded the wurmers. They clamped onto the insect-dragons. Tore off wings. Locked jaws on necks.

The stunned wurmers shrieked and spun out of control.

Several wurmers hit the ground.

Nath and Brenwar, quick to strike, pounded them with hammer and sword.

Above, the battle raged like fireworks in the sky. Light coursed through the bodies of the silver dragons, shocking the wurmers. The monsters fought back with their hot, glowing breath. Blasts of deep purple erupted from their mouths in balls of energy. The silver dragons slid by the attack, quicker than the wind.

One silver dragon, marvelous from the tip of his nose to the end of his tail, locked up in battle with the biggest wurmer. The dragon's tail coiled around the wurmer's neck, and its body charged like living light. Lightning fired from its mouth. The wurmer exploded. Smoldering scales showered the sky. A burnt, crispy smell lingered in the air.

Standing back to back with Brenwar, Nath said, "They're dead. All of the wurmers are dead." He blinked. "Those silvers really wiped them out." A couple more wurmers dropped dead from the sky. "Cloudy with a chance of wurmers."

The silver dragons circled like a spinning windmill.

Nath waved. "I guess this is the part where they save us and leave us. It would be great if once, just once, they'd stick around long enough for me to thank them."

"Aye." Brenwar gave a dwarven salute. He pumped his fist and thumped his chest. "Unlike you, they're not much for talking."

Nath eyed him.

Brenwar shrugged.

The circle of dragons broke. In a V formation, wings flapping in unison, they shot off toward the moon. All except for one. He landed, the biggest of the group. The leader. His lean, serpentine body clung low to the ground. His long neck undulated like a fish's body.

Nath spoke to the silver dragon leader in Dragonese—an ancient language, melodic, a combination of sounds and words. "Thank you, brother."

The dragon skulked forward. His eyes were bright blue. Penetrating. He had seemed bigger in the sky, but up close, the silver dragon was no bigger than Nath. Coming closer, he reared up onto his hind legs and stood like a man. He crossed his front paws over his armored chest. Holding his chin high, he stood a full head taller than Nath. Then he bowed and said, also in Dragonese, "I might be your brother, but you are my prince."

Nath's jaw dropped. He was speechless. He reached out and, with his hand under the dragon's chin, he lifted his eyes to meet his. "Slivver?"

"At your service," the dragon said in Common.

Nath hugged his brother.

Slivver hugged him back. It wasn't an awkward hug by any means, just two brothers embracing after a hard-fought battle. Slivver was all dragon but carried himself, at this moment, like a man.

Breaking the embrace, Nath exclaimed, "I've missed you!"

"Of course you have. Everybody has." Slivver's sleekness and charm matched the wondrous scales of his body. He held his elbow in one hand and gestured as he spoke with the other. "I have to admit, I've missed out on many exciting things." His ice-blue eyes drifted to Brenwar.

"Where have you been hiding, Slivver?" Brenwar said.

"Well, if it isn't my old, old friend Brenwar. Old, old, old friend." Slivver stretched out his arms. "Hugs?"

"Dwarves don't—"

"I know, I know, dwarves don't hug." Slivver laughed, shaking the bearded flap of skin under his chin. "Hugs, thugs. Watch out behind you."

Nath had completely forgotten about the nuurg sentry blowing the whistle and alerting the wurmers. It rushed the backside of Brenwar.

Without turning, Brenwar socked it in the gut with Mortuun.

"Oooof!" The monster sagged.

Brenwar cranked back for the finishing blow.

"No, wait!" Nath said. "Bind him up. Let's see what he knows."

"Still learning mercy, are you?" Slivver said.

"I've learned plenty since you've been gone."

"It's an abomination."

"I know, but I need information. I need to find Father. He's gone rogue."

"It wouldn't be the first time." Slivver's long tail swished behind him. "Tell me about it?"

Nath caught Slivver up with how their father Balzurth had healed Sasha of the wizard's dementia and then disappeared from the Temple of Spires.

Slivver shook his magnificent dragon head. "And ever since, you've been trekking the earth by foot and hoof? Why not call for the dragons?"

"I have called. They didn't answer."

"Just because they don't answer doesn't mean you stop calling." Slivver chuckled.

"Oh," Nath said.

Throwing his paw over Nath's shoulder, Slivver said, "I got here in the nick of time. Now let's go find Father."

CHAPTER

26

SELENE WAS BACK IN THE bedroom with all the murals. She wasn't alone. Grahleyna was with her, as was Sansla Libor. The winged white ape stood in front of one of the murals, staring at a distant view of Elome.

"Do you miss being among the roamer elves?" she said.

"I'm the Roamer King. It always hurts to not be among my people." His ape face was long. "It's not easy being an outcast, but I've learned to accept it."

"In time, your people will learn to accept you," Selene said.

"The elves aren't even accepting of one another at the moment. Their hearts have been twisted."

Grahleyna sat on the edge of the bed with her head down. She hadn't said a word in hours. "It's the titans' fault," she said under her breath. "Those evil spirits poison everything. I can only hope my overzealous husband puts an end to this. He went out there because he loves me, perhaps too much, if that's possible. But he hates Eckubahn even more. I can't blame him for what he did." She slapped her knees and stood. Pointing at all the murals, each as real as the next and divided by a network of honeycomb columns, she said, "You need to decide where you want to start."

"What do you mean?" Selene said.

"I mean, in what part of Nalzambor do you want to begin your search for Nath and Balzurth? It's not possible for us to fly you out of here, and it isn't safe to tunnel out." Grahleyna straightened and fluffed the pillows on the bed. She moved as if her mind was far away. "There is deep magic here. You feel it. With my aid, you can walk through to the place you see in an instant. You won't be coming back through once you cross, however. It'll be a one-way trip."

Selene gazed at all the different mural portals which filled the wondrous room. She could see the village at Dragon Pond. Tiny fisherman, like insects, fished from the piers. In a corner above her head, the orcen city of Thraag loomed. Part of its own mountain and carved from within, Morgdon of the dwarves waited with stark banners whipping stiffly in the wind mounted on enormous poles. Narnum, the Free City, was anything but. It stirred Selene within. She'd done horrible things there. Now it fared even worse than she'd left it. Giants of all the rogue races roamed the streets like men. Soaring wurmers crested the building tops.

"Where the trouble is, Nath will be." Selene stroked the tip of her tail, which rested over her shoulder. "That's the spot, but I don't want to be too close."

"That's not a problem. Just think of a spot you've been before and go."

Selene said to Sansla, "Are you coming with me?"

"I gave Nath my word I'd look out for you."

Selene hugged Grahleyna. "I'll stay if you wish."

"I'd like that, but under better circumstances. Now go."

Heart thumping hard in her chest, Selene grabbed Sansla and stepped into the mural.

CHAPTER 27

"TIMOTHY, YOU'VE BEEN BRAVE AND excellent. I thank you." Nath shook the veteran's hand. "Can you handle him?" He spoke of the last living nuurg. The nine-footer's arms and legs were shaking in heavy chains.

With a smile, Tim said, "I feel like I can handle anything. We'll put this monster to work back in the fortress if we have to. Probably let him bury his own dead. The people are happy. The fortress holds more supplies than I expected. It'll help us. Thanks, Dragon Prince. It's been an unbelievable honor fighting by your side. I might even have to come out of my retirement." He stepped forward, jabbing the air with his sword, but then he grimaced and held his shoulder. "Ohhhhh. I'll think about it."

Nath, Brenwar, and Slivver departed. Nath had allowed Brenwar to spend the better part of an hour interrogating the nuurg. That had been an ugly sight. Not so much the howls of pain, but seeing a cyclops cry was just uncomfortable.

Narnum.

Regarding the whereabouts of Eckubahn, all the slobbering crying nuurg could say was "Narnum." The very heart of Nalzambor.

It stirred a lot of bad memories for Nath. He'd seen the worst of the worst in Selene there. So much so, it made his heart ache. "I guess the titan den is pretty obvious," he said, rubbing the back of his head. "Evil seems to have an affection for the place. I wonder why."

"Location, location, location," Slivver said. He walked on all fours now.

"You always have a good answer for everything."

Brenwar huffed.

"No offense, Brenwar. You have good answers too. Sometimes."

Nath's thoughts drifted to the time he'd spent more than a century ago with Slivver. Unlike most of his brothers and sisters—who resented Nath for being named Dragon Prince when they were all older—Slivver was a friend and a mentor. The silver dragon had taught him much when he was younger about the different breeds of dragons and their ways. The two of them had even gone adventuring together, back when Nath was barely a century old, a youngster. Slivver shared Nath's fascination with the races. Like it was supposed to be for Nath, when Slivver didn't look like a dragon, he could easily pass for a man.

"So, Slivver, where have you been all this time?"

"Sleeping. You know how it goes." The silver dragon, now on all fours, moved more like a cat than a lizard. His lean body snaked through the bushes they passed. "When the dragon sleep comes, it comes."

"So you weren't part of the Great Dragon Wall?"

"I can say with glee my time on the wall has passed."

"Oh, I didn't realize. Of course, I never knew there was a wall to begin with. I can only imagine how many other secrets I don't know." He gave Slivver a look. "I don't suppose you're going to tell me."

"And let you miss out on the excitement of discovery?" Sliver flashed all of the fangs in his pearly-white teeth. "Fret not, Nath. For the most part I only know what I have seen. The rest of the dragons know even less than that. You know how they are."

"Yes, I know."

The odd group stayed on the country roads and wended their way through the rolling hills. It was still nighttime, and there wasn't a single passerby.

Nath had opted not to take the wrath horns along. The last thing he wanted to do was arouse suspicion. "Feel like picking up the pace?" he said to Brenwar.

"Aye."

"Surely you don't plan to continue walking to Narnum," Slivver said with his dragon face aghast. "That's preposterous."

"In case you hadn't noticed," Nath hitched his thumb over his back, "I don't have any wings."

"Then ride a dragon," Slivver suggested.

"No offense, but I don't think you're big enough. We tried before, remember? Ha ha."

"Oh, ho-ho," Slivver said. "My back still aches from it."

With moonlight shining on his face, Nath said, "Slivver, how did you come by me? By us, back there? Was it by chance? Because to me, it seems unlikely you'd show up at the right place at the right time so conveniently."

"Like I said, I've been asleep for quite some time. I've not been awake very long, and when I did wake, I sought you out." Slivver rose up on his hind legs and walked upright beside Nath. "Dragons are nestled all around. Some of them helped me. Besides, you've always been my charge, by Father's request." He whispered in Nath's ear. "I have to tell you, I'm surprised the bearded stump is still around."

"I heard that," Brenwar said. "Giants' whispers are quieter than that."

"As I was saying," Slivver continued, "I was close when all this happened. I caught up with you and have been watching since before you made your way into the small town of Timothy."

Nath stopped. "Why did you wait so long to reveal yourself?"

Oddly, Slivver rolled his ice-blue eyes. "I was waiting for a dragon call. I'm not supposed to intervene without the call. But you don't call. You're the Dragon Prince. Use the call." He huffed on his claws. "But there's nothing holding me back from ripping those dreadful wurmers apart whenever given the chance. Never seen such disgusting things." He eyeballed Nath. "Well?"

"Well what?"

"Will you summon a dragon so we can expedite this quest? You don't imagine the titan horde taking a stroll through the green valleys, do you? No, it's devouring everything in its path as fast as it can."

Nath cupped his hands to his mouth and took a breath.

"I don't want to fly," Brenwar interrupted.

"Of course you don't. If dwarves were meant to fly, they'd have wings," Slivver replied.

"For a change, I agree with you."

Slivver got back down on all fours and faced Brenwar, "I'll believe when dwarves fly."

"Enough of the bickering, you two. Here goes." In a voice with the strength of a vast and flowing river, he made the call. It was like the roar of the tide, blended in with nature. One would not know they heard it if they didn't know what they were listening for. Still, Nath tried to focus. His summons needed to be sincere.

"RrrrroooOWwwwwwfffFFFttTHhhhhrrrrrrruuuuUMmmmmmmmm-mmmmmmmm!"

After a minute, he stopped. The night skies remained clear. "Well, that's it. Should I try again?"

Slivver shook his head. "The call must travel. The dragon must travel back. It's not teleportation."

Moving on, Nath doubted anything would happen.

CHAPTER

28

BALZURTH WAS SUNK KNEE DEEP in mud thicker than ogre pudding. His hands were shackled above his head in dwarven irons. Scraped up and bruised, head pounding, he looked up at the light in the sky. Clouds drifted by the moon. Slow. Tedious. There was red—like blood—in them. He drew in the stuffy night air. The scent of evil was strong. The oil and sweat of giants. The presence of evil was even worse. Nearby somewhere, innocent blood had been spilled. Not of men and women but of dragons.

He snarled at the giants who filled the massive coliseum. It was the same group that had tried to drag the life out of him into the city of Narnum. Somehow, he had managed to make it back to his feet and walk into the town under his own power. The people's eyes were heavy on him, their stares familiar. He knew of the feats his son Nath Dragon had accomplished in the Contest of Champions. Now he was here. The people knew other things as well. How Nath, the form Balzurth had taken, had saved the world. He saw the hope fade from their eyes when they saw him shackled and broken.

Anger stirred within his breast. A deep hatred built. The titans were nothing but destroyers of everything good in the world. He had to put an end to them. It took everything he had to not burst free of his bonds, hunt down Eckubahn and Isobahn, and blast them into the netherworld once and for all.

I am close. So very, very close. Eckubahn, you will be mine. Vengeance for all the innocent is at hand.

CHAPTER 29

SELENE RUBBED HER SHOULDERS. THEY were ice cold from the teleportation from Dragon Home to where she'd just arrived. She'd known where she was the moment they arrived. After all, she'd targeted the destination. The towers of Narnum were a league away. Urns filled with fire burned on the rooftops. They hadn't been there before.

"The titans have a new home. Perhaps Urslay is abandoned." She laughed. "Maybe all the people should move there."

"What do you want to do?" Sansla shook the frost from his wings. The eight-foot ape stood with his knuckles on the ground. "I can't take to the air or waltz inside."

Selene's robes covered her wrists and ankles. "I can still pass for human. I should be able to go in. It's not as if the giants have any special defenses. There's nothing for them to defend against, aside from the dragons." She searched the skyline. Only wurmers passed overhead. "I'm only going in for a look. Maybe ask a few questions. Give me a day."

Sansla nodded. "There will be temptations."

"I know." Selene made her way out of the field and onto the road. Step by step, she headed back into the city she'd once conquered. A dangerous thought lingered in her mind.

Perhaps I can turn the titans on my own.

CHAPTER

30

NATH AND COMPANY HADN'T EVEN made it half a league when a great shadow blotted out the moon. Every head turned up.

Above, a massive dragon circled with wings spread wide. Gliding through the wind, he slowly spiraled downward. His front and rear legs bore great talons. A pair of tremendous horns formed a U on his head. An orange glow in his eyes resonated with what must have been a great fire within. He was a bull dragon, mighty in size and frame. He landed with the softness of a dove, blocking the entire road and then some.

Slivver somehow formed a smile on his nonexistent lips. "I told you so."

The bull dragon, red scaled with a hint of green, let out a snort and lowered his head. His body was scales over huge muscles, his breastplate like steel. His huge claws could rip a giant in half.

Nath approached on soft feet and rubbed the bull dragon's neck. It was like petting a hot anvil.

The dragon's eye remained fixed on him. The burning orb was as big as his head.

"Thank you for coming."

The dragon snorted a blast of heat.

That was as good an answer as Nath was going to get. Bull dragons weren't talkers at all. They were beasts of action. It was a temperamental brood too. Private. Difficult. Of all the dragons who could have arrived in reply to Nath's summons, a bull dragon was at the top of the list of least expected.

Nath had been in a fierce fight with them before, years ago, just outside of the Floating City. He eyed the sharp talons on the tips of its wings.

I hope he's not here to eat me.

"I'm Nath, and you are?"

The bull dragon clacked his teeth really fast and shook his head, knocking Nath backward.

"I see." Nath glanced at Slivver. "Could you make that out?"

With a nod, Slivver said, "Yes. He says his name is Waark. Well, for short. If you don't want him clacking like a beaver all night long, I'd stay with that."

"I can go with that. Waark, shall we ride?"

The big dragon's belly flattened on the ground. He held his head low. Nath used the hard, scaly ridges to climb on his back. He wedged himself between the armor scales running down the dragon's spine. Getting a grip on a dragon of such massive girth wasn't easy. Riding would be even more difficult.

"Uh, Brenwar, do we have a rope or something?"

Arms folded over his chest, Brenwar said, "No. You need to be walking."

Waark spread his massive wings. They flapped, and then, bunching back onto his back legs, the dragon launched himself up into the air.

"Whoa!" Nath yelled. He dug his nails and heels into the dragon's armor.

Up, up, up they went. Wedged between the dragon's ridges, it wouldn't be too difficult to hold on, assuming the flight was level and Waark didn't go into any barrel rolls, which was unlikely. Bull dragons weren't the fleetest. As a matter of fact, they were some of the slowest, if not *the* slowest—aside from the dragons who didn't have any wings at all.

Below, Brenwar shook his fist and screamed, "Get down here, Nath. Get back down!"

Nath shrugged and called out, "I'm just going to scout ahead. You know me. Do you want to ride?"

"No!" Brenwar became a speck on the ground, and in a few moments, the dwarf was out of sight.

Nath eased back into the strange seat, and before long, wind tearing at his face, he smiled.

Ah, it feels good to be part of the wind again. How I've missed it!

Before long, they were soaring through the clouds of the night, and Nath said in Dragonese, "We're headed for Narnum, but avoid the wurmers."

The dragon's wings beat slow and steady. There was enough power in them to hold at least ten more of Nath, if not twenty. The strength of the bull dragon fed him. Its heart beat in unison with his. They connected. Scaled brothers.

Out of the deep blue sky, Slivver came. His wings beat with the ease of a feather falling. He landed right on the back of the bull dragon, in front of Nath. "Enjoying the ride?"

"Absolutely."

"I don't think the dwarf is very happy."

"He'll catch up. Eventually." Nath chuckled. "He always does."

The bull dragon soared higher than the distant snow-capped mountains that spiked the drifting clouds. The chill air normally would brittle a man's bones, but it didn't. The bull dragon huffed out a warm wind, like off a campfire, every time his wings made a downward stroke. The fire from his belly was warm and soothing.

Taking a look at the quiet lands below where only sparkles of fires burned like fireflies in the night, Nath said, "This is really something, isn't it?"

"Adventure always is." Slivver managed to somehow make himself look extremely comfortable on the bull dragon's back, yet he seemed more man than dragon. "Sometimes it's fun to just enjoy the ride, though it is a slow one. For a dragon, Waark moves at the pace of a dwarf."

Waark's body tremored, jostling the riders.

Nath and Slivver clung on.

"Take no offense, Waark!" Slivver winked at Nath. "It seems no one appreciates being likened to Brenwar's sort."

Like Nath, Slivver was one of a kind among the dragons. He was a silver dragon, but there were many types. There was the larger breed, some of which grew to a size rivaling the bull dragons, and then there were the smaller, more petite sort, quick and powerful with their magic. Not all dragons were old because they were bigger, and not all dragons were young because they were smaller. There were fire bites and pixie dragons who were more than a thousand years old. But even among the rarest of rare was Slivver.

Unlike the rest of their kin, Nath and Slivver were both fascinated with the races. Most dragons didn't care at all. Ever. But Slivver did. If his brother could change into an elf, Nath had no doubt he would. For a while at least.

"Slivver, it's good to have you back. It makes me think of the good old days. You know, back when I was little more than a century. Boy, I was so cocky back then. It's a wonder I made it this far." Nath brushed away a lock of red hair that had drifted over his eye. "I really missed you when you left."

"I missed you too. Even in my sleep, I dreamed of our quests. Now they begin anew."

Nath glanced back. The bull dragon's tail swished behind them. Even at this slower flying speed, it wouldn't take much longer to get to Narnum. A few hours at most. He felt a little guilty leaving Brenwar behind. "Perhaps we should turn around."

With a flip of his paw, Slivver said, "Do as you wish. I can do the scouting ahead if you want. Besides, if the wurmers catch wind of Waark, he won't be able to escape them, but they'll never catch me."

"Eh, he'll be fine."

CHAPTER
31

SELENE DONNED HER HOOD JUST before she entered the formerly Free City of Narnum. She'd almost forgotten the people would recognize her. Thinking back on all the atrocities she and the other Clerics of Barnabus had committed, she had no doubt the people would mob her if she showed her face.

She walked by a pair of giants, each of whom was covered in coarse hair and patches of armor. They were full bloods. Twenty feet high, their bodies filled half the stone-paved street. They poked at one another, jesting and laughing. Their bellies shook when they laughed. Women scurried back and forth, rushing in and out of a tavern. They held pitchers of ale in their arms and filled the huge tankards the giants set on the ground. Every time a giant spoke, the women shouted praise. Their painted eyes were wild with adoration in most cases, but not all.

Music, exotic and dark, blared from horns, voices, strings, and drums. It echoed throughout the city. Sounds from band after band collided with one another.

Selene weaved her way toward the sound of where the masses gathered, fighting the urge to cover her ears and moving with the flow of the raucous crowds filling the once-glorious streets, now rough and shambled. Above, nested in the spires and lying on rooftops, were the dark-scaled wurmers. Their eyes bright, bodies never resting, they were like lizards bathing in a moonlight sun. She could see dozens, but there must have been hundreds.

She pressed through the knots of people who waded among the giant men as casually as they did their own. Men and women who stood ten and more feet tall. Each had a flock of followers behind them, and for every ten small giants, there was one full blood. They lounged and frolicked with one another. The normal-sized people behaved with wild abandon.

This is insanity.

A woman caught Selene by the elbow with both hands. "Come, sister! Come with me!"

Selene pulled away.

The young woman's grip remained firm. "Why do you hide your face, sister? We are all beautiful here."

A second woman blindsided Selene and jerked the hood down. "You're so beautiful! A true maiden for Eckubahn. He must see you!"

Selene shoved the women aside. Heart racing, she covered her head and ran.

The women called out after her. "Eckubahn will have you! He'll take your heart."

Ducking into an alley, Selene cut from one street to another and waded into a different sea of people. They all moved in one direction. Hands and arms waving, they were chanting and praising Eckubahn. The giants. The titans. She followed the sea of people into the arena where the Contest of Champions had been held. It was bigger than it used to be. The giants had expanded it to have seats to hold their kind. Within the entrance tunnel, Selene couldn't see what it was inside the arena that had the crowd so excited. Everyone pushed and shoved.

These people are wild!

Finally, the throng of cajolers squeezed out of the tunnel and filed into the seats of the oval ring. On ground level inside the arena, Selene looked up and caught her first glimpse of the colossal giants. There were many. Bare chested. Armed in some cases. All of them were full blood.

Seated on a throne made from the bones of dragons sat the biggest one of all, Eckubahn. His head was aflame. Beside him stood another titan with a long ponytail and burning green eyes.

A sick feeling stirred inside the pit of Selene's stomach. She made her way up the steps of the coliseum. The seats were filling fast. She made it up high enough to see down into the arena.

Time to see what all of this ludicrous commotion is about.

She turned. Immediately her heart jumped. She gasped and clutched her chest.

In the center of the arena, Nath was chained up to a wall of iron, waist deep in sludge.

CHAPTER 32

ECKUBAHN. THE TITAN KING.

Staring at him, Balzurth knew he was every bit the menace Gorn Grattack was, but worse in other ways. Gorn was a dragon. Even a good dragon once. He didn't hate dragons. He just hated the good in them. That's where Eckubahn and Gorn differed. Eckubahn hated all things good. The giants hated all things dragon, good or not. Eckubahn was the worst of all atrocities: an evil spirit in an evil body commanding an ever-growing army of oversized fiends.

"MY PRIZE. MY PRIZE."

Eckubahn's cavernous voice hushed the crowd. He turned his flaming head to face his fellow spirit, Isobahn. Together, the pair of titans was more formidable than every person and giant in the arena put together. Brawny and mystical, the titans emanated uncanny, wicked power.

"My servant Rybek did well. Did you send for him?"

"I did," Isobahn replied. He stroked his ponytail. Isobahn was the leaner of the two titans. His face, shaven and scarred, might have even been handsome at one time, for a giant. He didn't seem worried about a thing. "I imagine he'll be here soon. I see no reason to wait for him. Let the games begin."

Eckubahn shifted his focus to Balzurth, who was still disguised as Nath. The dark, glowing pits of the titan's eyes bore into Balzurth, searching. The titan's fingers gripped the dragon skulls that made up the chair arms. His long fingernails pecked the dragon-skull foreheads.

Two wurmers as big as horses lay at his feet like dogs. Their hungry eyes were fixed on Balzurth. Claws scraped at the stones below the dragon seat.

"Nath Dragon. Today your heroics end."

Time to sell it, old man. Say something smart-alecky like your son would.

Balzurth stared right back at the titan and said, "Why thank you, Eckubahn. I can't tell you how much I appreciate the celebration. And to think you went to all this trouble to throw a retirement party for me. I'm elated." He looked from side to side. "And a bit baffled. I don't see any cake."

Isobahn sat up, eyes wide, brows lifted. A confused expression filled his face. He chuckled. Others in the seats chuckled as well.

Eckubahn's flaming head brightened. His fists went up and came down hard, shattering the dragon-bone chair arms.

"SILENCE!"

As Nath, Balzurth shrugged. The chains on his arms rattled.

That's it. Get in his head a little. Distract him.

Sweat trickled down his cheek. Balzurth, as mighty as he might have been, could still worry. At the moment, he was faced with the two most powerful titans, Eckubahn and Isobahn. The rest of the spirits were scattered all over Nalzambor. In addition to that, a host of giants surrounded him. He couldn't fight them all. Not at once. Not without help. But he didn't need to fight them all. He only needed to take the fight to one, Eckubahn. Balzurth's nostrils flared. He had his wish. He was close enough to kill the titan king.

"I know what you're doing, Eckubahn." Balzurth jerked his head and blew at the long, red Nath hair in his eyes. Not having any success, he said, "You want to draw my father out. But let me tell you, he's too wise for that."

"He'll come," Eckubahn said. "He'll hear your cries. Feel your pain. The only way to save yourself is to get him to exchange his life for yours. Let me assure you, Balzurth is mine."

Balzurth shook his head, this time managing to get the hair out of his eyes. "No, no. I don't think it will happen. I'm my own dragon now. He knows this. I got myself into this, and I can get myself out. Besides, my father never listens to me. He's stubborn like that."

Eckubahn leaned forward and said with authority, "Call for him."

"Eh, my father is all knowing. If he wanted to be here, he'd be here by now. Sorry, but we'll just have to have the cake without him." Balzurth tried to cross his arms over his chest, but his restraints wouldn't let him. "Imagine me folding my arms over my chest right now."

Eckubahn sat back on his throne and gave Isobahn a nod. "You are a fool, Nath Dragon. For I am all knowing. Perhaps your father is not here, but someone else who cares for you is."

Isobahn's head swiveled over his shoulder. He pointed toward the audience in the stands and said, "Seize her!"

A commotion erupted in the stands. Men and giants converged on a single figure in the crowd. Oversized limbs and hands the size of shovels locked on the legs and arms of a lone robed figure.

Who is he talking about?

The giant men roughly dragged a woman kicking and screaming over the benches, but her cries were from anger, not fear. They dragged her in front of the throne. The giant yanked down the woman's hood. A black-scaled tail lashed out, smiting the giant in the head.

Balzurth got a glimpse of her face.

Selene!

Without holding back, the giant force of men clubbed her to the ground and dragged her across the dirt floor of the arena in front of Balzurth.

She moaned.

A giant hit her again.

"Quit, you monster!"

The giant drew back its club.

"Stop," Eckubahn said. There were no visible lips to be seen behind his speech; just his eyes showed on his face. "Harness her to the stone."

Standing twenty feet high, a cyclops walked over with a block of stone the size of an ox cart. The chunk of granite must have weighed tons. Rectangular in shape, the slab was bloodstained, like a sacrificial altar. With muscles bulging in its arms, it set the block between Eckubahn and Selene. The smaller giants shackled Selene by the wrists with dwarven iron and secured her to the pillar of stone. She lay flat on her back.

"What are you doing, Eckubahn?" Balzurth yelled. "You have me. Let her go! I demand it!"

Eckubahn's flaming head brightened when he spoke. "No one makes demands of me. I make demands of you. Your woman, this Selene, I know of her and her darkness. It still flows through her blood. I can sense it. But the good in her is strong. So much I don't like it." The titan nodded.

An earth giant hairy as a caterpillar walked over. It held a tremendous axe in its hand. It was an executioner's axe with a single, one-sided blade. Covered in dried blood.

Balzurth could smell dragon blood on the metal of the axe and on the stone slab. His temper rose.

How many dragons have died by this monster's hands? No more!

The giant executioner stood over Selene and the slab. Lifting the axe over its shoulders, it turned its head to Eckubahn.

"I don't delay, Nath Dragon. Call for your father, or she shall surely die right before your golden eyes."

The deranged crowd chanted, "Kill her! Kill her! Kill her!"

Every syllable the crowd said felt like a dagger in Balzurth's chest. It hurt. It angered him. His chin trembled with fury. For centuries, he'd been fully composed. There'd been no circumstance he couldn't handle. But the gorge of madness now surrounding him infuriated him. The twisted, evil minds disgusted him.

His temper, long dormant, rose some more.

And this time, he didn't tamp it down with wisdom.

Sasha's darkness now dwelled within him, and it stoked his fires. Fanned the flames. Urged him to let the rage against evil come forth.

It's time!

He locked eyes with Selene. The weary dragon woman's eyes widened.

He spoke into her mind. *Get ready.*

With a snarl, he spoke to the titan, "Fine, Eckubahn! Fine! If you want me to call my father, I shall call him!"

"Make it quick. Hope he arrives soon. The axe will fall at any moment."

Balzurth's golden eyes burned brighter than the stars. He said, "You don't have to worry about that. He's already here." Balzurth called out in an all-powerful voice that could be heard by the dragons to the five great cities and beyond.

"BAAAAAAAAAHHHHHHHHROOOOOOOOO!"

CHAPTER

33

FINGERS CROSSED BEHIND HIS HEAD, Nath said to Slivver, "You know, I'd probably have this adventure completed by now if I could get Brenwar to ride on a dragon. That's probably why, when I call, they don't come. Maybe my heart's not in it because he doesn't like it."

"Perhaps," said Slivver. The beard of skin under his chin waved in the wind atop the bull dragon's back. "But you need to remember you're a dragon, Nath. You can't do as the other races of people do. You're different. Being among them too much holds back your dragon development. That's been your problem all along."

What? Really?

This was exciting news that gave him hope, but on the outside, Nath played it cool. "I know. It's hard, though. After all, I was born a man. I've walked, eaten, breathed, and drunk as a man all my life. It's so hard to be something else." He stretched out his arms, letting the high winds caress his clawed fingers. "Besides, they're so entertaining. I tell you, Brenwar makes me laugh, and he's never even trying to be funny."

"Well, you know how I am about it. I share your fascination with the world of men. Much of that comes from my relationship with you. To mentor you, I've needed to comprehend your dilemmas. But Nath, the dragons, your brethren, are far from bland. You would find as much joy among us as anyone else. Take me, for example. Think back. You had friends back when."

"I know, but I'm so attached to people. I love them."

"There's no wrong in that."

"I'd hope not."

A sound filled with vibration rushed through Nath's body. His scales stood on end.

Waark lurched beneath him.

It was a dragon call. One much like the one Nath had used to summon the bull dragon, but at least a hundred times more powerful.

Nath was on his feet.

Slivver's eyes were staring into his. The silver dragon's jaw hung.

Waark's wings beat faster.

"That was Father! It came from Narnum!" Nath about jumped out of his boots. He'd never heard anything like that before. Nothing in the entire world could have equaled it. The earth-rocking bellow echoed through all the lands and stirred the snow in the very mountaintops. It was a dragon call for not just one dragon but all. It was a call to war. He could hear the voice of the people cry out in alarm as if the world were about to end.

Spreading his wings, Slivver hopped into the air and glided alongside Nath. "I'm going ahead. See you there." And with that, Slivver took off like he'd been launched out of a sling.

"No, wait!" Nath said.

Slivver was gone. His host of other silver dragons joined him, streaking through the air like bolts of lightning in a stormy sky.

Nath crawled up to the top of Waark's neck and said, "Faster! Faster!"

Waark moaned. His wings beat with new fury, neck stretched ahead.

Nath guessed it would take an hour to get to Narnum at this rate.

Might as well be an eon.

His muscles tensed and flexed. His body was ready to burst from his skin. He needed to get there now. Something big was happening, and he knew what it was. Balzurth battled Eckubahn. His father was ready to break the evil titan once and for all.

He needs me! I can feel it! Something's wrong. I feel he can't do it alone!

With the wind tearing at his face, he urged Waark on. "Faster! Faster! Balzurth needs us! The entire world needs us!"

CHAPTER
34

S ELENE COULDN'T BELIEVE HER EYES. It wasn't Nath chained to that slab of stone, it was Balzurth! His powerful roar strengthened her limbs and knocked the grogginess from her mind. She felt ready to fight every giant and wurmer in the land.

Axe in hand, the giant executioner quavered. The axe fell from its fingers.

Eckubahn shrank in his throne. The bones of its frame rattled.

Balzurth enlarged. The chains cuffed to his wrists popped and snapped. The body of Nath Dragon transformed.

The crowd screamed in terror.

The king of the dragons emerged. Forty feet of brick-red and bronze scales. His neck was a pillar of iron. His tail was a great cedar. A true natural-born behemoth of armor and brawn. The sun was a lantern behind his back. His shadow cast over both Selene and Eckubahn. Brilliant illumination came from his eyes, filled with anger and judgment. Balzurth shook his grand horns and said to Eckubahn:

"TODAY IS JUDGMENT DAY, TITAN! AND I AM THE JUDGE!"

The giant executioner's fingers stretched for its axe.

Balzurth's tail snapped like a clap of thunder, striking the giant dead.

Filled with a new strength she'd never imagined, Selene strained at the iron chains. The dwarven metal groaned. She didn't know if it was her newly scaled body or Balzurth's presence, but the strength in her limbs was that of a dragon. With a roar bursting from her lips, the chains snapped. She was free. Poised to strike from the slab, she surveyed her enemies. Giants and wurmers of all sizes converged from all directions in a maddened frenzy. It was her and Balzurth versus the world. She punched her fist into her hand. "To the end!"

The overwhelming sea of evil came by the hundreds.

And then it rained.

But it rained dragons.

In a wave of teeth and claws, dragons of all colors tore into the enemies with their tantalizing scales winking in the sun. Fire shot from their mouths, covering giants in flame. Blue razor dragons sent shards of lightning through the wurmers. Jaws locked on wurmers and tore them apart.

A sky raider dropped from the sky, crushing the giants in the stands. He stormed forward, horns down, stampeding a bewildered horde of smaller giants.

Indeed, it was judgment day on the back-biting citizens of Narnum.

Under a compulsion she could not explain, Selene grabbed the only weapon she could find: the giant executioner's axe. Somehow, she lifted the unwieldy thing and swung it into the back leg of an earth giant that was locked up with a bronze dragon. The giant toppled. The dragon blasted flames into its face. With a two-handed swing of the axe, she ripped into a flock of wurmers. Scales and claws were sliced and scattered.

All around, the ground shook and tremored. The battleground was hazy. Fire and smoke. Burning scales and sizzled flesh. Roars. Bellows. Screams. It was carnage.

Wave after wave of dragons dived down into the arena from the sky. They unleashed their breath weapons, pelting the giants with wroth heat and pain.

The enraged giants howled. They grabbed people and hunks of stone from the stands and hurled them at the dragons.

With ease, the dragons swerved in midair to avoid the huge flying hunks of stone, only to attack with more fire again and again.

So many dragons were there, and in such a multitude of colors, locked in a mortal battle. Blue razors, bulls, bronzes, green lilies, orange blazes, crimson dynamos, ivory sliders, yellow streaks, fire bites, grey scalers, and dozens of other colors attacked from all directions. It was an onslaught. They had the giants on the run.

An orange blaze was locked on a giant's head. The giant beat at it with fury. A second orange blaze unleashed a white foam from his mouth, coating the giant from neck to toe. The foam disintegrated the giant's skin to the bone.

A bronze dragon, grand in frame, swooped down from above. Its tail locked around a giant's neck like a whip. Wings pounding the air, the bronze dragon lifted the giant into the sky like a hawk snatching a rabbit from the prairie. Up, up, up the dragon went, a speck in the sky. The giant thrashed, arms flailing and legs kicking. The bronze dragon's neck bent, and it let out a gust of fire. The giant burned. The dragon uncurled his tail from the giant's neck. The burning giant fell like a falling star and crashed on two of its brethren.

Standing among the fray of chaos, Selene tossed the axe aside, pumped her arms high, and said, "Yes!"

The tide of battle was in the dragons' favor. Narnum was moments from being liberated.

And then a strange hum rose among the growls and the roar of fire. A storm cloud rolled in like a swarm of locusts. They came from the west. A deep purple glow was within the cloud.

A chill doused the fire in Selene's bones.

Evil's cavalry was coming. Wurmers. Not by the hundreds but by the thousands.

"Balzurth!" she yelled. "We need more dragons!"

Whether the Dragon King heard her she didn't know.

Balzurth, towering above all, battled Eckubahn. A crushed throne of dragon bones lay beneath them. Balzurth coiled his tail around the titan's neck. The titan king's fists hammered at Balzurth's body.

Boom! Boom! Boom!

Selene did a double take between the sky and the battle of kings. Balzurth needed to finish Eckubahn. He needed to finish Eckubahn now.

A second titan that Selene didn't recognize at first was on the move. Oh, it was Isobahn, the muscular, oily, tattooed brute with the long ponytail. The titan had slunk away from the fracas, only to reappear with a spear the likes of which she'd never seen before. At the huge spear's tip, six strips of twisted metal came to a razor-sharp point. The weapon was big enough to skewer three giants at once, more than capable of running Balzurth through, in one side and out the other. A dark aura flowed around the metal spearhead with a life of its own.

What is that?

But even though she had never seen the weapon before, in her heart she knew what it was. Before her time, her father, Gorn Grattack, had been the evil enemy in the first Dragon War. In the final battle, Gorn had been beaten and subdued by a man, a special man who wielded a weapon that could kill anything. A special man whose legendary name Gorn had twisted into a lie to turn the races against the dragons.

"Barnabus!" she cried out.

Selene knew she beheld that same weapon now. Isobahn had it poised at Balzurth's back. The titan had a gleam in his eye as if this moment had been planned all along.

Nalzambor, have mercy!

"Balzurth! Watch out behind you! He wields the Spear of Barnabus!"

CHAPTER
35

NATH HUGGED A LARGE FIN of armor jutting up from the bull dragon's back. His claws dug into the bull dragon's rocky hide. Jaws clenched, stomach in knots, he couldn't shake off the spiders crawling up his spine.

I need to be there! I need to be there now!

Still leagues away, he could make out Narnum from the sky. There was a deadly jubilation of fiery activity below. Dragons dive bombed from unseen heights. It sent a charge through his scales into his bones. He could sense the battle's full scale. The victorious shrieks of the dragons carried through the skies.

Nath couldn't imagine anything or anyone in the world surviving such an onslaught. What could possibly withstand a legion of dragons led by Balzurth?

The dark fear in his heart enlarged the moment he spotted a sea of wurmers moving in from the west like a rain-heavy storm. He clutched his head in his hands.

Oh no! Oh no!

The wurmers were on course to blindside the ranks of dragons. The foul insectoids not only had strength, they had strength in numbers.

Nath let out another dragon call, screaming a warning.

"MaaaaaaAAARRRrrrrrrrrrrOOOOooooooooooooooooooooooooo!"

It carried. But would it carry far enough, fast enough, and into the ears of the battling mad dragon fray?

"Faster, Waark! Faster!"

Nath felt his heart sinking in his chest.

I can't be too late!

CHAPTER
36

WITH THE SPEAR OF BARNABUS in hand, Isobahn closed in. Selene propelled herself into the towering titan's path, waving her hands above her head, shouting, "Take me, coward." Eyes fixed on Balzurth's back, the titan's steps did not falter.

Out of the corner of her eye, she could see that Sansla Libor came, blasting through the chaos. Wings beating, arms outstretched, the great ape's fists collided with the titan's jaw with ram-like force. The blow staggered the titan. The spear tip dropped. The metal bit into the ground.

Selene coiled her body around the spear and held it with all her dragon strength.

Growling, Isobahn lifted her from the ground along with the spear. He tried to shake her off, arms flailing back and forth, side to side.

All the while, Sansla Libor stood on Isobahn's shoulder, punching the titan in the face with blows that would have dropped an ogre.

The bone necklace on the titan's neck rattled, but he didn't flinch. "I will not be stopped!" Isobahn's huge legs churned forward again.

Selene called out in Dragonese, "Help! Help! Your king needs your help!"

A small host of silver dragons zipped through the battle. Bolts of white-hot light shot from their mouths, striking the titan.

Isobahn convulsed. Bellowed. His furrowed brow darkened his once-omnipotent expression. "Fleas! I am a titan! You are fleas!"

The silver dragons latched onto the evil giant from head to toe. Claws and teeth sank into the mad titan's skin.

Any normal creature on Nalzambor would have fallen. But this was no ordinary giant. He was a titan, fueled by more than just flesh and bones; he had an ancient dark and evil magic as old as the world itself.

Surging ahead like a juggernaut, the Selene-covered-spear-wielding titan said with sinister glee, "Ho-ho-ho, nothing can stop a titan like me." With a single hand, Isobahn wrapped his fingers around Selene's body and squeezed her like she was part of the spear itself. "Fledgling, prepare to witness front and center the death of the once mighty Balzurth!"

With her body being crushed like it was stuck in a blacksmith's vise, Selene let out one final cry:

"Balzurth, watch out!"

CHAPTER 37

THE TIME HAD COME. THE moment had arrived. Balzurth was locked up in combat with his mortal enemy Eckubahn. It had been more than a thousand years, and the hatred they harbored for one another had only grown.

It showed. The two thrashed through the arena like a pair of rabid savages. Balzurth's claws sank into the flesh of the earth giant's body that hosted the evil spirit of the ancient titan. Balzurth's tail coiled around the flaming neck of the fiend. The kings conversed silently, from mind to mind.

"It's over, Eckubahn! I showed mercy before, but I show mercy no more!" Balzurth drove the titan into the ground, smashing a wurmer and giant beneath him. "And all of your foul brood are going down with you!"

"Never!" Eckubahn's fist slugged Balzurth in the jaw with thunderous impact.

The Dragon King's talons held firm, sinking deeper into the titan's thick hide.

Eckubahn squirmed, twisted, and wrestled with all his might. He threw dirt in Balzurth's eyes. Spat fire in his face. He clawed at the ground, straining. The titan couldn't escape Balzurth's grasp.

The Dragon King locked on with fire in his eyes and a volcano ready to erupt from his chest.

Striking Balzurth with anything and everything he could get his hands on, Eckubahn unleashed another deadly defense. "You cannot win, Balzurth! You are already defeated! See my wurmers! See my giants! They are turning back your pathetic surprise attack!"

Balzurth sensed the presence of the swarm of wurmers. He'd even anticipated it. That was why he'd put his plan in motion long before he arrived. The dragons had gathered high above, far from sight and suspicion, the moment he'd arrived in Narnum. It was all on account of a very tiny dragon who had been with him all along, hiding behind his locks of hair. A lizard wisp. Small but faster than a hummingbird with wings that beat a hundred times faster than an eye could blink, the tiny creature had carried out Balzurth's orders. The dragons had come and waited for his call. Now he just had to do his duty. Finish off Eckubahn. If not, he'd be lost. All of the dragons who had come would be lost as well.

"Again I say it's over, Eckubahn! Stop squirming and accept what's coming!" Balzurth rolled on top of Eckubahn. He pinned the titan's shoulders down to the ground. "Look me in the eye and face your doom!"

Eyes squeezed shut, the titan pushed back, shoving Balzurth's face up with his palms. "You can't destroy me, Balzurth! You weaken! I strengthen! You couldn't destroy me before. You doubt you can destroy me now! I can feel it!"

"I DOUBT NOTHING!" Balzurth drew his horns back and head butted Eckubahn in his flaming face.

CRACK!

The titan's body shimmered. His mighty limbs loosened.

Balzurth freed his front talons from the titan's body. Faster than a wing, his talons seized Eckubahn by the throat and squeezed.

The titan's head turned from orange to red to purple flames. His hands chopped at Balzurth's powerful arms. "You will not win, Balzurth! You will not win! You have a blind spot!"

Balzurth dug his talons deeper into the mounds of neck muscle. He searched for the titan's evasive eyes.

The fiend wriggled and thrashed. His huge head rolled from side to side like a spoiled child trying to avoid healthy food.

"You will face the truth, titan! You will face it now!"

"Never!" Choking, the titan's eyes popped wide. Balzurth's eyes bore right into him. "No! No! Never!"

Balzurth, fully aware of the chaos that surrounded him, sent out a silent message to all of the dragons.

Go! Far and fast!

He sent another message to his son, Nath. Mind to mind, Balzurth's final thoughts mingled with his son's. "Nath, save Selene. Save yourself. Get out of here. That is my final wish. Live on, Son. I love you. Live on."

CHAPTER 38

"FATHER! FATHER!" NATH CRIED OUT. The message his father had sent confused him.

What's going on?

For a moment of the fleetest sort, he and his father had been connected, mind to mind. He had felt Balzurth's fury and rage building. Had sensed the deep love within his father too. There had been that final command from father to son, and then the connection had just gone.

Nath barked an order. "Dive, Waark! Dive!"

Narnum rested in their path, only seconds away now. He'd be in time to help his father win the battle. But Selene was in danger? Where was she?

The dragons scattered in the air in all directions.

The wurmers gave chase.

Nath's keen dragon eyes zeroed in on the battleground. The arena of the Contest of Champions. More than half of the arena's stonework stands were nothing but dust and rubble. Thousands of bodies of giants, dragons, and wurmers lay still, but many others still battled. In the middle of it all, his grand and glorious father Balzurth had the titan held fast to the ground.

Nath pumped his fist. "Yes, Father! Yes!" Balzurth had Eckubahn right where he wanted him: in an unbreakable death grip. His father's plan had worked.

I should have known!

"End it, Father! End it!"

Wurmers came at him like bats bursting from a cave.

Waark plowed through them.

The wurmers cracked against his mighty frame. They spiraled toward the ground with their wings busted.

"Go, Waark! Go!"

Scanning the ground with the winds ripping at his face, Nath caught a glimpse of another battle. Another titan stormed toward Balzurth with a monster-sized spear. A woman hung onto the shaft. The ugly ponytailed titan plucked the female from the shaft and slung her hard onto the ground.

"Selene!" Nath cried out.

The titan lifted the spear over its head.

"Waark!" Nath ordered. "Attack! Now!"

The bull dragon shifted direction the slightest bit, maneuvering away from Balzurth and toward his and Selene's attacker.

Now I know what Father meant. But I want to help him.

Nath caught a glimpse of his father's grand breastplate turning the color of flame. Time stopped around him. In his mind, he got it. He understood.

Waark plowed into the spear-wielding titan, knocking it flat on the ground.

Nath hopped off Waark's back, rushed over to Selene, and picked her up in his arms. "Selene, Selene!"

Blinking, she said, "Nath?" She wheezed, coughed, and shook her head.

Sansla Libor landed by his side.

A wurmer rushed in.

Sansla cracked its skull with his fist.

"We must go!" Nath said. He ran toward Waark carrying Selene, Sansla with him. "Father is going to turn this place into an inside-out volcano!"

"Understood." Sansla gave a nod and leapt into the air, flying away.

With Selene in his arms, Nath climbed back up onto the bull dragon's back. "Go, Waark! Go!" It ripped him up inside, not rushing to his father's aid. He wanted to help with the victory. But he understood what his father was doing. And he needed to obey.

Finish him, Father! Finish him so I can celebrate with you!

The bull dragon lifted them into the sky.

Selene came to her senses. "What are you doing? Let me go, Nath! Let me go!" She fought in his arms.

With great effort, he held her fast, saying, "My, you've gotten stronger. Now stop squirming, will you? My father's victory is at hand. Watch it unfold. But you might want to shield your eyes."

"No, Nath, no!" Her eyes were filled with terror. They got bigger the higher they went. "You don't understand. It's a trap! The titan has the spear!"

"No spear can pierce my father's hide."

"That's no ordinary spear. That's the Spear of Barnabus!"

Nath watched the titan pick up from the ground the huge spear that had fallen from its grip. The titan resumed its march on Balzurth's exposed back.

It all came together. The doubt that had been pushing at his mind blossomed. Eckubahn was ready. The vile monster was ready for anything.

Nath slapped Waark on the neck. "Down! Down!"

Fire erupted from Balzurth's mouth, filling the arena with blinding, white-hot flames.

CHAPTER
39

BALZURTH LOOSED ALL OF HIS power.

BOOOOOM!

His fury. His fire. Wave after wave of orange, yellow, blue, and green flames blasted from his mouth. The fires pounded into Eckubahn. A blast wave of his raw power tore through the arena, shattering the stonework and beyond. The closest surrounding buildings of Narnum collapsed. Everything the mighty dragon's breath touched caught fire. It spread. The wicked turned to ash.

Eckubahn screamed, writhed, and howled. The flames exposed everything he was and the harm he meant to bring on others like those who already suffered a thousandfold. The flesh of the giant body he inhabited flecked away like paper, burning in Balzurth's fire.

The titan's spirit fought against the flames consuming it. It clawed and squealed, trying to tear away from the inescapable fires.

"Mercy, Balzurth! Mercy!"

The flames kept coming.

"I will do anything! Anything!"

The endless stream of unbridled disintegrating heat did not slow. Balzurth would not let up. He had to destroy the evil spirit once and for all. "You still spin lies in your last moment of life. You lived a liar, you'll die a liar, forever."

Eckubahn swam in the flames. Separating from the body, the titan's spirit bucked and flailed. Its energy crested over the fire only to be pulled down again. Eckubahn shrank in his futile struggles.

Sensing the end, Balzurth huffed out the final gust where his flames were hottest.

In the very back of his mind, he heard someone yell, "Watch your back, Balzurth! Watch your baaaaaaaa....."

The Spear of Barnabus pierced Balzurth's scales and bore right through his heart.

His fire extinguished.

Only his last cry remained.

CHAPTER 40

THE BLINDING BRIGHTNESS CLEARED. NATH could see the battle of a lifetime unfold. His father's fire destroyed everything but the titans. Isobahn dropped to a knee on the shaking ground, but in a moment the titan was back on his feet, poised to strike.

Eckubahn fought against the dragon flame but could not overcome it. The titan was like a man drowning in a storming sea. Doomed.

With the artifact over his head, Isobahn drove the Spear of Barnabus right through Balzurth's heart.

Nath clutched his head again and screamed. "Noooooooooo!"

Balzurth's flames turned from fire to the fury of sound.

"MAAAAAAAAAROOOOOOOOOOHHHHH!"

The Dragon King's voice sent shock waves through all of Narnum. Its tallest tower cracked in half. It toppled. Five hundred feet of stone crashed on top of the city.

"Get down there! Get down there!" Nath ordered Waark. He pumped his finger at the ground.

Face white as a sheet in his arms, Selene said, "He's gone, Nath. He's gone. We must go."

The wurmers thickened in the sky.

Nath could barely see the ground beneath them. The last thing he saw was his father's body. The Dragon King lay still, surrounded by smoke and flames for a grave.

Nath jumped off Waark.

"Nath!" Selene yelled.

He sailed toward the ground like a falling meteor, hair billowing over his shoulders like the meteor's tail.

The ground rushed up to meet him.

A wurmer glided into his path, jaws wide.

Fang out, he split the beast in half. Still falling, he saw more wurmers coming after him.

Sansla Libor swooped in. The roamer king caught him under his arms and bore him away. Slivver flew nearby. The silver dragon and his host battled away the wurmers.

"Let me go! Let me go!" Nath screamed and kicked. Tears streaked down his face. "Release me!"

"I am sorry for your father, Nath," Sansla said. "But you are the Dragon King now. Take it from one king to another. You must be protected. The world still has hope so long as it has you. We can't lose you too." Sansla dropped him back onto Waark's back and then joined a regiment of dragons to fight off the wurmers.

Waark flew on. The distance between them and the enemy lengthened.

Now Selene held Nath in her arms.

Head down, Nath sobbed and sobbed.

CHAPTER
41

ECKUBAHN BREATHED. THE TITAN'S SPIRIT remained in the same body it had been hosted in. He stood, a mountain of a person, more skeleton than flesh. He peeled off the smoking skin from his forearm and flicked it aside. His eyes burned with deep orange flames. He faced Isobahn.

The brother titan glowered down at Balzurth's dragon body. All of the hair was burned from the titan's body. Boils covered his skin.

"That was close," Eckubahn said.

Isobahn nodded.

Eckubahn took a knee in front of Balzurth's face. By the horns, he turned the Dragon King's eyes toward him. "Finally, my greatest enemy has fallen. I told you that you had a blind spot. The sacrifice you made for a woman. Compassion. Mercy." He spat. "For weaklings." He eyed the spear. "Make sure he's dead."

Isobahn took the spear in hand, set his foot against Balzurth's body, and gave it a twist. The dragon body didn't move. The titan yanked out the spear. With a grin, he said, "We did it." Spear high, he shouted. "WE DID IT! WE KILLED BALZURTH!" He pounded his smoldering chest.

Only the wurmers were gathered. All that remained of the others were dead piles of ash and bone.

Still talking to Balzurth, Eckubahn said, "And you called me a liar. Well, I didn't lie about everything. I told you to watch your back, didn't I?" He stood, grabbed the Spear of Barnabus from Isobahn, and stabbed Balzurth himself. "Didn't I!"

EPILOGUE

S HARING A SADDLE BEHIND SASHA, Bayzog the elven wizard swooned and fell from his mount.

Sasha jumped off the horse. "Bayzog!" She grabbed him up in her arms. His limbs trembled.

Birds scattered in the trees. Vermin darted back and forth. The horses whinnied and nickered.

"Bayzog, what is it?" Sasha said.

A dragon's roar, like a spirit, ruffled the leaves with a wind of its own.

Dismounting, Ben's nape hairs stood on end. Sadness filled him.

Bayzog's violet eyes moistened.

Sasha started crying. "Oh my, oh my," she said. Her chin quivered. "What happened? What happened? Is Nath all right?"

"I did not foresee this. Who could have?" Bayzog cradled the Elderwood Staff in his arms. He closed his eyes. A tear dripped down his chin and fell to the ground. Mystic words formed on his lips for several minutes. The clouds darkened, and Ben didn't feel it was because of Bayzog but something else. A buzzing *ree-rah, ree-rah* sound permeated his ears. It became louder. Covering his ears, he watched above.

A flock of wurmers soared overhead, heading south.

In a loud voice, Ben said, "That's not good! Not good at all!"

Sasha shook her head. Her hands were on Bayzog's. "I don't like this."

The wurmers passed.

Ben's hands fell from his ears.

Bayzog's murmurings stopped, and he spoke once more in Common. "He's gone. He's gone."

"Who's gone?" Ben demanded. His blood rushed through his ears. All he could think of was Dragon. "Is it Dragon? Tell me it's not Dragon!"

Bayzog's spacey violet stare cleared. "No, it's not Nath." The wizard's shoulders sagged as the truth became too much to bear. "It's Balzurth. The Dragon King has fallen to the titans."

Sasha gasped.

Ben fell back on his haunches. "Impossible," he whispered. "That's impossible, isn't it?"

"Death is the enemy of all who live, even Balzurth."

Sasha began crying uncontrollably. She babbled. "It's my fault. It's my fault. I know it. He lifted my curse and took it upon himself. It weakened him. It must have." She clutched clumps of grass and ripped them from the ground. "I did this. I did this."

Setting the staff aside, Bayzog hugged her from behind. Holding her fast, he said, "Balzurth was wise. He would not have done something without knowing the consequences. This is not your fault, Sasha. Do not think of it like that. What he gave you is a gift. Accept it. Enjoy it. Live right by it."

Shuddering, she said, "I didn't deserve it."

Ben took her hand in his. He rubbed her palm with his thumb and said, "Sasha, just like Nath, Balzurth would have done the same for any one of us. Now is the time to be strong."

"Why?" she said, half hysterical. "Why?"

"Nath is the Dragon King now. He's going to need us."

She wiped her nose and eyes. Sitting up straight, she said, "Forgive me. I know you're right. Nath will need us, but what about Rerry and Samaz?"

Bayzog kissed her on the cheek. "It's been revealed to me he'll need them too." He helped his wife to her feet. "Every one of us. You know how he is."

She giggled a tiny bit. "How can you make me laugh at a time as dark as this? You never make me laugh."

Bayzog cupped her face in his hands and thumbed the tears from her eyes. "There's hope. There's always hope. That's why we laugh at death."

Ben slapped Bayzog on the back. "I like it! I don't know where that came from, Bayzog, but I like it!" He pointed toward the sky with his sword. "It's time to avenge Balzurth! Come back, insects, come back." He winced. His hand went to his ribs. "Something still hurts. Something everywhere still hurts."

Bayzog patted Ben softly on the back. "That's a good thing. It wouldn't hurt at all if you were dead."

"I don't know if he's being cynical or funny," Ben said to Sasha.

"Me either, but it's refreshing." She climbed into the saddle. "Let's find our sons before the world ends."

OTHER BOOKS AND AUTHOR INFO

Craig Halloran resides with his family outside his hometown of Charleston, West Virginia. When he isn't entertaining mankind, he is seeking adventure, working out, or watching sports. To learn more about him, go to: www. craighalloran.com.

Check out all of my great stories ...

CLASH OF HEROES: Nath Dragon meets The Darkslayer

The Chronicles of Dragon Series
The Hero, the Sword and the Dragons (Book 1) Free eBook
Dragon Bones and Tombstones (Book 2)
Terror at the Temple (Book 3)
Clutch of the Cleric (Book 4)
Hunt for the Hero (Book 5)
Siege at the Settlements (Book 6)
Strife in the Sky (Book 7)
Fight and the Fury (Book 8)
War in the Winds (Book 9)
Finale (Book 10)

The Chronicles of Dragon: Series 2, Tail of the Dragon
Tail of the Dragon
Claws of the Dragon
Eye of the Dragon
Battle of the Dragon
Scales of the Dragon
Trial of the Dragon
Teeth of the Dragon

The Darkslayer Series 1
Wrath of the Royals (Book 1) Free eBook
Blades in the Night (Book 2)

Underling Revenge (Book 3)
Danger and the Druid (Book 4)
Outrage in the Outlands (Book 5)
Chaos at the Castle (Book 6)

The Darkslayer: Bish and Bone, Series 2
Bish and Bone (Book 1) Free eBook
Black Blood (Book 2)
Red Death (Book 3)
Lethal Liaisons (Book 4)
Torment and Terror (Book 5)

The Supernatural Bounty Hunter Files
Smoke Rising (2015) Free ebook
I Smell Smoke (2015)
Where There's Smoke (2015)
Smoke on the Water (2015)
Smoke and Mirrors (2015)
Up in Smoke
Smoke 'Em
Holy Smoke
Smoke Out

Zombie Impact Series
Zombie Day Care: Book 1 Free eBook
Zombie Rehab: Book 2
Zombie Warfare: Book 3

You can learn more about the Darkslayer and my
other books, deals, and specials at:
Facebook – The Darkslayer Report by Craig
Twitter – Craig Halloran
www.craighalloran.com

Made in the USA
Columbia, SC
27 February 2019